THE HILLS OF GOLD
UNCHANGING

THE HILLS OF GOLD UNCHANGING

BOOK TWO OF THE LONG TRAILS

LIZZI TREMAYNE

Lizzi Tremayne / Blue Mist Publishing

Franklin Road, RD 2

Waihi, New Zealand 3682

www.lizzitremayne.com

Publisher's Note: This is a work of fiction. Names, characters, places, and incidents are a product of the author's imagination. Locales and public names are sometimes used for atmospheric purposes. Any resemblance to actual people, living or dead, or to businesses, companies, events, institutions, or locales is completely coincidental.

Cover design and photos by Jessica Cale at Safeword! Author Services and Lizzi Tremayne with assistance from Elliot Thompson.

Author photos by Kajai Lang | Artwork by Made by B 4 U

Book Two of The Long Trails series

The Hills of Gold Unchanging / Lizzi Tremayne 1st Edition February 2017

Draft2Digital Print Edition V19 Reprinted 2022 08 16

ISBN 978-0-9951157-7-4

DEDICATION

To Kate and Matthew...

*You told me there was another book in between
Book One and its epilogue.*

I didn't believe you.

You were right.

CONTENTS

LIZZI'S BOOK LIST AND SERIES ORDERS

The Long Trails Series
A Long Trail Rolling (Book One)
The Hills of Gold Unchanging (Book Two)
A Sea of Green Unfolding (Book Three)
The Long Trails Box Set: Historical Western Family Saga: Books 1-3

Multi-Series Samplers
Lizzi Tremayne First Chapter Sampler

The *Once Upon a Vet School* Series
~*Vet School 24/7*~
Fifty Miles at a Breath
Lena Takes a Foal
~*Practice Time*~
Greener Pastures Calling

Boxed sets with Bluestocking Belles
Follow Your Star Home

Sign up for Lizzi's VIP Club to hear about new releases and specials, plus get your free sampler gift here:
www.lizzitremayne.com/VIPHills

PRAISE FOR LIZZI TREMAYNE

With her debut **A long Trail Rolling,** *Lizzi was:*

Winner 2016 True West Magazine
Best Western Romance
Winner 2015 RWNZ Koru Award
Finalist 2015 Best Indie Book Award
Winner 2014 RWNZ Pacific Hearts Award
Finalist 2013 RWNZ Great Beginnings

"vivid, light and fast-paced… a ripping good read. " *–Deborah Challinor, #1 bestselling author and historian*

"An authentic, emotional story of one woman's fight for survival in an unforgiving landscape." *–Leeanna Morgan, USA Today bestselling author*

"An impressive debut…a romance, a western, and an adventure story, all rolled up into a compelling read." *–Booksellers NZ*

The Hills of Gold Unchanging:

"The pace is fast, there's plenty of action and adventure and a few twists I didn't see coming. Good characters plus excellent history equals a great read." *–Deborah Challinor, number one bestselling author and historian*

"…superb storytelling." –*Judy Knighton, editor*

"I particularly liked the attention to historical detail… an author who does her homework… a cracking good yarn." –*Shelagh Merlin, NetGalley Reviewer*

A Sea of Green Unfolding:
"the historical research is excellent…well-integrated into the narrative." –*Deborah Challinor, number one bestselling author and historian*

"A lovely combination of historical accuracy and adventure…beautifully researched and engrossing." –*Shelagh Merlin, NetGalley reviewer*

"Loved this book. The characters draw you in on a story filled with interest and suspense." –*Kate Le Petit*

Fifty Miles at a Breath
"Lizzi Tremayne is a born storyteller. The characters…[are] three dimensional and you can feel Lena and Blake's emotions." –*Lori Dykes*

"a wonderful series about…becoming a veterinarian, the love of horses and sweet romance. Lena and Blake will grab your heart." –*Teri Donaldson*

Lena Takes a Foal
"This book is for anyone with a passion for horses… or loves a story about strong, independent young women finding love!" –*Stacey*

"The story… displays Lizzi Tremayne's ability to develop strong characters… with a nice strong black moment to challenge our heroine and prove her worth." –*Shelagh Merlin, NetGalley Reviewer*

"…perfect blend of sweet romance, horses and real emotions with fascinating info…about the medical care of horses." –*Teri Donaldson*

Greener Pastures Calling

"A young female vet, in rural NZ, tell of the trials and tribulations of being the first female [horse] vet in the area… The romantic aspect… runs hot and cold. Outside interference doesn't help, but it all comes to head on Christmas day… Good story, with interesting look into rural New Zealand." –*Rosemary Hughes*

"I adore Lizzi Tremayne's writing and in this Once Upon A Vet School series, it gets better and better… even though it was a novella, it packed a lot into every word and I highly recommend this story as I do anything written by this author!!" –*Lori Dykes*

UTAH TERRITORY, 1860

Central Portion of
(Central Overland California and Pikes Peak Route)

(Nebraska)

(Wyoming)

(Colorado)

(Utah)

(Nevada)

(California)

Fort Laramie

South Pass

Great Salt Lake City

Deep Creek

Carson City

Fort Churchill

Sacramento

San Francisco

KEY
—— Utah Territory Boundary, 1860
‑ ‑ ‑ Existing State Lines
(xxx) Existing State Names
‑‑‑‑ The Central Route

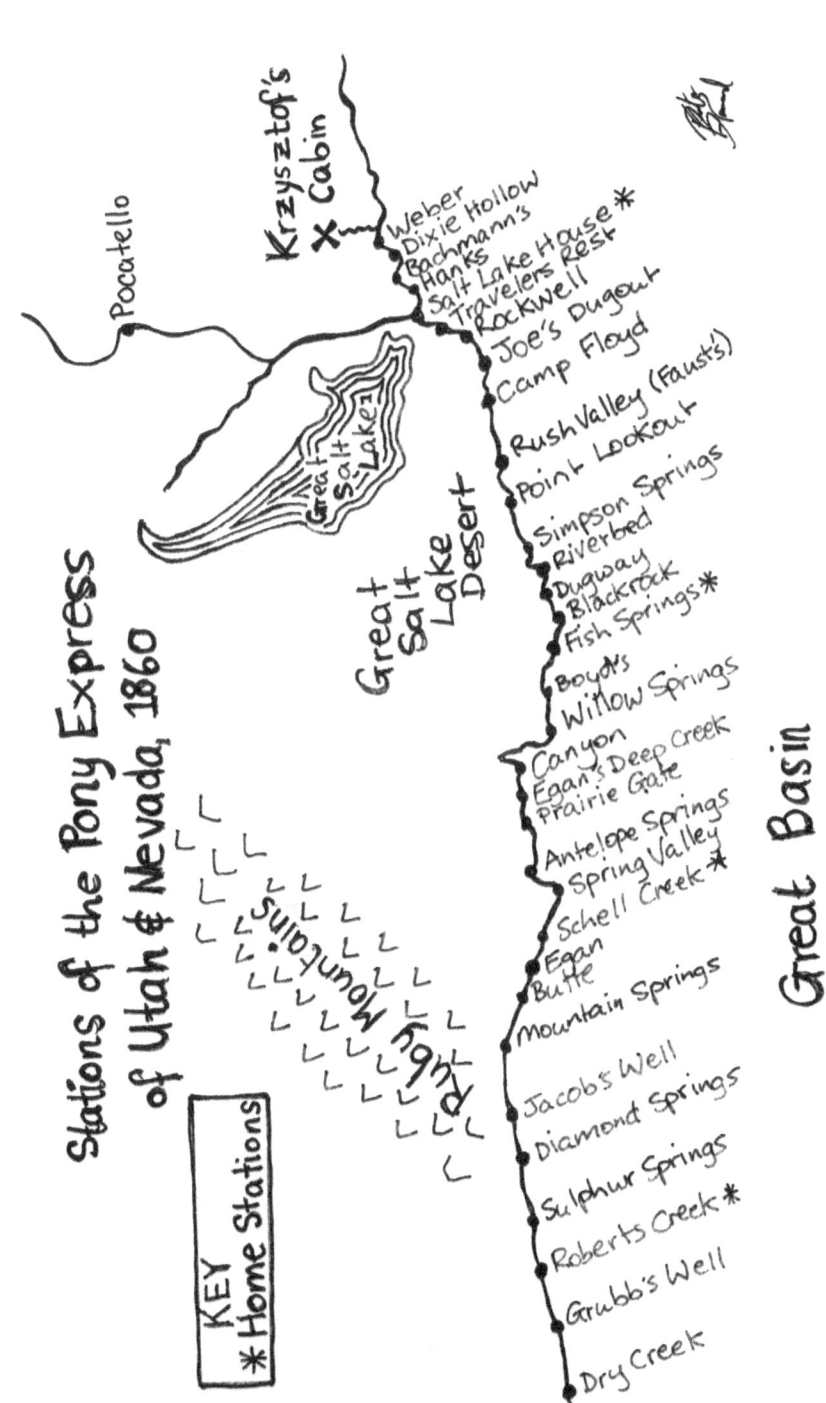

Stations of the Pony Express
of Utah & Nevada, 1860

KEY
✳ Home Stations

Pocatello

Krzysztof's ✗ Cabin

Weber
Dixie Hollow
Bachmann's
Hanks
Salt Lake House ✳
Travelers Rest
Rockwell
Joe's Dugout
Camp Floyd

Rush Valley (Faust's)
Point Lookout
Simpson Springs
Riverbed
Dugway
Blackrock
Fish Springs ✳
Boyd's
Willow Springs
Canyon
Egan's Deep Creek
Prairie Gate
Antelope Springs
Spring Valley
Schell Creek ✳
Egan
Butte
Mountain Springs
Jacob's Well
Diamond Springs
Sulphur Springs
Roberts Creek ✳
Grubb's Well
Dry Creek

Great Salt Lake

Great Salt Lake Desert

Ruby Mountains

Great Basin

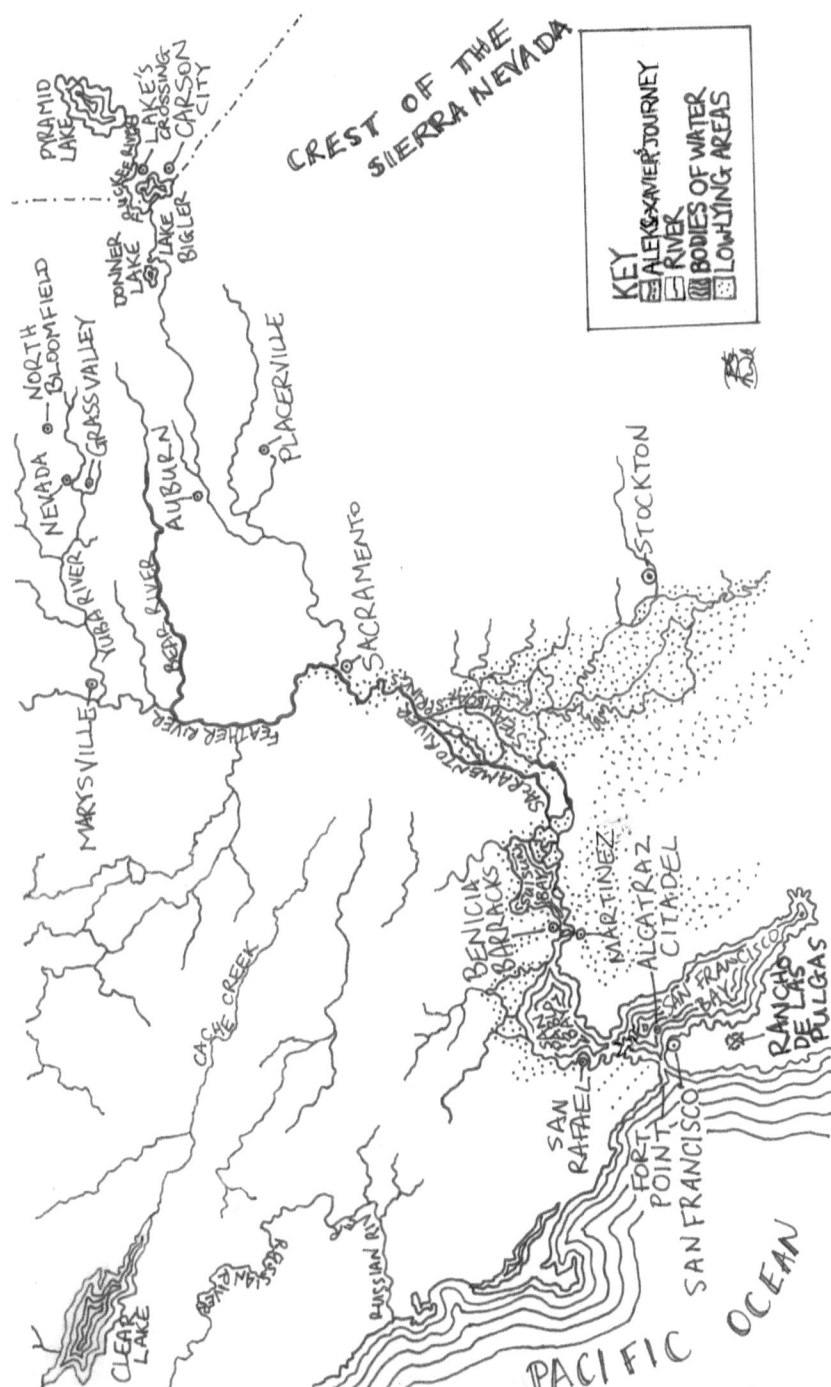

PART I

1860 ~ ECHO CANYON, UTAH TERRITORY

1

June 1860, Echo Canyon, Wasatch Mountains, Utah Territory

His blade glinted in the sunlight as he lunged toward her, but she ducked and spun, her own sword flashing in a figure eight while she retreated, and his strike met with only air. He recovered and prepared for the onslaught he knew would come, coughing as the dust kicked up by their boots thickened.

Blade up, he parried the blows she rained down upon him. He managed to get in one of his own and retreated for a moment, breathing hard. She stepped back as well, her breast heaving beneath the thin linen. Blue eyes glittered below brows narrowed with concentration, before her sword returned to action with a vengeance. They circled, dodging and striking in turn. Her skill was far greater, but the girl's injuries from her last fight, combined with his greater reach and fitness were beginning to tell. A movement caught the edge of his vision—he glanced up from her sword to see her hat tumble off. Her hair cascaded down in a tangle to her thighs, and his heart surged.

She's mine now.

He offered the ghost of a smile as he moved in to disarm her with a passing lunge and struck at her sword arm.

The air left his lungs and he tasted dirt in his mouth as he hit the unforgiving ground face-first. He groaned and rolled over, expecting the worst.

Above him, her laughing visage met his eyes. Her glorious curls, molten gold, fell around his face like a veil as she bent to wipe his face and kiss his lips. She slid the hilt of his sword from his hand.

"All right, *halte*, hold, you two," their instructor said, in his heavy Russian accent. "There's still work to be done, Xavier, but you've done well."

Xavier Argüello took the hand his opponent offered, hopped to his feet and dusted off his clothes.

"Well done, *Querido*," said his intended, Aleksandra Lekarski, as she returned his sword.

"Xavier, come here, please," Vladimir Chabardine said, from the doorway of the cabin, where he was propped up in his sickbed. "You have worked hard. I am impressed, and it is rare that I am compelled to say that. That *shashka* now belongs to you. Use it in good health."

Xavier stared at him, then at the Don Cossack saber in his hand, its leather grip smooth with years of use. He was silent.

"But it's yours, Vladimir," he said.

"It was one of mine, yes. Now it is yours. Tatiana brought my other two *shashkas* with her from Russia. One is for Nikolai, when he is ready, and this one is for you. It's the least I can do, after my part in," he looked at Aleksandra and grimaced, "your papa's death."

She nodded grimly in acknowledgement.

"Thank you, from the bottom of my heart," Xavier said, shaking his head at the Russian, as he ran a finger from the tooled embellishment on the pommel through to the rawhide bouton and strip they used for their practice sessions. He slid the protectors off and his new shashka whispered into its scabbard. He turned to face Aleksandra, and bowed to her. "Thank you," he said, then turned to Vladimir, "and again, to you."

She returned the bow and smiled at them both.

"You're not quite done," Vladimir said. "Xavier, replace the guard."

"What would you like?" Aleksandra asked.

"One more bout. *En garde*," he said, and they prepared. "*Prêt*." They nodded. "*Allez*," he snapped, and they began. Aleksandra feinted, then moved to strike, but Xavier saw a hole in her defense and lunged. She twirled way, with a laugh, then drew back, looking frightened, her body twisted strangely to the right.

Was she injured?

His gaze lifted to her face. What a chance! Her whole left side was open. He went for the opening. Before he could alter his course, she unwound and her *shashka* flashed toward him. For the second time in his life, he froze as he found her blade across his throat.

"*¿Recuerdas?* Remember this?" she said, her eyes merry.

"How could I forget, *Querida,*" he spoke for her ears alone, "our first meeting?"

Hands clapped behind them and they spun as one, their own hands gripping their sword hilts.

"No need fer that, no need fer that," said a man, mounted on a chestnut horse. Beside the horse walked a black man, tied by the wrists to the rope in the rider's hands.

"What do you wan—" Xavier began, then clamped his jaw, as his breath came short. Blood pounded in his ears and his face heated. "What can I help you with," he finally managed, past gritted teeth, as he walked away from the house door, toward their callers.

"Well, hello theah," the rider said, his Southern accent heavy. "Good fightin', and fer a girl, too." He looked sideways at Aleksandra.

"Aleks," Xavier hissed, as he felt, rather than saw, her bristle beside him. He glanced at her knuckles showing white on the pommel of her saber. He reached out and covered her sword hand with his own and she took a deep breath and stilled.

"We're yer new neighbors down th'road. Y'all wanna buy a slave? We've jus' done come West 'n now we've done finished buildin' the house, he's," he nodded at the man at the end of his tether, "jus' 'noth'r mouth t'feed. Ca'int use 'im to grow nuthin' in this rock y'call dirt around heah." He stopped and looked at the yard and cabin. "Nice place y'all got here."

Xavier nodded, silent.

The man's brows narrowed, then he continued. "Well, ah wondered if y'all had a breedin—ah, a woman slave I could trade fer him. The missus wants help in t'house, an' I could use a little...too." The glint in his beady eyes turned his grin into a leer.

Xavier closed his eyes and clenched his fists. "This territory may allow slavery, but nobody holds with it around here."

The Southerner was silent for a moment, then answered with a voice dripping with sarcasm. "Now that's mahty neighborly of ya. Are y'all some o'them ab'litionists we come West to git away from?"

"As you wish." Xavier raised a brow at him, then shifted his gaze to the man on foot, staring at the dirt. "I apologize to you, sir, but you'll have to go home with him again. May you find yourself a better life soon."

The corners of the slave's mouth lifted briefly. His eyes flickered up to Xavier's, brightened, then dulled again as he dropped them to the ground.

"C'mon Jordan," the rider growled, "we're not welc'm here, by all accounts." He jerked his horse around and they retreated the way they'd come.

Xavier stood silent, watching them go, then began to shake. He closed his eyes, willing himself to control the anger and the deepening darkness. He inhaled sharply. When he opened his eyes, Aleksandra was staring at him.

"Are you all right?" she said, her brow furrowed.

"Yes." Xavier nodded.

"More Southerners," Aleksandra scowled as she wiped sweat from her brow with the back of her sleeve, "running from home before the government takes their slaves away?"

"That'll never happen," Xavier said, from between clenched jaws. "Too strong, too wealthy—cotton—slaves. Poor beggars down South." He peered around. "Even here. I can't believe it."

"Believe it," she said. "They're coming."

He shook his head. "I just wish we could stop it—the abuse, the owning."

Aleksandra wrapped her arms around him, held him close until the tremors quieted. She leaned back in his arms and studied his face, then seemed satisfied with what she saw.

"Having you here with me makes it bearable, I think." He kissed her.

"I'm so used to you being the strong one...sometimes I forget the demons that still eat at you," she said.

"So, when do you leave?" Nikolai Chabardine asked, a frown marring his features, as he sat with Aleksandra at the barn table piled with sweaty harness.

"It'll be at least a few weeks," Xavier said, sponging water down Rogan's neck and over his back. "Your papa must be able to get around before we go."

"We'd stay longer," Aleksandra glanced up at Vladimir's son from the saddle soap can at she was trying to open, "but I'm worried about my Mustang Dzień. He's back at the Fish Springs Pony Express station. We don't know if the Indian attacks out West have continued, or if they've—" She uttered an expletive, then reached for a screwdriver to pry off the lid.

The sixteen-year-old's eyes widened. "Mama said I mustn't say that, when I heard the teamsters say it." He beamed. "I'll practice when she cannot hear."

Aleksandra shot him a look. "Not your best idea, Niko. I'm sorry, I shouldn't have sworn," she said, with a wry grin, as Nikolai turned back to Xavier.

Nikolai got up and handed the sweat scraper to Xavier. "May I come with the two of you?"

"Sorry," Xavier smiled at the boy, "but you're needed here to help with your papa and the new garden. No *Moskva* stores here—you'll have to grow or catch your own food." He ducked, laughing, as the boy swung a hand at his shoulder. "Can you shoot that rifle of yours?"

"Yes, I can, and I love it here. It is very different from *Moskva*. Fewer people, and much warmer." He quirked a brow.

"Staying here and helping your family keep an eye on this place is a big help to us, Nikolai." Aleksandra was silent for a moment. "We might not be coming back for a while." Her eyes filled, and she glanced at the sponge in her hand to hide her tears.

Her heart ached for her father, dead only a month, and the rest of her family in their little graveyard in the orchard.

How can I leave this—them—here?

She gulped and forced herself to attend to the conversation.

"It is our pleasure," the young Russian was saying, with a slight bow—a glimmer of his father in his action. He glanced at her face. "Are you OK, Aleks?" His forehead creased.

"Yes, but this has always been my home... you'll understand about leaving home." She tried to swallow past the lump in her throat. "You've come a long way, too."

"Yes, but we came to find Papa." He smiled softly.

"And you've found him." Xavier said briskly. "As for the time remaining to us here, your father said you may join into my *shashka* lessons, now that I'm no longer a danger to you."

"Really?" The boy's eyes lit up, then he laughed. "You, a danger to me?"

Xavier's lips twisted. "His words, not mine."

"How long have you been taking fencing lessons?" Aleksandra said.

"Five years, it has been." The boy stood taller as he replied. "Mama desired that I should know something of the art at which my papa excels."

"Wise woman," Aleksandra raised a brow at him, her hands full of soapy sponge and harness. "She told me you were accomplished. It's but a small step up to handling a *shashka*."

"You'll try not to hurt me too much, eh Niko?" Xavier asked, with a sheepish grin, and turned back to the colt to scrape the last water from his rump.

"Never."

"Would you like to walk Rogan cool while I help Aleksandra clean the harness?"

"I should be happy to," Nikolai said, as he took the leadrope and walked out into the spring sunshine, chattering to the big bay.

"WHAT DO YOU PLAN TO TAKE?" Tatiana Chabardine asked.

"We take only what we can carry on the horses," Aleksandra said, staring at her mother's oak secretary, then gulped and turned back to Vladimir's wife.

"Your delaine will stand you in good stead," Tatiana said, smoothing a hand over the blue woolen muslin. "It's just the color of your eyes." She moved it aside to lift another bolt of fabric from the chest, then paused. "This is lovely," the Russian woman murmured as she fingered the bolt of fine material beneath her hands.

"Oh, the lawn. Yes," Aleksandra said. "Papa brought it back for me from Great Salt Lake…" frozen, she gripped it in her hands and tears flowed onto the fabric, darkening its sprigs of lavender flowers, "…City," she finished, trailing into silence. Tatiana wrapped her arms about her and hugged her to her chest.

"I'm so very sorry for the loss of your papa, and at Vladimir's hands, albeit accidentally. We cannot ever make that up to you—but I thank you with all my heart for what you have given to me and Vladimir, not to mention Niko." She tilted Aleksandra's chin up and smiled into her eyes. "He idolizes you, do you know? I'm afraid he will never find a woman to compare to you, so we should have him around for a good, long while."

Aleksandra laughed through her tears and gave the woman one last hug before stepping back and wiping her eyes. She picked up the lawn and held it to her face for a moment. "I'll use it to make a dress to be wedded in, as soon as I find the time," she whispered, then placed it back into the trunk with care.

"I wish I could be there for your wedding." Tatiana gave her a wistful smile. "One is never sure where one will end up, no? In the meantime, we will begin on the gown before you leave."

"Thank you. I was afraid to cut into it myself. I've only made muslin dresses and shirts for Papa since Mama died."

"We'll surely have it well in hand before you leave," Tatiana said, "and thank you, again, for letting us stay here. It is a dream come true for all of us."

"I'm happy you'll be here to take care of it. We're not sure whether we'll return or not, nor when, so it is helpful to know you'll be here—" Aleksandra paused, her hand gliding over the surface of the secretary, "—and that things like this will be kept safe for a little longer. There's no way to carry this with us, and it has no place in the goldfields. I'd hate to see Mama's dream cut up for firewood." She tried to swallow past the lump in her throat.

"We will care for everything as if it were our own. After Vladimir's healed…" Tatiana's face lost a bit of color, but she carried on, "…we will find you, wherever you are."

"We'll keep in contact." Aleksandra bit her lip. "We've been watching over our shoulders for Vladimir for the past few decades. I wouldn't know what to do if we lost track of him now."

"I've never been so far from a hospital before, although," she gave her a wry grin, "that could be a blessing in disguise, with the spread of disease in them."

"Vladimir will get better..." Aleksandra bit her cheek, wishing she could be sure, "...surely." Tatiana reached out and gripped her hands and opened her mouth to speak.

Rogan's trumpet echoed from the orchard, his hooves beating a tattoo on the packed ground of his field. Over the tumult, Aleksandra heard hoofbeats coming at speed down the wagon trail toward them. Raising an eyebrow at Tatiana, Aleksandra grabbed her rifle from its deer-antler rack on the wall, checked it was loaded, and slipped to the side of the open doorway as an Indian on a painted pony enter the clearing at a run.

2

The Indian's Mustang returned Rogan's call.

"Dancing Wolf!" Aleksandra bolted back to return the rifle to its rack, then raced out the door with a laugh. She reached the pair as the Indian slid from the horse. He pulled the thong serving as a bridle from the pinto's mouth, and the horse trotted away to trade scratches with Rogan over the gate.

The scowl on her childhood friend's face stopped her for a moment. She peered at him from the corners of her eyes. His frown finally cracked into a half-hearted attempt at a smile.

She hunched her shoulders. "You've heard, then...about my last scrape, with Vladimir?"

"That, and your last Pony ride, all the way to Roberts Creek and back? Dead men, burning stations and *Pah-Utes* on the warpath? Can't you stay out of trouble for even a week?"

His grip on her shoulders hurt.

"I do try." She winced.

He shook his head and wrapped his arms around her for a few moments. "Tell me about it, *Kwahaten*" he murmured, then dropped his hands to his sides and turned toward the cabin.

She smiled briefly at his use of her Indian name—*Shoshone* for the graceful antelope—then shot after him and grabbed his arm. "Wait, Dancing Wolf." She stopped. "Umm...Vladimir's...inside."

The Indian whipped the bow from over his shoulder and she lost her grip on him. An arrow was nocked on the string before could reach him again.

"Inside?" he hissed. "What is your father's killer doing here?"

"It's OK, wait," Aleksandra said. "In his condition, he couldn't hurt anyone. His wife and son are here, too."

"From Russia?" His eyes bulged. "Tell me all," he said grimly.

She half-led, half-dragged the *Shoshone* warrior away from the house to a seat in the barn. Once she was sure he'd stay put, she told him the story, or part of it, anyway, of her abduction by Vladimir, her and Xavier's plot and deception to escape him, their escape, Vladimir's downfall, and his redemption. The hard lines on Dancing Wolf's face slowly relaxed as she spoke.

"So he didn't kill your papa, after all," he said, his voice heavy with doubt.

"No, he didn't." She wished she sounded more certain. "If you knew nothing of them before today—"

"—is he responsible for this?" he interrupted, and held up her bandaged wrist.

"Well…"

"He is." The Indian jumped to his feet. "He will pay."

"He has paid," she said dryly. She lunged forward to grab the hem of his shirt and pulled him back to sit beside her. "He's half dead in there. His horse collapsed on him and he's quite broken, but not dead yet."

"And won't be, if I have anything to say about it," Tatiana said, as she walked toward them, with an edge to her accented, but clear English.

Tatiana stretched out a hand to him. "You must be Dancing Wolf. Aleksandra has told me so much about you."

He stood frozen, looking at her. His frown finally softened as she continued to smile at him, fingers still extended.

"As I was saying," Aleksandra continued, "if you knew nothing of them before today, you'd think they were some of the nicest people you'd ever met." She raised a brow at him and walked away, leaving him to Tatiana's tender mercies.

The three of them walked into the cabin half an hour later, the Indian ducking his head to miss the sill, seemingly without noticing its presence. Aleksandra chuckled.

A lesson he'd learned years ago.

He frowned at her for a moment. "Oh, the doorway," he said. The corners of his mouth turned up, as he lifted one hand to touch his head. His brows narrowed again as he turned to look at the man propped up in Aleksandra's father's bed.

"You are responsible for the killing of my friend Krzysztof?" He enunciated with care.

"In that I trained him to fight, as a young man, and that an arms master should have been able to prevent his opponent from falling upon his own sword, yes, I am. I am prepared to make amends, if at all possible."

"Dancing Wolf, it's over." Aleksandra stepped between the pair and introduced them. "Thank you for protecting me, but it's done."

"I cannot hope for your forgiveness," Vladimir looked from the Indian to Aleksandra and back, "but I will ask anyway," said the pale man, leaning back against the headboard.

"It is my father, Krzysztof's brother by blood, from whom you must seek forgiveness."

Vladimir stared at Aleksandra, one brow raised.

"Chief Golden Hawk of the *Shoshone*. Papa's blood-brother," she said.

"When I am able to seek him, I will hasten to do so," Vladimir said clearly. "If he wishes, he may visit here, as we will be staying indefinitely. As you can see," he waved an arm, indicating the bandages and thick splints running the length of his leg, "I'm not going anywhere soon, unless it be to Heaven."

Tatiana's sharp intake of breath filled the silence, then Dancing Wolf took a deep breath and walked closer to Vladimir.

"If it is as you say, you may live. If I find out otherwise…"

"Dancing Wolf!" Aleksandra growled. He turned and moved toward her, standing near the door. "Forgiven. Not forgotten, but forgiven. He has made amends, and will continue to do so. For my sake, please bury it?" She turned on every bit of pleading guile she knew.

He shook his head at her. "You always get away with it, don't you?" he whispered. "You have me wrapped around your finger." His frown cracked again.

Vladimir smiled wanly from his place while Dancing Wolf seated himself on a bench.

"We're about to eat, will you stay?" Aleksandra said.

The Indian smiled at her as she carried hot soda bread and *kielbasa* to the table. "I've missed your bread. No one makes it in our village."

"Sorry, it's not sourdough. At least there was some of the *kielbasa* I left with Scotty at the trading post," she said. "The *zakwas* and sourdough starter are at Fish Springs Pony station…" she sobered, "…if it still stands, anyway."

Dancing Wolf cut some bread and added crispy, curling slices of the sausage, then got to his feet. Aleksandra swallowed hard against the lump forming in her throat.

He's leaving already…

He looked at her and grinned, proceeded to the bed, and handed them to

Vladimir. He and the Indian locked eyes, then Vladimir nodded ever-so-slightly.

"Thank you, Dancing Wolf, for your consideration." The Indian returned to the table and took another slice from Aleksandra. He brought it to his face and inhaled deeply. "Sourdough or no, your bread is the best."

"That's only because you haven't tasted Tatiana's." She quirked an eyebrow at him. "It's like Mama's."

The man pivoted slowly to face the Russian woman and smiled his best smile.

"So I'll expect you regularly, shall I?" Tatiana smiled. "Another friend in America, even if it is just cupboard love."

He protested, but another piece of the steaming loaf quieted him.

After they'd all eaten their fill, Dancing Wolf stood and once again approached the invalid's bed.

"I'm glad to find my best friend in the world alive here today. Be sure your dealings are honorable," the Indian said.

"You have my word on that," Vladimir said, his lips in a grim line. "Thank you for your understanding. I already offered Aleksandra a sword, and my neck, but she didn't take them."

Dancing Wolf's eyes widened. "You're a braver man than I, for I've seen her with a *shashka*. Go well, Vladimir. I shall return."

"I hope to see you soon," the Russian returned, with a nod, and a smile.

Dancing Wolf, Tatiana and Aleksandra walked down the steps together.

"After all these years, I finally understand why your father has trained you like a man," the Indian said.

"What do you mean, like a man?" Aleksandra hissed.

He blinked, and looked from her to Tatiana and back. "You had a need to protect yourself. A valid one."

"Yes, I understand," she mumbled, then picked up her head and sighed. "But it doesn't mean I can't fight as well as any man."

"Never said you couldn't." Dancing Wolf raised one brow at her and scanned the orchard. His pony walked the fence, ears pricked, gazing from side to side. "Where's Dzień?" He turned to Aleksandra, a frown marring his smooth forehead.

"*Dzień*? Day?" Tatiana's brow furrowed.

"Yes, 'day' in Polish." Aleksandra said. "I was quite young on the beautiful, sunny day when I named him. No one liked 'Beautiful' for a colt." She nodded at the Indian's Mustang. "He and my Dzień were raised together, as we were." She looked at her friend. "At ten years old, we were each given a colt by Dancing Wolf's father to raise and train for our own, up there." She waved a hand toward the mountains to the north, and tears blurred her vision.

Tatiana glanced at her with a soft smile.

"I'll leave you two to say goodbye," the Russian woman said, and shook the Indian's hand. "Thank you for your understanding. There will be bread waiting." She grinned over her shoulder and headed for the house.

"You leave soon to pick up Dzień?" Dancing Wolf asked. She looked away from him until he reached out a finger and turned her face to his.

"Sad again?"

"I miss your family, and Papa. Your father was so good to me, to Papa, to all of us."

"Every day he regrets sending you away," Dancing Wolf sighed, "but his love for you would not permit him to keep you with us. The *Pah-Utes* are inciting even the peaceful tribes to join them on the warpath against the settlers…and the Pony Express. You would never be safe with us when they come to talk war, no matter that you were allied with the family of the Chief —even if you were married to his son—" His voice dropped to a whisper.

"I understand, my friend." Clamping her jaw tightly, she wiped the tears from her eyes in one rough movement and looked up at him.

Sometime in the past, unbeknownst to her, Dancing Wolf had asked for her hand, but her father had believed her to be too young. She'd only been told of it after she'd found her father dead and gone to their village, hoping to be taken in. By then, it was too late. The chief knew her life would be at risk with the Indians, and had tearfully sent her back to her own people.

"I am told you've seen the carnage on the trail, on your ride to Roberts," he said. The cold lump in her stomach which she'd tried to forget returned with a vengeance. She reached out and took his hand, then set her jaw.

"All the Pony Express stations between Roberts Creek and *Ibapah* have been destroyed by Indians. I rode past them all. I stopped and looked," she shuddered, "where there was any chance of a survivor, and kept going." She looked at him and swallowed hard against the rising gorge in her stomach. "I saw men…" She fell silent.

"Killed?"

"S…s…"

"Scalped." He whispered, then hugged her close. "It's unspeakable."

"How could Indians do such a th—"

"—it's not just the Indians." He frowned. "The colonists and their government used to pay for Indian scalps, ever since they came to America."

"I d-d-didn't know that," she stuttered, staring at him.

"Doesn't make it any more right," he said. "The Indians do it and the white men do it." He paused and looked hard at her. "Are you OK?"

"I think so," she said, straightening, and he let go of her.

"And I hear you rode over three hundred miles in one run?"

She nodded. "There were few replacement horses. Some went further than I would have ever asked them, if I had a choice," she said, to her boots, then froze. She held her clenched her fists to her mouth against the nausea, her head spinning. "The dead men and stock, riddled with arrows...and tomahawk—"

"-stop," he cut in, and grabbed her fists, opening her hands and holding them together between his. "You'll make yourself ill."

She gritted her teeth and pulled herself together. "I was nearly discovered by the Indians as they raced down the hill towards Roberts Creek station." Her teeth were chattering by the time she finished.

"You cannot continue to put yourself in such danger, *Kwahaten*." He gripped her fingers, as if willing her to look at him. "You are too special to die."

"We don't know when, or if the Pony will resume." She took a deep breath and continued, like she hadn't heard him. "We thought we'd head for the big silver strike at Virginia City for a few months. It's unlikely the Pony will start up again in that...that...time." Her voice quavered off toward the end. She stopped and dropped her gaze again.

"What is it you don't wish to tell me, *Kwahaten*?" he asked softly.

He knew her too well.

"Dancing Wolf," she said, in a small voice, "Xavier asked me to become his wife, and I accepted." She glanced up to see the Indian look away, his face tight, before turning back to her.

"I wish you both the best," Dancing Wolf said formally, then stopped. "You know I wished you for my own, but Spirit has decided it is not to be. I truly wish the best for both of you."

Aleksandra's heart leapt at his acceptance, and she hugged him quickly before turning toward the sound of an approaching horse. Charro, and Xavier.

Xavier.

He rode toward them, staring in silence at his intended and the Indian standing side by side, the *Californio's* jaw rigid and his eyes hard as flint.

3

Aleksandra went to meet Xavier, riding on his gray stallion. She gave Charro a pat, then reached up for the packages Xavier held before him, her eyes on his stony visage.

"Good trip?"

He made no answer, and she glanced back over her shoulder at her childhood friend, then back to Xavier.

"Dancing Wolf has come to make sure, once again, that I'm OK," she said, at his continued silence, as tears cooled on her cheeks.

Xavier shook his head, inhaled deeply through his nostrils and stared at Aleksandra's face. He turned to the Indian. "Thank you, again, for seeing to her," he said, and gritted his teeth.

"I am here for her anytime. You know that, Xavier," the Indian said quietly.

Xavier dismounted and walked toward the Aleksandra and Dancing Wolf.

"This time...it was me who should have listened," Xavier said. "Aleks knew Vladimir was a danger and I didn't believe her. Because of that, I almost lost the one who is most special to me," he glanced at her "and to you as well." He reached out to Dancing Wolf and shook his hand. "Please, I have behaved atrociously. To friendship." He squeezed the man's hand and they looked at each other for long moments.

Aleksandra held her silence, struck by the strength of their love for her, despite the trouble that seemed to follow in her footsteps, and by their new mutual acceptance.

"The more I learn about Aleksandra," Xavier said, raising a brow at Dancing Wolf, "the more I see it will take both of us to keep her out of trouble. Come on into the cabin. I'm sure you've heard the story? The man Aleksandra's family feared the most, and rightly so, now seems to be…not an enemy, but a friend."

"Yes. In the past few hours, I've gone from desiring to revenge Krzysztof to making friends with Vladimir. I've been invited back, so I must've done something right." He gave Xavier a wry grin. "Speaking of which, I wish to offer my congratulations to you both. If I cannot have your woman in my life, I can't think of a better man for her."

He whistled for his pony, slipped the horsehair loop around his jaw and vaulted on.

"Take care, all of you. I'll see you soon," he called over his shoulder, as the skewbald loped away.

XAVIER PULLED BACK the quilt and slid into bed beside Aleksandra. "I'll get over this someday, but when I saw you standing with Dancing Wolf…my heart hit my boots again." At her look, he hurriedly began again. "I know the situation. You were raised with him, but I also understand you were nearly promised to him—"

"But—"

"I know, I know," he held his fingers to her lips to stop her protest, "you weren't told of it. I believe you, but it still scares me. I trust you and I keep trying to remember that everything will work out."

"It's OK." She looked down at her hands for a moment, then closed her eyes.

"I'm just trying to be honest, as you've asked of me."

She sighed and looked him in the eyes. "Yes, I did, and it *will* all work out." She tried for a smile and nearly won.

"I just wanted you to know. It shocked me for a moment, I had my panic and then I got over it. I may win this one yet."

"You will, we will."

"It's so good to know I've made another friend, and that he's also looking out for you, because Lord knows, I need the help. You're a handful, *Chiquita*."

She shook her head as he took her into his arms and held her close.

"ROGAN IS BEING SO GOOD, is he not?" Nikolai tried hard to whisper. The colt tipped an ear back, listening to the boy who held the reins.

"Yes, he is, but let's not push our luck." Xavier looked sideways at him, then past him to Aleksandra on the wagon bench seat. Nikolai smiled and held the reins firmly, but with a deft touch. The boy was a natural. He glanced ahead at the wagons parked outside the trading post.

"There are people at Scotty's trading post today. I've never seen so many," the young Russian said, as they neared the log cabin beneath the lofty red obelisks of Weber.

"Yes, there are." Xavier frowned. Rogan skittered sideways as raised voices came from inside the building, his eyes bugging.

"How about you give me the reins, Niko, and you can go in with Xavier?"

He nodded and carefully handed the lines to her.

"Maybe we'd best stop back here a ways, Xavier? I'll keep Rogan moving," Aleksandra said. "Neither of us like crowds."

"Ok. Let us off here then?"

She nodded, then turned all her attention to the nervous young stallion. "I'll go past and walk him toward the river. You don't need more than a few minutes, do you?"

"No, that will be fine. Take care." He frowned. Rogan had only been driven to the dogcart a few times and was still pretty unpredictable.

"He'll be fine when we get away from all the shouting in there." She glanced towards the trading post as the wagon passed it, then turned back to the horse, crooning to him all the while. Xavier watched her go, her slim, upright body swaying with the gentle movement of the wagon as the horse settled into his regular ground-eating walk. They'd be OK. He smiled and walked up the steps to Nikolai, who danced from foot to foot on the porch.

"I said no, and I mean no," the voice of Scotty, the proprietor, came to them through the open door. "I'm not normally rude to customers, but you've gone too far."

"Stay behind me, Niko," Xavier said, as he stepped into the store and sidled to the right, his back to the corner, to see what was upsetting the normally-placid Scot.

He didn't have far to look. A couple near the flour barrels to his left stood stock still, staring at the disturbance at the front counter.

"I wanna sell 'er t'ya. She'll make ya a good housekeepah, she's been a good help fer m'wife here." He gestured to his left at a thin woman in a tidy blue muslin dress and pinafore standing beside him, her back to the door. To his right, head bowed toward the ground, stood a negro woman. Her dress was several shades less tidy and new than that of the Southerner's wife. And she was pregnant. Very pregnant.

"She'll warm yer bed too," continued the man, grinning at the red-faced Scotty like an idiot, and his wife turned away. "She's a good breedah, too."

Scotty took a step toward him, fist raised, as the man's wife spun away toward the door. Her face was pinched, mouth in a hard line. The wife's head shot up, her eyes wide, to see she had not one, but two groups of observers. She gritted her teeth and turned back to the men.

"You'd better get out, before I—" the shopkeeper growled.

"Kin I talk alone fer a minute with the man, Georgia? Please?" he said to his wife. She stomped away to finger a bolt of calico halfway to the door.

"I've nothing to say to you," Scotty growled.

"Now see here, suh, I don'wanna let this Mary go, but my missus, she's makin' me. Seems she ain't gettin' wi'child herself, an' when she sees how'as Mary's breedin', well, it makes her a bit crazy-like."

"Livin' with you would make anyone crazy-like," Scotty growled. "Now get out." He gave an apologetic smile to the colored woman still standing beside the pathetic man. "I'm sorry fer you, miss, but I don' hold with slavery, Utah bein' a slave state or no."

"But wait," the Southerner said, "look here." He pulled the drawstring holding the slave's blouse together at the neck and the fabric dipped below her full breasts. She looked like she wanted to die. "Ain't they somethin'? Wouldn't you like—"

"Get out," Scotty roared, and the man blinked and finally backed up.

He turned to his wife. "Ah, Georgia, I tried, but it ain't no use. I did try," he whined, as he looked at the slave's exposed breasts while she tried to recover the cord and tie it with shaking hands.

"You're not trying very hard," she hissed. "I won't sleep another night in her presence, even if she's under the wagon. I just won't. And soon there'll be a baby, then what will you do?" She rounded on him and he cringed. "Be back in her bed?"

"Come on," he said, and the two women followed him toward the door. His gaze met Xavier's and his eyes lit up. "Say, suh, could ah interest you in this fine—"

The man froze and went pale as Xavier neared him, then he grabbed the hands of the two women and ran from the store as if pursued by the hounds of hell.

"Xavier, was that man…" Nikolai whispered.

"Forget him," he said. Nikolai took one look at his face and took two steps back, his hands held up before his face.

"Xavier, come back," Scotty said, in a firm voice.

He took a few deep breaths and the darkness lifted…a little.

"Sit down, lad," Scotty said. "Close your eyes. It'll go away. He's gone."

"*Dios mío*. My God, I can't stand it, Scotty," he managed. "Isn't there anywhere we can get away from the abuse?"

"Xavier?" Nikolai whispered from three feet away and he picked up his head to look at him. "I've brought you some water. Will you have a drink?"

He reached out a hand for it. "*Gracias*, thanks, *mi amigo*. I'd rather whisky, but water's probably safer right now."

"You OK?" Scotty hunkered down beside him. "With all the Southerners comin' West, we're seein' more and more o'this. I don't like it one bit."

"Me either. Aleks and I are considering our next move. This is making California look better and better."

"Plenty o' Southerners comin' through here, talkin' 'bout makin' California a slave state, too." He twisted his lips. "'Secessionists', they're callin' themselves."

"So I've heard, but it can't happen there, surely."

"For your sake, let's hope not. Now, young Nikolai, how's your papa faring with his broken bones?"

He'd gone rather pale, but perked up to speak with Scotty. "He's doing well, and teaching Xavier and me how to fight with *shashkas*. Aleksandra already knows, and she's helping."

"And that lovely mother of yours?"

"She's well, trying hard to keep Papa to his bed," he gave the Scot a crooked grin, "it is difficult, she says, so she must stay there with him often."

"Wise woman." Scotty chuckled. "Now, I suppose you came to pick up the tools you need to grow your family's food this year?"

The boy stood taller. "Yes, sir."

"Let's get those loaded up, then. Xavier, you just come out when you're ready."

"I'll be right there. Aleksandra should be along soon, if she's not already."

They left him sitting on a chair contemplating the relative merits of guns vs. *shashkas* for men like the one who'd just left the trading post.

"I wish I could make it all go away for you," Aleksandra whispered. The sheen of sweat sparkled on her skin in the early morning chill as she slowly leaned forward and took his face in her hands. She kissed him thoroughly, deeply. As deeply as he'd been into her as the dawn broke.

"*Dios mío*, but how you do. If you only knew," he murmured, her tears salty on his lips.

"I can't fix it, it's here to stay," she said, and sat up, astride him, narrowed brows marring her face.

She rose and fell with his deep breaths.

"The abuse, I cannot—" He closed his eyes. "*No puedo*, I can't stand the abuse. I lose control completely."

"I can't abide it, either," she hesitated, "and you know more of it than I, with your—"

"—father...it makes me think of my father."

"Your stepfather. At least you know that now."

"*Sí, gracias a Dios*, his blood does not run through me. At least I now know I will not turn like him, and do unspeakable things..." He fell silent. "But it's not that alone...growing up on the *rancho*, there were so many servants—slaves, I now know—whom I have taken for granted."

"And now you know, you can help them, no?" she said, and gripped his hands tightly before her.

He frowned. "I've been thinking. Maybe we should go on to California."

Her face lightened. "To your *rancho*?"

He nodded, scarcely daring to smile. Fear squeezed his heart until he had trouble breathing, but it had to be better than the paralyzing emotions he encountered almost daily here now.

Can I really go home again?

His mother wanted him back there, but his brothers? To inherit it, as the eldest son, out from beneath them after they'd worked it for so many years? His jaw tightened. He couldn't go back with nothing to show for his time away.

Aleksandra drew a deep breath and his thoughts fled.

"I'll miss—" she hesitated, and paled, "our ranch."

"Where your family lies." His eyes held hers, and he gripped her suddenly-cold fingers.

She blinked as her eyes filled, and tears dripped cold onto his belly.

He pulled her down on top of him and held her close, their bodies entwined in every way.

"I can't return them to you, but we'll never forget them, and," he pulled his head back and tilted her chin up to meet his, "we'll teach our children about them. Every day."

He went rock-hard as he spoke, and began to move again. The intensity in her eyes matched the fire in his loins, and soon, all words were forgotten.

THE DAY of their departure finally dawned, clear and bright.

"Goodbye," Xavier called back toward the family in the cabin doorway, as they rode away.

"Vladimir," Aleksandra shouted, "you behave for that lovely wife of yours.

Your sorry hide won't be worth a penny if I hear you've not been a perfect saint for this woman who's traveled halfway around the world to find you!"

"That I'll do, that I'll do," he replied, and smiled at Tatiana.

They headed for Great Salt Lake, the horses snorting in the morning breeze, keen to be on the trail again. They snatched at tufts of spring grass, just beginning to grow.

Aleksandra took a deep breath of the sharp air.

They traveled light—*pemmican*, two bedrolls, a few bags of herbs, food, horse feed and their weapons. The horses could trot freely, and they made good time, until Xavier's horse suddenly went dead lame in his right fore as they slithered across a patch of loose rock. They both dismounted and led the horses to firm ground, then Aleksandra watched as Xavier pried the start three-sided stone from beneath Charro's shoe.

"Lucky that didn't puncture his hoof," Aleksandra said, and Xavier nodded.

The horses flung their heads up at the sound of rifle shots echoing up the canyons from the meadow far below.

"That's no hunting party." She glanced at Xavier. "Who could be out here, of all places? There's not that much game around."

"I don't know, but we'd best find out," Xavier threw over his shoulder. He mounted his Andalusian and set off at a trot down a wagon trail so treacherous, the emigrants had to go down with their wheels locked. Aleksandra clucked to the big bay colt and vaulted on as he struck up a guarded canter behind Xavier's stallion.

His shout made her turn. He pointed down the hill, just north of the trail they followed. Below them, a cloud of dust teemed with swirling horses and men bristling with rifles. Xavier's gray slid to a halt, and Aleksandra swore as her bay swerved to miss him, then jolted to a rough stop beside them.

"Who is it?" Xavier shaded his eyes with his hand.

"Ummm…oh my dear Lord." She gulped and took a deep breath, feeling suddenly faint. "It's Ephraim Hanks and his men, and a black woman…and someone's on the ground. Quick, Xavier, we need to get down there."

4

Aleksandra gave Rogan his head and they bolted down the hill. She buried her fists in his thick mane and let the colt find the fastest way down.

Four of the riders spun, training their guns on them as they neared them.

"Mr. Hanks, Ephraim! Stop! It's me, Aleksandra!" she shouted at the top of her lungs.

"Hold fire, boys!" The Mormon's low growl cut across the distance and the muzzles lowered. Rogan cut across the distance in a matter of seconds, and bounced to a halt, granite chips flying, a few feet before the leader.

"Mr. Hanks, what's happened?" Aleksandra said. She looked past him at his Avenging Angels vigilante band gripping the arms of three white men. The remainder of them surrounded a black woman on the ground, holding a limp body in her arms.

"Aleks, Xavier." Ephraim acknowledged them, then turned back to glare at the trio standing still, their arms twisted behind their backs. "I want to know what's happening here," he barked.

"Is that man all right?" she called to him, as she slid from Rogan's back and hit the ground running.

"He's dead, you can stop racing around, Aleks. As for these men, they've not opened their mouths yet," he scowled, "but I'm beginning to figure it out."

Silence reigned, other than the sobs of the colored woman.

Aleksandra turned to her. "Are you all right, miss?"

The woman stopped crying and stared at her, the negro woman's tears making tracks down her face and onto the dusty and tattered muslin dress she wore. She glanced at the two sorry-looking bays standing beside the trail. Her whole body tensed as if she would run, then she took a breath and stilled. "This is my man, that thoose others haf just shot," she said, her voice oddly accented.

Aleksandra stepped back to keep her in her field of vision and still see the rest of the group.

"She's ours—" one of the captive men began. His comment, with a heavy Southern drawl, ended in a whimper as his arm was wrenched higher behind his back.

"That gives you the right to shoot a man, does it?" Ephraim said, and turned his back on him.

"They're escaped slaves," said another of the men, also from the South, by his accent.

"Be that as it may, you men aren't going anywhere 'till we get this sorted."

Two of them opened their mouths to answer, but flapped them shut again.

Ephraim backed up, motioning Xavier and Aleksandra to follow.

"What's up?" Xavier's brows nearly touched.

"Truth be told, we were on the way to see you, Aleks," he turned to her, "and here you are." He reached for her and gave her a quick hug. A longtime family friend, Ephraim was also a Pony Express station keeper. "A bit bruised and battered, by the looks of things, but you're OK?"

"Sure am, but this here, what's this about?" She frowned at the woman standing beside Ephraim's men.

"Not sure, but I'll get to the bottom of it. We heard shots and came to investigate. They might be runaway slaves, but we'll see."

Ephraim moved back to the three captive men, in varying stages of discomfort. "Right, who's in charge here?"

None moved.

"Righto, you there," he poked the end of his rifle at the closest one, "supposin' you start?" It wasn't a question, and the man jumped.

"Them'r escaped slaves, from our wagon train 'n they stole horses 'n guns."

"Your slaves?"

"Nope. A friend's ones."

"So why is one of them dead?"

The three men all looked at each other, but none spoke until Ephraim prodded him again.

"He shot at us first, it was self d'fence."

The black woman gasped, but said not a word. If she was pale before, she went positively white and slumped against the man on the ground beside her, eyes wide and staring as she bit her lips together.

"So where's his gun?" Ephraim said, past tight lips.

Silence. "Ahh…ahh've got it here," said one man, drawing his own gun from its holster.

"That so, is it?" Ephraim's face was thunderous.

The narrowed brows and bared teeth of the three men menaced in the slave's direction.

She dropped her head and swallowed hard.

Aleksandra closed her eyes as her stomach roiled from the sickly smell of fear-sweat, heavy in the air.

"Are these men telling the truth, miss?" Ephraim stared at her.

"If they say soo," she murmured to her lap, "it must be…trrue." She looked at the ground, her voice fading away at the end. She had an odd accent.

Dutch?

"So who do you say this woman and man 'belong' to, if not to you?" The Mormon turned back to the Southerners and glared.

"A business 'ssociate o' ours, never you mind who. This here's a slave state, so don' be botherin' 'bout us, we kin jus' take 'er back with us."

Ephraim gritted his teeth. He could do little more, if the woman wouldn't contradict them.

Aleksandra leaned back against Xavier and he wrapped his arms about her, tightly.

"That so, miss?" Ephraim said, more softly this time. "Do you know these men?"

She looked at the ground and nodded.

The three Southerners jerked their arms away from the Mormon's men and strode toward the woman. One took her arm and half-led, half-dragged her to the thinnest bay horse and tossed her up. Hunched over, she fumbled with her stirrups and stole glances at the man lying in the dust as she wound her hands into the horse's mane. Tears flowed like rain, without a sound, as they took her horse's reins and dragged it and the other exhausted horse away.

"What about this man?" Xavier yelled after them.

The men pulled up and turned back to them. "What man? Oh, him? A slave? Whatever y'all want. No good t' us anymore," he sniggered, and other two laughed. The three kicked their horses into a lope, dragging the bay with its reluctant passenger behind.

"Well, that went well." Aleksandra looked at the ground and shook her head, then flicked her gaze to the dead man lying in a pool of blood. She turned in Xavier's arms and squeezed him tight.

"Jesus, how can people think they own another person?" she whispered into his shirt.

"I don't know, *Querida*. Every day it eats at me...thinking about our Indian servants. Some of them loved us, the children, *y mi madre*, but they were still slaves, though I didn't know it, then."

Aleksandra glanced up at her man's face. His body was strung tight as a bow. She reached for his hands and held them.

He buried his face in her hair. "I'm sure my brothers still have servants, for which they have many uses." He finished on a growl. "I cannot help them until we return, but at least this man we can give a Christian burial." He squeezed her hands and let them slip from his, then turned to face Ephraim. "Do you have a burial ground on your place?"

"Sure do, and he'll be welcome there."

BURYING the man in the rocky ground on Ephiram's ranch let the men release some of their fury and pain at his needless death, as well as the hopeless situation of the female slave, still in the hands of the Southerners.

"We don't even know his name for the cross," Xavier said, an edge to his voice. Aleksandra took his hand and squeezed it. She looked into his haunted eyes and wrapped her arm around him.

"This can only get worse," Xavier said, "with all the unrest we're hearing from the Southern states." He sank down to sit on a log and pulled Aleksandra down beside him.

"I'm not likin' it any." Ephraim wiped his sweaty forehead with the back of his sleeve.

"Me either." Aleksandra frowned at Ephraim and continued, with a shudder. "The trouble in the South and out West...the Pony being shut down...we don't know how long it'll take to rebuild the burnt stations, or if they'll even be rebuilt." She bit her lip and looked up at him. "The Union needs that route open. The other stage route passes through too many Southern states to help keep this country together."

"You can't do much about the Pony for now," Ephraim said, "so what are you going to do in the meantime?"

"We're going to Virginia City until the Pony starts up again, and maybe someday," she flicked a glance at Xavier's back, "back to Xavier's family's *rancho* near San Francisco. Surely the whole secession idea will have blown over by then."

"No doubt," he said, but his furrowed brow and pursed lips belied his words. "Did you know," he threw over his shoulder to Xavier, behind him, "the *Californios*, almost to a man, are siding with the secessionists?"

Xavier froze, and paled beneath his tan. "Seriously?"

"Yep." Ephraim nodded grimly.

"We won't be seeing you for a while, then," Aleksandra dragged her eyes from Xavier's face and gave him a crooked grin.

"Well, gal, the boys and I," he glanced at the gang of toughs behind him who looked to be anything but boys, "will be heading to Virginia City sometime in the next year to have a little talk with a blasted buyer who seems to have forgotten he owes me money for a ranch north of Fort Churchill. We'll look you up then."

Aleksandra shuddered inwardly and looked away. She wouldn't want to be that man.

"We'll look forward to it." Xavier smiled.

She faced Ephraim again. "There'll be a meal waiting. I'm not sure where, but we'll make it happen." She grinned up at him. "And thank you, again," she said as he pinched her cheek and turned away toward his massive black stallion.

Xavier turned to Ephraim. "Anything else we can do to help you here?"

"No, son. We're all fine here. You two just head off, you've a long ride ahead."

"*GRACIAS A DIOS* FOR THE OPEN TRAIL," Xavier said, and let out his breath.

"*Sí,*" Aleksandra said. "It lets everything even out, puts things into better perspective?"

Xavier reached across and took her hand. "A little better now, eh? I could even consider eating again," he said, smiling at her.

Aleksandra opened the pemmican bag and offered it to him. "I might even be able to eat without feeling nauseous. She sighed. "I guess we just need to help those we can, when we can."

He grimaced and swallowed hard. "Yes. I kept control of myself with those Southerners. A near thing, but I did it. Good thing Ephraim was there."

"You can control it. I know you can."

He said nothing for long moments, just stared at his hand, gripping hers between the two horses.

Finally, he spoke. "Did you hear what Ephraim said, about the *Californios* backing the secessionists?"

"Yes." Aleks gritted her teeth.

"I'm thinking I don't want the *Rancho de las Pulgas* to back it. We need to get home. Mama would never countenance that, and she might need us—that's treason."

"Shall we go straight there?" A chill grew in the pit of her stomach as she spoke.

He hesitated. "I want to go back—for Mama's sake, and the rancho, but…I don't want to go back empty-handed, after all these years."

"Seven years is a long time."

"Seven years of my brothers' running my inheritance. I have to bring something back to make up for it."

"But you never thought to return and claim it."

"No," he shook his head, and whispered, "I never thought to see it again, ever."

"I'm glad your mother found you and helped you see the truth—and how much you are still loved."

The shadow of a smile flickered over his face. "If I can only get past the shadow of the abuse and learn people can be trusted—"

"—women, you mean?"

Xavier flushed and smiled. "Yes, women. Starting with you." He reached across to kiss her.

"THE TOP," Aleksandra breathed, as she slipped down from Rogan. "One of my favorite views." Great Salt Lake spread out before them, far across the horizon. The patchy, white desert surrounded its far borders, while snow-topped mountains behind and to the south framed the picture.

"Mine too, but I can't decide whether I like the view from here or Lookout better." Xavier said, as he dismounted. "Let's put that last scene away. We'll revisit it soon, but let's enjoy this time together."

"Sounds good to me." She closed her eyes and sighed.

"Back to Lookout," he murmured, "perhaps I just have the association in my mind with the lovely evening spent with you there."

She gazed at him. Her face grew warm and butterflies danced inside her belly. She reached for his hand and then grimaced. "My most recent experience at Lookout wasn't quite so pleasant. Dodging arrows at a full gallop down that rocky gully is something I'd rather not repeat too often."

"We need to look up that Mustang, Scout."

She smiled and reached up to kiss him. "He's usually ridden between here and Faust's and Lookout station, so hopefully he'll be at Doc Faust's and I can give him a good groom or some treats."

"I'm eternally grateful to him, and to Dancing Wolf's friend, who stopped the others from firing more arrows at you. Thank Christ they didn't have rifles. I owe that man and the horse more than I can say."

"Thank you for accepting the truth. Dancing Wolf and I have always been friends. He poses no threat to you, or us, in any way."

"Yes. I'm grateful he has the grace to accept my apologies and friendship, despite my past behavior." He dropped his chin to his chest.

"'All's well that ends well,' my mama always said," Aleksandra said lightly. "Are you ready to race me down the hill?" she said, as she turned away and set off. With a flick of his black tail, Rogan trotted down the grade beside her, while she grinned over her shoulder as the older stallion laid back his ears at being left behind.

THE TRAIL LED down the mountain to the Great Salt Lake flats. The immense body of water shimmering in the sunlight, and the tall buildings of the main street soon came into view.

"Is Johnny here?" Xavier asked the stable lad at the Great Salt Lake Pony Express station.

"Yes, but he's at his dinner." He pointed across the street at a saloon and returned to grooming the palomino stallion. Aleksandra gave him a pat as she walked past.

"I've ridden him, he's a 'good un', as they say," Aleksandra said.

Xavier smiled and took her hand.

"Aleks! And Xavier!" The grizzled station keeper stood up from his salt beef and biscuits so fast he nearly knocked the table over. A large fading bruise spread its way down one side of his face.

"Johnny." Aleksandra threw herself into his arms and he swung her around.

"Lass?" he blinked. "You were a boy last time we met. I must have missed something." When he let her down, even Xavier gave him a heartfelt hug.

"Are you OK? We heard what happened to you from Vladimir—"

"—Vladimir?" he spat out. "So have ye found the scoundrel, then?"

"Well, actually, he found me," Aleksandra grimaced, "and it wasn't pretty, but we wanted to thank you for your letter alerting Xavier of his whereabouts. Vladimir told us he did you a bad turn, too. In the end, we discovered he didn't actually murder my papa. His wife and son have shown up from Russia, and—"

"—lets talk through the whole story over a drink, OK?" Johnny said. "Are you two here for the night?"

"No, sorry," Xavier shook his head, "we're on our way to Doc Faust's, but we'd be glad to sit somewhere besides a saddle for a few minutes. The horses will appreciate a rest and a feed. I've put them in your stable, I hope you don't mind."

"Not at all, Xavier, not at all." He gestured to his table and motioned to the serving girl. "Funny thing was, other than the bump on the head he gave me," he paused and touched his face, his eyes narrowing, "I don't think he really meant me much harm. He dumped me quite a way away, but there was a road half a mile from the big rock he hid me behind."

"He'll be coming to visit you to apologize formally, and to turn himself in to the authorities if you wish to press charges, once his fractures are healed," Aleksandra said.

"I see you've had *quite* a conversation with him," Johnny's brows shot up as he took his seat. "Do tell," he murmured, after the girl took their order.

Aleksandra glanced at Xavier, who nodded. "You're due an account of the story. Vladimir has pursued my family for nearly two decades, upon orders from the Russian tsar, to find a secret formula my grandpapa and papa discovered when they still lived in Poland."

Xavier interrupted her. "Excuse me, but would you mind if I left you with Johnny for a few minutes? I have an errand to run."

She raised an eyebrow at him and cocked her head, then smiled. "Meet you back here?"

"*Sí*," he murmured, and squeezed her hand as she returned her attention to Johnny.

"Long story short, he tracked us to Utah and he and Papa fought. Papa," she gulped and steadied herself, "fell upon his sword and died. Vladimir didn't get the information he wanted, and knowing no one would believe his story, he kept pursuing 'Krzysztof's son.'

"Vladimire saw me ride away on the palomino that day. He apparently sat at this very window," she nodded at the panes before them, "with you." From what he said, he kidnapped you that evening," she grinned, "and told us you led him a merry chase way up north to the City of Rocks."

"Sure did, but he still found you, eventually." He frowned.

"It wasn't pretty, but it's done now. Vladimir's quite broken, but seems to be recovering. His wife and son showed up, from Russia, and all is forgiven. You'll no doubt meet him again—hopefully on better terms than before."

"I'm just thankful you're well, Aleks—"

She smiled. "It's Aleksandra, if you were wondering. More thanks to you, Johnny. Without the message you sent to Xavier, he might never have found me in time. I was on my way to Russia, else. I owe you one."

"Think nothing of it, happy to help," he said, but he flushed bright red with the praise.

"Excuse me sir." Xavier looked up from his perusal of the items in the glass-topped case in the general mercantile store. "Wasn't there a haberdashery near here for women's items, like fine under-things and, and…"

The man waited a moment, his lips twitching a little. "Rings?" he said.

Xavier took a breath, feeling it might be his last. "Yes, please, r-rings," he managed.

"It's one street over." The man smiled as he led the way to the door and pointed out the directions. "Don't feel bad, son, it's always a bit like that, no matter how much you care for a girl."

"Thank you, sir," he said with a laugh.

Chrissake, I've already asked her to marry, why is this so hard?

He upbraided himself as he stalked the block to the store in which he might lose his life as he knew it.

What if women truly can't be trusted? What then?

His feet found the store and he stood before another glass-topped case, this time in a room smelling of roses and feminine comfort. An extremely comfortable-looking woman approached him, a smile covering her face.

"Good day, sir, how may I help you?"

He opened his mouth, expecting words to exit, but none came.

"Would you be perhaps looking for some pretty trinket for a special girl? A figurine? We have a lovely china shepherdess, just arrived from back east, or… no," she waited a moment more. At his apparent inability to speak, she smiled. "A ring, perhaps?"

Am I really that obvious?

He gulped.

Be a man!

Xavier kicked himself. "Yes, please." He closed his eyes for a moment, concentrating on filling his lungs with air. When he opened them, he wanted to shut them again at the display of rings upon the tray before him. He stared at the rings, the glittering splash of silver and gold upon their bed of emerald velvet.

"This is our selection. Would she prefer a simple ring or one with more decoration? Silver or gold? With a stone? A colored stone or a diamond?"

Xavier pulled his eyes up from the endless array in time to focus on her last question.

"And what size is she?"

I can do this, really I can.

"Perhaps I may assist?" Her fingers roved over the rings. "What is she like? Is she highly decorative, preferring to be flamboyant, or is she a simple, active girl?"

Xavier began to relax. He could handle this.

"She's active, very active. I think those she would prefer the simple rings, otherwise it would get hung up in a horse's mane or something." He found himself smiling, but at his next thought, he frowned. "But she likes beautiful things as well."

"That helps a great deal. We can ignore this whole side. Well done, sir. Now, would she like a stone? Brightly colored or diamond?"

Xavier looked at the remaining rings. She might like a diamond. She liked the crystals her papa had brought her from the cliffs near Camp Floyd. A diamond ring in a gold setting caught his eye. Smoothly curving, diagonal ridges enfolded and protected the inset stone. It was perfect. She could have this symbol of his love, with its glittering crystal, and still be able to wear it every day without risking her fingers.

"How big are her hands?" The woman knew all the questions.

"Well, they are about this big." He measured the size of her hands against his own on the counter. He stopped, his mouth open.

She's become a part of me, without my even knowing.

He gulped. Perhaps this was what it was all about, this getting married. Maybe it would be OK…trusting. He swallowed again. Maybe, just maybe, he could do it.

"Perhaps this size?" she continued.

"This one will fit her," he said. "It's perfect. I'll take it. We're leaving town now and I wish to give it to her at a special place on the trail."

"I certainly hope you're right," she smiled, then pursed her lips and her brows narrowed. "I suppose if it doesn't fit, you can get it sized to fit her, wherever you are going."

"Oh, and would you perhaps know if there is a Catholic Priest in Great Salt Lake City?"

"No, I don't believe there is, I'm sorry."

"Thank you…and thank you for more than just the ring. "

She smiled at him as he bowed and turned to go. Did all men searching for a ring feel like this? From the responses of the man in the mercantile and the haberdashery assistant, probably so.

He felt different. He wasn't sure how, but suddenly it grabbed him. He finally knew what it was.

It was hope.

Maybe Aleksandra could be trusted, even if he had taught himself to believe no woman could be. Maybe he could go past his fear, his disbelief in others. Not everyone would abuse him as his father had. Many others in his life hadn't. Perhaps it was time for him to trust a little. He felt the familiar fear again, the clutching at his heart, but for the first time, he held the clutching hand in his…and the panic eased.

Trust.

He needed to try. He had to give her this much.

Feeling like a new day was dawning, he breathed it in. He laughed, and nearly skipped down the boardwalk to get back to her sooner, instead of walking like an adult. How would he keep Aleksandra's gift, wrapped in its colored paper and ribbons, a secret for days, when he wanted to rush to her and place it upon her finger on bended knee?

He closed his eyes and stifled a laugh, thinking of the wedding vows to come...love, honor and obey. Obey? Aleksandra?

5

The horses trotted through the rolling hills west of Great Salt Lake and onto the level plains again. Aleksandra and Xavier kept a close eye out ahead and behind. Johnny hadn't heard of any Indian trouble this far east. It had eased Aleksandra's mind that Fish Springs station was untouched, "last time a rider went through there, anyway," he'd added as an aside.

Travelers Rest and Rockwell's passed without incident and ahead, the low roof of Joe's dugout showed on the horizon.

"Haloo, Joe!" Xavier called out, not wishing to become afternoon target practice. A rifle muzzle, followed by Joe's head, appeared as he climbed out of the dugout.

"Oh, it's Xavier, and Aleks! Aleks? Where did that hair come from? Are you..."

"Yes, I'm a girl, sorry, and it's Aleksandra," she said.

"So you've been a girl all along?" The look on Joe's face was priceless, and they all enjoyed the laugh. As they left the station after watering for the horses, though, Aleksandra's glossy hair glinting gold in the sun made Xavier reconsider.

"Xavier! Welcome home," the sentry posted at the outskirts of Camp Floyd called out, a few hours later. "Do we finally get you back from Fish Springs?"

"Sorry, Jason, nothin' doin'. We're on the way back now, just passin' through," Xavier drawled.

"Miss." He nodded his head to Aleksandra, then his brow scrunched up as he stared at her in silence.

"Good day to you, sir," Aleksandra said, in her girl's voice as they passed, then sat frozen, holding her breath.

"What's the matter?" Xavier looked sideways at her.

She glanced over her shoulder at the private two hundred yards behind them and erupted in a flood of giggles.

He stared at her.

"He was one of the boys in the group that took Aleks-the-Express-rider boy to the saloon last time I was here—when I was beat up. He looked like he nearly recognized me, but not quite. It wouldn't do to be recognized." She sobered and they were both silent for a long moment.

"Aleks, it might be a good idea to keep your hair under a hat. I know you're in buckskins, but we don't know who we might run into, and you might be too tempting for some highwayman."

She frowned, but while they rode, she quickly braided her hair into a thick rope and coiled it up beneath her grubby ten-gallon hat.

"I wonder how the louts are that you cut with the broken glass?" Xavier said, his brows nearly touching.

"Let's not find out, and say we did?" She raised a brow at him.

"I'd like to see Desiree and thank her."

Aleksandra smiled. "Me too." The saloon girl had probably saved her life when she'd run out of the saloon, the entire room full of drunken men in pursuit. Desiree sheltered her and they'd shared stories and comfort—for the first time since her father had died. She owed her more than a simple thanks.

"We've not seen any Indians since we left Traveler's Rest," Xavier said, as he scanned the horizon.

"I wonder if the attacks will continue?"

"I don't know." Xavier thought for a moment, then continued. "It might be a good idea to see if any troops are heading west that we could join. We're not riding fast Express ponies."

Topping a rise just before the fort, they came upon a medium sized wagon train camped beside the trail, its Conestoga wagons parked in a defensive circle. Grazing on a long picket line just outside it, their horses stood to attention and called out to Rogan and Charro. The bullocks staked further out never even raised their heads from the sparse grass. Faded women in even more faded calico dresses and sunbonnets tended a group of children who quietly wrote on slates or recited their lessons.

"I wonder how they got across from the East this early?" Xavier glanced across at a group of men standing beside a gig. Their raised voices hushed when they noticed Xavier and Aleksandra on the trail nearing their camp. Two army officers, their bright blue uniforms a sharp contrast to the dull and dusty clothes of the travelers, extricated themselves from the cluster and walked around the circled-up wagons with one of the men.

"They must've left late in the year and overwintered somewhere in the Midwest," Xavier murmured.

A man patrolling the perimeter of their camp kept narrowed eyes upon them as they rode past. He gripped his rifle, lips set in a hard line.

"Aren't taking any chances, are they?" Aleksandra's brows raised. "And they're not even a minute from Camp Floyd."

"A man could barely squeeze in between those circled-up wagons. They look pretty worried." He shook his head and they continued into town.

Aleksandra kneed Rogan closer to Charro as the buildings crowded closer on both sides of the road. She removed her ten-gallon hat, tying it behind her saddle.

"What are you doing, woman?"

"Last time I was here, that hat got me into a heap of trouble. The big towhead who attacked me in the saloon, or someone else, might remember it. I'd rather that didn't happen." She bit her lip as she glanced around the busy streets.

"Despite the buckskins, with that hair, no one could mistake you for the grubby urchin in there," he nodded his head at the shiny gold-lettered sign outside the saloon as they passed, "not so long ago."

She looked at him from beneath her brows as their horses walked side by side.

"Keep an eye out for men resembling big, blond locomotives."

"Why don't you go see Desiree while I find out if any detachments are heading West? Are you OK on your own?"

She glared at him, then softened when he took her hand and squeezed it. "I'll be fine. I'm just not used to being looked after," she said, the ends of her lips finally turning up. "I'll see you soon."

THE US ARMY encampment was a flurry of activity, with blue-coated men scurrying past and rowed-up tents in every direction. The thunder of hooves and shouts of drilling men carried from the practice field beyond. Only the smell of cooking fires lent the scene a touch of homeliness.

Xavier finally found the commander's tent. Raised, angry voices carried from behind the dropped front flaps.

"You can't expect me to be a nursemaid to every snotty-nosed Easterner looking for the land of milk and honey," a gruff voice growled.

"But we need protection," a man with a high pitched Boston accent said. "We have women and children with us. We've paid our taxes to the U.S. Government, and we expect to be looked after. Besides, this letter," paper rustled from inside the commander's domain, "says the United States Army will take care of us as we cross the territories, to the best of their ability."

"Where did you get this?" the deeper voice queried.

"My cousin is the Governor of Kansas State. He said you would help us."

"Governor, eh?" He was silent for a moment. "I'll see what we can do to assist," he said on a long exhale.

"That's it, then, is it?" the Easterner said brightly.

"I'll see what we can do and get back to you shortly."

A man, dressed in civilian clothes, exited the tent and walked with a jaunty stride towards town, a smarmy grin on his face. He never looked at Xavier as he walked right past. Xavier shook his head. This couldn't be a good time to ask the commander for anything.

You don't ask, you don't get.

Xavier took a deep breath and closed his eyes for a moment, then tapped on the canvas. "Excuse me, General, sir, are you available to speak for a moment?" Xavier called out in the direction of the tent flap.

"Enter," he shouted, his booming voice anything but welcoming.

"Good afternoon, sir, Brigadier General Johnston," Xavier said as he ducked beneath the tent flap and hurried on. "I won't take much of your time. I'm Xavier Argüello and I used to be the Express station manager here. My fiancée and I are returning to Fish Springs, and I wondered if there are there any troops heading that way we can join?"

The general held out his hand. "Johnston is quite sufficient. I don't believe we've met, Mr. Argüello, but I've seen you about town. If you'd spoken with me a quarter of an hour ago, I'd have said no, but it appears," he pinched the bridge of his nose and took a deep breath, "the wagon train out there will be getting an escort, so you could probably tag along with my men."

"Thank you, sir."

"I don't imagine," a grin broke through the man's visage and his eyes brightened, "you'll be going quite the pace you're used to, but at least there'll be protection for you both." He waved Xavier toward a camp chair as he took a seat behind his table, piled high with rolls of missives and his writing implements. "Take a seat, man. Drink?" he said, pouring two glasses of water from a jug beside his feet. "So who's the lucky girl?"

"Someone I met back at Weber." Xavier looked down at his toe, digging a hole in the dirt floor of the tent.

"Congratulations. I'm sure you'll be very happy together." He sighed. "I'm glad you stopped by, gave me a chance to settle down a little."

"I appreciate your consideration, sir." Xavier stood and held out his hand. "Thank you for the drink, I must be off."

"And I must organize a small unit to..." he stopped, then continued beneath his breath, "...mollycoddle those blasted settlers. Governor's cousin, indeed..." The commander scowled at the ground, silent for a moment.

"When are we to leave?" Xavier's voice sounded loud in the silence.

"I expect they want to leave as soon as possible, so most likely at first light."

"Suits us. We'll be there."

"You should have time for a sleep-in, then, before they get going. They don't move very fast, with their entire life packed into those wagons."

"We can take our time, for once, then."

"And," the general continued, his voice dropping low, "prepare yourselves for a long trip. For the most part, the men of the land have stayed East—and few of them understand their conveyances require maintenance."

Xavier's brows shot up. "We're talking wheel and axle disasters?"

Johnston grunted.

"This should be an...interesting trip, sir," Xavier said, with a smirk. "Call out if I can help. Growing up ranching might come in handy after all."

ALEKSANDRA TIED Rogan before a general mercantile and walked back toward the saloon. Peering from the corners of her eyes at the double doors of the saloon, she gave it a wide berth and walked down the far side of the road. She crossed the street and headed for one of the doors set into the wall of the same building, then took a deep breath and knocked, hoping Desiree was alone.

"Just one moment, who's there?" Desiree said, through the door.

"It's Aleksandra. Xavier and I are passing through and I wanted to come by and say hello."

"Aleksandra, please come in!"

The door flew open and a petite brunette, her hair curling down past her waist, reached out a hand and drew her into the room. Glancing both ways outside the door, she pulled the door to and latched it, then spun to face her.

"I'm sorry, my hands are all wet." She glanced at the freshly washed dishes on the sideboard. "What brings you back to Camp Floyd? I was sure you wouldn't be..." She stopped, her mouth dropped open as she gripped Aleksandra by the shoulders and held her at arm's length "You're traveling as a woman!"

"I am now. I no longer need to hide, and can be myself. It's a relief," Aleksandra said, with a sigh. "Riding for the Pony was an answer to a dream, but it became a nightmare in the end. I'm thankful everything has sorted itself, but I came here to thank you again, and to see how you are."

"I'm fine, actually," she said, in a surprised tone, then her voice dropped to a whisper. "Can you keep a secret?"

"Of course," Aleksandra replied, *sotto voce* in return, intrigued.

"There's a wagon train just north of town, you'll have seen it, I expect?"

Aleksandra nodded.

"I've met a man there. He lost his wife while they overwintered on the prairie. He has three young children to care for, and he's asked me to come along to mother them." She looked at the floor for a moment, then lifted her face back up to Aleksandra's.

"Oh, that's wonderful, Desiree!"

"I'm sure, knowing how he met me, with my profession, there'll probably be more to it then just caring for the children," she flushed prettily, "but one man after many would be a blessing."

"Does he know about your condition?" Aleksandra had to ask.

"Yes, and he still wants me to come. I suspect that was what his first wife died of, by something he mentioned. He didn't think I'm any more likely to die on him than anybody else, pioneering, anyway. He seems a kind man, and it has to be better than what I have here." She looked around the room with raised eyebrows and took a deep breath.

"I'm so pleased for you, Desiree, and I'm sure Xavier will be as well."

"You're traveling with Xavier?" Her head shot up.

"Yes, he's asked me to marry him and we're on our way to Fish Springs. The Pony Express is on hold between Carson and Diamond Springs, so no work."

"I'd heard about the Indian attacks and the closure, but didn't the Pony keep running when there were attacks before?" Her forehead wrinkled.

"I guess they didn't put out the details. You want the truth?"

She nodded.

"There aren't any stations left standing along that whole stretch—no stock, no ponies, and no station keepers."

"But that's...that's..."

"Just so. Plenty of dead men and stock, and no ponies left there."

" All those men... and..." She stared at Aleksandra blankly, then shook her head and took a deep breath. "So, what are you going to do next?"

"We're heading for Virginia City for a while. We'll wait to see what happens with the Pony."

"Will you be traveling with the wagon train?"

"Xavier has just gone to ask if—"

A loud knock sounded and Desiree jumped. They swung toward the door and Desiree's face blanched. Aleksandra touched her arm to steady her.

"Aleksandra, are you in there?"

"It's just Xavier." Aleksandra let out her breath as Desiree rushed to lift the latch.

"Xavier, so nice to see you again," she said, with delight. She took his hands in hers, her knuckles white.

"It's good to see you, Desiree, how have you been?" He smiled down at her.

"I've been well," she said loudly, then closed the door, dropping the latch and pulling in the latch-string. With a glint in her eyes, she lowered her voice so she was barely audible and told him her news.

"The answer to your prayers," he whispered. "That's wonderful. Even better," he winked at Aleksandra, "we'll be traveling with your party. The sergeant I just spoke with is arranging an escort for the train."

Desiree's eyes glinted, then she bit her lip. "It might be tricky. The saloon owner won't be best pleased about my leaving."

"You're not telling him you're leaving?"

"You're kidding, aren't you?"

"Will you have any trouble getting way?" Aleksandra frowned.

"I don't think so. He sleeps late in the morning and the wagon train leaves at first light. We should be well away before he discovers I'm gone."

"Is there anything we can do to help?" Aleksandra whispered, wincing. A man on a horse could catch up to a wagon train in no time.

"Maybe just hide me, if he should come looking."

Xavier and Aleksandra both nodded.

"I don't think I'm worth that much to him," she said, with a shake of her head. "He probably won't bother sending anyone after me."

"It's not likely he'll give up so easily," Aleksandra said. "You're probably worth a fortune to him."

"Do you owe him money?" Xavier raised a brow at her.

"Not a thing, and he doesn't own me..." Desiree's voice trailed off.

"What?" Aleksandra frowned at the terrified look on her face.

"He's hurt those who tried to leave before." She stared at the floor. "It wasn't...pretty. He's vicious."

"Desiree..." Aleksandra gripped her hands and looked at Xavier from the corners of her eyes.

"But leaving a few of these dresses behind should appease him a bit." She lifted her head and set her jaw. Taking a deep breath, she plucked at one of the stained scarlet satin gowns hanging over a chair. "He'll have them to put on the other girls."

"You have some more plain dresses to take, I hope?" Aleksandra asked with a crooked grin.

"I have two calicos and a warm cape, so I should be should be well started," she said. "My new employer still has his wife's clothes and she was a trifle bigger than me, so I should be able to wear them."

"I can help you fit them in camp," Aleksandra whispered.

"Thank you. I look forward to spending time with you." She glanced from one to the other.

"I can't wait." Aleksandra said. "We'd better get out of your way. I'm sure you have things to do."

"Yes." She stared around the room. "I need to pack, though it mustn't appear as if I've done so, and there's not much time left before men start heading to the saloon." She gritted her teeth. "I won't have any time to myself after that until nearly dawn," she said softly, with a wan smile. "But that will soon be over."

"Is there anything you'd like us to take to the train for you?"

"Oh, could you? Would you please take this for me?" She pulled a small canvas bag from under the bed and handed it to Aleksandra. "Special mementoes and the money I've saved up," she hesitated, "in case something goes wrong."

"Nothing will go wrong. If you don't show up tomorrow morning, we'll return and demand your release," Xavier growled. "We can make up some story. If I have to say you're my wife, go along with it. Whatever we have to do will be done."

"Such friends as you…" Desiree shook her head and turned to hide the tears that filled her eyes.

Aleksandra and Xavier exchanged a glance as the brunette threaded the whipcord back through the door and lifted the latch to show them out.

"Goodbye for now," Aleksandra said.

"It was lovely seeing you both. I hope to see you again someday!" she called loudly as she waved them out the door.

"*Hasta luego.*" Xavier tipped his hat to her and she closed the door with a smile.

"Rogan is at the mercantile," Aleksandra said, taking his hand in a firm grip.

"So Charro told me, as we passed." He smirked. "I left him beside him. Seemed the wisest thing to do."

"We need food for the trip." She shook her head. "I forgot about it in Great Salt Lake."

"We had other things on our mind." He smiled and led her down the muddy road. "The Express station keeper invited us to eat with him before we leave."

"Such memories…your first station."

He cocked a brow at her. "The office where you and I really first began."

The place where he'd stopped her from nearly making a dreadful mistake, and then acceded to her request to become a Pony Express rider. It seemed forever ago, although it was only two months.

They purchased dry-goods, then collected the horses, stowing Desiree's sack in Charro's saddlebags. At the army camp, they stopped at a row of barrack tents to find the leader of the troop accompanying the wagon train. A private pointed out a tent, and the horses picked their way between tent tie-downs to the pavilion on the far side of the encampment.

"Captain Moore?"

At his nod, Xavier introduced himself and Aleksandra. "Thank you for allowing us to accompany you," he added. "We'll be ready to join you at dawn."

"Happy to have you along. An extra sharpshooter or two is always welcome," he said, glancing it the rifle holsters slung across both stallions' shoulders. "A hunting party will leave the train at midday, if you'd both like to join it?"

Xavier looked at her, brows raised. "I'd go along. Aleks?"

"I'll stay behind and talk with Desiree, but you go on.

"You're sure?" he asked.

She grinned and dropped her hand to the hilt of her *shashka*. "We're sure."

He shook his head. "Yes sir, I'd be happy to do my part. Until tomorrow, then?" Xavier touched the brim of his hat and they rode back to the Express station.

"I can't say I feel comfortable heading into Camp Floyd, anymore," she said, thinking about their last, surreptitious, exit from town. While she escaped the saloon brawl with only bruises and grazes, her opponents met the sharp end of her broken glass, and she wasn't keen to wait around to see if they would press charges against the 'boy' Pony Express rider she'd appeared to be at the time.

6

"Oh, no." Aleksandra froze, and Rogan danced sideways beneath her, ears back.

"What?" Desiree said, from her seat on the wagon box.

"I can't find my surgical kit." She made her body relax, and the colt sighed and walked on. "I took it out of my saddlebags last night to sharpen the scalpel blades...and left it behind."

"Do you need it?

"Only if I want to do some surgery," she said, through gritted teeth, and shook her head. "I'm going back to get it."

"Alone?"

At the look of horror on Desiree's face, Aleksandra smiled, but then she remembered the girl's previous boss. "I'll speak with the commander, you'll be all right."

She didn't look convinced. "It's you I'm worried about."

"I'll see if Xavier will come," she called over her shoulder as she rode toward the front of the train.

Captain Moore shook his head. "Sorry, Aleks, the men headed off early for their hunt. Xavier was showing them a place he knew..."

Aleksandra took a deep breath and held it.

"Anything I can help with?"

"I left something at Floyd. I came to tell him I was going back to pick it up."

"Alone?"

She rolled her eyes. "Desiree just said that. I'm the daughter of a trapper. I've spent most of my life alone out here."

"I don't doubt for a moment you're capable of it," he lifted a brow, "but I've a small troop of men headed that way in a few minutes." He glanced at her sword and gave her a wry grin. "They'll appreciate the protection, and I'm sure Xavier would appreciate the fact you were with a troop of soldiers."

She dropped her eyes, and couldn't keep the corners of her mouth from lifting a little. "Yes, thank you. Xavier would have my hide if he knew I'd been offered an escort and not taken it."

"They'll find you at your friend's wagon on their way past?"

"Yes, please. Oh, and about that…" she said, "Can you keep a secret sir?"

"Of course."

"Can you please keep an eye out for my friend, Desiree? There may be a man who comes from Floyd to try to claim her, but he's only her old employer, from the saloon. She owes him nothing, but he may insist. Feel free to say she's Xavier's wife, if you need to."

His brows shot up as high as they could go. "Of course. I'll watch out for both of them."

"Thank you, sir. I appreciate your confidence. Desiree would hate the exposure of her past life on this train."

"Any time, madame. You have my word." He tipped his hat and she spun Rogan back toward Desiree's wagon.

⌁

"IN TRUTH, I was annoyed to have an escort foisted upon me today, gentlemen, but you've all been rather entertaining," Aleksandra said, as she slid from Rogan's back outside the Camp Floyd Express station.

"We appreciate the opportunity to spend an hour in the captivating presence of a lady such as yourself, Miss Lekarski," said one of the soldiers.

One of the older soldiers closed his eyes and shook his head "You are appreciated, even if you are affianced, Miss Lekarski." He glared at the flirt. "Our apologies, madame. You'll have to excuse him, there's a shortage of women in camp," he said, with a twist of his lips. The rest of the men nodded with enthusiasm.

Aleksandra bit her lips together to keep from laughing.

"We'll meet you here in three or four hours for our return trip," said the first man, a swarthy blond man with relatively clean hair.

"That long?"

"Yes, I'm sorry. I should have said."

"I'll just trot back on my own, then, but thank you, anyway."

"Are you sure that's…the best thing to do?" He hesitated. "My captain—"

"—your captain is very kind, but it's not necessary. Thank you for your concern."

The blond's brows lowered, but he took a deep breath and saluted her. "I'll see you back at camp this evening, then, madame. Please...be careful?"

Aleksandra laughed at his tone, then sobered. "I'll be fine. See you then." She waved them off and went inside, holding the end of Rogan's reins.

The kit was where she'd left it, but no one was at the station. She scribbled a quick thank you note to the keeper on his blotter pad and headed toward the shortcut through the trees she and Xavier took last month when they left, or rather *snuck*, out of town. Rogan shook his head and Aleksandra let him rock into a gallop across the open plain as soon as they were out of town, but she slowed him to a trot when they entered the trees heading up the little canyon.

She drew in the clean, fresh smell of water and willow and reached forward to pat Rogan. "We'll stop for a munch of willow, eh boy? Would you like—"

The horse's head shot up and he stopped in his tracks at the sound of a man swearing blue murder ahead of them.

Aleksandra peered through the trees at a burly man, mounted on a chestnut horse, following the same trail. It stumbled and he jerked its head, then it stumbled again over the exposed roots crossing its path. The horse swerved to avoid the hand he swung at its head, and he swore some more.

She growled in her throat and gritted her teeth to stop herself from calling him to task. People like that deserved to walk—without a horse.

Soon the man was clear of the trees and the ground levelled out before him. Aleksandra kept a safe distance, but when she and Rogan exited the glade, the man's horse threw up its head and whinnied, then spun on its hind legs and tried to bolt back towards Aleksandra.

"Who's there?" he barked.

It was the saloon owner. He had a face you'd remember, even if you'd only seen him once.

Aleksandra scrambled for a name, as she rode closer. "Mrs. Parkes," she called out. "I'm with the wagon train. I forgot something at Camp Floyd."

His face glowed like a just-cooked lobster and the anger still boiled off him. "Wagon train, eh?" he muttered, his free hand gripping a large coil of rope slung around the saddle horn before him. "I'm off to get my...wife. I can't find her. She must've run off with someone on the train."

"Really? Oh no, imagine that," Aleksandra said, moving the hem of her buckskin shirt aside to free her *shashka* grip.

"Are you from Camp Floyd?" he said, eyeing her sideways.

"Oh no, we've just come from the East."

He peeked at her again, scrutinizing her from head to hip. His brows narrowed. "You look familiar. I may have my shortcomings, but I never forget a face."

"I can't imagine where we might have met, maybe at church in Illinois?" Aleksandra's face grew hot. Lying was not her forte. "That's a nice chestnut you're riding."

"I have a saloon in Camp Floyd." He frowned. "You haven't been there?"

"Saloon?" She blinked. "Surely not. My husband wouldn't approve, I'm sorry to say." She smiled at him and gulped as she remembered her hat. She'd been so wild at the man's treatment of his horse that she'd forgotten. When he turned away from her, she slid it from her head and fumbled to crumple it beneath her. She prayed he wouldn't notice it was the same hat the 'boy' who visited his establishment only a month ago had worn.

She looked up to find him watching her.

"Ahhh…" He nodded once, and his eyes gleamed. "Now I remember you."

"I'm sure we haven't met." Aleksandra shook her head.

"You're the boy…or whatever you are…" his eyes narrowed at her chest, then shot daggers from beneath bushy brows. "You didn't have tits then, but like I said, I never forget a face."

"I'm sure you're mistaken," Aleksandra said, backing Rogan away from him.

"You cut my best customer, with a broken glass." He kicked his horse toward her. Rogan sidled away and bolted at Aleksandra's urging, but the chestnut came fast after them.

What is closer? The fort or the train? It would have to be Camp Floyd.

She turned hard and her pursuer followed, back toward the trees. At the very least, Rogan could make up time through the trees. She glanced over her shoulder and her blood chilled. His horse was faster than it looked. The trees loomed closer, but he'd be onto her before she reached them. She had to do something else. She bit her lip and rode.

But what?

Dzhigitovka.

Aleksandra had never performed the Cossack military moves on Rogan, and neither had anyone else. She'd have to trust in Papa's good basic training of the young stallion to track straight and pray he didn't toss her into the next century. She urged him to gallop straight for the willows, then glanced back.

The saloon keeper was nearly upon them, his great ham fist grasping at the empty air behind her. She'd have to risk it.

Biting her lip, she took the chance he offered, praying they didn't find a badger hole. She slipped a split rein beneath her horse's neck to the right and twisted one foot into a stirrup leather, then let the man come a little closer, staying just far enough ahead that he couldn't reach Rogan's reins. Her bet paid off and he lunged, throwing his body toward her. As he began his leap, she dropped into a Cossack Hang, low to Rogan's right side. Her attacker overbalanced and scrabbled for a hold on the cantle of her saddle.

"Yah, yah!" she called to Rogan, and the horse turned on a rush of blistering speed.

The saloon keeper disappeared. Five more strides and she flicked herself back into the saddle.

The clink of metal on stone rang out and she turned back to see him crumpled on the ground. Aleksandra pulled Rogan to a bouncing halt, then saw the gun, its blue-black body glinting dully against a rock.

Everything in her screamed to keep going, but she needed to stop him. She couldn't let him take her friend. Desiree saved her life, and it was time to return the favor—she owed her that, at least.

The man sat up, rubbing the dirt from his eyes and cursing, then reached behind him for his pistol. His face contorted when his hands found the empty holster, and he scrabbled around on the ground beside him, searching, then froze as he caught sight of it, a short distance away.

She had to get the gun before he did. Glancing down at the hang loop always attached to her and her papa's saddle cinch rings, she sent thanks to her papa in heaven as she shoved her right boot into it and twisted her body around so that her toe pointed upward, then kicked Rogan toward the gun. Dropping her reins, she turned in the saddle and tucked her left knee up, then kicked her left leg over her head as she lay backward and hung head-down from her right leg off Rogan's side in a Cossack Death Drag, fingers reaching for the ground. She'd learned *dzhigitovka* on her well-trained, but smaller Mustang, so it was a stretch to reach the ground. Rogan swerved as she grabbed for the gun, and her fingertips just grazed its grip. Flicking herself back up, she pulled the horse to a sliding halt, then spun him around and tried again. The saloon keeper was moving toward the gun, and Rogan headed straight for him as she dropped down into the Drag again.

Aleksandra's heart lurched as the cool grip of the pistol slid into her fingers and she pulled herself back into the saddle. Rogan screamed to a halt, shaking his head. A glance forward showed the man gripping and dragging on the cheekpiece of the young stallion's bridle.

Rogan really hated that.

He reared and struck with both forelegs. She trained the gun on him, but the man let go and slumped to the ground. Aleksandra gritted her teeth as Rogan rose higher and higher. He'd never fallen over backwards before, but he was more excited than he'd ever been, so all bets were off.

Afraid she'd end up beneath him, she stepped off as he rose still higher and drew her *shashka*. Rogan shook his head again and landed back on solid ground beside her with a thud of his huge hooves.

She froze for a moment, considering. She hadn't a chance in hell of tying the saloon owner up without help, unless she shot him first.

Tempting...

Her lips turned up, then dropped into a frown. The burly saloon keeper would have no difficulty relieving her of the weapon, so better it was out of the picture altogether. With a glance at the man's still form on the ground, she flung the gun as far as she could into the willows. It landed with a satisfying splash in the distant creek. The man jerked at the sound, then sat up slowly, holding his ribs and scowling.

She didn't want to risk Rogan to the possibility that the man carried another pistol, so she gave him a shove and he trotted a short distance away to browse on the willows, keeping a wary eye on the sitting man. The chestnut followed Rogan and joined him in the feast.

Papa hadn't taught her to fight with a *shashka* for nothing. Vladimir's training had brought her up to speed and she was ready. She eyed the saloon keeper while she stuffed her long braid down the back of her shirt.

Sunlight glinted off the Cossack sword as she held it toward him.

He looked up and glanced at it in derision.

"What's that, a play sword?"

She gritted her teeth and waited. He would learn how it felt to play with it.

"Come here, girl. We can do this the hard way or the easy way." He wiped his glistening forehead with his sleeve and stood up. "You come back and turn yourself in for attacking my friend and it'll go easy on you. Make it hard and you'll end up the worse for wear."

"I've seen how well you treat women."

He went on like he hadn't heard her. "No one will believe your story. You're just another girl on the make." He moved toward her. "Come over here and play with me with your little sword."

He was no slouch fighter, though she had a blade. They lunged and feinted. He swung for her with open hands, as she dodged and parried. Grateful her hair was tucked away, she managed to keep out of his way, just, with the help of her *shashka*.

If only I could immobilize him, but how?

"I'm my own bouncer...I toss drunken...men around my...establishment...every day." He was panting now, his movements not as fast, but then again, neither were hers. "Every day...for years. Do you...think you can..." puff, puff "evade me..." puff, puff "for long?"

She kept her face emotionless, and said not a word.

"And I've killed many of them…let's see, there's Joseph, Sarah…"

What kind of a man was this?

She stopped listening as he rattled off names of men and a woman he'd killed, dragging her attention from his words back to his actions.

"What kind of sword is that, a little girl's one?" he taunted.

She couldn't resist. "A sharp one," she said, and slashed at his groping hand. She had no idea what to do with him. A sharp sword made it difficult to stop a person without killing him.

They circled, again and again. She had many opportunities to kill him, but she only wanted to detain him for a few days.

He babbled while they fought, spinning, whirling. She took the slashes she dared, making the occasional contacts, trying just to dissuade, not kill. Blood soaked his shirt in patches where she'd made contact. If only he'd give up and go home.

"Maybe I won't go after Des—my wife…" he puffed. "What a hellcat you are. You're worth more than three of her. Imagine what you'd make upstairs at the saloon for me. I don't need that wife after all."

She gulped as her heart froze in her chest. Papa's words came back to her:

'Never get excited in battle. Keep your heart slow and your brain will keep you alive.'

She breathed, and focused.

"You'll soon learn who your boss is." His leer was pure evil.

She tried to focus, but fear slipped in. She needed to end this. He was a huge man, with a long reach. Her wrist was not yet healed from her fight with Vladimir, and she was beginning to feel it.

She had to risk getting in close and dropping him…but could she do it?

7

Aleksandra took another deep breath. For courage?

A coolness came over her. She seemed to be watching from above. Smelling the scent of exertion and anger…and a little fear from him. The girl below stood still, then advanced toward him. A pretend trip over a nonexistent rock.

He grabbed for her and she struck at his outstretched hand. The smooth slice of fine steel through a joint of meat, then the jar of metal on bone—but meat doesn't scream.

His shrieks filled the air as he clutched at his bloodied hand with the other. Her training overrode her rising panic as her stroke followed through and the sword wheeled back to strike his head, pommel first.

He dropped like a stone and she stepped away, leaving him where he fell.

Aleksandra fought for air and held her bad wrist as she stood looking around for any moment, but nothing stirred except the two horses. Her stomach lurched at the violence of the act, hands clammy as she automatically wiped the blade and slid it into its sheath. Her healer's heart recoiled and she turned away to retch until her stomach was empty.

Through all the years of her training, it was the first time swordplay had resulted in blood and pain. She looked at the man on the ground. His rasping breaths were the only sounds she heard over her pounding heart. Even the birds in the willows were silent, no doubt astonished by the carnage in their usually-peaceful glen.

She whistled to Rogan. He came at a trot and the saloon owner's gelding followed, the long rope dragging from his saddle. She rinsed her mouth from her canteen and breathed deeply until her pulse slowed.

Aleksandra spoke softly to the chestnut. It stood while she untangled the rope from around one of his forelegs and removed it to tie the man's bloody hands in front of him. The wound still seeped blood, but wasn't bleeding badly. She managed to drag him by the heels deep into the willows to a hidden hollow by the stream. The trail looked relatively unused, likely no one would find him for a few days, at least. She checked him for knives and weapons, then untied his hands and hogtied him. With a momentary pang of misgiving for leaving an injured, unarmed man in the wild, she pulled out her medicine kit. The blade had sliced cleanly between the second and third fingers, missing the major vessels and nerves. If it didn't get infected, he'd probably regain use of the hand.

Not that he deserved it.

She mixed a poultice of honey and thyme, smeared it liberally into the wound, and bound the hand tightly. She'd bandage his hand, but damned if she'd give him a weapon. He'd already hurt too many people. She wrapped the free end of the rope around a tree and knotted it firmly, washed her bloody hands in the stream, and left him.

Approaching the saloon keeper's spooked horse again, she unsaddled him, slid the bridle from his head, and set him loose. The gelding wandered deeper into the willows to munch the new shoots while she tossed his bridle high into the treetops. She called to Rogan and he eventually came to her, sidling sideways and snorting at the blood on her buckskin shirt. She quickly checked him over. He'd torn one corner of his mouth but appeared otherwise unharmed. The man's ribs would hurt more than Rogan's mouth, so it was probably only fair. She found her hat and jammed it on.

She spun Rogan around and swung up as he loped off.

Might as well let him start getting used to dzhigitovka moves now.

Aleksandra smiled wanly. He'd made a good start today. She let him run, and soon the white billowing wagon covers of the train showed against the darkening late-afternoon sky. Xavier rode toward her at a walk on Charro. She shoved her hat low over her forehead and ducked her head.

"I was about to come find you. What took you so long?" Xavier said lazily, reaching for her hand. "Trouble finding your kit?"

"Had a little difficulty on the track down by the willows," she muttered.

His eyes jerked up to her face and then down to the front of her shirt. "You're covered in blood."

"We won't be going back to that saloon," she said, picking up her head and looking straight ahead.

"What have you done now?" He stared at her.

"Umm...fell off," she mumbled.

"You don't fall off." He shoved Charro closer. "That's blood, and a new graze" he said, gently wiping some of the seeping fluid from her cheek.

"Most of it isn't mine," she said.

He frowned at her. "Start talking, please. I thought you had an escort?"

"I did, but they weren't heading back for another four hours, you were off hunting, and Desiree was in camp."

"Oh."

"Let's just say the saloon owner won't be coming after Desiree, at least not until he wakes up and figures out how to untie himself, and if his hand doesn't get gangrenous and kill him. Unless, of course, some carnivores find him first and give themselves indigestion. He's tied with his own rope—the one he planned to use to drag Desiree, or maybe me, back with him."

He looked heavenward. "*Dios mío*, they'll send the army after us."

"I don't think so. He was talking about how easy it was to kill. He must've been sure he was going to win—and was stupid enough to name names. I don't think he'll be coming after us. Hardest fight I've ever fought." She closed her eyes for a moment. "Harder than Vladimir, and he had a *shashka*, but then Vladimir had honor, at least a little. This man has none."

He slid from the saddle and stopped Rogan, then drew her down into his arms. "You've got to stop risking your life. I know you can win, but could you please just stop?" He hugged her tightly against his chest. "I've just found you—I don't want to lose you now."

"You don't understand—he would've taken Desiree. I couldn't leave her to him. I owe her a life."

"There is a whole wagon train here. We could've all saved her."

"You were away, and their wagon is near the end. He might have simply said she was his wife and dragged her off. Who'd believe a runaway wife, even if she wasn't one?" Her voice dropped to a whisper. "And he had a gun."

He paled and pulled her in tighter, if that were possible. "What happened to it?"

"It's in the stream. Heard it splash."

He began to laugh while he shook his head. "You're amazing."

"And his bridle is in the trees." She grinned. "The horse will probably stay there forever, with the willows, so hopefully no one will look for him." She began to shake.

"Delayed reaction," he said, as her teeth began to chatter. He put his forehead against hers and closed his eyes. His lips moved, but no sound came. He finished and looked into her eyes, then took her lips with his.

The kiss started soft, but urgency borne of fear tugged at her, harder and harder, as his tongue sought hers. A tightening in her belly and she pressed against his hardness, and looked up in surprise. He nodded and deepened the kiss. When she could no longer do without air, she pulled her head back and gazed into his eyes. Her body still shook, but now it was her mind that was unbalanced. She gave a shaky laugh.

He smiled grimly. "Yes, the train is out of sight, but probably not far enough away. We'd best go, shall we?" He wriggled and tugged at his trousers. "We can revisit this tonight after dark, eh *Querida*?"

"That's a promise," she breathed, and let Xavier lead her back to Rogan and lift her into the saddle.

Desiree clasped Aleksandra to her chest and held on like she'd never let go.

"But did he hurt you?"

"Not much, but he wore me out a bit." Aleksandra smiled with more confidence than she felt. Hoofbeats approached behind her at a canter. She glanced over her shoulder to see Captain Moore on his big gray.

"Miss Buchanan, back to your wagon, if you please."

With one last hug, Desiree scurried away.

Aleksandra turned to face the commander and Xavier.

"Xavier says you've had an 'altercation' with Miss Buchanan's previous employer," the captain said abruptly.

She flicked a glance at Xavier and winced. "My specialty," she muttered, to her boots.

"Pardon?"

"Nothing." She looked up at the captain.

"Supposing you tell me what happened," Moore continued.

Aleksandra nodded, and began. Their leader's brows lowered, then lowered some more as Aleksandra skimmed over her encounter. She cringed inwardly and stared at the ground as she finished her story.

There was a long silence. She glanced up to see the officer shaking his head at Xavier.

"I know. I live with this daily," Xavier gave them both a twisted smile.

"He'll be mad as a hornet, and may be in trouble from that wound, but as you suggested, those people he said he's killed will probably keep him home...and hopefully, quiet. I know at least one of those he named was reported missing last year. He clearly planned to win that fight." He frowned. "Even so, I'd stay out of Camp Floyd, if I were you, at least until he's locked up, if there's anything to what he told you." He looked hard at Aleksandra.

"I will, sir," she murmured.

"I thought I sent you with an escort. Have you dispatched them, as well?"

She looked up at that. "Oh, no, sir. They were going to be three or four hours, so I—"

"—came back on your own. I see."

She nodded slowly.

"Next time someone sends you with an escort, please do them the courtesy of staying with that escort? Then everyone will know you're safe, and no harm can befall you," he sighed, "or less, anyway. No telling out here." He frowned as he scanned the horizon.

"I will, sir." She gritted her teeth. "I promise."

"I'd appreciate that, too." Xavier raised a brow at her.

"Good night, soldier," Moore nodded to her, with a quick grin. As he wheeled his horse, he added: "I'll move Jensen's wagon closer to the front before we start tomorrow. The train'll be circled up tonight and I'll keep them close."

The cold knot in her stomach dissolved at his words. "Thank you, captain," she said, as their eyes locked.

Desiree was happy to welcome Aleksandra and Xavier for supper at Mr. Jensen's wagon than night. Captain Moore joined them as they finished.

"I hope that's the last we see of him, ever." Desiree said, shivering as the hairs raised on her arms and down her back.

"He won't bother you anymore," Aleksandra said, leaning back against a barrel.

Despite the assurance, Desiree's knees threatened to buckle and Mr. Jensen put an arm around her to support her.

"We'll be keeping an eye out for him," Captain Moore growled. "I'll report the names of the people he bragged of killing to the authorities back in Floyd when I return, or sooner, if we meet any troops. He won't be bothering anyone for a good, long time, if he somehow manages to survive a long drop with a short rope."

Desiree shuddered. "Couldn't happen to a nicer person. I even left my own three gowns for him to sell to his other girls. I hoped that would placate him."

"Some people are past placating," Xavier said. "You were probably the best thing to happen to his saloon. He should've taken better care of you."

"Anyway, it's over," Aleksandra said, as she gingerly touched her abraded cheek. "He won't disturb you ever again."

Desiree looked around the circle of people—new friends—and her heart warmed.

"It's been a long time since anyone cared. Thank you all," she said.

"*Ja*, Miss Desiree, and you haf a new life to consider on this wild wagon road to the West with my family." The look in Jesper's eyes was pure happiness. It matched the feeling in Desiree's heart.

THE FIELDS OPENED out before them as the horses splashed through Meadow Stream, far ahead of the lumbering wagon train.

"Just about a mile from here, now," Aleksandra said. "Can't wait to see Doc."

"Me neither. He's the father I always wanted." Xavier took a big breath and let it out slowly.

The horses stopped mid-stream and drank deeply, then Rogan began to paw, splashing water all over Charro and Xavier.

He flicked the end of his rein at Rogan's rump, and the horse desisted and walked on.

"We'll have the whole morning to play with Charro's colts."

Xavier grinned, a look of contentment spreading over his visage.

"You saw Major Egan before we left?"

"Sure did."

"Did he say how long it would be before the stations are rebuilt and the run resumed?"

"No, but he said to take a long honeymoon," he replied with a smile, and then sobered. "But if the owners of the Pony don't pay their creditors soon, they won't be opening it up at all."

"That bad?"

He nodded.

"Frankly, I'm more worried for the Indians. They'll be driven west until there's nowhere left to go." Aleksandra sighed.

They rode in silence for long minutes, her heart heavy.

The sun was setting over Lookout Pass, outlining Doc's ranch. Even in the dimming light, the valley floor showed pale green with new grass.

"They should get plenty of hay this year," she said.

He chuckled. "When I worked with Doc last summer, we made enough hay to see most of the Express horses and stock through the winter."

She raised her brows at that. "That much?" She turned her gaze back west to Lookout, a cleft in a solid wall of mountain some three or four miles past the station—the pass of her fateful first Pony Express ride—the arrows—the poison. She shuddered and dragged her thoughts away from that day, and turned to face Xavier.

He reached out a hand and squeezed hers. "So glad you survived," he said softly.

She had no words, and clung to his hand in reply.

Barking dogs heralded their arrival at Doc's ranch and Pony station. Charro and Rogan replied to the cacophony of whinnies filling the air.

"Those are your foals out there, Charro, my man," Xavier said, slapping the stallion's neck, as proud as if he'd sired them himself.

"Aleksandra, Xavier!" The grizzled man scurried from the barn to meet them.

"Hello Doc, good to see you again in one piece," Xavier said.

"That goes for both of you too," Doc said, narrowing his brows at Aleksandra. "Glad to hear you're OK, miss. Xavier sent word down the line."

"We'll tell you the whole story later." Aleksandra smiled.

"That, I want to hear." The station keeper rubbed Rogan's forehead while she dismounted.

"Is Scout here, or up at Lookout? He's OK, isn't he?"

"Sure is, missy. He's done right well and he's getting fat up on the mountain," he replied, in his German accent. She and Doc had together treated the Express Mustang Scout for the poisoned arrow wound he'd received on that frightening trip down the pass last month.

"I'm so pleased. He'll be getting some treats when we see him."

Doc grinned. "What are you two planning to do while the Pony is out?"

They told Doc their plans. "And we've hooked up with an army unit accompanying a wagon train across this next portion of trail." Xavier raised an eyebrow at his old friend.

Doc sobered. "A good idea, lad."

"So, on to better things," Aleksandra said, "we left the train behind today. They'll catch up in a few hours, which leaves us time to give you a hand if you need it, and to spend time with these colts."

"Go ahead and put your horses away—you know where they go, stallions down the end, and I'll lay out a couple more plates." He grinned. "You aren't staying the night?"

"No, sorry, we leave when the train passes."

"Too bad you won't be here for supper—it's Aleks' favorite—wolf mutton."

Xavier's eyebrows shot up, and he stared at her. His face said it all.

Aleksandra laughed. "It's good."

"See?" Doc chuckled as he headed back into the station.

"Wolf...mutton..." Xavier said, as he led Charro away into the barn, followed by Alex.

"Breakfast!" Doc called from the station door, a short time later.

Aleksandra knocked the curry and the dandy brush together a few times, put them out of Rogan's reach, and let him loose. "You done there, Xavier?"

"Sure am. Wouldn't miss one of Doc's breakfasts for the earth."

"Eggs, steak or sourdough pancakes?" Aleksandra rolled her eyes.

"My bet's on the pancakes," he said, holding open the door.

"You win," she whispered, as the tangy aroma of sourdough filled her nostrils.

"No, we both win, it's sourdough."

"What're you two whisperin' about?"

"Just betting on the magnificent breakfast we're about to enjoy, Doc." Aleksandra grinned. "Whatever we bet, we both win."

"It's just sourdough pancakes," he grumbled, "but that has to be the best breakfast in the world."

"I hope my sourdough starter and *zakwas* at Fish Springs survive a month of starvation." Aleksandra twisted her lips.

"They're tough, they'll be fine." Doc smiled. "Couple of feeds and they'll be good as new. So, you two ready to go down and have a go with these colts?"

"Can't wait," Aleksandra said. She forked a wedge from a stack of dollar-sized pancakes, dripping with maple syrup, into her mouth.

"Do you have enough halters for all three of us to use at once?"

"Of course, Xavier. We have plenty."

"We're not sure exactly how long we'll be gone, Doc," Xavier said, with a frown, "but would you mind keeping these colts for us for a couple of years, if need be? Mining camps aren't really the place for two stallions, much less two stallions and two colts. Vladimir can pick them up from you when his leg is healed, and start their training, but I'd prefer they return to you to live in a herd, where they'll learn manners."

Doc chuckled. "Fancy Vladimir being part of your lives now, after all the years of worry. I look forward to meeting him and learning his methods. Haven't had the chance to practice my Russian in years, either."

"I'm sure he'll be happy to teach you anything he can. He's trying to make amends," Aleksandra said.

"Aleksandra, you never did show me that *dig, dij, dig*, whatever it is," Doc said.

"*Dzhigitovka?*" She smiled at him.

"Yes, that."

"I need my pony here to do it. Rogan's too green, although he did a pretty good job when I needed it earlier this week, bit that's another story. I promise to show you when I'm here next with Dzień."

The foals were wonderful to handle—interested, willing and fearless without being aggressive—and cooperated while the three groomed and led them around the yard.

After setting them loose, Doc, Xavier and Aleksandra stood together, elbows on the rails of the youngstock's pen.

"Doc, I can't thank you enough for your work with these colts." Xavier shook his head.

"Nothin' I wouldn't do with my own."

"Know that it's appreciated by both of us," Aleksandra murmured, her eyes on a stunning black foal as he nosed at her fingers, then pressed his forehead against her fingertips when she raised her hand to scratch him on his white star. She glanced up at the sun and looked east. "No sign of the wagon train, but they should be here soon. I'll go in and pack up, if you two have anything else that needs doing."

"Matter of fact, Xavier, I could use a hand. I gave my worker the day off today and I'm having a little trouble fixing a chute gate," Doc said, with a wave to Aleksandra.

"AND SO," Xavier said, shoving the final bolt home into its slot, "things might be changing in my life soon."

"Thanks for that, son. Haven't been able to line up of those bars on my own." He glanced sideways at Xavier. "Hmmm, changing, eh?"

Xavier squirmed, then straightened his shoulders. "I've gotten her a ring."

"Well congratulations, Xavier." The smile creased his whole face.

Xavier twisted his lips and scrunched his brow. "I've already asked her, but I wanted to let her know I really mean it…so why am I so nervous?"

"I don't think you need to worry about it, son. That girl adores you, and she's been waitin' for you to understand that."

"I'm going to ask her up on top of Dugway."

"Sounds like a fine idea. Be sure to send me a note when you get to Virginia City, so I can send my congratulations." Doc clapped him on the back so hard he nearly choked.

"Without your help and your good advice, my life wouldn't be what it is today, and for that I thank you."

"Anytime, Xavier. You know that. Always."

8

Aleksandra looked up from her coffee at the sound of Rogan's whinny. Through the open door, a cloud of dust showed over the horizon. If she listened hard, she could hear the creaking wagon wheels and shouts of the men.

"The train?" Xavier raised his brow.

"Sounds like it," she replied. "Can't see them yet."

"They'll stop at Meadow Stream for a drink. I don't imagine the oxen will move very fast, once they get to the water," Doc said, as he stood up and collected their cups. "I don't think you'll need to saddle up just yet."

Saddlebags over their shoulders, they wandered out to the broodmare field again, stopping to rub the mares' withers and scratch the foals' ears.

Aleksandra scratched the rump of the little bay standing before Xavier. "Wish we could take them with us, but it just wouldn't work."

They returned to the horses and saddled up. Xavier tightened Charro's cinch *latigo* with a tug. "All set?" He looked at Aleksandra.

"As ready as I'll ever be to join a train full of Easterners," she said with a chuckle, "but at least I'll get to spend time with Desiree."

"Something I suspect you need. How long has it been since you've had female companionship?"

Aleksandra was silent, looking at her fingers tying the feed sack to her saddle horn. "Since Mama died...many years."

"I thought as much," he said and pulled her close. "Soon we'll be living in a town, if only for a short while, and there will be plenty of women."

Her breath caught in her throat and she swallowed hard.

Xavier gripped her shoulders and held her at arm's length, his brows narrowed. "What is it?"

"Town...I think I need to sit down," she whispered. The saddle before her seemed to shimmer as Xavier took her in his embrace.

"I didn't know you were afraid of anything. Are you afraid to live in town?"

"I don't know if...if afraid is the right word, but the thought of being near so many people makes me feel like a wild animal in the cage. Claustrophobic, I guess you'd call it."

He wrapped his arms around her again. "We'll make sure we get out of town for a ride every day. Will that help?"

"I don't like towns either, Aleksandra, if it helps." Doc gave her a sheepish grin as he walked up to them.

The Army men at the head of the column were close enough to make out their faces now.

"Goodbye Aleksandra. Until I see you again." Doc gave her a bear hug, then stepped back. "Xavier," he clasped his hand, and gave him a hearty hug as well. "You go well, eh, son?" He winked at him, then stepped back, with a pat for each horse while she and Xavier mounted.

"Until we meet again, my friends," he called, as they rode off.

Doc was still staring after them when Aleksandra glanced back to wave a few minutes later.

"What was that look between you and Doc?" Aleksandra raised a brow at Xavier.

"Look? I saw no look." He sent a lazy grin in her direction, then turned his attention to the approaching troops. "Good morning captain, men."

"Gentlemen." Aleksandra smiled her greeting.

"Glad to have you along," one of the soldiers said, then nodded to them both, his gaze lingering on Aleksandra a little longer than necessary.

She felt, rather than saw, Xavier's hackles rise at the intrusion, and kneed Rogan close enough to Charro that her and Xavier's legs touched. When she lifted her head, their eyes locked. She couldn't remember having felt so safe in ages.

"Aleksandra, Xavier!" Desiree waved from Mr. Jensen's wagon as it drew abreast of them. At a nod from her employer, Desiree hopped down from the box and ran toward Aleksandra.

"We've had a lovely time with Doc Faust," Aleksandra winked at her, "and we've just seen Charro's first foals!"

"I wish there was time to see them now." Desiree gazed with longing at the paddock of mares and foals, and then back at her wagon.

"You'll see them someday, when you visit in California. Now you'd best run, or you'll lose your wagon."

"OK." Desiree beamed, looking happier than Aleksandra had ever seen her. "Thank you again, for giving me my life back," she said, taking Aleksandra's hands.

"Nothing you wouldn't have done for me." Aleksandra grinned and squeezed her fingertips.

"See you soon!" her friend said, as she dashed off and leapt into the Jensen's wagon. Six little hands reached toward her as she climbed.

She turned to wave, and was soon lost in the dust.

WHEN THEY REACHED the top of Lookout Pass, they stopped to gaze out over the panorama before them.

"With a troop of Army men and an entire wagon train at our back, Lookout Pass doesn't look nearly as threatening as I've found it to be," Aleksandra said to Captain Moore. The boulders and scrub cedars, big enough to hide several men, were today pretty parts of the scenery. No arrows flew, and the horses swung along, nodding their heads.

"This is General Johnston's Pass, isn't it?" he replied.

"The Pony boys have taken to calling it Lookout," Xavier said. "Not sure if it's due to this view, or because the riders needed to 'look out' for threats."

They rode ahead of the wagon train to see Scout at Lookout station. Aleksandra found him in his corral, while Xavier took the horses and went to find the keeper. The Palouse stallion shook his head at Aleksandra she approached, then rubbed his forehead up and down against her chest.

"I see you found him, Aleks," Mr. Jackson said, as he and Xavier walked up.

"You're doing him proud, sir," Aleksandra said, stroking Scout's glossy neck. "That wound over his trachea," she pointed it out to Xavier, "was where Doc and I cut away the poisoned tissue and sutured the wound."

"Good job that was," Xavier said. "It's healing well."

"The arrowhead went in between the tracheal rings, so we didn't have to remove any."

"This would've put most men off from riding the Pony, but you didn't even think of quitting after that, did you?" Xavier shook his head.

"'More guts than brains', Papa always said."

"And I see you've had a wee change as well, miss. Last time I looked, you were a boy." The station keeper laughed.

"Ahem...Aleksandra and I are to be married," Xavier said.

"Congratulations to you both," he said. "A better pair, I cannot imagine."

"Thank you," he said. "And how are you faring without Pony riders coming through?"

"It's rather quiet, but I have time to do things I've never finished in the past," Mr. Jackson said. "I've had a lot of my Indian friends in. They're pretty worried, and their plight upsets me no end. For years they traded with me, and now their lives are going to pieces. I do what I can to help them, but I don't think it will be enough."

"I understand completely," Aleksandra said softly. "I grew up in the middle of a band of *Shoshone*. My father was their Chief's blood brother, and until recently, I was one with them."

Xavier pulled her close against of his side and reached out to shake Mr. Johnson's hand. "Thank you for your good care, both of your Indian friends, and of Scout. That pony means the world to both of us."

"And to me as well," the keeper said. "You two take good care of yourselves, and congratulations once again. You're welcome back here anytime. Let's get some water into your horses while you wait."

"Yes please," Aleksandra said, as they turned to follow him toward the barn.

Davis Mountain showed on the right as they came down off the pass and onto the floor of Skull Valley.

"The name still bothers me." Aleksandra shuddered.

"The sheer number of skulls littering the valley bothers *me*," said the young soldier beside her.

"Not much water, for an awful lot of miles," she said.

"None through Skull Valley, nor Government Creek Wash," Xavier added, "other than the little spring at Government Creek station."

The soldier frowned. "So, if a station doesn't have a spring, how do they water the horses, and the keepers, for that matter?"

"Water's carted in, if you can believe it," said Captain Moore.

The soldier looked at him, aghast. "Stations every ten miles, and they have to cart the water?"

"And feed. There's fresh water at Simpson Springs, anyway" Xavier said, "and there might even be grass."

"Enjoy it while you can," Aleksandra said. "Once we hit Riverbed and Dugway, the water carted from Simpson gets pretty brackish in those barrels."

The miles passed slowly as a biting, cold wind whipped across the salt flats. Only pale green tufts of sagebrush and cheat grass broke up the grey and white flatness as they passed Government Creek Wash station. The wagon train's oxen were still fresh from the relatively easy terrain, so they pushed on to Simpson Springs.

"I love this trail, but I've never passed through it at oxen-pace."

Xavier twisted his lips. "We don't have to stay with the train, but I think it's a good idea."

"At this pace," she murmured, "we'll only make two stations every two to three days."

"It'd be faster," said the captain, "if they all had horses or mules, but we're out of luck, because there are too many oxen—and you can only push them to two or three miles per hour."

"But they don't eat as much, or need such good quality feed as horses and mules to keep working," said one of the men.

"Trust a farmer boy to know that one," jibed another.

"Either way," Aleksandra grimaced, "I think I'll go mad if we have to keep to this crawl until Carson City."

"We might have to alter our plans a little," Xavier said. "Even Charro's getting bored. Let's see how we go after the worst of the Express stations. Why don't you go see Desiree? Take the children for a run?"

She smiled her thanks, and turned Rogan back toward the wagons.

"Desiree," Aleksandra said, "would you and the children like to run ahead with me to visit the keeper at Simpson Springs station? It might be dark by the time we get there, and I'm sure the children would enjoy the change."

"Would that be all right, Mr. Jensen?" Desiree quirked a brow at her employer, seated on the wagon box to her right.

"*Ja, ja,*" he said, as he changed his mules' reins from one hand to the other.

The looks exchanged between them seemed to hold more than they had last time she'd seen them together. Aleksandra hid her smile as she dismounted, then led Rogan beside the woman and the three bouncing children.

"I'm sure I'll need to carry the little one soon," Desiree said, "but the freedom is worth it."

They walked in silence as they passed the other wagons, and then the troops and Xavier. The soldiers tipped their hats to the ladies and Xavier called out a greeting to Desiree.

"Things are going very well with Mr. Jensen," Desiree said, looking down at the ground as she strode down the trail in front of the train.

"I noticed you two look…happy together," Aleksandra said, with a smile.

"We've decided not mention we're more than employer and employee," she glanced up at Aleksandra, her eyes glowing, "but there's much more to our relationship now. I don't think I'll be leaving him and the children once we make it out West."

Aleksandra gave her a swift hug. "I'm so happy for you. He seems lovely, and the children are adorable. They'll be a lot of work, but they seem to be kind, and willing."

"They're even teaching me to speak Danish." Desiree chuckled. "And here I thought I was meant to be teaching *them*."

"Where did you live, before your family went West?"

"As I'm sure you can tell, I'm a Southerner. Long story short, my mother fell in love with my father, but he was not the husband her wealthy, plantation-owning parents envisioned for their only daughter. They eloped, and were never welcome back in my grandparents' home. My family had a small farm, barely enough to subsist on, in South Carolina. Times were hard, so my parents decided to take us West."

"On a wagon train."

"Yes," she hesitated, then went on. "Unfortunately, on the way across the plains, they were all taken with a fever, and I was left to the tender mercies of a man who disliked one of my brothers, raped, and left for dead. I survived as best I could, and finally ended up in the saloon where you and I first encountered each other."

Aleksandra's eyes met hers. "We are survivors, we two."

"Speaking of survival," Desiree said, "what do you think of the rumors about California seceding from the Union?"

Aleksandra gritted her teeth. Desiree was her friend, but she'd asked. She'd get the truth, Southerner or no. "I abhor slavery. I think any state seceding from the Union to join the South is in the wrong."

Desiree was quiet for some time, then she spoke. "I grew up with slavery being the norm. It was all I knew. My experiences, after being left alone on the wagon train, became more and more like slavery, and they taught me something entirely different. Now, even the thought that a person would own or control another repels me, so I too, would fight against California becoming a Southern slave state."

Aleksandra let out the breath she didn't know she'd been holding and smiled. She'd fervently hoped the accent was the only part of the South her new friend had retained. In the distance, the stone walls of Simpson's Springs Express station stood out against the pale green of the springs and the distant salt flats below it.

"Excuse me, miss, is that Simpson's station?" asked the elder girl.

"It sure is. If you want to run on ahead, you may—no, wait. Perhaps you should stay back with us, until we know it's safe." Aleksandra looked over her shoulder to be sure the troops were close enough, should anyone be lying in wait at the station.

The sound of dogs barking came from the station, and the door opened. In the distance, a man stepped out over the sill, his rifle over his shoulder. She breathed a sigh of relief. It was George, the keeper.

"OK, away you go. His name is George," she called after the already-running children.

"WAIT A MOMENT, while I check the descent," Xavier said, and trotted Charro toward the edge of a precipice. He peered over the edge, then turned the horse hard to the left and disappeared from sight.

"Where'd he go?" A young soldier's brow wrinkled as he stared at the drop off just ahead of him.

Alex's smiled. "Down into Old Riverbed."

"He's checking there isn't an ambuscade waiting," Aleksandra said.

His mouth formed an 'O', as he waited with the others.

The *Californio's* head appeared above the edge. "All clear," he reported, then turned back down toward the riverbed.

"That's some river to create a bed a couple miles wide," one trooper said, raising both eyebrows.

"Sure must've been, though it was probably a long time ago," Xavier said.

"Isn't it haunted by desert fairies?" another trooper asked, looking at them out of the corners of his eyes.

"And it flash floods," said a third.

"I spent a few weeks at the station when it was just built." said Xavier, "It's a little dugout." He pointed at the smoke coming from a hole in the ground on the far side of the riverbed. "It's right there beside the far bank. You might start to think strange thoughts, too, with no view of approaching danger, and the ever present chance of a flash flood, but perhaps the volume of *tequila* you'd down just to stay out here might make you believe in fairies, too." He grinned at the other men.

"These rock formations out here," said the captain, "I've not seen the like anywhere else. Like that strange mountain on the other side of the far bank."

"That one?" Xavier pointed. "Table Mountain."

"Yes."

"They're odd, aren't they?" Xavier said. "If you dig around in the hills, or look closely at the walls of the mountains around here, you'll find figures in the rock that look like the shells of ocean creatures I've picked up on the beach in California. I wonder if this was under the sea in ancient times?"

The men shrugged.

"Does it really flash flood?"

"I've heard it does, but a highwayman is probably more likely to kill you." Xavier laughed and waved to Riverbed George, who came out to greet him. "I'll catch up with you men at the top. Remember to send someone ahead to check the top of the trail on the desert floor before the rest go up, eh?" He looked at Aleksandra. "Shall we go?"

Aleksandra grinned. "I'm amazed he's still here, after his brush with Vladimir."

"That makes two of us." He touched Charro with his heel to turn toward the Old Riverbed Pony Express station.

"George," Aleksandra called out as she slipped from Rogan's back, then trotted the few steps to him, "how are you?"

"You don't look like an Aleks anymore. You look more like an Aleksandra."

"Well," she winced, "that's true. I've always been an Aleksandra. Do you still love me?" She laughed. "I'm so sorry for what happened with Vladimir. It was me he was after. I thought he was the keeper, and he caught me when I tried to change horses."

"So whatever happened to the bastard, and how did you get away?"

"It was a bit of a rough time, George, but we escaped together, and by some odd turn of events," Xavier closed eyes and shook his head, "he's now become a friend."

"Really?"

"And I'm sure if you are still here the next time he comes through, he will be groveling with his apology." The *Californio* laughed.

"I can't wait to hear this story," the keeper grinned. "Do you two have time to tell it now?"

"Considering it'll probably take a good hour or two for the wagon train to get down into the riverbed and another to get up that bank," he nodded at the exit from the riverbed, "we should have time for that, and a cup of your good *mocha Mexicano*."

"Ahhh, *recuerdas*, eh, Xavier?"

"How could I forget? As good as my mama makes." The *Californio* smiled at the Mexican keeper.

"That'll be a new one for me." Aleksandra's eyes lit with anticipation. "What makes it so special?" she asked, as she slipped the cinch and pulled Rogan saddle off.

"It's *chocolate de Mexico* with coffee, which includes, of course," he grinned, "cinnamon, *chocolate*, ground *chiles* and milk, if you're lucky."

"Ooooh, my mouth is watering already." Her eyes sparkled.

"We have time for the whole story, if you want to tell it." He glanced at the wagon train. First wagons had reached the base of the steep trail descending from the desert floor to the bottom of the riverbed.

"After what he's been through, he deserves to know," he said, gesturing for her to climb down the stairs into the dugout before him.

"So whatever happened?" George's brows shot up. "All I remember is throwing a metal curry and seeing it hit his cheek, and the blood. Vladimir knocked me over the head, and that's all she wrote."

"Good shot," Aleksandra smirked. "He'll carry that scar forever. It'll remind him to be nice."

"Well it went like this…" Xavier said, as he sat down beside Aleksandra on the bench before the fire.

9

"The front of the column with the troops is definitely the best place to be, unless the wind is blowing at our backs." Aleksandra pulled up her bandanna, which had hung about her neck for most of the day, as they started up Dugway Pass.

Xavier agreed, glancing around them at the flying dust. "The wind should turn soon, *Querida*."

The troopers stopped and turned to check the progress of the wagons behind them. The train spread out for nearly a mile behind them. Twenty wagons, all told. It was a good sized group.

"You'd think if they wanted safety, they'd close up their line and stay together," one soldier muttered into his mustache.

"Guess they figure that's our job," another said softly, with a crooked grin, "even if it turns us into a pretty big target."

Their voices hushed as Captain Moore trotted into their midst.

"I've asked them to tighten up their train and travel closer together, especially when their wagon wheels are in the dugway," he said. "The rear half of our troop is going to give them a hurry-up."

One of the men who'd been speaking turned away to hide a smile.

"Good idea, sir," said another, nodding emphatically.

"Ever seen a wagon train go over a dugway, boys?" He looked around his group of mostly young men.

"No sir," a few of them said, shaking their heads.

"We went over dugways with the wagon train we emigrated with, sir," said one of the troopers. "I mostly remember the noise." He shook his head.

"Wailin' women and children, while the wagons tilted and jolted their way to the top. There's a trench dug into the uphill side of the roadway to anchor the wagon and keep it from slipping and tipping over the side of the mountain into the gully below."

"That there is, boys," the captain affirmed. "Worse, though, the trenches make it hard for the stock to pull the wagons up, but it's got to be better than falling over the edge. It keeps those wagons on the track."

"It does, sir, no disrespect, but it strains the wagons somethin' terrible, too," the man to the right of the leader said.

"We came out in a wagon train, too, sir, when I was young," said a towheaded man, who still looked young to Aleksandra, "and the axle on my uncle's Conestoga broke in a dugway going over the *Sierras*. My pa said it happened because my uncle didn't care for his wagon. He never soaked his wheels when they were near water, or kept them greased in between, neither. A bunch of them broke, too, on the trip. He had to ditch the wagon and trade his oxen for mules. He rode one and led the other, loaded with whatever he could carry, all the way to California."

"Well, gentlemen," Captain Moore said, "let's hope we don't have any of that today.

Aleksandra had heard enough. "Shall we trot up to the top? Rogan's getting bored," Aleksandra said, through gritted teeth.

"I think Aleksandra's getting bored," Xavier said, beneath his breath. "We'll meet you at the top, men, after we check out the other side."

"Thanks for that, Xavier, Miss Lekarski," Captain Moore nodded at her. "Just give us a whistle to show the coast is clear once you get to the top and we'll bugle back. Three short blasts, repeated."

"Will do," he said, waving as the horses put their heads down and trotted up the steep grade.

"I'd love to let them gallop up, but under the circumstances—" Aleksandra fell silent.

"—saving the horses seems a good idea, right about now," Xavier finished.

Just before the top of the pass, Xavier turned onto a trail that snaked off to the right, and Aleksandra followed. They climbed until they reached a small grassy clearing.

"I suspect they won't be up here anytime soon," Aleksandra said as she slid from Rogan's back and, handy as a goat, climbed atop the big boulders to the chest-high, turret-like vantage point. She was on top of the world as she turned full circle, holding out her arms to encompass it. From the lookout, she could see everything—from the desert to the west, the mountains at the north and south, and finally to Riverbed, barely visible to the east.

Xavier wasn't far behind her. He looked west, while she scanned the gullies the wagon train had yet to pass on its uphill climb.

"This side looks good," Aleksandra said. "How about over there?" she said, slipping an arm around his waist.

"I don't see any movement, other than some antelope near the bottom," he said, pulling her around so she stood before him, her back against his chest, and wrapped his arms about her.

"That's good," she said. "They wouldn't be there if anyone was hanging about."

"Let's go unsaddle the horses. They've plenty of time for a roll and a rest," he said softly. She looked up to see the corners of his lips turning up and his eyes beginning to glow.

She cocked her head at his sly smile, and smiled back. "We need to call down to the captain," she said. "Do you want to whistle, or shall I?"

"Considering your four-fingered shriek beats mine hands down, I think it'd better be you. You bring down the heavens with yours," he said with a laugh and covered his ears. Aleksandra wet her lips, slammed four fingers into her mouth and whistled for all she was worth. Shortly, three short blasts from a bugle, repeated, echoed their way up the canyon.

"Is it safe now?" he asked, hands still over his ears.

She laughed and turned away, slipping back down the rocks to untie Rogan's cinch and pull the saddle from his sweaty back. The big bay didn't wait for an invitation and managed to get three steps away from her before he dropped to his knees and rolled from side to side, scratching his itchy back on the rough, wispy cheat grass.

The older Charro was more sedate. He waited until after Xavier had removed his saddle and curried him before he rolled, then stood like a gentleman while the *Californio* brushed the dirt off his back, before nosing for a feed of grain.

XAVIER JOINED ALEKSANDRA up at the vantage point as the wagon train begin to creep its inexorable way up the side of the Dugway Pass. The wagon road rose gradually from the desert flats, then steepened as a rocky bank rose sharply on its right. On the left, at the edge of the trail, the ground dropped away just as abruptly to the ravine far below.

"Oh my God," Aleksandra said, "They're not even halfway up, and look at them strain." The oxen and mules drawing the wagons struggled to draw their loads. They sweated and staggered, pulling overloaded wagons, their efforts made even more difficult by having their uphill-side wheels in the deep trench. The women and children walked alongside the wagon, putting a shoulder to their wagon, and then to their neighbors' ones, when the beasts were unable to budge them.

"That's Mr. Trenton-White, the one who demanded the escort at Floyd," Xavier pointed to a man riding back and forth beside the wagons, stopping and cracking his whip at intervals. "Even then, he didn't seem a pleasant sort of a man."

"I'd have to agree with you there." Aleksandra gritted her teeth, while her hands gripped the buckskin at her sides.

"I guess that's why they chose him," Xavier added. "It might just take a pushy, bully Bostonian to ensure they get through the *Sierras* before the first snows fall. Moore said they started too late last year and had a weak leader. They had to replace him."

"These people aren't even to the *Sierras* yet," Aleksandra's said, in a strangled voice, "and they already look exhausted, not to mention their stock."

"They may have started out like this," Xavier said. "Most of them didn't have much to begin with, so this is a big push for them—a chance at a new life."

Xavier was silent for a long minutes, lost in thought.

"Scotty said the government back east is trying to push through a homesteading act, so people who can make a go on the block of land they register for a certain number of years get to keep it—Indian land." Aleksandra's face clouded.

"I've heard about it. The Indians stand to lose even more. And you're right," he winced, "the Homestead Act property is in Indian Territory—land the Indians were promised."

"I can't even imagine how bad it will be for the Indians." Aleksandra's eyes brimmed. "Even so, should we be down there," she peeked over the edge at the wagons, "lending a hand?"

"We probably could, but they seem to have plenty of help already, and they did choose to make this trip."

"That's true. I just hate to see anyone struggle," she said.

"People choose to struggle, it seems," Xavier said. "Let's go have a look at the other side of the mountain." He reached out a hand to her.

They walked across the top of their little castle and looked west. The panorama spread out across the desert. The Black Rock Hills showed dark against the Fish Spring Range. Xavier sat on a boulder beside the drop-off and pulled her down beside him.

"Aleksandra, I have something for you." From his shirt pocket he pulled a paper-wrapped parcel.

"But it's not Christmas, nor my birthday." She raised an eyebrow at him.

"Just open it," he said.

She untied the twine and unwrapped the plain brown paper of the packet to reveal the small box wrapped in colored paper and bound with bright ribbons. She looked at him, brow furrowed.

"Open it," he repeated.

She unwrapped the last layer, to find the box, and inside, the golden ring with its exquisitely-set diamond.

She only stared at it, and Xavier's heart froze.

Maybe she didn't want it.

"Put it on?" he murmured.

She looked up at him, eyes aglow, and gulped.

"Shall I do it?" he asked, and at her nod, slid it onto her finger. "It's a bit big," he said.

"Xavier!" she yelped, and threw herself onto his lap.

"You've already promised to be my bride, but I wanted you to have something of me to hold until we find a priest to marry us."

"I promise to be the best wife to you I can possibly be," she said, between kisses.

"Stay here a moment," Xavier said, as he stood to check the desert floor and the mountains around them, then returned to lower his lips to hers. They kissed with abandon, then kissing led to touching, and they lost themselves in the warmth of the sunny afternoon, under the watchful eye of the two grazing equids.

Afterward, he pulled her tight into his arms.

"Are you hungry?" she asked.

"Always, for you," he said, and kissed her lips again.

She shook her head. "For food. It's way past dinnertime."

He grimaced. "Yes, and the train is still making their way up here."

"We should probably go help." She raised a brow at him and he chuckled.

"Okay, we'll go. Let's get some sustenance first. Could I interest you in some...*pemmican?*"

"Oh, of course. I'd love to have some, it's been ages since I've had any." She winced. "Can't wait to have a real meal at Fish Springs," she said, then froze, and the smile ran away from her face.

He took a deep breath. "Everything will be fine there." He wasn't sure if he was trying to convince her or himself.

IN THE END it took four hours to get all the wagons over Dugway Pass.

"Glad you came back," one of the men said, as Xavier and Aleksandra helped him drag his reluctant ox up over the top of the pass. "This has been a plaguing crossing, what with that broken axle back there."

"Did anyone have a replacement?"

"No, and there's not much timber anywhere to hand, is there?" He gazed around him at the low scrub and rocks.

"So, how did they fix—come *on* beast." Xavier swore as the ox dug his toes in and started going backwards. "How did they fix it?"

"The man's brother is a blacksmith back East. They were able to jury-rig it."

Xavier raised a brow at him.

"They splinted it with some pieces of wood and bolted it together with a couple big U-bolts the man's blacksmith brother made for him, just in case he needed them on the trip."

Aleksandra sent blessings the way of the smith who'd enabled these wagons to keep going today.

"Just to the north, that's Granite Mountain," Aleksandra pointed off to the right, and waited for it, flashing a quick grin at Xavier.

The soldiers looked where she'd pointed. They stared at it, but said nothing. One narrowed his brows, looked at his captain, than back at the peak. Others alternately looked, closed their eyes, and looked again.

"Um, captain?" said one.

"Yes?"

"Ahhh, that mountain," he said, looking back at it, "it doesn't look right."

Aleksandra, Xavier and the captain broke out laughing.

"It's a mirage, boys," the captain said with a laugh. "It only looks like it's floating over the desert." He turned to Aleksandra. "You can always tell who traveled here during daylight hours, or on a warm day. Most of these men passed through here with me when a frost was still on the ground, and the mirage wasn't there." He turned back to the men. "Do you boys remember those hills?"

"Sure do, captain. Those are the Black Rock Hills," said the young man who'd put his foot in his mouth about the mirage.

They rounded the northern reaches of the ebony-streaked hills and Black Rock station came into view.

"Rock House," said Xavier. Beside it stood the great black basalt outcropping from which it had received its name.

"Can't say I'm not pleased for the respite from regular duties, but traveling at oxen pace is beginning to wear on me," a soldier said, beneath his breath.

"You're not alone," Xavier said.

"We're so close now, Xavier, can we head off on our own to Fish Springs?

I can't wait to check on Dzień and pack up whatever else we want to take before we head on." She held her breath as she looked at him.

"Let's check with James at Rock House, make sure there hasn't been any trouble," he replied.

Aleksandra took a deep breath and faced forward again, counting slowly in her head. "I'll go mad, staying at this pace until Virginia City," she said.

"We're with this train for a reason, Aleks." He raised a brow at her.

"I know, I just miss Dzień, and I want to make sure he's OK," she whispered, her heart clenching.

Xavier reached over and squeezed her hand. "I promise. We'll go as soon as we've spoken with James."

The keeper's barking dogs brought him out of the station, rifle in hand. He lowered the rifle when he saw Xavier and Aleksandra trotting ahead of the column.

"Aleks, Xavier! You've still got your hair." The towheaded man laughed, then he frowned, looking at Aleksandra's long braid. "I suspect I've missed something."

She chuckled. "Yes, it's Aleksandra, not Aleks, sorry."

He grinned. "You don't look sorry."

"James, has everything been quiet out here? Aleks is climbing the walls to get back and see her Mustang."

"Sure has, I'm pleased to say. Bit of water for your horses, and you can be on your way." He smiled at her. "I rather like you as a girl," he said.

"That was meant as a compliment," Xavier said, at her frown.

"Most assuredly." James' eyes lit up.

"Well thank you, then," Aleksandra said with a smirk, taking the bucket from him and filling it at the barrel.

"James, this is Captain Moore," Xavier said, as the officer rode up. "He's providing an escort for this wagon train." He snorted.

"Xavier, I'll leave you with them if I see you laugh at me again like that," he grumbled. "Nursemaiding pioneers."

"Sorry Captain," Xavier laughed, "but I need to warn you, in case you don't know, it gets boggy a little way ahead. Unless you want to spend the next few days pulling wagons out of the muck, I suggest you take the train far to the south just before you get to Fish Springs."

"Howard Egan and I were thinking of starting a new business there," Aleksandra said, biting her lip, "with some draft horses to pull pioneer wagons out of the mud. It'd be a great income producer, but I'd rather not start it up today."

"Thanks for that," the captain said dryly.

10

"Charro hasn't forgotten where home is." Aleksandra said, as the big gray quickened his pace shortly after they left Rock House.

"He never does." Xavier grinned.

The dark-striped hills eventually receded, leaving only large expanses of flat, salty ground broken by tufts of cheat grass.

"I can't wait to get home," Aleksandra said. "Let's have a little run."

"OK, away you go."

Rogan laid back his ears and fairly flew. Charro followed, easily keeping pace with the younger horse. They let them run for about a mile, then Aleksandra pulled Rogan back to a walk.

As they neared Fish Springs, her heart grew heavy at the thought she needed to be on the lookout for ambuscade.

"Even after I was attacked at Lookout by the Indians," she said, biting her lip, "I'm finding it hard to believe the peoples with whom I was raised would actually want to hurt me." The wind cooled the streaks down her face, as her tears fell.

Xavier reached across and held her hand. "We'll do what we can for them. You have my promise."

"Thank you," she said, her heart in her words.

"We're nearly there." He smiled at her. "Let's track south, or we'll be digging our own horses out."

They topped the last rise before home and Aleksandra stopped her horse.

"Now this," she said, as she looked across the great slough-filled valley ahead, "is my favorite vista." At this time of year, its purple sheen almost glowed against the dark backdrop of the Fish Springs Range.

Rogan's head jerked up, his ears pricked hard forward. On the wind she heard the high-pitched whinny of a pony.

"DZIEŃ!" Aleksandra shouted, at the same time as Rogan screamed and began dancing on the spot.

"What are you waiting for?" Xavier said.

She flashed him a smile and loosed the reins. Rogan raced off, as if shot from a bow.

By the time they got to his corral, the Mustang was beside himself, whipping back and forth along the rails. Rogan reached over the rails to the pony, and they frantically scratched withers over the fence.

"Just a minute," Aleksandra said, as she pulled off his saddle, then led him to the gateway, where she could drop the rails to let Rogan hop in. They'd always been together, since Rogan had been bought as a foal, and hadn't ever been apart for this long. Aleksandra laughed and shook her head to see the massive bay stallion flapping his jaw, in a submissive foal-chew to the diminutive pony.

"I don't think you'll get them apart again." Xavier chuckled, as he slipped the cinch and unsaddled Charro.

"They'll sleep well tonight."

"As will we," he said, his eyes shining.

"Welcome home, you two," said a man they'd never met before. " I'm Luke. You must be Xavier and Aleks," he said, as he walked over to shake Xavier's hand.

"Good to meet you. Howard's not about, eh?"

"He's gone back to Deep Creek to see the lie of the land, but he told me to watch for you two, and especially," he glanced at Aleksandra, "to take exceptional care of that Mustang." He nodded at Dzień. "Said my life wouldn't be worth living if I didn't."

"Got that right." Xavier laughed.

"You two ready for a meal?"

"Any time," Xavier said, and turned back to finish the horses.

"Not much sense in trying to brush Rogan until after he and Dzień have finished grooming each other," she said.

"True," he said. "Happy now? Your beloved pony is safe and well."

She reached up and kissed him long and hard

"We'd best let Luke know what's going on. When I last saw Egan, it was as a boy."

"Egan read Scotty's letter before I shot out the door to find you, so I'm sure he's put two and two together." He quirked a brow at her.

"OK, let's go in."

A box of ammunition and several rifles were laid out on the table.

"Have you had any trouble?" Xavier nodded at the arsenal.

"Not as yet. We have quite a few men, and plenty of food over at the farmhouse, so we'd be one of the best places to raid."

"Oh, the sourdough and *zakwas*! I hope they're still alive," she said, wincing.

"Hope you don't mind, but I've used your sourdough. Thought it could use feeding. I wasn't sure what the brown one needed, so I've left it."

"You wonderful man." Aleksandra could only stare at him.

"I've lived on my own a long time now, and it sure makes life taste better. Living with a bunch of men, cooking gets me out of doing dishes," he said.

"Because of you, there'll be sourdough biscuits tonight and pancakes in the morning," Aleksandra said, as she pulled down the *zakwas* and trotted to the cupboard for rye flour.

"It's a deal." Luke beamed.

They told him their plans "—that is, if Egan doesn't mind," Xavier finished.

"I'm fine to stay. You can tell the major when you pass through *Ibapah*."

"Thanks," Xavier said. "We'll give the horses a few days to recover while we do some fishing and salt down some little brown fish from the Springs."

"No need to bother yourselves." Luke snorted. "I've been doing that for weeks now. Even dried some as well. You're welcome to them, especially since I'll be staying. Having to fish most of the day is the easiest job Egan's ever given me."

DESIREE NODDED at the stranger as he walked past their wagon, then turned back to kneading bread. She jumped when she heard his voice at her elbow.

"Ah've seen you b'fore," he said. He gazed at her with that look in his eyes she'd rather forget.

"I don't believe we've met," Desiree said, glancing up as she shook another handful of flour into the bowl and pushed her sleeves up.

"Oh yes," he said, raising his brows.

"What may I help you with, Mr..." She waited, then when he didn't continue, said, "Well sir, Mr. Jensen will be back presently. May I let him know you called?"

"Oh no, you prob'ly shouldn't tell 'im. You prob'ly shouldn' tell 'im anythin' a'tall. Not if you don't want word o' yer profession t' get out."

"I make no secret of my life," she said confidently, but the air left her lungs and it was hard to draw a breath.

"Yer life maht get a little hard here if all the wimmen knew." He flashed her a knowing smirk. "They wouldn' let you anywhere near their men, and they'd certainly keep their youngsters away from yer charges. It's a long trip west."

"What about your wife, Mr...ah...oh yes, Mr. O'Rourke, is it? I do seem to remember hearing your name."

His brows shot up, then he recovered. "Ain't got no wife."

"Well then, if you'll excuse me, I mustn't neglect my duties, so I'll wish you good day. I must attend to the children's arithmetic."

"And b'sides," he dropped his last bombshell, "I'm sure that saloon owner maht come lookin' fer one o' his saloon girls. I'm sure he'll pay nicely fer word o' yer...safety."

Picking up the bread bowl, she cradled it in one arm and scrambled up over the wheel into the wagon bed, to the safety of the little ones scratching their sums onto a shared slate.

"Pia, are you nearly ready to recite to me?" She gritted her teeth and tried to smile at Mr. Jensen's eldest daughter.

"Yes, Miss Desiree," she answered.

"Well, I'll listen while I finish the kneading, and then you can all help shape the bread. How does that sound?"

"Oh yes, oh yes!" The two youngest children clapped their hands, while Pia smiled as she picked up her slate.

The woman risked a glance behind her. O'Rourke stood, brows narrowed, lips set in a hard line as he watched her.

After he'd gone, Desiree closed her eyes, hands clasped. When she opened them, Pia was looking at her, biting her lip.

"What's the matter, Pia?"

"That man is evil," she said, and glanced out the front of the wagon.

"Which man?" Desiree replied, as she saw the direction of the girl's gaze.

"That yellow-haired man, Mr. O'Rourke, the one who was being nasty to you while you were trying to make bread," she said in her Danish-accented English.

"He doesn't bother me, but I wouldn't like it to bother your papa."

"I don't like him trying to hurt your...feelings," she struggled for the right word.

Desiree smiled at her. "Thank you, but everything will be fine. Don't you worry."

"I hope he doesn't come back anymore."

"He might be a friend of your father's, so it wouldn't be right to keep him away," Desiree said. "Let's get back to your lessons. I believe it's Søren's turn, yes?"

Pia sat close beside her. The eleven-year-old's protectiveness warmed her heart. It'd been a long time. To the rest of the wagon train, she was simply the hired nanny, there to care for the children and cook Mr. Jesper Jensen's meals, but in truth, they'd become closer, and now slept together as man and wife. She smiled at the children. They were loving, and has accepted her completely.

She gripped her hands together in the folds of her skirt. She'd never seen any women from the train before she joined it, but several of the men had been in the saloon while the wagon train was in Camp Floyd. It was only a matter of time, or a matter of how much they feared their wives, before her history would out.

"Mmm? I'm sorry, Søren, you said? Three plus two is…"

"Three plus two is…," he counted on his chubby fingers, "is *fem*, five," he said, with a wide grin.

"Well done, young man. And now you, Kirsten. Tell me what you have been practicing."

The smallest child, a lovely girl with rosebud lips and blonde curls, lisped out her numbers, to the clapping of her older brother and sister.

Truth be told, if Mr. O'Rourke's information became common knowledge, it would make Jesper's and the children's life difficult. It was already hard enough for them, with Danish as their first language. As well as they were doing with their studies, they'd soon speak better English than most of the American-born children in the train. Desiree had been taught by her mother, who'd been educated to a high level before her fall from grace in marriage to a man beneath her station. She could do this for them, at least.

Dzień spun around and whinnied, head up, ears pricked.

"The wagon train already?" Xavier pulled the last nail out of his mouth and positioned it carefully in the crease of Charro's new shoe.

"I see dust, anyway. The saddlebags and bedrolls are all packed. It'll only take us a minute to saddle up," she said, as she called Dzień back and finished grooming him. "I'll put the pack saddle on Rogan."

"Any last-minute instructions, boss?" Luke drawled, and raised a brow at Xavier.

"Nothing you don't already know. Any messages for Egan?"

"Just tell him the fishing is shocking, and how much I miss the ranch work. That'll get a laugh out of him."

Xavier chuckled and clapped him on the back. "Ready, Aleks?" At her nod, he turned and stepped out into the late morning sunshine, leading Charro. Aleksandra followed, leading Dzień and Rogan.

"Thanks again, Luke," Aleksandra said, as they rode through the willows trailing over the road from the barn. The trees were just beginning to leaf up, and the shoots colored the midday light a dappled spring-green. When the dust of the last wagon dissipated, Aleksandra and Xavier turned the horses heads to follow the train and waved goodbye to Luke.

Just after they left the station, they took a shortcut over a high outcropping of the range. The view from the top was brilliant. The rocky plains behind them had given way to salt flat desert, which continued all the way to the high, snow-capped Deep Creek Range to the west. To their right shone the whitest of the pure salt flats, their glittering expanses like so much snow, spreading far to the northwest.

The wagon train was still far to their right, following the main trail as it circled the far end of the Fish Springs Range.

"WHERE DID YOU COME FROM? You were behind us at Fish Springs," the captain said, when the train finally reached Aleksandra and Xavier.

"There's a shortcut over the top just after the station, but it's not suitable for wagons."

"Ahhh. Good to know." He nodded.

"I'll drop back to see Desiree for a while," Aleksandra said. Xavier waved her goodbye and turned to speak to Captain Moore.

Desiree walked beside the wagon with the older two children, while Mr. Jensen drove his mules from the box, with Kirsten beside him.

"Good morning, miss," the two older Jensens chimed as one, and the youngest sat staring beside her father, her fingers in her mouth. At a nudge from her father, she managed "g'mornin' miss."

"Good morning, Aleks," Mr. Jensen said.

"Good morning." Aleksandra smiled.

"Someday, I would love to have a horse," Pia said.

"Would you like to ride my—ahh, Jesper," Aleksandra turned to the girl's father, "would you permit? He is very well-mannered with children."

"*Ja*, of course," he said.

"Pia, would you like to ride Dzień? I'll walk right beside you." Aleksandra dismounted and stretched her legs.

"Oh, please!" Her eyes shone and she scrambled into the saddle.

Aleksandra and Desiree walked together, periodically switching children on and off the Mustang.

Pia and Søren were both off running ahead when Desiree glanced over her shoulder, then bit her lip.

"What's the matter?" Aleksandra frowned.

"We'll have to talk another time," Desiree said, beneath her breath. "Too many people about, and I can't say it in front of the children."

"Are you OK?"

"For the moment, just stay away from the men in the third wagon ahead of ours. The driver's a snake." Desiree's lips curved up at the ends as the children returned to them, but her eyes weren't smiling.

"Let's catch up after supper tonight," Aleksandra said loudly, and asked Søren if he'd like another ride. "I don't think Dzień would mind at all, especially with all the hugs and rubs you two give him."

"He looks pleased with himself," said Pia. "Look at his pricked-up little ears and his jaunty stride."

"Your English is excellent, Pia," Aleksandra said. How long have you been speaking it?"

"Only since we came to America two years ago, but we are improving quickly with Miss Desiree's help." The girl looked up at Desiree, her eyes glowing.

The former saloon girl reached down to hug her, and Pia returned it with enthusiasm. Aleksandra's heart swelled for her friend.

When the captain called a halt to rest the stock, Aleksandra farewelled her new friends and rode toward the front of the file. A negro woman walked on the other side of a nearly empty Conestoga wagon. Her head was bowed and bonneted and she dragged her feet as she made her way along the rough trail. One man, head lolling, slept on the wooden boxes in the bed of the wagon, but the driver looked Aleksandra up and down as she rode past in her buckskins. He nodded slowly to her, smiling, but the glint in his narrowed eyes raised the hairs on the back of her neck.

11

Aleksandra dipped her head in brief acknowledgment of the man on the wagon box and quickened Dzień's pace.

"I should be more charitable—I don't even know the man, but he gave me the creeps when he looked at me," Aleksandra said to Xavier as they ate their dinner. Captain Moore walked up to them just as she finished speaking.

"Which man, Miss Lekarski?"

"I'm sure I was just imagining it," she said.

"Nevertheless, we don't need problems out here," said the captain. "Was it Mr. O'Rourke?"

"I'm sorry, I never got his name."

"The driver of the wagon with nothing but a few boxes and some blankets in the bed? Two men, with a black woman walking beside them?"

"That's the one. I'm sure he's very nice, and I'm just being silly."

"You're being perceptive, not silly. We've had trouble with him already. He's a Southerner, says he's carrying printing press parts, but I have my doubts. His attitude to women in general and to the free and slave negroes on the train...leaves much to be desired?" He gritted his teeth as he looked back at Mr. O'Rourke's wagon. "You'd be advised to keep your distance, miss."

"Thank you, sir, I will." Aleksandra moved closer to Xavier, who reached an arm around her waist and drew her against him.

BRENT O'ROURKE TURNED his head aside and spat over the side of the wagon, readjusted the quid of tobacco in his cheek, then turned back to his partner with one brow arched. "Shore wouldn't mind a piece o' that pie," he said, nodding at the back of the pretty girl riding ramrod straight on the buckskin Mustang, her long blonde braid brushing the horse's back behind her saddle.

His partner blinked and stretched, then looked where O'Rourke indicated. "I'm pretty shore her man might have somethin' to say about that," his partner drawled in a heavy Southern twang.

"That him up there?" O'Rourke said.

"Yep."

"He's just a Mexican or somethin'. Wouldn't pay 'im no mind. Lots o' accidents happ'n out here, 'specially out huntin'. I think we just might be needin' t' get us an antelope fer supper soon." He grinned evilly.

"Now don't ya go makin' trouble fer us both, ya hear?" O'Rourke's partner lowered his voice, "that man that's payin' you'd skin us alive if you was to make trouble, an' someone were t' find out what's in these here boxes."

"I ain't afraid o' him," O'Rourke muttered between gritted teeth. "We got us a big chunk of land and we're gonna make us a town. There's nobody fer nearly a hunnert miles around it. Nobody'll know what we're gittin' up to, till it's too late. Yep, too late."

THE MEN of the troop had come to realize she probably knew this trail better than most, and deferred to her.

"This station seems pretty defensible, with all those rifle ports, what's it called, Aleks?" said the captain, as they neared it.

"This is Boyd's. Keeper's named Bid Boyd."

"We can fill our canteens and water the horses from their little spring," Xavier said, then called out to the keeper, who'd just put down the hoof of the Mustang he was shoeing.

"Xavier, Aleks!" he called out, walking towards them.

"Would Mr. Boyd perhaps be willing to sell some hay?" the captain said, eyeing the huge barn filled with hay and firewood.

"Probably, especially since the Pony isn't running. He might not need all the hay he's stored."

Aleksandra turned toward the station keeper. "Bid, great to see you again!"

His eyes narrowed as he looked at her, then at Xavier, and then back to Aleksandra's hair, and finally her chest, and then he broke out into a belly laugh.

"I see things have changed," he said, when he got his breath back. "Welcome back, you two, and the rest of you. I'm Bid," he said, holding out his hand to Captain Moore.

After Aleksandra cared for the horses and she and Xavier had eaten, she gathered her dishes and sought out Desiree. The children had gone with Mr. Jensen to play at the next wagon, so Aleksandra added their dishes to her dishpan and smiled at Desiree.

"Let's go do these," Aleksandra said. "I know a place to sit and talk," she added in an undertone.

"Mr. Jensen," Desiree called to him, "would you be able to keep an eye on the children while I clean up?"

He smiled at her and nodded, waving her off.

"If he keeps smiling at you like that, you won't keep your relationship a secret for long," Aleksandra said, when they were well out of the camp, heading for the spring behind the hay barn.

"I hope he does keep smiling like that," she looked around to be sure no one could hear, "even if it *does* make 'Evil O'Rourke' try to stir up trouble."

"O'Rourke… he frightens me too, and all he did was look at me. Has he said something?"

Desiree told her of Mr. O'Rourke's visit.

"I'm afraid of what Mr. Jensen will do. I'm happy for the first time in years, and I don't want to risk that."

"I've always found honesty to be best. At least you won't be frightened he'll find out," Aleksandra said, with a twist of her lips.

"I'm so afraid," she said in a small voice. "Please don't say anything until I decide what to do."

"I promise." Aleksandra gripped her hand until she looked up from where she'd been staring at the ground.

A Mrs. Brown, from another wagon, came around the corner of the barn.

"Why Miss Lekarski," sneered the woman, "what are you two doing back here all by yourself?"

"Washing the dishes?" Aleksandra raised a brow at the woman.

"Why aren't you caring for your charges, Miss, ummm… your name's not Jensen, is it, Desiree?" she said, in a snide voice.

"Mrs. Brown, is there some problem?" Aleksandra raised both brows at her this time.

"We're not liking what we're seeing here." The woman's face was pinched with bitterness as she spun on her heel and stalked away.

Aleksandra faintly heard her comment on the breeze.

"No better than a whore. Taking up with that black gypsy, with his high handed ways, and that other one, unmarried. The shame."

"Did she say what I think she said?" Aleksandra said.

"I believe she did. I wonder what she's heard, and from whom." Desiree shuddered.

IN THE DISTANCE between Dzień's nodding ears, a verdant flash on the horizon slowly became a fresh green stand of cottonwoods, shining against the ever-present Utah starkness of salt, sand and sage. As they drew closer, it grew into the valley of spring-fed grasses, cottonwood and willow she knew as Willow Springs station.

Aleksandra and Xavier rode ahead to the Express station, calling out for Peter to get the heck out of his dugout and come see them.

"Xavier, Aleks…ummm…" Peter stopped, staring at Aleksandra's hair.

"Guess you haven't heard. I'm alive, anyway." She raised her eyebrows at him with a sheepish grin, and told him their news.

"The train can circle up their wagons over there," he pointed, "where there's plenty of grass for them on the river banks."

"I'm sure they'll want to hunt, is there anywhere you would like them to stay out of?" Aleksandra asked.

He gave his instructions, offered water for their horses, and sent them back to intercept the wagons before they trampled his hay fields.

After the horses were settled, and Desiree's charges had been fed, Aleksandra and Desiree walked toward the stream to fill their buckets.

"Oh, look," Aleksandra whispered, and grabbed Desiree's arm to stop her. A little way upstream, near a gurgling waterfall stood a doe and two tiny spotted fawns. They stood watching them for a few moments in silence, while the mother drank deeply from the pool below the fall.

Out of the corner of her eye, Aleksandra saw a movement—O'Rourke. Her heart stopped as he lifted his rifle to his shoulder to take aim. She screamed his name at the same time as she threw the buckets in his direction. They landed harmlessly, and noisily, on the shingle. As the doe flung her head up, then melted into the willows with her fawns, the Southerner swung in their direction and raised his rifle again.

Aleksandra and Desiree stood stock-still, scarcely daring to breathe.

"Well, well. What have we here?"

"We have a doe, with two live fawns," Aleksandra gritted out. "What kind of hunter are you?"

"That's not how ah see it." The man's eyes glinted. "What ah see, is I've got the two whores alone to m'self now. What I see, is that you two'll be making' up for my havin' lost that doe." He smacked his lips. "I've the real whore," he looked at Desiree, "and you, '*Miss*' Aleksandra, with yer highfalutin' airs. Nothin' but a whore, sleepin' with a Mexican."

"Desiree," Aleksandra said, under her breath, "turn around and walk with me. When I say, run."

As one, they turned and began to walk away. With each step, Aleksandra tried not to think of the crazy Southerner behind them in the stream bed, his rifle aimed at their backs. She counted ten steps, and whispered "*run.*" They ran like rabbits, and only stopped when they were behind the station dugout.

"Aleks, please don't tell anyone about this," Desiree said, desperation in her voice.

"You can't mean that." Aleksandra closed her eyes and pinched the bridge of her nose. "This man could hurt somebody, and it looks like we'll be first."

"I'm afraid I'll lose everything if Mr. Jensen find out."

Aleksandra shook her head. "How long will you let him run you around —and what are you willing to do to maintain his silence? It's not worth it."

"I just don't know. Just give me a few days, and I'll figure out what to do."

"Is that you, Aleksandra?" Peter's voice came to them from inside the dugout as they walked past.

"Sure is, Peter, and my friend Desiree. Are you busy, or would you like some visitors?"

"Come on in and sit down for a while," he called. "I'm at the stove just now."

"There was a nice doe with two tiny fawns down at the stream just now," Aleksandra said, as slid onto the bench at the station keeper's table. "It would be a shame if someone accidentally shot her. Some of these Easterners might take a shot at her, even with her babies, not naming any names, you understand." Aleksandra raised a brow at him and he returned it, as he banged a wooden spoon on the rim of a cast-iron pan.

"That's true, I've seen those deer down here most days." He took a long hard look at her and returned to the fire to pull the pan off the coals. "Good thing I don't have to saddle ponies for the Express right now. I'll spend some time down by the water hole with my own rifle and keep that doe away from anywhere close to the wagon train hunters." He gave Aleksandra a wry grin. "Thanks for that, girl, I owe you one."

"Just keep a close eye out and stay out of the path of bullets yourself, eh?"

"That I'll do," he said, as they stood.

"It's been great to see you again, Peter," Aleksandra said, and they made their goodbyes and started to walk out of the dugout.

Desiree grabbed Aleksandra's arm, her nails digging in. She nodded ahead of them at O'Rourke, stomping back to the campground, rifle slung over his back. From time to time, he glanced from side to side, but he never looked back.

"Aleksandra," Peter growled, "is that him? Did you get in the way of his shooting them?"

"I think the doe was scared of our buckets. I…dropped one." She raised a brow, daring him.

"She was probably more frightened of your shout, Aleks." Desiree jabbed her in the ribs and gave her a wide-eyed look.

"Was that you I heard, Aleksandra?" Peter shook his head. "Xavier needs to keep a closer eye on you. That'll just get you killed."

"Peter, please say nothing. Desiree has something she needs to work out, and I said I'd give her a few days. Please?"

"This goes against every ounce of better judgment in my body, but OK," he said. "You'll take care of it soon, before you get hurt?"

"We promise," they both chimed together.

"Thank you, Peter." Aleksandra turned her face up to him, her eyes wide and pleading.

"THAT GIRL IS GONNA PAY. She's gonna pay, and pay, and pay." O'Rourke slammed his fist into a sack of flour.

"What girl?" his partner ventured.

"That uppity one, that Aleks Lekarski, the one sleepin' with the Mexican."

"What'd she do t'you?"

"It's ever'thin' she does. She stopped me from shootin' a doe today down at the crick…I nearly shot her instead, but she had that saloon girl from Camp Floyd with 'er, an I wanna have a bit o'fun with that one, first. The blonde one, I just wanna teach a lesson. Can't cross an O'Rourke and get away with it, no siree, can't. Won't let it happen."

"Whatcha' gonna do 'bout it, boss?"

"Well, its gonna go a little like this…" O'Rourke said, and continued on about it far into the night.

12

"This canyon is one of the main reasons we wished to travel with you," Aleksandra said, as they began the ascent. The sides of the canyon closed in as the trail twisted its way along a tiny stream, the way becoming narrower and higher on both sides as they progressed, until they were traveling between sheer rocky ledges with windblown turrets and pockets. One cavern high on the left was big enough to hide several men, bent upon ambush.

Nothing moved in the landscape today, except for the breeze through the sagebrush.

"Blood Canyon," Aleksandra pointed out a defile opening out to the left, its sides even higher and narrower than those they had just traversed.

"Don't think I'd want to go in there and find out how it got its name," Xavier said, with a shudder.

"Amen to that," said one of the soldiers riding beside them, shaking his head.

After a long climb, the canyon opened up into a sagebrush-dotted landscape that spread out on both sides.

"Is that what's left of Canyon station, Aleks?" Xavier said, nodding to their left at a pile of cinders in a patch of blackened ground.

"Yes," Aleksandra said, through clenched teeth, then looked away. "I'll go see how Desiree's faring."

"OK, Aleks, see you soon." He reached across and squeezed her hand.

Xavier took a deep breath, and waited till Aleksandra was out of earshot. He had to tell the captain.

"She rode the Pony Express until a few weeks ago," he said, in an undertone.

His brows shot up. "But she's female!"

"She got away with it. She's lost her entire family and is a fearless horsewoman. She's been trained in Cossack trick riding. She's the best little rider I've ever seen."

"Why would a woman—"

"—because she had nothing left, and because she could," Xavier finished for him.

"Ah, well," Captain Moore sighed.

"She rode this whole stretch from Salt Lake to Roberts Creek and *back*, because there were no live riders. The sights she saw on that 340-plus mile ride were past shocking. Stations burned, men and stock butchered. She saved a lot of men—"

"—say, was he, uh, *she*," the young private cut in, "the one that saved all the men at Roberts Creek—went back to get the Army detachment she'd just passed?" His eyes were aglow.

Xavier groaned. He'd spoken too loudly.

"Sure was, but don't you men go telling anyone. She'd get into a heap of trouble."

"Cross my heart, hope to die," he said with reverence. "She's my new hero!"

"She'll die of embarrassment, but I'll tell her anyway. Not a word now, eh gentlemen?"

"Her story's safe with me," said another man.

"And me."

"And me," said the captain, "but I'm still going to congratulate her," he said with a grin.

"OK, I'm sure she'll accept that," Xavier said.

After the stock were rested near a prospector's cabin beside a small stream at Clifton Flat, the wagon train readied itself to move again. Two men called out a greeting to Aleksandra and Xavier as they rode by.

"Lucky they didn't recognize me from my last ride." Aleksandra said. "Probably moving too slowly this time."

"You probably didn't have that whopping great braid down your back then," he said, and tweaked it.

"OK lads," the captain called out, "one more incline, then it's a long downhill run to Egan's Deep Creek Ranch. We'll spend the night there."

"Dancing Wolf said the Indians call Egan's place *Ai-bim-pa*, which means 'White Clay Water'. Sounds a lot like *Ibapah*."

"There's white clay at one of the waterholes. Slippery." Xavier said.

Sagebrush dotted the landscape in all directions on the gradual rise from Clifton Flat, and extended up to the higher reaches of the surrounding Deep Creek Mountains.

"I never tire of this view," Aleksandra said, with longing. She gazed at the panorama opening before her eyes as they topped the hill. Deep Creek Wash, a wide valley which ran from horizon to horizon, bloomed with greens and purples along its length. Smoke puffed from the Pony Express station and the big ranch house at the bottom.

Egan's Deep Creek Ranch, a scattering of buildings and fields, was surrounded by a huge patch of green.

The captain smiled at her. "It's a sight for sore eyes, isn't it? All that verdure."

"Set your brakes, men," he barked back to the first wagons following them, as they set off down the two mile straight-as-an-arrow road down the mountain.

The call echoed back down the line as the immigrants prepared for the steep descent.

"We'll go ahead and find out where they want us to camp," Xavier said. "Shall we?" He raised a brow at Aleksandra and they moved off at Charro and Dzień's ground-eating walks.

"Dzień really hates oxen-speed." Aleksandra chuckled.

"We all do."

The miles slipped by quickly at their new pace, and soon they were on the flats, with greening fields on both sides of the trail.

As they neared the ranch buildings, the ring of hammer blows from the blacksmith shop pinged through the air and the smell of baking wafted from the cook shack behind the house.

"Egan," Xavier said, as he dismounted and took the man's gnarled hand in a firm grip.

"Xavier," he said, thumping him on the back, "so you found her." He turned to Aleksandra. "Well, miss," his eyes shone, "I think you have a story to tell me."

"Well, about that," she muttered, looking down at her feet, "it might take a few minutes."

"It'll take that long for that wagon train to get down that hill, anyway," Xavier said.

Egan tipped Aleksandra's chin up with his forefinger and smiled at her, then grabbed her in a bear hug. "You don't know how happy I am to see you in one piece," he said. "As worried as Xavier was when he shot out of Fish Springs after he got Johnny's letter from Salt Lake House, I thought you'd be a goner for sure. I read the letter he dropped on the floor," he glanced at

Xavier sheepishly. "Begging your pardon, but I put two and two together and figured out you were a girl. Toughest damn girl I've ever seen in my life," he said, shaking his head.

"That's what the army commander said, after she saved the whole lot of them at Roberts. Said he wished he had more men like her, then told me he wanted to join her up on the spot."

"You never told me that." Aleksandra rolled her eyes.

Xavier smirked. "I was choking when he told me that, thinking what he'd say if I'd told him Aleks was female."

"Male or female, you're still my favorite rider, bar none." Egan smiled and tweaked her braid. "Your horses can go down in the two pens on the end, plenty of feed and water in there already. When the wagons arrive, I'll come out with you. Coffee, anyone?"

"MAJOR EGAN SAID the train can camp over in that field. There's a good track to the water right beside it."

"Thanks, the feed looks good. Their stock are pretty stressed, after the steep downhill." The captain's brows narrowed.

"I'll go help Desiree make camp," Aleksandra said, and headed for the woman holding hands with the two older children as they walked beside the wagon.

"Aleks, could you please pass the word back that there's a meeting for the whole train tonight after suppertime?" Moore said.

Aleksandra quirked her lips at him for a moment. "Is it for the whole train, or just for the men?"

At the officer's silence, she raised a brow at him and shook her head before she turned away. "I'll never understand."

"Aleks, how has your day been?" Desiree said. "I love it here."

"It's been lovely."

"Miss Lekarski, is there an Express station here?" Pia asked.

"Yes, it's right over there." She pointed to a small building by the edge of the creek, surrounded by pens full of Mustangs of many colors.

"You're all to camp over there," Aleksandra said to Jesper, "so if you'd like to follow me, we'll find you a good spot."

"Thanks Aleks," Desiree said, as Mr. Jensen turned the sweating mules to the right and headed for a spot shaded by cottonwoods beside the swiftly running stream.

"I can help you set up camp, if you like," Aleksandra said.

"We have it all sorted, Mr. Jensen, the children, and I, so go spend some time alone with Xavier." Desiree gave her a sly grin. "There's not much room for privacy with a wagon train. Take advantage of it while you can."

Aleksandra laughed. "We get plenty of time alone, but I'm glad you're enjoying your new family."

"I haven't had such good times since before my family died. I'll never go back to that kind of unhappiness again, whatever it takes," Desiree said, beneath her breath.

"Good to see you happy," Aleksandra said, her eyes filling with tears, and she headed back toward her man.

She had nearly reached Xavier when hoofbeats sounded, becoming louder as a single horse approached at a good clip. Her head shot up as a bugle sounded. Around the bend in the trail, a young man raced up to the station and flew off his black Mustang and into the farm kitchen. After a few moments, the door slammed back against the adobe wall of the station as he left the building and headed for the barn.

Xavier raised a brow at Aleksandra and they turned to watch.

"That's James," Xavier frowned, "one of the stableboys from Salt Lake House."

Scarcely two minutes later, Egan walked out of the building with his saddlebags and a buckskin jacket thrown over one shoulder. He glanced around and saw Xavier and Aleksandra, spun on his heel and almost trotted towards them.

"James came from Great Salt Lake to get me. Something of importance, but he wasn't told what it was."

"Do you need help?" Xavier's brow furrowed.

"James doesn't expect any danger, but it's urgent. I'll get a message to you to let you know what's up," Egan said, as he slung his saddlebags over the back of the pinto Mustang the stableboy had just brought around for him.

"James," Xavier nodded, "good to see you."

"Xavier, Aleks," he said, grinning from ear to ear, as he held the bridle while Egan mounted.

He must've heard, too.

She smiled wanly back at him, then turned her attention to Major Egan.

"You take good care, eh old man?" Aleksandra reached up to him for a quick hug.

"Not so much of the old, please," he said as he returned it. "You two take care of each other, you hear?"

"Hold on to your hair, Egan," Xavier said, shaking his hand.

"James, I'll see you back at Salt Lake when you've had some rest," Egan said as he loosed the piebald's reins and the Mustang shot off.

"I don't think that horse's had much exercise since the Pony stopped running." Aleksandra chuckled and shook her head.

"What's the news at Salt Lake House?" Xavier said, as they walked together back toward the station.

"The Indians have been pretty peaceful," James' brows knit together, "but something's going down tonight. We've had a warning, and we hoped Egan could defuse things a little—maybe keep a few more people alive."

"Pia, can you please keep Søren and Kirsten in the wagon with you while I collect water from the creek?"

"Of course, Miss Desiree. Shall I do spelling with them?"

"Thank you," she replied, "and later, I'll braid your hair up 'specially, if you'd like."

"Oh yes, please." She glanced around, and frowned. "I don't see the evil man. Watch out for him."

"Nothing will happen," Desiree shook her head and bit her lip, "I will be back in a few minutes."

The poor girl was so worried.

She'd lost her mother, and taken on more responsibility than she should have had to, at her tender age. Desiree would keep reassuring her until she believed she wouldn't be abandoned again. Despite her confident words, Desiree hurried to be back as soon as possible.

The soft, young green shoots of the willows lining the creek were like velvet to Desiree's fingers when she reached up to touch them. As she stepped with care down the wet clay bank, she heard an unwelcome voice growl behind her. She slipped and fell the rest of the way down the bank, landing on her bottom at the edge of the creek. Somehow she'd managed to keep hold of her buckets and quickly filled them without turning around.

"I *said*, good afternoon." O'Rourke jumped down the bank and grabbed her arm. "When I speak t' you, y' answer me, ya hear?"

"Unhand me, sir," Desiree stared into his eyes, unflinching as her own.

"Where you and I come from, women obey men, don't they?"

"I no longer live in the South."

"Girls in your profession—"

"—and I am no longer in that profession." She enunciated each word.

"What ya were, is what y'all always be. A Southerner from a poor family'll always be dirt. A whore'll always be a whore. And remembah, you'd best not be tellin' yer man 'r anyone else I'm consortin' with ya. I'll just tell it was all your doin', an' I had to push ya away from me. If ya don't want him to find out about us, you'd best be takin' a walk with me afta supper tonight. In *private*." He gave a final jerk to her arm and spun her about, then disappeared up the stream.

Desiree closed her eyes. She took deep breaths until her heart stopped pounding. After years of being a saloon girl, she'd thought no man could upset her anymore.

She was dead wrong.

↳

"WHATEVER IS that gray stuff down the back of your skirt, Desiree?" Aleksandra shook her head. "You're usually so much tidier than I could ever be," she said with a laugh, then slapped her mouth shut at the tears threatening to spill from her friend's eyes.

"I slipped going down the bank to fill the water buckets at the creek. It's clay," she said with enforced cheerfulness, as she stood behind Pia and braided her hair into a style worn by women, rather than by children. She stared over Pia's head at Aleksandra, and shook her head.

Pia frowned.

"My, my, Pia, don't you look the grown-up young lady with your hair up?" She smiled at the girl, and took her hand. "You'll be the prettiest woman at the campfire tonight."

"Please, Miss Desiree, may I keep it up for the campfire?"

"You certainly may," Desiree said, with a look of gratitude to Aleksandra, over the girl's head. She finished the job and tucked the last pin into place. "Now run and get my mirror, and you can see what it looks like. We'll be over here behind the wagon."

"What's going on, Des?" Aleksandra stared at her.

"Nothing."

"Nothing won't work with me, Des, and what's happened? Where did the clay come from?"

"I slipped and fell when O'Rourke found me down by the river. He told me I had to go with him tonight, alone, or he will tell everyone...everything."

Aleksandra shook her head.

"I have to meet with him tonight, or he'll make those children's and Mr. Jensen's lives miserable. They have shown me nothing but kindness. I cannot allow this to happen."

"Can you trust me? We can fix this, but you'll need to trust me, and Xavier, completely."

She stood in silence for long minutes, her emotions warring in her face, then took a deep breath, stood up straight, and agreed.

↳

XAVIER MOVED over to the other side of the campfire to keep Jensen's wagon in view. His fists clenched and unclenched in his coat pockets as he waited for a sign from Aleksandra that Desiree had gone to meet with O'Rourke.

"I vote we push on for at least two Express stations every day, mountains or no mountains," said the Boston leader.

"You've asked the Army for an escort, and escort we will, but I won't be responsible for your stock being so exhausted we can't get out of a tight spot if we need to." Captain Moore said, unruffled.

"The hills between here and Carson can't be that big," the Easterner said, with disdain.

"Just how high do you think they are?" The captain toyed with the hilt of his saber, and it glinted in the firelight.

"Not that high, and we could go around them, like we're going around most of the others in the last hundred miles."

"They run a long way north and south," the captain said, then tried another tack. "Ever been at 6,900-plus feet? With snow? With no feed or water for the stock? I encourage you to think about it before making decisions which will result in deaths, deaths which will be upon your own head," the officer's raised brow showed in the light of the campfire, "with all due respect, of course, sir."

He turned on his heel and walked away, glancing at Xavier as he left. He nodded his head to the left, and Xavier and Jesper rose to follow him.

"Captain, Aleksandra hasn't come me yet, and it's well past the agreed time." Xavier looked at Jesper. "I don't like the look of this. We'd best check out your wagon."

"*Far, Far, kom med mig!*" Pia ran towards them through the darkness, then glanced from her father to Xavier and the captain. "Father! Come with me, please, all of you," she whispered.

"What's the matter, Pia?" her papa said.

"No time, time there isn't, you must now come," she said, words jumbling together, and grabbed her father's hands. A flood of Danish ran from her mouth, but her father's English wasn't up to the translation. After a moment's hesitation, she reached for Xavier's as well and tugged with all her strength.

"Tell us, Pia," Xavier said softly, ducking down to get closer to her height.

The girl took two deep breaths, then concentrating on every word, she got it out. "The evil man has taken Miss Desiree."

"Who has?"

"Mr. O'Rourke. Miss Desiree put the other children and me to bed, then Miss Lekarski and she sat outside the wagon in talking. I wasn't sleepy and was sitting up in bed watching the flames of our little campfire, when Miss Desiree stood up, twisting her hands together. Her face in the firelight was so sad. I started to get up to go to her, when that nasty man stepped up behind her and held a knife across her throat. He said they were both to come with him or Miss Desiree would die. He made Miss Lekarski go ahead of them. I came to you as soon as I thought he wouldn't see me, and it was safe. Please, please hurry!"

13

"Where have you positioned your men, Captain?" Xavier said, then took a deep breath.

"They are all off to the north, where Desiree was to lead him when she went to him."

"Jesper, are there other men in the train you trust?"

"There are three. Two have already left the meeting, so they should be at their wagons," the quiet Danish man said.

Xavier thought for a moment. "Captain, if you go straight west to check the riverbank, I'll check the farm buildings, then go to the south and do the same. You know how to make the sound of a barn owl?"

Jesper nodded.

"If you find them, hoot three times, silence then repeat."

"Are the women armed?" the captain asked.

"Aleksandra will be, but I don't know about Desiree," Xavier said, shaking his head.

"We'll have to gather the men we can and stick as closely to our plans as possible," Captain Moore said. "The biggest unknown is O'Rourke's partner."

"He must be silenced, above all," Xavier said grimly, his own words barely audible to himself over the pounding of his heart.

Grabbing a rope and two of Aleksandra's scarfs, Xavier followed the captain to O'Rourke's wagon, but his partner was nowhere to be found.

"Damn," the captain whispered under his breath. "On to plan two."

"DON'T EVEN TRY T' protect 'er, Aleks, ah'll just cut her throat. Ah've done it before, when a woman didn't do what they were s'posed to, and ah'm happy to do it again."

While he spoke, Aleksandra had been working her hand beneath the waistline of her skirt, freeing up her *shashka*. It shouldn't be too hard to deal with O'Rourke, as he sat on Desiree, pinning her body to the ground. He had only so many hands. With one, he shoved up her skirts, and the other was tied up, holding his knife to her throat.

"You can have her when I'm done," he said over his shoulder into the darkness, "and then I'll have the blonde."

Aleksandra whipped her head around to see O'Rourke's partner step out of the trees into the moonlight. She gritted her teeth, but kept the grip of the short sword in her hand.

So he has backup.

She scowled.

"That don't sound very fair t' me," he said, and his brows narrowed. He turned his glance from the white legs showing behind O'Rourke to look at Aleksandra. "Why can't ah just have the blonde now, and then we kin swap?"

"Ahh *said*, ye can have a turn with the blonde after ah'm done, that is, if there is anything left by the time *ahm* done. Ah definitely owe her one, and she has a few lessons t' learn 'bout a woman's place. Ah'll be pleased to teach 'er. You kin watch—ya might learn somethin'."

The partner glanced around and listened carefully. Satisfied, he walked toward Aleksandra and took her arm, his knife at the ready.

Desiree was past being stoic, and started to whimper, but then she gave a great kick and nearly bucked him off her abdomen. "If you don't let me up and let us go, I'll scream, and all the men will him be here in a second," she whispered with fury.

"Oh no you won't, girl," he growled.

O'Rourke's knife glinted as he flicked it up near Desiree's face. "Women in your profession need their looks, so you'll be quiet. You wouldn't want me to rearrange your pretty face, now, would you? Come on, it's not like I'm your first." He laughed.

A barn owl hoot three times, then again. A moment later, she heard the sounds, but from the other direction. Without moving her head, she glanced at both of the men, but they didn't seem to have noticed. She took a deep breath and peered around again.

Xavier and the captain were here, but how could they help without getting Desiree killed?

"Let me go, leave me alone!" Desiree squirmed, then bit at his hand when he tried to cover her mouth.

"Like it rough, do ya?" he said, with grim pleasure. "I know yer sort o' woman."

"No," she said, firmly and steadily, calm once more. "I've changed my life. I don't do that any more."

"Ya will with *me*, otherwise yer life'll be hell on this wagon train."

Desiree swung with one fist and something crunched. She grimaced.

"Fight me, will ya?" he roared. Throwing down the knife, he backhanded her and continued to grope between Desiree's exposed thighs with the other.

His sidekick gripped Aleksandra's arm, but his eyes wandered to the scene playing out before them. Only for a moment, but that was all she needed.

As Aleksandra spun around the arm he held, *shashka* raised, crashing resounded in the bushes all around them. He turned, seeking the source of the noise, still trying to grip her arm, and she hit him hard on the side of the head with the pommel of her sword and he went down in a heap.

"You're OK?" Xavier bit out, and hugged her hard and fast.

"Yes, go," she said, and pushed him toward the captain and Jensen, heading for O'Rourke, while she knelt beside O'Rourke's partner to make sure he was out. Two other angry men, death in their eyes, were close behind Xavier.

He and Captain Moore dragged O'Rourke backwards off Desiree and held him up against a tree for Jesper to take Desiree's revenge for her. Over their captive's shoulder, Xavier watched Aleksandra. She relinquished custody of the O'Rourke's unconscious sidekick to the other two men and raced to Desiree's side. Pulling the brunette into her lap, she rocked her silently.

"You about done there, Jensen? Want us to take a turn?" one of Jesper's friends offered.

"I think he'll remember," Jensen said, puffing.

O'Rourke slumped between the men, his face a bloody pulp, the front of his shirt stained dark in the moonlight.

"Just dump him next to his partner," Xavier said to the captain. "Can you hear me, O'Rourke?"

When he made no answer, one of the men kicked him in the ribs for good measure. "Wake up, man."

"I repeat, can you hear me?" Xavier growled.

Eyes closed, he lifted his head an inch or so, and nodded once.

Xavier started. "This wagon train—"

"—and I," the captain took over, his voice ringing out in the darkness, "order you and your partner to take your wagon and be gone before dawn. We could kill you both now and no one would ever be the wiser, or we can let you go on the condition you never show your face again to anyone on this train. You are no longer welcome here."

The Southerner's head slumped again. His accomplice still hadn't moved.

Xavier hunkered down beside Aleksandra after the men dragged O'Rourke and his partner away and held her tight, lips against her hair. He picked her up and carried her back toward the train. She was shaking, and clutched at his arms. He shook his head with a smile. "You probably could've gotten both of you out of there without our help."

"I planned on it, before his blasted partner showed up. We'd have been in trouble if you men hadn't arrived. Sorry we didn't stick to the plan, but he had a knife to Desiree's throat, so I thought maybe we'd go along with him."

"So said Pia. She alerted us you'd both been taken." He pulled her close again.

"Is Desiree OK?"

"She's with Jesper," Xavier said. "I believe he's asking her to become his wife, as we speak."

Aleksandra managed a smile at that. "I never did thank you for coming to save us." She turned her face up to him and he kissed her lips.

"While I love being your knight in shining armor," he said, "I fear someday I won't be in time."

"It's a good thing, then," she chuckled low, "I'm so good with a *shashka*."

"No, I mean it," he said, gritting his teeth for a moment. "How can we keep this from happening?"

"I haven't the faintest idea," she said. "Trouble keeps finding us."

He sighed. "Let's get some rest, not that I'll be able to sleep until those Southerners leave camp. Maybe not even then."

After the children had been settled into their beds, the four adults sat around the fire and kept watch for any movement from the shadowy heap on the Southerner's wagon bed.

"Another story to tell our children," Aleksandra said.

"Never before have I been so happy to have been raised on the *København* docks as tonight." He gave them a haunted grin. "It required of me that I learn to use my fists. I hope our Mr. O'Rourke remembers, because I will not forget." He wrapped his arms about his new fiancée, her eyes glowing in the firelight.

Few people in the camp slept well that night, and most were still wide awake for the scene in the morning.

"Ye'll pay for this, y' Northerners, all o' ya," Brent O'Rourke growled as he drove his mules away in the predawn light. His partner lay rolled in a pile of blankets in the wagon bed, on top of the long wooden boxes, all they carried besides food and the black woman in the travel-worn calico dress, her bonnet still pulled down low over her face.

Women peered out of their wagons, nighttime braids hanging to their knees, while their men stood before the wagons, clutching rifles before them.

"Get on with it," the train leader returned. "Go, before we change our minds, O'Rourke."

"Ye'll pay fer this with yer lives," he shouted back, and drove his team west.

"That should keep everyone looking over their shoulders for the rest of the trip," Aleksandra commented dryly to Desiree.

"Probably not a bad idea if they do," she returned, one brow cocked.

"All right, people, let's get on the road," Captain Moore barked. "We've got an easy trail today, and if we make Prairie Gate early enough, we might push on to Antelope Springs Station."

"We'd better go pack up then," Desiree grinned and wrapped her arm around Pia, who stood close beside her.

"Pia, thank you again for coming to our aid last night," Aleksandra said. "It was very brave, and I'm proud of you."

"I would do it again, if I had the opportunity, or the need," the girl said, pulling Desiree even closer.

"Hopefully, there won't be any more need," Desiree said, "with O'Rourke gone."

THE SUN SHONE, Pia's evil man was gone, and Aleksandra's world looked bright, riding beside her man on his gray along the flat valley floor, surrounded by high mountains.

As the afternoon wore on, the alluvial plain turned to dry sagebrush flats.

"What do you think O'Rourke was carrying in that wagon, Captain?" the young private asked.

"What do you think, men," Captain Moore looked around the group, "and ladies?" he added, as his eyes ran past Aleksandra.

"Guns," she said promptly. "Guns for the California secessionists."

Everyone was silent for a moment.

"I should've checked," the captain murmured. A muscle twitched in his tensed jaw.

"O'Rourke said they were machine parts, for printing presses," said one of the other soldiers.

The captain laughed. "They could've used them to rebuild *The Monitor's* printing presses. The crowd threw them into the bay."

"They what? Into the San Francisco Bay?" Xavier said, wide-eyed, and slack-jawed.

"*The Monitor?*" Aleksandra tilted her head at them.

The officer nodded, then turned to her. "*The Monitor* is the Roman Catholic Archdiocese's newspaper. Their articles have been getting a bit Southern-oriented over the past few years, and many believed they were printing the secessionist flyers around town. The loyal Union citizens decided they'd had enough of their treasonous activity."

Xavier locked eyes with Aleksandra. "It's really heating up, then, isn't it?" he said.

Moore agreed. "With the presidential nominations to be announced any day, the friction between the Union and the South is getting so hot, it's about to combust."

"Hold up, hold up, hold up," the shout rang up the line, and the beasts of burden stopped and stood still.

"I'll see what's up," the captain said, as he spun his horse and loped back down the line. He returned a few minutes later, his mouth a firm hard line.

"A wheel," he said, his words clipped, "on that big wagon, the one owned by our fearless Bostonian leader."

"The one who doesn't maintain his wagon." Aleksandra raised an eyebrow at him.

The captain gritted his teeth. "And the one who doesn't carry a spare."

Aleksandra winced, then turned to Xavier, who shook his head.

The commander shook his head, then ordered his men to break camp for the night. With a set jaw, he turned his stallion toward the rear of the file. "I'll be back as soon as I can. Taylor, McCabe, you two come with me and help them circle up the wagons. Their boss is going to be busy for a while. A long while."

In the distance, Aleksandra could see Prairie Gate station.

So close, and yet so far.

They dismounted and picketed the horses. Dzień stared at her as she left him.

"I know it's early yet, boy, but we can't go on today."

The wrinkles over his eyes deepened and his muzzle clenched for a moment, then he sighed and lowered his muzzle to the ground, seeking wisps of grass.

They camped, within sight, but not within hearing distance, of Prairie Gate station.

"I'd actually feel safer camped away from the wagon train. How about you?" Xavier raised a brow at her.

"You must've been reading my mind." She smiled as she pulled her rifle from its saddle scabbard. "Let's go for a hunt and scout out a place with at least some brush for shelter."

They walked toward a clump of brush about a mile from the camp, looking for signs of game.

"It's a buffalo wallow," she said, when they reached it.

"I've never seen one," he said, looking over the rim of the big depression inside its ring of sagebrush. The oval hollow was filled with green, if patchy, grass.

"They probably started out as springs where buffalo and antelope walked through the mud, over the ages. They hollow out, maybe by the animals tracking the mud out when they leave, and the dirt packs down. Animals like them. They must hold water, because grass grows in them, even when it's too dry for it to grow just outside the sink."

"It's like a magical fairy ring," he said in a soft voice, and his eyes took on a faraway look. "Mama used to talk of them—" he broke off with a sheepish grin.

"It is." Aleksandra smiled and put her arm around him. "Especially with the new little flowers peeking out from beneath the brush."

"The horses will love it, too," Xavier said.

"It's nearly deep enough to hide them inside it."

He turned her in his arms and pulled her close, his lips finding hers.

"Matter of fact, I rather like all this grass too," he said, dropping to his knees and pulling her down beside him. He sat up and tugged off his buckskin jacket, his eyes never leaving her face, and her heart caught in her throat.

There hasn't been much time to be alone lately.

She nodded at the question in his eyes.

With a final glance about them, he slid her doeskin shirt over her head and placed it on the ground beside his. Lifting her onto them, he lowered his bulk over her, supporting himself on his elbows.

Aleksandra looked up into his chocolate eyes as his lips took hers, and an ache grew down low in her belly, becoming stronger as his hands began to flow over her smooth skin. She was kissed by the warmth of the afternoon springtime sun, and its light made a halo around her Latin lover's head.

When she came to her senses again, the sun was low, and the warmth had quite disappeared from their magic circle. Xavier held her close and kissed her again, then dressed her with slow languor.

"We'd best see about catching some supper," she murmured.

"We were just waiting for the perfect dusk for hunting," he said, his eyes still glowing.

WITH TWO JACKRABBITS slung over their shoulders, they returned to camp an hour later, just on dark. It was a quiet group around the communal campfire, and as the night wore on, men often rose and left the fireside to check on the sentries posted beyond the edge of the flickering light. They'd sent the Southerner away, but he couldn't be very far away yet, and they weren't taking any chances.

They slept peacefully in the wallow that night. Their trio of four-legged sentries stood through the night, with only the sounds of ripping grass interspersed with the occasional blow through soft nostrils punctuating the starry night. Aleksandra hated to rise from their magical den, but leave they must. One last long kiss for Xavier, then she stood and folded her *serape*.

Back in camp she was lugging two canvas buckets of water, kindly supplied by Jesper, toward the picketed horses, when a cloud of dust appeared over the rise between them and *Ibapah*.

"Captain!" Aleksandra shouted at the top of her lungs.

He swung about from where he stood speaking with two of his men and looked in the direction of her pointed finger.

"Get the stock, women and children inside the wagon circle, we've got visitors. Now!" his voice boomed over the sounds of breaking camp. Men and women scurried to do his bidding as Aleksandra and Xavier saddled and bridled their horses, then stowed their excess gear beneath Jesper's wagon.

By the time the ears of the first thundering horses showed over the ridge behind them, every rifle and Colt revolver in the camp was trained in their direction.

14

The oncoming group's leader's head showed first. He waved his arm as a bugle call rang out, and the men by his side slowed their galloping horses to a walk.

The blue uniforms of the US Army troop appeared, and the wagon camp breathed again, lowering their weapons. A few made light of their fear, while others wiped their brows, covered in beads of sweat, despite the chill late afternoon air.

The commander signaled to his troops and they stayed behind while he and a vaguely familiar man closed the distance between them at a trot.

"It's Egan." Xavier grinned at Aleksandra.

"I've never seen him riding towards me on a horse, and with a *mochila*, no less!"

They rode with the captain to greet the newcomers.

"Captain Moore, Xavier, Aleks," Major Howard Egan said, " this is Major Jackson."

"Gentlemen." Moore nodded. "We're stuck with a broken wheel." He raised a brow at them. "Glad to see you're not raiding Indians."

"You were prepared, anyway," Jackson said.

"As prepared as this lot can get," the captain grumbled.

"What are you doing out here, Egan? Thought you were in Salt Lake?" Xavier cocked an eyebrow at him.

"Didn't quite make it there, this troop met me halfway."

"What's so urgent?" the *Californio* asked.

"Four lots of Express mail to go West, and big news from back East—Lincoln's been nominated for President of the United States."

Aleksandra looked at the troop of twenty hardened-looking men behind him—no boys in this lot.

Her eyes swung back to Egan and she took a deep breath. "Hence the escort," she said. "That ought to stir up the hornet's nest between North and South."

"Precisely." Major Jackson said. "Despite the destroyed stations, we couldn't risk losing these Express shipments and mail on the Butterfield southern route, so we've been asked to see it gets through." He flicked a glance at her again. "It won't be as fast as you'd get it through, Aleksandra, but it'll get there."

She cringed as she stared up at him, then recognized the man who'd commanded the troops at Roberts Creek when she led them back to save the station keepers there. She swallowed as the world swam around her.

Word must have really gotten out.

Major Jackson glanced around to be sure no one heard them outside their circle of five. "Your story's safe with me, lass—"

"—sorry Aleks," Egan interrupted, "I had to tell him."

Xavier flushed, then smiled and shook his head. "Thank you, men."

"I thought it'd be easier to tell him," Egan grinned, "in case you two want to ride West with us. Figured you'd be going crazy at this pace somewhere around now."

Aleksandra looked at Xavier. His ear to ear smile matched what she was sure showed on her own face.

"Please, gentlemen. We'd be grateful," Xavier said, with a heartfelt sigh

"Are we leaving now, or are you taking a break? We need to collect our gear and say our goodbyes."

"We'll have a short stop now, then continue on to Prairie Gate in a half hour." He smiled at her.

Desiree and Pia were waiting for them just outside the circled-up wagons.

"They're going West, and they've invited us. Will you be OK on your own, now O'Rourke's gone?" Aleksandra asked.

"How can I be on my own?" Desiree grinned and hugged Pia to her side. "I have my new lovely daughters and son, not to mention husband-to-be."

Pia smiled up at her, then at Aleksandra and Xavier. She hugged them both together. "Thank you for saving our Desiree. We are forever in your debt," she said, choosing her words with care.

"Pia, we're grateful to *you*. Without your quick thinking, both Aleks and Desiree would have fared much worse," Xavier said, and looked up to see Mr. Jenkins and the two younger children, their hands clasped together.

"Yes, to you both we are grateful, and we wish you the very best," Mr.

Jenkins said in his soft Danish voice. "If we discover our train will be delayed, we will return to overwinter with you in Virginia City. We have no wish to share the Donner's fate." He closed his mouth abruptly.

Aleksandra stared at the little man. She'd never heard more than five words from his mouth at once before.

He looked at her and chuckled. "Yes, I can speak when something means as much to me as you two do. Thank you for being such a friend to my fiancée." He broke off as he and Desiree exchanged a soft smile. "I never thought to love again. I sought a mother for my children, but for me, no, or so I thought." He wrapped an arm around Desiree and Pia, then the little ones ran for Aleksandra and Xavier, before they were joined by Desiree and Pia.

"Travel well, and we'll see you soon. If not on this side of the *Sierras*, perhaps at Rancho de las Pulgas, eh Xavier?" Desiree arched a fine brow at him.

"Perhaps." He smiled.

Pia wrapped her arms around Dzień's neck. "You'll take good care of him, won't you?"

"I'll guard him with my life. You'll take good care of Desiree, won't you?"

"I promise. *Mange tak,*" she said, as Aleksandra mounted.

Aleksandra thought for a moment to recall the Danish words the girl had taught her. "*Tak i lige maade,*" she said with a wry grin.

"Goodbye, all, take care." Xavier called, as they rode back to Captain Moore's troop.

"Please farewell your men for me," Aleksandra said, when they reached them. "I'm not used to being with many people at once, but they made it fun."

"The pleasure was all ours," he assured her. "You two livened up what could have been a long, arduous trip. Perhaps our paths will cross again." He wheeled his horse about and returned to the wagon train.

"Thought you'd appreciate the faster escort." Egan raised his eyebrows. "Aleks, are you OK to see the stations ahead?"

Aleksandra sobered, then nodded, with a gulp.

They soon reached the blackened, burned-out shell of Prairie Gate station, sad in its solitude. No keeper with gun primed came to greet them, and there were no animals to be seen. They approached carefully, refilled their canteens and let the horses drink their fill from the remaining barrel beside what was left of the pens, then went on.

"We'll break for dinner at Spring Valley and let the horses a feed, before heading over Shellbourne Pass. They'll need it. After the pass, we'll head on until dark," Major Jackson said as the troop mounted up, "then break camp for the night."

Aleksandra was looking decidedly green. "You know Schell Creek station is burned out too, don't you, sir?"

He nodded and gritted his teeth.

"When do you expect we'll get to Nevada station?" Xavier asked, trying to draw Aleksandra's attention away from the vision of charcoal and death before them.

"Ummm…that's Chinatown?" The major looked across at one of his men.

"Yes, sir, that's what they're calling it now," the soldier replied.

"It should take us about five days to get there, all going to plan," Major Jackson said. "Where are you two headed?"

"Virginia City," Xavier replied.

"I've got a sister there, runs a rooming house with her husband. She might be able to put you up."

Aleksandra and Xavier looked at each other. "We might take you up on that, thank you," Xavier said, and looked sideways at Aleksandra. Her color seemed to be coming back.

"Are you OK?" Xavier asked her, when they were out of earshot of the others. "Is it Schell Creek?"

"Yes, just the thought of…of the men there…" She gulped.

"They were dead, yes. I wanted to bury them, but I was afraid I'd be too late to find you, *Querida*."

She glanced up for a moment at the endearment. "Not dead. Yes, they were dead, but they were…were…*scalped*."

She was white as a sheet, and it chilled him to the bone.

"Aleks, you've done all you could; you saved the men at Roberts Creek, didn't you?" he pleaded.

"I'm terrified to see it again, but it'll be OK," she said, gripping his hands for grim death, and offered him the parody of a smile.

The terrain continued easy. They trotted most of the time, slowing to a walk for a rest, and letting the horses run on for short distances when they'd gotten their breaths back. They passed the blackened and charred Antelope Springs station and headed for the Antelope Range just ahead.

"The pass isn't that high, but the rocky ground is still tricky. I'm glad it's light," Aleksandra said.

They traversed the divide, traveling four abreast, and brushed through the branches of the close-growing *Piñon* pines and cedars hanging over the trail.

"It smells like Christmas," Xavier murmured through gritted teeth, thinking of the ones he barely remembered, and his stomach clenched.

Aleksandra looked at him with the ghost of a smile and shook her head.

They kept a close eye out around them, but saw nothing other than startled antelope and hawks circling on the air currents.

Dinnertime came, and with it, a forlorn, destroyed Spring Valley station.

"Big pass up there." Major Jackson nodded at the snow-topped peaks flanking the Shellbourne Pass. "Good thing we're crossing it in the daytime."

"Last time I rode over," Aleksandra said, "it was just on dusk. Boy, did the temperature drop."

"Well, we best be off," their leader said as he stood and stretched.

"Major," Aleksandra took a deep breath, then dropped her eyes to the ground as she continued, "we don't have to go near Schell Creek station, do we?"

He frowned at her bowed head, then his eyes met Xavier's.

Xavier shook his head.

"We need to water the horses, but you needn't go near the station, eh lass?" the officer said.

She nodded at him gratefully, then went to her horse.

They reached the ascent to the pass and set a slow, but steady, pace for the 7000-foot summit.

"Keep an eye out about you, men," the major repeated. "The trees are thin, but it wouldn't be hard to hide in there."

Aleksandra slid from Dzień and walked beside him up the mountain. He reached his ears towards her and she obliged, scratching him around their base, where he so loved it. When she stopped, he gave a great shake, starting at his neck and progressing to his whole body.

"Good thing your saddle's cinched up tight," Xavier chuckled, and dismounted as well.

"All right, Rogan, leave my saddle in one piece," Aleksandra growled at the colt, tied to the buckskin's saddle horn. Without Aleksandra sitting in the saddle, the big bay seemed to think it was a scratching post. Dzień laid back his ears and bared his teeth as the bigger and heavier horse nearly pushed him over. Rogan ignored him until the Mustang nipped him on the shoulder, then he backed off, looking sorry for himself.

View from the summit was breathtaking, and the air crisp. The snow stood deep in the shelter of the boulders beside the trail, but melted softly beneath their feet. Aleksandra took a deep breath and trotted down the hill beside her pony.

"I'll take the horses and your canteen, if you like, Aleksandra," he said, as they neared Schell.

When she turned to face him, her face was ashen. He reached for her hand and squeezed it.

"Thank you, Xavier," she muttered beneath her breath. She picked up her head and stared straight at the adobe wall of the stable, away from the station building, whose door swung at a crazy angle. Flies buzzed in the bloodstained and hacked-up doorway.

ALEKSANDRA TURNED AWAY from the stable and the desecrated Schell Creek station, where she'd found the scalped men on her last Pony Express ride. She shuddered. She'd been so close to danger herself—the men's blood wasn't yet clotted when she'd found them. Deep breaths seemed to help, but in the end she dropped to her knees and put her head down to keep from vomiting as the scene ran again and again through her head.

"Come on Aleksandra," called the major, "let's go on ahead."

She scrambled onto Dzień, her reins all anyhow.

The company trotted along the sagebrush flats near the Cherry Creek Range, then turned up a gentle slope into the mountains. Egan Canyon, a beautiful, wide-open valley surrounded by rugged, snow-topped mountains, was stunning.

"This was the first time I've seen it in full daylight." Aleksandra spoke for the first time since the station. "There aren't many valleys like this out here."

"If you like this, you'll love Rancho de las Pulgas," Xavier said.

"I'm sure I will," she said with a tentative smile, and reached for his hand.

The station at Egan Canyon promised to be no better. Buzzards flapped away and lifted into a holding pattern as the troops approached, and as they neared it, they saw the remains of a cow before the door.

"We have enough water, don't we?" Egan softly queried the commander. Major Jackson's eyes met Aleksandra's, and he waved them on the next station. Ten miles on, Butte Creek appeared untouched from a distance, but the bullet holes and tomahawk marks on the remains of the plank door soon showed. They did what they needed to do and moved on west down a long valley and through a low pass.

They followed the eastern slope of the Maverick Springs Range before them until they came to Mountain Spring station in the dusk.

"Half of you come with me, the rest go ahead and set up camp," the major said, beneath his breath. The troops were so silent, his orders were clearly heard by all. Aleksandra slumped in her saddle, seeing little of the trail ahead.

The morning found them headed over the top of a high pass into Ruby Valley. They clattered into the echoing and empty yard of Ruby Valley station, then stopped to restock at Camp Ruby. Aleksandra curled up beneath Dzień's hooves and lay still until she fell into a fitful slumber. Whenever she'd waken, she'd see either Xavier or Egan standing near. She'd lost count of the stations, and shuddered at visions of the charred remains, and at the burnt smell that remained, even after three weeks. The Indians? Why? And what would become of them in the retaliation? She drew herself further into her shell, safe.

She awoke fully to Xavier kneeling beside her. "Time to go, *Querida*," he said. "Are you ready to go on? I know what seeing these stations is doing to you, but were almost out of it."

Her heart wrenched. "Most of the men got out," she murmured, and swallowed hard, "those who aren't dead," and the stations can be rebuilt."

"What's worrying you the most?" Xavier said, as he sat down on the ground and pulled her onto his lap.

"The scalping, and…the Indians. A whole people is on the way to being destroyed. How will they survive the retaliation? When will it end? Will it ever?" her voice dwindled to nothing.

He shook his head and held her close. "I don't know. I don't think anyone knows."

"I think we do, and that's the worst of it."

He clamped his jaw and stood, then helped her to her feet.

Soon they were on their way again, the snow-covered Ruby Mountain range looming tall before them.

"How much snow was at the summit when you went through last, Aleks?" Major Jackson's brow furrowed in her direction.

She shook her head to clear it at his question. "About a foot, and we haven't had any storms since."

The trail remained good over the top, with half a foot of hard-packed snow at the crest. Aleksandra dismounted again, and walked down the steep slope beside her pony, while the big bay pranced along beside them, snorting in the crisp mountain air. They passed Jacob's Well station and crossed Huntington Valley, then rode toward the Diamond Mountains.

O'ROURKE SCANNED the horizon behind him again. "Oh-oh." He swung around and the wagon shuddered as he jerked the mules to a halt.

"What?"

"Dust cloud behind—riders—coming along fast." He slapped the rump of the wheelers with the reins. "Yah, get on," he growled to the mules as he glanced around, looking for a place to hide the wagon. They were still a good way from the mountains just ahead, but he pushed the mules to a gallop, and they drew the bouncing, rattling wagon there in short order and raced on into the foothills at a good lick.

"Lucky we were near these here mountains," his partner said, as the pass narrowed around them and the mules began to tire. "Just up ahead there, off right." He pointed.

"Yep, good thing we foun' a place to hide this lot," he murmured. "If them Union boys caught us and d'cided to open these boxes, we'd be swingin' from the next tree fer sure, or mebbbe the top of a wagon-bow."

"Don't ah know it," his partner said, his face grim as he leaned over the side of the box, looking for holes in the ground ahead of them. "Too many badgers out here," he muttered.

15

"Excuse me Major, can we please stop?" Aleksandra glanced around, then swung down to inspect the wheel tracks and hoof prints leading off the main trail into a deep, rocky side-canyon with sparse trees and high sides. The hairs raised on her forearms. The perfect ambuscade.

"Aleks?"

"Dust still settling in the tracks," she muttered. She shaded her eyes with her hand, but could see nothing. "Mules, four, one's lost a shoe." She mounted and nodded at the officer.

"Good. That'll slow them down a little," Xavier murmured.

The major lifted his binoculars as the troop settled into a ground-eating walk. "Yep, a lone wagon—drawn by mules."

"Three bays and a chestnut?"

"Yep."

"That'll be them." She raised a brow at Xavier.

"It would be best, Major, to avoid them completely," Xavier commented. "They're as nasty as they come."

"No problem. We'll go around them. If we weren't carrying this vital information, we'd go after them," the major said, "but this news must reach California immediately, if not sooner." He waved the troops forward at a trot, into the foothills.

They all watched to their rear for quite some time, and only stopped when the were off the mountain. The horses chomped their nosebag rations at Diamond Springs station while Aleksandra and the men took a moment to rest at the empty station house, with its the plentiful water and shelter from the wind and sun, while they ate dinner.

"Is this escort to run on a regular basis?" Aleksandra said, then took another bite of *pemmican.*

"This mail had to go through." Egan scowled around at the group. "It's been sitting there for six days already. Somebody needed to put their neck on the line just keep the lines of communication open, and I thank you kindly for that, Major."

"Let's just say, we're not yet officially approved, but with the impending unrest between the states, we must maintain communication between California and Washington." The commander glanced around before he continued. "The southern route is untenable for the Union, and this route must be kept open, at all costs. We had to provide an emergency army escort." He stood and pulled his gloves back on. "I carry the orders for the Union Army in San Francisco to supply escorts for the Pony every five days."

Xavier squeezed Aleksandra's hand.

Aleksandra stood and began to saddle up Rogan.

"Let's go, men." The officer smiled. "Aleksandra is showing us up again."

They set off at a brisk pace. The horses were fresh from their rest, and the terrain rolled along flat and easy. Aleksandra pointed ahead to a patch of disturbed ground.

"There it is," she said, turning to Xavier, "the badger hole the Express mare fell into and bowed her tendon." She turned to Egan. "Do you know how she's doing?"

"Pinto?" Egan asked. "Right fore? Bandage with an astonishing amount of padding?"

She nodded, holding her breath.

"She was at *Ibapah* last week, and was being walked slowly east by her devoted keeper. Seems he won't let anyone else take over her care... something about you having his guts for garters if she didn't get the care you ordered, after you limped her into the station for four hours during the Indian raids," the older man said with a laugh.

THE WAGON TRAIL continued along the flat plain, with only Roberts Creek Mountain rising on their right to ease the monotony of the skyline. The road began to rise and fall before them as they entered its foothills.

"This is where I met your troops, Major Jackson, the ones who came back to save the men at Roberts Creek."

"It wasn't looking good when we arrived, but those keepers've gone on to live another day, thanks to you, missy."

"I didn't think I was going to survive the troops," Aleksandra said. They had their rifles aimed at me before someone recognized me as a Pony rider."

Aleksandra looked up to her right at the steep slope of the mountain and her heart stopped in her chest. She could almost see again the *Pah-Ute* warriors, resplendent in war paint, racing down through the scree toward her. She shook her head. Best not to think of it.

She caught a snatch of a conversation and returned her attention to the men beside her. "Pardon? Afraid I was somewhere else."

"Was the station burned completely?" Egan raised a brow at her.

"I don't believe so, but don't quote me on that," Aleksandra murmured as they passed over the next rise.

"And there it is, people," the major nodded his head forward. "Roberts Creek station."

"Pretty lucky, all right." One of the soldiers shook his head and grinned as he looked her way. "Good thing you were coming through."

"All right men, we have pretty good visibility here, let's set up camp," the commander said. "We need to sleep light, double sentries, and keep everything you don't need tied to your saddle in case we need to leave in a hurry."

The morning came too soon.

Aleksandra snuggled deeper against Xavier's chest as the dawning day intruded against her eyelids.

"Waking on the trail has never felt so warm," she murmured, and kissed him in the valley in the center of his chest.

"Nor so lovely." There was a smile in his throaty voice before his lips met the top of her head. He drew her up to kiss her lips, and she stole quick breaths between his mind-blanking kisses until he relented and chuckled down at her.

"I think breathing's highly overrated," he said.

"I can tell." She giggled, then turned her head to where the troop and Egan slept—No one moved, but they would soon.

"Hey, you two, behave," Egan barked across the camp.

"Always, sir," Xavier said, laughing. "OK, woman, time to get going, now Major Egan has seen fit to awaken everyone else in camp who wasn't already awake."

"Wasn't me," Egan protested, "It was Aleks."

Dzień whinnied, near at hand.

"Whoever it was, the pony's up and wants his breakfast now," she said, grinning at her man as she sat up.

THROUGHOUT THAT DAY, they followed the canyons, dry gullies all. No rain threatened and the days remained hot and dry. Grubb's Wells station was intact, but an hour later saw them staring at the broken door of Dry Creek station.

The stench and buzzing of flies hit them before they got anywhere close.

"I left two dead men in there and jammed that door shut just like that." Xavier's jaw was so tight the words could barely slip out.

"And how long ago was that, soldier?" Major Jackson gritted his teeth and peered sideways at the barely-closed door wedged shut with a thin strip of kindling. "I'm afraid I might know the answer."

"The same day as the attack on Roberts," Xavier winced, "three weeks."

"Mmm..." the major managed, "in this heat..." His brow wrinkled and he closed his eyes.

"Just so."

He sighed heavily. "Scott and Nelson, cover me. Arnott and McCabe, go around the back. The rest of you stay aware. I'm going in. If the men, or what's left of them, are there, they'll need buryin', so snap to it." He swung down from his horse and approached the station, a revolver primed in his right hand. Calling out loudly, he rapped the butt of the pistol on the door. No answering sound met him, so his two men covered him as he swung open the door and threw himself against the outside wall.

The flies buzzed louder, but nothing else moved. The major looked inside briefly, then spun on his heel and returned to the troop, his face green.

"Men, dismount and find some digging tools—there's bound to be something near the barn—you five start moving rocks over there," he pointed to a rocky bank. "We may not be able to dig deep, but we're not short of rocks, anyway. Start hollowing out a grave."

"Their names..." Xavier choked out, "were Ralph and John."

"Good men," Egan added. "Didn't deserve this end." Even his visage was ghostly when he turned back to where Aleksandra and Xavier still stood beside their horses.

"Aleks, can you go look after the horses? The spring's over there." Xavier turned her away from the cabin and shoved the reins of all three horses at her. "I'll help here. You stay away, keep an eye open for us all and get a bite to eat." He dropped a kiss on top of her head. "Just stay away. You've seen enough of this for your whole lifetime."

She gave him a vague look and wandered away with the horses. He stared after her for a moment. Her light seemed to have been snuffed out gradually, as they'd passed one after another burnt station. She'd seen each of these men alive, only a short time before, and the burnt facades—not only did these men die horrible deaths, but it was the end of a way of life for two peoples—both of them her friends and family.

The dead men were bloated beyond recognition. The burial detachment dug and shuffled rocks as fast as they could move.

"Glad they were wearing buckskins, else we might've never finished this job—they held everything together," said one of the red-faced soldiers, after he returned from behind the station building, wiping his mouth and gagging.

Aleksandra glanced at the man from the corners of her eyes.

"Now man, that's no way to speak of the dead," the major growled, in an undertone.

"Sorry sir, ma'am." He nodded in Aleksandra's direction and touched his forelock.

She looked away from the soldier and ignored him. Xavier wrapped an arm around her, drawing her back against him.

"Can we go?" she whispered into his shirt front. "I don't know if I can stand to be around these men much longer."

"We've a bit more dangerous country to get through, then we might be able to head off on our own sometime late tomorrow, if you still want to."

"How many more burnt stations?" she said, in a rush.

"One, that I know of, Dry Wells, but I don't know if there are more—no one's been through here since…"

"…Roberts Creek."

"Yes."

"Let's go men," their commander barked.

"I've never seen them move so fast," Aleksandra remarked to Xavier, with the ghost of a smile, when they were on their way, moving at a slow lope down the track.

"They were afraid we'd find more bodies to bury." Xavier looked at Aleksandra. The gray mask hadn't lifted from her face or her demeanor, and the band constricting his heart tightened.

"How far to Dry Wells?" She spoke so softly, he barely heard her.

"Four stations—probably mid afternoon, all going well."

She took a deep breath and stared straight ahead between her pony's ears, then absently scratched his withers as they rocked along.

"ALEKS, BWA BRA…" she heard, as if from a distance. She turned her head and shook it a little, then looked at him sideways.

"Aleks, give me your canteen," Xavier said, this time. She fumbled with the cord and he gently moved her hand away and lifted it from the saddle horn himself.

"Thirsty."

He frowned at her. "*Querida*, it's still full, haven't you had any water today?"

"Don't remember."

Xavier held a canteen to her lips. She drank, then closed her mouth when she'd had enough. It spilled down the front of her buckskins. He was speaking to her, but she didn't understand what he was saying—and she didn't really care.

At the next Express station, he took her canteen and offered her water and *pemmican* upon his return.

It was dark when he gently pulled her from the saddle and held her close. She didn't argue when he wrapped her in his *serape* and slid her into their bedroll, then snuggled down beside her, his arms tight around her, and her head pillowed on his arm.

She dreamed...dreams of dead men, flies and stench, stations hacked by tomahawks and bullets, and Indians fleeing from villages...and blood.

16

Xavier gently disentangled himself from Aleksandra and joined the silent men at the fire.

"Is she any better?" Egan's brows were nearly touching. "Don't like it one bit."

"Me either." Xavier shook his head. "She's never been like this before."

"She was OK after her long ride and seeing all the dead men before?" the major asked.

"She seemed fine—upset about the scalped men she saw, but nothing like this."

"Shock," Major Jackson returned. "Too many deaths. She was probably too tired to take in the deaths three weeks ago, and it's preyed upon the back of her mind since then, and this has brought it out. Seen it in a lot of men after battles—"

Xavier nodded.

"Keep her close, Xave," Egan said grimly.

From the edge of the firelight came a bloodcurdling, feminine scream. Xavier ran back to find her sitting bolt upright, looking around in terror.

"It's OK, Aleks, I'm here," he said, in the voice he used to quiet frightened young horses. She stopped her frantic movements and sat staring at him, her eyes wide in the flickering firelight.

He lay down beside her and slid into their bedroll, taking her into his arms again, and brushed her hair with his fingers until she slept.

"WAS THERE ANYTHING AT DRY WELLS?" Aleksandra murmured, when she awoke in the morning.

"Blackened timbers and a pile of rubble. No bodies."

"I hope they got away." She spoke slowly, her eyes dull.

"So it would seem..." He hesitated. "Are you OK, Aleks?"

She was silent for a moment. "I think so—I don't remember much of yesterday after the major went into the station to check on the dead men at Dry Creek. Were we there long?"

Xavier looked sideways at her. "A while." He didn't detail it, or tell her she'd ridden beside him for another forty miles afterwards.

She dropped her head and didn't ask.

Aleksandra became progressively more alert as the day went on, and by mid-afternoon, she even smiled at the antics of some lizards on a rock during a break in the riding. Edwards Creek and Middle Gate passed without incident. Eerily desolate, but without incident. Most of the bigger mountains were behind them, and ahead was only the flat, empty Carson Sink.

"Is that water?" Aleksandra nodded towards a blue-black shimmer near the center of the sink.

"Yes, it's Carson Lake." Xavier smiled, but she only pursed her lips.

They camped that night in the shelter of a jumble of boulders and left for Sand Springs as soon as the sun spread its early tendrils across the sand and sagebrush. The water at Sand Springs proved to be relatively fresh, and they filled canteens and moved on.

Topping a small rise, Xavier pointed ahead to a gleaming ribbon snaking its way west.

"And that?" Aleksandra queried.

"The Carson River."

"Real water, clean?" Aleksandra actually grinned, and his heart stilled in his chest. It was the first real, positive emotion he'd seen from her in days. He let out the breath he didn't know he'd been holding and beamed back at her.

"That it is, and we follow it right to Nevada station."

"Is Virginia City on that river?" Aleksandra looked at him, her eyes glowing.

"No, sorry, it's several miles up the side of a rocky mountain...rather like a big pile of scree...straight up."

"Trees?"

"Nope."

"Bushes?"

"No, *lo siento*."

"Rocks." She stated flatly.

"*Sí*, yes."

Aleksandra's face fell. "Oh."

"But there's plenty of silver, I hear."

"That's something," she said, but she didn't look impressed.

"And people, plenty of those." He smiled, then watched emotions flit across her face—none of them good—fear, anxiety, maybe—before she hung her head and turned away. "What is it, Aleks?"

"Do people live close to each other, like right next to each other?" It was barely a whisper and her visage had turned the color of the Carson Sink sand.

"Aleks, are you all right?"

She turned a tear-stained face to him. "Yes...no...I don't know," she finally offered.

He reached a hand to her, wiping the wetness from one cheek with the back of his fingers. "It's the people, isn't it?"

She nodded without speaking.

"You've never lived in town, have you?"

Aleksandra shook her head.

"It'll be OK, really, it will."

She swallowed noisily.

"What are you worried about?"

"I feel like I'm drowning, when I'm in town—trapped—like I can't breathe." She took a deep breath, and her color began to return.

"It gets me here." She made a fist in front of her belly and squeezed it tight, hunching herself around it.

He caught her hand and held it. "If it helps, there's wilderness all around." He gave her a crooked smile.

She gave a half-chuckle, half-sob, then wiped her eyes. "It'll be OK, if you're there with me," she said softly.

"Yes, it will. I love you, *Chiquita*, and we can do this together."

Their eyes locked.

"And with all the Irish miners in Gold Hill and Virginia City, there's bound to be a priest as well."

He nearly laughed to see her, usually so tough and self-reliant, blush and drop her eyes at the thought of their upcoming nuptials. He shook his head. "So Aleks, have you thought about what you might to do in Virginia City?"

"I could work in a livery, maybe, and keep our horses fit."

"You could, but they might not hire a woman. What else would you like to do?"

"Sew? Cook? Clean?" She frowned. "None of them are my forte, as you know." She gave him a rueful grin.

"What about teaching?"

"I've never taught anything," she stated flatly.

"Sure you have. You taught Dancing Wolf to read and spell in English."

"Yes, but it wasn't formal or anything. I never went to school. Mama and Papa taught us."

"It's got to be better than cleaning houses."

She lifted a brow. "True," she murmured and leaned back.

"Truth be told," he looked deeply into her eyes, "I wouldn't want you in a livery. I'd rather you were teaching. Much safer."

She swung the end of a rein at him and he ducked, laughing. Charro danced away sideways as she blew him a kiss, with real pleasure on her face this time

"I don't need to be coddled," she spat, her eyes sparking.

"Just wanted to see if you were really better," he said with a chuckle. "*Sí*, you are."

Far across the desert, row upon row of white tents rose slowly from the desert floor.

"Fort Churchill?" Aleksandra asked.

"Yep," Egan answered, "after we cross the Carson." He nodded at the river between them and the army camp, lined with scrubby willows.

"You're sure you don't want us to escort you all the way to Carson City?" Major Jackson asked.

"That won't be necessary," Egan said. "I'll be with these two," he looked at Xavier and Aleksandra, "and then, I'll only have another ten miles to Carson. Carson Station can wire the good news out west and I'll be back before you know it with more mail, so be ready to ride in five days, eh gentlemen?"

"Thank you for the escort, Major," Aleksandra said, with a wave.

"*Que le vaya bien*," Xavier said.

Egan tipped his hat to the commander, then turned to follow Aleksandra and Xavier.

"You three take care," Major Jackson said. The rest of the troop called out their goodbyes as they rode north.

"What could possibly keep you busy in Carson for the next five days?" Xavier raised a brow at Egan.

"I'll buzz over to Carson, but I really need to go check on some land Ephraim Hanks and I were selling up north of Churchill. Selling, but not getting paid."

"Ephraim mentioned something about that," Xavier said.

"Can't rightly say I trust anyone from south of the Mason-Dixon right about now. Wouldn't do to have a hornet's nest in our own house."

"Nope, especially if they want to support the secessionists in California."

"Where's the land?"

"North and a little east of here a ways."

"How did you end up with land up there?"

"Well...let's just say someone left it to us," Egan said. He turned his face away and looked far to the north for long moments.

Aleksandra and Xavier exchanged a glance—and left it.

Xavier cleared his throat. "*Bueno*, so next station," he looked hard at her, "is Coate's Wells, then Reeds, then we're at Chinatown."

Aleksandra frowned. "I thought it was Nevada station."

"Yep," Egan agreed, "it is. Nevada station sits at what was called Gold *Cañon* Flat, but so many Chinese miners came down from the California goldfields after they started taxing, it's mostly Chinese there now, and they've changed the name to Chinatown."

"So Virginia City is up the mountain from there." Aleksandra said.

Xavier nodded, and turned to Egan. "Do you need an escort to Carson?"

He rolled his eyes. "It's a whole ten miles. I think I can ride that far on my own."

They followed the river and stopped for water at Coate's Wells. Relieved to find the station still occupied, they reported the news from the East, then rode on along the Carson through the desert, the pancake landscape broken only by the scrubby willows and nondescript brush along the muddy shores.

The keeper at Reeds peered out the door of his station, and flung the door wide when he recognized Xavier. "Argüello, Egan, I wondered when I'd see you again! Come in for some dinner, men," he said, then glanced at Aleksandra and hastily added "and ma'am. If you take care of your horses, I'll put together a feed."

"Good to sit at a table, for a change," Xavier said, sliding onto a bench seat beside the table.

"Good to have some company," the keeper replied. A quarter of an hour later, he placed steaming bowls of beef stew before them. "It's been quiet since the Pony shut down, with only the riders carrying dispatches between Carson and Fort Churchill to keep me occupied."

"Been a lot of those?"

"They're increasing in number, with the secessionists trying to get a foothold out in California—lots of orders coming through from the Presidio in San Fran to Fort Churchill, but the military is hamstrung—cooling their heels at Carson and Churchill because they can't get the messages conveyed back East."

"We can't get them through as often as before," Egan said, breaking a chunk from the loaf in the center of the table, "but we've been given Army escorts to take the mail just over once a week. We have to go at troop pace—not as slow as oxen, but not as fast as the Express. The mail, however, *will* get through."

"Hallelujah for that," the keeper tugged at his beard and a sliver of his grin showed through. "Best news I've heard in weeks."

"Hasn't been a lot of good news lately." Egan scowled.

"Nope." The keeper's smile faded and the silence at the table lengthened.

"Great stew, thank you," Aleksandra murmured into the stillness. The man jumped on an excuse to talk. "Why, thank you, Aleks. Made it myself," he said with forced enthusiasm. "Good to still have our stock—" he said, then came to an abrupt halt. "Sorry, all. Just can't get over it. It's good to be able to talk about it—I think my horses are getting tired of listening to me."

Aleksandra reached out a hand and squeezed his. "We've been in the middle of it, and it's not pretty."

Xavier brushed back his stray forelock with one hand. "Yep, we all do, so how 'bout we talk about it, so we can get it all out?"

Heaving a combined sigh of relief, they began, each adding what they'd seen, heard, or felt about the raids on the pony trail, with each person adding their own thoughts and fears.

"We might have done some good for each other," Aleksandra said. "I grew up in a close family, but we never did anything like this before."

"I sure feel better about it now," the keeper said, running his fingers through some deep grooves in the table before him.

"Me too." Xavier muttered. "Surprisingly so."

Aleksandra sat up straight beside him and took a deep breath. The last of the tension left her body with her exhalation.

Major Egan closed his eyes and nodded.

Waving their farewells, they left the man alone at his post and headed west on the last leg of their journey. All too soon, they were at Nevada station.

"None of those sloppy goodbyes, now." Egan hopped off his horse like a man half his age and reached up to hug Aleksandra. When he drew away, tears glistened in his eyes. She pinched her lips together to avoid embarrassing the man.

"We'll be fine; it's you still riding the Pony," Aleksandra said, shaking her head. "You'll let us know when the Express starts up again, won't you?"

"Sure will, missy. You two take good care of each other, you hear?"

"*De veras*, we sure will, sir," Xavier said, clasping the older man's hand in his firm grip. Egan mounted up, his eyes threatening to spill over, and turned to wave.

"Old softie," Xavier muttered.

"And I want to hear," he shouted over his shoulder as he loped away, "you've found a priest and made an honest woman out of my Aleks!" He waved, and he and his stallion slowly faded away into the distance.

"Well," Xavier raised a brow at her, "guess we've been told. Let's go find that priest," he said, and they turned their horses toward the foothills of the gray mountains before them.

ALEKSANDRA'S HEART sank as she looked up the steep slopes ahead. "A bit gray and forbidding, aren't they?"

"Yep, like I said, rocks and rocks."

The trail began to slope upward. An hour later, they passed a handful of shacks. Away from the wagon track, a few men swung picks in rhythm. The road became steeper. After another hour of climbing, it levelled off at a small settlement.

"I thought Virginia City was further." Aleks frowned as she looked around them at the cluster of roughly-thrown-up shanties, with a few bigger buildings mixed in, lining the wagon tracks ahead of them.

"This is Gold Hill, I believe."

A large group of men hammered away at the most ambitious-looking structure she'd seen since Salt Lake City, on the far end of the settlement.

As they approached, a boy ran out from between two of the cabins.

"Mister, mister, can I pet your horse?" He called, and ran straight for Xavier's huge stallion.

A dark haired man jumped off the roof of the under-construction building and raced towards them. "Billy, get away from that horse!" he shouted.

PART II

1860 ~ VIRGINIA CITY, UTAH TERRITORY

17

July 1860, Ophir Mine, Virginia City, Utah Territory

THE TOWHEADED boy slowed his rush toward them and stopped, biting his lip.

"I'm sorry, sir, he won't do that again," the builder said. He wrapped an arm around the boy and leaned over, puffing from his sprint from the roof.

The boy took a deep breath, then burst into tears.

"We just lost my wif—our old horse, and Billy's been pining for him," the man continued, then turned to the trembling boy. "You can't just run up to strange horses, Son. They're not all like Storm, and these big ones are stallions. You could have been killed, or caused one of these fine people to have been thrown."

"I know, but I miss Storm, and…and…he looks just like him…" the boy got out, between sobs, then stopped.

Aleksandra slid off Rogan, holding Dzień's lead. The pony strained at the end of the rope, ears pricked, trying to get to the boy. She handed her reins to Xavier.

"May I?" Aleksandra looked at the boy's father, who stepped back as the Mustang nearly dragged her to the side of the weeping boy. "Dzień will be your friend," she said.

He looked up from perusing his dusty boots.

"He might not be the same color as Storm," she whispered, as Dzień shoved his nose toward the boy, "but he wants to talk with you. He helps me when I'm sad."

Billy looked up into the big brown eyes of the dun pony and gave one last sob, which turned into a tear-streaked giggle. He reached for Dzień and the pony whuffled softly into his outstretched fingers. Holding his breath, he walked to the pony, slid his arms around his neck and hugged him. Dzień nosed his trousers, his neck over the boy's shoulder.

"He likes you already," Aleksandra said, "don't you, Dzień?" The pony flicked an ear back in answer and stood like a rock.

The man's eyes glowed, and he turned to Xavier. "You two new in town? Jason, Jason Steen," the stranger said, eyeing their packs and the two stallions as he shook Xavier's hand, "and my son, Billy."

"Just arrived. Xavier Argüello, and this is my fiancée Aleksandra Lekarski."

She smiled a greeting at him and returned her attention to the boy and Dzień.

"What are you building? It's a more significant structure than," he surveyed the rough shacks ahead of them, "the rest of them," Xavier said.

Jason gave a rueful glance at the smaller buildings. "They're rather temporary, aren't they? But this," his chest puffed out proudly, "will be something to see! I'm calling it the Gold Hill Hotel. We should be ready to open early next year."

"Quite a project," Xavier shook his head, "but it's well on its way. How far it is to Virginia City, please?"

"Only about two miles, but it's straight up." He looked briefly at the steep incline up ahead, then back to the child, who beamed at Dzień and Aleksandra. "We're just about to knock off. Would you like to stop for a meal with the boy and I?"

"Thanks, but we must get to Virginia City to find a place to stay before it gets any later."

"You're welcome to stay the night with us, we've plenty of room. For both you and your horses."

"Aleks, what to do you say?"

"*Please?*" Billy pleaded, as he clung to the pony.

"We live just over there, the place with the stable out behind," Jason said in a rush. "If you like, Billy can show you where your horses could stay for the night."

It was clear Billy wanted their company, even if only to keep Dzień's company a little longer, but Jason sounded just as wistful. Aleksandra couldn't refuse. "We'd be pleased to take you up on your offer, Mr. Steen."

"Please, call me Jason," he said, his lips turning up at the ends. "Son, will you show them the stables? I'll be there as soon as I can."

"Sure can, Papa."

His father flashed a grin over his shoulder, trotted back to his edifice and scrambled up onto the rooftop again.

"It's right this way, miss," he turned to Xavier, "and sir."

"Do you ride, Billy?"

"I used to ride Storm all by myself," he said, a proud tone in his voice. "Storm was Mam—" he broke off and gripped Dzień's mane, silent.

"Would you like to lead Dzień?" Aleksandra said, and the boy reached for the rope with alacrity.

"Of course," he said, folding the lead properly in his off hand as he led the little group away.

"Tell me about Storm," Aleksandra said, as she led Dzień toward the barn Billy indicated. Xavier followed along with the two stallions.

The boy took a deep breath and held it, then slowly let it out. "He was Mama's hunting and carriage horse. Papa said when they went out West from Pennsylvania, Storm was all Mama had left of her old life. She gave it up for him." He finished on a whisper.

Aleksandra swapped a worried look with Xavier as they watered the horses from the trough beside the building.

"This is a lovely barn, Billy. Did you help build it?" Xavier laid a hand on the rough-sawn wall and raised a brow at the boy when he lifted his tearstained face to answer.

"Sure did, me and Papa built it for Storm and the team."

"Storm was one lucky horse," Aleksandra said, as the boy then showed them into the wide aisle of the barn.

"He was," he replied, then added in a whisper, "I sure miss them."

"Would you like to groom Dzień for me?" Aleksandra said, touching him on the shoulder to draw him back from wherever he seemed to be sinking.

"Could I? Yes, please," he said, spinning around to a shelf on the wall opposite the tie-rail. Grooming implements were laid out with care on the smoothed plank, all in a neat row. Each brush and comb was clean and free of dust.

He reached for a brush, then hesitated. "I'm sure Mam—Storm wouldn't mind," he murmured, almost to himself, then reached for a curry and a soft body brush, and finally, a hoof pick.

Aleksandra peeked around Rogan's rump, watching Billy from the corners of her eyes as she untacked the bay. The barn really was lovely, and swept completely clean, with not a trace of its former occupants. The lad slipped Dzień's bridle over his ears and buckled his halter, then tied him with a careful slip knot to a ring bolted to the wall. He picked out his hooves, then curried and brushed the Mustang until he shone.

"You sure know what you're doing, don't you? How old are you?" Xavier smiled at him.

"Ten years old, sir."

"Where did you learn all this?"

"Mam—" He took a deep breath and carried on, more firmly this time. "My mama."

"She must be a wonderful woman, to teach you to care for horses so well." Aleksandra smiled at him. "I can't wait to meet her—"

"—please, let's not talk of it," he interrupted, gritted his teeth and turned back to brush the preening pony.

It was all Aleksandra could do to not hug the child. The flood of sadness for him punched at her heart.

"Look, here's your papa," she said.

"Papa, we're nearly done here, would you like to see?"

"Hello again, Xavier, Miss Lekarski—oh Billy, you've done yourself proud. I can almost see my face in that pony's hide," Jason said, reaching out a hand to scratch Dzień's withers.

Billy ducked his head to hide his proud smile. "It's sure easier to groom a Mustang than Storm. Storm was a huge horse, as big as your Charro!" He turned to Aleksandra with a grin, "I needed to climb on a partition to reach his back."

"You've done a great job, Dzień's happy to have found a friend." Aleksandra winked at the youngster.

"Tidy barn you have here," Xavier said. "Looking a bit lonely, though."

Jason started to speak, then glanced at Billy. The boy cringed against Dzień's side and hugged him tight. The man shook his head at Xavier and went to the boy's side.

"Billy, there should still be some hay in the loft, if the mice haven't eaten it all. Would you please clamber up there and throw it down to me?"

He flashed a grateful smile at his papa. "You'll let me go up there by myself?"

"You're big enough now."

He grinned and raced for the ladder. When he was out of sight, Jason turned to them. "I'll tell you about the horses and his mama when he's abed," he murmured, then turned to catch the neatly-tied shock of hay. "You can't jump to me anymore, though, you're too big now!" he called up to Billy. The lad grinned and scarpered down the ladder.

Horses fed, they walked across to the house, one of the more substantial buildings in the township.

Aleksandra slid her fingers along the glossy door jam as she entered the parlor and her mouth dropped open. Brass lamps adorned the smooth oaken sideboard and table, and the matching chairs were padded golden velvet. A braided rag rug covered nearly the entire floor, and a cast-iron stove completed the room.

"Please, make yourselves at home," Jason said, with a sweeping gesture, suddenly formal.

"Oh." Aleksandra stopped, lost for words. "I couldn't possibly. We're filthy from the trail. Could we clean up, somewhere less..." she struggled for words, "...pristine? This is the loveliest room I've...ever...seen."

Jason twisted his lips in the shadow of a grin. "It is special. It was..." He stopped, glanced at his son and hurried on. "Come on through and I'll show you your room. It's not much, but it's a roof over your heads, more than you've had, I daresay, in a while."

"'It isn't much...'" Aleksandra repeated to Xavier, when they were alone. "Every room, even every hallway in this place is exquisite."

"I wonder what that's about..." Xavier said, nodding his head back toward the parlor. He took her into his arms and held her tight, lips in her hair.

"I'm afraid we won't hear a very happy story tonight," she whispered.

"No, not happy at all."

"What a heavenly smell," Xavier said, as he closed the kitchen door behind them.

A pot bubbled on the massive cast iron cook stove, the letters 'Reliance' in raised relief on its front door. Beside it, Jason and Billy stood, flour up to their elbows.

"Billy is teaching me to make biscuits," he grinned ruefully, "but I'm not doing very well."

"'Course you are, Papa," the boy said, as he finished patting out his round of the soft dough.

"It's sourdough, you know," he said in a conspiratorial whisper to Aleksandra.

"Ooooh, my favorite," she said, smiling at him. "I have a starter in my saddlebags. I even have one made of rye meal, if you'd like some of it?" She raised her brows at him.

He frowned "I don't know how to use it, though."

"Where did you learn to cook, lad?" Xavier asked.

"My auntie taught me, when she came to stay, after..." He gulped, and stopped.

"That's a great skill to have, cooking." Xavier cut in, "You'll never go hungry if you can cook."

"That's what Papa says. He doesn't know what he'll do when they find a new schoolmistress and I have to go back to school."

"There's a school, *here?*" Xavier's brows shot up. "It's hardly a big enough town to have a school?"

"Up in Virginia City," Jason said. "It's only a few miles. Mind you, it's straight up, but nothing for a fit young lad!"

Aleksandra and Xavier exchanged a glance.

"Looking for a teacher, are they? What are the requirements to teach here?" Xavier said.

"I think they're…rather keen to find someone, so the ability to read, write and cipher are probably the most important. I think they have an examination the applicant must pass, but they've been seeking a teacher for several months now."

"Miss Parker was there one day and gone the next. We all wondered why she left us. She was nice," Billy added. "She boarded with us for a term, because Papa's on the school board."

"Ah, well, let's get these on the griddle, shall we, boy?" Jason redirected his son's attention to the biscuits.

"Please, pour yourselves some coffee," he waved his floury hands at the stove, where a spatterware enamel kettle steamed.

"It's awfully nice of you to put us up, Jason," Xavier said. "Do you know of anyone hiring in the mines?"

"Matter of fact, I do. The Ophir is looking for a man run the assay office and keep records. You any good at that sort of thing?"

"I've had a pretty good education and I've been a station manager for the Pony Express. I might have the skills they need."

"I thought you might." Jason dusted his hands and tipped the lid on the stew, then turned to them again. "The job comes with a house and stable—one of the nicer ones in town."

In town.

A cold lump formed in Aleksandra's stomach at his words.

"Sounds too good to be true." Xavier gave him a wide grin.

"That's what the last man employed for the job thought, until he was caught with his hand in the till. They've been trying to fill the position since then, but they're being a mite more choosy about who they hire this time."

"So is this common knowledge, about the fired worker? I assume he was let go?" Xavier said.

"Sure was, but you're right, it's not common knowledge." Jason raised a brow at them. "Mob justice is a bit rough around here, so publicly, he's been 'transferred' to a different place. We haven't told the men he's lodging with free room and board behind bars."

"If the miners knew he'd had his fingers in their pies," Xavier said, "he might have been found at the end of a short rope."

Jason nodded. "The mine shareholders want blood, but at least he'll get a fair trial this way."

Xavier took a deep breath and exhaled slowly. "I'd be interested in that job. Whom do I see about hiring on?"

"That'll be my brother. We'll go see him in the morning." He grinned. "Finding him his man should put me in his good books for quite a while."

"Why hasn't he filled the job?" Xavier's brows drew together. "There must be plenty of educated men hanging about the mines."

"They've been a bit more particular this time. Educated men abound, but 'trustworthy' and 'reputable' seem to be chief requirements."

"You seem pretty educated yourself, why aren't you taking it on?"

"Oh, no." He backed away, his hands held up before him. "I'm not working for my brother again. I've got my hands full with my new hotel, and Billy and I like it out of town."

"My thoughts exactly," Aleksandra murmured, then bit her lip.

"It won't be forever, Aleks, and we can ride every day. Have to keep the horses fit and hunt, so we'll get out."

Aleksandra took a deep breath and endeavored to smile. It must've worked, because the other two grinned back at her.

"Aleks, may I ride with you sometime?" Billy looked up from his griddle, between turning biscuits.

"Of course you may, I'd appreciate the help. That is, if you don't mind, Jason."

"Any time," the man returned, as he reached a ladle from its hook.

"The team was sold when we got here, and since Mama..." Billy trailed off, then started in a rush. "There's been no horse to ride."

"We'll ride as soon as we see about work, OK?"

"OK," the boy said, with a sigh. Aleksandra winked at him.

"We'll all go to town tomorrow and see about work for you two." Jason turned to Billy. "We need more nails, so we'll go to the mercantile too."

"Yes, we're nearly out of flour," said the lad.

"And now, for my masterpiece," Jason said with a grin, as he handed out the bowls full of steaming stew. Hungry, they ate supper in silence, as soon as Billy said grace.

"Is there anything else you two need to do tomorrow?"

Xavier looked at Aleksandra, his eyes warm. "Yes," he said.

Her cheeks heated as he hesitated, and then continued.

"Find a priest."

"Aaah." Jason's eyes gleamed. "Aren't you two the lovely couple?"

Aleksandra ducked her head, but Xavier took her hand and nodded.

"We'll find Pastor Clay tomorrow as well, then."

Yawning, Billy said good night and made his way to bed. When the boy had quit the room and his bedroom door clicked closed, Jason turned to them.

"As you may have surmised, my wife died last year," Jason said in an undertone.

"I thought that might have been the case. I'm sorry for your loss," Aleksandra whispered. "You must both miss her very much."

"Unimaginably so." He swallowed hard. "Billy and Sarah were inseparable and she was a magnificent horsewoman—taught the boy all she knew." He was silent for long moments. When he spoke, it was barely audible. "I found the love of my life on her favorite ride, dead beside the horse she loved so well. The big gray stood over her, one leg held up in the air, and wouldn't let anyone but Billy get near her, not even me."

Aleksandra's heart broke for the man, and it was hard to swallow past the lump in her throat.

"His cannon bone was shattered. Following his footprints, we found the rabbit hole." He shook his head. "Amazing how something so small can make such a big gap in so many lives." He looked up at them, tears in his eyes.

"Oh Jason, I'm so sorry." Aleksandra reached out to grip his hand.

"It can't be helped," he took a deep breath and steadied himself, "but with no school, I feel for the boy. I can't be with him all the time and still finish the hotel."

"So our next step is to the school board?" Aleksandra locked eyes with him, and Jason sighed in relief.

"You two must've been sent to help Virginia City in its time of need, or my family's need, anyway."

"Glad to be of assistance." Xavier nodded to him, his eyes glistening too.

Jason turned to Aleksandra. "You'll find Billy a competent horseman, for all his age." He returned his gaze to Xavier. "Seeing your stallion, Xavier, was too much for him. Charro is the spitting image of Sarah's horse. We were looking for a horse for Billy before the accident, but he hasn't shown any interest in *any* horses...until you two arrived today." A soft smile lit his visage.

"We'll have a ride tomorrow and see how he and Dzień mesh."

"I trust you'll sleep well tonight," Jason said as he stood. "I begin work with the sun, but we could perhaps go to Virginia City around ten. Will that suit?"

"Yes, and it will give us time for a ride with Billy beforehand."

"I'll borrow a horse from one of my men for the day and we can all ride to town. Billy can visit some of the friends he's seen only rarely, of late."

"Until then," Aleksandra murmured. "Thank you for sharing Sarah's story with us."

Jason stood stock still, halfway through the door, looking at the floor.

"We'll do what we can to help," she said.

"Bless you," he said, and glanced at them both, then the door whispered closed.

"Well," Xavier murmured into her hair as they stood before the stove, "so tomorrow will be a big day…bigger than we could have hoped."

She lifted her face as his lips reached for hers.

18

Xavier smiled as Aleksandra's mouth dropped open at the panorama of Virginia City spreading out before them.

"Bigger than you expected?"

She stared at him. "I thought Great Salt Lake City was big. There's no comparison." She finally laughed, then sobered. "It's a good thing I didn't expect this. Wild horses couldn't have dragged me here."

"You still willing to give it a shot?"

"I said I would."

He reached over and squeezed her hand as a loaded wagon rumbled past. Its driver lifted a hand in greeting, then grabbed for the brake as the conveyance started down the steep hill behind them.

"You have a nice touch on the reins, Billy," Aleksandra called back over her shoulder. The Mustang swung along, his relaxed, rocking walk easily keeping pace with the bigger horses. His ears swiveled around as he took in his surroundings.

"He's magnificent, and just my size," Billy said. His smile lit the morning.

"We'll have to see about finding a horse for each of us, then we can ride together."

A shadow flicked across the boys face for a moment, before it was replaced by grim determination. "I'd... like that, Father."

"Really? You're not just saying that?"

"No, Papa, I mean it. Mama wouldn't have minded," his voice dwindled, "would she, that we're doing it without her?"

"She'd have been proud, Son. We were looking for a pony for you just before she... died."

"Oh." His chest rose and fell a few times. "Then it sounds grand."

"For now, Dzień might like some rides after school." He glanced up at Aleksandra, who nodded.

"On the right, there, Xavier. That's the mine office." Jason turned to Aleksandra and Billy. "Would you two like to go along to the mercantile," he said, as he and Xavier dismounted, "while I introduce Xavier to my brother? I'll be right along."

"Good luck, my love," Aleksandra whispered, her eyes glowing, as she leaned down to kiss him.

"See if you can find a pretty dress to get married in, if you can." He slid a few coins from the pouch at his side into her palm.

"Do we have enough?" Her eyes widened.

"Of course, for you." He kissed her again, and turned away.

Just down the street, big, bright silver letters on a deep blue field ensured 'The Ophir Mining Office' sign stood out against the muted browns of the wooden buildings and boardwalks. Xavier ducked his head beneath the big, swinging placard and followed Jason through the glass-paned door.

Xavier blinked. The man seated behind one of the desks could have been Jason. Jason looked back over his shoulder and grinned at him.

"Yes, he's my twin." He laughed. "We always get that."

"It's remarkable," Xavier said with a grin, glancing from one to the other.

"Jeremy," Jason said as the seated man glanced up, "this is Xavier Argüello. I think he's the answer to your prayers."

The furrows in Jeremy's brow smoothed as he took a breath and leaned back in his chair, his eyes on the newcomer, then stood and extended a hand.

"Good to meet you, Mr. Jacobs. Your brother says you're looking for someone to manage the assay office. What would you like to know?"

"Please, take a seat, Mr. Argüello." He motioned to the chairs opposite his desk. "You're keen to do it? It's a big job."

"Might need to learn a few new skills, but I grew up on a big *rancho* in California and worked with the books for years. I've mined in Placerville, and lately acted as station keeper for the Pony Express. Ephraim Hanks will give me a reference."

"Ephraim?" Jeremy's brows shot up. "Well, then, the job's yours. Comes with a house and barn, salary, plus bonuses if you can save me money and not cheat me or the miners."

"I'll try to save you money, and I'll surely not cheat anyone. I've worked too hard for my living to do that."

"Yep, you're my man," he said, then turned to Jason, "and you're the best brother a man could have." His brows narrowed. "Out with it, what else?"

"Xavier's intended is interested in teaching our school."

"No, really?" Jeremy's mouth dropped open. "Where did you find these gems?" He shook his head and stared at them both.

"Billy ran out to Xavier's stallion—spittin' image of Storm, so you might imagine the scene."

Jeremy took a deep breath and bit his lip.

"The horse is just outside and Miss Lekarski is at the mercantile with Billy now. Do you want to interview her or should I ask Simon?"

"I'm happy to." He pulled a glittering watch from his pocket and glanced at it. "What do you say we meet at my house at twelve? Dorothea will feed us all dinner and we can give—"

"Miss Lekarski," Jason responded.

"We can give Miss Lekarski her interview and teacher's examination."

"She'll appreciate that, sir. She's never taught in a schoolroom, but you'll find her…extremely learned and accomplished in many areas," Xavier said.

"Please, call me Jeremy. We don't stand on ceremony out here. It's not like New York." He stood and gripped Xavier's hand.

"Thank you, sir, call me Xavier."

His new boss opened a desk drawer and extracted a set of keys. "For your house and the office door," he said, identifying the keys. "You'll find a loaded pistol locked in the bottom right drawer. Pray you don't need it. Pay is twenty-five dollars per week, plus the house. Acceptable to you?"

Xavier blinked. "Excellent."

"See you all at dinner," he said, dismissing them. Before they were out the door, he was already engrossed in the columns scrawled down the ledger page.

"Thank you for that." Xavier shook his head at Jason as they walked down the steps into the street.

"And we get dinner out of the deal as well," Jason lifted a brow. "Dorothea's the best cook I know. My Sarah could cook but she'd have rather been cleaning stalls in the barn."

"I know how that is. Aleks, too." He chuckled.

They found Aleksandra near the doorway of the mercantile, fingering a scarf of the sheerest azure silk.

"Mama would have loved this on me," she said, with a wistful smile.

"Then let's have it," Xavier gently slid it from her fingers and held it, then took her hand. "So where's the young man?"

"That boy of yours, he's trying to rob my shopkeeper blind." The rotund mercantile owner looked ruefully at Jason. "He's just talked her down by a good twenty percent on that bag of flour. I should know better than to let her assist when Billy shows up. She adores him."

And someone adores her.

Jason gazed with longing at the woman. By the time she finally turned in their direction, the flush that had pinkened the woman's cheeks when they entered the shop had extended down her neck.

Jason saw Xavier looking at him and raised a brow, wincing. "Caught, am I?" he murmured.

"Appears so." Xavier said, beneath his breath.

"I'd best go rescue her, else Billy'll make her lose her job." Jason walked toward his son, stopping briefly to speak with a balding man. The man hurried from the shop, a packet in his hands.

"We'll come back and shop after we move our belongings into the house, but let's buy the silk now. Were there any ready-made dresses?"

"I've already started a dress, but I won't have time to finish it, if we're to be married right away," she whispered. "It'll have to be before I begin teaching, if it comes to that. Normally, they wouldn't have a married teacher, but I guess they're desperate. I can wear Mama's best and do it up with this scarf."

"I'm sure we can get someone to help you finish the gown. You say it's nearly finished?" He locked eyes with her.

"Let's find the priest first, and see when he can do it."

"That was him I was just speaking with," Jason piped in, "or rather, our Methodist Pastor, Reverend Clay. He was on his way to visit a sick parishioner, but said he'd find us tomorrow."

"That was lucky." Aleksandra glanced at him, then at Xavier.

"Oh Aleks, you have an interview at my brother's home at dinner." Jason pinched his lips together, at Aleksandra's slack jaw and wide eyes. "His wife Dorothea makes the best dinner in town."

"Onward and upward." She shook her head. "Nothing happens by half around here, does it?"

The men shook their heads.

Aleksandra nudged Jason as they crossed the road. "So who's the pretty lady in there who made your eyes glow?"

"Soon, soon," he said, looking at the ground and smiling.

"Cousin Billy, Cousin Billy!" A girl and a boy near his age squealed when they saw him at the door. They each grabbed one of Billy's hands and dragged him away down the hallway.

Dorothea's cooking spread the full length of the table. It looked as good as predicted, and her home was lovely.

"However were you prepared for such a feast at this short notice?" Aleksandra shook her head.

"He does this all the time. I've gotten used to it." Dorothea gave a hearty laugh and pointed out the window, to where they could see the front door of the mine office. "I keep an eye on the people coming and going at the office to get a general idea, then send the children to ask an hour before dinnertime."

"You amaze me," Aleksandra said, gazing at the rows of food heaped before them on the table."

"We grew up on farms in New York, so I'm used to feeding big crews." Her long blonde braids swung as she finished setting the table. "It's part of my upbringing."

The men came in from the barn and sat down on the long benches before the feast table.

"Miss Lekarski, shall we eat first and have our interview after that?" Jeremy asked.

"That would be fine," she said, "and as I said before, please call me Aleksandra. I'm not used to being called by my last name."

The children tumbled in, glowing and still dripping from their wash at the pump outside.

"Towel," Dorothea said. Billy caught it in midair and they shared it, amidst more giggles, then sat. Jeremy said grace, and they tucked into the best meal Aleksandra could remember in years.

The interview went well, and soon only the examination remained.

"But Xavier, I don't know if I can pass it," she whispered through gritted teeth when they went outside for a short break. "I only know what Mama taught me before she died."

He raised a brow at her. "Fluency in English, French, Polish, some Russian and German, ability to do math in your head and write beautifully. *Really*? I don't think they could possibly do better."

"We'll see." She still wasn't convinced.

An hour later, Jeremy grinned and held out his hand to her.

"Congratulations, Aleks. You have the job. Schools usually offer room and board plus a salary, but this one now comes with a house and salary. However, it appears you may have no need of it, with Xavier's mine position offering the house and barn," he hesitated, raising his brows at them both until they nodded acquiescence, "so we can rent it out on your behalf and offer you the value of its rental, in addition to your salary, which is five dollars per week."

She was struck dumb and stared at Xavier. Five dollars per week, and a house? Just for teaching? Not what the Pony had paid, but still, a fortune. She shook her head and blinked. Other than her brief employment riding for the Pony, she'd never had a job. Her trapper family had only seen money when the fur buyer came to purchase their year's worth of tanned hides from trapping, and most of that stayed right there in the trading post for their supplies for the year.

"Seeing as it's Thursday," Jeremy continued, "will you start the school on Monday?"

It was Aleksandra's turn to blink, then she nodded.

"Everything you need should be there, and we'll drop more coal and wood there before Monday. Here are your keys to the schoolhouse, so you may prepare for next week." He turned to Xavier. "I seem to be handing out a lot of keys lately."

A short while later, she preceded Xavier out through the front door. Too late, worries set in.

Her guts clenched at the thought of standing in front of a room full of miner's children, teaching.

"I'm not so sure," she whispered to Xavier, "this is a good idea. I've only taught one person before, Dancing Wolf." She shivered, as she untied Dzień. "How will I cope with a whole schoolroom full of students?"

Xavier shut his eyes and shook his head. "You're an Express rider—you've ridden through Indian wars, had arrows shot at you, and you never thought of giving up—how can you possibly be frightened of a room full of children?" He squeezed her hand and smiled, but her hands still felt cold in his large, warm ones.

THE NEXT TWO days passed in a blur. They moved into the new mine house, settled the horses into their new stables and Aleksandra prepared her lessons for school.

The roll showed thirteen children, ranging from five through sixteen years, and the older ones were all female, so she presumed the older boys worked in the mine. Her heart squeezed still further when she visited the schoolhouse—books were few and there was only a blackboard and a handful of chalk.

The smell of chalk hit her hard, as she cleaned the dusty blackboard, with memories of her mother patiently teaching her and her older brother. A tear rolled cold down her cheek and she sat down hard in the teacher's seat—her seat now. After a surreptitious glance about the room and out the windows, she allowed herself a little cry. After a few deep breaths, she remembered the same woman taught her she could do anything, if she was willing to make it happen.

She bit her lip. She'd do it, if only for the memory of her mama. She smiled wanly as she locked the schoolhouse behind her and walked the few blocks to their new house.

"What do you think?" Jason was saying to Xavier.

"I'll have to speak with Aleks," he said.

"I'll leave you two to talk it over. Let me know when you decide. How did you find the schoolhouse, Aleks?"

She gulped. "It's grand, as Billy would say."

"You'll do fine," he said soothingly.

She winced and tried to smile.

"Anyway, Jason, thanks for the offer. We'll let you know soon," Xavier said, and waved goodbye.

Xavier took her in his arms and hugged her close.

"The horses have never known such luxury," Aleksandra said, her gaze taking in the interior of the four-stall barn. "Enough room in the center aisle to park a Concord coach."

"Hang the horses, what about us?" Xavier waved at the home beside the barn and dragged her towards it. "Six rooms in the house, it's nearly the size of *la hacienda* at the *rancho*!" Xavier said.

"But what will we do with all that room?" She took his hands and looked up at him. "We certainly don't need it all. I'm sure there are others with big families who need it more."

Xavier grinned. "My thoughts exactly, to be truthful. Jason thought the same, which is why he's invited us to stay with them until the hotel is finished."

"Really? We don't have to live in town?" She leapt into his arms. "Please, can we stay in Gold Hill with them?" She stopped like she'd been shot. "What happens after the hotel is finished?"

"Too many questions. No, we don't need to live in town. Yes, we can stay in Gold Hill. After the hotel is finished, we get to keep the house on our own."

"Fantastic!" Aleks squeezed him even harder around the neck. "Oh thank you, thank you, thank you.".

"He's already checked with Jeremy, and we may rent this one out, and put that money away as well. We're on our way to saving up a nice nest egg."

She took a deep breath and let it out slowly. "I can teach, as long as I can leave town in the evenings. I can do this."

"Are you trying to convince me or yourself?"

"Me," she said softly.

"What's wrong?" Xavier caught her by the waist and pulled her against him.

"Monday."

"But think about Sunday." He brushed her lips with his, then deepened the kiss. She relaxed against him and slid her arms about his neck, entwining her fingers in his glorious ebony mane.

"Sunday?"

"The pastor."

"Are we to go…are we to go to the church?"

"He's coming here, and Jason and Billy will be our witnesses."

"Sunday will be fine," she managed a smile. It's Monday that worries me —I wish I had your confidence." She clenched her jaw and breathed deeply. "I'll do," she said, eventually. "As Mama always said, 'I'll do.' Let's go down to Gold Hill and tell Jason and Billy we'd love to stay with them, then Billy can show us around on Dzień."

"You know what?"

"What?"

"I really love you. I can't wait to have you as my wife."

"THAT'S THE OPHIR MINE." Billy pointed. "Uncle Jeremy says they are making inuf—enufa—" Billy stopped, his brow creasing.

"Innovations?" Xavier raised a brow at him.

"Yep, innovations. Anyways, it means they are doing things different."

"What sort of things?"

"Things so they can get more silver out, I guess."

"So it's only silver that's mined here?" Aleksandra asked.

"Uncle Jeremy said the men who first mined here were looking for gold, but all this heavy, gray clay kept blocking their rockers. They finally figured out the sludgy stuff was full o' silver, everywhere! They were standing right in it, and it was all over their boots and clothes!"

"Standing in silver, imagine that," she said, with a big smile for the boy.

The wail of a siren rent the air, not fifteen feet from where they stood. The stallions jumped, but Dzień, beneath the young boy, stood like a rock. Aleksandra's heart glowed, watching the quivering pony. His heart thumped visibly beneath his girth, but he never moved a single hoof.

"Cave in," Billy said, the color draining from his face.

"Is there an accident team?" Xavier asked.

"Oh my—I'll go get Father—he needs to be here." He spun Dzień on the spot. "May I?" His eyes, suddenly hard, flicked to Aleksandra.

"Of course. We'll stay here to help," Aleksandra said. Billy flew back the way they'd come, as she and Xavier dismounted and tied up the horses.

A handful of women, some carrying babes, ran toward them at the mine entrance. They said little, but their white faces told of the fear that resided in their hearts every day.

Glass rattled as the door of the nearby Ophir office slammed back against the wall. Rogan jumped and whirled to face the men racing from the building toward them. Carrying ropes and shielded lanterns, they shoved helmets on their heads and ran for the yawning maw of the mine, just as the first group of miners stumbled out, squinting in the brightness.

"Are you OK, man? What level were you on?" barked a big man to one of the exiting miners.

"We're from level two." The miner swiped at the black grime covering his face and winced, then turned to count the men stumbling from the entranceway. "Boys, over here," he croaked, leading them to a spot twenty yards away. "All accounted for—seven men." They slumped to the ground and sat, taking deep breaths and coughing, as their womenfolk ran to them.

"What happened?" A slight man with a German accent stepped toward them. Several of the miners glanced at him and their eyes lit up. The rescuers from the office hesitated to listen before going underground.

A red-haired man lying heaving on the ground, not more than a boy, answered, between gasps. "We heard a great cracking sound. The rock around us began to shake and we heard a slithering, then the siren."

Jeremy was in the group of men from the Ophir office. Aleksandra elbowed Xavier and nodded at Jason's brother.

"So, the cave-in wasn't at your level?" the German persisted.

"Nope. Somebody else rang that siren." His questioner patted him on the back and moved on to the next group of men.

More miners half-stumbled, half-dragged their mates with them out through the wood-framed mine entrance and found their work gangs. They, too, were accounted for and questioned. Finally, the German left them and raced into the mine, against the tide of miners.

The rest of the miners' woman and children continued to appear, most of them at a run, crying aloud prayers of thankfulness, tears streaking down their faces as they held each other like they'd never let go.

"Are any of you hurt?" Aleksandra called out to them. Xavier moved among them, talking with each one.

Another group of seven men looked around at each other, then one answered. "Nothing more than the normal cuts and bruises, Lord be thanked," one of the men remarked, his Irish brogue thick, and the rest shook their heads.

"Is there a water bucket here somewhere?"

"Office," one blackened man said.

Entering the Ophir office, Aleksandra glanced around and found a water bucket and dipper, plus a box of medical supplies. Filling the pail outside at a pump, she ran back and offered it to the thirsty miners.

"How many men were down there?" Aleksandra asked a lone man, as she counted those sitting around her.

"Maybe fifty or so." He glanced about him at the group of miners. "The boys from Level 3 South are still down there. Probably six or seven men."

Xavier was suddenly beside her and their eyes locked. Her heart thudded in her chest at the determination in his face.

"You're not," she whispered.

"I have to."

"Come back to me safely," she somehow managed.

He kissed her, his lips hard against hers, and he was gone, down into the darkness.

The first group of miners stood. "We're going back in. Anyone else can join us," one said. Carrying picks and shovels, they followed Xavier down the ladder.

The waiting had to be the hardest, both for the tense women above ground and for the miners trapped beneath, yet to emerge. The remaining men on the surface had long gone home, but for those who kept the vigil, the hours tripled.

19

The small army of men filed out, stumbling and filthy.

Xavier.

Where was he? Men kept filing past, but he didn't appear, nor did Jeremy. Her heart pounded in her ears as she searched the faces of the men coming to the surface. Again and again she wiped hands sweaty with fear on her buckskins.

Finally they came—they were the last two men to walk out, carrying two severely injured ones. Jason rushed to help lower the silent man Jeremy carried to the ground.

"How'd you stay so clean, brother?" Jeremy said, puffing, as he collapsed on the ground beside the man he'd carried.

"No one would let me go down there, for Billy's sake."

Jeremy closed his eyes and nodded, clasping the hand his brother offered.

Xavier's passenger groaned as two men lifted him gently from Xavier's back to a blanket spread upon the gravel.

Xavier was covered in gray, sticky mud, from nose to tail, but Aleksandra pulled him hard against her in a brief embrace before facing the bloody man he'd carted out. The other rescuers were muddy, but clearly hadn't been immersed. A cold fear clutched at her belly.

"You didn't...what..."

He set his jaw and said nothing.

She shook her head. She'd ask him later.

She turned to the miner on the ground before her. Mud and blood smeared every exposed surface of his body and the toe of one boot faced in the opposite direction to the other.

Her stomach roiled as she squeezed his hand. He looked up at her, conscious, but somewhere far away.

"Can you hear me?" she asked.

"Yes," he croaked. "We're really out, aren't we? I told the boys they'd get us out—did you find Adrian? He was under the cave-in, or maybe beyond it, we hoped," he muttered, his eyes brimming, and he glanced around until his eyes fell upon his silent comrade, surrounded by men, and then he broke. "Oh my God, it's Adrian—my boy Adrian—I sent him back toward the entrance so he'd be safe—we knew it wasn't stable.

He moved toward him and cried out.

Aleksandra touched him on the arm. "Hold still, your leg is injured," she said, her eyes scanning the rest of him, trying to see what injuries lay beneath the thick layer of gray grime. "Just lie back," she said gently, pushing him back down to the ground.

"My leg—under a big rock—think it's broken—but Adrian?"

"Xavier, will you go see? Then I can begin with Mr...?"

"Thank you, lass." The man laid back down, his breathing shallow. His unfocused eyes never left the still form of his son.

Aleksandra pulled his torn pants leg aside and surveyed the mess just above his boot. What was left of his grossly swollen leg below the knee didn't bear contemplating. It oozed blood but it was dark. Very dark. She swallowed hard. He must be in shock to not be raving from the pain. She whipped off her jacket and covered him.

"Blankets, can someone fetch blankets?" she called out softly, and there was a rustling behind her. She repositioned herself so the man before her couldn't see his damaged leg.

She jumped at the hand on her sleeve, and turned to find Xavier beside her again, his face drained white at the sight of the leg before him.

"I'll need my kit, the mine's kit has no laudanum," she murmured.

"'You see to the boy, Adrian, and I'll get the kit," Xavier said.

"He's alive?" The man on the ground struggled to sit up, biting his lip as hope dawned in his eyes.

"Unconscious, but alive," Xavier said. "Here, lie back down...he's your son?"

"Yes—" The injured man seemed about to continue, but clamped his mouth shut.

Aleksandra leaned toward Xavier. "Be back soon, I don't like his chances," she breathed into Xavier's ear, and slipped away.

"Can someone sit with this man?" Xavier called loudly, and a miner hustled to his side. In a softer voice, he said, "this man will stay with you, I'll return shortly."

He only nodded and fixed his bleary eyes on his son, while the *Californio* ran for Charro, and galloped off for Gold Hill.

Adrian's breath was shallow, his face pale, but he was alive. Bruises and swellings covered his body, and a few ribs were broken. A greenstick fracture of one arm and a gaping head wound needed attention, preferably while he was still unconscious. Aleksandra lifted his eyelids with her thumb to see normal pupillary reflexes. Hopefully no severe brain injury, then? One could only hope.

"Before he wakes up, can someone get splinting materials?"

Two men bolted for the office and Aleksandra returned to older man.

"Your Adrian's alive." She said, and told him of his boy's injuries. "We'll set the arm as soon as we get the splints, then I'll be back with you."

He returned her smile with the ghost of his own as she turned back toward his son.

On her way, she heard the German's voice in a conversation.

"—and I wanted to do more testing, but we need to get the square-set timbering going. We have to do it now. We cannot continue to risk men's lives needlessly."

The men surrounding him were nodding, with many murmurs in agreement.

Aleksandra was crouched down beside young Adrian when she heard the same man again, this time from beside her elbow.

"How is he?"

"*Guten tag,*" Aleksandra replied automatically to his German accent, and placed her ear to the unconscious teenager's chest to listen to his heart. Straightening, she took in a dark-haired man, about thirty years old. "Pardon?"

"*Guten tag,*" he said. He faced her. "You have some medicine—medical training?"

"Yes."

What are his injuries?"

"He has a few fractures, and a head wound, but he's stable, at this point. Are all the men out?"

"All the rostered men are accounted for, thank God, and if there was anyone else in there, we've not found them."

"What happened?" she murmured, her eyes and fingers nimbly running over the rest of his body, seeking other injuries.

"Cave-in." He gritted his teeth and stared at the boy, silent for a moment, then continued. "These mountains are a mining accident waiting to happen. They're just a pile of loose rubble. It's not like California, where the gold lies in veins within solid rock. The Comstock is made up of great spherical masses of loose rubble with all the goodies mixed in."

"So it's unstable?"

"Very." He looked back at her. "The normal T-supports we use elsewhere, with two side-supports and a crossbeam, cannot hold the rock back after the men have dug into it. Slips and cave-ins are all too frequent for my liking," he looked down at the boy, "and fatal."

"Is it worth continuing to mine here," she glanced around and lowered her voice, "if it's killing men?"

"The miners and mine owners seem to think so," he said, glancing down. "That's why they've brought me over here from Grass Valley, in California. Philipp Deidesheimer," he stuck out his hand to her, "Mine Engineer." She shook it, then frowned up at him.

"Don't the mines here have engineers, Mr. Deidesheimer?"

"Call me Philipp, please, and yes, they do, but they are…how do you say…flummoxed? They want me to solve this problem. I'm so close with my models…" His face lit up, and then he stopped, looking at the boy beside him, and his brows drew together again.

"Models?"

He took a deep breath and went on. "I've made a small replica of what I think will work to hold open the area in which the men will work, and also to support the areas from which they've already removed the ore."

Aleksandra raised a brow at him, then smiled her thanks at the men who handed her bandages and a pile of smoothed sticks. She bit her lip, considering the best way to splint the boy's arm.

"What is broken?" he asked.

"So far as I've found, both the radius and ulna, as well as several ribs, and he has a nasty lump on his head."

"Can you fix them?"

"I can set it and splint the arm. Luckily, he's young, and his bones are still soft. They're greenstick fractures—not completely broken—so they should heal soon. How old is he, do you know?"

"I'm not sure, I'll ask—"

"Nearly fourteen," his pa spoke across the distance. "Will he be OK?"

"I hope so," Aleksandra told him, and his face contorted.

"Not another one," he whispered. "Too young to be in the mines. His ma would have murdered me to even see him in there. Please, God, keep this one alive," he muttered to the sky, then turned back to face her.

Aleksandra bent the angled bones back toward straight with some difficulty, and splinted them. "We'll leave his ribs alone—my papa said bandaging them can do more harm than good."

Philipp frowned. "How is that?"

"Pressure on broken ribs can make the broken ends stick inwards—and puncture the lungs."

The German raised a brow, but was silent. "Was your father trained in medicine?"

"Yes, by his own papa, who was a doctor in a big *schlacta* household in Poland."

He turned to stare at her. "Bit of an international, aren't you? You speak German, what else?"

"I was born in Vienna, but we came here when I was young. My family trapped in Utah and taught me languages—Polish, German, French, and a little Russian, amongst other things."

"And medicine. Impressive."

"It's come in handy." She sighed and tied the knot in the first bandage, then tapped on it. It sounded firm. Hopefully, it would be enough. Raising her eyes, she saw Xavier trotting toward them with her kit.

"Can you stay with him, Xavier? I'll get that laudanum into his papa now, and then stitch Adrian's head wounds."

"May I help?" A female voice came from above her. "I can stay with him, and he knows me well."

Looking up, Aleksandra saw a girl of about her own age. Luminous brown eyes stared steadily at her from beneath a furrowed brow.

"Is he going to be all right?" she asked.

"I hope so. His arm and ribs will mend. He's got some nasty head wounds, but his pupils seem to be OK."

"I can help you stitch him up," she said. "I help my mother."

"Your mother?"

"She's the midwife. I'm Molly."

"Thank you, Molly. Can you find some boiled salt water and scissors while I tend his pa? We need to do this before he wakes."

Aleksandra met Xavier beside Adrian's pa. He handed her the saddlebags and she pawed through them. She located the bottle of precious mindlessness-inducing liquid and pulled the cork. "Here, drink this. It will help the pain," she said, pouring a small bit into the miner's open mouth.

He grimaced and shook his head. "All my fault," he whispered, "should've just waited until they found a new schoolmistress, not taken him into the mines," he rambled, as if he was already full of laudanum. "Boy like that—no business in the mines—he'll be OK? Please tell me he will—" The hand gripping her arm was surprisingly strong, though he shook like a leaf. "I can't bear another one—" His voice dwindled to nothing.

"Unless his head injury is too severe, he should survive. He's young."

"Too young. All my fault." He was shaking. He squeezed his eyes shut, but not before a tear rolled from each, down the side of his face, staining the dust on his face a dark brown.

Aleksandra took a deep breath and looked again down the man's body toward the twisted leg.

"What's your name?" The man's voice was weakening.

"Aleksandra."

"Aleksan—," he struggled with the words, "tell him I'm sorry, so sorry. It was all my fault. He was not meant for the mines...tell him...to get educated, become a doctor like he wanted..." His voice wavered.

"You can tell him yourself," she murmured, "after he awakens."

He turned to face her, and his eyes focused on hers. "I saw my leg. My papa was a doctor. I've seen enough wounds to know this might be the last time I see my boy." He inhaled deeply. "Please let me touch him one more time?" His eyes pleaded with her.

With one hand on the man's rapid, thready and irregular pulse, she couldn't help granting what might be his last request.

"Xavier? Let's move him."

Several men carefully lifted the blanket already beneath the man and ferried him to lie beside his son. His eyes closed and a smile settled onto his face as he placed his arm over his boy's chest. As the laudanum carried him away, his groans ceased and he became still.

Too still.

Gently moving his foot, she winced at the crepitus, but the look on his face never changed.

"OK, gentlemen—" she looked around at the circle of worried faces about her. "Isn't there a doctor here?"

"He's gone to Fort Churchill."

"Guess I'm it, then?"

"You seem to know more medicine than anyone else here, I think," Molly said in her soft voice.

"If the shock doesn't kill him, infection might," Aleksandra murmured. "I suspect that leg is in too many fragments to knit together."

"No doubt of that," the girl returned.

"All I can do is clean it up, then bind it up tightly with a poultice and see what happens."

Molly nodded her approval. "He has trouble with his heart, too."

Aleksandra stared at her. "Seriously? It felt irregular, but I thought it was just from the shock." She turned to Xavier, but he was already on his way to her saddlebags, wiping his hands on a cloth someone had handed him. He returned and silently handed her the stethoscope.

"It didn't bother him all the time," Molly shrugged, "Adrian told me it only got bad when he was excited or worried about something."

Aleksandra raised a brow at her and placed the head of the scope over his chest.

Dunk-a-dunk-a dunk-a dunk.......... dunk... dunk...... dunk...... dunk-a-dunk-a-dunk-a-dunk, in rapid succession, dunk.......... dunk.................... dunk-a-dunk-a-dunk.................. dunk-a....

She slumped for a moment and shut her eyes at the implications of the irregular rate and rhythm.

Get on with it.

She filled her lungs once more. "Molly, can you please clean up Adrian's head? Cut the hair away from his wounds and clean them up with salty water?"

"I've put a handful of salt in, good?"

"Yes." Aleksandra nodded and smiled her thanks, then turned back to the man before her. At least they were close enough she could take care of them both at once.

Jeremy ducked down beside them, brows raised. "Schoolmistress *and* doctor?"

"Close, but I wish I could hand this man to a real one." She gritted her teeth. "He has a problem with his heart, shock and his leg probably needs to come off, but I haven't the skills, so the best we can do is turn the foot around the right way, poultice it and bind it up. There's probably no blood supply to that foot, so it's likely to go gangrenous and kill him, if the shock doesn't do the job first."

"And that's the good news, I take it?" Jeremy's face was blanched to the color of fine porcelain.

"No, that's the bad news. Good news is he knows it'll probably kill him. Seems his pa was a doctor."

"Yes, he was," Molly murmured.

"And his only concern is for his lad—" Aleksandra stopped, unable to go on for the tears choking her. "Wants him to follow his dreams and become a doctor—told me to tell him that..."

Xavier put his arm around her and held her tight. She shook her head and swallowed, then reached into her saddlebag for the herbs.

"Boiling water, please?"

Another steaming pot was to hand, and a pile of clean cloths. She dumped a handful of comfrey and a handful of thyme in and covered it, then turned to see Xavier slitting the man's pants up the side seam of his bad leg.

It only looked worse for being exposed—the purple and bloody tissue was swollen beyond recognition from knee to boot, made all the more surreal by the sight of his foot facing the wrong way.

Aleksandra bathed the wound with saltwater and picked out pinkened ivory chips with forceps while Xavier sawed at the leather of his boot. She gave thanks for the blessed laudanum-induced unconsciousness. The pain they'd be causing him otherwise was incomprehensible.

Finally, she was satisfied. The wound was clean and free of obvious bone fragments. "Turn his foot the right way, please, Xavier?"

He gulped. Gripping the swollen, pale foot, he slowly turned it, amidst the crunching of bone on bone, until the toes lined up with the knee.

Aleksandra's stomach rolled at the sound, and breathed deeply to will it to stillness. "There may be more fragments in there, but I can't get to them."

"Are the bone ends overriding?" Xavier asked.

"A little, but then I'm not sure what's a bone end in this leg anymore. Is his foot warm or cold?"

"Colder than I'd like." Xavier swallowed hard.

"Let's get the poultice and under-bandage on, then we can distract it and see what happens."

"Splints and more bandages," Jeremy said, handing them to her.

"Thanks," Aleksandra said. "Oh, honey. Can you get some, Jeremy?"

"Sure thing." He wheeled about and disappeared.

"Aleksandra flushed the wound with the comfrey and thyme tisane, then filled a piece of muslin with the soaked herbs and left it in the hot tea while she packed the wound with honey. Placing the poultice bag atop the honey, she bandaged it in place.

"Now pull apart, gentlemen," Aleksandra said. Jeremy gripped the man's thigh while Xavier clung to his foot, applying traction for all the was worth. She felt what she could through the swollen tissues for the bone ends, to see if they were positioned well. By the time she was satisfied, the men were sweating with the exertion.

"That will have to do, but it's a jigsaw puzzle in there," Aleksandra said. Molly added more padding and together they firmly bandaged the splints in place from hip to ankle.

"He can drink some of that tisane…after he wakes up," Aleksandra said, gritting her teeth against the roiling of her guts.

If he wakes up.

THEY WERE SETTLING both men into Molly and her mother's house, a short walk from the mine office, when the door burst open and a lad of around five years ran in, shouting.

"Mama, mama, there's been a—" He stopped like he'd been shot, at the people surrounding the beds before the parlor fire. "—mine accident," he finished, his voice dwindling to a halt.

"Yes, darling, I know," Molly murmured and closed the space between them. She picked him up, her brows drawn together and mouth tight. "The injured men are here. Sebastian, it's your Uncle Adrian and Grandpa."

Aleksandra stared at her. She'd handled it all with calmness and competence, and they were her *family*?

"If you no longer need us here," Jeremy glanced at the slumbering men, "we'll see to the other men and make sure they're OK, then we're going to begin the new shoring-up system tonight. Philipp is keen to begin and the men are more than ready." He looked at the ground, then back to her face, and then to Xavier. "We're more grateful than you'll ever know to the two of you. Thank you." Jeremy headed for the door, then closed it from without.

20

Aleksandra was white as a sheet, her legs unsteady, as she walked across the uneven boards of the kitchen floor. Xavier moved to her side and held her, then sat her down in a chair in front of the fire, before she fell down.

"Emergency's over. I can take care of you, now. Are you all right?"

She looked up at him and their lips met briefly as he squeezed her icy hands. "Yes, a bit queasy. It always gets me after the pressure's off."

"Have a drink," Molly said, handing her a mug. "Some good Danish bitters will do you good."

Aleksandra sipped at the liquid, winced, then turned to the girl. "Molly, they're your relatives. I'm so sorry, I didn't realize…"

"It's OK," she said, looking away and holding tightly to her son. "I want to help anyone who's injured…" she gulped, and continued, "especially in a mine accident." A tear coursed its way through the dust on her cheek, smearing as she brushed it away. She turned to ladle soup from the pot on the stove and placed it on the table before her boy. "Sebastian," she said, "This is Aleks, and Xavier," she said, and the boy looked around at them, tears in his eyes as he took up his spoon.

Molly moved back to her father-in-law's side.

"What are his gums like?"

"Pale as his face, sorry."

"Can you use a stethoscope?" Aleksandra's color was returning to her cheeks, as she held the instrument toward the girl.

Molly's hands shook as she took the stethoscope in hand. She was bent over the unconscious man when a soft knock came upon the door. A moment later, it opened to admit Jason, Billy and a tall, balding man, his face and frock coat pale with dust.

Molly looked up, and nearly ran toward them.

"I'm so sorry." The stranger gripped both of her hands, and she crumpled and began to cry. He wrapped an arm about her shoulders and led her to a bench against the wall. "I came as quickly as I could. Didn't even stop for a wash." Crouching down before her, he wiped away some of her free-flowing tears.

Xavier looked down at Aleksandra, brows narrowed. She shrugged and turned back to the pair before them.

Billy sank down onto the bench beside the quietly sobbing little boy and put his arm about him, too.

"First your husband, and now his brother and pa. The Lord works in mysterious ways," he continued, "we just cannot know…"

Xavier's heart skipped a beat. He gripped Aleksandra's hand, remembering other times he'd heard those words.

Molly cried harder. Her son broke from Billy, ran to her, then clung with all his might.

"I wondered when you'd let it all out. There, there, darling…you've never really done that after Jack, have you?" the man said.

"Oh Reverend, why? Why? Why take them all?" She shook her head and glanced at Aleksandra and Xavier. Seeming to gather her wits, she took a deep breath. "I'm sorry, Aleks and Xavier, this is Reverend Clay, in case you've not yet met."

Xavier stood to shake the pastor's hand. "Good to meet you, sir, though I'd not planned to meet you under such circumstances."

"But well-met, all the same." The pastor's eyes shone into his, even if his mouth was still grim. "We'll talk later about your matter." He looked from Xavier to Aleksandra.

"Thank you for all you've done for them." Jason glanced at Aleksandra, then nodded at the two men on the bed. "You've probably saved their lives."

"I wouldn't speak too soon," Aleksandra whispered. "The boy's still out, and I'm afraid to let his pa awaken—I'm not sure he'll survive, with his heart and the shock he's had."

"The fear of losing his last son is shock enough, without the damage his leg has sustained," Molly whispered.

"Oh my God, his other son, too?" Aleksandra said, stricken. "Your…"

"Yes," Molly barely got out, as she stood and wrung her hands. "My Jack. My husband. My world."

Aleksandra shook her head and enclosed Molly in her arms.

"I want us away from here, far from where Jack's son would be raised in a mine."

"Yes, now, well, we'll have to see about that, Molly," Reverend Clay's voice intervened. "For now, you have plenty to think about, so let's be about it. But I've interrupted. How is his heart?"

"Irregular, and his pulse is weak. Can't really count it well enough to even tell…" Molly said, looking at the ground.

"You can still count it," Aleksandra said. "Tell me when you're ready with your watch, and I'll start."

"ALEKS, there's plenty. Come and sit down before you collapse," Molly said, shaking her head.

"Aleksandra stopped pacing and acquiesced. They were alone in the room. "You have enough to do without feeding us too." She smiled at the girl. "Where are the rest?"

"They've gone to put the horses up. You're both to stay the night. Maybe you should get some sleep? You didn't even notice them leaving. You're in a daze." She put her hands on Aleksandra's shoulders and pressed her gently onto the bench at the table. She placed a horn spoon into her hand. "Eat."

The stew brought her back to her senses.

"I can't remember when I last ate…breakfast, it must have been," Aleksandra said, and looked out the window. It was dark.

"No wonder you were fading. Off to bed with you," Molly said, "it might be a long night. I'll wake you if there's any change. Shall I give my father-in-law another spoon of laudanum if he wakes?"

Aleksandra's heart clenched. "I've no idea, Molly. With his heart, I've really no idea." She shrugged and winced. "I wonder if it's kinder that he doesn't awaken, just to die later from the shock and infection, in pain…" She looked up to see Molly looking at her in horror. "I'm just rambling now," Aleksandra murmured.

"You really were a hero out there, you know."

The shocked look had gone from Molly's face and Aleksandra sighed with relief.

Molly squeezed her shoulders and gave her a peck on the cheek. "Now you rest. I promise to wake you."

"And Molly, pray. A lot. I think that's all we can do."

Molly tried to smile, and failed. She closed the door, leaving Aleksandra to her dreams.

"Wake up, *Querida*," Xavier murmured, from above her. "His pulse is weakening and Jason says his heart is becoming erratic, no, he said sporadic...I think we're losing him." Xavier brushed her forehead with his lips.

"What time is it?"

"Just before dawn. His color seemed to be getting better and he was breathing easier, then all at once he began breathing fast, shallow breaths and he went horribly gray in the face."

She closed her eyes for a moment. "Who else is up?"

"Only Jason."

Her heart squeezed in a vice. "Send him for Reverend Clay," she heard herself say.

Adrian awoke with a blinding headache, just before the pastor arrived to give his pa his last rites.

Tears leaked from Adrian's eyes as he hugged his father with his one good arm. "Please don't leave me, Pa," he whispered into the candlelit darkness, willing his father to hear him.

"I'm so sorry...can't..."

Aleksandra could just make out the older man's faint words spoken from between parched lips.

"School...doctor...never told you...love you...proud..." His eyes closed for the last time.

Adrian wept over his body. Reverend Clay held him until he stopped, and blissfully, slept again.

The morning found Adrian awake. He was barely responsive, and lay staring into space. Aleksandra sat by his side, but he didn't, or wouldn't, recognize her presence.

"You know, Adrian," she said, "he asked me to apologize to you. Said he was so sorry, that you should never have been down in that mine."

Adrian gritted his teeth and growled as he rolled toward her. "He made me go, put me in what he thought was the safe place, and now he's dead, just like Jack," he spat out.

"Yes." There seemed little else to say.

"So what am I to do now?"

"Your pa asked me to tell you to get off to school and become a doctor, like you've always wanted."

The boy sucked in a breath and froze, his good hand flying to his ribs, then lay still as a statue.

"I think that was what he was trying to say just before...just before he died."

"What did you say?" His voice was barely audible.

"You heard me. You heard right."

He let out his breath slowly and moved his injured arm a fraction, setting his jaw.

"Last night," Aleksandra continued, "while you were still unconscious, he begged your forgiveness and asked you to follow your dream."

He rolled his head from side to side for a few moments.

"I want that more than anything, but I'd give it up to have him back, alive, by my side."

"Then take the gift he's offered."

Emotions flitted across his wan face.

"I'll teach you all I can about medicine, and I'm sure Molly's mother will too. When you're able, you can go back to school."

"We've got no teacher," he said flatly.

"You do, as of Monday. Me."

"Really?"

"Yes, so go back to sleep and let that head of yours repair. It appears you'll need that brain intact if you're going to be a doctor—no don't." She reached out and stopped his hand that was headed toward the new sutures in his scalp. "You have stitches there."

"I thought the doctor was away."

"He is. I did it."

His brows narrowed, and he cocked his head.

"Long story. I'll tell you soon," she said with a smile. "Anyway, you need to eat a little, then you can rest. Can't get better without that."

He gave her a wry grin, then cautiously rolled to his side, clamping his jaw and grunting.

"You can start with some willow bark tisane. It'll dampen down the pain in your chest. How's the arm feeling?"

"Not so bad as the blessed ribs," he groaned, then sobered.

"No more pain for your pa," she said softly, and he glanced up with a look of surprise.

Silence. "How did you know?"

"I've lost my whole family. I know how it feels." She squeezed his good hand. "Now, eat."

"I will," he said, then took a gulp of the tisane, "if you tell me how Papa..." he gulped, "died."

"With a prayer for you on his lips."

"Yes," he said, frowning. He swiped the hair from his face with a quick gesture, and winced. "But I want to know, could a doctor have made a difference?"

"Maybe yes, maybe no."

He sat motionless. "Elaborate, please, miss."

"What do you want to know?"

"I suspect you have some physician training."

"I'm not a trained doctor, but I learned what I could from one who was," she said, sighing deeply. "My papa."

"I'm sorry." He looked genuinely chagrined. "Can you please tell me of Pa's injuries, which you perceive to have been reparable by a well-trained doctor, and those you would have to leave to God?"

She blinked. Whatever she'd expected to hear, it was not this, and certainly not in language more formal than she'd heard from anyone but her mother.

"Well," she said, gathering her thoughts, and began.

ALEKSANDRA SAT on the edge of the Molly's spare bed, shattered, but she wasn't about to go to sleep before she had it out with Xavier. She eyed him. His borrowed clothing barely buttoned across his chest. Her anger grew as he unbuttoned the shirt to expose raw, seeping patches of skin all over his upper body.

He raised a brow at her. "What?"

"You did it, didn't you?" She whispered, but the accusation in her voice was clear.

"*¿Cómo?* What?"

"You were the only muddy one there." Her voice rose. "You didn't just fall and get a little muck on you, did you?"

"Well," he raised both brows this time and took a deep breath, "no."

"You promised!"

"I promised," he stated flatly and his jaw clenched for a moment, then turned away. "What did I promise?" His voice was edged with steel.

"You promised to come back to me safely, not be a hero," she spat, clenching her fists, her whole body shaking as she jumped up from the bed.

He spun back toward her and gripped the bedstead with both hands, his knuckles white. "I went to help save that boy in there," he growled, and motioned with his chin toward where the two injured men lay, just beyond the door. His eyes were on fire.

"You're ready to sacrifice yourself in an instant!" She didn't care who heard.

"You're big enough and tough enough to survive this world, even if you don't think so. Adrian needed me, then and there. A promise, if you can call it one," Xavier scowled at her, "not to risk my neck become null and void, at a time like that."

"So I don't count? I suddenly cease to exist every time someone else is in need?"

Xavier rose up before her, menacing. "*No tiene catorce*—he's not even fourteen yet. He had a rock on his chest the size of my body." Xavier enunciated every word, every syllable. "I'm grateful he has any ribs left at all, or has survived this long, for that matter!"

The force, the anger, and the righteousness emanating from Xavier's whole being shattered every shred of Aleksandra's resistance, and her fury crumbled, all the way to the terror at its roots.

Her knees wobbled when she dared to look up at him. "I...know...," she said, tears blurring her vision.

"It took every man jack of us to move it, and I was the only one tall enough to reach the little mite. How selfish can you be? There wasn't time to consider my safety. It was what it was, and I won't be coerced into regretting it."

"I'm sorry, Xavier. I...I didn't think." She shivered. Hugging herself, she looked at her feet. "I was so... so scared... I'd lose you down in the darkness, that I'd never see you again. I've never felt this for anyone before and it's frightening in its... immensity. You did what was right," she looked up at him, "as you always do. Maybe that's why I love you so much."

He pulled her to him and took her in his arms, hard. They were both shaking, and stood in silence for long minutes.

"I'm proud of you," he finally said. "You did more than anyone could have ever guessed for those men tonight."

She clung to him, her face buried in his chest. "Thank you for saving them, and for loving me enough to stand up to me," she hesitated and squeezed him as tight as she could "I'm so, so glad you're safe." She pulled her head away, sniffed and wiped her eyes on the back of her muddy sleeve. "Maybe you'll understand why I do some of the things I do, too...the ones I think are important, and you think are just dangerous."

He smiled and sighed, then kissed the top of her head as he crushed her to him. "*Sí, sí,* always the last word," he said, and pressed his lips to hers.

"You're freezing, Aleks," he said, with a start, at the touch of her cold hands on his back.

His hands, running up and down her body, burned like fire. She reached for his kiss again.

"Warm me up, then," she whispered, and melted into his embrace, hot and cold mixing to a glow that warmed her to the core of her soul.

"AND SO," Aleksandra said, "after I gave him my honest assessment of his father's injuries and possible care, he sat up very straight and vowed to God and his father to do everything to become the best physician possible, and do everything in his power to help those in need, especially miners, from this day forth."

Molly, Xavier and Jason stared.

"I guess you have your first serious student." Xavier gave her the ghost of a smile and looked ahead of them at Billy and Adrian walking together in the funeral procession.

The funeral was attended by almost every miner from all of the nearby camps. Reverend Clay's voice was soothing as he spoke of Mr. Jamieson and his family to the assembled, then he stepped aside for others to offer their words.

No one spoke when Philipp Deidesheimer moved to stand before the lectern. His clear voice rang out across the fully packed church, reaching even those miners outside the door, unable to find standing room within.

He offered his condolences, and commended this leader of men, then went on.

"I promise you to create a safer environment for all miners." You could have heard a pin drop as he continued. "The owners of the Ophir mine brought me here to help solve the problem which has plagued the silver miners of this lode. I'd like to dedicate the new square set timbering method we've developed to Mr. Jamieson, and to all miners and their families," he nodded at Adrian, "in hope many injuries and deaths may be prevented."

A low murmur went around the crowd.

"Mr. Jamieson's last thoughts were of his son, Adrian," Philipp continued. "Adrian, will you please come forward?"

The young man, one arm in a sling, took the lectern and Philipp stepped a short distance away. "Thank you all for being here today to farewell my father," he said. "Last year, you all helped us farewell my brother after his untimely death in the same mine."

Tears sprang to Aleksandra's eyes as Adrian continued, speaking of his father and brother, and the bond they'd shared, since losing their mother many years previously. He repeated the vow he'd said to Aleksandra days earlier, and the miners clapped their approval, most with tears streaking their faces. Thanking them again, he turned to return to the crowd.

"One moment, young man, if you please." Philipp put a hand on his shoulder. Jeremy and several of the owners of the Ophir Mining Company walked to the front of the church and faced the crowd. Adrian raised a brow at them and wiped his eyes.

"Your father's last wish," Deidesheimer looked straight into Adrian's eyes, "was for you to follow your dream to become a physician. To that end, I would like to offer to pay half of your upkeep and schooling."

Adrian stood silent and bit his lip. The miners held their breaths. He composed himself and shook Philipp's hand. "Thank you, sir, from the bottom of my heart." His tears flowed freely now, but he didn't seem to care. "It will help me make good on my promise to my pa.

"Not only that," Jeremy stepped forward and stood beside Philipp, "but the Ophir Mining Company will make up the balance."

The miners hooted and cheered as one.

The young man faced his benefactors and shook each of their hands, a serious look upon his face. A tumultuous ovation erupted, with a great clapping of hands across his back that shook even the floors of the church as he made his way back to his seat.

"I'm going. I'm truly going,"Adrian whispered, as he slid into the chair beside Aleksandra.

"Of course you are. We begin your preparation on Monday."

"I'm ready."

By the look on his face, he was.

"GOOD OF YOU TO come into town, Miss Lekarski," Reverend Clay said, motioning her to a seat opposite his desk.

She smiled. "I'm sorry Xavier couldn't make it today, but he was needed in the office, after all."

"I wanted to discuss the ceremony, and any particular wishes you may have."

"Thank you. Xavier and I wanted to know if there were any impediments to our marriage. You realize we're both Catholic?"

He bit his cheek. "I'd wondered, him being of Spanish descent." He steepled his fingers and looked at her over the top. "It can be done. If there were a Catholic priest anywhere near here, I couldn't perform the service. As it is, there are no priests closer than Sacramento. I believe we can proceed, provided we receive a dispensation from the bishop in..." he closed his eyes for a moment and pinched the skin between his eyes, "...the closest would be San Francisco."

She blinked. That would take months.

"But, sir, Reverend, we wish to marry now. We've waited longer than we likely should have," she quirked her lips at the pastor and continued, "and I've been offered a job teaching at the school."

"Ah, I see. So it cannot wait."

"Not if there's any other way."

He inhaled slowly, then let it out. "Perhaps we can stretch the rules a little, and perform the ceremony, and when the dispensation arrives, all will be correct."

She winced. The visiting Catholic priests she'd met when their family journeyed to visit them on their circuit of Utah several years ago were stiff, stern and forbidding. They couldn't possibly approve.

"Will it be OK?" she murmured.

"We should be fine. We really have no choice, do we?"

"No." She gulped. "I appreciate it very much, sir."

"No problem at all. So do either of you have any concerns, before the big day?"

"What about reading the banns? Is it not necessary?"

He grinned. "At least in this, I can satisfy you. Most of the settlers haven't been here long enough to know each others' histories, so banns are of no use. Some churches have their own rules, but there are actually no laws regarding marriage in Utah Territory. They're considering instituting them, if only to ward off polygamy, but they're not even close to drafting any laws, much less implementing them."

"Well, that's a relief."

"So it seems the ceremony will need to be held tomorrow or the day after, if school begins on Monday."

Aleksandra winced. "They've put school off for another week, with the mine accident."

"Well then, shall we say Tuesday?"

She inhaled sharply and tightened her jaw. "Yes, that will be fine."

"You're sure you have no concerns?"

"Nothing more, thank you, Reverend."

"Well then, go and make ready. Some time in contemplation will be necessary for both of you to free your hearts to accept the joining."

"I will, we will, sir."

He smiled. "Until then," he said, and guided her to the door.

"Thank you, Reverend. We will be there."

We will be there…of course we will. Wasn't that a daft thing to say?

She shook her head at herself as she stepped down the stairs to the boardwalk and headed toward Dzień, tied to the hitching rail beside the little clapboard church.

Xavier had already left for home by the time she reached his office, but he was still in the barn unsaddling when she arrived home.

He smiled at the news. "So he'll write to the bishop in San Francisco?"

"Yes. It's a good thing, too." She looked down and smoothed her hand over her belly, then reached up for a kiss. Charro nudged his nose between them and she drew away.

"He wants his supper, and so do I," he said, and gave her a peck on the forehead.

"A student gave us a half-dozen eggs. Shall we have them with *kielbasa?*"

"Thought you'd never ask." He swung a hand at her bottom and she yelped. Her face warmed as he held on to her, his other hand wrapped around her waist. "And then, while you're washing up, I might have to...help."

"Oh, might you, now?" She squirmed as her pelvis tightened.

"*Sí, Querida*...and it might," he hesitated, "take quite some time to do those dishes."

She raised a brow at him as her knees seemed to unlock. He held her tightly against him.

"They might not even get done..." he ran a trail of nibbles from the corner of her mouth, past her earlobe and down her neck.

"What dishes?" she said, faintly, as her legs melted. "We might not even make it out of the barn."

He released her slowly, then held her by the shoulders at arms length. He chuckled deep in his throat. They were both already panting. "*Va a la casa,*" he said, an edge to his voice. "I'll be in as soon as I've fed the stock." His cocoa eyes were black. "I'd suggest you make those eggs, else we might not get any supper tonight."

She fled.

21

Like my mother.
Aleksandra started.

She must have made a noise, because Molly looked up from the shoe she was buttoning. Aleksandra looked in the mirror again.

"What is it?" Molly asked, her brow furrowed as she stood and reached out a hand to Aleksandra's shoulder.

"This was Mama's favorite dress. I've tried it on over a petticoat before, but never with a crinoline and stays, or with my hair up." Tears filled her eyes and she wiped them away. "I look just like my mother…" Aleksandra's voice dwindled. "She and Papa would have so loved to be here today," she whispered, one saline drop discoloring the fabric of the new scarf Xavier bought for her. She watched the stain spread, navy against the sky blue silk.

"Well then, she must have been the loveliest woman I've ever seen," Molly replied with a smile and hugged her tight. She stepped away and adjusted the scarf to cover Aleksandra's bosom more demurely.

Aleksandra tried to take a deep breath, gave up, and quirked her mouth.

"Can't breathe with stays." Molly grinned.

"I've never worn stays or a crinoline before." She smoothed her hands over her unfamiliar figure. "Thank you for the loan of them," she said, then looked in the glass again. "For all the discomfort," Aleksandra wriggled against the restraining whalebone and cotton, "I must say it pushes… things…up a bit, doesn't it?" Her face heated.

Molly chuckled low in her throat. "Xavier will choke when he sees his wild Pony rider walk up the aisle."

Aleksandra's heart stopped and she bit her lip.

Molly glanced up and laughed.

"No, silly. What hot blooded man wouldn't?" She laughed. "OK, spin around for me, there's the girl. Perfect. Now we go," she said brusquely.

"Go? Go where? We're to be married downstairs?"

"Aah…no. Surprise. That's all I'll say."

There was no one downstairs. Not Xavier, not Billy, not Jason. She froze.

"Come on, you don't want to be late for your own wedding, do you?"

"Where are we—"

"—never you mind. Just let Xavier do this for you?" Mollie's eyes pleaded with her as Aleksandra clung to her new friend's hands like a lifeline.

Aleksandra followed where Molly led. She frowned—the streets were oddly deserted, for this time of day. When they turned the corner toward the little Methodist church, Aleksandra stopped and stared.

There must be some mistake.

"Molly, are we going to a church?"

"Yes," Molly said, and kept walking, Aleksandra's hand gripped firmly in hers.

"This couldn't be the right one, then." Every tie rail near the little church was filled, and overfilled, with horses; some saddled, some hitched to wagons or gigs.

"Surely." The girl looked askance at her.

"Perhaps the wrong day?"

Molly looked around, then turned back to Aleksandra, her brow furrowed.

"What are all these people doing here?"

"You and Xavier are getting married today," she said slowly, enunciating slowly.

"Yes, but…" Aleksandra chewed on a fingernail.

Understanding dawned on Molly's face and she grinned. "Miners are a tight group. Your assistance to their own hasn't gone unnoticed—both of you are already in their hearts. Take credit where credit is due and enjoy it." Taking Aleksandra's hand, she led her up the steps to the closed door.

"Just a moment, Molly, let me gather my thoughts," Aleksandra murmured, smoothing down Mama's dress. She closed her eyes and tried again to breathe, and couldn't. The big wooden door before her swam, and Molly grabbed her arm and held her up.

"It's time, dear. Don't struggle against the stays, it won't work. You'll be out of them soon enough." She leered. "I'm sure your man'll see to that."

A laugh bubbled from Aleksandra and then everything was fine again. She gave Molly a weak smile and sighed. "Thank you for your help and care today. I'm ready."

Molly muffled a laugh and pulled open the heavy door.

Aleksandra took one look at the packed pews and the men standing at the back of the church and stopped stock still, her jaw slack. A million pairs of eyes seemed to stare.

"Come on," Molly smiled at her and beckoned.

"I can't," she whispered, shaking her head. "Too many…many…"

"What is it?" Molly let go of the door and it swung shut with a muffled thump. Her eyes wide and her brow furrowed, she reached out a hand to Aleksandra.

Aleksandra closed her eyes. "I've never seen that many people in one place, other than at the funeral, only then, they weren't looking…at…me.

"They are here to wish you well and show their respect," Molly said in a soft voice. "Your man awaits."

Aleksandra blinked and tried to breathe again, and let out a half-laugh, half-sob. "You're pure gold, Molly."

"Go on, girl, show 'em what you've got."

She straightened her spine and together the girls opened the door. Just inside, Jason's scrunched brow relaxed and a smile softened his visage as he took her arm to lead her forward.

Xavier.

She looked straight up the aisle and into the warmth of his eyes. He slowly perused her up and down and shook his head slowly, his grin fit to split his face. A warm tingling began deep inside, and suddenly it was only the two of them in the room. Her steps somehow took her to his side and he clasped her cold hand tightly in his big warm one.

Even later, she didn't remember what was said during the ceremony, or by whom, but she did remember the gold, warm from Xavier's pocket, sliding up her finger, and his lips hot on her mouth. He held her closely to his side as they left the church, to a roar of applause. No quiet piety, this lot. Ribald jokes were thrown Xavier's way when they descended the steps and he lifted her into the air, preparing to put her and her voluminous skirts into the waiting surrey.

"Dzień!" Aleksandra grinned at Xavier.

The pony turned his head to her, craning to see around the blinkers of the fancy patent leather harness. He snorted at her skirts, but stood.

"He'll be embarrassed to pull me in these silly skirts, and wear patent leather. Where did you get the harness?" Aleksandra murmured into Xavier's shirt front.

"How could he be embarrassed? You're the most wonderful and beautiful woman I've ever known, and he looks pretty flashy too."

She could lose herself in those eyes—and she finally realized it was OK.

Everything. They were bound to each other, forever, and it was fine. She closed her eyes and inhaled his scent.

"What?"

She shook her head, their eyes locked. "We really do belong to each other now—really, and truly—till death do us part. I thought that would terrify me, but all I feel is warm."

"I was thinking the same as you glided up to me in the church. No more fear. It just isn't there anymore."

"I do wonder, though, about the love, honor and *obey*." She frowned briefly.

He chuckled. "I wondered, but you did say it."

"Hmm, well, yes." She tightened her grip around his neck to kiss him, and applause exploded around them. Dzień jumped, but stayed put. "Good boy, Dzień," she crooned.

"Get her in there and away before you two embarrass yourselves, for crying out loud." Jason laughed. "Remember, she's our new schoolmistress." He stood beside the trim brunette from the mercantile. "We'll see you at the hotel."

Dzień drew them down the road towards Gold Hill, and the crowd followed.

Xavier set the brake on the gig as Dzień negotiated the steep gravel road down to Gold Hill with care. At the bottom, Aleksandra shook her head, mouth open at the red and white crepe ribbons flapping in the breeze from the frame of Jason's unfinished hotel.

"Who decorated it?"

"After I left you at Molly's, a bunch of us did it last night after work. Like it?

"Love it." She laughed. "And I love you."

"I love you too. When I said you were the most wonderful woman I've ever known, I meant it. We'll have our ups and downs, but I can't imagine a better person to have them with." He gently kissed her forehead.

"I just wish I could breathe…" She tried to draw a full breath. "How do women wear these all the time?"

He looked toward her chest.

She peered down to where his eyes had lit. The silk scarf, so carefully placed, had blown from the front to somewhere down her back. Her breasts bulged frighteningly above the trim of the bodice.

"I'd have to say I approve of the stays, if there were a way you could breathe in them." He slid his fingers down her face, past her neck to her bulging bosom. With a glance back up the hill, he smiled and returned to his slow perusal of her bodice. He rubbed the tip of a finger over her taut nipple, just beneath the lace edging. "Unfortunately, I'd never get anything done around you."

"What about you?" she said, her face heating, as his fingers roamed. "Where did you get this beautiful outfit?" She touched the fine linen ruff at his neck and the silk vest showing between the jacket lapels over his wide chest. The side-striped black linen trousers appeared to have been cut to his measurements—skin tight over the torso and thighs, and flared over his glossy boots. "And this exquisite work," she said, and shook her head, leaning closer to examine the tiniest embroidered silk swirls embellishing the coat and pants.

"Mama gave it to me when we met in Carson City. It was my Papa's Spanish Grandee suit, and his father's before that, from the last century. She saved it for me." He swallowed noisily and sniffed, then continued. "I wish she could have been here today. She told me to wear it at our wedding."

"You told her about me?"

"Yes. And she made me leave immediately and race back to save you from Vladimir."

Billy called out from behind them, then his face appeared as he caught up to their wagon. Xavier jerked upright and took up the reins again.

"Good morning, Billy!" Aleksandra called, laughter in her voice, as her husband's blush showed through his darkly-tanned skin.

"Congratulations to you both! Would you like me to care for Dzień and take him home after you alight at Pa's hotel?"

"That would be grand, Billy, as you say," Xavier said.

"I'm glad they put the school opening off for another week so I could go to the wedding," he said, with a smug grin.

"If there'd been school this week," Xavier said dryly, "there wouldn't have been a wedding to attend."

The boy glanced at him, brow furrowed, then he chuckled as a light dawned. "Fair enough, you got me. I owe you one."

They danced, danced and danced some more. Everyone she knew wanted a turn, and she partnered them all. "My waltzing is a little rusty," Aleksandra said, lying back in Xavier's arms as he swirled her about, "but it's wonderful to dance with you," she said.

Xavier's eyes glowed. "I haven't danced in...it must be nearly ten years."

"The new planks on the floor do little for 'lightness and grace,'" Aleksandra chuckled, "as Mama used to encourage, but it works a sight better than rocks and grit would."

Women were a minority in the camp, and they obligingly turned around the floor with many men, their husbands good-naturedly sharing for this brief time. By the time the party was well-started, men began dancing with other men, just so they could keep dancing. The fiddle and piano players might be lacking in finesse from the hours wielding pick and shovel, but everyone clapped and sang along to the old tunes.

THE NEWLYWEDS LEFT while the party was still in full swing, before the miners got too drunk.

"Billy's gone to Jeremy's tonight, and I won't be home for hours," Jason shouted as they tried to leave. "Make all the noise you want!"

Aleksandra's mouth dropped open and her face grew hot once again.

"Get used to it, *Querida*," Xavier murmured into her hair, "you're married now."

She gave him a wan smile.

"I owe you one, Jason," he called over his shoulder. They both waved to the cheering crowd as they left and headed across the street.

"Oh." Aleksandra stopped short in the doorway of their room and gripped Xavier's hand.

They slowly entered and stared around the bedroom.

Candles flickered on every surface. On their pillows sat two homemade, cut-out paper doilies, each beneath half of a piece of maple sugar candy. Between them sat a carefully lettered note in a young hand.

> *Felicitations on your wedding. I hope your lives together last forever, much longer than Papa had with my mama. I'm glad you both came to Gold Hill. I'm glad Dzień came, too.*
> *Sincerely,*
> *Love,*
> *Billy*

A soft voice came from behind them. "I promised Billy I'd light the candles before you came home."

"He did all this?"

Jason nodded, his eyes brimming. "He meant what he wrote. That Christmas candy was his most prized possession."

"From his mama?"

He nodded.

"We can't take it from him," Aleksandra whispered.

"I wish you would," Jason said, and gulped, looking at the floor. "He thinks the world of you both, and he thinks this bit of his mother will make your marriage last a long time..." He closed his eyes and took a long, slow breath before continuing. "He doesn't want either of you to suffer the way we have."

Aleksandra took his hands and squeezed them tightly. "I understand," she said. "When did it happen," she stumbled, "the accident, I mean…"

"Last year, February, as soon as the snow began to melt. She and the horse were both so fresh and keen to escape the town—she would have never seen the…hole."

"She must have been very special," Xavier said.

"She was my reason for living—but life goes on. She would have been the first person to tell me that. In fact, she said—" he hesitated and gulped "—that if something happened to her, I needed to move on and find someone else to love, and to care for Billy and our other…" He fell silent.

"Other?" Aleksandra breathed into the stillness, after long moments.

"She was pregnant that day…that day…" He doubled over like his guts were being wrenched out. Aleks hugged him while he pulled himself together. He finally looked up and disentangled himself, then stood back and looked at them both, a tear glistening in the candlelight on one cheek. "Our most profound thanks to both of you—you've given both of us our lives back."

"You were nearly there without us."

"I guess I have to go forward now."

"You said she'd have wanted it."

He swallowed hard. "I still didn't think it right."

"You have someone who's clearly taken a shine to you," Aleksandra smiled, "and Billy adores her—your brunette at the mercantile."

He looked at her, hope dawning on his face. "Do you genuinely think it's the right thing to do?"

"Yes," Xavier said. "I nearly lost this one," he pulled Aleksandra back against him, "because I wouldn't let her in. Learn from my mistake."

The first real smile she'd seen on Jason's face in days spread over his face. "Thank you both, again," he said, backing toward the door. "And like Billy said, may your marriage be long and fruitful. Enjoy your wedding night."

The door closed behind Jason with a soft click.

"*Ven aqui, Querida, mi mujer.*"

She turned slowly toward him, and their eyes locked.

ALEKSANDRA'S EYES glowed soft as the candlelight filling the room. Something deep in Xavier's core pulled tight into an intense ball. It was like the first time, only so much more—just more.

Uncertainty didn't enter into it now—only a heart-stopping, gut-wrenching certainty that the fearful times were passed. This woman, shimmering, surrounded by flickering flames, was his—to have and to hold, not just for this hour, this night, but forever.

He'd honestly never thought a woman could, *would* give him this.

Yet, she had.

With reverence, Xavier kneeled before her, pressed his face to her belly, and kissed it. His vows flowed again from his lips and a tear from above wet his forehead, as he looked up and took her hands.

He rose and picked her up, one arm beneath her knees, holding her tightly against him as he slowly circled in the candlelight. He shook his head, still scarcely believing this woman was his for all time, then lowered her gently to the bed and began to honor her.

With a wry grin skyward, Xavier gave thanks she'd removed her boots with her damned button hook when they'd entered the house. He slid silken stockings down even silkier legs. Aleksandra's breath came faster as his fingertips slid up toward her waist.

Her hair cascaded, molten gold in the flickering light, as he pulled the restraining pins from it, one by one. She turned away and pulled her locks aside for him to unbutton her bodice. Slowly, slowly. One button for one kiss on her neck, for one on fingertips, a touch on an already-hardened nipple. Her breathing, already short with her tight stays, raced and she made little sounds like a kitten, louder with every touch.

She reached for him, but he shook his head.

"It's your night, *Querida*. You'll have to wait."

She shuddered.

He pulled her to her feet and she stood, shaking, while he slid the gown up and over her head and lay it on a chair. He crooked a finger at her, and she came. Her already-full breasts were...he blinked and sucked air into his lungs...incredible, bulging above her stays. The rosy hue of nipples just showed. He ran the tip of one finger along the top of the restraining fabric and she whimpered as his nails found one, then the other, and her knees began to buckle.

One tug on the knot behind her, and she sighed as her stays released. He chuckled deep in his throat and turned her to unlace them.

Aleksandra grabbed his hands, challenge in her eyes, and he stilled. She slid off his vest, then the shirt from his body, then they were skin to skin. Warm silken touches, cool sheets, warm featherbed. Time ceased as they climbed higher and higher. He heard sounds that might have been her, might have been him. Louder, stronger, harder, then the oneness, drifting down and down to rest.

Spent, sheen covering their bodies, they returned to this plane and he pushed the hair back from Alexander's face for another kiss.

"Loving you has always been wonderful, easy, but never have I felt so loved in my life," she whispered.

"Yes, exactly. You're truly mine now–as never before–and I want to revel in it, like a horse rolling in a green pasture—it's that kind of joy." He smiled at her, heart full to brimming. "You stay here, I'll get the candles."

She smiled at him as the sound of laughter echoed from the party, still in full swing, at Jason's saloon.

22

"Married life suits you." Molly smiled at her.

"I don't know why a few words spoken in a church makes such a difference to us," Aleksandra reached up to place the last plate away in its rack, high on the wall and hung the dishcloth on a hook, "but it does. I guess it's the commitment given before a representative of God. The fears of loss I had before are gone. Xavier feels the same."

Molly took a deep breath, opened her mouth to speak, then clamped it shut.

"Oh my God, Molly," Aleksandra whispered, wrapping her arms around the other girl, "I'm so sorry."

"It's...OK." She gulped. "He's been gone over a year now, I should be getting on with my life. Sebastian needs me to be strong for him."

"It doesn't make it hurt any less when someone talks about loss, especially when they still have their special someone." Aleksandra was silent for a moment. "Have you any plans, other than helping your mother in her practice?"

"Not yet. I'm trying to hold it all together here. I can't even begin to look at another man, certainly not a miner." She shivered. "I can't face it again, watching them go down the pit every day, knowing many of them won't be alive five years on."

"Oh Molly." Aleksandra's heart ached for her.

"When the men walk past my window on their way to the mines in the morning," she mumbled against Aleksandra's shirt, "I put my head under the covers so I can't hear them shuffling past. Whenever the alarm bells ring for a cave-in…" She shuddered, and Aleksandra tightened her arms.

"Molly," she held the girl at arms length and willed her to look into her eyes, "have you gained your high school certificate?"

"No," she dropped her head and continued in a whisper, "I got married, and then I had Seb. After that, there didn't seem to be any need, or time, for that matter, and I expected my husband to live." She ended on a wail and burst into tears.

"You're sad, but are you also a little angry?"

Her head shot up and she stared at Aleksandra. "Sometimes I'm so angry at him for leaving us, but then I get even angrier at myself. He didn't ask to die in the mine, and then I get angry with the mining company, but it's not their fault, either…I no longer know what to think, or do, so I just carry on," she mumbled, and sank into a kitchen chair.

"Seb is five now, isn't he?" Aleksandra hunkered down beside her chair and took her hand again.

"Yes, last month."

"What do you say you come along with him to school and finish your schooling, as much as your mother can spare you from working?"

Molly sat still, silent. "Yes," she said slowly, "I could do that."

"If you want to escape from a town where nearly every man and boy goes underground every day, education will give you choices."

Molly let out a long breath, then stared at the floor for long minutes. She finally looked up, and a glimmer of a smile lit her face. "Bless you, Aleks, for coming here. I needed to be dragged out of this slump I've been in for far too long. This last mine accident was a nightmare, but it encouraged some needed changes, and I thank you."

"Think nothing of it." Aleksandra looked away, but she smiled just the same, her heart full.

"Surprised, really." Aleksandra shook her head as she stood before Xavier, her long curls glistening in the early dawn light peeking through the window.

"I knew you'd be a fantastic teacher, and it's only been a month," he said.

"I never thought I could do it, but I guess Mama and Papa taught me more than I knew."

"More than most people here will ever know." He kissed her atop the head as his hands slid from their resting place on her bottom.

"Stay out of that mine, please, will you?"

"Can't promise that, *Querida*, but I'll do my best." He smiled. "Speaking of which, Philipp Deidesheimer asked if you and Adrian would be free to accompany him into the mine on Saturday."

"Into the mine?" She turned a wrinkled brow to him. "Do you think that's wise? Adrian's just beginning to get over his pa's death."

"I don't think that'll ever happen," Xavier said softly, his heart like lead in his chest.

"Well, of course." A tic started in Aleksandra's jaw, and she slowly let out a breath. "OK," she said finally. "Why does he want us down there?"

"To show you the progress on his square-set timbering."

"Oh," was all she said, but her demeanor lightened.

"So, shall I tell him you accept?"

"Yes, and I'll bring Adrian along. He'll be glad to see it."

"How is he coming along? I've not seen much of him lately."

She paused before speaking. "I've never seen anyone dig so hard into their study before. The boy is obsessed." She twisted her lips. "He puts me to shame."

Xavier frowned. "Is that OK? I mean, is it healthy for him?"

"He needs an outlet. He's getting through his lessons so fast, I'm using the extra time to put some of Papa's medical theory his way. He's eaten halfway through one of Papa's medical books already."

"What else is he doing, I mean, outside school?"

"A widow from the town has moved into his family home and he's turned his papa's bedroom into his study hall." She smiled up at him. "She's making sure he's getting plenty of exercise and eating well."

Xavier's hands unclenched from the door frame. "That sounds good."

"He's also spending time with Dr. Bayes and Molly's mother when they see patients. The local patients appreciate his presence. He's taking every opportunity he can create for himself."

"Doesn't get much better than that."

"No. I'm sure he'll be keen to see the new timbering; I'll ask him this morning."

He pulled her close again. "And I'll stay out of the mine whenever possible, but occasionally I need to check on things for the boss."

"I know." She bit her lip and hugged him, her face buried in his chest.

"I'll take care, and remember, I spent much of my young life in mines. I know what I'm about."

"You spent time in California, where the lodes were only a hand span wide," she said, her brows narrowing and voice sharpening. "The Comstock is dozens of feet wide in places. Once the ore is removed, there can be no stability. There's no comparison, and you know it."

"Hence Philipp's presence." His jaw clenched tight as she gave him a last hug.

"That doesn't make you invincible, *Querido*."

With a deep sigh, he gave in and smiled. "I guess not. I promise to be careful, and of course, I'll be down there with you on Saturday."

Aleksandra turned him around and smacked him playfully on the rear. "Off with you then, you'll be late."

She yelped when he spun back and picked her up in a bear hug.

"Let me down, you big oaf." She laughed and pounded at his chest with her fists.

"You've not done that before, have you?" His chest tightened and his abdominal muscles clenched.

She turned a furrowed brow to him in answer.

"It pushes my buttons." He raised a brow at her, and started for the stairwell.

"Xavier, we'll both be late..." Her eyes glowed dark into his, and she fell silent as he took the steps two at a time to their bedroom.

"You know what you do to me when you do that?"

"Do what?"

"Handle me there." He felt hard and tight against her body, cradled in his arms. He had to have her, now.

"Not yet, but I'm beginning to think I might do it more often," she breathed.

He only smiled as he laid her onto the bed. Turning her over, he flicked her buttons open with one hand and caressed her bottom with the other, then rolled her back over and peeled her dress, then her petticoats off, revealing her body, resplendent in only stays.

"Oh." She gazed at him as he shucked his trousers. He pulled his shirt over his head in one movement and her eyes locked with his for a moment, then focused downward on his huge erection, her face flushed. "Do we have time..."

"Yes." Hard.

She took a deep breath. "If this is being married—" cut off as he took her lips in his.

ALEKSANDRA GRIPPED the hands of the two men on either side of her. A bit disoriented, she stumbled again over another uneven railroad tie. The light from their mining helmets never quite eliminated the darkness shielding the ground before her feet.

"Are you all right, Mrs. Argüello?" Adrian stopped and turned to her, turning his head away again and reaching a hand toward his forehead to block the light of the flickering head lamp.

"Pardon?"

"You just tripped."

"Oh, yes. Thanks for that." She motioned towards her own forehead. "Even a candle flame seems too bright in this darkness. It's a little hard to breathe, isn't it?"

"It is hard, when you first enter the mines." He squeezed her hand. "We're nearly there." He gulped and stood still.

His solicitousness of her was touching, in such a young man. She was glad the utter darkness behind her lamp concealed her smile.

Xavier, behind her, tightened his grip on her fingers and lifted them to his lips. He kissed them silently.

"Are you sure you want to do this, Adrian?" Aleksandra gripped the boy's hand in return.

He breathed in through his nose, a long breath, let it out. "Yes."

"Then lead on, man." There was a smile in Xavier's voice.

A glow showed around the next bend, growing into a brightness that illuminated everything in the passage as they advanced.

"Oh." Adrian stopped dead. He dropped Aleksandra's hand and walked toward the cluster of candles and objects lying on the floor before a pile of loose rubble extending toward the roof. "They've kept it going," he whispered. A sob escaped him, as he fell to his knees.

They both hugged the boy close and watched him.

He pulled a candle from his pocket and touched its wick to one of the long ones glowing on the ground. From inside his shirt, he drew a head lamp, lit it as well, and kneeled before the cluster of candles left by other well-wishers. Bowing his head, he whispered for many minutes, then placed the head lamp, its light illuminating the darkness beyond the circle of light toward the slip that must have imprisoned him and his father, stood, bowed to the shrine, and turned back to them.

Aleksandra reached for his hand again before she and Xavier moved forward and lit their own candles, offering a prayer for Adrian's papa.

"Shall we," the boy's voice caught, then strengthened, "go on?"

"Yes." Xavier looked up at him and his light shone on the pale glow of the boy's face. "You know where we're going, Adrian?"

"Been to that level many times," he said flatly.

"I'm glad your pa encouraged you to go—" Aleksandra broke off, swearing softly as she stumbled again, "—with your dreams."

"Yes, well," he murmured, "it helps."

Tears showed on his cheeks in the illumination from the candles, before he turned to leave the shrine.

"I've never seen anyone study so hard. You'll do it, Adrian, I know you will."

A brief flash of a smile showed. "Thanks."

Aleksandra heard the voices before she saw the lights ahead. They entered a cavern so large that the bright light from its many lanterns barely reached the further reaches of its expanse.

"I never imagined it could be so big," Aleksandra breathed, and a cold chill ran up her spine. Despite the lights, it felt like a mausoleum—anything over a whisper seemed sacrilegious.

"And therein lies the problem." Xavier motioned to a few piles of rubble which had escaped the boards stacked against the walls and ceiling in an attempt to keep the sides from caving in. "The whole Comstock lode is loose rock mixed with clay, rather than solid rock with narrow veins of color."

She shivered, remembering the feeling of scree rolling loose beneath her feet out hunting. "Not a good place to mine," she said.

"Enter Philipp Deidesheimer." Xavier said. They approached the men, straining to drag huge square beams into position on the far side of the open area. "Philipp, I've brought Aleksandra and young Adrian to see your workings."

"Excellent. We're just about to fit in a diagonal," he said, drawing a deep breath and wiping the moisture from his brow with the back of his blackened sleeve. "Take a break, men," he told them, and they silently removed to the other side of the clearing, flexing arms and shoulders as they walked.

"We can't wait to see your square-set timbering in action, Philipp. Do you really think it'll work?" Aleksandra said.

"I believe so." He nodded. "The structure of the Comstock makes these mines more dangerous than others. The sheer size of the Ophir ore lode makes it even more so. I mentioned to you, Aleks, at the time of the cave-in," he winced at Adrian, who bowed his head, "about the masses of rubble making up the lode?"

Aleksandra nodded.

"The miners call it porphyry. What I didn't say was that it contains much clay, which absorbs water from the air when it's exposed. So, when the men extract rock during the mining process, the clay swells, and the working stopes, or the cavities from which the ore has been extracted, collapse."

"That's why the normal T-supports don't work." Adrian narrowed his eyes at Philipp and slowly shook his head.

Philipp nodded "Cap rails over uprights won't cut it here. Worse, with the seasonal changes, the clay alternately dries and becomes waterlogged. More stress to the supports. The farther they dig, the more dangerous it becomes."

Silence reigned while Aleksandra fingered the end of a carefully finished beam lying on the floor of the cavern, surrounded by wood chips and shavings, and thought of the joints of their log cabin back in Utah.

"These beams are shipped in at no small cost. Few big trees grow locally, so we have no choice, really." He smiled ruefully. "When they arrive, they are cut, then a mortise and tenon joint is created on each end. We join them into square structures, as you see here." He walked toward the unfinished cubes, like massive, empty box-frames, standing against the wall.

Adrian turned to Philipp. "They look strong, but how do they keep it from collapsing as we dig it?" He gulped, and his voice trailed off.

The engineer put an arm over his shoulders. "That's the key, lad. As the ore is removed, the timbers are set into place in these cube-shapes. These four-foot-wide base timbers," he pointed them out, "are locked into six-foot-high supports, then they're capped with a six-foot header, and so on, and so on." He waved at the honeycomb of hollow cubes extending from the newest one beside them.

Adrian frowned. "But how—"

"The cubes are back-filled with rubbish rock from this and other mines, after the silver's been extracted.

The boy's mouth formed an 'O' and his eyes began to glimmer.

"You're looking at the first full-sized model."

"So the waste rock holds back the pressure from the expanding wall—" he stopped.

"Yes, son. In high pressure areas, we can strengthen the cubes with diagonals, like we're fitting here. It won't hold the rock back forever, but certainly it should for long enough to extract the ore we want. Eventually, the pressure will crush even these massive beams, but by then, we should be long gone."

"How big a cavern do you think you can support?" Xavier asked.

"It seems limited only by the amount of waste rock we can get down here," said Philipp, "but there's talk the Savage Mine is developing a sort of a big cage to take men out, and water, rather than de-watering via the buckets we all use now. If they can make it work, we'd be able to get a lot more fill rubble down here quickly."

"You're a genius, Mr. Deidesheimer," the boy said, shaking his head, "a genius." Tears glistened in his eyes.

"I only wish," Philipp's voice was heavy with sorrow, "this had been in place early enough to have saved your father, lad, but there are other things that kill miners, and you'll be able to help them."

Adrian's face glowed in the lamplight. "That I will. Thank you for all your help." He clasped the engineer's hand.

"See you up top, all?" Philipp was already turning back to his obsession— a good one, by all accounts—and motioning for his men to join him.

23

Philipp Deidesheimer was as good as his word. Within the week, all hands at the mine were employed shoring up the inside of the biggest cavern in the Ophir.

"I've worked harder than I've ever done in my life," Caleb McIntyre shook his head, "but never have I felt like it'd make such a difference."

Xavier smiled up at him and handed over his chit for the week. "It's good to know you can make everyone's life safer in the mines."

"Have you been down in the mines?" The man wiped at the black smeared over his face, his brows narrowed and lips tight.

"Sure have," Xavier said smoothly, ignoring the snub. "I worked a Long Tom in the California goldfields for many a year and spent time underground as well."

"Oh, did ya now?" McIntyre's eyes widened and his Southern accent thickened as he spoke. "Nobody said *that*."

"My life isn't anyone else's business," Xavier said flatly.

"Ah, well…" he hesitated, then said in a rush, "a few of the boys and me 'r gettin' together for a game o' cards tonight, if you'd like to come?"

Xavier gritted his teeth. "I'll see if I'm free," Xavier hedged, "not sure what the wife has planned. In case I can, where will you be meeting?"

"Out at the Skinner place," he pointed out the window, "last house down the hill, on the edge of town."

The office door opened behind him and McIntyre spun around, his hand flashing toward his hip, then with visible effort, he turned back to Xavier and thanked him. He nodded to Jeremy as he walked past him and left.

"What was that about? Wasn't he a little touchy, going for his absent gun like that when I walked in?" His brows raised, he looked at Xavier.

"I'm not so sure, myself." Xavier told him about the invitation.

Jeremy sighed and sat on the edge of Xavier's desk. "Some of the boys are up to something, I'm not exactly sure what it might be."

"Windup to a strike?"

"I can see you're not all that interested in going to their card game, but could you go along there tonight, just to see what you can find out?"

Xavier stretched his arms over his head, taking a moment to think. "Can do, if you think it's important."

"I wouldn't ask it, otherwise. Where is it? A few good men and I will keep an eye on the place, in case you need anything."

The card game turned out to be just a card game, with a bunch of Southerners. They mostly talking about the South, women, guns and their dogs, not necessarily in that order.

"So here ah find Xavier, sittin' behind his payments desk in the Ophir office, lookin' all clean an' shiny, an' I figgered he'd never got his hands dirty b'fore," McIntyre sniggered, then snorted. "Seems I was wrong, boys. He's been minin' fer longer'n most of us."

A few surreptitious looks went around the group, then their attention returned to their cards. A fair bit of Southern whiskey went down as the night wore on.

"Do you men do this often?" Xavier indicated the cards laid out on the table and the third bottle of whisky.

"Shore do, ev'ry week." McIntyre's young sidekick grinned.

"Someone's got a big whisky stash, then." Xavier smiled at him.

"Oh no, we got friends comin' from—"

"—my brother recently came West," a big man with bushy brows cut in, silencing the boy with a look, "and brought us a load of his good Southern drop."

The lad sat back and gulped, then clamped his jaws shut.

"Very nice, very nice drop indeed," Xavier remarked, rolling his glass between his fingers.

He made his excuses shortly thereafter and met with Jeremy and a few of his managers outside the Ophir office.

"So what news?" Jeremy murmured.

"No talk of strike, but something's not right. Can't quite put my finger on it, but it's something, something to do with a brother who's just come out West and brought whisky."

"Whisky?"

"Yep. Seems they meet every week and I'm invited."

Jeremy raised his brows.

"Sure, I'll go along." Xavier twisted his lips. "Now I'm curious, too."

Soon he was playing cards most weeks. Everything seemed above board, and he enjoyed the occasional night out. They spoke a little of their families, drank more than a little and gambled. Xavier played the games they didn't gamble on, drank little and kept his mouth shut about his family and everything private.

"I'm glad you spend time with Molly when I'm carding with those Southerners, best they know you're not alone. I don't trust them as far as I can throw them."

"You know I can take care of myself, but like you say, they seem to have their own agenda, and I don't want to be part of it." She smiled. "I love spending time with Molly, anyway. Maybe she can come to California when we go."

"Not a bad idea at all." Xavier replied.

"Sometimes I wish I'd gone to school," Aleksandra said one morning, as she laced her stays, "then I'd know how to teach students who don't understand. Teaching mathematics on a blackboard is nothing like how Papa taught me while we were out trapping together." She bit her lip and looked away.

His heart clenched. "You miss him, I know," he said, and took her into his arms.

"Every day," she mumbled into his shirt front. "I've been trying to use what he taught me in the schoolroom."

Xavier held her at arm's length. "How?"

"Instead of just sums on the board or their slates, I'm using examples—like Papa used—number of traps we needed, how many streams, how many per stream, things like that."

"Ah, practical questions."

"And money, different denominations and such. Using examples that interest them." She smiled. "Even some of the older boys listen."

"Sounds like you're winning."

She smiled at his praise. "The summer's been hot and difficult, but the schoolhouse is well-situated, and the children work well on the days the wind blows through the schoolroom."

"Soon the winter storms will hit. Hard to imagine we've been here nearly four months." He reached an arm around her and pulled her to him. "Are you happy to stay here through the winter?"

Aleksandra was still, considering. "I actually enjoy teaching now, but have you heard from Howard Egan yet?"

He turned her around, taking the moment as he gathered up her laces to think. She wouldn't be pleased.

"He left a message for me at the Ophir office. Said the Pony's running again."

She spun about and he dropped the laces and thought quickly. She'd be ropable if she knew how long ago he'd received the message.

"Hold your horses, Aleks. Turn around so I can tighten your stays."

She did as he bid, but turned her head and looked over her shoulder at him.

"Breathe out," he said. She let out her breath and grunted as he pulled them snug. "OK, you can breathe now."

She took a deep breath against the lacings and her breasts swelled above the corset. "So what did he say?"

"He said there's still a lot of unrest with the Indians, and begged you to stay where you are for now. He doesn't want you hurt. And neither do I."

Aleksandra bit her lip and tried to inhale over the top of her stays. She remained silent for a moment. "OK, let's stay for the winter," she acceded, "then we'll talk about it again."

Xavier sighed and pulled her into his arms again. "I'm so glad you said that, *Querida*. Thank you."

She tied on her crinoline and Xavier dropped her dress over her head.

"Never thought I'd get to be a lady's maid," he said.

"Never thought I'd be *dressing* like a lady." She smirked, and presented her back for him to button the long row of buttons from below her waist to her neck.

When he'd finished and she'd slapped his hands from her breasts, he stripped out of his chore clothes and began dressing himself for work. She fumbled around under the bed, hampered by her skirts, and uttered a word a lady shouldn't know.

"What have you lost?"

"The button hook."

"Can't you do up your boots without it?'

She raised her brows at him. "Have you ever tried? No."

"Here it is." He fished it out of a drawer and handed it to her, with a flourish.

"Thank you." She curtsied to him, then made short work of her buttons, crushing her skirts.

He winced. "Why didn't you put them on first?"

She winced back. "Forgot. You mentioned the Pony and my brains fell out."

He shook his head and chuckled, pulling her to her feet.

"We'd better get going," she said, "or we'll be late."

"*Vamos.* Let's go."

"Billy, are you ready to go?" she called down the hallway from the kitchen.

"Yes ma'am, I just need my dinner bucket," the boy said, as he trotted into the room, grabbed his pail and raced outside.

"This has been a good place to live," she said in an undertone, "with them, and out of town."

"You can handle being in town during the day?"

"As long as I can leave it at night."

He smiled and took her hand as they stepped down into the yard before the house to Dzień, already put to the gig.

Life was good.

"You know what?" Aleksandra said, as she slipped her leg over Xavier's hips and sat astride his smooth, tanned body in their bed.

"What?" A lazy smile grew across his face, warm as the sun just peeking through the frost-edged window panes.

"It's going to be another chilly one."

His eyes perused her, from head to waist, and his callused hand slid down her thigh. He nodded slowly and she shivered.

"Do we have time this morning?" he murmured.

Her face grew warm. "No, I mean, yes—no, we don't have time." She stumbled through the words.

He laughed deep in his throat. "You're getting my hopes up again."

"You know what else?"

"No," he said, with a resigned sigh.

"I'm starting to think I like this marriage thing."

"That makes two of us." He took her hands and kissed her fingertips, one by one, then slowly sucked on her index finger, rolling his tongue about it. She quivered and her nipples hardened and grew erect. He reached to touch one of the taut areolas, and her insides contracted.

"What you do to me..." She swallowed hard. "Maybe we shouldn't..."

"No," he gave her a lascivious grin, "not if we're going to have Billy knocking on our door to drag you off to school in half an hour."

"Oh," she said, at the feeling of him hard against her nether regions.

"That's what happens when you sit on me—things wake up," he said, wriggling his pelvis.

"Best I climb off?"

"Sadly, yes, but we'll revisit this later, eh *Querida*? Maybe a little work-talk will settle us down?" He shook his head as he lifted her off and placed her beside him.

She sighed, rubbed her hands against her aching breasts and acquiesced. "So...tell me how Philipp's timbering is progressing."

"It seems..."

She chuckled. He seemed to have difficulty gathering his thoughts. "Continue, continue," she said, smiling and waving a hand at him.

"Oh, ok. It seems sound, the men are pleased with the safety it'll afford them, and they're hustling to get the waste rock back down to backfill the honeycombs. Over the past few months, that cage we've built, like the one in the Savage, has made it much easier—seepage water can go up in the cage in barrels, instead of in little buckets."

"So the men can do the same, ride the cage?"

"Sure can. See?" He picked up the bedcovers and showed her. "Changing the subject works on me."

She closed her eyes and shook her head. "So they use the cage to transport—"

"*Sí, señora,*" he murmured, rolling her over so she was beneath him. He braced himself above her, then took her lips again.

"So," Jason looked down at his coffee mug and placed it on the kitchen table between them, "do you think it's too early? For Billy, I mean..."

Xavier waited, his eyes on the fingernail he was paring with his pen-knife. The silence lengthened.

"...to begin...courting?"

The *Californio* grinned, then sobered. "You mean for you to begin courting, not Billy, I take it?"

Jason scowled at him.

"Sorry, ahem." He sat up and looked at his friend. "If you mean young Emma, I can't see that being a problem for Billy. He adores her." Xavier smiled and his friend's face softened.

Jason sighed and drew a long draft on his mocha. "Thanks, I hoped you'd say that."

"Anytime, *amigo.*"

"How's the job coming along?"

"It's a job, nothing too difficult about it, but I miss managing a station, miss the horses and the riders—don't tell Aleks— but I miss being out in the wild." He looked at his friend from beneath his brows and gave him a twisted smile.

"Nary a word, man."

"She wants to go back riding for the Pony, now it's started up again. There was a bit of a final showdown with the *Pah-Utes* somewhere near Ruby Valley in August, and the Indian attacks since then have abated, but I simply," he gritted his teeth, silent for a moment, "don't want to lose her. If I forbid her to go, that'll just add fuel to the fire—she'd be gone tomorrow."

Jason raised a brow at him, then winced. "I'd say you're right."

"I'm hoping she finds enough pleasure in teaching to want to stay. I don't know what else to do." He swallowed hard and looked squarely at Jason.

A light tread on the porch stairs, then Aleksandra stepped into the room.

"Brrr..." She rubbed her arms and planted her buckskin-clad bottom against the fender of the stove. "It's getting cold."

"It'll be Christmas before you know it."

"Christmas?" Billy burst in, a step behind her, carrying an armload of firewood.

"Less than a month, Son." Jason smiled at him. "Thanks for remembering the firewood."

"Another load and we should be good, Pa." He looked sideways at his papa. "Can we invite Emma—ah—Miss Clark to Christmas supper? She's very nice. I think she likes horses too," he said, and turned to wash his hands in the bucket near the door.

Xavier and Jason shared a long look and they smiled.

"I've done it." Jason's eyes glowed.

"Really? Have you told Billy yet?" Aleksandra asked.

"No, but I will soon. I wanted to give him time around Emma before he learns she'll be a permanent part of his life."

"I don't think it'll be a problem," she said. "He talks about her all the time."

"Thought we'd marry in February."

"So soon?" Her thoughts raced, and her stomach clenched. "So...you'll want your house back." She tried to smile, but didn't quite manage it.

"Oh no, we'll need to be at the hotel, for now," he grinned, "and you can stay in the house."

"Oh, can we?" She breathed again, as she carried fried eggs and salt pork to the table.

"Sure can. It'd help me out, actually. I don't want to sell it and I'd rather see you two in it."

"Thanks, Jason," she said as Xavier entered the room.

"Evening, Jason." Xavier said, stamping snow from his boots.

"Still snowing, I see," Jason said, dryly.

"Can't wait until winter's over," Aleksandra shook her head, "then we can have fresh meat again. I'm so tired of salt pork, just smelling it makes me queasy."

"I'm getting that way, too," Xavier said.

Jason glanced her way, his brow slightly wrinkled, but he said nothing. *Odd.*

"Oh." Jason's face fell. "I have some bad news. Just came through. I'd imagine haven't heard?" His jaw tensed as he slid onto the bench beside Xavier.

"From...?" The *Californio* raised a brow.

"South Carolina seceded last week."

"Seceded." Aleksandra blinked. "From the Union? They've really done it." She placed Xavier's supper before him, then sat. She closed her eyes, elbows on the table, chin on hands. "And so it begins. Not a surprise, with Lincoln's election."

Xavier frowned. "Wasn't the Crittenden Compromise meant to stop the Southern states from seceding?"

"That was the idea," Jason shook his head, "but apparently there isn't enough in it to satisfy them."

"What *will* satisfy them?" Xavier looked sideways at them both.

"A country that's all slave, probably." Aleksandra gritted her teeth.

"So we wait," Jason muttered, "to see what the rest will do."

"And if they go, too?" Her voice sounded small to her ears.

"Then it's war. Civil war. North against South, brother against brother. I'd hoped it wouldn't come to this." Jason got up and put more wood onto the fire, then sat staring into the flames for a long time.

No one was hungry anymore.

ALEKSANDRA CLAMPED her mouth shut and spun back to the dishpan.

What's wrong with her?

She'd agreed not to ride for the Pony until after the winter, but here she was going on about it again. She must be getting cabin fever, she was so irritable lately.

Xavier closed his eyes and shook his head. Before winter turned to spring, he hoped she'd have forgotten all about it, but it was looking far from likely.

"Why not?" she gritted out in the general direction of the wall before her.

"It's too dangerous."

"But I've ridden through the worst part of the Indian attacks. It can't," she turned her head to glare, "be much worse."

"Aleks, it was spring when you rode the Pony."

"So?"

"So now it's winter. It's bad enough you riding to the schoolhouse in a blizzard, much less through seventy miles of it every working day…and I thought you liked teaching."

"I'd be fine." Abruptly. No mention of teaching.

"Did you ever stop to think," Xavier's stomach churned and he stopped, then continued slowly, "that despite your abilities, I might fear for you? I have no desire…to lose the best thing, the best person, the best love… I've ever found in my life."

Somewhat mollified, she stilled, as he slid his hands around her middle and pulled her back against him, his lips against her hair.

"I just don't want to lose you."

"All I can promise is the winter," she finally said.

"*¿Cómo?*" He shook his head to clear it. "What?"

"The winter. I want to ride after that."

Dios mío…what am I to do with her?

Xavier took a deep breath. He could only squeeze her tighter, and pray.

24

"You're going the wrong way." Xavier frowned as Aleksandra walked toward the house, an armload of straw before her.

"No, I'm not." She raised a brow at him.

"Are you OK?"

"Yes, why?" She looked at him, wide-eyed.

"The stable..." he said, "it's behind us." What could she be up to? She'd been acting strangely. Maybe he should have a talk with the doctor.

"You'll see," she said, lips twitching.

Xavier held the door open for her. "You've been baking." He sniffed, closing his eyes for a moment. Glimpses of holidays past flashed behind his eyes, and his stomach clenched. They always started out so well, but then— he opened them quickly. "It smells heavenly." He squeezed her waist as she moved to the table and began spreading the straw over the surface of the table.

She smiled over her shoulder.

"*¿Cómo?* What are you doing?"

Aleksandra handed him two corners of a tablecloth, pristine as fresh snow and motioned for him to back up, then together they placed the fabric over the straw.

"Setting the table for *Wigilia*, Christmas eve supper."

"So this is what you've been doing in here all day." He stared at the plates and bowls spread over every surface of the kitchen, and shook his head.

"Yes."

"So many dishes. I didn't know we even had that many plates and bowls."

"Twelve, one for each of the apostles."

"Ah." He thought hard, trying to remember his catechism, and whether his family ever did this. "I don't recall seeing this before," he finally said.

"Maybe it's only in Poland that we do this? A dozen meatless dishes." She looked about the room and frowned. "Could you find another chair?"

"Are more people coming to eat?"

"No."

He looked at her sideways, then searched the house for another, returning with their bedroom chair.

She stood still for a moment, transferring some tiny pies from the griddle to a plate, and he slid his arms about her from behind. Inhaling her scent, he kissed her neck. She wiped her hands on her apron and turned in his embrace. Their lips met, and he froze. Her eyes watered as she kissed him fervently, then drew away. A liquid drop of silver slid down her cheek.

"Why the tears, *Querida*?" he murmured.

"I'm so thankful you were given to me." She buried her face in his shirt. He listened hard to make out her words. "I miss my family so much on these festival days. We always baked and prepared together."

He took a deep breath. "Holidays growing up…Mama tried to make them special, but my fa—my stepfather would begin to drink, then our world would come crashing down. It is for this reason I have avoided holidays, and people, in general. I cannot bring them back, but I'll do all I can to make up for their absence and be your family. You just need to tell me what to do."

"You already do." She snuffled and raised her head to look into his eyes, her blue ones sparkling through the tears. He wiped them and kissed her again. "What can I do to help?"

"Go get cleaned up. I think the boys will be back soon and then," she peered outside, "it will soon be time to eat. I hope they hurry." Her brow furrowed for a moment.

"Why?"

"So we can sit down on time."

"On time?"

She stopped in her tracks and stared at him, then smiled. "Oh, sorry, you don't know." She laughed. "*Wigilia* begins when the first evening star appears. Now go, it is soon!" She shooed him from the kitchen and turned back to her plates.

Xavier and Jason were seated when Aleksandra and Billy rushed back from the window.

Billy slid into his seat, looking at the empty chair beside him, and frowned. "There's an extra one."

"Yes," Aleksandra smiled, "in case someone else comes to share our supper."

The boy gulped and his eyes glistened. "Maybe it's for Mama, or your pa," he whispered to Aleksandra.

"Perhaps." She swallowed hard as her own eyes filled. "Billy, will you go peek at the sky again to see if there are any stars yet?"

He hopped to the floor and trotted to the window again. Peeking out, he stood still for a moment. "Yes, yes, there's a star! Can we start now?" He gazed with bright eyes and glowing cheeks at the first course before them.

"Yes," Aleksandra said, and nodded at him.

The boy bent the *opłatek,* and the traditional wafer broke into three pieces. He glanced at Aleksandra, who nodded. He passed one piece to her, and the other to his papa, seated on his other side. He kept the small piece himself. "I wish you all blessings on this Christmas Eve," he said in a formal tone and the others continued the breaking of bread and offered their good wishes around the table.

"Thank you, Billy." Aleksandra squeezed his hand. "Well done. Yes, you may begin, after a bit of wafer."

"What are these?" Jason took one of the small dumplings from the platter Aleksandra offered.

"*Pierogies,*" she said. "These ones are meatless, but they can be filled with anything, on other days. They're boiled, then fried on a griddle."

"Mmmm..." Jason and Billy said, as one, tasting the spicy filling enclosed in its chewy-soft covering.

"Yummm..." Xavier murmured as the first bite of a delicately browned and crispy potato dish melted on his tongue.

Aleksandra grinned at his expression. "I love those too. I don't know why I don't make them more often."

"A very good question," Xavier said. "Be my guest."

"Wherever did you find fish?" Jason shook his head.

"I bribed one of the local boys to go fishing in the Carson a few days ago, and they managed it."

"I hope they didn't get into that freezing water!" Jason looked at her, his eyes wide. "And the rest, Aleks," he gazed at the remains of the laden table, "how did you do it all?"

"I made the sauerkraut a few months ago, the potato salad today...and... dessert I made today," she said as she placed the poppyseed torte before them with a flourish. They stared at her agog.

"You're one lucky man, Xavier." Jason raised a brow at him.

"Don't I know it," Xavier said as he locked eyes with his wife. "Don't I know it."

They sang carols and there were tears in many eyes—for those they'd lost, and in this new year, found.

"Ooooh, it's lovely," Aleksandra breathed at the sight of the sitting room on Christmas morning.

The table had been set again, this time for breakfast, and beside each plate was a small wrapped packet tied with twine. A fire roared in the stove, louder even than the storm buffeting the walls of the house. Beside the cookstove a great bowl of sourdough pancake batter bubbled.

"Happy Christmas," Jason looked up from the bacon sizzling on the griddle.

"Smells heavenly," she smiled. "Happy Christmas to you, too."

Billy trotted, bleary-eyed, through the open doorway. "Has Father Christmas come?"

Jason nodded at the table and the boy came to a screeching halt beside his chair. He gazed at the present behind his plate.

"Off to your chores, then breakfast will be ready."

Billy spun on his heel, dived into his boots and grabbed his jacket. A swirl of snow swallowed him as he shot out the door.

"Button it up!" his pa called out after him, as the door slammed.

Aleksandra set their presents beside everyone's seats and took the plates down from the rack. "You want them there?"

"Yes, please." He nodded and turned the first stack of pancakes onto the top plate.

The enticing aroma tickled her nose and made her mouth water. Xavier and Billy entered, shaking snow off their coats outside the door.

"You've got to use the clothesline in this weather, Billy, Christmas or no," Xavier growled. "You'd be lost in a storm like this and freeze before we found you."

Jason gritted his teeth and turned back to the stove, probably glad for the chance to have someone else to tell his boy what he'd repeated till he was blue. "Sit down and eat, all. We honor the cook here, so eat while they're hot." By the time he'd turned to join them after pouring another batch onto the sizzling griddle, he'd regained his composure.

The tangy pancakes dripped with maple syrup as she forked the first bite into her mouth.

Exquisite.

"You make a mean pancake, Jason," Aleksandra murmured, as soon as her mouth was empty, and that wasn't for long.

"I'd better, after your amazing supper last night."

"Least I could do for my family." She smiled around the table at them all.

Jason and Aleksandra took shifts at the griddle and there were long silences while they ate batches of the luscious pancakes to their hearts' content.

"I couldn't eat another bite," Billy finally groaned.

The rest nodded and blinked. The boys cleared the table while Aleksandra beat milk, oil, flour and yeast into the remaining batter, covered it and left it to set for the evening's bread.

Billy's fingers drummed the table. "Is it time yet?"

"Yes, lad." His father tousled his hair and grinned.

Aleksandra's eyes overflowed again when she opened a calico-wrapped package to find a flat braided latigo bridle.

"It's from Mexico," Xavier said, as she wrapped her arms around him to thank him properly.

"Where all good things are made?" She teased his lips with hers.

"Apparently. Now let me open mine." He smiled at her. "This is heavy." He hefted the slightly floppy package with one hand.

"Well, open it!" Billy squirmed, sucking on the largest lump of maple sugar candy Aleksandra could find.

Xavier unwrapped the brown paper slowly and shook out the velvety-soft buckskin shirt.

He looked at her, then glanced down again at the Indian beadwork decorating the front. "You did this, all of it, didn't you?" He looked into her eyes, his eyes soft.

"Yes, I'm not much for sewing dresses, but buckskin and beadwork, I love."

"Well, it's magnificent," he said, as he slid it over his shirt, then took her into his arms.

Billy sat before the glowing wood stove, his eyes threatening to spill over onto the hand-plaited reins Aleksandra spent so many hours making.

"Now I even look like a real builder." Jason laughed, then hugged Aleksandra, still staring at the hand-carved tool belt Xavier and Aleksandra had agonized over for weeks.

A series of knocks came upon the door, loud enough to be heard over the storm battering the little house.

"Who would venture out in *this*?" Jason frowned and hurried to the door. Two completely bundled up figures stumbled in, accompanied by an arctic blast of swirling snow.

"Emma!" He unwound the muffler from about her head and exposed his beloved.

Aleksandra was already unwrapping the bigger form beside her. "Jeremy?"

"*Dios mío*, but what *are* you two doing out in this?" Xavier shook his head as he took their wraps. Billy dragged two chairs closer to the fire for the newcomers.

"Your horses, are they outside?" Aleksandra said, starting for the door.

"In the barn," rasped Jeremy.

Instead, she gathered two mugs from the shelf and filled them with mulled wine, hot from the top of the stove.

"Ahhh," Jeremy murmured. "Thank you, Aleks."

"Whatever are you doing out in this storm?" Jason's voice had an edge to it. "You could've been—"

"—she couldn't stay away from you, little brother, and I wouldn't let her go alone," Jeremy cut in.

Emma took his hand. "Please, don't be angry," she bit her lip, her eyes wide. "We made it. I couldn't go without seeing you on Christmas day."

He shook his head. "I was going to come see you later, you silly woman…" He took her into his arms and kissed her.

"You didn't tell me that…" she whispered.

"You didn't ask."

"Will you stay here forever?" Billy asked, and stood still, very close to the pair. Emma and Jason wrapped their arms about him, including the boy in their circle.

Aleksandra and Xavier turned away, hiding their smiles, and joined the still-frozen Jeremy.

"The wife will miss me, but I'll go back in a few hours, after my horse is rested. Nasty day for Christmas," he grimaced, "but I don't think any of them will notice," he nodded at the trio by the table, "and I couldn't miss seeing you two today, either."

"I'd have done the same for my brothers." Aleksandra gave her new almost-brother-in-law a swift hug to stop the tears from falling.

Aleksandra and Xavier fed the stock and returned to their room early to snuggle beneath the quilts.

"It's so soft, I hate to take it off." Xavier ran his hands over his new buckskin shirt.

"Papa helped me tan the hides last winter." She closed her eyes for a moment, then went on. "The skins were from two bucks I shot. I thought they'd never be finished."

Xavier's brow wrinkled. "How do you tan buckskin? I've tanned deerskins, but they never turned out like this." His hands were still smoothing the surface of the leather.

"I soaked the hides, then scraped all the hair off and stretched them on a rack, then rubbed brains into the rough hides."

"OK, I've done that…"

"And then," she smiled, "the work begins. They're scraped and stretched some more on the rack, and then rubbed over a log...for hours and hours, to break down the fibers and make the skins tough, but elastic and soft. They're soaked some more, and rubbed over the log again...for several days."

"Seriously?"

"Not a word of a lie. One of the hardest things I've ever done."

"Oh." His eyes were large and his fingers, appreciative before, became positively reverent.

"But that shirt has to come off," she continued, in a soft voice, "so you can feel this beautiful silk."

"It's not as silky as your skin," Xavier murmured.

"Of course it is. Wherever did you find it, by the way?"

"The seamstress had it hidden in the back of her shop and she was only too happy to drag it out. She thought the schoolmistress should have something lovely beneath her working dresses," he said, sitting up to pull the buckskin shirt over his head.

"Mmmm..." she murmured, "nice."

His fingers traced from her neck, down her front. His fingertips brushed lightly over the peaks standing out beneath the silk, shimmering in the candle light. Rolling onto his back, he lifted her to sit astride. "Now, you were saying?" He murmured, and pulled her down for a kiss.

"Don't bother. I'm sure it wasn't imp—" cut off as he deepened the kiss.

All thoughts fled.

His heart nearly stopped when he saw the woman before him on the Virginia City street. Even dressed in fine women's clothing, he'd recognize that hair and figure anywhere. Golden curls glinted in the winter sunlight and his fingers almost reached for her long braid.

His jaw tightened.

She'd cut it. It used to be longer.

It only went to her backside now.

That would be remedied.

She wouldn't cut it again when she was his. She turned to go into a shop and he saw her face. It was Aleksandra, all right. There was an ache in his groin, and he promised himself it wouldn't be long.

That Mexican must be around.

No matter. He'd deal with him. He slipped deeper back into the alley as she came out of the shop and walked down the street. She'd pay. They all did when they crossed him.

He smiled.

25

"Look Aleks, it's done!" Billy jumped to his feet and deposited the newly-plaited halter and lead in her lap. "It should fit a big pony."

Aleksandra shook her head and smiled. "Well done, lad," she said, turning it over in her hands. "You've done a beautiful job."

Jason looked up from his book. "So you're ready for your own now?" Jason asked, his voice soft.

"Yes," he said, standing tall. "I am, Papa."

"You've earned it, Son."

"Thank you, Pa."

"This sure has been a grand winter with you two here." Billy looked at the ground. It's been good to laugh, and—" he looked up at his pa with a soft smile "—ride again."

"Same for me, Billy." Aleksandra hugged him. "Winter nights beside the fire have been like having my family back, too. Now, you wanted some help with homework?"

Billy winced and gathered up his slate and books from their shelf, seating himself beside Aleksandra.

"More states have seceded," Xavier said to Jason, in an undertone. "That makes six now, South Carolina, Mississippi, Florida, Alabama, Georgia and Louisiana. Jefferson Davis resigned from the Senate and has been elected provisional President of the Confederate State Constitution."

"But it should stop now, shouldn't it?" Aleksandra frowned. "Today's newspaper said the House passed a resolution that would guarantee...how did they put it? 'Non-interference with slavery in any state'."

"I'd like to think it's the end, but I wouldn't hold my breath. The Southerners have the bit in their teeth and want to rule themselves."

"Guess we'll just have to wait and see." Xavier took a deep breath and looked around at the grim faces surrounding him.

Aleksandra picked up her sewing and put it into the basket at her feet. "All done, Billy? See, wasn't as hard as you thought it would be," she said, as he packed it up. "I'm for bed. I can't seem to get enough sleep lately."

"I'll check the stock and be right there," Xavier said, and donned hat and jacket before stepping out into the cold.

She pulled the covers up under her chin and waited for Xavier.

"Cold one out there," he said, as he entered and closed the door a short time later.

"Funny, but even as cold as it is, I seem warm most of the time, hot, actually. It's unlike me."

Xavier looked sideways at her, then stripped, blew out the candles and slipped into bed. "My hands are cold."

"Put them on me, I'm hot."

"Are you OK?" He searched the darkness for her face.

"Seem to be, why?"

"You've also been queasy a lot lately."

"Yes, I ha—" She blinked, lost for words.

His hands slid to her breasts and he cupped them. "And these have grown."

She gulped.

"Are you…"

She was silent, the old fear stopping her heart. His hands slid to her flat belly, then returned to her breasts. She groaned.

"I think you are," he murmured and took her lips gently with his.

"I don't know," she whispered when he released them. "I've never been before,"

"We'll just have to see, then."

"I'm in no hurry to find out—they won't let me teach if I'm pregnant. They usually don't even let married women teach, but they've no one else."

"Either way, *Querida*, if you are pregnant, I'll care for you, and our child, forever, and to the best of my ability." He took a deep breath. "How very sobering," he added abruptly.

"I'm not sure what to think, it's so new," she said, her head spinning at the implications, "but it's special to think I may have part of you inside me."

He pulled her close. "Yes, that's the best part…the best part."

Sleep was a long time coming, but the morning began abruptly with a dash to the chamber pot. Xavier kneeled behind her, holding her hair out of the way. He left her briefly, returning with a wet cloth to wipe her hot forehead and wipe her mouth.

"Yes," he said, and held her close. "I'm pretty sure we're expecting. Maybe you should speak with a midwife. I'm sure you could find one who won't say a word to anyone?"

"I spoke with Molly yesterday," Aleksandra looked at the floor between them, with a hint of a smile. "She says we're going to have a baby."

"Guess that puts an end to your riding for the Pony."

"Why? Indian women ride until they deliver."

Xavier stared at her, his eyes wide. He opened his mouth to speak, but nothing came out. Finally, he found his voice. "You cannot possibly be thinking..."

She grinned at him. "Gotcha. Just wanted to see the look on your face."

Xavier shook his head. "Some days, I want to bend you over my knee..."

She laughed and sidled away to turn the biscuits on the smoking hot griddle.

"It sure is nice," he slid his arms about her waist and held her against him, his hands cupping her still-flat belly, "to have this place to ourselves today. Soon Jason will move over to the hotel and we'll be all alone here."

She flashed him a lewd grin. "Sure is." She flipped the little breads onto a plate and he reached for one. "Hot," she said.

He held it carefully on the tips of his fingers, but didn't let go of her waist. "Can't wait, sorry," he murmured and nibbled one edge. "Mmmmm..." He rolled his eyes. "You're the best cook, ever."

"I'm getting plenty of practice. It helps."

"Let's go for a ride. I know of this place..."

She looked over her shoulder, and her insides tightened. She gave him a long look. "A picnic ride?"

"Yes, hot biscuits and you."

"Oh." She gulped, then smiled softly. "You go get our quilt, would you?"

"You're looking pink."

"It's just the heat of the stove," she said, fanning herself as she turned back to finish baking the rest. He laughed and headed for the bedroom.

The horses were saddled by the time she finished packing their meal and they rode out into the sunshine.

"What's on your mind, Xavier?"

He relaxed his face with an effort, and turned to her. "There seem to be an awful lot of Southerners here."

"By the accents of the schoolchildren, I'd agree."

"We're our own territory now, in case you hadn't heard. Nevada Territory, cut out and dragged from the grips of Utah Territory."

"Will it change anything?" she asked.

"Not sure. Either way, I'm thinking it might be a good idea to head on toward California," he said. "I haven't heard any secession talk from the California gold mines. Their miners just seem to be trying to make a living, but maybe I'm wrong. I'd hope it would be more peaceful there."

"I can't teach once I start showing, anyway, so I'll be free to go soon. Even out of the mouths of babes, the bigotry and talk of slavery from some of my students are shocking."

They rode in silence for a while.

"It's a good thing the Pony's back running, or we wouldn't get the news till everything was long past," he said.

"Nice for the riders," she twisted her mouth in attempt at a grin, "that it's warmed up."

He kneed Charro closer to the pony, reached across and took her hand. "I know you wanted to ride," he said softly.

She laughed. "I did, but even this staid jaunt has me nauseous. This little one," she looked down at her still-tiny waist, "doesn't seem impressed by riding."

Xavier let out his breath. "That's a relief. Sorry *Querida*," he grinned at her, "but I was afraid I'd wake up one morning and find you gone, run off to be a Pony rider."

"*Un*likely." She swallowed hard against her suddenly-roiling stomach. "Are we nearly to your magic spot yet?" She peered around the corner as they climbed up the side of the peak.

"Just around the next bend, promise."

The trail wound higher and higher up the mountains above the town and opened up to a flat, if rocky, place. Aleksandra sighed as her feet touched the ground, willing the horizon to stay level. Closing her eyes, she slid down Dzień's foreleg and sat frozen where she'd dismounted. Dzień nosed her hair, blowing wisps of it into her eyes.

"Tired, love?"

"A bit sickly. I'll be OK after I sit on solid ground for a moment." She gave a shaky laugh. "Not that I ever thought I'd say that." The pony was watching her, his muzzle and eyes wrinkled. "Not your fault, Dzień," she said to the Mustang and reached up to rub his nose. Relieved of his bridle, he wandered off to fossick for cheat grass around the boulders.

Xavier stared at her for a moment, then unlaced the blanket from behind his saddle. Kicking aside the the stones, he spread the quilt upon the ground and led her to it. "How about some food?"

Her stomach flipped over and she covered her mouth with her hand.

"Oh, no food," he murmured.

"Cuddles."

"That, I can manage. Let me tie Charro. It's a long walk home."

"Yes," she managed.

By the time he'd wedged Charro's rein between some big rocks and returned, her guts had settled a little.

"Sitting still helps, and the view...I haven't been around this side. It's beautiful."

The mountain dropped away at the edge of their perfect tryst, leaving just enough room for the horses and them. The panorama was exquisite, with the flats to the west rimmed by the snow-topped Sierras at their furthest reaches.

He followed her glance west.

"They're still finding a lot of gold out there, even though the gold rush is mostly over, aren't they?" she murmured.

"Yes," he sighed, "pretty destructive, though."

"Hydraulic mining?"

"*Sí*. Huge money in it, though, so no doubt it'll continue."

"Where are they doing it?"

"At the Malakoff Diggins, on the California side of the Sierras. It's just a little way past Lake Bigler."

"You're happy here, aren't you, for now?" she said.

"Other than the increasingly disquieting Southerners, yes. Teaching is going well for you, isn't it?"

"I love my little ones, and even the older boys are listening now." She chuckled. "Though I did like confiscating the pen-knives the boys used to peg the braids of the girls seated before them to their desks."

Xavier's mouth dropped open. "Little beggars. Not really?"

"They hadn't planned on losing their toys for two weeks. It seems to have sunk in, finally. Reciting from their slates in the front of the room with the youngest children might have helped, too," she said, with a smirk.

"They were probably expecting the strap or ruler."

"I'm not big enough to cane them—they're twice my weight, some of the big boys, and this seemed effective." She winked at him.

"Now you have me worried, punishing the big boys."

"They're just overgrown little boys, and they're figuring out it's for their own good. I think the death of Adrian's father, and watching him follow his dream has impressed many of them. They're studying harder now, too."

"They're lucky to have you."

She winced. "They won't think so when they find out I'm pregnant, married or no. Who ever heard of a pregnant schoolmistress?"

"How long do we have? Before they figure it out and make you quit?"

"Molly thinks I won't show much for another month or two, if I take out the waists of my dresses and keep wearing a shawl."

"The weather's warming up." He frowned.

"I have some lovely Spanish lace your mother sent. It'll make a nice shawl, without the warmth of my woollen one."

Xavier looked unconvinced, gazing at her breasts, already straining the muslin of her dress.

Aleksandra glanced down. "Oh. I'll take out the bodices too." She smiled and drew him down beside her. She took his hand and they sat, looking out over the cliff to the desert far below. "It's beautiful, Xavier, thank you for bringing me up here."

"Yes, beautiful," he said, and turned her chin toward him. She leaned across for his kiss and then her fingers found the laces of his shirt. He pulled her closer and deepened the kiss, exquisite in the warm spring sunshine.

"ALEKS, ALEKS! XAVIER!" Billy screeched as they rode into the yard, scattering chickens in his wake.

"What's the matter be, boy?" Xavier sat deeper as the stallion sidled sideways.

"Express rider's just gone through Chinatown and told the news—they've done it, it's war!"

"¿Cómo? What?"

"The Southerners are calling themselves the Confederate States and have fired on Fort Sumter—um—" he hesitated.

"So it's war, then…" Aleksandra's blood went cold in her veins.

"Dios mío. Brother against brother—this cannot help anyone." Xavier shook his head. "Thanks Billy," he called after the boy, who waved and ran to spread the news.

"It's not like we didn't see it coming, but I'd hoped it wouldn't happen. This should make the Ophir situation interesting…" Xavier fell silent.

"The Southerners?"

"Sí, muchos de…lo siento. Yes, many Southerners."

"Will they leave to fight?"

"I don't know. Maybe they won't have to travel far to fight…"

"What's that supposed to mean?" Aleksandra's breath caught in her throat. Xavier looked away from her, over her shoulder.

"What do you mean, Xavier?"

"Later," he whispered, bending down to inspect Charro's cinch buckle. "Ah, Branden," he called, looking up at the man riding in on a fancy-looking thoroughbred, "my wife, Aleksandra. Aleks, meet Mr. Branden Stark, recently of Charleston."

He nodded to her.

She somehow managed to smile at the Southern gentleman, as he approached. "Pleased to meet you. North Carolina? You're a long way from home, sir."

He swept off his hat. "Pleased to make the 'quaintance of such a lovely lady out heah in this wilde'ness," he murmured in a slow Southern drawl, "so different from civilization as ah know it." He picked some imaginary lint from his immaculate lapel.

Aleksandra remembered to drop a curtsy in his direction.

"Begging your pardon, ma'am, but may ah speak with yer husband alone fer a moment please?"

"Of course." Aleksandra gritted her teeth and turned for the barn, leading Dzień.

When she came back outside, the Southerner was nowhere to be seen. "Where's he gone?"

"Left." Xavier frowned. "Wanted to invite me to a card evening tonight— bit of drama for a simple card game. Wonder what they're up to?"

"Not sure I like it. Why did he want to speak with you privately?"

"No idea."

"Odd." She shuddered. "He gave me the creeps, for all his polite talk."

"What trouble could they get up to at a card game in the middle of town?"

Aleksandra looked sideways at him as a shiver ran up her spine.

FINALLY, *things were coming together for him.*

The Mexican didn't know it, but he was in the same room with him, just on the other side of the curtain. The card-players were in bright lamplight, and his side was in darkness, so the semi-sheer curtain gave him a good view, without anyone being aware of his presence.

That blonde of his...she'd be alone every night the darkie was away playing cards with his own boys. Just the thought made his mouth water and his nuts tighten. He tugged at his too-tight crotch and gritted his teeth.

Soon.

If he played his cards right, with a little patience, she'd be his plaything for as long as he wanted to keep her alive.

26

—————

"See? Nothing to worry about." Xavier smiled as he slid into bed and blew the candle out, then took Aleksandra into his arms.

"Still, I'm glad you're home," she said, as she pulled him against her backside under the comforter.

"Just a card game, after all."

"How many men?"

"Nine or ten, all told. Southerners, all but one."

"You?"

"How'd you guess?"

"Secession talk?"

"Not a word."

"Strange, given the Confederates have just declared war on the Union…I take it Mr. Stark was there? What rock did he slither out from under?"

"Branden? After Charleston, he was in Los Angeles, in southern Calif—" he stopped like he was shot. "*Dios mío.* I just remembered something." Xavier moved back and turned her to face him, his brows narrowed. "The secessionists have been mustering near Los Angeles. El Monte, I think it was. The Union troops put pressure on them, and many of them headed north to Nevada Territory." He was silent for a moment. "I hadn't heard any of them made their way this far."

"I can't imagine they'd want to announce their presence." She twisted her lips. "Stark seems awfully pushy."

Xavier raised his brows. "The men defer to him…I think you're right.

Something's up, but I can't put my finger on it yet. Other than Branden, all the other men there tonight work for me."

She tapped his chest with a fingernail. "You take care, please?"

"Always. Wouldn't want to leave you alone," he murmured, and pulled her close.

"What were you about to say when Stark rode up yesterday? About them not having to go far to fight." She shuddered at the thought he might put her fear into words.

"With the southern California secessionists gathering, the army might have to send Union forces south to fight."

"So what'll happen out here if the troops are all down south?"

"Guess we're about to find out. Another good reason to head west."

"And your Southern friends have nothing to discuss in your presence." It was a statement, not a question, and she shook her head.

Xavier took a deep breath and held it.

"What *do* they say?"

"Just what we already know. War's been declared, Sumter under fire…and that's it." He fixed her with a stare. "With surprisingly little emotion, especially for Southerners. Come to think of it, Stark was the only one speaking. The others just gritted their teeth and clenched their fists."

"They'll bear watching." She cradled her belly in her hands. The knot in her guts tightened.

"I'll be watching, *Querida*, I'll be watching."

"I'M OFF, Xavier, off to join the Union troops," Johnny Fry fairly hooted at Xavier across the table.

"But Johnny, the Pony needs you, more than the Union Army does," Aleksandra protested as she walked into the kitchen.

"There are plenty of riders. Why don't *you* join up again?"

Aleksandra and Xavier exchanged a glance and Xavier nodded.

"We'll let you in on a little secret. You can only tell Doc and Ephraim on your way east."

The boy's eyes lit up. "Course you can. On my honor."

"Well…" Aleksandra looked at her stomach and then at the Pony rider.

"*Are* you?"

"Yes, due in November."

"Congratulations to you both! Johnny said. He jumped up to clap Xavier on the back and squeeze Aleksandra's hand. He sat back down and shook his head. "Now I'm even more glad you two are out here, out of the trouble."

"What trouble?"

"Blinkin' secessionists—they've been causing trouble out in California. Do you have any of those fool Southerners out here?"

"Quite a few. Several of them quit and went East, presumably to fight, but it hasn't made much difference. They're always in the office, looking for work."

"None stirring up trouble?"

"No, well..." Xavier's eyes flicked to Aleksandra, then back to Johnny, "...there's a group of men I've been playing card with most weeks—they've begun talking about how great the South is, and one of the younger men started to ask me if I'd join—" he stopped abruptly and rubbed his shin.

"You never said—" Aleksandra growled and shot him a look.

"—I know, but it's not happened since, so it's no problem...Anyway, Johnny, no apparent trouble."

"What's the trouble in California?" Aleksandra asked.

"The secessionists have been holding public demonstrations, not sure how they're getting away with it."

"The Knights of the Golden Circle," Xavier muttered, "hold the highest places in San Francisco society—plenty of money—and probably hand-placed most of the 'elected officials' into office."

"Let's hope the Union commander can keep it under control, then," Fry said, and stood up from the table. "Well, anyway, you two," he clamped his hat down on his head, "congratulations again, and take good care. I'm off to join the circus. I'll be back soon, when we've beaten these Southerners back down where they belong."

"Sure you won't stay for supper?"

"No, thanks, I'm off."

"You take care of *your* self, Johnny." Aleksandra smiled and gripped his hand before Xavier took it.

"Hold on to your hair, boyo."

"That I will. Haven't lived this long as a Pony rider just to die now!" He tipped his hat with a flourish, hopped down the steps and was gone in a flurry of hooves and dust.

"Replace Johnston?" Xavier's jaw nearly hit the floor.

"Yep, says right here," Jeremy tapped the *Territorial Enterprise* on the desk before him, "in the news from the Nevada Territory capital at Genoa. Colonel Johnston, the US Army Commander headquartered at Benicia, met with Southern secessionists."

"Seriously? Publicly?"

"It gets better. Apparently, he told the rebels he'd heard of some foolish plans to seize the strongholds of the government under his charge, like the arsenal at Benicia and the forts at San Francisco, and that he'd prepared for emergencies and 'would defend the property of the United States with every resource at his command, and to the last drop of his blood.' He told them to tell that to all their Southern friends."

Xavier blinked. "He sounds honorable, but blood's thicker than water. The Union Army won't believe a word of it, Johnstone being a true blue-blooded Southerner from Kentucky," he said dryly. "So what's the Army done about it?"

"They're sending one General Sumner out. He should be here late April."

"That's fast." Xavier raised a brow.

"Via Panama." Jeremy read further. "There's more...seems California's Governor Downey sent a large shipment of arms to southern California, 'where the pro-Confederate sentiment is high'—but he sent them to the secessionist militia in El Monte."

"You can't be serious...is he a Southerner?"

"Born in Ireland, but he spent time in the South and his policies have been...shall we say, questionable?"

"So now they're well armed down there..." Xavier's fingers drummed on the table.

"Nope—it says down the page, the army intercepted the guns at San Pedro."

"Well, that's something. So what's happening in northern California? Haven't heard anything about that."

Jeremy frowned. "There are plenty of Southerners up there, probably a third of the population—the white population, anyway—so it's hard to say which way it'll go. What's your interest in northern California?"

"My family," Xavier winced, "has a *rancho* on the other side of the San Francisco Bay."

"Really?" Jeremy's brows shot up. "Then you're holding with the secessionists?" His knuckles went white on his pencil and a tic started up in his jaw.

Xavier snorted. "Hardly. Absolutely not."

"Glad to hear that." Jeremy let out his breath. "From what I hear, most of the *Californios* are siding with the secessionists, who've promised to restore the lands the government or squatters have taken from them over the past twenty years."

"My brothers'd better not be siding with them," Xavier said through gritted teeth. "Might have to pay them a visit."

"What's your interest, then?"

He held his breath, silent for a moment. "Eldest son of the Argüello family, holders of the biggest old Spanish land grant in the San Francisco Bay Area," he murmured, "at your service." He swept him a low, formal bow.

The mine manager stared, fingers steepled before him, his elbows on the desk. "What, in God's name, are you doing here, working for me?" he finally asked.

The *Californio* looked away, then closed his eyes. "Long story, but I don't want to go back empty-handed, despite what *mi madre* says. My brothers have worked it all this time, it's only right."

"Okaaaay," Jeremy drew it out on a slow exhale, "so how are you going to make this fortune?"

"I don't rightly know—work here for a while, maybe go further West, back to the California goldfields—they're mostly worked out, but now they're hydraulicking near Grass Valley, there's potential to do pretty well out of it."

Jeremy sighed. "While I should tell you to stay here, for our sakes, I understand. Just remember to give me some notice, not that we could ever replace you. Far from it. You'll have a glowing reference from me."

Xavier smiled his thanks and moved toward his own desk. "*Gracias*, I appreciate that, now I'd best get back to work."

Riding home with Aleksandra that afternoon, he brought up the news. "Oh, and you know about Colonel Johnston?"

"He led the Army troops to put a non-Mormon government into place in Utah, didn't he? About five years ago." Aleksandra said, "I hear he's in command of the Department of the Pacific at Benicia."

"Yes, well, it's heating up in California, especially down south. Arizona Territory voted to separate from New Mexico."

She blinked. "Ouch. They're serious."

He told her what Jeremy said about the colonel.

"Sounds like he meant what he said, anyway. You've got to give him that." Despite her words, she still looked dubious, and flicked the end of her rein at an early fly on Dzień's neck. "If I were him, I'd be clearing out and heading south before anyone gets any ideas."

"He might be doing just that. He resigned last week."

"It's all on, then. Will they let him go? Southern California's not that far away. He could so easily lead the rebels from there."

"He could, and he's got his family here to think about, so I guess we'll see..."

SHADOWS HID the two men's faces from passers-by as they stood in the alley behind the mercantile.

"We won't do it, he doesn't know nothing yet," drawled the dark haired man.

"Oh yes, ya will. He knows too much an' he's kept me fer too long from what ah want." The second man spat in the dust, his eyes narrowed dangerously.

"Ah tell ya, he knows nuthin'. Leave 'im alone."

"'Y'all do as I say," he patted the pistol in his belt," or thing'll get mahty noisy around here. I'll just hold 'im at our headquarters 'till things quiet down and all the guns'r passed out where they need t'go t'help our great cause, then ahl release him."

"Ah don't like it none. He ain't done nothin' t' us."

"This is war, boy, war. It'll be ovah soon, them lily-livered yank boys'll run an' it'll be a rout."

ALEKSANDRA PLACED a bowl of porridge before Xavier and sat beside him.

"Aleks, remember when I said the Southern boys haven't asked me again, about joining them?"

Her brow narrowed, but she nodded and said nothing.

"Well, they asked me again last night. I didn't want to disturb your sleep."

"And?"

"They didn't look pleased, especially Stark, and the employees who work closest to me looked mighty uncomfortable."

"Well, at least they know you're not interested, anyway."

"Yes, but…"

"*But?*" Aleksandra stared at him, mouth open.

"One young hothead reached for his hip as I was leaving, and I turned toward him in time to see Stark mutter something at him. When I arrived, they were talking about some guns."

"Guns?"

"Something along the lines of *wagonloads* of guns, and they mentioned Churchill."

"Who was speaking?"

"Stark."

She sat frozen, clutching her belly.

"I pretended I'd heard nothing."

"Do you think they believed it?"

"I don't know," he said, pulling her close against his side, his lips against her hair for long minutes.

They spoke little on the way into Virginia City. Xavier left her and Billy at the schoolhouse and went to work. He pored over the employment lists.

There were more missing Southerners every day from the Ophir's rolls, but other than these absentees, all ticked along until he heard gunshots a short distance away.

"Jeremy, I'll go see what's up." Xavier was already moving.

"Think I'm going to let you have all the fun?" Jeremy grinned. "You lock the back and I'll meet you out front."

More people than Xavier believed existed in Virginia City were gathered around the flagpole in the center of town. The Stars and Stripes was gone, and in its place, a new one was being raised as they approached the square.

"What the heck is that?" Jeremy spat out.

"Must be the new Confederate flag," Xavier growled. "Let's get out of here."

"Whad'ya mean, a 'hold on mah funds'?"

"You'll have to speak with your lawyer, sir," the teller apologized. "It appears a hold has been placed on your funds due to lack of payment on a mortgage held by you. The seller appears to have presented a court order to this effect. I'm sorry, I can't do anything about it but request its rel—" cut off as the man grabbed him by the throat.

"Get it r'leased, by the close o'work today, or there'll be no more bank by mornin'," he snarled, then released him. The man slithered to the floor, blubbering.

The Southerner turned and left the bank, while patrons looked away at the floor, their fingers, or anything else handy, other than him.

He needed money to equip himself for the trip over the Sierras to the mine, after a little detour east. Lord knew the guns in the wagon would more than pay for it, but his uncle paid for the guns, and for him to bring them across from the East...less, of course, what he was going to keep for himself....

Who'd risked his life to get them here, after all?

His uncle would get some, but he'd make sure he got his fair share, and then some.

He chuckled beneath his breath, striding down the rutted street. He'd go find Julia. She was just what he needed to let off some steam. The tall, slender brunette with the dark eyes liked to call herself a courtesan...but she was just like all the rest.

The doorman at her establishment said she was unavailable.

He gritted his teeth. "Whad'ya mean, unavailable? You jes' go an' give 'er mah name. She'll see me."

"I'm sorry, sir, she's gone off to a fire."

He blinked. "A fire?"

"Yes sir, she's an honorary member of Virginia Engine Company Number 1."

The idiot had the gall to grin.

"When'll she be back?" O'Rourke puffed himself up, disconcerted.

"Doubtless after the fire engine returns to the station. I'm sure she'll see you then. She's the darling of the fire department, you know. She rides the fire engine in her hat, and runs the pump for the firemen."

His jaw tightened further as he imagined her servicing the whole fire crew. "Ah'll wait."

The man hesitated for a moment.

"What is it?" O'Rourke said from between his teeth.

"Well, sir, after that she'll be tied up for the evening fundraising for the Union Army, but you can buy a ticket if you wish."

"Tell 'er I stopped an' expected to see 'er. Let 'er know she missed out on a heap o'fun," he said, as he stomped off down the street. "An' a whole lot o'money," he threw back over his shoulder at the door, already shut behind him.

27

"What's going on, Xavier?" Aleksandra pulled the door of the schoolroom closed behind her and stood in the anteroom with him. His face was thunderous.

"The fools just unfurled a Confederate flag and hoisted it up the flagpole in the main street of town. They're spouting their gibberish for all to hear, looking for people to join them against the Union—saying they're acting on the authority of the Confederate government.

"Oh no," she said, glancing at the door, and her pupils. "Who's leading them?"

"Never seen him before."

"Was Stark in front?"

"No, but I caught of glimpse of him in the crowd. Let's get the children home. The men are drinking, and who knows what they'll do."

"We can take them down the back streets and deliver them home," she said, and opened the door. "Children, please gather your books and dinner pails. Get your coats and wait quietly with Mr. Argüello until he says to follow him."

The children eyed each other sideways, but her demeanor brooked no objections and they obeyed with alacrity. She sent those living to the north and east of town home in groups with the older students and together she and Xavier escorted the rest. They delivered Billy to his aunt and uncle's house, as Jason and Emma were in Carson City, selecting lamps and furniture for the hotel.

"What now?" Aleksandra said, as they sat around Jeremy and Dorothea's big kitchen table.

"We'll see what the rabble does." Jeremy shook his head. "I sent a runner to the Express station at Chinatown with news for Sumner at Benicia, and another to Fort Churchill, asking for backup. Guess we lock up the house and hope they drink themselves out."

"Heating up way too fast here." Xavier's brows were nearly touching.

"The secessionists are way ahead in California. I'll bet we get the backlash from the mess they're having in southern California out here soon," Dorothea said. "Old Mrs. Severn said Mrs. Bowers predicted this would happen."

"Who's Mrs. Bowers?" Aleksandra asked.

"Haven't you heard of her?" Dorothea stared at her. "They call her the Washoe Seeress, she's the one who predicted about Gold Hill and the Ophir Mine. She hires herself out as a speculator...seems she's made herself and many others rich."

"Dorothea," Jeremy winced, "that woman's just taking advantage of others' gullibility."

"Well, she did predict all those things, and now this about down South."

"What now?" Aleksandra changed the subject, before an argument erupted.

"Seems when Sumner arrived to take command at Benicia, Johnston had handed over the reins, all properly," Jeremy said, "but when the authorities went looking for their previous commander, he wasn't to be found. Seems he'd packed up his family and bolted south, joined up with a secessionist militia, the Los Angeles Mounted Rifles...as a private."

"A private?" Aleksandra snorted and looked at Jeremy blankly.

"Doubtless he's not a private by now." Jeremy stared at his fingers, drawing circles on the table.

Xavier nodded. "And now they have one of the Union's best commanders on the secessionist side. Not ideal, for us, anyway."

"Well, gentlemen, as there doesn't seem to be any trouble out that way, I need to go back to school and close up properly," Aleksandra said.

Xavier frowned. "I don't like the thought of you being out there alone."

She rolled her eyes at him. "It's all clear out by the schoolhouse. They're all hanging around the flagpole."

"I'll go with you," Xavier said, standing up and grabbing his coat.

"You don't have to do that, really, I'll be fine. I've just a few things to do, then I'll be on home.

He wasn't convinced, and she shook her head.

"OK, OK." Xavier tried to smile at her. "I've a few things more to do at the mine office, so can you meet me there in an hour, unless you've got a lot more to do?"

"They seem to be quieting down, I can't even hear them now," Jeremy remarked from the doorway. "I've got more work to do today, too."

"Are you sure you'll be OK, Aleks?"

She looked heavenwards, then grinned. "Of course. I'll come by your office when I'm done. If you finish before me, you can go home and make supper. Deal?"

"Deal. Just don't trust anyone, eh *Querida*? You don't know who you can trust out here anymore."

"Got it." She kissed him and sashayed toward the door. He took a breath, then laughed at her. She glanced back from the next street and waved at him and Jeremy as they walked back to their office.

Aleksandra skirted the town center, no need to look for trouble. She sighed as she unlocked and entered the schoolroom. *Her* schoolroom. She had no idea she'd love teaching so much.

When she lifted her head from her papers, the light was beginning to fail. Locking the door behind her, she collected Dzień and saddled him. She wasn't sure she liked her new side-saddle, but at least she could ride, rather than drive the gig, in full skirts.

Town was silent as she rode the streets, eerily quieter than usual. The drunken louts of the afternoon must be home sleeping it off. She shook her head. They'd have sore heads tomorrow.

No one answered her knock at the door of the darkened mine office. She was sorry to have missed riding home with Xavier, but a hot supper would be waiting. Dzień strode with purpose toward home, the barn, and his own waiting feed.

THE SOUND of men and milling horses came from around the front of the barn as Aleksandra rode up behind it. Dzień planted his feet, his ears pricked and his body tense.

Heart in her throat, she slid off and backed away, one hand over the Mustang's nostrils, praying none of the horses would give them away.

She peeked through a wide crack in the back wall of the barn, out through the open barn doors, to see a crowd of men. She scanned the crowd, but didn't see Xavier. Maybe he was still in town? She looked amongst the tallest men for his figure, but he wasn't there.

There he was...hunched over. She closed her eyes for a moment as her guts turned to ice. He'd never give them what they wanted without a fight, whoever they were. Blood ran from the corner of his mouth and one eye was nearly closed.

What have they done to him? And who...

Her stomach lurched when she focused on their speech and heard the Southern accents.

She counted…fifteen men.

No chance of stopping them with one pistol.

She gritted her teeth and willed her rising gorge to stay down.

"You've heard too much, you're joining us now, like it or not," Stark growled over the sound of the gathered men.

Aleksandra's heart froze at the sickening thud as he struck Xavier over the head with his reversed pistol. Through hot tears, she watched the men bundle Xavier onto Rogan's back and tie him firmly in place. He didn't move a muscle. With one last look around the barn and the house yard, the men of the band rode down the hill toward Chinatown at a trot, shouting congratulations at each other and passing bottles between them. Their horses were heavily laden, each man's saddlebags filled to overflowing.

She listened in silence and held her breath for what felt like an hour, then tied Dzień behind the barn and snuck inside. From behind a stall divider, she watched the house windows. Fighting down panic, she crept through the deepening dusk to the back of the house and peered in the windows, then slipped in through the back door. No one lurked and nothing was disturbed.

Food was the last thing on her mind, but she'd been trained to survive.

Who knows how long before I'll see food again?

She managed to get out of her dress and stays and donned her buckskins, between bites of Xavier's blessed stew and packed provisions for several days. Aleksandra glanced across the road at the darkened hotel, wishing Jason were home. She stared at Charro, considering. The stallion strained against the stall door, looking in the direction Xavier had gone, nostrils flared and entire body tight as a bowstring. She swapped her sidesaddle for Dzień's regular one, then tied her saddlebags on. She saddled the gray stallion as well and filled the spare bags with grain. She could move nearly twice as fast with a second horse over a long distance, and who knew where these men were headed; they were packed to travel.

She slipped out of the yard, ever watchful, and loped down the hill behind the kidnappers. Only a few minutes had passed, just enough time to let the kidnappers get out of sight. There were only so many trails they could follow once they hit Chinatown. She should see them on the Carson Valley floor while she was still up the mountain, even in the rapidly falling darkness.

The moon peeking over the eastern ranges glinted on the rifles of the mob below as they took the longer road down the mountain and turned east. Aleksandra let out a breath and closed her eyes for a moment. At least they were going east. She took the horses straight down the mountain on the shorter route and followed. Half an hour on, the band cut left, avoiding the Pony Express station and the row of shacks comprising Chinatown. She turned Dzień's head toward the Nevada Pony Express station just before her, and her stomach chilled.

Trust no one.

Xavier's words came back to her. Whom could she trust? The men traveling before her, packing her husband, were employees of Xavier's mine, or fathers of her students. Not for a moment had she ever considered they could be kidnappers.

"But come to think of it," she mused to the horses, "they *did* have Southern accents."

The horses flicked their ears and turned their heads forward down the hill toward their quarry.

Nope. She couldn't trust anyone yet. She'd follow and stay out of the way, find out where they were taking Xavier. If she couldn't secure his release, she'd get help from somewhere. Fort Churchill wasn't too far away.

Three hours later, the band had slowed a little, alternating between walk and trot. Aleksandra switched horses every half hour to stay awake and give the horses a break. The fires of Fort Churchill shone in the distance, accompanied by the moonlit ghostly glow from the rows of white tents.

They won't make it past Churchill undetected.

She frowned when the mob turned off the trail, just before the fort, and headed north.

North?

There was nothing up there, as far as she knew. Nothing. No one.

A perfect place to hide.

She closed her eyes for a moment.

"Oh Dzień, should I follow or go for help? If I went for help, I should still be able to track fifteen horses after that, for goodness sake." She shook her head. "Dancing Wolf would be appalled I'd doubted my ability, after he taught me."

The pony shook his mane.

"But what if they split up? For all I know, they've switched Xavier to another horse and I'd never find him."

Even just whispering to the horses made her feel less alone.

She stared into the darkness around her, then up at the waning crescent moon, wishing for an answer, and then followed.

Half an hour later, the mob stopped and made camp. She found a rock big enough to hold Charro's lead rope, unsaddled and fed them both grain from her saddlebags. Dzień meandered, finding wisps of cheat grass around their makeshift campsite, while she watched Xavier's captors light a fire and bed down for the night.

"Where can they be heading?" she whispered to Dzień as he whuffled near her head. She reached out to rub his muzzle and he stood quietly for a moment, then wandered away to forage. She curled up in Xavier's *serape*, her hand guarding the life inside her, wondering what he had to wear tonight against the cold on the hard ground somewhere ahead of her. Aleksandra's heart clenched tight in her chest. What would they do with him? And why out here? There was nothing up this way, other than rocks and a few old prospectors. Nothing else for hundreds of miles.

ALEKSANDRA TOOK another bite of *pemmican* and chewed slowly, as a shooting star lit the heavens. They were in a big flat wash, well away from the mountains ringing the valley, so she'd have to retreat a long way before dawn to avoid being seen by the secessionists. In the pre-dawn light, a clump of what looked like cottonwoods appeared. Maybe there would be water?

She shook her canteens, though she knew they were empty. She'd already shared her last water with the horses the previous evening. She saddled up quickly, then hurried them into the trees. Sure enough, there was a spring. Small, but fresh, and with enough water to fill the canteens and her hat for the horses. She lay back down to get what rest she could, while the horses nibbled willow leaves and twigs in the darkened glade.

Aleksandra awoke to the vibration of hoofbeats coming through the ground beneath her cheek. She rose slowly, keeping low and out of the line of sight of the oncoming rider. Grabbing the saddlebags, she went to Charro while she whispered to Dzień. The pony came, even as their heads swung around toward the oncoming rider, ears pricked, but then their noses were at her fists, begging for the grain she held. She gave them only a few grains at a time, and they were silent, though they each kept an ear pointed in the direction of the intruder. Breathing a sigh of relief, she peeked up a little higher and saw the rider...

O'Rourke!

Blood pounded in her ears and her knees began to give way. She scrabbled for more feed, and fair shoved it into the horses' mouths. It wouldn't do to be found by him, anywhere.

What, in God's name, was he doing here?

She closed her eyes and sank to the ground, giving thanks for the glade, and the escape, when she realized he had to be involved.

Vengeance.

Her world swam about her, but she shook her head and forced herself to breathe deeply. O'Rourke's presence changed the situation. This man would think nothing of killing anyone who'd crossed him. She and Xavier had done just that.

The rebel group ahead, previously still, became a flurry of activity. As

O'Rourke neared them, they scrambled to order, two of them dragging a standing, but wobbly man between them.

Xavier!

Granted, he was alive, but even from this far away, he looked like a mess. Across the distance, she heard raised voices. O'Rourke stood before him, then her husband slumped to the ground.

The Irishman strode back and forth between the men, waving his arms and shouting. She couldn't make out the words, but he wasn't happy.

With a sinking heart, Aleksandra knew, for dead certain, that O'Rourke was in charge.

XAVIER'S HEAD THROBBED. He licked his lips and tasted the metallic tang of blood. His hands were numb. Tied. From afar, urgent voices.

"... keep an eye out...far from Fort Churchill...sentry..."

He slept.

Voices again.

"O'Rourke said to hurry."

"Shhh—" Another voice. "He said not to use his real name."

"Oh." He imagined the crestfallen look on the lad's face.

Xavier's heart sunk at the name. He had to have heard wrong. He opened his eyes a little at a time to see a bunch of men on the ground around him in the early dawn.

They'd lured him from the house and attacked him. Some of them he recognized as his new 'friends' from card nights and work. His stomach knotted.

"Best keep an eye out, Harker. Don't think we've been followed, but we're still close to Fort Churchill." Stark's voice stood out.

So he's the ringleader.

Xavier stopped himself from shaking his head and sighing at his own gullibility.

"Rider coming!" one man growled.

"Who is it, Harker?"

"I can't see..." he gulped, "damn me, it's O'Rourke. And he's alone."

The world around Xavier exploded as the camp came to life. Men scurried to catch and saddle mounts. He was left lying in the middle of it, peeking about as he had the chance. They paid him no mind. He remembered nothing after he went out to meet the group, other than the punches and kicks from many men, a final pain in his head, then darkness. It was far too late to wish for his *shashka*.

The men were lining up in some sort of formation, then someone approached him and dragged him to his feet.

"Somebody help me," said the man they called Harker.

"Comin' boss," answered another of the men.

"I know you're awake, I saw you watching us," Stark's voice boomed in his ears.

"Not very," Xavier managed, from between swollen lips. "Some welcome you give a friend."

"Blood's thicker than water—blue blood especially."

Xavier raised a brow at him, and it hurt.

"Blue blood. Good, Southern, blue blood. It will prevail."

Xavier said nothing.

"Now stand up, man, here's the real boss." He nodded at the approaching rider.

"Who's that?"

"Just call him Boss."

"*O'Rourke?*" Xavier spat out.

"Where'd you hear that name?" Stark's eyes scorched their way up and down the line of men.

"Oh, we've met. No time for him," he whispered.

"You'd better *make* time, or your life will have very little *time* left." Stark elbowed him in the ribs with his free arm. It hurt there too, everywhere in fact, he noted as he moved his joints around a little. They must have pummeled him good.

"STARK" O'Rourke's voice boomed out.

"Sir." The man snapped to attention.

"Where's the girl? Ah told ya t'leave 'er there, but she wasn't there when I went t' git 'er."

"She wasn't there when we found him. I don't know where she was."

"Didja bother t'ask *him?*" O'Rourke nodded at Xavier.

Stark gulped. "No suh. He's just come around."

The leader glanced at Xavier, then narrowed his eyes at Stark. "Ah told ya t'capture 'im, not kill 'im."

"Yes, sir. He wasn't going to come with us, otherwise."

Xavier shook his head to clear it. "I wasn't asked."

"That true?" O'Rourke glared at Stark, who stared at him in silence.

"It's clear ah need a new lieuten'nt. Git t'the back, Stark."

"Sir." He let go of Xavier's arm and turned on his heel. Xavier stumbled, but kept his feet.

"Where is she?" he snapped at Xavier.

"Who?"

"Miss Lekarski."

"Gone."

"Gone? Ah've bin watchin' 'er in Virginny City. She was with you."

"Yes, Mrs. Argüello. We're married. Miss Lekarski is gone."

O'Rourke reached out and clipped him across the ear.

"While ah admire yer pluck, yer smart mouth has t'go. Where's she?"

Xavier scowled, and even that hurt.

"Where?" he repeated.

"She was working late."

"Well, she mus' be doin' some fancy sort o'job in a saloon to not be home bah the time ah got there—say, midnaht?"

"Gone?" Xavier's brain struggled. Was she all right?

"Not a soul in the place." He clouted Xavier again and he hit the ground, hard. "Now, where is she?"

"*No sé. De veras, no*—I don't know," he replied, through the fog.

"When she gits home, mah men," he raised his voice and scowled at the assembled Southerners, "mah *trusted* men, will bring 'er here." He leaned down to murmur to Xavier: "Bin waitin' to have her waitin' on me an' servicin' me fer ages now. *Me*, ya hear? *Me*, not you. Maht even let ya live a li'l while, to watch-like. You two've done me bad, an' y'all'l pay. Rememba that."

"You'll be dead if you so much as touch her," Xavier growled.

"Sez you?" O'Rourke sneered at him. "Cain't even git yer hands untied. You, a threat?" He laughed. Turning his back on Xavier, he walked back and forth before his men. The world slowly dissolved before his eyes again and he knew no more.

THE HORSES of O'Rourke's group seemed to be tiring. They managed only a jog-walk during the day and early evening as they rode north through the wide wash. Aleksandra continued to switch and feed the horses, so they were still fresh. The rebels ahead, with no such luxury, continued north-east, staying at the base of the high mountains rimming the flats. A valley opened up before them to the north, and they followed the wagon road in its center as it climbed into the mountains.

Aleksandra took a deep breath. She'd need to be more watchful—the steep sides of the canyon ahead were perfect for sentries, and by the way the men were suddenly pushing their horses faster, they must be nearing their destination. They were soon lost to sight, and she followed slowly, watching the big boulders along the sides for any movement. The horses snatched at any grass they could reach as they walked, interested in their surroundings, but not announcing the presence of others.

Several miles up the valley, she topped a small rise, and froze.

Atop a pole...a flag, fluttering in the breeze—same colors as the thirty-three star flag her students raised every day up the flagpole, but there the resemblance ended.

She clutched at her abdomen, and her heart clenched tight.

The flapping silk couldn't be anything but what the secessionists called the Stars and Bars...a gross caricature of the flag of the Union—seven white stars on a blue field and three fat stripes, red, white, red.

She slowly advanced a few feet, and the sight before her nearly knocked her off her horse.

28

All she could do was stare, while her world tumbled down around her. Over a hundred tents littered the area around the Confederate flag, in no particular order, and it teemed with men in various standard of uniform.

How could she, alone, break Xavier free from this many rebels? She couldn't see any way Xavier could come out of this alive, and she wasn't likely to live through it, either. She might as well just hand herself in and die right now.

Except that she couldn't.

For the first time, there was more at stake than just herself: Xavier, and their unborn infant.

A gray fog enveloped her as the term 'secessionists' evolved from an obscure idea to an actual armed force, in the blink of an eye. She shuddered, slid from Charro's saddle and backed away, dragging both horses behind her.

Hoofbeats.

Still a long way off, but coming, from the direction they'd just come. There was nowhere big enough to hide herself, much less two horses. She checked that her hair was hidden, then tugged the ten-gallon hat low over her eyes as she considered the horses. No way Charro could ever look like a prospector's horse, but she could try. She switched to Dzień and rode back down the trail towards the oncoming man. Soon he was upon them.

"Sir," she said in her best boy-voice, and nodded to the grizzled prospector and his mule.

"Good day to you, young man. Mighty fine horse you have there," he waved at Charro. "Care to sell him?"

"No, thank ya, he's m'Pa's."

"And where might he be?"

"Just over that ridge, I think. Told me to wait, but I'm goin' off t' find 'im."

"You just do that. If you don't, come find me, off that way." He indicated the way ahead of him...toward the rebel encampment.

"Ah, thank ye, sir." She said in a rush and pushed Dzień on, her back ramrod straight. She risked a glance back to see him waving at her.

A dusty Confederate flag lay draped over the panniers on his pack saddle.

It took every fragment of strength she possessed not to push the horses into a gallop and get far, far away as fast as possible. She let the horses trot for an hour, then they cut west up a gully full of cottonwoods. Their dappled light camouflaged the horses and sheltered a cool, freshwater spring. She and the horses drank their fill and ate their trail rations, then slept the sleep of the truly exhausted.

Aleksandra awoke at first light with a pang for Xavier. She shook herself and nibbled *pemmican* while she fed and saddled the horses. At a trot, switching horses as before, she made Fort Churchill by early afternoon. She'd never been so happy to see the uniform rows of tents, with their timber central command. She stopped to pull her hair out of her hat, taking out the braid and shaking her head to let the mass of curls tumble down her back.

"You thea," called a sentry on the outskirts of the camp, as they approached, "what's yer business?"

He turned to his companion and they laughed harshly, then resumed speaking, heads together.

Southern accents.

Her heart tried to leap out of her bosom as the hair raised on her arms. Nausea threatened to overwhelm her.

Report a rebel camp to a couple of Southerners?

She had to be mad to even consider it.

She glanced up at the flagpole to reassure herself the American Flag still flew above the fort, then let out the breath she didn't know she'd been holding. Could she trust an army full of Southerners? Xavier might only have one chance, and she didn't want to waste it. Who else? Xavier's brothers? She should be able to trust them, but by the time word reached them it would be too late. Much too late. Besides, if it were true that the *Californios* were pulling for the secessionists...who knows what that could mean for Xavier?

Ephraim Hanks

The only man she knew with the guts, brains and men of undoubted loyalty to pull it off. He'd planned to come to Carson City and Genoa to check on a land sale, and also, Xavier had told her, on behalf of the people of Utah, to protest the loss of nearly half of Utah Territory to Nevada, Colorado and Nebraska earlier this year.

"It's OK, sorry, I'm looking for the Express station," she said in the men's general direction and spun the horses about, heading at a trot for the station, but she hesitated again. They were still too close to Fort Churchill, and all it held, so she pointed the horses' heads east, along the wagon trail on the Carson. Swinging along at their ground-eating trot, the horses brought her to the station at Carson Sink in a few hours.

This should be far enough from Churchill.

"Hi—be just a minute." The towheaded, harassed-looking keeper said. He reappeared a few minutes later as Aleksandra watered the horses. "Hello." His brow wrinkled, taking in the buckskin Mustang and Charro. "I've seen you before."

"Sure have," she said, glad her hair was up. She stuck out her hand. "I used to ride for the Pony out of Fish Springs."

"Ah, thought you looked familiar. What are you doin' out West?"

"Came out when the Pony shut down, but I'm looking for Ephraim Hanks. You haven't seen him? He was meant to be out this way."

"Ephraim? Sure thing? He left yesterday."

"Was he alone?"

"No, he had a dozen men with him."

"Riding fast?

"Moderately, as he does, but not topped."

She breathed again. "You wouldn't need a rider, would you? I need to find him, fast."

"Matter of fact, I do." He flashed her a grin, "Rider's just come in vomiting. He's pretty unwell. I was going to have to ride for him, but if you're sure?"

"Can you take care of these two until I return?"

"Yep. How much time do you need? Pony's saddled."

"Give me two minutes." She was already off her horse and untying his cinch as he walked toward the barn.

"Leave your gear in here," he threw over his shoulder as he entered the station. "I'll get you some grub. You've got sixty miles to ride yet."

Aleksandra rubbed her abused posterior. She was out of shape, with teaching school.

School.

How were her students faring? Her heart clenched, thinking of Adrian. She quashed the thought and focused. Sliding Charro's saddle to the ground, then Dzień's, she led them to an empty corral, rubbing the nose of the palomino Mustang waiting for her as she passed him.

"I'll be back for you soon, Dzień," she murmured into his mane, her arms around his neck. He dribbled water from the trough down her front as she backed away from him. A kiss on the nose of the gray stallion and she turned away with a wave. "Be back soon, my darlings," she whispered.

"I'll rub them down," the keeper said as he walked up, handing her a waxed-calico wrapped packet. "Your feed. You ought to catch the old man before your ride's done."

"Thanks, I owe you one."

"Not at all. You're doin' me a favor."

She clicked her tongue to the Mustang, who jumped forward. Aleksandra vaulted onto the surprised mare, waved at the even more astonished keeper and they flew off.

Her abdomen cramped and nausea threatened to overcome her.

That's the last vault I'll do until I've had this baby.

She shook her head. Showing off would get her nowhere.

A few miles out of the station, they slid down the cottonwood-lined bank of the Carson River and splashed through it, the golden horse taking a good drink as he walked. The trail east was busier than she'd ever seen it. She passed two wagon trains in that leg of her journey. Most of the emigrants would have turned north earlier in the trail, but many still went this way, heading for California via Placerville. Thankfully, the last spring rain was a month ago, and the deep ruts still evident beside the trail were now flattened in the center, making the going easy, at least between wagon trains. The second wagon train must have planned for enough feed and overwintered somewhere part way across, by the look of their stock. They'd have the advantage of reaching the base of the *Sierras* at the best time of year, after the snow, and before the worst heat of summer. The mules and oxen were light, but not too thin, and they pulled with a will. Drovers, mounted outriders, women and children cheered and waved hats and bonnets at the pair as they loped past. She saluted them, and rode on through the miles of sage, cheat grass and sand, changing horses every ten miles or so. Small mountain ranges rose and fell to either side as she rode.

"All quiet out there?" asked the dark-haired station keeper at Edwards Creek.

"Other than the wagon trains, nary a soul, that I could see." This time, Aleksandra remembered to lower her voice.

She'd forgotten at the previous stop, and the keeper had given her more than one sideways look. She grinned at him. "You've not seen Ephraim Hanks lately, have you?"

"Matter of fact, he left earlier this evening. Lookin' fer him?"

"Shore am," she drawled, her heart quickening, as her belly cramped again, and she flinched.

"You OK, boy?"

"Yes." She swallowed, noisily, to her own ears.

"Only one more ride to go for the day," he grinned, "then supper and bed, unless of course, there's no rider to go on."

She tried for a grin and suspected it failed, as she was gripped by another spasm.

The man's brows drew together. "You're not OK."

"I'm fine," she managed, and jammed her foot into the stirrup. She gritted her teeth. Vaulting into the saddle wasn't even an option now, with her guts tied up in knots and cramping. She must've had some bad water.

"Take care, Aleks, he's pretty green, and fresh to boot."

Her face burned. She turned to wave and threw the reins at the black colt. He bolted and for a moment she forgot the agony in her belly at the exhilaration of the flight.

The colt *was* fresh. He was uncertain about her aids, and she suspected the Mustang was newly off the range. Station keepers tended to buy just-broken horses from the Indians, roped them down to get shoes onto their flailing hooves, put a few rides on them and let the Pony riders rip. It went against everything she believed about good horsemanship, but most of the Pony riders considered it great fun and reveled in the keenness and spirit of the more-wild-than-tame Mustangs. Today was a different story. The hours felt like days, as she let him race along the cottonwood and scrub lining the Carson at his own—fast—pace until he began to tire. Mesmerized by his rocking horse lope, she dozed in the saddle.

A sudden nauseous feeling—the world was upside down, or her stomach was upside down—and the hard packed desert floor hit her body with a vengeance, filling her mouth and nose, a blinding pain in her belly, and then nothing.

HOT BREATH TICKLED HER NOSE, then a warm, rough tongue licked her cheek and something dribbled onto Aleksandra's face.

The *pain*—never like this before. She curled around her throbbing belly and groaned. A hoof nudged her leg and she opened her eyes. A faint trail of red ran from the commissure of his mouth. She glanced at her fist, still holding the end of the reins. She closed her eyes and thanked her papa.

"Sorry, pony," she managed, after spitting out the dirt and sneezing.

"Hold on to your reins, Aleks!" she'd heard more times than she'd like to admit, in fact, every time she'd fallen off in his presence. *"It'll be a long walk home in your riding boots if you fall off alone, far from home!"* He'd laugh and help her up, handing her back onto her pony. Most of her unplanned

dismounts were when she was tiny and the ponies were closer to the ground. As she'd grown older and progressed to Dzień, then to her father's big horses and *dzhigitovka*, her papa had taught her how to fall safely.

Being asleep, she hadn't controlled her fall, but at least her reflexes from years of repetition let her keep hold of the reins and still have a horse to ride —that is, if she could get up. She tested out her limbs. Nothing broken, but the cramping in her abdomen was worse. Between spasms, it was OK, and during a lull in the pain, she slid her fingers into the Mustang's mouth and along the bars. A little bruised, but not cut by the bit. The torn corner of his mouth should heal soon.

"Good of you to stick around," she murmured against his muzzle, and he snuffled at her face. She managed to mount, and loosed the reins. A walk proved nearly unbearable. Each step found her gripping her belly and she finally had to stop the horse and slide to the ground.

How would she keep going?

She had to find Ephraim—he was her only hope. She leaned her head against the sweating colt's neck and wrapped her arms around his neck, tears flowing.

Papa's secret formula.

Sweat broke out on her brow. The secret for which he'd died—an old Siberian folk medicine—might help her go on.

With shaking hands, she pulled out the beaded leather pouch she always carried from inside the neckline of her buckskin shirt.

No syringe.

She couldn't have hit a vein if she tried, with the tremor in her hands, so she'd just have to drink the stuff. It should work, but probably not as quickly.

Unstoppering the vial, she raised it to her quivering lips and let the honey-gold liquid fill her mouth. She held it there, under her tongue, hoping it would work that much sooner, and sat down, closing her eyes, to let it take effect. She'd never given it by mouth, but its effects in a vein were immediate and rather spectacular. Her lips curved into the ghost of a grin, remembering.

Her hands gradually ceased quivering and even the cramping diminished.

"Let's go, boy. I don't know how long it'll give us, but we've got to find Ephraim."

The black sniffed at her and snorted, dancing away a little, but let her mount.

A trot was punishing, but he was happy to lope, and it was bearable.

Odd, sweat doesn't normally stick me to the saddle.

The seat of her trousers *was* stuck to the saddle, though. She shook her head. Could it be her courses? Of course not, she was preg—her heart clutched in her chest.

Our baby—what have I done?

A sob escaped her and she glanced downwards. Blood soaked her pants down the inside of her legs—and all over the *mochila*.

"It'll be interesting explaining that one to the next station keeper," she murmured, "no wonder you were unsettled, boy. Not keen on blood, eh?"

The colt flicked his ears back at her.

"That makes two of us," she said. She had no idea how far she'd gone, nor how far she had yet to ride.

Ephraim.

She set her jaw, and her resolve, and rode on.

At his ground-eating lope, the Mustang scented the wind and turned his head to the right. Through bleary eyes, a creek appeared, not a quarter mile off the trail. Aleksandra roused herself to hold his mane as the Mustang turned off the trail and picked his way through the brush. While he drank, she picked up her head and looked around.

Like I should've been doing the whole time.

The latigo *mochila* over the saddle tree was stained with blood. She daren't dunk the sheet of leather in the creek—even though the letters in the locked cantinas at its corners were wrapped in oiled silk, immersing them wouldn't do them any good. At four dollars per half ounce letter, it didn't make sense to soak them. She slid off, pulled the *mochila* from the saddle and rinsed it as best she could, pouring water from her hat over the seat portion. The Mustang peered at her from the corners of his eyes, standing as far away from her as possible at the end of his reins.

"Get over it, boy. Can't be helped, sorry."

He shook his head and tugged at the reins, then swung his head around, ears pricked.

Hoofbeats again, in the distance.

A group of some dozen horses raced past her on the trail, led by what looked like Ephraim's stallion. She swung up and set the Mustang off at a canter.

"Ephraim!" she called out, but no one turned, and then she was falling, falling.

The ground hit her like a hammer, as it stopped her body's headlong flight, and then there was only darkness.

29

"Holy Moses, it's Aleksandra! Riding the Pony?" Ephraim threw himself from his horse and hit the ground running. "Aleks?" he whispered, touching her face, blanched white as a sheet.

She groaned and blinked, then shut her eyes again.

He began to check her over for injuries. Something slippery under his hands.

Blood. Everywhere. Down her legs, her trousers.

He looked up at his men, standing in a half circle, one wringing his hands as he stared. He nodded at them and they turned their backs while he slid her trousers down to reveal dark blood coming from between her legs.

"A clean cloth, someone," he barked, and three men ran for their saddlebags, returning with a bundled shirt and several handkerchiefs. He folded them into a wad and packed it against her.

He opened her eyes one at a time. Her pupils were constricting normally, but he daren't move her. Who knew what injuries her head and neck had taken? There was an almighty great lump on her head. He sat back on his heels, silently begging for guidance.

She uttered an un-ladylike word and doubled over.

"Aleks? It's Ephraim. Where are you hurt?"

She rolled her head from side to side, but opened her eyes and winced at him. "Xavier…"

"No, sorry love, it's Ephraim. Xavier's not here."

She turned her gaze to focus on him. "Ephraim," she struggled to speak, "thank God I found you. They've got Xavier—you've got to save him.

"Southerners...north of Fort Churchill...hundreds. I can't...too...many..." she trailed off. She curled up in a tight ball, moaning.

"Aleks, are you pregnant?"

She nodded, and the tears began rolling down her face. "Probably...not now," she whispered, "my fault, but needed to...find you...save Xavier."

Ephraim squeezed his eyes shut for a moment. He gripped her shoulders and tried again. "Can you hear me?"

She nodded.

"Are you hurt anywhere else?"

She straightened with an effort and wriggled hands and feet. "Just sore," she mumbled, but this..." she reached for her abdomen, and cringed as another wave hit her.

"How long have you had the pains and how far along are you?"

"Four or five months."

"Oh, my God." He slid a dusty hand over his face. She needed a doctor. She was losing a lot of blood.

"Searle," he said over his shoulder, "you're a sworn rider, aren't you?"

"Yessir," he said, scurrying closer.

"You'll need to take the *mochila* on to Smith's Creek station. Ride yours and lead the colt. Come find us when you've handed it over, and tell them I sent you. By the time you return, we should be back to the Pony station at Churchill."

"Yep, boss. Go safely with her." He frowned, then led his mount toward the Express colt. The black Mustang eyed up Seattle's chestnut mare and rumbled deep in his throat, while the mare gave a low whicker. "None of that now, you two, we're off," he snapped. He took the colt's reins, then he swung up onto his mare and galloped east.

"Let's go boys." Ephraim stood. "One of you lift her up to me, carefully," he said, and mounted his stallion.

Alternating between a walk and a rocking-horse lope, they made their way back west. Aleksandra drifted in and out of consciousness, sometimes more lucid than others. By the time they reached Fort Churchill, he had the information he needed to find Xavier.

"Halt there," a sentry shouted at them through the darkness.

"It's Ephraim Hanks," he growled, "with a woman who's miscarrying. We need the doctor. Take me to him, now." At the ensuing silence, he added "Please."

"I'm sorry, sir," the soldier moved closer, "the doctor left for Virginia City yesterday. He's probably still there."

Ephraim spat out an expletive only a sea-going Mormon would know and sat still, considering. "I need to speak with your commander, please."

In the moonlight, the man raised a brow, turned on his heel and left them.

"Aleks, are you awake?" he murmured into her hair as she sat slumped against him on the front of his saddle.

"Mmmm…"

"The doctor's at Virginia City and I need to get you there, Xavier will have to—"

Aleksandra snapped awake. "No! Please, go get him. I can—"

"—excuse me, Ephraim," one of his men interrupted as he rode up close to them, "I can't shoot my rifle with this damned broken hand, but I can make sure she gets to Virginia City, all right."

Aleksandra held her breath, then slumped again.

Ephraim let out the breath he didn't know he'd been holding and reached out a hand to the man. "Thank you, James. I'll see if I can get an escort for you. I'll send them after you. Find the doctor and the midwife. Tell her I sent you. When you return, head north with a few more men on the trail I told you about. We might even still be here when you return, or at least the troop I plan to raise will."

"Yessir," he said. Two of the other men dismounted and handed Aleksandra across. He settled her before him on his horse.

"Ephraim?" Aleksandra murmured, her eyes glazed again.

"I'm here, but you're on your way home."

"You can't take me, you need to go get…you're the only one I can…trust"

"That's right," he soothed. "James will take you and I'll go into the fort to—"

"*No!*" She jerked upright and her eyes stared. "There are Southerners in there!"

"The commander is a good Northerner. It'll be fine, see, James has got you now, and we'll bring your man home to you soon as we get him out."

"Are you sure?" she whispered. "No Southerners?"

"Promise. I want to get out of there alive, too."

"Thank you, Ephraim, for everything," she gasped and tucked up, "from the bottom of my heart. Ride, James." She lay back, panting.

"It's nothing. I owe you one, girl," Ephraim said. "You saved my favorite pony, remember?" He reached up and touched her cheek. It was hot and dry. "You be a good lass and listen to James. He'll have you home in no time."

"Ephraim," she whispered, and he had to lean close to hear her, "please be careful. There are a lot of them."

"I know. We'll take care and not risk his life." He glanced up at James, whose face was nearly the same color as hers in the moonlight.

James lifted his canteen to her lips. "Drink," he said softly, and she did, then they were off, heading for the Comstock. Ephraim watched them until they were swallowed by the darkness.

"Mr. Hanks, the commander will see you now. Right this way, please." The sentry led him towards the lights of the encampment.

IT WAS FULL DARK. Xavier tried to move, but couldn't. A little strip of light showed, and he craned towards it. No, it was daytime and he wore a blindfold. It had slipped a little. He tried to pull it off, but couldn't get his hands up to it—couldn't feel them, for that matter, other than the pain where the rough rope cut into his wrists.

Damn.

Thoughts flashed in and out of his brain.

Aleksandra, O'Rourke, sticky gray mud, blood.

He ground his teeth. His tongue was furry and thick and his empty guts growled.

He pushed his face across the packed dirt floor to try to move the blindfold and was granted the view of a wedge of his prison. A four by six foot outbuilding of some sort, mostly filled with crates of ammunition and the stench of rats. By the ache in his shoulders, his hands must have been tied behind his back for some time.

He'd kill for some water. He tried to focus on the door to see if there was a guard, but the darkness returned and he slipped into oblivion again.

IT WAS the scratching that woke him.

"*Meneer?*" a feminine voice whispered, then the scratching came again.

Xavier rolled his head from side to side. Surely he was hearing things. He shook his head and it throbbed—more, if that were possible—and pulled himself to a sitting position against the rough crate behind him.

"*Meneer,* are yoo alif in therr?" More scratching.

"*Sí, estoy*—yes, I am. Not so good," he managed through parched lips.

"Look, I haf dugh a little hole at de back herr, ant dere's a knife, food an' vater. You ant your vife tried to help me back in Udah ant I never have gifen you tanks forr it. *Sterke,* gut luck. I must go now, before somevone sees me."

He sat stock still. Another dream? Skirts rustled, and then nothing. His ankles were bound, but he struggled to his knees and managed to scrape the blindfold off against the nearest crate. It didn't change much, so it must be full dark.

Light showed between the cracks on only one wall, and when he focused, the light flickered. Campfire or torches. Two parallel bands of the glinting light—a door?

He really needed his hands. Beside him was the wall from where it seemed the woman had spoken. He lay back and carefully slid his boots along the wall until one of them caught on something. A nail?

Kneeling again, he scraped his arm around on the wood until the nail scored his flesh. Could he cut the rope with it? He'd have to try. Backing up to it, he rubbed the rope against it, somehow not screaming with pain as he moved his hands. The square sides of the forged nail were sharp and bit into the strands of the frayed rope. The fine rope finally cut through, but it didn't come loose. By the feel, it was stuck in crevices in his swollen skin. Catching the loops of the rope on the nail, he swore beneath his breath as he pulled the rope away and slowly brought his hands to the front to feel what had become of them.

Rubbing brought some feel back into them—and not in a good way. He bit his lip to squelch the yell trying to escape. It felt like hours, but surely it was only minutes before he could control his fingers and drag a few of the ammunition boxes away from the wall where he'd heard the voice.

"Bless her," he breathed as his hand closed on the hilt of a knife beneath the wall of the shed. He scrabbled in the hole and found meat, bread and a canteen full of water.

She'd die if they found her out.

He pushed the box back to hide the breach and drank deeply of the water, then tore at the meat. While the bread was soaking up water, he began to cut the rope binding his ankles, then shook his head with a grim smile.

Untie them, fool.

He'd heard no sound from near his prison, just the occasional raised voices from afar, and the crackling of fire.

They couldn't have left me unguarded?

His eyes had adjusted to the light now, and he stood and stretched his limbs, then inched toward the lit side of the shed. It was a door. He pushed softly, but it didn't move. He listened again for any sound, but heard nothing but several owls calling back and forth. He gave it a shove. Something heavy clunked against the door and he jumped backwards. A lock, or at least a heavy latch. What now?

He sat down on a box to think. How to get the door open without attracting attention? And find a horse?

Something tugged at the edge of his consciousness.

The owls called again, closer at hand this time. They repeated again, farther away. Different birds.

Xavier was done for. He didn't know how much time had passed, but one thing was certain. He wasn't going to live through whatever O'Rourke had planned for him—he only hoped he wouldn't drag it out too long.

Great Horned Owls are solitary. They don't hunt together.

He caught his breath when the realization hit, and stared at the walls.

Maybe…maybe someone knows I'm here…

He shook his head.

Don't get your hopes up, Argüello.

Owls again

…maybe?

He could do a reasonable owl call, with his fingers—he tried, but they were too swollen to make any useful sound. Perhaps just a whistle, it wouldn't hurt to try, much. His lips were swollen too, but not as badly as his hands.

After a few lisping attempts, a passable screech filled the shed and one of the other owl calls cut out mid-sound. Repeated again, both of them, closer to hand, then silence. He made his owl call again and jumped at a soft scratching against the wood of the shed behind his head.

"Xave?"

"Ephraim," he breathed. "Thank Christ."

"Thank Aleks," he whispered. "Are you guarded?"

"Not in here, but I've no idea about outside. I'm untied now, anyway, but the door's locked or latched. It's on the other side."

A muffled chuckle and scuffling sounds around the side of the shed, then the front.

Shouts rang out from far away and gunshots rent the night. A rifle shot, close at hand, filled his head and choking dust flew. "*Dios mío*, there's ammo in here!" Xavier whispered. "Watch the bullets!"

Then Ephraim was there, and he half led, half-dragged him to a horse. Charro snorted, then snuffled at him, dancing sideways.

"Idiots locked my shed, didn't they?"

"Your shed?" Xavier's heart stopped.

"Later," he whispered. "Stand, ye daft bugger," he growled and the stallion stood. Ephraim fair threw him into the saddle, but kept the reins as he swung up onto his own stallion and led them away from the sound of men scrambling for guns and horses. Just behind them, shouts echoed.

"Where is 'e? Where's the Mexican? Find 'im, he cain't have gotten far."

They were already gone, headed away at a gallop.

"How're your hands, son? Can you take the reins yet?" Ephraim called back.

"Rubbing them for all I'm worth, nearly there. Who's doing all the shooting back there?"

"My men—your diversion."

"How'd you find me?"

"That woman of yours is gold. Found her riding an Express pony to find me." He slowed the horses and turned to listen behind them. The gunshots had stopped, only the men's yelling continued.

Galloping hooves approached and Ephraim drove the horses off the track into the shelter of some willows along a creek.

Xavier placed a hand over Charro's nostrils and kept his attention on him. "Shhh, not a sound, old man," he breathed.

"He's gotta be heah. They cain't've gone far." O'Rourke's voice carried to them as the sound of their horses' hooves stopped.

"How many do you think, Xave?" Ephraim breathed.

"Not more than four, I'd say," Xavier returned, behind his hand.

Xavier slid off and laid a hand on the ground, wincing when it touched.

Hoofbeats.

Many of them, coming at speed, from far away. Whose? O'Rourke's or Ephraim's?

"Those should be my men," Ephraim whispered. "Wait for the owl's call, then we'll go huntin'."

Xavier could just make out the grin creasing his friend's face. Suddenly Ephraim's hand dropped onto his arm, and he nodded back toward Fort Churchill. Faint in the darkness, he saw them. Coming at speed.

Troops.

Moonlight glinting off bayonets.

Ephraim made the sound of a whippoorwill, his hands cupped over his mouth and the oncoming hoofbeats to the north stopped. The call was returned, twice.

"Quite a system you have there." He caught Ephraim's shrug, and the glint of teeth. "It works. They'll melt into the trees and meet us up ahead, around behind the army troops."

Xavier jumped. "Troops?"

"Churchill. The commander knows what, and who, they're lookin' for, thanks to Aleks. We'll wait 'till they engage, then we're off."

"But—"

"You're in no condition to fight and those men mean business. You can take your revenge in court, if he lives that long."

The troops were close enough to hear their thunder.

"Why is O'Rourke still here? Maybe he thinks they're his own—"

Ephraim gripped his arm again and Xavier clamped his mouth shut.

"You there," a rough shout cut across the distance, when the head of the troops appeared around the corner.

O'Rourke's head shot up. As one, his men spun around and bolted back toward their camp, the troopers in hot pursuit.

Ephraim released his arm and headed his horse back out to the road, leaving Xavier to follow.

"Why didn't we stay to help?"

"Aleks—" his rescuer drew a deep breath and was silent for a moment, "—I can't think of a good way to say this, man, but she's lost the baby—or is losing it now."

Xavier swung to face him, his aches forgotten. "What?"

"She was in pretty bad shape, lost a lot of blood—I wanted to take her to the doctor at Virginia City, but she wouldn't hear of it, wanted me to go find you, so I sent her back home with my second in command and an escort. He'll find the doctor and Molly."

"What, how?" Xavier could hardly draw a breath. "What was she doing out here?" he managed.

"She was coming home late and saw the men taking you away. Trailed you to that camp," he flicked a glance over his shoulder back the way they'd come, "and headed back for Fort Churchill."

"Fort Churchill? But that's way out—but—where'd she find *you*? And," he frowned and stared at his own horse beneath him. "How did Charro get here? They packed me in on Rogan...so he's got to be here somewhere..." Xavier gritted his teeth. Aleksandra would have his guts for garters if he'd lost the horse. "We need to go back and get him."

"You're doin' no such thing," Ephraim growled. "We'll get him later. Not as if a horse lookin' like that's easy to hide. Your woman needs you, bad." He stared at Xavier.

Xavier took a breath and blinked.

Aleks not OK? She was always OK.

"What did you say about Aleks?

"She's miscarrying; can't you hear me?"

His heart hit his boots as the pain hit.

"Not Aleks," he said, "that couldn't be right."

Ephraim looked at him strangely. "Did you take a hit to the head?"

"Quite a few of them. Everything's a bit...blurry. Don't remember anything of the trip here. I don't even know where we are."

"She took both Charro and Dzień from home," Ephraim continued, "but when she got to Churchill, the sentries sounded like Southerners and she panicked, and headed east for the next Pony station. She knew I might be in the area, and they needed a rider, so she left the horses there and riding an Express pony, set off to find me. She fell off and started bleedin'—bin bleedin' pretty badly ever since." He stopped.

Xavier shook his head to clear the last cobwebs. "Well, let's go. How far are we from there?"

"We're about a hundred miles from Churchill, and Dzień, and then about twenty-five miles to home."

30

"Hey, boss," the station keeper grinned at Ephraim, then turned to Xavier. "Good to see *you* back. Looks like Mr. Hanks got you out all right?"

"Sure did, thanks. We've come to pick up Aleks' buckskin," Xavier said, then swallowed hard, thinking about Rogan. He couldn't explain losing the last living thing of her father's.

"And you can take that blasted bay thing too." He frowned at Xavier. "Nice looker, but I don't need him around with my mares."

"Rogan?" Xavier's jaw dropped.

"Is that his name? Your Rogan showed up just after Ephraim picked up Charro and I figgered he must be yours—that Mustang of Aleks' knew him all right."

Xavier glanced at Ephraim and shook his head. A whinny came from behind the station and he grinned. "That'll be Dzień. Thanks for looking after them both." Charro trumpeted in return, followed by Rogan's shriek.

"No problem, well, other than that I owe you a stud fee…he found one of my mares out loose."

"Nothing doing, glad to be of help," Xavier said.

"I'll get his saddle, I know you guys are in a hurry. Please give Aleks my best when you see him? James stopped on his way by," the keeper said, as he took them around behind the building. "Your Rogan was wearing his saddle, and most of a bridle. His side was a bit cut up, but he let me doctor him— he's OK as long as you don't try to hold too tight onto his head," he added with a wry grin.

"It's a long way from his heart," Xavier said, as he took in the long scrape down the colt's side. "Must've taken that in his exit from the camp." He rubbed Rogan's forehead and the colt stepped closer to rub his head vigorously on Xavier's chest. "Bet you've got a story to tell, eh boy?"

He threw the saddle over the bay's back and cinched it up, then assessed what was left of the bridle. The noseband was decimated, and one rein was only a foot long, but there was enough to work with.

"Don't have time for that," Ephraim snorted. "Thomas, get us a bridle, if you can find one big enough. We'll bring it back on our way through. Aleks is in bad shape and we need to go."

He shot away before his boss finished and returned with a wide bridle he used on the working horses. "Not very nice for a horse of his class," he winced, "but everything else would only fit Dzień."

Xavier laughed. "He won't care. He just wants his buddies." He deftly swapped the draft horse bit on the working bridle for Rogan's snaffle, handed the massive draft bit back to Thomas, and slipped the bridle over the bay's ears.

He mounted Charro and turned to the station keeper. "Thanks Thomas, we'll see you soon."

"Hope Aleks is OK," he called after them as they loped away.

Xavier turned to his benefactor. "I appreciate everything, but I can go on from here if you want to head home."

"Leading two horses?" He raised a brow at Dzień, on a lead beside his own mount. "With two stallions in the mix? It's OK lad, my man took her to Virginia City. We'll at least ride with you until we meet up with James."

"Happy for the company, and the help."

Ephraim's crooked grin showed in the early dawn's light.

"What?" Xavier asked.

"Remember I said I had some trouble with a man who was buying some land from me up north of the fort?"

"Yes?"

"That's how I knew to look for you in that shed, and where the door was. I built it."

"That's *your* place?"

"Mmmm…bunch of hornets. Don't think I'll need to see them again."

"O'Rourke kept talking about his uncle—sounded like it was his place—some bigwig in a California mine somewhere."

"Knew the name sounded familiar when Aleks talked about him."

"Sure glad you got me out of there—his methods didn't sound a pleasant way to die."

"Not a nice sort of a man, by all accounts. I'd never actually met him before we met on the wagon train, and hadn't a clue he was the man who bought my land. The lawyers did it all." His brows drew together and his lips formed a tight smile. "I'll catch up with what's left of him when I get back to Churchill."

From the steely glint in the Mormon's eye, Xavier wouldn't want to be O'Rourke. Then his heart clenched at the thought of Aleksandra on the trail alone and bleeding.

As if he heard his thoughts, Ephraim went on. "She was already cramping before she dozed on the Mustang and fell off. She knew she was pretty bad and drank some of her pa's secret formula."

"She took his formula?" Xavier stared.

He nodded. "It let her get back on, and then she fell off again. I think she must have passed out. I carried her on the front of my saddle for nearly seventy miles back to Churchill and sent her on with James, the same way."

"She couldn't even ride? Aleks?"

Ephraim just looked at him.

Xavier closed his eyes, and his gorge rose.

"I told you she was bad," the Mormon said. "She is. Doctor had left Churchill for Virginia City. I only hope he was there."

"Can we go any faster?"

"You go on ahead. I'd switch over to Rogan and lead Charro, if I were you. The young bugger needs the work, and I'll lead Dzień home. It's only twenty-five miles, so we'll see you later this morning. I want to see how she is. Tell James to rest up."

Xavier slid from Charro and mounted Rogan. "I'll see you shortly." He waved and loped off. Just out of sight of Ephraim, he knotted Charro's reins up over his ears and let him loose. He let Rogan rip and called back to the great gray Andalusian, who galloped easily behind them as the two massive horses ate up the miles. He waved, but never slackened as he passed an encamped wagon train and the Pony stations along the way.

Climbing the steep track up to Gold Hill, the horses hit a long trot and powered up the rocky mountainside.

Billy ran out of the house as Xavier rode up. "Xavier, Xav—" his voice dropped to just above a whisper. "I'll take care of the horses."

"Aleks?" He glanced towards the door. "Is she OK?"

"She's in there with Molly and Emma."

"Thanks lad." Xavier frowned at the heaving, frothy horses as a man stepped from the barn.

"James," he said, and shook Xavier's hand.

"Thank you for getting her here."

"We'll cool the horses out properly," Billy said. "You go look after Aleks —she's been asking for you—crying, actually."

He took the steps two at a time, stopping briefly at the door to take a deep breath before entering the open door. The sitting room was empty, but at a noise from the hall leading to their room, he tiptoed down the hall, his hands cold as ice, his jaw clenched.

Molly and Emma stepped away from the bed. Aleks lay back against the pillow, her eyes closed, pale beneath her tan.

He knelt beside her and took her cold fingers in his hands. Her lashes fluttered, but she didn't open her eyes.

"How is she?" he whispered to Molly.

"Sleeping now, but she lost a lot of blood. Thank Christ she went to sleep, she couldn't stop crying." She looked at Xavier. "She thinks she's killed the baby and you. You look very much alive, if a bit battered." She gave him a tired smile.

"I'm fine. Ephraim saw to that, but how is she? Is the baby..."

Molly glanced at Aleks, then looked squarely at Xavier. "The baby is most likely dead. She's what, four months along?"

"I think so," he whispered, sick to his core, "four or five."

"She's lost a lot of blood, and...probably the baby."

"But Aleks is going to be...all right?" He closed his eyes, afraid of the answer.

"She's resting quietly now, and her fever has abated a little. All we can do is hope. Mother will come again soon to see if there's anything she can do."

"Can I do anything?"

"She's just gone to sleep," she looked him over, her gaze pausing at his face, and she bit her lip. "You'd best go get cleaned up and get a meal into you—you don't look much better than she does."

"I imagine not," he murmured, as he left the room, watching Aleksandra over his shoulder.

He stumbled down the hall and out the door, heading for the pump.

She could die.

He carefully splashed water on his face, swearing softly.

She's the best thing that's ever happened in my life. She has to be OK.

"I'll have breakfast for you in a few minutes," Emma said, as Xavier entered the kitchen, but her smile changed to a wince when he turned to face her. "It looks worse without the dirt," she said, handing him a towel.

"If it looks as bad as it feels, I must be a mess," he said, but he was unprepared for the black, blue, grazed, and swollen visage staring back at him in the looking glass. His 'friends' must have really had the time of their life. He grimaced, then gulped. Even that hurt, but it was nothing to the feeling in his heart, or what Aleksandra was going through.

It was heart wrenching that they'd lost their first baby, but they could try again—and Aleks had to live. He shut his mind down, as he'd learned to do early on—to not feel—as he rubbed his head with a towel and pulled off his shirt, the cold morning air bringing out goose pimples everywhere. His head slowly cleared as he finished scrubbing at his body with the dampened towel.

In the kitchen, Molly told him about Aleksandra's homecoming and her care since then. He gave them an abbreviated version of his attack, kidnapping and rescue as he ate, sitting beside the sleeping Aleksandra.

She awoke with a start. "Xavier," she cried out before her eyes opened.

"I'm here,"

"Tell me I'm not dreaming it again?" she whispered in a pitiful voice.

He gripped her hands, then wrapped his arms around her and held her close, lying beside her.

"I killed our baby," she sobbed.

"None of that, now. You did your best to save its father, and I thank you, *con todo mi corazón*, with all my heart. I'm so sorry we lost the baby, but we're both safe now. You'll be OK, and I am too."

"I fell off," she mumbled. "Twice."

"But you did it."

"Yes, I found Ephraim," she said, her eyes beginning to droop already.

"You sure did, and he found me. Turns out that was his own property, the one he wasn't being paid for."

That got a hint of a smile from her wan face.

"Thank you for giving me my life, *Querida*. O'Rourke's plans for me were not for the faint of heart."

"That's why I kept going. Wonderful black stallion I rode out of Churchill," she gave him a shade of an impudent grin.

"Yes, Aleks, you got to ride for the Pony again." He shook his head and grinned.

"Four and a half months pregnant wasn't a good way to do it." She frowned.

"No. How are you feeling?"

She was silent for a moment. "Sore and bereft. After I came off the first time, I used Papa's formula."

"What happened?"

"It stopped the shaking and let me get back on again and ride."

"And then what happened?"

"Ummm…a little while later, I must have passed out, but it let me find Ephraim, which I wouldn't have been able to, otherwise, so thank you, Papa." She looked up at the ceiling and closed her eyes for a minute.

"Well, that's something, a big something."

"He always said it was a tonic. Maybe I should take it a little a few times a day and see if it helps."

"Sounds reasonable, but no riding, you hear?" He looked hard at her. "How did you inject yourself?"

"Drank it." She motioned at her medicine bag on the table beside the bed and he sat up and gave it to her. She reached for it and winced. After she'd sipped a quarter bottle of it and recapped it, she handed it to him. "You look as pale as I do, other than the blood and bruises." She gave him the ghost of a smile and squeezed his hand.

"Hard for a *Californio*, so I must not look so good."

"Nope, drink up. Half of that."

He sipped. A strong alcohol tincture. "It doesn't taste too bad. A little like honey." It burned a trail down from his throat, and a minute later, his heart began to pound.

She smiled faintly. "Feel it?"

"Sure do." He raised a brow at her. "Is it meant to make my heart race?"

Her brow raised. "Yes, remember Vladimir's chestnut? But it got me back on my horse to get you saved, so it must be good."

He nodded. "Have you stopped bleeding?"

"Pretty much," her face fell, "and the cramping only happens occasionally now. That must mean the baby's dead, truly." She gripped his hands in hers, her jaw tight. "Sometimes I cry and can't stop. It's got to get better."

"It will, I'm here for you, we're all here for you. Ephraim will be here soon too, with Dzień."

"You've got Dzień?" She sat up straight and peered out the window.

Xavier smiled. "Yes, all of the horses. Dzień will be here within the hour."

"Even Rogan?"

"Yes, the beggar must've turned himself loose from the rebels' camp and headed back to the Pony station and found Dzień."

"And O'Rourke?"

He gave her a grimace of a smile. "Last I saw, him and three of his men were running from the entire force of Fort Churchill. The army should have O'Rourke, plus his whole gang, so things ought to get back to normal now. I wonder how many men will be missing from the Ophir?"

She raised a brow at him.

"Aleks, did we ever do a negro woman a special favor in the past, other than the one we found clutching her dead man back in Utah? When Ephraim and his gang were there?"

Her brows drew together. "No, I don't think so."

"Must've been her, then."

"Why?"

He told her of the woman who brought the food and knife to him in Ephraim's shed.

"The importance of kindness," she whispered. "Always, as Mama and Papa said. The woman must have belonged," she shuddered, "to O'Rourke."

"She must have been on the wagon train with us too, but I don't remember seeing her."

Aleksandra considered for a moment, then picked up her head, brows narrowed. "There was the woman always walking beside his wagon. She kept her head down, so I didn't recognize her."

"Must have been. Anyway," he said, taking her hands, "she might have saved my life."

"Yes," she smiled and squeezed his hands in hers. "I'm very lucky to have you back. Come lie down beside me again." Her eyes pleaded. "Tell me what else I've missed while I've been lying about," she said, reaching for him.

"That, I can do. I've missed a bit of sleep, myself." He carefully fit his body onto the bed beside her and murmured into her hair, "but you'll be safe now, *Querida*, safe…" he mumbled, put his forehead against her, and slept.

Unnoticed, Molly slipped out and closed the door, a smile and a tear on her face.

31

"The South won't be happy with the news from England," Molly said, wiping flour from her cheek with the back of an even more floury hand.

"England?" Aleksandra swung to face her and winced at the pain.

"Yes, from Queen Victoria."

"What does the queen have to do with anything? I thought we were free of England sometime after 1776—we aren't exactly friends with them, history being what it is?"

Molly laughed. "It seems the new Confederacy thought the mother country wouldn't be able to survive without the cotton they export to them. They expected her to break the North's blockade and support them in the war. Quite the furor about it in England, so my London uncle wrote to tell my mam."

Aleksandra scrunched up her brow and looked up from the seam she was stitching in one of Xavier's shirts. "So she wouldn't break the blockade?"

"No," Molly said. "A few months ago, she signed a 'Proclamation of Neutrality', and won't back either side. The Southerners are not impressed. Unfortunately, by her recognition of the blockade, she's given the South 'belligerent' rights."

Aleksandra pricked her finger and swore, putting her finger in her mouth. "What are those?"

Molly's brows drew together and she stopped kneading. "International recognition as a real entity, undermining Lincoln's insistence that the war's only an internal battle, not a war between sovereign states."

"Ahhh…" Aleksandra nodded. "So…now the South can search neutral vessels for the North's messages."

"Yep." Molly grimaced, as she absently finished kneading the bread, then began forming the sourdough into loaves.

"One rarely knows what the full effect of one's actions might be," Aleksandra said. She knotted her thread and stood, then folded the shirt and placed it beside the others. "At least, being homebound, I'm getting through our repairs. Xavier will appreciate having more than two shirts without holes."

"How are you doing, really, Aleks?" Molly looked sideways at her. "I saw the 'ouch' when you moved back there."

"I'm doing all right." She looked away from Molly, out the window.

"When do you think you'll be ready to go back to school?"

Aleksandra shuddered and took a moment to answer. "Soon, I hope. I'm a bit stiff and sore, but nothing exercise won't help. No more bleeding, anyway." She reached up to the goose egg still on her head. "A few bumps and bruises, but nothing that won't mend…"

"…but?"

Aleksandra tried to swallow past the lump in her throat, her heart constricting, and she hunched over, hugging herself.

"Are you still crying all the time?"

Aleksandra gulped and stared at Molly. She didn't think anyone knew. "Sometimes," she said, in a small voice.

"Sometimes, or a lot?" Molly put her fingers under Aleksandra's chin and lifted it, then looked straight into her eyes.

"The tears, Molly," Aleksandra shook her head, "they just keep coming, and I don't," she paused to wipe the drops suddenly raining down her face, "know how to make them stop."

"Is it about the baby?"

She nodded, her heart breaking. "I think so," she got out, between sobs.

Molly wiped her hands on her apron and wrapped her arms around Aleksandra. "Ma and I see this all the time after women lose babies," the midwife's daughter looked her in the eyes, "because the feeling of loss is so strong. It's a rotten, 'abnormal' sort of 'normal' situation. I know that doesn't help you right now, but it will get better, it always does."

Aleksandra cried harder.

"Many times, the woman believes it's her fault, that she's killed her baby," Molly stated bluntly.

Aleksandra closed her eyes. Maybe the floor would swallow her, if she was lucky.

"Aleks, is that you?"

"Yes," barely a whisper.

"You did what you had to do. Nothing more, nothing less."

"And worse," Aleksandra sobbed, "Xavier thinks it's *his* fault, when it's *mine*. I shouldn't have gotten on that Express horse and ridden off to find him. He didn't want me riding for the Pony when I was pregnant."

"Sure, and then you'd be pregnant, and your babe without a father, or worse, you'd be trying to raise it somewhere in the scrub as a captive of that creep O'Rourke. You'd probably lose the baby anyway, or maybe both of you would be dead by now," she said gruffly.

That stopped her in her tracks. Aleksandra sat up as her stomach turned over and she clutched at Molly. "I hadn't thought of that, Molly."

"That man's just plain crazy." She glared and shook her head, then was silent for a moment. "Did you know, they were calling that little tent-town 'Dixie'?"

Aleksandra looked up at that. "Seriously?"

She nodded. "The doctor said not to talk about it with you, for fear of upsetting you more, but I think you need to get it all out."

"So...what happened after they got Xavier out?" she asked, her curiosity piqued, as the tears dried on her face.

"The commander of Fort Churchill rode O'Rourke and three of his men down, dragging them off their horses, and left them tied up while they encircled and captured the whole camp—about four hundred men and enough guns and ammunition to fight the whole Union Army."

"Xavier was held in a shed full of crates of ammunition." She gritted her teeth at the bruises all over his body, only now beginning to fade.

"I'm pretty sure a whole wagonload of them came west with O'Rourke in our wagon train."

Molly shook her head.

The cold feeling in the pit of Aleksandra's stomach got colder. "Molly, back up a step," she said. "What you said before, about my being a captive of O'Rourke?" She frowned. "What was that about?"

Molly was silent for a moment. "Me and my big mouth."

Aleksandra stared hard at her, mouth open.

"Apparently," she leaned close and whispered, "seems he went back to your place to collect you after his cronies had taken Xavier, but you must've already gone, thank God. When he was tied up by the Army troops, he was raving about a woman—long blonde curls—and about how he was going to find you. Some rather unsavory things he had in mind. I imagine that'd be you."

The room swam around Aleksandra and she shook her head to clear it. Xavier hadn't told her. "Really?"

"Really. Ask Xavier."

"Why wasn't I told?"

"The doctor was worried it be too hard on you, in your condition."

"I'm glad you told me." She swallowed hard. "So he's locked up?"

"I've heard nothing to the contrary." Molly attempted a smile.

Aleksandra looked around the room, her glance pausing at the windows and door. "I don't want to be looking over my shoulder all the time."

"He's locked up. Don't make me sorry I told you, please?"

"No, I needed to hear that. Maybe it's time we moved on."

"I'll miss you terribly," she grimaced, "but why are you staying in Virginia City, anyway? Doesn't Xavier have family with a big *rancho* in California?" She led Aleksandra to a chair at the table. "If I did, I sure know where I'd be. I don't want my boy to grow up in a mining town. Besides, everything here," she paused and swallowed, "reminds me of my husband."

"Xavier has this idea he can't go home empty-handed, so he wants to go back to the California goldfields on the way."

"If his family loves him, I don't think 'empty-handed' would be important."

"Neither do I, but he does." She bit her lip, considering for a moment. "Molly, sometime next year when we get to the *rancho*, surely there'd be work for a midwife around there?"

Molly looked up at her, and tears filled her eyes. "Do you think so? Would you..." she hesitated, "...have us with you?"

Aleksandra reached out to Molly and nodded. "You're family to us now, and you've made the past weeks bearable. What about your mother?"

"She can handle the practice fine on her own, and it looks like her beau is about to pop the question, so she'll be fine."

"What about Adrian? I promised to help him."

"He's learned so much from you already. My ma and the doctor will let him work with them, and soon enough he'll be off to a fine medical school back East, like Harvard, Chicago, or one of several in Georgia. I hear there's even one to open soon in California. Maybe it'll be ready by the time he's ready to go. Either way, thanks to you, his goal is set in stone, and he'll not be dissuaded."

Aleksandra smiled. "Molly, I sure appreciate the help you've given me since...Xavier's kidnapping..." She wrung her hands in her muslin skirt and looked around the house. "I don't know what I'd have done without you—all credit to you this house is even livable, much less that I'll be able to teach again soon," she said.

"Adrian will be pleased, though he hasn't missed much with your tutoring him," she smiled. "He won't miss teaching the rest of the students, though. That was inspired, Aleks, putting his name forward to teach."

"He offered, actually." Aleksandra said. "I couldn't see any other choice for it." She found her eyes on the loaf pans, with a start, then shook her head and handed the rest of the greased bread pans to Molly. Picking up a lump of the sourdough rye dough, Aleksandra formed it into a loaf, turning it over in her hand and pinching the bottom and then the end seams, then slipped it into a pan. She smiled at the loaves filling the pans before them. "It's nice to feel well enough to do even this, Molly. It's been hard not being able to do for myself."

"Here's to California," Molly said, and reached for Aleksandra's hand.

"To California," she returned, as they shook on it.

"I'M NOT WINNING HERE, XAVIER," Aleksandra stood and turned a tear-streaked face up to him.

He wrapped his arms about her and inhaled her wonderful scent. "What's up, *Querida?*"

"It's been nearly a week back at school, and still, all I can do is cry. Nearly everything sets me off."

"Don't the midwife and doctor say it's to be expected?" He brushed a few strands of hair back from her face and kissed her on the forehead.

"I think I need to get away, go somewhere totally different," she paused, "somewhere without the triggers. Maybe it's time to go to California, as you've been saying."

He inhaled slowly. "Are you sure? I want to go, but I want you to go because you want to."

"I'm not sure about anything anymore."

He looked at the floor before answering. It was getting harder and harder to watch Aleksandra's wrinkled brows framing the lost eyes in her pale face. Maybe it was time to go. Running might not be the answer, but maybe she was right.

"Jeremy put some feelers out for us around Grass Valley. Seems the Malakoff Diggins is looking for an assay manager, and they're interested in talking with me."

She glanced up with the first hopeful look he'd seen on her face in weeks. "Really? When?"

"As soon as we can get there, ideally by the middle of next month."

"Maybe it'll even be cooler there." She fanned her perspiring face with her hand.

"Don't count on it." He winced. "It's even hotter in the Sierras, but there are plenty of rivers near where we'd be."

"I'll take rivers," she said, and laid her hand against his chest. "Wait, that only gives us two weeks to get there." She sighed and leaned back in his arms to look into his eyes. "Can we make it?"

"Sure can. Jeremy's also come up with a schoolmaster. He's just come to town and is ready to start tomorrow, if need be."

Aleksandra sat down in her chair again, hard. Her face tightened for a moment.

"Careful, there."

"Yes." She sighed. "If that's the case," she glanced at the grandfather clock on the wall behind her, "since school's out for the day, I'd best go find the new teacher, let him know who's where and transfer some records and then pick up my teaching things."

"I'll go with you. I need to let Jeremy know we're going."

"We'll tell Jason tonight." Her brow wrinkled. "I hope it doesn't create difficulty for him—I know he wanted us to stay."

"I don't think he ever asked his wife-to-be if she wanted to live upstairs from an unfinished saloon." He laughed.

"I was thinking the same. We might save his marriage by letting him have his house back—before he even gets married."

He gently helped her into her stays and skirts, then they set off for town on Charro and Rogan. Dzień was sleeping in the sun and didn't seem bothered at being left with the house cow.

"I won't miss the noise," she said, looking around them as they entered the town. It was in full roar, the steam pumps and stamp mills running for all they were worth, while men walked to and fro to keep the mining town running around the clock.

"I can't promise it'll be quiet there, but I hear the manager's houses are away from the mine at the Malakoff."

Her eyes lit up at that.

"It will be better soon," Xavier nodded at a tired looking whim horse walking in circles to power the capstan at one of the smaller mines, "to see all the mines with cages, rather than the men having to climb ladders with sacks of ore on their backs, even if they still have to use a whim."

"It'll be even better when they can replace the horses with a steam engine," Aleksandra gave him a wry grin. "I'm just glad you rarely need to go underground." She looked into the yawning maw of a mine, and shuddered, then told him Molly would like to come to California.

He smiled. "She's been a good friend to you, and will make a fine midwife. She can make a name for herself in her own territory."

"I was thinking that too."

"Here's the new teacher's place," he nodded at dusty white house on the roadside. "Shall we meet in, say, an hour at Jeremy's?"

"You beggar, that'll be dinnertime."

"Really?" He flashed innocent eyes at her. "She loves having us, and soon we'll be gone."

"We can't just show up at dinner time." Aleksandra shook her head.

He rode closer to kiss her. "She invited us. I just wanted to surprise you. Billy and Jason will be there, too."

Aleksandra returned to Jeremy's just as the whole family sat down for dinner.

"I have no idea how Jeremy's going to replace you at the Ophir, Xavier," Dorothea said, passing the plate of buttered bread.

"We'll get by. You've spoiled us, Xavier, but we'll survive."

"At least we have a new teacher," she looked at Aleksandra, "but the children will miss you terribly."

"The new teacher will be fine," Aleksandra said. "I spent time with him just now. He's all I could have asked for: keen, experienced, young, yet old enough to command respect from the bigger boys. He's written down where all the students are in their learning, and he's promised to come to school tomorrow morning to be introduced to the pupils."

"That was fast," Jason said, his brows shooting up.

Aleksandra smiled, then looked down at her lap.

"So when are you leaving?" Billy asked.

"We," Xavier squeezed Aleksandra's hand beneath the table, "will be leaving as soon as we can pack up. Probably the day after tomorrow, if the new teacher's ready."

Silence filled the room.

Billy finally broke it. "Can we come visit you in the goldfields?"

"You sure can, but you'll have to come all the way to California," Xavier said. "It's near a town called Nevada and they do hydraulic mining." He glanced at Aleksandra. She was biting her lip, her fingers clenched on the table.

"We'll miss you too, Aleks," Dorothea murmured.

Aleksandra took a deep breath and looked around the table. "It's been wonderful being in a family again. I've missed mine." Her voice trailed off, and her eyes glistened.

"We've lost more than one child," Dorothea said, her voice soft, as she stood and went to Aleksandra. She kneeled beside her and wrapped her arms around her, rocking her slowly.

Xavier's guts tightened and he struggled for the right words. The rush of warmth for Jeremy's and Jason's family threatened to overwhelm him and he gripped Aleksandra's hand tightly.

"I…thank you all," Xavier looked from Billy to Jason, then from Jeremy and Dorothea to their children, one at a time, "for welcoming us into your homes and hearts and giving us, for a time, the family neither of us have had for a long, long time."

Dorothea unwrapped an arm from about Aleksandra and reached one hand to him.

"You've both added to our lives, and to the lives of so many in this town," Jason said.

One of the children was fairly dancing in her seat, looking expectantly at her mother.

"Yes, Gemma, you may get it now," she said, with a smile. "We were going to wait until after dinner, but now seems a good time."

Aleksandra glanced up at her, brow furrowed. A lone tear ran down her cheek at the gaily decorated packages the girls held, and the bigger wooden escritoire Billy handed to Xavier.

The girls went straight to Aleksandra and pushed one of the presents into her hands. She pulled the ribbon holding the muslin into place and it unfolded to reveal a crystal inkwell. The other gift was a packet of nibs and a pen, rolled in tissue-thin writing paper. Aleksandra beamed. "Until I became a teacher," she said slowly, "I'd never even had my own nibs, and now we have a whole pack of them." She hugged the girls and smiled her thanks to the rest of them, then looked at Xavier.

He turned the dovetailed writing desk between his hands and smoothed his hands over its satin surface. "Where did you get a thing of such beauty?"

"We made it ourselves," Billy whispered over his shoulder, "Papa and I— from pieces of the saloon paneling. Do you like it?"

"I've never seen such fine work. Is this truly for us?"

"Oh yes, it's a special thank-you," he looked back at his father, who nodded. "You helped us both to believe again—to believe life is to be lived. Right, Papa?"

Jason nodded and sniffed a little.

"It's not like we'll never see you all again," Aleksandra gave them a warm smile, through her tears. "We'll make our fortune, or so Xavier says, then we'll be for San Francisco. I'm sure you'll need to go out West someday."

"Hence the escritoire and writing implements," Jeremy said, with twist of his lips. "We figured it'll be a while, so we'd all best write."

"I guess so." Aleksandra leaned back against Xavier. "We'll write, we promise."

32

Once the decision was made, things happened quickly. Before she knew it, their saddlebags and bedrolls were packed and they were ready to leave. Leaving their new friends, however, was the most difficult of all.

"I've never had friends my own age, except for Dancing Wolf," Aleksandra said to Molly, with tears in her eyes. "You've become so special to me."

"You to me, as well, Aleks." Molly wrapped her arms around her. "I'll begin organizing my life to go to California next year, so don't you go changing your mind on me," she said.

"I promise, Molly."

"And no more tears."

"No more." She turned to Billy and he flung himself at her and wrapped his arms about her waist, tears streaming from his eyes. "You won't forget about us, will you?" he whispered.

"Of course not, my love. We'll see each other again, but until then, we can write, can't we?"

He nodded and Aleksandra was passed to his father, who hugged her and handed her to his wife-to-be, thence to his brother. By the time they'd made the rounds, she was crying, too, and Xavier had to take her hand and lead her over to Dzień.

They mounted up amidst a clamor of goodbyes and headed out, Dzień's head turned to stare behind him with his worried look.

"It's OK, laddie," Aleksandra said, through her tears, "We'll see them all again, someday."

Xavier took her hand again, and they rode on, together.

"You know," she looked up at Xavier, "People really aren't so bad after all. I think I'm starting to learn to trust."

"Aren't we both?" He smiled and reached down to kiss her and the crowd behind them cheered.

ALEKSANDRA'S HEART clenched as she stared down the grade ahead of them, thinking of the last time she'd trotted down the wagon track out of the hills from Gold Hill to Chinatown, of her loss, and of her terror that she'd never see Xavier alive again.

"We owe Ephraim a lot." She looked across at Xavier.

"Don't I know it, and I'll always be grateful he saved your life."

She snorted. "What about yours?"

"Well, yes, but you're more important to me," he smiled and gripped her hand tightly.

She shook her head, glanced down at Dzień's head nodding before her, and scratched his withers. He flexed his neck from side to side as she scratched.

As they cleared the hills, Chinatown came into view. A few of the pigtailed men hanging laundry on lines between their tiny shanties glanced up as they passed, and returned Aleksandra and Xavier's waves.

An hour later, the buildings of Carson City came into view.

"Do we need anything from town?" Aleksandra asked.

"No, but we can go see the stores if you wish."

"I'd rather go around, if you don't mind." She shuddered. "Carson's bigger than Virginia City, isn't it?"

"It is." Xavier said, and nodded at a trail heading off the main tracks. "We can go that way."

Later that day, riding north from Carson, she stared at the mountains blocking out the afternoon sun—mountains upon formidable mountains. "How far is it to the other side?"

"Of the Sierra Nevada? About a hundred and fifty miles."

"It can't all be mountains like that?"

"Nope," shortly.

"That's a blessing." She let her breath out slowly and turned to see Xavier grinning. "What?"

"Nope, they're not like that—they're higher than these, steeper, and rockier."

"You can't be serious. They cannot be rockier."

He raised his brows at her and quirked his mouth.

She said nothing for a long while.

"Xavier," she frowned, "remember we spoke of Samuel Clemens the other night?"

He nodded.

"Well, I'm wondering about a little adventure here...should we go all the way up to Lake's Crossing and then cut west on the Truckee Trail, or should we," she cocked a brow at him, "try the shortcut Samuel found past Lake Bigler and aim to end up at *Welganuk*?"

Xavier stared at her. "*Welganuk?*"

"Truckee Meadows, in the *Washo* language."

"Oh. We don't need to go near Lake Bigler. About Clemens, he only said he *made it* to Lake Bigler. He didn't say he went on from there. *If* we could get to the lake—and that's a big if—and *if* it were possible to go far enough around the lake, we could eventually get to the Truckee River, which *if* we were able to follow it, would bring us up to Truckee."

"Do you know where his trail splits off this one?"

"Somewhere just near here," he said, peering up at the heights.

"Where?" Aleksandra stared. A few ravines led up into the steep mountains, but nothing resembled a pass.

"There it is." Xavier pointed to their left. "Just there."

"But it doesn't go anywhere. It just runs up into that steep sidling."

"It does. Did you hear the rest of Clement's story?"

Aleksandra winced. "No."

"Well," he gave her a wry grin, "he said he climbed over two of those big ridges before he even got a glimpse of the lake."

"Oh."

"And he was on foot, able to climb rocks, not slither over them with horses."

"The Truckee Trail sounds better every minute." She looked at him sideways.

"Oh, and about Lake Bigler, Jeremy said the government is looking at changing its name from Bigler to something else."

"Why?"

"Bigler was California's Governor five or six years ago—but he's a raving secessionist. The Unionists don't want anything named after dis-Unionists."

"Sounds reasonable. What are they changing it to?"

"Not sure yet. It's already known by several other names, anyway. One map I looked over last week called it Mountain Lake, and another, Maheon Lake."

"It'd be nice to let it keep its *Washo* language name, *Da ow agato*." She glanced up at Xavier and gulped. "I wonder if we'll see Dancing Wolf again."

"I'm sure we will. He has a way of turning up when you get yourself into real trouble," Xavier's brown eyes danced as he caught her hand, "which happens too often for my liking. He grew up keeping track of you—the Sierra Nevada should pose no difficulty after that."

She tried for a scowl, but ended laughing with him. "All right, the Truckee Trail is it," she said, turning her face northward toward Lake's Crossing.

"Have you been this far west, Aleks?" Xavier said.

"This is the furthest I've ever been from home." Aleksandra's chest tightened at the thought.

"It's not very remarkable down here," he said, looking around him, "but you'll love it as we gain some elevation."

"I wish I had your confidence. The stories I've heard aren't encouraging."

"From people who crossed the Sierra Nevada with wagons?"

She nodded.

"It's a rough trail, but riding a good horse," he rubbed Charro's neck absently, "it's a lovely ride...as long as it's not winter, or the middle of the afternoon in summer."

"Should we break up our days around the afternoon heat?"

"That's what I usually do, if I'm not racing back to save you, ride from six to eleven—"

"—and take a *siesta*? The horses can feed until it cools off?" she interrupted.

"Yes, and ride until nine. Leaves us enough time before dark to make camp. That should get us there in about three days."

Dzień threw up his head and sniffed the air, ears pricked, then quickened his pace.

"Willows," Xavier said.

Aleksandra looked up and squinted into the distance. The band of pale green trees stood out in bold relief between the brown, round-topped mountains behind and the sagebrush-dotted sand flats at their feet.

"A river?"

"No, it's Washoe Lake. Probably dry at this time of year."

"It's pretty big."

"It's mostly dried, cracked up mud, but it's still lined by willows."

"Dzień's favorite." She grinned.

Rogan, loose, set off at a trot and she whistled him back. "I'd best ride him. Who knows what trouble he'll find." She slid from Dzień's back and nodded at him. "He'll stay close, even if he's not tied."

"Dzień doesn't seem to mind packing the gear," Xavier said, as Rogan nuzzled his foot in its stirrup.

"No, but the big horses are carrying nearly a much as he is now, plus us," she said, as she untied the bedroll from the seat of Rogan's saddle and secured it across Dzień's.

"*Pemmican?*" Aleksandra reached up to hand him a portion, then took one for herself and slung the bag onto Rogan's saddle horn. She swung up and drank from her canteen as they led off. Dzień alternately nosed the ground for wisps of grass and trotted to catch up. The pony fended for himself well.

Xavier glanced from her to Dzień and smiled.

"What?"

"You might be able to start doing *dzhigitovka* again."

She cocked a brow at him. "Now, that's a thought. I could teach riding, if there are any children about. Molly said both Nevada and Grass Valley are fair-sized towns with families."

"We'll be up at North Bloomfield. It's about fifteen miles from Nevada and twenty miles from the Empire Mine, just out of Grass Valley, so that could work," his face darkened, "but then again, I wouldn't want you riding alone between the mining camps—it's just not worth it."

She gritted her teeth for a moment, then took a deep breath and willed her body to relax. "I could teach school, I suppose."

"We'll see how the land lies when we get there. Shall we have a bit of speed?"

"Need you ask?" she flicked back over her shoulder as the colt struck up a three-beat gait.

Dzień snorted and bolted past them.

"Watch for holes, pony," she called out to the Mustang, as they broke into a gallop and the powerful bay's haunches drove them past the diminuitive Dzień. A short time later, spare energy spent, the horses dropped down into a trot again, flecks of foam flying from their mouths as they champed their bits.

"You said we'd stop at Lake's crossing," Aleksandra puffed a bit, "is it at a lake?"

"No," he looked around for a moment. 'Lake' is for Mr. Lake. He's built up the settlement around his ferry crossing, hence its name. Last time I was through here, he'd already built a livery stable, kiln and a grist mill. The community's growing up around it, servicing the emigrants. It's the last stopping-off point before the Sierra Nevada on the California Trail. We should be there in three hours."

Aleksandra digested this and nodded as she looked around. "Not much grass. Should we let them have a browse on the willow and cut some to take along?"

"Good idea." He laughed as Dzień trotted away from them toward the stand lining the dry lake and ripped into the new green leaves. "He approves, anyway."

"SAFELY DELIVERED," Xavier said, dismounting before Lake's livery stable just on three hours later.

"Busy place," Aleksandra looked at him from the corners of her eyes. Wagons and horses filled every available space along the main road through the new town.

Xavier led Charro and Dzień into the barn and she followed.

"I have room for your two stallions back here." The ostler clumped, bowlegged, toward two hefty-looking stalls at the back of the barn. "You can store your gear in my office." At a nod from the ostler, Aleksandra put Dzień into the stall beside Rogan's.

The horses didn't turn their heads from their new hayracks when they left them. Aleksandra and Xavier humped their loaded saddles and bags back to the front of the barn.

"How long will they be staying?" the wife of the ostler said, pencil poised over a ledger.

"We'll be leaving at four p.m., thanks," Xavier replied.

"Oh," she blinked, "that'll still be a full day's board, anyway."

They only smiled at her flustered face.

Aleksandra stuck close to Xavier as they walked down the street. She'd gotten used to Virginia City, but the proximity of so many strangers still made her stomach turn.

"Last time in civilization." He raised a brow at her. "Shall we get a room at Lake's Hotel?"

"Oh, let's." She was far from tired, but it might be a while before they slept in a bed again. At his look, her insides tightened and her face warmed. She squirmed a little as he took her hand, and the bag she carried.

"Maybe even a bath?" He raised a brow at her.

She nodded, and her face grew hotter. "I brought clean clothes, anyway," she said.

Half an hour later, the metal hip bath beside them was nearly full of hot water. She slowly unbuttoned his shirt, letting her fingers trail down his chest. Xavier's glossy, black curls sprang back after her touch. He shivered, although the room was anything but cold. His nipples tightened, standing erect as she encircled them with light fingertips, then touched their tips with her tongue, one after the other, as he groaned and gripped her shoulders.

He reached for the hem of her buckskin shirt and pulled it up over her head. "You've far too much clothing on, Mrs. Argüello." He slipped the knot in the drawstring of her buckskin pants and they slid to the ground. Lifting her medicine bag from about her neck, he laid it with care onto the table beside the bed. His arms came about her and held her close against his hardness for a moment before he lowered her into the steaming water.

By the time he'd soaped and rinsed her, they were both panting. She somehow got him clean and they made it to the bed before they ended up tangling on the floor. The tub wasn't big enough to take them both—even though most of the water had sopped over the low rim onto the floor.

"I love making love with you," Aleksandra said, some hour later, her eyelids heavy as she ran fingertips over Xavier's chest, the sweat still glistening on its broad expanse.

"And I, you," he whispered, capturing her hand and kissing it, then turned her and pulled her backside against his front. "I'm so glad we're back to this, nothing between us."

"Yes. If we're blessed again, so be it." She swallowed hard. The fear was still there, but she knew she could survive it now, with Xavier beside her, whatever happened.

They slept.

"WE'RE REALLY OFF," she said, watching the last of Lake's Crossing disappear as they followed the Truckee River west. "How far is it to Truckee Meadows?"

"This is part of it," Xavier said.

"Meadow? Looks just like desert."

"It greens up as we climb into the mountains."

Within an hour, the desert scrub gave way to a wide, grassy valley with meadows on both sides of the river. As they climbed higher, the banks of the Truckee River steepened to sheer cliffs, first on one side and then on the other, requiring wagons on the trail to cross and re-cross the rough water multiple times over the next twelve miles.

They stopped on a grassy knoll beside one of the crossings to let the horses graze and watched the already-exhausted emigrants lower wagons with ropes over a six-foot drop into the river and pull them up the other bank with tripled-oxen teams.

"Sure glad we're riding," Aleksandra said, handing *pemmican* to Xavier.

He nodded. "You'll be even happier about that when you see the rest of the trail."

As the shadows lengthened, the green swales gave way to gray-brown granite cliffs, large rock falls and the smallest bits of grass beside the tumbling Truckee. Pines grew in crevices and higher up the mountainsides. Most of the easily accessed trees were already stumps, likely cut for fires or building over the past few decades.

"You know," she said, as they snuggled beneath their *serapes* inside the bedroll, "I could travel on and on with you like this, and never stop."

He rolled over on top of her. "*Sí, Querida,*" he murmured, taking her lips with his. "Never, ever stop, because I won't."

She looked past his face, ghostly in the moonlight, and vowed to the stars.

"Never, ever stop."

33

Morning brought mists over the river, as the water tumbled down its rocky bed.

"Swim, Xavier?" Her eyes twinkled.

He winced. "That's snowmelt."

"Oh, but it's melted. Come on, I'm dusty."

"*De veras*, but how nice the dust," he said, snuggling his face between her breasts as she half-lay, half-sat beside him.

She jumped up. "Wagon train's coming soon, and you wouldn't want them to catch me swimming, would you?"

"Aleks," he glanced all around them and got to his feet. "You don't know who's around."

"Oh, I do...you!"

"*Ai...*" he grumbled, shaking his head. "*Sí, sí, vamos.* Let's go."

She danced down the narrow path before him to the deep spot where they'd fished the previous night.

"You'll scare the fish," he murmured.

"I didn't last night, did I?"

"Well, no."

"Then come on," she said, ripping off her nightshirt as she ran. She dropped the shirt and her bath linen, and dived in. He shook his head as she came up spluttering and laughed, her teeth chattering. "It's fine, a little chilly," she said, with a smirk.

His testicles tightened at the thought and his waking erection melted. Seeing no way out, he dived in beside her. Circling back, he dragged her under with him, then let her go, so they could both scramble out. There was no ice on the surface, but it was a near thing. "Aleks?"

She paused from rubbing her pinkened skin with her bath linen to peer up at him.

"I'm sorry we lost the baby, but I'm so glad you've found pleasure in life and me again," he said, clasping her hard against him.

"I'll never let it go again, Xavier. I promise."

"I'm so happy to hear you say that," he said, and tilted her chin up to place his lips softly on hers. "Now let's hit the road before we end up back in bed."

The sides of the banks grew steeper and the river rocks gave way to huge granite boulders. Their surfaces glinted with shimmering white flecks in the sunshine as the trail continued to crisscross the riverbed. The trail climbed higher, and when Xavier dismounted and walked to spell his horse, his breath came shorter.

"Oh," Aleksandra said, her eyes wide, at the meadows opening up before them.

The grass beside the wagon trail was hard-grazed by the stock of countless wagon trains, but further away, the grass grew lush.

"Neither of mine have ever seen grass like that," Aleksandra said.

"Charro hasn't for some time. We'd best limit their time on it, or they'll founder for sure."

They grazed the horses for half an hour, then went on.

"I SEE what you mean about the sheer rock faces," Aleksandra said, looking down beneath Rogan's feet. The boulder-studded dirt farther down the mountain had given way to mounds and slopes of solid granite. The horses could gain little purchase on the slippery trail, and their iron shoes skidded on the steeper surfaces. Rogan slipped and nearly fell near the edge of a sheer drop to the river, and she glanced back at Xavier. They stopped and listened as a loosened rock bounced again and again down the bank and splashed in the river below.

He winced. "I forgot to put borium on their shoes before we left. Good time to remember." He closed his eyes and sighed.

"Can't be helped now. We'll just have to be careful where we walk." She looked over the edge. Just ahead, a lake appeared, stretching as far to the west as the eye could see.

"Donner Lake," Xavier said.

"Where the Donner party was trapped." Aleksandra shivered, and couldn't help scanning the sky for storm clouds.

"Wrong time of year, *Querida*." He smiled at her, albeit grimly. "The leaders of their wagon train listened to Hastings about his new trail, made some bad choices, and nearly didn't even make it across the Utah deserts. They reached the *Sierras* too late in the year, with exhausted stock and depleted food stores, took a risk and were caught here in that snowstorm."

"The snow came early, didn't it?"

Xavier winced. "In October."

"Papa said there were twenty-two feet of snow?" Aleksandra shuddered. "That's as high as that cluster of pinecones."

He nodded. "After they ran out of food and began dying of malnutrition and starvation, they began looking sideways at each other—" he hesitated.

"—and eating their dead," she added softly.

"So you've heard the whole story?"

She made a face. "Yes."

"Hard to imagine it, on a day like today."

Sunlight filtered down through the spring-greening pines. Squawking jays hopped from limb to limb and squirrels chased each other as they romped thorough the branches.

Aleksandra took a deep breath and gazed about her. "Dancing Wolf told me there are old drawings up on the rocks above the lake."

"Drawings?"

"Well, carvings. Covering the flat rocks up on top of the mountains just south of the lake. Very old." She looked up the mountain to the south. "The trail goes up to the summit there, he said"

"Oh," Xavier said, "That's where our trail goes. I've not heard of them, but surely we could find them."

Charro was the first to prick his ears as they rounded the next corner. Before them was the tail of a wagon train. There was room to pass the slow-moving wagons, pulled by gaunt, glassy-eyed oxen. Several of the wagons were pulled by teams of four, rather than six, oxen.

"We lost two back in the desert," the woman handling the reins answered, in reply to Aleksandra's question, "and my man's been sick since he drank some of the same alkali water the oxen did."

Aleksandra murmured something suitable about condolences and they hurried past.

THEY WERE HALFWAY past the train, when the long line of wagons stopped. Xavier pointed forward.

"Here's trouble."

Aleksandra's head snapped up and she stared toward the front of the train to see the leaders standing before a sheer cliff, which rose almost straight up in front of them.

As they watched, several oxen scrambled up the steep rocky face, driven upward by shouts and whips until they reached a level spot. The men already at the top threw down the ends of the ropes they'd used to help the beasts up and the men at the bottom of the cliff tied them beneath the bed of a dismembered Conestoga wagon. The oxen at the top were then hitched to the ropes and strained at their yokes to drag the wagon bed upwards until it reached the top as well. The undercarriage, with its wheels, followed next.

"I wonder how much they've left behind on the trail so far?" Aleksandra said, beneath her breath, as they passed the last of the intact wagons. The pioneers' piles of household goods littered the area below the cliff.

"There must be a trail around this mess." Xavier scanned the rocks above them, as their own horses scrambled up the bank beside the string of wagons.

"Up there, Xavier." Aleksandra nodded ahead to their left.

Sure enough, there was a trail. Though narrow, it was a good one, and disappeared behind one of the massive boulders comprising the cliff up which the wagons were being dragged. Rogan and Charro scrambled up the narrow defile, with Dzień bounding up behind them, and eventually gained the top of the cliff.

"That pass the wagon train took is Summit Canyon, which goes over Donner Pass." He shook his head. "I don't know why they came this way. It's the hardest traverse of Donner Summit for wagons, out the three common trails." Xavier said. "Roller Pass has been used for about fifteen years and it's only a few miles south."

"Can you drive a wagon up any of the trails?"

"You can drive most of the way up Roller Pass, but it's incredibly steep. They can only ascend the final climb by pulling the wagons up with long ropes or chains from the wagons on one side to the oxen on the other, just below the summit. They pass the ropes over rolling logs at the top."

"That would take some time to rig up." Aleksandra quirked her lips.

He nodded. "Coldstream Pass, between here and Roller, is a better choice. It's much less steep than the others," he pointed to the southeast at a cleft in the range, "and it's between Donner Peak and that next mountain south, Mt. Judah. On a horse, this way is fine, and it's the shortest."

"How far will we go today?"

"We should make Yuba Gap before it gets dark, which should get us to the Malakoff by the next evening." He nodded up the trail. "The summit of the pass is just ahead."

"The stone carvings are meant to be down on some flat rocks just north of the main trail," Aleksandra said.

They rode in silence for a few minutes, the horses' hoofbeats on rock the only sound. The scent of pines wafted on the occasional puffs of breeze. "That sun still holds some heat, even at this altitude," he said. The air shimmered over the rocks as they rode out of the shady side of the boulders into the full glare of the afternoon.

"And this," he said, dropping his reins on Charro's neck and spreading his arms wide, "is the summit."

Aleksandra stared at the range upon range of mountains, stretching away to the west as far as the eye could see. Donner's azure depths glittered far below them.

"Donner Lake again."

"It's beautiful, but it looks different from here. *Datsa' shut.*" She nodded her head at it and closed her eyes for a moment.

"Pardon?"

"*Datsa' shut.* The Washo name for Donner Lake." She looked all around her. "I've never seen this much green and blue in my life." Her brow wrinkled. "But where do the mountains end? Where is the sea?"

Xavier laughed softly. "The ocean's a long way from here, *Querida*, but we're at the top now, so it's mostly downhill from here."

"I thought the ocean was just on the other side of the Sierras," she said, staring west.

He gazed out across the ranges. A few mountains opposite them still showed unmelted snow on their peaks. "The ocean's still a long way away, but there's nothing like the Sierras between the base of these mountains at Sacramento and the *rancho*, I promise you."

She smiled over her shoulder and reached out to rub Dzień's withers as he stood beside Rogan. "I'm sure the horses will be happy to be done traveling."

"Except for Rogan," he said. "He seems to love the excitement of new places."

"I think he just likes finding new mares. I don't think he cares about much else."

"Can't blame him for that." He laughed.

She raised both brows at him. "You want many women?"

He stared at her. "Oh, I don't, but just the part about being keen for females—"

"—I'd stop while I was ahead, if I were you," she interrupted. "The hole's getting deeper."

Xavier's face heated and he kneed Charro forward. Gripping Aleksandra about the waist, he kissed her. "Only you, *Querida*, only you."

"That's more like it," she laughed, with a satisfied smile on her face, "much more like it." She looked around her. "Oh," she said, pointing a way back down the hill. "Look at those big flat stones down there." The smooth, nearly level granite bench to the right of the trail sloped gently away from the summit trail toward the north. "I'm sure that's the place." She slid from Rogan's back and scurried back down the way they'd come, then off the trail, pulling the horse behind her. "This is it," she called over her shoulder, then dropped to her knees beside the first etchings. Her fingers traced the figures as she stared, mesmerized.

Xavier dismounted and crouched beside her.

"Look at them all," she whispered, "there must be dozens."

"I'd double that," he said, as he walked around them, careful not to step on the figures etched into the solid stone. Circles nested within circles, simple circles attached to lines of all descriptions, complex combinations of wavy lines, figures that looked like people or animals. "I wonder how long they've been there, and how they were made."

"Dancing Wolf said they used a—, a hammerstone, I think it was. The figures were made by the *Washoe* Indians, or a tribe that came before them. They'd stop here on their yearly travels from the Western Sierra Nevada, over the top to *Da ow agato*, which we call Lake Bigler, and on east to the Great Basin."

"All that was their territory?"

"Yes."

"Do you know what the symbols mean?" he asked.

"Some of them." She turned her face to him, brows together. "I think these are tracks: deer and bear, stick figures of people and another four-legged animal. There aren't many of these, though. These others, like these squiggles, might be snakes, or these multiple ones," she moved to another slab, "water...but the rest of these," she shook her head as she moved between rocks and examined the oddly symmetric concentric circles joined together with straight lines, "are unfamiliar. They could be symbols of another tribe, but most of them use roughly similar figures."

"Perhaps they're very old?"

"Probably. Do I have time for a quick sketch? Dancing Wolf would love to see them," she gulped, "if we ever—"

"—yes, meet again," Xavier cut in. "Go, get your sketches done."

His guts wrenched, but he reached out to squeeze her shoulder anyway. "He still means a lot to you, doesn't he?" he said, and tried to unclench his jaws.

"I love him as a brother, Xavier, and I probably always will," she said, her voice soft. "I thought you understood that."

"I do, Aleks." He sighed. "I'm getting better."

"It's you that I married," she smiled up at him briefly, "but I worry about him and his family in the wars, and with the settlers taking over. Their way of life is being destroyed. I wish there were something I could do."

"There isn't. The government is determined to open up this land for settlers. If the Southerners have their way, it will be for intensive slave-agriculture. Either way, the Indians will be pushed up north, out of the way —rounded up and killed, pushed up or folded into what the American government wants them to be—devoid of their culture, their livelihoods, their languages. I fear for him, too, Aleks, and all of his people."

By the time he finished speaking, Aleksandra had unpacked the escritoire from Dzień's pack saddle. She got comfortable, sitting cross-legged next to the ancient markings, and dipped a nib into the ink. With swift decision, she sketched several of the figures on one sheet of paper.

"You're quick, have you drawn a lot?"

"On my own, mostly horses, but Dancing Wolf taught me the figures used by his tribe." She sketched a few more figures across the bottom of the page. "This signifies a horse, this one's the sun, and a river, and a bear. This one's a dog, and this one, maize, or corn."

"Those are quite different from the carvings. He taught you well." Xavier squelched the thought that the Indian might have taught her other things, but still, he wondered.

She flicked him a glance. "If you keep gritting your teeth, they'll wear out. What do you want to know?" Aleksandra regarded him with narrowed eyes and half-stood, then sat back on her heels, waiting.

34

"It doesn't matter," Xavier said.

"If it didn't, it wouldn't upset you so. Out with it," Aleksandra said.

He was silent for long moments. "Well, did you...were you..."

"Intimate?"

He could barely look her in the eyes. "Yes."

"One kiss, Xavier. One kiss. And that was after his father just told me Dancing Wolf had asked for my hand in marriage, and then told me I couldn't stay with their tribe because of the danger to me. It was a pretty rotten day all around. A bit rough to find out what he'd wanted for so long was never to be, and that we might never see each other again."

"And what about you?" He wiped his sweaty palms on his trousers. God help him, but he couldn't stop. "What were your feelings for him?"

"As I've told you before, I always thought of him as a brother. I thought we'd shared all our hopes and dreams. It seems we had, other than the little detail that he wanted me for his wife." She twisted her lips and looked like she was about to cry, and bit her lip. "We were so close, I'd never even considered it. There were no other families with children of our age around, outside his tribe. It was such a bittersweet goodbye, a chaste kiss seemed the rightest and purest thing in the world." She finished on a whisper, and a single tear traced its way down her face.

Xavier reached for her and held her. "I can understand how he might have felt," he murmured in her ear. "I'd have done the same."

"I'm never leaving you, Xavier. You've got to believe me. I meant every word of my vows."

"I know, and so did I."

"So can you bury this hatchet, so we can go forward?"

"Yes," he sighed, "it's done." He sat for a minute, still. "Anyway, you seem to find enough trouble that he'll probably always be able to see you again."

"I guess I'll be too far away for him to save me anymore. You'll have to rescue me on your own."

"Perhaps you could try to stay out of trouble, so no one would have to."

"I do try, really," she said, then dropped her head at Xavier's look. "Truly." She raised a brow at him.

He could only laugh and hug her tight.

When he released her, she sat back down to finish her drawings. He was lulled by the chirping birds, the rhythmic munching of horses eating their grain and the soporific warm granite. Aleks' nib scratched at the paper, with an occasional 'tink' of the metal tapping the inkwell as she drew. He closed his eyes.

Hoofbeats rang out on stone. Xavier's eyes shot open to see the horses spin to face the sound, and he jumped to his feet. Aleksandra was already heading for Rogan and he stepped quickly to Charro's side to release the strap securing his rifle. A moment later, a mounted party of three men came into sight.

"Hello," called out one of the approaching men, in what sounded like a Cornish accent.

"Dressed as gentlemen, but they could still be highwaymen," Aleksandra whispered, as she slid her *shashka* from its scabbard.

He nodded.

"Heading for the mines?" the same man said, as the group approached them.

"Yes, and you?" Xavier answered, talking over the horse's back, holding the rifle low on his side of the horse.

"We're on our way back to the Empire." He stopped his horse a half dozen feet away and nodded to them both. The other men stopped by his side. Their horses shone and their fine quality tack was in pristine condition. The newcomer looked around at the view. "Always love this spot. The lake, the mountains." He took a deep breath and closed his eyes. "So much nicer than the mines, don't you think?"

Xavier lifted a brow at that.

"We're about to stop for a bite to eat. Mind if we join you?"

"As long as you're not highwaymen," Aleksandra said dryly.

"Nope, never that. I'm John Carpenter. Manage the assay office at the

Empire. These men are Richard Curnow and Nick Spanger, some of the mine foremen," he said, as the men stepped down from their horses.

Xavier lowered his rifle and walked forward, as he introduced them both. Aleksandra slid her *shashka* back home and walked forward, letting her braid fall down from under her hat.

The men blinked and grinned. "Ma'am," said one of the two others and all three nodded at her.

"We're heading for North Bloomfield," Xavier said.

"Ah, the illustrious Malakoff Diggins," Mr. Carpenter's replied.

"I believe they need someone in their assay office," Xavier said.

Carpenter had been perusing Rogan, but at that, his eyes flicked back to Xavier. "Assay office, did you say? Are you experienced?"

"I've been mining, a bit here and a bit there." He cracked a smile. "I used to work underground in the Empire. We just left the Ophir in Virginia City."

"What did you do there?"

"Managed the assay office." He couldn't help grinning.

"And did you leave under good circumstances?"

"Left with the mine manager's friendship, blessings and a reference. My wife and I wished to travel further west and eventually, to return to my family's holdings in California," Xavier said.

Carpenter looked from one of his companions to the other, the grin on his face widening. "See, gentlemen? Didn't I tell you the good Lord will provide?" He turned back to Xavier. "Didn't you consider going back to the Empire?"

"I didn't want to go back underground, and I heard about the assay office job at Malakoff."

"You haven't asked him yet, have you?" Curnow gave him a crooked smile and Carpenter turned back to Xavier.

"So did you say you've taken a job or just been invited to view one?"

"It's not certain, if that's what you mean, sir."

He chuckled. "Well, in that case, please consider a visit to the Empire Mine prior to accepting a position at the other one."

"Didn't you say you were the assay manager?"

"Yes, but I need to go back to San Francisco. Seems my wife isn't as keen as yours to spend time in, as she calls it, 'the backwater of Nevada County'."

Xavier nodded to him as a smile broke out on his face and he looked over his shoulder to see Aleksandra grin. "So we make a detour, do we?"

"Let's say it would behoove you. I'm sure your lovely wife would prefer the sophistication of Grass Valley over what you'll find in North Bloomfield."

"Aye, but most importantly," Mr. Spangler said, "there aren't any pasty shops up there, but we have many in Grass Valley."

"Pasty?" Aleksandra's brows drew together.

"Ahhh…as good as me old mum used to make in Cornwall," he said with a wistful look.

"You've come all the way from Cornwall?" she said.

Mr. Curnow laughed. "Most of the Nevada County mines are full of Cornishmen, and women," he said as an aside to Aleksandra. "Just the other day, the Grass Valley Union, our newspaper, said the town could be called the 'Cornwall of California.'"

"Seems we're in demand," Mr. Spangler said, with a cheeky smile. "Placer mining isn't much good after the above-ground gold is gone, but there's plenty underground. That's where we Cornishmen come into our own. We're the best hard rock miners around."

"Oh, are you, now?" Aleksandra couldn't help mimicking his accent.

He laughed. "Seriously, it's true." He looked to the other two miners. "Isn't that true?"

"Truth," said Mr. Carpenter. "Unfortunately, the boasting of the Cornishmen doesn't endear them to the rest of the miners."

"I'd imagine," Xavier said.

"Ten of us from Cornwall came over on the Cultivator about four years ago, and a good trip that was," Mr. Spanger said, his eyes lighting up. "Some of the boys went to Lake Superior, not sure what they're going to do there, but the rest of us came out here."

"You'll find the majority of miners in the Grass Valley, Washington and Nevada area mines are Cornish. And thankfully, many brought their families, so we have pasties. Keeps the mutinies down," Carpenter said with a laugh.

"My Jane, though, she makes the best in town, and keeps all our babies fat on them!" Curnow said, as he unwrapped a lightly browned pasty "Mmmm, good."

"Have you never had one, Aleks?" Xavier asked her.

She shook her head.

"Oh, you'll have to try some," Curnow said as he broke off a hunk and handed it to her. "This will make them come to the Empire, if nothing else, Carpenter."

All eyes turned to Aleksandra.

She chewed slowly, barely noticing Dzień sidling up to her. His muzzle was nearly to the pie remaining in her hand when she noticed. "Dzień, you scoundrel," she said, and handed him a bit of the crust. He turned up his lip at it.

"She brushes the crust with meat broth. He won't like that," Curnow said.

"Thank you, Mr. Curnow," Aleksandra nodded in his direction. "Xavier, we must go immediately to Grass Valley. This is the fare to which I wish to become accustomed." Her grin nearly split her face in two.

After their dinner, the three men took their leave. "We need to get back, but we hope to see you later today? I'm sure Mr. Rowe will put you up. Come by the assay office when you arrive," Mr. Carpenter said.

"It'll be good to see him again. We'll see you this evening, then. Thank you for your kind offer," Xavier said, as they men waved goodbye.

Aleksandra hugged Xavier when the others were gone.

"Things are looking up," he said. It was wonderful to see her smile. The haunted look still returned from time to time, but not so often, and it was going away sooner, when it did appear. His girl was coming back.

He helped her replace the escritoire back into Dzień's pack saddle. She gave the Mustang a good rub between the ears and then they were on their way again.

THE SMOOTH GRANITE boulders might have been slick on their ascent, but they were treacherous on the steep downhill trail. Aleksandra and Xavier tried to keep to the dirt beside the massive rocks, but in some places there was no way around, and only granite met their eyes.

"We were going to go north on the Nevada Road where it splits off in Bear Valley to get to the Malakoff, but since we're going straight to the Empire, we'll stay on the Truckee Trail 'till we get to Grass Valley," Xavier said.

"How far will we be from North Bloomfield?"

"It's only a half-day's ride from the Empire, but it's straight up, and the horses will be tired from the steep ride the day before. We'll have time to pick up supplies in Nevada or Grass Valley on the way, and still get to North Bloomfield by mid afternoon. We've plenty of time."

She tried to smile and he shook his head. "They're not big towns, really. They're…mining towns that've grown up."

"Like Virginia City?"

"Well," he hesitated," let's just say they've had time to mature. About the same population, but these towns have been around for longer and become more established, and civilized."

"You're digging that hole deeper, again." She looked at him from the corners of her eyes, and gulped as Rogan slipped again, then recovered his balance.

"OK, OK." Xavier grinned. "It's not forever, anyway. We'll build up some capital and head for the *rancho*."

Aleksandra lifted her chin and managed a smile.

"You survived Virginia City, didn't you?"

She sighed and smiled at him. "Yes."

"And you can do it again."

She held her breath and tried to stay balanced as Rogan's hooves slid on a patch of rock concealed by only a thin layer of dirt and gravel. He scrambled to keep his feet and lost, then they were falling, falling...

I've lost my reins.

Her face smacked into gritty hardness and motion ceased. She took a deep breath, and opened her eyes.

Rogan?

"*Gracias a Dios,*" Xavier muttered, "*Está bien, Querida?* Are you OK, Aleks?"

"I think so," she said. Her own voice seemed far away. She struggled to sit up, and her world spun.

"Lie still, *Querida.*" Xavier's voice echoed through a dim fog.

She lay back on the hard boulder. "Yes," she breathed. "Rogan?" the word came out a strangled cry.

"He slipped and rolled, thank Christ you weren't beneath him."

"Is he OK?" she nearly screamed.

"He's up. Shaking, but standing on all four... oh..."

"What?" Aleksandra struggled toward a sitting position, looking around wildly.

"Lie *down.*" Xavier gently pressed her back down. "I'll go check on him, if you'll lie still. He's got all four legs on the ground, but he's cut his leg."

"Oh no, all my fault, I shouldn't have—"

"Stop. You couldn't have known he'd slip. You stay there and I'll look after him."

"OK." Closing her eyes was bliss, and by the time she opened them again, the heavens had finally stopped spinning. Irregular hoofbeats approached and she turned her head to see Rogan coming toward her. "How bad is he?"

"It's only skin-deep, and it's bleeding, but his tendons are intact. He hasn't cut any big vessels."

Aleksandra sent up a prayer of thanks and took a deep breath, willing the pain to go away.

"Where are the bandages?" Xavier asked.

"In my right-hand saddlebag," she said faintly.

"I'll get it bandaged up and you can lie there. I daresay it won't be as pretty as if you'd done it, but it'll have to do today."

She nodded. Her head hurt too much to argue.

"OK, your turn." Xavier finally said, kneeling beside her. He gently wiped the dirt from her face. "Nasty graze," he said. She shook her head at the whisky fumes, just before the cloth touched her cheek.

"Ouch!" she yelped and tried to squirm away.

"Nothing for it, love, it needs to be done. Rogan didn't like it either."

She gritted her teeth and lay still. Tense, but still. "Yes, but it's usually me with the alcohol in my hand."

Xavier gave her a wry grin and leaned across to check all her limbs. "Can you move everything?"

She wriggled hands, toes and torso. "They'll hurt tomorrow, but nothing's broken."

"Good thing you've a tough head." His face blanched a little. "I thought you were going down underneath him. I've never been so scared in my life, since the last time, anyway."

"I've fallen off a lot. I'm pretty good at it." She glanced up at him and reached for his hands. "I think I can get up now."

She sat for a while, taking deep breaths, while her stomach churned. "Please stay down," she murmured. Eventually, it settled and she turned her focus past Xavier, sitting beside her, to Rogan. "Good job on the bandaging."

"You haven't seen it up close yet."

"I can see it from here." She smiled at him.

"Let's call it a day. Give you both time to rest."

"You'll get no argument from me there."

"Let's get you somewhere a little more comfortable than that rock, eh?"

"Thought you'd never ask."

He picked her up, one arm beneath her shoulders, one under her knees, and carried her toward Rogan.

"Then I'll get a fire going, so you can brew some willow bark and whatever else you've got to put into it."

She raised a brow at him. "You *are* learning."

"I've got a good teacher," he said, kissing her carefully on the nose before setting her down on Rogan's saddle blanket.

"Was I unconscious?" She frowned at the pile of saddles and blankets he'd already pulled from the horses.

He frowned and bit his lip. "Yes. Let's see how you are in the morning, before we make any plans."

"I'll be fine."

"I'm sure you will be," Xavier said smoothly, but his jaw was locked tight.

"Really, I'll be OK," she said, gripping his hand. "I've had much worse falls than that."

"I'll bet. I imagine one couldn't learn *dzhigitovka* without it."

"True. The other horses—"

"—are fine," he interjected. "Dzień's tied up. I had to tie him to keep him from nuzzling you awake."

She looked over at the Mustang. His muzzle and brows were tensed and he nickered softly at her. "I'm awake now, Xavier, could you please let him go?"

"Can do." He picked up another piece of kindling and loosed the pony, with a pat on his rump. The pony trotted straight to her and nosed at her belly, then moved to her face. She gripped his halter and rubbed his nose.

"I'm OK, pony," she murmured. "I'll be fine. You go find some grass. I'll be right here."

He gave her a long look, then turned and began foraging around the boulders, but kept one eye on her.

35

Aleksandra awoke with sunlight on her face. She shivered and snuggled closer to Xavier, then winced at the pain in her limbs and skinned face. A hoof crunched in the gritty soil near her head, then warm breath heated the back of her neck. She slowly turned to find Dzień's nose against her head.

"Good morning to you too, pony." She guarded her face with one hand and reached up to rub his muzzle with the other, then gazed past him toward the flat rocks bearing the marks of Dancing Wolf's people. The granite already shimmered in the mid-morning heat. They'd slept in after yesterday's events, and last night.

Her face heated. Last night, she'd felt good enough to snuggle with Xavier, and more. Her body still glowed. She rubbed her swollen lips, with a smile, and tried not to touch her sore, weeping cheek.

High tensions and the risk of loss gave their lovemaking a new fervor—and raised them higher than ever before. She sighed and reached over to kiss Xavier atop the head. He murmured something and closed his eyes again. Dzień stood, slack-hipped, and watched her closely as she sat up with care and crawled a few feet to pull the bag of feed from a pannier.

She stood up slowly and stretched, biting her lip against crying out as sore muscles screamed. She rationed out feed in nosebags to all three horses, then checked Rogan's leg above and below the bandage.

No heat.

Aleksandra managed a wan smile. She checked the rest of him, flexing her way down his spine. His whole body swung with every small, rhythmic push.

All good. The bony parts of his pelvis and head were covered with grazes, but otherwise, he looked pretty good.

Gathering their remaining bandaging materials, she crouched to remove Rogan's bandage. Xavier had done his job well. The leg was cool, the wound clean and it was barely swollen. The laceration was mid-cannon, off to the side, thankfully with only bone beneath. He shrank away a little when she wiped it clean with whisky, but stood his ground. "Good boy," she whispered. He nuzzled at her hair with his empty nosebag, as she rewrapped the wound, covering it first with a honey-soaked muslin. "You're a lucky man, Rogan." She removed his nosebag to check his muzzle and teeth, and he snorted at the scent of the bandage she'd removed, then licked the remains of the honey from her fingers.

Xavier's footsteps crunched behind her. "I'm a lucky man, too, *Querida*." He slid his arms around her from behind. "I am, too."

Aleksandra turned to him and wrapped her arms about his neck. "That makes three of us." She smiled up at him. "I'm ready to go on."

He looked hard into her eyes and seemed satisfied at what he saw. "How's the head?"

"Hurts a bit," she said, "and there's an egg on my forehead, but no more dizziness or nausea, and I can see straight today."

Xavier let out a breath and held her tightly. His lips moved against her hair and her heart glowed.

"I'll saddle up. Can you organize something for us to eat?" He raised a brow at her.

"Easy. Thank you."

"Then we'll be off. I'd like to get you to civilization. I nearly lost you last time, and I don't want to do it again."

She squeezed his hand and flashed a grin his way. "I'm pretty hard to kill. Look how hard Vladimir tried."

Xavier shook his head at her. "He wasn't trying, and you know it. Else you'd be dead."

She laughed, then winced. "OK, OK. Yes, I know. I wonder how they're getting on?"

"Oh, sorry. We had a letter the day before we left, but I forgot to tell you. It's here." He fumbled in his saddlebag and produces a battered envelope with a flourish.

Aleksandra unfolded the thin pages with care and scanned it. "So they're happy to stay there for a while."

"Seems so." Xavier tugged at Charro's cinch and tied it off.

Her heart twinged. "I miss the old place. It's so lovely this time of..." She couldn't finish.

Xavier came to her side and enveloped her in his embrace. "And your family too, I'll bet."

She could only nod and cling to him, before the sobbing began. He held her like he'd never let her go.

"I can't make up for your family, but I'll do my best," he murmured against her hair.

"You always do," she said, squeezing his hand. "Anyway, the place is being looked after. I sure would have liked to take Mama's secretary to California, if we're staying out there."

Xavier looked at the three horses and gave her a crooked grin. "I don't think any of them would want to carry it over this trail."

She sighed. "No, they wouldn't. I guess I have to let go of it all, and go on with my life. A desk won't bring my family back, as much as I want it."

"No, but together we can build a strong, new family."

She pressed her face into his chest with care and breathed in his unique man-smell.

"I'm not the cleanest," he murmured.

"You're just fine. The river swim was what we both needed. The fall, however, was not." She flexed her right arm and held her sore shoulder.

"Yes, you landed on that arm when you rolled off."

"Good thing I was wearing buckskins, or my shoulder would look like my face." She touched the still-seeping grazes on her face. "I did Rogan's leg, but forgot to put honey on my own face."

He kissed the top of her head and nodded at the letter in her hand. "Sounds like they'd be interested in coming out to the *rancho* once we've settled there."

"I'd love to have them with us," she said.

He gave her a wry grin.

"Yes," she chuckled, "it's a complete turnaround, I know. Now I see where some of Papa's mannerisms came from. I wish Papa'd been here to share the time we all had together—but then, nothing would have happened like it did, would it?"

He sobered. "No, but let's put all that behind us. Is Rogan OK to travel?"

"He looks well. He's tough. There's only a little swelling at the wound, and none further down the leg," she glanced at Xavier, "thanks to your bandaging it so quickly." She hugged him.

His eyes shone. "If you pack the panniers, I'll start saddling."

She carefully refilled the pack saddle boxes, including the escritoire with her new drawings, then carried the packs toward Dzień to be loaded onto his pack saddle. She'd send some sketches to Dancing Wolf when she got the chance.

"I thought we'd put you on Dzień today," Xavier said, coming around from the other side of Charro, "and Rogan can carry the packs—give him some time off."

She smiled. "You just want me safe on Dzień."

Xavier flushed. "Well…yes," he said firmly. "He's the most sure-footed horse we have."

She shook her head at him and turned toward Rogan, who already wore the pack saddle. She laughed. Xavier had clearly planned to win this one.

She swung a heavy pannier upwards to sling it from the saddle tree and yelped at the pain shooting through her shoulder.

Xavier was at her side. He grabbed it, before it hit the ground. "I'll get it, why don't you go bridle your Mustang?"

Aleksandra took a deep breath and relinquished the pack. It stung to have others do things for her, even now.

Dzień, however, whickered at her approach with bridle in hand, and opened his mouth for her to slip the bit between his teeth. He lowered his head and let her pull his headstall over his poll, then stood still to have his ears scratched. She turned to get his saddle, but Xavier already held it in his hands. He swung it over him, and cinched it up. She stood, uncertain what to do with herself.

Xavier glanced over his shoulder at her and closed his eyes for a moment. "It's OK, you're injured. I'm happy to do these things for you. Grateful, in fact, that you're alive for me to do these things."

She sighed, then took the rein he handed her.

"Do you want a leg up?"

She tried to stick her foot into the stirrup, but her knee wouldn't bend far enough without her wanting to scream. She turned to him and gritted her teeth. "Yes, please."

"Happy to help," He said, taking her shin in his right hand and cupping her knee with his left. "Always. One, two, three." On three, she hopped while he lifted her clear of Dzień's saddle and she slid lightly into the seat.

He motioned to her and she leaned down for his kiss.

"More of that tonight, please," she whispered.

"Again? You're insatiable," he said, shaking his head as he untied Rogan's lead rein and led him to Charro's side. Charro laid back an ear and lifted one hind leg in the direction of the colt. Rogan dropped his head and stepped lightly to the side, away from the older stallion.

"He's still got respect for Charro," Xavier said, as he mounted his stallion.

"He sure does," Aleksandra said. "They had a set-to a few days ago, just before we left. Charro reminded him who was boss."

"I saw no marks?" He cocked a brow at her.

"Nope, he bumped him in the chest with his heels, just hard enough to make him sit up and take notice."

"That's good. I'd hate for him to be truly damaged."

"Colts..." Aleksandra paused. "Guess he's not really a colt anymore. He's got to be four years old—he's a stallion now."

"He's acting like it, anyway. Thank Christ we didn't select fillies from Doc Faust. Oh, I heard from him last month, too. He's still happy to hold onto the colts until we decide whether we're returning to Utah or staying in California.'"

Aleksandra stared at him. "Is there any chance of that? Why wouldn't we stay at the *rancho*?"

Xavier looked away for a moment before he answered. "It's been a long time, Aleks—Mama wants me to return, but my brothers may not be so keen on the idea. I don't know what we'll find." He turned Charro's head toward the trail west, Rogan's lead gripped loosely in his right hand.

She followed.

AFTER A BIT more scrabbling down the faces of the omnipresent black and gray flecked stone, the sheets of rock gave way to smaller boulders, which were gradually replaced by scattered rocks as they left the higher altitude. Instead of making up the whole landscape, the rocks interspersed themselves with more and more numerous pine trees. The stiff, tense movements of the horses on the uncertain footing became their regular relaxed, rolling gaits and they made better time as they headed down the mountain. A little lower, and the brown dirt changed to a sienna, and manzanita grew beside the pines.

Dzień's ears pricked and he turned off the trail.

"Where's he going?"

"Not sure, but he wants it," Aleksandra said, then heard the tinkling of water. "It's a creek," she said over her shoulder.

"Is it safe to get down to it?"

"It's a pretty good deer trail. We'll see." They rounded a bend. A creek tumbled over small rocks, forming a big pool just below the trail, where they now stood. "There's a track right to it."

The trail was well-traveled, but not meant for two horses abreast. Behind her, Rogan snorted and bounced at the brush and young manzanita bushes between his legs. "Just let him go, Xavier. He'll get into less trouble that way."

Xavier unclipped the lead and the horse leapt toward Aleksandra, then spied the water and dove straight in.

"Never be subtle when you can make a spectacle of yourself, Rogan," he called out to the bay, who flicked an ear at him before he plunged his whole face in, past his nostrils, then pulled his muzzle out and drank properly.

"Papa always said you could tell it was a good horse if they plunged their whole muzzle in like that." Aleksandra grinned at Xavier, as Dzień did the same.

"This is Bear Creek," he said. "I forgot it went this far up."

"Does the trail follow it?"

"Yes, most of the way, until we meet the road that goes up to Nevada and Grass Valley, then we leave the creek and climb uphill for the best part of the day." He reached for Aleksandra's canteen and ducked down to fill it with the cool, clear water.

She took a long drink after he handed it back. It chilled her gullet going down and she shuddered. "Cold. Cold, but so good."

"Tastes like snowmelt," Xavier said, as he lowered his canteen after his drink.

"It will be," she said. "Plenty of snow still up there, despite it being summertime."

They stopped for a mid-morning rest high above a dark blue lake, nearly as big as Donner, then headed on. The trail improved as they descended. Scrub oaks and undergrowth now dotted golden, summer-dry grasslands. The steep mountains became rolling foothills as they cascaded down from the high Sierra. The horses grazed while they walked and they made good time. When the turnoff to Grass Valley and Nevada showed to their right, they turned up the hill toward the mining camps.

"There are an awful lot of wagons on this road," Aleksandra murmured, and bit her lip.

"This area's been growing steadily for years. It's even bigger than when I left."

She looked at him, her jaw tight.

"It's very civilized," he said, with a smile.

She wasn't convinced. Degree of civilization didn't matter to her. Either way, it was a big town.

A few hours later, they rode into Grass Valley.

"I can see it's been here for awhile," Aleksandra said, looking from left to right, and back again, at the rows of pretty houses that lined the road. Others perched side by side on the gentle mountain slopes nearby, their bay windows glinting in the sunlight.

"They've been here for a while, so they're not just miners' cottages," Xavier said, with a sideways look at her. A building was going up, its bright red brick standing out against its painted neighbors.

"Must have been some money in the Empire," Aleksandra said.

"Plenty. Some of the people here made their fortunes in mines all over this side of the *Sierras* and moved here afterwards."

As they walked the horses further up the hill, the road became a busy main street, with stores on both sides. Horses, some hitched to conveyances, dozed at their hitching posts or between their shafts from every available space along the road. Even at this early hour, music came from the saloons and a dance hall.

"Already?" Aleksandra said, glancing up at the sun.

"It never ends for some."

Aleksandra's heart lightened at the profusion of mercantiles, milliners and bakers on both sides of the muddy street. "Well, you're right about something."

"What's that?"

"It's civilized, but the pasties help. Immensely."

That made Xavier smile.

"Shall we stop for said pasty?" Aleksandra asked. "There's the shop one of the men up at the summit mentioned."

"Thought you'd never ask," he said, and turned off the road and dismounted.

After they'd eaten their new treats, Aleksandra licked the last pasty crumbs off her fingers and grinned at Xavier.

"I told you you'd like Grass Valley, once you got used to it. Thought it might take a little longer. Pasties to the rescue." He chuckled.

She took a deep breath and turned to him. "I like it. So help me, but I like it," she said.

"Turn right, just up there." Xavier nodded at a turnoff, onto a well-traveled road, that wended its way through tall trees. "I'm pleased. I'd hoped you would."

They rode through the tall pines, then came out into a clearing and headed toward a cluster of large buildings.

"And, this, madame," Xavier waved his arm with a flourish, "is the Empire Mine."

"Impressive," Aleksandra said, gazing at the cluster of mine buildings to their right. The rhythmic, dull thumping noise of a stamp mill echoed through the trees.

"Those buildings are made from the mine tailings."

"They look like the old photographs I've seen from England, of the buildings made from flint."

"They'd be made the same way, and probably by men who knew how to work flint and other stones, from Cornwall. That's the mine office to our left there," he nodded, as they walked past it, "and that one on top of the hill," he pointed to the right, "is the manager's house, Empire Cottage.

"That's the biggest house I've ever seen. That can't be for one family?" Aleksandra had to slap her mouth shut.

"A lot of money comes out of this mine." He cocked a brow at her. "It's one family, plus servants," he murmured, as they rode toward it. "On our right now is Ophir Cottage, the engineer's house."

"Even that's massive," she said under her breath. "That's the biggest stamp mill I've ever seen!" She nodded to the huge structure surrounded by men, with its great beams going up and down.

He smiled. "I'll take you over there later."

She smiled and glanced again at the behemoth.

"The Rowes live here." He looked ahead of them. "We'll stay at the big house tonight, and head on to the Malakoff tomorrow."

"Stay here," she blinked, "in that house?"

He grinned at her as they rode up to the mansion. "Yes, here. We've been invited," he said, and dismounted, then held her knee.

"Really?" Her uncertainty must've shown in her face. Her chest squeezed tight. It was the grandest house she'd ever seen.

"Would I lie about that?"

She shook her head.

Xavier climbed the steps to the massive door. An equally massive door knocker thumped hollowly, and a woman in a starched and frilled apron opened the door.

"May I help…" she began, her painted-on smile melting as she appraised Xavier, and then Aleksandra. "…you?" she finished, in a haughtier tone.

"*Sí*, madame. I'm here to see Mr. Rowe, please."

The maid gritted her teeth. "Servant's entrance is around the back," she said shortly, and began to close the door.

"*Perdón*, but please give Mr. Rowe my name. Xavier Argüello," he said, in a tone Aleksandra had never heard him use. "He will be expecting me."

The servant's head shot up, brows narrowed, and her voice was less certain this time. "Mr. Argüello, is it? One moment please. I'll see if he's in." Leaving the door ajar, she turned and trotted down the hallway, her shoes clacking on the wooden floor.

Xavier turned back to Aleksandra. "Servants."

She snorted behind her hand. "I didn't know you could speak like that."

"I grew up in a house full of servants. Snooty maids always annoyed me," he said, then his stern visage melted and he laughed. "I'll bet she's changed her tone about now."

Heavy footsteps approached the door.

"Xavier!" The door swung open and a voice boomed from the doorway. "You finally made it back."

"James, good to see you," Xavier said, clasping the mine manager's hand. "Let me introduce my wife, Mrs. Argüello."

He took Aleksandra's hand. "Charmed, charmed, madam. Welcome to Empire Cottage." He held her hand a moment longer than necessary, and

Aleksandra's face heated as she pulled her hand from his, ostensibly to gather the reins connected to the stone-still Mustang, who eyed him sideways. She flicked a glance at Xavier but he didn't seem to have noticed anything untoward.

"Long ride?" Was he staring at her long braid, lying over her shoulder?

"Yes, sorry we took so long," Xavier said. "We intended to be here yesterday, but Aleksandra's horse rolled down a granite boulder near the summit yesterday."

The manager's brows shot up and his gaze flicked up to her grazed cheek. "Are you hurt?"

"I'm fine," she murmured.

"Aleks is pretty lucky," Xavier said. "She rolled free and escaped with a mild concussion, grazes and her fair share of bruises. The horse finished up with only a cut on his cannon and plenty of scrapes, so we're grateful, all around."

"Let me know, madam," Rowe looked intently into Aleksandra's eyes, "if there's anything I can do to assist."

She couldn't shake the shiver that ran down her spine, all the while telling herself he was only being friendly, and to stop being a fool.

PART III

1861 ~ GRASS VALLEY, CALIFORNIA

36

August 1861, Empire Mine, Grass Valley, California

"Welcome back, Xavier," Mr. Rowe said, as they sat down to supper. "I'm sorry Mrs. Rowe is away, but she's visiting her sister in San Francisco, so we'll have to make do with Mrs. Abbott, our housekeeper." He smiled at the surly maid they'd met the front door, then frowned as she set the soup tureen down with more vehemence then the fine bone china deserved.

"Will you be wanting bread with that, sir?" The housekeeper stared at her employer.

He looked at her sideways, his brows raised. "Of course."

"It's just that... I just made... there's only..."

"Bring what we do have, please," he said. She spun and left the room.

Aleksandra blinked.

Mr. Rowe smiled at them.

"She puts on airs when the wife is away. Went so far as to set herself a plate at this very table yesterday. I was so surprised, I couldn't say a thing." He shook his head. "Perhaps she fancies herself the mistress here. Anyway, now that you're cleaned up and rested, we can get down to business. Are you ready to come back and work for me?"

"Well," Xavier hesitated, "I've been offered work up at North Bloomfield, at the Malakoff."

"Really?"

"I met one of the owners in Virginia City when I was working at the Ophir's assay office. He offered me a job managing their assay office, if I wanted to leave Virginia City."

"That's a good offer. I hear they pay well. Just remember," he steepled his fingers and looked over them at Xavier, "you've always got a job back here."

"With all due respect, sir, I don't want to go underground anymore."

"I wouldn't think of putting you back down there—you're much too valuable a manager for that, if what Jeremy says is correct."

"You know Jeremy?"

"That boy and I go way back. He sent me a note the other day, just to let me know that you were comin' this way, in case you decide you'd rather be here than at the Malakoff."

Aleksandra and Xavier exchanged glances. "That was kind of him."

"He had nothing but good to say about both of you."

Xavier raised a brow at him. "What did you have in mind?"

"Second-in-command in the assay office for now, with promotion to manager when John leaves, probably within the year." His eyes glittered.

"That's a generous offer, and I'll consider it. For now, I've promised to be at the Malakoff before next week, so we'll front up there first."

"You've always been a man of your word."

Xavier twisted his lips. "Not always the easiest thing to do."

"And what do you do to occupy your time, Mrs. Argüello?" His eyes perused her, his face pinkening a little as he shifted in his seat.

Aleksandra gulped. Did she dare reveal she been a Pony Express rider?

"Aleks is a schoolteacher," Xavier said into the silence.

"Yes, I was hoping to teach at North Bloomfield, if there's a school."

"A teacher, now that's a noble profession. I detected a slight accent, madame, are you from around here?"

"I was born in Europe, but my parents came here when I was an infant. We've been trapping in Utah Territory for my whole life, until I met Xavier."

"Aah, a woman of many talents." He smiled at her. "My children are turning into little savages, and my wife has been seeking a governess. If you return, perhaps we could work something out?" His smile seemed genuine enough now.

"That was a splendid meal." Aleksandra nodded at Miss Abbott when she retrieved the cut crystal dessert bowls. "The peaches in cream were an exquisite cap on an exceptional supper."

"Thank you, madame, I'll tell Cook," she murmured from beside Aleksandra's head, a faint smile cracking her polished visage.

Aleksandra leaned back against the tatted antimacassars and surveyed the room. The dark mahogany dining table for twenty was polished within an inch of its life, as was every other piece of furniture in the room. The lingering scent of cigars competed with the men's hair cream and beeswax. Standing lamps shone, their light reflected in the polished brass of their bodies, and hand worked doilies took pride of place on every surface. No spatterware here, every plate and bowl was bone china, and the tableware was silver.

"Will you be wanting port in the drawing room, gentlemen?" the housemaid asked.

"We'll all take it in there, thank you Miss Abbott," he said, an edge to his tone, and she scurried out, her face set.

"Don't know what's gotten into her this week," he said, in an aside to Xavier. "Women—begging your pardon, Mrs. Argüello. I'm sure you'd never be testy like that."

"On the contrary, I'm sure I would, given the right circumstances." She grinned at them both.

Xavier shook his head. "Aleksandra can be full of surprises."

"Shall we retire?" Mr. Rowe said, and they rose together. He indicated the comfortable chairs on the other side of the large room serving as both the formal dining room and drawing room. "I apologize for the lack of a fire, but as you can see," he waved a hand at the window, "it's still far too hot to light one. You'll understand when you go upstairs. You wouldn't sleep a wink."

"Not at all," Aleksandra murmured.

Miss Abbott had already laid out the crystal decanter and glasses. Mr. Rowe poured out and handed the glasses around.

"To your success at the Malakoff, and to your eventual return here," he nodded to Xavier, and the three clinked glasses.

Mr. Rowe passed a hand over his face and closed his eyes as his smile vanished for a few moments, before his pleasant host demeanor returned. Aleksandra and Xavier's eyes locked for a moment.

"Is something the matter, sir?" Xavier asked.

"Nothing, well..." he hesitated, then continued, "I'm just tired. We've been pulling incredible hours, cleaning up from the last fire in the shop, while still running to full capacity. The damage was...extensive."

"Got away from you, did it?"

"Sure did, like most of the fires around here in the past few years."

"Isn't there a fire department in Grass Valley?"

"It used to be the most advanced one in the state, but since '56, when the local government went to pot, we've had nothing you could call effective town government. We're just getting reincorporated now. Maybe soon we'll be able to stop the big fires that are destroying the industry up here."

Xavier winced. "So it's been eating into profits?"

"They're up and down like a yo-yo." He looked up from where he was fraying the edge of an antimacassar, and dropped it, with a guilty look. "A lot of mines won't make it unless we do something soon."

"So, no fire department. What about the hospital?"

"It's not looking so good, either."

"So, will you be running for mayor?" Xavier grinned at him.

"Unlikely. I'm not nearly diplomatic enough, nor even socially acceptable."

"Me either." Xavier chuckled, as their host filled the glasses again.

The port was as fine as the furnishings, and before her second glass was finished, Aleksandra's eyes were closing. As she sank deeper and deeper into the luxurious sofa, her head began to throb again.

Her husband looked at her. "Ready for bed, Mrs. Argüello?"

"You men continue, by all means. I'll find my way upstairs."

"No, I'm ready too," Xavier said. "It's been a long day. Thank you for a lovely supper, James. I'll get my wife off to bed. Is your head still paining you?"

"It is, rather." She looked at him in surprise.

"Good night to you both. If you don't have to rush away, you're welcome to stay another night—I'd like to show both of you around the mine tomorrow."

Xavier raised a brow at Aleksandra. "We have time, would you like to stay another day?"

The prospect of a real, clean bed and the fine stable for the horses? Definitely. "That would be lovely, thank you," she said with a sigh, and Xavier grinned back at her.

"Such opulence," she murmured, fingering the shiny brass figures atop each corner of the four-poster bed in the center of the bedroom, "but at what cost in men's lives?"

Xavier took her in his arms. "The Empire is a pretty safe mine, as they go, at least it was when I was here before. It's very different from what you saw at the Comstock. This is hard rock mining, which has its own dangers, but nothing like the unstable rubble at Virginia City."

"You won't go underground?" she whispered.

"It'll be part of the job, to check on conditions, and men...and yes, cave-ins."

She closed her eyes, as her heart clenched. What would she do if she lost him? Without her noticing, he'd become an essential part of her life, of her essence. "You'll be careful, won't you? No unnecessary risks?"

He laughed, then sat down on the bed and pulled her against him. "Did I just hear you say that? Are you the only one who can take risks?"

She gave him a crooked grin.

"But no, I won't. I don't want," he wiped stray strands of hair from over her eyes, "to lose you, now that we've finally found each other."

She smiled and reached for him. His lips took hers in a crushing kiss, their bodies craving each other as much as their minds did, tongues meeting, reaching, giving and taking. Talk of risks reminded her of what she stood to lose, and created an urgency that could only be satisfied by the rough loving she, and he, both craved.

"GLAD THEY DIDN'T LIGHT the fire," Aleksandra said, untangling her hair from Xavier's hands when they awoke in the morning sunlight. "It was warm up here last night."

"Sure that wasn't just you?"

She grinned. "Might have been, but I had help."

"So you did. Want some more?"

Brisk footsteps sounded in the hall outside their door and Aleksandra froze. The treads stopped for a moment, then continued. "Tempted, but I think that's our housekeeper. Might not be a good idea," she whispered.

He grinned at her and ran a finger down one side of her breast. "Sure?"

"You want to face her afterwards?"

His grin disappeared. "Not entirely, but it's a nice thought."

"Ok then, let's get up."

They dressed in clean clothes and went downstairs.

Miss Abbott still seemed to resent their presence, but her demeanor had thawed a little.

"Breakfast will be served as soon as the master is down, which should be any minute."

"Thank you," Aleksandra and Xavier said together.

"You keep a lovely house here," Aleksandra ventured.

"I've been with the Rowe family for nigh on twenty-nine years, I should know what it's about," she said, and returned down the hall toward the kitchen. Sharp voices issued from there a moment later.

"She doesn't look old enough to have been in service for that long," Aleksandra said.

"She must have been born in their household. A lifer."

"Do you think we should sit, or stand here?"

"Don't worry about her. Let's take a look around outside," Xavier said, opening the front door and taking her hand.

The houses stood on the highest hill, overlooking the mining operations.

"Those are the mine offices and workshops," Xavier said, nodded to their left at the sprawling cluster of buildings they'd passed when they entered the compound.

To their right were the rest of the mine buildings and the thumping stamp mills, their beams towering high into the sky. At chest height, big metal cogs turned, pushing the great beams upward for several inches before releasing them to land on the platforms below, only fractions of a second later, with a great thump and a crunch of metal splitting rock.

"Gold veins run along and within the quartz seams in the rock that's mined here. They have to crush the rock to expose the gold, which can then be more thoroughly extracted."

"They were pounding until we finally went to sleep last night, and they're still going now. Do they run all the time?" she asked.

"The mines run 'round the clock. The stamp mills have to do the same, to keep up with the rock coming up from the mine. They run full time in Virginia City, too. You didn't have to hear them all night, there, because we lived down in Gold Hill."

She shuddered.

"You'd get used to the sound and vibration, and you'd sleep, especially after working in the mines all day."

She shot him a look. "I don't think I'd ever like it."

"Probably not." He grinned.

"Good morning!" Rowe's voice thundered behind them. "Showing the little lady around already, Xavier?"

"Does he always talk like that?" she whispered to Xavier as they turned to face James.

"Yes." Xavier chuckled.

"Sleep well? The stamps can keep people awake sometimes when they're not used to it."

"We were just talking about that. We were so tired, we could sleep through anything, I think." Xavier squeezed her hand.

"Come on in to breakfast, then I'll give you both the full tour. Plenty of improvements since you were last here, Xavier."

"Looking forward to it, sir," Xavier said, and they followed him in.

Breakfast was another exquisite affair.

"I could get used to this," Aleksandra whispered to Xavier, while they waited for Mr. Rowe outside on the porch.

As they walked down the hill from what Rowe called his 'cottage,' he pointed to their right, just past the row of stamp mills. "That's where the rails go down into the mine. We've just finished it," he said, beaming. "It's got to be the best mine entrance around."

"You were talking about it last time I saw you. You've done it!" Xavier sounded as excited as James.

"Yep. We'll look at it later, but the men sit on a long 'railcar' at a sixty-degree descent and get a ride up or down. They love it, and it sure makes their life easier, and safer."

"It's got to be better than going down in a bucket." She mumbled.

"Aleks, you've seen how they work at the Comstock?"

She nodded.

"It's a little different here. We hard rock mine, because the gold is in solid rock." Rowe glanced around at the crowd of workers just leaving their shift. "Most of them are Cornishmen, who grew up doing just that in Cornwall. Men are lowered into deep coyote holes, like wells. They drill into the rock, fill the drill holes with black powder, scurry out, then detonate the charges. The blasted rock is hauled out in ore carts and—" He broke off as a man in a clean white shirt and trousers strode purposefully to Mr. Rowe, then stopped and waited for his attention.

"Excuse me, you two. I'll be right back," Mr. Rowe said.

"This mine's been going for eleven years now, and they've worked out a lot of glitches," Xavier said, as the manager walked away. "The other owners are mostly big businessmen in San Francisco, so there's some capital to play with. James holds the major interest in it, so he makes most of the decisions."

"This is miles ahead of the Comstock. Granted, it's been operating a lot longer."

"Let's go in, James won't mind. He could be hours." Xavier took her hand and led her to a door in the center of the long row of connected buildings, and ducked under the 'Assay Office' sign.

The manager of the assay office they'd met at the top of Donner Pass jumped up to greet them, clasping Xavier's hand in a great handshake, and then hers. He told them to make themselves at home, then turned back to his work. "Sorry, but I'm behind today," he murmured.

Xavier glowed as he showed her a shiny new gold balance. He fingered the brass weights like they were old friends. Aleksandra supposed they were.

"Did you work in here when you were at the Empire?" she asked.

"No, I was underground, but I spent any free time I had in here. Something about it." His eyes went soft and he took a deep breath.

"Sounds like this is the place for you then, if the Malakoff doesn't work out."

"The idea is sounding more and more interesting, I have to admit." Xavier twisted his mouth. "Seems a good way to make some good money so we don't go home empty-handed."

"A governess position sounds better than a schoolroom, but then, I've not done it before, either."

"Let's see what the Malakoff holds. At least we have this to fall back on," Xavier said, as James rejoined them.

Rowe led them up the outside stairs of the building and into the manager's office. Aleksandra stopped and fingered the ordered rows of stones making up the walls.

"They're all made from stone chips from the mine waste," James said, over his shoulder. "We have some men who learned flint work in Cornwall, too. It came in handy."

The building seemed to go on forever, with an ongoing pathway between offices and floors. At the far end stood the refinery room. It felt like the inside of a furnace. Aleksandra could only stare at the men bustling to and fro, stirring vats of strongly smelling liquids or standing before great furnaces, then pouring molten gold from the glowing crucibles into forms to set into bars. Despite the heat, she didn't want to leave the room. It was entrancing.

"No place for a lady, Aleksandra," James said.

She raised a brow at him. "I seem to do many things not suited to a lady."

His eyes grew warm. "Oh, do you now?" he asked.

She stepped closer to Xavier and grabbed his hand. "What are those buildings over there?" she said, and turned away.

"Now those," he turned away from her and walked towards another row of even bigger warehouse-looking buildings, "are the machine shops, blacksmith shop and the head frame." He pointed at a steel cart on rails, supported by the frame. "That's one of the ore carts I mentioned before. They carry rock from the mine to the crusher, where the ore is smashed up. The crushed ore is carted to one of those stamp mills." He pointed at the mammoth stamping monsters. "Compressors in the next building let us compress air to drive machinery and ventilate the mine shafts." He walked on to the furthest building to the left. "And finally, the hoist house, where men can be lowered into and raised from the mine, along with ore and supplies. We used that to bring up the waste rock used to create all these buildings."

He turned and glanced back at the refinery. "Over there, the crushed ore is mixed into a slurry with water and placed on mercury-coated copper plates to form an amalgam. After the impurities are washed away, the amalgam goes to the refinery to finish processing to become the pretty yellow stuff you wear." He looked at the ring on Aleksandra's hand.

"This is amazing," Aleksandra said. "What a feat of engineering, all these great buildings and machines. I've never even seen *buildings* this big in my life."

James grinned. "Glad you like the Empire. I hope you two come back here soon. Not trying to take a good worker from the Malakoff, but you'd both be welcome back here anytime, to stay."

"Thanks for that, James. We'll definitely keep that in mind."

37

The next morning, they packed up and waved goodbye to James Rowe and Miss Abbott.

"She sure warmed up in the end," Aleksandra said.

"Not sure if it was because we were leaving, or because she'd begun to like us."

"We may never know," she said, scratching Dzień's withers and edging Rogan away with her toe. "Back off, bucko." The bay ignored the first nudge and grunted when she gave him a good thump. "He needs more exercise, this horse. Can't wait until his leg is healed. It's time to give him some dressage and make him think a little—he's getting bored."

"Boredom isn't a good thing for a young horse," Xavier agreed.

"I'll ride him after we next stop."

"Good idea."

Another mile, and they were in Grass Valley.

"Pasties for our lunch?"

"We'd better, if there aren't any at North Bloomfield," Xavier said, with a laugh.

Soon they were out of the town and climbing. About an hour later, they entered the town of Nevada. It looked much like Grass Valley, with its stores, homes and saloons. A massive red brick mansion stood proudly beside the road.

"That wasn't there when I left," Xavier nodded at it. "They sure put it up fast."

They climbed on, turned east a few hours later, and rode into North Bloomfield by dinnertime.

"Not nearly as pretty as Grass Valley or Nevada," Aleksandra said, looking around at the rows of plain wooden houses lining the main street of the rough-looking town. There were some women walking together near the shops, and a few men talked on street corners. "There also seem to be a lot of Southern accents on the wind," she added, with a shudder.

"I noticed that, too." Xavier frowned. "I wonder what that's about?"

"Is that it?" She pointed ahead, to the only permanent-looking edifice.

"We should find the superintendent there," Xavier said, turning his horse's head toward it. He dismounted at the door marked 'North Bloomfield Gravel Mining Company Office' and tied Charro to the hitching rail, then disappeared inside. He soon returned, smiling, with a set of keys in his hand. "Let's get you to your new house, and I'll come back while you get settled in."

"Already set up?"

"Sure is. I'm told it's rather a nice house. It's up the road a little way, as promised. Definitely a plus."

"I'd say." Aleksandra nodded.

"Thought you'd appreciate it." His eyes glinted as he swung up on the gray and they left town, or what passed for a town, complete with a rough saloon and bar girls seated behind the saloon, eating their dinner outside.

"Wow," Aleksandra said, as she stared at the two-storied houses with picket fences lining the street before them. "This is a little different from the camp."

"Sure is, and the third one is ours. All ours." Xavier's face glowed.

"My opinion of this mine is going up by the minute."

"I wonder if you'll think so when you see what the monitors do to the mountains..." Xavier said in a quiet, almost reluctant voice.

"Monitors? What do they do to the mountains?"

"I'll take you out and show you later," he said, turning away. "For now, let's get you settled."

"Well, the house is nice, anyway," she said as she slid from the saddle and walked away with only a little limp. "Did you find out if there's a school?"

"No, but I'll ask." He dismounted, then pulled the packs from Dzień's saddle. "There are corrals and a few stalls out the back, I'm told. Seems they thought of everything."

"It looks too good to be true," Aleksandra said, gazing at the chairs set out on the front porch beneath the overhang.

"Well, it's true, so get used to it, Mrs. Argüello." He grinned and tipped her face up to kiss her. "We'll have our own little private house warming party tonight, shall we? There must be a store somewhere here."

"I'll find it. Like a bloodhound."

"I always said you were more than just a pretty face," Xavier said, and got a bump in the shins for his effort. "And the key even fits," he said, and swung the door wide. "After you, *Querida*," he said, and carried the packs inside and set them down in the spacious front hall.

"It's lovely. Not fancy, but it's clean, and has everything we need," she said, after they'd toured the house.

"And with that, I'm heading back to the office to see what I'll be doing tomorrow. *Ten cuidado, for favor.* Take care. I'm not sure how well behaved the men are here…"

She laughed. "You forget who you're speaking to…I always carry my *shashka.*"

"You take special care of yourself. I'll be back as soon as I can."

"I'll feed the horses and find us some supper," she said, then kissed him and sent him off.

After she found hay and buckets in the stables, it didn't take long to get the horses settled. She unpacked their meager belongings, then went down the porch steps and up the road to the next house to find out where to purchase supplies. This end of the road was lined with whitewashed wooden frame houses with window-ended gables. The picket fences lining the road and between the houses were built upon low stone walls, and it was all rather pretty. She smiled as she strode along the way.

No one was home at the first two houses. At the third, a maid dressed in black and white answered the door and took her name. Soon, a woman with a strong Southern accent greeted her. "Y'all must be the wife o'the new manager o'the assay office."

"Yes, that's me. I'm Aleksandra."

"Welcome to North Bloomfield. I'm Josephine. My husband is the mine superintendent."

"Nice to meet you. Thank you for organizing such a lovely home for us."

"No problem a'tall, not a'tall. Ah've put some food up for you in one of the cab'nets, ah hope y'found it?"

"No, I didn't, but I'll go look now, thank you. I was wondering where I could find a store."

"Y'all'll have to go back down t'the camp t'get food, but y've got 'nough for t'night, mos'likely."

"Thank you very much." Aleksandra beamed. "That'll be a great help."

"No problem a'tall. By the way, the men'r a bit rough down there, might be a good idea if you were t'take someone along with ya when y'all go down there," she said as she backed away from the door. "Ah need to get back to m'baby, but nice t'meet y'all."

"Thank you again, and we'll see you soon, doubtless."

"Y'all do that. Bye."

Aleksandra couldn't help feeling they'd finally done something right, coming to the Malakoff.

She found the makings of a reasonable supper in the top cupboard and went out to tend Rogan's wound. It was a little warm and red at the edges, so she lit a fire in the kitchen stove and set water to boil. She stirred salt into the pot of boiling water, then pulled honey, clean cloths and bandages from one of the packs. One cloth she smeared with honey and closed upon itself to keep it clean. The others she dropped into the salted water and boiled them for a few minutes. She carried everything out to the corrals behind the house in a basket from the kitchen.

She tied Rogan to a post beside his hay. Crouching on the ground beside him, Aleksandra hooked a cloth out of the pot with a fork and held it in the air for a moment to cool just enough to handle and fold. She held it against the wound until it had lost its heat, then pulled another from the pot and repeated the sequence. After twenty minutes, she wiped it well with another saltwater cloth, and bandaged it with the honey poultice, then heavy padding, and rolled a bandage into place over the top. "Now for a rest, boy. I wish we could have let you rest before, but we had to get here, sorry." He nuzzled her and lipped at her hair. "You get some sleep. You guys have earned it after the past few days." She stroked his neck as he munched his hay.

A SALT PORK and dumpling stew with vegetables was ready on the back of the stove when Xavier returned.

He grabbed her and swung her around in the front room. "It's perfect, what a job. Only five days on, with two whole days off every week!"

"Really? For that salary?"

"I can't believe it either. There's still time to show you around the mine before it gets dark. There won't be so many men there, either." He smiled down at her. "I know you hate strange men looking your way."

"I'd like that." She nodded. "Supper's ready. Do you want to eat now or when we return?"

"Let's eat now, then we can take the horses out to the diggings," he said, sitting at the freshly-scrubbed table. "Charro can stay behind and I can ride terror-horse. He should be OK to ride. I'll change his bandage again when we get home."

"Can we get some supplies at the camp?"

"Sorry, but the shopkeeper in town was closing up when I passed. Maybe tomorrow. North Bloomfield's pretty civilized, maybe not like Grass Valley or Nevada, but you should be able to go down by yourself."

"That's not what the mine superintendent's wife said." She quirked a brow at him.

"She doesn't know you like I do." He smirked.

After eating, they saddled up and left Charro to his hay. His only reaction at being left alone was a briefly interested glance as they rode out and left him.

Aleksandra watched the stallion as they rode away. "He's not too worried."

"He had a big ride today. I went with the superintendent all the way up to one of the big dams, where the water's sourced for the mines. He had to check on the new canal they're digging from a reservoir forty miles away."

"Forty miles away?" She stared at Xavier. "I'd like to see that."

"I can take you up there after we have a look at the mine."

They were nearly to the town, when she glanced up and the breath left her lungs. Above the rows of shanties and lean-tos were huge areas of denuded hillside. The once-pristine green hills covered with Ponderosa Pine were gone. In their place were jagged outcroppings of white clay and splashes of sienna topsoil.

They turned up the road leading to the mines, and as the open minefields opened up before her, Aleksandra could only stare in horror. Her insides grew colder by the minute as the extent of the devastation revealed itself.

Despite the setting sun, bearded and hatless men with white mud splashed high on their boots and trousers still scurried across the barren landscape, dragging heavy hoses and machinery from one area to another.

Xavier pointed higher up the mountainside to a handful of workers standing beside a machine that looked like a cannon. They wrestled with the thing as if it were alive until they seemed satisfied, then stepped away from the machine. "That's the monitor," Xavier said. "Watch what happens next," he said, with an air of expectation.

The men gave a call out to those working below, then two of the workers on the monitor tugged at a bar and a blast of water came from the end of it, shooting forty or fifty feet into the air. They aimed the stream at the edge of the forested area along the perimeter of the mine.

When the water hit them, great pines toppled and fell like matchsticks, followed by an avalanche of mud and water, down to the men working below it.

"Won't they be killed?" Aleksandra's guts clenched at the sight of the men below, and of the forest and mountain disappearing before her eyes. "It's not right...this destruction..." she whispered. She swallowed hard, willing her stomach to stay where it was.

This is your husband's new work. Pull yourself together.

She turned to Xavier. "What happens with all...that mud?"

He didn't seem to notice her distress as he watched the men at the base of the hill. He pointed to a confusion of wood and metal boxes surrounded by workers. "Those are big sluices, those boxes with high sides? They have riffles inside them, crosswise strips of metal or wood, to catch the heavier gold or gold bearing ore, leaving the lighter dirt in the mud to wash away, as fresh water is washed over it. An engineer and a tinsmith, along with another man at this mine figured out about ten years ago how to funnel water to the diggings, instead of carting the excavated gravel to the river for sluicing. The monitor was invented by turning the end of the hose around and aiming it directly at the hill itself."

"And they created a monster," Aleksandra breathed. The world spun about her, then settled.

He glanced sideways at her. "Are you OK? You're a bit pale."

She managed a nod.

He nudged Rogan forward, past the open mine toward a gully. Aleksandra followed on Dzień.

"This mine uses a huge amount of water," he said. "They already had a couple of big reservoirs high up the mountain, the Big Cañon and the Rudyard, made by damming up rivers early in the 1800's. Water was brought from those big lakes to the mines by flumes, like we saw going over the Sierra Nevada. When hydraulic mining was invented about eight years ago, even more water was needed, so they started building a new canal from another reservoir—the one I mentioned before."

Aleksandra focused on staying calm and breathing. A flash of red caught her eye, then another one. "What's that, Xavier, that red thing up on the bank?"

His brow furrowed. "It looks like…meat?"

She rode closer to see it. "It's a plant. And the whole thing is red, not just flowers! How odd!"

"Why don't you pick it and we can ask someone about it?"

She shuddered. "I think not. I'm sure we can describe it just fine. I don't think I want to touch it, for some reason."

He grinned at her. "Suit yourself. There couldn't be many plants answering that description. I'll ask someone at work." He turned back to the trail ahead. "Oh yes, and there's a school, but the boss didn't know if they needed anyone to teach. He said he'd ask."

"Thank you."

"There's the end of the new canal they're building. It's too late to get all the way to the reservoir, but we can see the men building, if you'd like to go up a little way. They'll be working until dark."

The trail switchbacked its way up the mountain, until finally, the working men came into view. Their pigtails swung as they worked in the darkening evening.

"They're all Chinamen, aren't they?" she said.

"Most of them. There are over three hundred Chinese, and a small number of European foremen."

"Seems the Chinese always get the hard work, but get kicked out when they are successful, like the men in Chinatown."

He nodded. "You're right.

They passed the first group of men digging a long trench in a higher piece of ground, and some turned to them and bowed, speaking in Chinese. She nodded to them and smiled, and was rewarded with the most delightful smiles she'd seen in a long time.

"They get the worst work, but they're still happy," she said, and took a deep breath. "Something for me to learn from that, I suspect."

"For us all."

They followed the flume as it rose higher and higher. In the elevated areas, the new wood of the canal lay in trenches, but over the gullies, the waterway sat atop frames that served as aqueducts.

"They've done an incredible amount of work," she said, looking up the mountainside at the miles upon miles of canal disappearing into the distance.

Dzień's ears shot up and he swung his rump around to look toward a man coming toward them on the narrow trail. An Indian, dressed in unadorned buckskins of an unusual design, walked toward them and nodded. As he set to pass them, Aleksandra called out a greeting in *Shoshone*. He stopped and slowly turned.

He returned the greeting, not in *Shoshone*, but in something she could understand. She told him she was raised with the *Shoshone*, near the land of the *Pah-Utes*.

He smiled and pointed at himself. "*Maidu*".

She asked him if that was his name.

He replied that it was his tribe. He nodded, turned and was gone.

"What did he say?" Xavier asked.

"He said he was of the tribe called '*Maidu*'."

"I was told they were the local tribe. It's rare to see them around the mines." He looked sheepish. "Some of the miners give them a hard time, so most of them stay away from the camps. I don't blame them. It's bad enough that the settlers and miners have taken their livelihood away, but to take even their land, and wreak such destruction…" He stopped.

"So it affects you too, the damage from the mine."

"How could it not, *Querida*?" he whispered, then gritted his teeth. "But I must make a living for my family, and to return home with something to show for my time away. I know no better." He hung his head and rubbed Rogan's withers. "Let's go home."

She reached for his hand and stood in her stirrups to kiss him as they turned as one to leave for their new home.

IT WAS dark by the time they returned to the house behind the picket fence.

"After seeing all that," she nodded her head back toward the mine, "I'm not as happy about being here as I was before, but I'll do my best. I'm sorry, Xavier, I know it's not easy for you, either."

He reached for her and they stood, clasped in each other's arms. "We'll get through this. It's won't be easy, but we'll make it work for us. It won't be forever."

"I'm here for you, *Querido*," she said.

"*Está bien*. Let's go to bed, *sí?*"

"*Sí.*"

Over Xavier's shoulder, through the lace curtains covering the window, two men appeared and walked past the house in the deepening dusk. A shiver ran up her spine. "No," she whispered, and froze, too scared to even shake her head.

"What is it?" Xavier frowned down at her and started to turn around to see what she was looking at.

"Don't move," she breathed.

"What?"

"It can't be…" she said, and started to shake.

She closed her eyes, then opened them and looked again.

It was.

It couldn't be, but it was.

"O'Rourke," she whispered.

38

"He's here. O'Rourke," Aleksandra repeated, beneath her breath. "He can't be. They caught him. I'm sure they'd have shot him," Xavier said.

"Come away from the window. Let's see where he goes."

They crept upstairs to the bedroom and watched as O'Rourke walked straight up the porch steps of the supervisor's house, then walked in like he owned the place.

Aleksandra sank onto the bed and Xavier sat beside her.

"Xavier, you met the mine supervisor today, didn't you?"

"Yes, why?" he said in an undertone.

"Is he a Southerner?"

"I'd say he had to be, by his accent."

"That's his house. I met his wife this afternoon."

"What's O'Rourke doing at their house?"

"What's the supervisor's last name?

"*Dios mío*," he said, and put his head into his hands. "It's O'Rourke."

"This gets worse... I remember him saying, back on the wagon train, that his uncle managed a mine in California."

"This can't be." Xavier gritted his teeth.

"Maybe shouldn't unpack." Aleksandra closed her eyes. For the second time tonight, the bottom had just dropped out of her life.

Xavier pulled her in tight against him. "We need to leave tonight, before O'Rourke figures out who his uncle just hired. I'll just have to leave a note for him...with no forwarding address."

"Will the Empire be far enough away?"

"For now, it'll have to be. I'll let James know the story and maybe someone'll pick him up and deal with him."

She shuddered.

"You can keep watch for now, then after dark, I'll go saddle up and we'll head out."

"Why don't you watch now," Aleksandra said, "and I'll pack up our belongings. I know where I put everything, and then I can watch while you saddle up. If he stays there, we don't have to pass him. I'd sure like to know where he is, in case he figures out we're here."

"With his uncle as the mine manager, and all the Southerners here, we wouldn't have a show in hell."

She kissed him and slipped down the stairs, returning with a steaming bowl of stew. He smiled his thanks and returned his eyes to the window, as she began to assemble their belongings.

ALEKSANDRA HADN'T THOUGHT James Rowe was capable of looking so grave.

"That's some story," he said, closing his eyes and pinching the ridge between them. "But why the hell did they let him go?"

"We assumed they caught him, and by the mood around Fort Churchill, that he'd been shot by now.'

"But we didn't check." Aleksandra stared out the window, but saw nothing. "With my training, how could I have not—"

"—Aleks," Xavier said in a tone that brooked no disobedience, "you were half dead from blood loss, I wasn't in the best shape myself, and survival was our only concern at the time. Yes, we should've checked, but we didn't, *sí?*"

"*Sí.*" She took a deep breath and look straight at James. "So, do you still want us here? Trouble seems to be following us right now. There's no telling what O'Rourke'll do."

"Bring it on," the mine owner said. His eyes could've cut stone. "He won't find a welcome here. Now let's get you two settled." He led the way upstairs to their previous room. "Nobody from around here'll be makin' trouble for you, or they'll deal with me. I've got an old army buddy coming to visit sometime soon. We'll see what he can do. In the meantime, make yourselves at home and we'll get you moved into John's house when he heads back to San Francisco."

"THIS IS EMILY, SHE'S TEN," Mrs. Rowe said, upon their return home two weeks later. The little girl curtsied prettily and smiled at Aleksandra. "Tobias and Theodore, Toby and Theo for short. Say hello to Mrs. Argüello." She pushed the two boys toward their new governess.

"We're twins," Toby said.

"We're eight years old," added his brother.

"I'd never have known." Aleksandra shook her head.

They beamed.

"Welcome to our home, Aleksandra. I hope Miss Abbott's been taking good care of you." She shot a sharp glance at the housekeeper, who raised a brow at her.

"Of course. She's been wonderful," Aleksandra said. Truth be told, the woman was being more helpful than she'd been upon their arrival.

Mrs. Rowe looked toward her husband's office. "Is Mr. Rowe at home?"

"No, madam," said Miss Abbott. "He's been away a lot lately."

What was she on about?

Aleksandra glanced at the housekeeper from the corners of her eyes. She and Xavier had only moved out into the assay office manager's home yesterday, and Mr. Rowe had been at home every evening, and for dinner every day. She narrowed her eyes at Miss Abbott. The woman caught her look and gritted her teeth. She glared at Aleksandra, daring her to say otherwise.

"Well, Aleksandra," Mrs. Rowe took a deep breath, her hand gripping the back of the carved chair-back before her, "shall we see you and your husband at supper tonight?"

Miss Abbott gave her mistress a hard look, before Mrs. Rowe turned to face her. "Miss Abbott, there won't be any problem with that, will there?"

"Of course not, I'll set extra plates." Her tone was civil, but only just. She spun about and stomped toward the kitchen.

Aleksandra blinked. Out of the frying pan, into the fire.

"May I help you unpack, or take care of the children while you get settled?" Aleksandra asked.

"No, thank you. That won't be necessary. Your duties won't start until tomorrow. As soon as I let the children go, they'll be entertaining cook with stories from their travels. You go ahead and let your husband know you're coming to supper, and I'll have a rest before you arrive."

She looked like she needed it. She'd gone very pale, and looked like she was about to cry.

"Madame, are you all right? You don't look well."

"I'll be fine, thank you." She tried for smile, but didn't quite pull it off.

"If I can be of assistance, please let me know. I'll see you at supper. Shall I tell your husband you're home?"

"That would be nice, thank you."

"I'll see you at supper then. And welcome home."

She smiled at Aleksandra, a sad little smile.

IF ALEKSANDRA WAS WORRIED THERE WAS a problem between Mr. and Mrs. Rowe, the excitement with which he received the news of her arrival negated it.

He jumped up from his desk and trotted from his office, with a brief word to his secretary.

"And thank you, Aleksandra. We'll see you tonight." He sprinted down the steps, humming a tune.

She leaned out over the second-story railing, taking in the activity below. Men milled about the head frame at the mine entrance, on the far side of the yard from Aleksandra. The shift change bell rang and soon a horde of men dismounted from their rail seats, blinking, but laughing and joking. A far cry from the exhausted men of the Ophir and so many of the others, when they stumbled out after climbing every ladder on the long way from the depths of the mines at the end of their long shifts.

With a smile, she headed down the steps and entered the assay office, the bell over the door jingling at her entrance. Xavier looked up from the journal into which he was entering row after row of figures from a scrap of messily-scrawled paper.

"Well, aren't you a sight for sore eyes?" With one more glance at the column, he lay down his pen and corked the inkwell.

"Hello there. How is it going today?"

"Much better, now you're here."

"We're to dine with the Rowe's tonight. Mrs. Rowe has returned, with the children."

"Excellent. I only have a little more left to do here, then I can go home with you."

"I'll wait outside." She went outside and back upstairs to a bench placed against the wall of the manager's office. She looked back at the head frame. Two men stood there, looking around. She didn't know what it was, but they didn't seem to belong there, for some reason. They both turned to look at her at the same time. When they saw her looking at them, they turned away and walked toward the blacksmith shop, as the hairs raised on her arms.

She was still staring in the direction they'd gone when Xavier found her.

"You look like you've seen a ghost," he said.

She told him about the men.

"I think you're getting worried about nothing," he said. "Most of these men haven't seen a real woman in a long time. If Rowe's housekeeper and cook are the only women they get to see, you'd be like a breath of fresh air. Come on, let's go." He wrapped his arm around her and gave her a kiss on the forehead before they headed home to clean up for supper at the Rowes.'

"Who are you? What are you doing here?" Miss Abbott called out in a sharp voice, poised to run back up the steps into the kitchen. She peered into the semi-darkness and gripped her laundry basket full of antimacassars.

"I'm hoping for another glimpse of you." His voice was deep and smooth as honey. A beautiful blond man stepped out into the lamplight, shining through the kitchen window.

The half-smile on her face froze. She was entranced, but her fear won out. "Was that you out here last night?" she said, her voice dropping to a furious whisper.

"It was, my darlin'," he said, "and every other. I watch out for you always, when you hang out the pretties from the house."

She opened her mouth to speak, but no sound emerged, as her heart pounded. She should, by rights, be angry at his insolence, but his flattery won out.

He rushed to her side, his fingers to his lips. "Shhh…please say you'll be mine, and I'll give you anything."

"I don't even know you, sir. This is most…improper." She finished on an unwilling whisper.

"All right, I'll leave you then, to dream of me. Only say I can see you tomorrow."

"Sir, I must protest," she managed, in a weak voice.

"What is there to protest? Only say I can see you again tomorrow. Say the words, please?"

"But I don't even know your name."

"'Tis Delaney, only please call me Courtney."

"Oh, I mustn't—this is sinful."

"How else must I profess my love to you?"

She hoped he couldn't see her face flush hot in the dusky dimness. "I mustn't, sir." She picked up her basket, without even hanging the fabrics on the line. "Be on your way," she nearly shrieked, then turned tail and bolted up the back stairs into the kitchen.

Cook stared as she ran in and nearly slammed the door behind her, placed a hand over her heart and leaned back against the door, trying to catch her breath.

"Are ye runnin' fra the faeries, Miss Abbott?"

"No, no. Nothing. Just slipped on the stair and gave myself a fright."

Cook looked into the washing basket and glanced up to Miss Abbott's face. Her brows narrowed. "Are ye hangin' out the rest tomorrow, then?"

Miss Abbott glanced down, then inhaled sharply. The antimacassars still covered the bottom of the basket. "Oh, yes," she said, then turned and raced from the kitchen.

In the privacy of her room, she drew the drapes, but couldn't resist one last peek out to see if her admirer still stood guard. Did she imagine it, or did a white face glow softly near the trees at the edge of the lawn? Miss Abbott squelched the smile that threatened, then pulled her head back and snapped the curtains together.

In her bureau mirror, by the light of the flickering candle, the lines on her face were clear to see. Did Mr. Delaney—*Courtney*—see them in the half-light, and would he still love her in the light of day? She bit her cheek and looked at her hands, tightly gripped in her lap. If she were truthful with herself, other than Mr. Rowe's old stablemen and the occasional delivery boy, all of whom were far below her station, no man had ever spoken to her like she was special, and no man had ever said the word 'love'. She swallowed her bitterness. There was someone watching out for her now, and professing love. Perhaps, just perhaps.

Her heart clenched. Would the Rowes keep her on? Mr. Rowe's father, who employed her mother as housekeeper in San Francisco, said she'd always have a position with the family. Would they still want her if she was married to someone outside the home? The young Mrs. Rowe didn't like her, that was certain. Granted, Miss Abbott hadn't made it easy on her when she came to this house as a new bride, but she should be over that by now. She pursed her lips. It could prove difficult if Mrs. Rowe wanted to return the favor.

She thought about Mr. Delaney, *Courtney*. She quivered when she thought of his Christian name. Who knew if he was toying with her affections or not? She had no personal experience of it, but the novels secreted away beneath her dowry linens were full of men who spoke as he did. She took a deep breath. If only she could find it in herself to trust.

Time would tell, but truly—she gritted her teeth—the only way to guarantee her future was to ensconce herself here, in this very house. To become 'closer' to the master. She knew how to do it, or had seen others do it, anyway. She frowned.

She'd been trying, but he wasn't having a bar of it. He didn't even notice when she tried to act the wife, but maybe that was part of his game. She knew he had women outside the home. She'd just have to try harder the next time his wife was away. It was a good thing the mistress visited her family in Sacramento with increasing regularity. She gloated. Soon, she'd see her position was guaranteed for life—*but what about Mr. Delaney?*

If only Mr. Rowe treated me like that.

She thought about it while she unwound her braids, long enough to wrap around and around her head, and slipped her hair loose. She brushed it her nightly one-hundred strokes until it shone in the lamplight. She untied her skirts, removed her bodice and stays, then sat back down at the bureau and arranged her hair artfully over her breasts, so only the nipples showed. She blushed in the mirror. There was still plenty to like, and she was still a virgin.

Her gaze flicked to the covered window. She considered standing before it and opening the curtains, but her nerve failed her.

Her mind in turmoil, she tumbled into bed. With Mr. Rowe, she just wanted security, and this home of course, but with her as its mistress.

Mr. Delaney, now, he was a real man. She wondered what he did for a living. With his fine way of speaking, he must have a grand home. Envisaging herself walking up the aisle of the big Episcopal church in Grass Valley, she slid into sleep.

THE NEXT EVENING, as Miss Abbot stood in the kitchen, she finally heard the front door close behind Aleksandra. The girl had left later than usual, on the Master's pretense of needing her to help him with some of his more difficult accounts. She shook her head. Anyone could see he wanted her.

Why her and not me?

She seethed.

The lateness of the hour had its advantages, though. Cook was already up in her room above the kitchen. Miss Abbot glanced around the kitchen with a smile, before slipping out the door and gliding down the back stairs..

He was there again, intently gazing down the path toward the mine office. She dropped the basket on the ground and it made a crunching noise as it landed on the pine needles. He flicked a glance at her, then returned his attention down the hill.

She followed his gaze to the lighted area outside the mine offices, where Aleksandra was just opening the door to the assay office. She frowned, then cleared her voice. Mr. Delaney jumped, then straightened and rushed to her side.

"You were watching the governess?"

"The governess? I only saw an impediment to our privacy. It seems," he glanced at the offices again, "it is gone." He smiled at her. "We are safe now, my love."

"I am not, in truth, your love, for I hardly know you," she finished in a rush, "but sir, what are your intentions?"

"Only the truest ones, my love. Only say you'll be mine and I'll carry you away from this drudgery to my mansion in the sky."

"That doesn't sound very practical." She had to ascertain his intent.

"Oh, I can be practical, and do whatever is necessary," he said in a serious tone, maybe even a menacing one. "Say you'll drive out with me soon, in my fine carriage."

"Sir, I could not. It wouldn't be seemly."

"Oh, but for a chaperone. Do you know anyone who could accompany us?"

"No one," she whispered.

"What of the governess? What could be more proper than a governess for a chaperone?"

"I don't believe I could talk her into it." Her brows drew together. Aleksandra would be sure to tell the Rowes. That would spoil everything, if it didn't work out with Mr. Delaney.

"I'll... I'll ask her."

"And may I have the honor of calling you by your Christian name?" He whispered, close to her ear. She shuddered, and a funny feeling started up in her belly and spread to the tips of her breasts.

"It's... Bertha," she found herself murmuring.

"Then until tomorrow, sweet Bertha. Your name is honey on my lips." He took her fingers and kissed their tips, then melted into the night.

39

The weeks passed quickly as the summer gave way to autumn. Xavier's enthusiasm for his job only deepened and Aleksandra adored the little Rowes. They were keen to learn, especially when Aleksandra taught their lessons with examples from real life. Mrs. Rowe, however, sank lower as Miss Abbot's insidious comments cut deeper and deeper. Aleksandra considered speaking with Mr. Rowe about it, but every time they were alone, he seemed to try every possible trick to move his body closer to hers. She finally avoided being with him unless the children were present, and always carried her *shashka*.

"You're just being silly." Xavier shook his head.

"You've said that before, Xavier, and look what happened, not once, but twice."

He had the grace to look abashed, but still argued. "This is different. Mr. Rowe is an honorable, married man who loves his wife. You're his family's governess, and he'd never mess that up."

"I don't think that's the whole story."

"Oh Aleks, what proof do you have?"

"Just a feeling, mostly the 'feeling' of his eyes and hands on me when they shouldn't be."

"Oh, that." He smiled and pulled her into his arms. "I'm sure you're imagining it. You'll be fine."

She shook her head.

"Trust me," he said. Everything will be OK. We haven't seen O'Rourke, so maybe he's gone away."

"Just like a bad penny, he keeps turning up."

"Go out driving? With whom?" Aleksandra said.

"It's a surprise. A friend of mine," said Miss Abbott. "A secret." She glanced over her shoulder, then turned back to Aleksandra.

"Thank you for the invitation, but I've promised my evenings to my husband, sorry. I'm sure you could find someone else. Maybe cook?" She smiled at the housekeeper. Perhaps she was courting. "I must return to my charges. They are working sums on their slates this morning, and the twins cannot be left alone for long."

"Well, dinner will be served in half an hour."

"Thank you," Aleksandra said, and hurried back to the children.

"Walk on," called the driver, to the pair of matched bays.

"Goodbye children, mind Mrs. Argüello and I'll see you in a few days, as soon as Grandmama is better." Mrs. Rowe waved from the gig, as her driver guided the horses down the steep driveway.

There were tears in Toby's eyes and Aleksandra took his hand. The other two ran up the steps.

"Cook said she was making biscuits!" Emily said.

Aleksandra laughed. "OK, go ask her for one each, if they're ready, and meet me back out here. We're having riding lessons today on Dzień.

"Really?" Emily said, eyes wide.

Aleksandra had never seen them move so fast.

Dzień was exemplary for their first lessons, aided no doubt by their administration of small bits of biscuit and cookie donated to the cause by Cook. The children glowed as they ran up the steps again, after un-tacking and grooming the preening Mustang, looking all the happier against the frown on Miss Abbott's face.

"It's nearly dinner time and you're all filthy," she said to the children, but she glanced sideways at Aleksandra.

"That will soon be remedied." Aleksandra scowled at her. She wouldn't let the housekeeper rain on their parade today. It was too lovely a morning. Even Dzień was in heaven, trimming the lawn before the cottage.

Aleksandra herded the freshly-scrubbed children into the dining room just as their father entered the house. The children stood beside their chairs until their father pulled out his own, then they all sat down, one twin on either side of Aleksandra.

Miss Abbott hustled in with a terrine of soup and ladled it into the bowls, then trotted back to the kitchen, to return with a freshly baked and cut loaf of bread. She had removed her apron. After handing round the loaf of bread, she sat at the remaining table setting.

Mr. Rowe sat bolt upright and stared. Aleksandra held her breath and busied herself with the children, waiting for the explosion.

It never came.

"So how was your riding lesson, children? I saw you from my office." His voice sounded unnaturally high and breathless.

Aleksandra murmured to them when they all began to shout at once, then they took turns speaking to Mr. Rowe in a reasonable tone of voice. She glanced at him. His color was dangerously high. He never looked in Miss Abbott's direction.

"That's one hell of a nice pony you've got there, Mrs. Argüello," he said. "Willing to sell him? He's worth his weight."

"Sorry, but he's not for sale, for any price."

"Don't blame ya, lass. He's great with the children, though."

"Yes, he is. So you're happy for us to continue riding lessons?"

"By all means, by all means." He'd relaxed a little, thankfully, but then his gaze strayed to Miss Abbott, silently spooning soup into her pinched mouth, and he froze, then sniffed loudly. "Well, I must be off," he said as he stood, nearly knocking over his chair.

"But we've not had dessert," Miss Abbott frowned, then pasted on a smile.

He scowled, kissed each child goodbye, then hesitated for a moment beside Aleksandra, as if he'd do the same to her.

She shrank away from him and reached down to pick up a hastily-dropped napkin. When she looked up, he was gone and Miss Abbott's eyes shot daggers at her. "Finish up, children. I'm sure Miss Abbott is ready to tidy up now. Miss Abbott, can we please have that dessert in a few hours, after our lessons?"

Her grim smile answered. Aleksandra and the children fled.

AFTER PUTTING the children to bed that night, Aleksandra led Dzień down the hill toward Xavier's office. Dzień pricked his ears toward the trees to the left of the drive, and from the corners of her eyes, she thought she saw someone duck behind a tree, a blonde someone. She watched the tree until it was gone from sight, but saw no more of the mystery person.

Now I'm seeing things. Xavier's right.

She shook her head at her fears, opened the door of Xavier's office and stepped into the brightly lit room.

Xavier turned as she entered the room, and his face took on a guarded look.

She raised a brow at him.

He winced. "You're not going to like this."

"Try me."

"Just got a letter from Howard Egan."

"What is it?" She stepped quickly to his side.

"The Pony...it's been closed down."

"Closed?"

"Yes. Permanently."

"No...it can't be," she whispered. "All that...effort, blood, guts...all for nothing?" Her heart felt drained of blood and she placed her hands on his desk as the room wobbled around her.

"Sit down, Aleks." He came to her side. "You're a bit pale."

"But why?"

"The telegraph's through."

"And...?"

"Seems the owners of the Pony got themselves into hock pretty deeply, and the government bailed them out, because they needed the communication, but..."

"But?"

"The bailout was on the proviso that the day the telegraph lines were complete, the Pony would cease to exist."

She could only stare at Xavier. "But...but...the keepers, the ponies...the riders...?"

"They're done, unless they can get a job with the company which took over the route and stagecoach contract. They have the telegraph for the communications that need to be sent quickly, and the stages will have to suffice for the rest."

She took a deep breath and sat still for long minutes. He kissed her on top of the head and rubbed her shoulders.

"Well, I guess nothing's holding us here anymore, then," Aleksandra said, in a voice she herself scarcely recognized. We can take our nest egg and head for California whenever you want."

"I'm sorry, Aleks. I know what it meant to you, and to me, too."

She clenched her teeth for a moment. "Are you so sure you wanted it to start up again?"

He ducked down to meet her eyes. "I'll admit I feared you'd ride for the Pony again. I didn't want you to do it, because I didn't want to lose you, but I can honestly say I'm as gutted as you are to know it'll never run again." He was still as a statue for a full minute. "One thing for sure, though, we were blessed to have been a part of something that held so much importance for our country. Blessed indeed."

She grudgingly had to admit it was true, and told him so. He pulled her to her feet and wrapped his arms around her. They held each other like they'd never let go.

"It's home time. Where's Dzień?"

"Just outside." She opened the door and he whickered softly.

Xavier locked the door and they headed for home.

As had become his habit, Courtney was waiting for her again, just beside the stairs this time. He was becoming bolder, as her heart slowly softened.

Why, oh why, did he have to press his suit now, when Mrs. Rowe was gone, and it was her only opportunity to try to latch onto Mr. Rowe? It appeared to be feast or famine. She laughed weakly.

"Oh, to see you smile like that for me," Courtney whispered and reach for her hand. She let him hold it, his fingers making hers tingle. "Can it be your heart yearns for me as mine does for yours?"

"You flatter yourself," she said softly, but her face heated.

"So can we take our drive soon?"

"The governess' time is all taken by her husband, so I must ask Cook."

His face darkened. "The Mexican?" he growled.

She shot him a look. "Pardon?"

"Oh nothing, my love," he said, smiling down into her face.

She quivered as she watched his lips, felt his hands on her shoulders, and she could do nothing to stop him. Those lips lowered to hers and an electric shock tingled where they met hers. "Oh…" Her legs jelly, she was happy for his strong arm about her waist. When his lips met hers again, her arms reached around his neck and she pressed her body to his. Her face must be flaming, for the heat she felt.

"Say you'll be mine," he murmured against her neck, "and soon, my love, for I don't think I can contain myself much longer."

"Yes…soon…" was all she could manage.

"Now go back, before we are discovered." He stepped back and she stumbled, devoid of his support. "Where do I find your father, to ask for your hand?"

"He is dead, sir, so we needn't ask, but we would have to ask Mr. Rowe."

"I'm sorry to hear that, but it gladdens my heart," he breathed, "that there is less impediment to our marriage. But isn't Mr. Rowe just your employer?"

"I guess we don't need to ask him," she said. As excited as she was at the thought of his making love to her, a voice of reason still whispered in her ear.

Take the master.

She couldn't decide.

"We need to get that governess to chaperone you. Perhaps if she thought you were ill? Just so you can get off the mine without risk to your reputation," he said. "It will be dark, after all."

She shivered with delight at Mr. Delaney's nearness, but she wondered again which man she should choose.

ALEKSANDRA LED the children into the house to get cleaned up for dinner. A peek into the dining room showed an additional place once again set at the table. She let out the breath she'd been holding. Mr. Rowe tolerated it yesterday, but then he'd had a day to consider what he might do if it happened again. As dinnertime approached, Aleksandra tried to think of any excuse not to be present for the disaster waiting to happen at the table, but none was forthcoming.

She didn't have long to wait. The master was seated when she and the children filed into the dining room, each child as tidy as Aleksandra could make them. They kissed their papa and sat down. Aleksandra kept her distance, and tried to remember to breathe.

The dinner was served and Miss Abbott made a show of removing her apron and folding it away before seating herself. There was a roar from the head of the table and the housekeeper leapt to her feet as if she'd been stung.

"*Miss* Abbott, I will see you in my office," Mr. Rowe glanced around the table, "privately. We are not to be disturbed, for any reason."

There was a low, but insistent, feminine murmur from the office for quite some time before the volcano erupted. They needn't have removed to the office; every word he shouted reverberated throughout the house. His voice may have even been audible from deep inside the mine.

40

M iss Abbott couldn't remember having ever been this angry before.
"And what, sir, is the reason I cannot sit at table with you? That tart of a governess sits beside you and your children, and you simper over her," she said, in a terse whisper. "Doubtless she favors you with whatever you want when your wife is gone. Who is it that looks after your household, has always done so, and keeps you happy? Certainly not your pale shadow of a wife. She's getting more and more nervy. She might even be getting a nervous disorder. Then where will your children be? I could make you happy, warm your bed," her face heated, "and bear you more children. Why Aleksandra, and not me?" She finished on a wail.

He sat frozen for a few moments, pinching the bridge of his nose.

Finally, he's coming to his senses.

"My father has always had extramarital affairs." Mr. Rowe finally said, as he lifted his eyes from the desk before him to fix upon her face.

She stopped smiling and stared at him.

He looked straight into her eyes. "So you're to be just like your mother?" It was more a statement than a question.

"Pardon?"

"You want to be the master's mistress."

"Oh yes, more than anything. I would be the best mistress of your house that you could ever imagine."

"I don't believe we're talking about the same sort of mistress."

The silence stretched out between them and her smile faded.

"Like my father, I also have extramarital relationships. And like my father, I take care of any consequences of those affairs."

"What do you mean?" Uncertainty crept into her voice. "I wouldn't want to—"

"—we took care of you, didn't we?" His voice cut into her consciousness.

Her mouth dropped open and her gorge began to rise.

"Yes, you're my half-sister. I will never take you to my bed. Live with it or leave. We've given you a forever home and position, but your disparaging remarks regarding those under my roof will no longer be tolerated, regardless of any promises made by my father." This last was uttered at earth shattering volume. It was impossible to miss its impact.

She fled.

⌒

"COME IN," Rowe shouted to Xavier's knock on his office door.

"—and some ruffians torched the printing shop overnight," a stranger said. "They don't know what they did, or maybe they did. They destroyed a printing press that was the first one ever brought to California, way back in 1834."

"I'll come back later," Xavier said.

"No, it's fine, stay. Xavier, this is Philip Sanders, from over at Columbia, and you remember Captain Moore?" He turned back to Mr. Sanders. "So you think it's arson?"

Xavier nodded at Mr. Sanders, then grinned at Captain Moore and shook his hand.

"Sure do," said Sanders, "and I think I know who's done it. Could be the same ones who burned the schoolhouse in Union Hill last spring."

Rowe frowned. "Any motive?"

"For the printing shop? They'd reportedly been printing secessionist handbills, so likely that."

"Ah, yes. Things are certainly heating up. When you figure it out, we'd sure like to know, if he's the one who fired the Union School last spring." Rowe gritted his teeth. "All right, then. We're done with our business? I'll see you next month. Thank you for your help," he said, as Philip left.

"Good to see you, Captain," Xavier grinned. "Did you know, Rowe, this man may have saved my life?"

"Don't believe he mentioned it, but it doesn't surprise me."

"That's actually why I've come here today, Mr. Rowe," said the captain, and turned to Xavier. "I understand you've seen O'Rourke?"

"Sure have. Was a bit like seeing a ghost. We thought he'd have been dead after your boys found him in Dixie." He gritted his teeth.

"Slipperiest bugger we've ever tried to keep hold of," Captain Moore said, shaking his head. "I'm sorry, but we let O'Rourke get away." He shook his head. " Mr. Rowe says you saw the bastard at Malakoff?"

"Yes, but his uncle's the supervisor there, and the place is littered with Southerners," Rowe said.

"That makes things a little tricky." He looked at his hands gripping the desk. "I've no troops at my back, but I'll get help as soon as I get back to Benicia Barracks."

"I'd sure appreciate that," Xavier said, with a sigh.

"So Aleksandra is here? She's OK after losing the baby?"

"She's doing well, now…" he hesitated, "and I'm sure she'd want to send her thanks to you and your boys for going after that Confederate hornet's nest," Xavier said.

"You're welcome to supper at the cottage, Moore, then Aleksandra can thank you herself," Rowe paused, "but I can't be sure what's on the menu—or if there's a menu at all. Our housekeeper ran out this afternoon and I'm not sure she's returned. Cook's still there, though. I daresay we could carry our own supper from the kitchen." He grinned for a moment, before his face fell again, and he exchanged a worried look with Xavier. "Come on up. Supper'll be served just before dark and we'll eat—whatever it is."

MISS ABBOTT RETURNED to the cottage before supper and thankfully served in silence, then retired to the kitchen. When the door closed behind her, Aleksandra breathed a sigh of relief and exchanged glances with Mr. Rowe. Xavier and Captain Moore were deep in conversation. After supper, Aleksandra took the children upstairs to bed while the men took port. On her way back to the drawing room, Miss Abbott tapped her shoulder as she passed the kitchen door, a pleading look in her eyes.

"I'm not well. I can only turn to you. Can you please chaperone me? My friend is going to take me to the doctor."

Aleksandra gave her a hard look. Something didn't ring true. "But why do you need me to go?"

"You are the only one I can turn to. My friend is male, and it wouldn't be seemly to drive alone with him."

Aleksandra hesitated. The housekeeper was correct, but why her, and why now? "Can't Cook go with you?"

"She's gone to bed early with a headache. Please? Just to Grass Valley and back, I promise. We can be back in an hour, before we're missed."

Aleksandra wavered. She had her *shashka* after all. She sighed. "OK. Let me get my coat."

"I'll be back shortly," she whispered in Xavier's ear. "Miss Abbott needs my help with something." He reached up and squeezed her hand, then returned to his conversation.

She stepped out into the night. A carriage waited halfway down the drive, and a white hand from the figure standing beside it urged her to hurry. She ran to the gig and placed her foot onto the step. Before she took her seat, the carriage shot forward, throwing her back against the seat.

"What are you—" cut off as a hand came over her mouth and a familiar voice spoke into her ear.

41

Aleksandra closed her eyes for a moment to still her rising panic.
O'Rourke.

"What are you doing, my love?" Miss Abbott said, in an astonished voice.

"Can you drive?" He asked, his voice impatient.

"Yes, of course."

"Then take the reins. I need to hold her."

"But—"

"Just drive," he snapped.

"But you said—"

"Stop your whining. You think I could want the likes of you, when she's available? Shit—" he growled and Aleksandra yelped as he twisted her arm. "Biting isn't nice, Aleksandra."

"You know her?" Miss Abbott said.

"Sure do."

"Then…why…?" Miss Abbott's voice dwindled.

"Because I needed *you* to get *her*." He nodded at Aleksandra.

"Why, you, you despicable liar!" She swung at him with the heavy butt of the whip and he flinched.

It wasn't much, but it was enough for Aleksandra to free her mouth and right hand, then pull her *shashka* from inside her skirt while she shrieked his name. The road from the mine doubled back toward Grass Valley, so maybe Xavier would hear her. It wasn't a big chance, but it was all she had. She swung the sword toward him and missed.

The already-nervous horse swerved and leapt forward at the unintended lash of Miss Abbott's whip and the gig swayed as O'Rourke lunged for Aleksandra. She ducked to the floor of the gig and he overshot her, flipping head-first out of the fast moving conveyance. He landed in the road with a shriek of rage and pain.

"Give me the reins," Aleksandra barked. Miss Abbott fumbled with them, but only succeeded in dropping them. She shook her head. "Just sit still and hold on," she said to the housekeeper, and spoke calmly to the shaking horse. She managed to get him stopped and turned in the narrow road, then dashed back the way they'd come.

"We're going back towards him?" Miss Abbott shrieked.

"No choice. Move over and be quiet," Aleksandra hissed. She leaned forward so the housekeeper could move across. "Where's the whip?" Aleksandra shouted at the housekeeper.

"I don't know, I think I dropped it."

"Oh, hell," Aleksandra said. O'Rourke stood in the middle of the road, whip in hand, its long lash snaking beside him in the moonlight.

"Stop, Aleksandra," he barked.

"Get out of the road, or I'll run you over," she growled, and pushed the horse on as fast as he would go. O'Rourke never wavered, but swung the whip towards the horse's face. The beast shied away from him, but kept running. O'Rourke grabbed for the reins and the horse slid to a halt and reared, O'Rourke holding on for grim death.

He turned his head at the report of a rifle, and Aleksandra swung the end of the reins toward his head. He grabbed them as they hit his face and jerked, pulling Aleksandra from the wagon and onto the ground. She hit the ground rolling and jumped to her feet, *shashka* held before her, and stood facing him in the middle of the wagon track.

Galloping hooves, headed their way.

O'Rourke looked at her, hate in his eyes, then turned back to where the horses raced toward him. The moonlight glinted off rifle barrels and a bayonet.

"I'll be back," he said, "for you," then turned and dived off the road down the sheer embankment into the trees.

Aleksandra looked back to the gig to see Miss Abbott's face, white against the blackness of the forest behind her. "Whatever could you have been thinking?" she asked the maid.

"I'm sorry," her voice quivered. "I never thought—"

"—I can see that. Move over," Aleksandra said again, and hopped into the gig. She steadied the white-eyed, heaving horse. He whinnied frantically to the approaching horses.

Xavier vaulted from Charro's back. "What happened?"

"O'Rourke. He just shot off down there." She pointed to the steep canyon down which the Southerner had disappeared. "He saw you coming and ran."

"Are you hurt?"

"Tumbled out of the gig, my fault, but I'm OK."

He leapt up beside her and enveloped her in his arms. Captain Moore's and Rowe's horses crashed through the undergrowth, but soon returned.

"We lost him," Rowe said. It's a sheer face down there, and too many foxholes to follow him in the dark. We'll send out search parties tomorrow. Are you OK, Aleks?" He looked up at his dumbstruck housekeeper and his brows narrowed. "Did you have something to do with this?"

She nodded, slowly, as his question sank in.

"We have some talking to do," he muttered beneath his breath.

"Who's horse is this?" Aleksandra asked.

"Courtney, Mr. Delaney—" Miss Abbott stuttered.

"First names, now, eh?" Mr. Rowe growled.

"—he brought it," she said, more steadily.

"And what were you—"

"Why don't you talk to her back at the house, Mr. Rowe, she's in shock. I'll drive."

Miss Abbott sat back silently. After a while, she reached out a hand to touch Aleksandra's arm. "I am so sorry, Aleksandra. I never meant you any harm. I was eloping with him, or so I thought. I honestly had no idea of his plans."

"I believe you," Aleksandra said, her voice gruff to her own ears. "He's the devil's spawn, that one."

"My vanity has brought me to this. I have need of—much contemplation."

Aleksandra glanced over at her, then back to the still quivering horse. It appeared Mr. Rowe had just obtained a new horse and carriage.

Two weeks later, Miss Abbot knocked on the children's schoolroom door. "Mrs. Argüello, someone here to see you. It's Mrs. Davies, the mine engineer's wife from next door."

"Whatever can she want?"

"I can't say I know," the housekeeper's voice carried from her retreating form.

"Children, please continue with your letters," Aleksandra said, "I'll return in a moment." They returned to scraping away on their slates, as she followed Miss Abbot.

"...and so I thought, as long as you were teaching three, you might as well teach another three." Mrs. Davies, the mine engineer's wife from next door looked expectantly at her.

Aleksandra waited for her to finish.

"Well, what do you think?" the overblown matron said, peering down her nose at Aleksandra.

She considered for a moment. "I've been hired as a governess here. I cannot govern that many more."

"Oh, just for their lessons."

"Have you spoken with Mr. and Mrs. Rowe? I am in their employ."

"I'm sure they'll agree."

"I'll discuss it with them, if you wish," Aleksandra said.

"Yes, please. I'd like my children to start with you right away. No time like the present."

"I'll speak with my employers and let you know," she said firmly. "Now I must return to my charges."

"Well, best hurry up with it," Mrs. Davies said. "I'll hear from you without delay." She nodded and turned on her heel. Her bustle wiggled from side to side as she sashayed down the hill toward her two-story house.

Mrs. Rowe bit her lip when Aleksandra told her of the visit.

"I told her I'd ask your opinion."

The superintendent's wife took a deep breath and exhaled slowly, while she looked around the sitting room. She finally answered. "Her children are…shall we say, indulged? At the very best, I don't want them in the house. Worse, they might prove challenging to teach."

Aleksandra raised a brow at her.

"Their last three governesses have run screaming from the house." Her lips twitched. She was too much of a lady to laugh.

"So, then—shall I refuse her?"

"I'll do it," Mrs. Rowe said. "She's venomous. You'd not like to have her as an enemy."

Aleksandra gulped. No, she didn't need any more of those.

Mrs. Rowe visited at the house down the hill later that day, and went on down to her husband's office afterwards. A short time later, Aleksandra heard shrieks from down the hill, followed by the sight of Mrs. Davies stomping down the path toward the mine offices.

Aleksandra was grooming the horses when Xavier rode Charro up to their barn just before supper.

"Just what did you say to Mrs. Davies?" Xavier's brow furrowed.

"Why?" Aleksandra turned away from Rogan to face him.

"She was in her husband's office next door to mine, raving about the uppity wife of the new assay officer refusing to teach her children."

"What?" Aleksandra nearly dropped her brushes.

"What was that about?" he asked.

She told him, finishing with "...that was a close call, I might have taken her children on. I'm sure she couldn't ever be satisfied."

"She seems like a nasty piece of work." Xavier's brows narrowed. "You'd best watch your step around her, *Querida*."

"I promise you," she shuddered, "I shall."

ALEKSANDRA unpinned and folded the last sheet from the line, then placed it on top of the others. It was good to have a whole day without rain. There'd been precious few of those in the past few weeks, and she smiled as she picked up the wicker basket. An all-to-familiar voice made her spin around.

"Well, lookee what I've found... If it ain't the uppity bitch—'Uppity Aleks.'

O'Rourke.

She peeked sideways in the gathering darkness, praying for Xavier to appear. No such luck.

"Even before our little ride last month," she said from between gritted teeth, "I thought I'd never have to see you again. And now you're here."

Had anyone else returned to their cabins, close enough to hear her if she screamed? No lights lit their windows. She'd have to bluff.

"Oh, you mean after Fort Churchill?" He chuckled. "They caught me, but can you believe, they were stupid enough to leave me under the guard of a Southerner? He was easily convinced I'd be less trouble if I wasn't his prisoner. There was a dead Southerner who looked enough like me to be passed off as such, so I took his identity papers, and...just left. Here I am. Glad to see me, sweetie?"

She gritted her teeth and placed her hand on the hilt of her *shashka*, then eased back a step, keeping the basket between them, hiding the sword.

"Have you left that no-good husband of yours yet?"

She glared in silence.

"You know, mine accidents—they happen all the time. It'd be easy. Pity 'bout the rest of the men."

"Stay away from me and mine, and never return," Aleksandra growled.

"Oh, I'll return, and you'll go with me, willingly or not. I'll just wait until we have a little more privacy." He laughed, low and evil, as he backed away, then melted into the night. "I promise you that, and I always keep my promises." His voice carried to her as the squelch of his footsteps on sodden pine needles retreated.

ALEKSANDRA RAN BACK into the house and pulled in the latchstrings, counting the minutes until she heard Charro's hoofbeats on the path outside. She peeked through the window just to be sure.

She bolted out the door and reached for him.

"Hey, what's this?" Xavier asked, "missed me?" He smiled and slid from Charro, and she wrapped her arms around him, her face against his chest.

"O'Rourke was here again tonight, Xave." She didn't sound nearly as calm as she'd hoped she would.

"Here?" He jerked his head back and looked her in the eyes.

She shook in his arms. "He talked about mining accidents, presumably to get rid of you, and of taking me. He's a lunatic."

"How did he know where our house was?"

"I don't know."

"Did he say anything that might tell you?"

She sat in the nearest chair for long moments, then her head shot up. "What did Mrs. Davies say?"

"*Perdón*? Pardon me, what?"

"When she raved in the office next to yours, last week?"

"About the 'uppity—"

"Yes, that was it. That's what he said…O'Rourke called me the 'uppity bitch.' I think I know where he got his information. Mrs. Rowe said she wasn't a woman to cross."

"We're done here. Start packing, we're going home," Xavier said, his jaw so tight it could have been a drum.

"WE'RE LEAVING. I cannot continue to risk Aleksandra's life. That man won't take no for an answer," Xavier muttered.

"We're do our best to keep you both safe," Mr. Rowe said, in a soothing voice.

"Like that night last month? Like tonight? That lunatic's still out there. Tonight's shown just how much safety we have here. I'm sorry, James, but we can't stay. We need to go home."

"You can't *get* home," Rowe reasoned. "It's been raining solidly for the past month, the snow's even melting on the mountains. You've seen the swollen creeks. The Sacramento River is impassable and the whole central valley's flooded."

"We leave as soon as the waters drop." Xavier wouldn't be dissuaded this time.

"That's fair. You've done well to stay as long as you have with that madman still running free."

"The troops Captain Moore sent haven't found him?" Xavier growled.

"Nope, and his uncle at the Malakoff sent his apologies to you for his nephew. Says he knew nothing of his activities."

"He would say that, even though the guns were for him, or so O'Rourke said when he had me kidnapped."

"Anyway, his uncle says he hasn't seen hide nor hair of him since that night he was last here."

"We'll be watching."

Miss Abbott slipped into the room to pass around tea and cake.

"Please, sit down and have dessert with us, Bertha," Mrs. Rowe said.

The housemaid glanced up, her pale face lighting up for a moment, then she sat on the edge of her chair. She looked as if she might run away the slightest provocation. She ate her cake and thanked them for the invitation, then cleared the plates and took them back to the kitchen.

"That was kind of you, darling," James said to his wife, and squeezed her hand.

"We're the only family she has left, and she's changed her tone since that dreadful night," she glanced at Aleksandra, "hopefully for good."

Mrs. Rowe had recovered her poise and smile, and Aleksandra was pleased as she could be.

Brent O'Rourke grinned. Turned out it wasn't hard to find out where the Mexican's celebrated family lived.

There were plenty of *Californios* willing to talk, with a little greasing of their palms. It seems the Rancho de las Pulgas was one of the biggest old Spanish land grants in the San Francisco Bay area, owned by the Argüello family for three generations.

A place that big shouldn't be hard to find.

His uncle was sending him west to recruit support for the Knights from amongst the old *Californio* families anyway, so he'd just look them up. Might be a while before he got there; his uncle wanted him to visit southern California first and work his way north, but he'd get up there, all right.

"Tell them if they support the Confederates," his uncle told him, "we'll get their old land grants restored to them. They're losing them piece by piece, hand over fist in the courts, now that the real Americans want that land. To sweeten the deal, tell them we'll kick out the squatters trying to take ownership of their land, too. That should do it." He grinned. "With their help and a little politics, we'll get California into the Confederacy. Once the Southwest and the West are tied up, the Union will be nothing but a memory, and the Stars and Bars'll flutter over the entire country. And we'll be rich."

"You can trust in me, Uncle."

"See that I can." His voice had an edge. "You made a fiasco of our name last month, not to mention losing one of my best horses and gig. I had to swear up and down I hadn't seen you. Good thing everyone around here's loyal to me."

"I've apologized," O'Rourke growled.

"Time for action, not words." He turned to go. "And stay away from that girl. We can't risk alienating the *Californio* contingent by your stupidity."

O'Rourke bit his lips together to hold in the retort his uncle's comment deserved, but he knew better than to anger him further. Without his support and concealment, life could get hard. Very hard. As it was, he'd be seeing Aleksandra again soon. And this time, he'd make it clean. She'd be his for sure, and her husband wouldn't get out of it alive.

"I'M NOT LEAVING you alone, Aleksandra, so get used to it." Xavier stomped down the hall to their bedroom and started stuffing his clothes into his saddlebags.

"I only meant you should go put your affairs in order at work. You can leave me off at the Rowes'," she said.

"And have him whisk you off in broad daylight? Beneath the nose of the ladies of the house and two children, all within sight of my office? No, thank you. You're staying with me until we leave."

She sat in a chair and watched him.

"I have my *shashka*."

"You had it the last time, when you got into his gig." He stopped his pacing and looked at her, his mouth open.

No, it couldn't be.

"What?" Her brows came together and she froze.

Did she encourage these men?

He shook his head.

A tiny voice, the one he'd stopped listening to months ago, whispered over his shoulder: "You know, women can't be trusted. Maybe she isn't what you think. You're being played for a fool."

He shook his head again.

The voice was insistent. "Dancing Wolf—O'Rourke—Vladimir—"

Maybe I'm going mad.

Aleksandra jumped up from her chair and rushed to his side. "Xavier, what's the matter?"

He flinched when she touched him, and she let go like he was a red hot poker, then stood staring at him.

He stared at her, motionless.

She stepped toward him, her eyes locked with his, and slowly reached for him.

He shook with the effort of holding his body still, not sure if he wanted her to touch him or not. He closed his eyes and tried to suck air into his lungs.

"What is the matter, Xavier," she repeated, as she clung to him. "You look like you've seen a ghost."

Of their own volition, his arms reached around her, crushing her to him. "I won't share you."

He wanted to drag her upstairs and show her he was her master and lover, both—at the same time.

She stared at him and pulled back, but he had her locked in. "What?"

"I won't..." He blinked.

What was he doing? He slowly pulled her in again, resting his head on hers. He kept trying to breathe, and slowly the fog dissipated.

"Xavier, I'm here. I'm not going away." As if she sensed his desperation.

He kept dragging air into his lungs and his mind began to clear.

What could he be thinking? These men weren't drawing her—she'd been taken. Taken.

He had to get control of his fear. She wasn't going anywhere—without him.

She tugged at the back of his hair and he opened his eyes and looked down into hers. Tears fell from the corners. He kissed them away and lifted her in his arms. Kissed her beautiful lips and carried her to the bedroom. Proved to her and himself that it was him she loved, and only her he loved. Their lovemaking was hurried, desperate, then tender. Time drew out until it was only them, together, flying high, then drifting low, still in each other's arms.

They slept.

Xavier awoke a short time later and gazed at her, slumbering. This fear—of being abandoned—it still hadn't gone away. She wasn't to blame. He needed to get over this.

Christo.

She didn't deserve this. She'd never done anything but try to love him, again and again.

Time to trust her, or forever stay away from women.

He pulled her close, spooning his body around hers, and lay awake for long hours.

He promised himself it wouldn't happen again.

42

Xavier wanted nothing more than to pick up his woman and take her home, but the cold storms buffeting the Sierra Nevada and its foothills made their prospects grim for the fifty-odd miles down to Sacramento, at the confluence of the American and Sacramento rivers. From there, they could get a steamer to San Francisco.

Reports of fifteen-foot snowfalls in the mountains behind them were not encouraging. Finally, the frigid rains and snow gave way to warm ones, and although everything was wet, from clothes and bedding to the muddy roads, he was happy. At least they could get on the road now and he wouldn't be putting Aleksandra through any more discomfort. As Rowe said, the streams and rivers were still up, but he wanted to get on the road.

"Aleks, what do you say we head out tomorrow?"

She glanced up from the blouse she was stitching, then looked out the window at the deluge outside. "Mmmm…" she mumbled. She stabbed her needle into the fabric and left it, then removed her mouthful of pins. "Sounds good. I can't wait to get out of this rain. At least it's stopped snowing."

He glanced out the window for a moment. "The rivers are still up and a crazy man somehow made it here from Truckee. Says he's never seen so much snow."

"Doesn't surprise me, with all the snow we've had this far down the mountain."

"Problem is, that traveler says it was *raining* up there yesterday and again this morning." Xavier frowned.

" And that's a problem because…?" Aleksandra's brow furrowed.

"It's melting the snow. It's only December. It shouldn't be melting until late in the spring. The streams are already in flood and it'll only get worse. I'd like to get out while we still can, else it might be February or March before we can get out."

Aleksandra paled. "So it's now, then?"

"It's a risk, but if we don't want to be stuck here, it's a chance we may have to take."

She was silent for a minute, then took a deep breath. "Let's do it. Nothing ventured, nothing gained."

"That's my girl. Let's get packed and say our goodbyes."

"We leave as soon as that's done?"

"Yes." He leaned down to kiss her lips. "I'll go get the horses' gear together." As he spoke, the heavens truly opened up and the rain sheeted down, obscuring everything outside the windows of the little cabin.

Aleksandra winced. "Well, maybe we wait 'til the downpours stop."

The rain didn't stop. It continued at deluge proportions for days, but when it finally ceased toward dawn, several days later, they were ready. A small crowd waved them on their way. Through blurry eyes, Aleksandra waved goodbye to the little Rowes, the flowers they'd picked for her from the garden filling her other hand. Dzień still munched the carrot they'd slipped to him, while Rogan nosed the ground for the orange bits the pony dropped.

She locked eyes with Xavier. He smiled and she pulled Rogan's head up and they turned to go down the hill. A few men waved from the mine office as they rode out the gate and to the left toward Grass Valley, Dzień matching Charro's strides as they set off on their last stage home.

"Maybe we'll be home for Christmas?" She looked at Xavier beneath her brows.

He winced. "I wouldn't count on it. It's a long way, and I don't know how long we'll have to wait at Sacramento for a steamer. The reports lately haven't been good." He fell silent.

The rows of stately homes lining the Grass Valley streets were incongruous with the muddy streets, their window glass still dripping from this morning's downpour. Although the road was a quagmire, the normal stench coming from the back streets, of raw sewage and animal slaughter, was absent. She grinned. It would be back.

After a brief stop for supplies at the dry goods store, they headed down the hill. Once out of town, they could ride beside the road and the footing was reasonable. A quarter of an hour later, they rode through Union. Its busy Union Hill Mine was in full swing.

"That was the schoolhouse," Xavier pointed at a pile of blackened timbers beside the road, "that burned down last year."

Aleksandra's brows narrowed. "On purpose?"

"Seems so. Plenty of stories floating around. Disgruntled student who didn't like a punishment meted out by the schoolmaster, a parent who wanted his boys to mine with him, a prank gone wrong. Nobody knows for sure."

She shook her head. They rode on until a muddy torrent, raging down the mountain in a ravine, crossed their path.

"That's...Wolf Creek. It usually wouldn't even cover the horses' fetlocks," Xavier said.

Aleksandra frowned and took a tighter hold on Dzień's lead as she squeezed Rogan forward with her legs. Charro didn't even look sideways, and walked on into the water, past the middle of his forearms. Rogan and Dzień followed, the pony holding his nose high to keep it out of the water.

Half an hour later, the Bear River tumbled across the trail before them. It wasn't quite as nice as Wolf Creek. Aleksandra and Xavier looked at each other. "I'm worried about Dzień. I don't want him to be swept away."

Xavier considered for a moment. "How about we put two ropes on his halter, with Charro furthest up river, then Rogan, and then Dzień."

"Let's give it a try," Aleksandra said, and dismounted to find their extra rope. "It'll be fine, pony. We'll get you through."

Their plan worked, despite the large log that flew past them, narrowly missing Rogan's rear as it twisted end-for-end in the current. Dzień had to swim, but the ropes kept him from being swept downriver by the torrent.

Half an hour later, it started to rain.

"Again?" Aleksandra looked skyward, her buckskin leggings still dripping from their last swim.

Xavier raised his brows. He untied the *serapes* from behind his saddle and tossed one to her. She wrapped it tightly around herself to keep out most of the rain and pulled the brim of her ten-gallon hat lower on her head.

They passed *Alta Sierra*, Higgins Corner and several other small mining camps. The inhabitants who could escape work huddled inside their shanties, while the rest dripped with water as they trudged around the quagmire of their workings.

When their trail met with the churned-up mud of the Truckee Trail at Auburn, Aleksandra was ready for a stop, since the rain showed no signs of doing so.

"Xavier," she said, "any possibility we can get a room for the night and some shelter for the horses?"

"You're reading my mind, *Querida*. I feel like a fish."

"A fish would be having an easier time of it," Aleksandra grumbled.

"We'll be on a ship soon enough," he murmured. "It's only 100 miles on the steamer, downstream. The river'll be a bit high, but what could be easier?"

"Aaaah, blessed warmth," Aleksandra held her hands toward the fire in the grate. Their room at the Auburn Hotel was small, but toasty warm. A tinny piano downstairs plinked out a tune and already, drunken miners were shouting along with the music.

"The horses looked pleased, with their heads in a manger full of hay, in a warm barn."

"At least we're warm, from rubbing them down."

"True, but my hands might be cold forever," Aleksandra said.

Xavier nodded. "We should be able to make Sacramento by tomorrow night, unless the weather's truly horrible. If it is, we can probably stay at George Cirby's place at Grider's. I helped him out for a few weeks about five years ago. It's a couple hours before Sacramento.

After a good supper of roast beef and potatoes, they fell into bed. Aleksandra wriggled her body firmly into the front of Xavier's and slept like the dead.

In the morning, the sun peeked fitfully through the clouds, but it wasn't raining. An hour and a half down the slippery slope towards the big city, they rode through Newcastle.

"The country up here used to be winter grazing for the ranchers down on the flats," Xavier said. "Man named John Sutter ran some massive holdings, courtesy of the Mexican government, with his own army of Indians. Unfortunately for him, in 1848, this all became part of the United States and Sutter started losing his hold on it. To top it off, he sent Marshall, his partner, up to Coloma to build a sawmill on the American River. The rest is history— he found gold on the site of the new mill. Word leaked out, and the 'Argonauts' seeking gold flooded the area, and pretty much wrecked New Helvetia, as he called his holdings, as a functional ranching property."

"Is that the land we're passing through?"

"No, his biggest holdings were along the Yuba and the Feather Rivers, and the land around his fort, where Sacramento now sits. Since then, with all the miners up here, it's not safe to leave your stock to roam. They'll just turn up as somebody else's supper. I imagine it's getting a bit like that back at the *rancho*." He winced.

"We'll be back there soon, and we can see how the land lies," Aleksandra said, reaching for his hand. He gripped it and gave her a wry grin.

"That we will." He smiled.

Aleksandra nodded at the three men arguing by the side of the road when they rode through Penryn a few hours later.

"I'm tellin' ya," said a man in stained miner's garb with a Cornishman's lilt, a frown furrowing his brow, "those jobs should be held for 'Cousin Jack'.

The mines in Cornwall are dead and they need the work. 'Sides, they're the best. You won't get the gold out o' the mines without 'em."

"But there are other men here already, who need the work now, too," said a nattily-dressed man, likely a mine manager.

The first man began to reach toward the businessman, but his hands dropped and he clenched them together tightly at his sides. "The Cornish grapevine'll hear o'this," he growled, beneath his breath.

"Let's trot, shall we, before they come to blows and start a riot?" Aleksandra whispered.

"Don't mind if I do." They pushed the horses into a trot and were soon past. Behind them, the men shouted something about the tommyknockers avenging them. "Those Cornishmen want to fill the mine with their friends and relatives from back home, even though they're not here yet," Xavier said.

"One of the cleaning maids at the Rowes' said men've been talking about stopping work all at once," she said, "and refusing to work until they're offered better pay and working conditions. She said it was mostly the Cornishmen leading it."

Xavier stared at the reins in his hand a few moments before he spoke. "They're out for better working conditions and pay for themselves, and they know the mines can't run without them because they have the experience needed for hard rock mining. They'll bring the rest with them because they know there's strength in numbers. Rowe's been watching, but nothing's come of it—yet—but it's only a matter of time. They're pretty persuasive."

A shiver ran up Aleksandra's spine. "The management won't like that much. Would they force the men back to work?"

Xavier sighed. "They'll try, but the Cornish know what they're doing. They've done it for years back in Cornwall. It costs a lot of money to keep a mine running, and many are running on a shoestring between big gold strikes, especially after the fires they've had in Grass Valley and Nevada."

"And the investors and owners wouldn't like it."

"No, they want their ongoing profits. Even if they're not paying the miners during a stoppage, the running costs continue, so they'll try to bring in outside men to work the mines."

"Is that a problem?"

"Apparently so. I haven't seen it, but apparently the 'striking' miners, as they are called, form solid lines which the incoming new men have to pass. They harass them and try to prevent them from getting to the mines."

Aleksandra stared. "Knowing some of those men, I'd imagine things could get nasty."

Xavier nodded. "Everything from fights to murder. It's not pretty. Rowe tries to keep the men as happy as the rest of the investors will allow, but the dollars only stretch so far and some men'll always make trouble."

"I'm glad we're out of the mines," Aleksandra said, and rubbed Rogan's withers.

The rain started again at midday and the already-soaked clay of the wagon trail turned more greasy, if that were possible. Aleksandra turned Rogan off to the side of the road, but it wasn't much better. "At least the horses can grab a bit of grass," Aleksandra said, shaking water from her dripping collar.

The rain poured down as they passed the Placer Post Office, a lone building near a forlorn cluster of miners' shacks.

"There's a stage stop just ahead in Secret Ravine, at the Hawes Ranch. We should be able to get a hot meal there," Xavier said, shouting over the deluge.

Aleksandra smiled. Dzień plodded along, head low, his ears fanned out to the sides. "Look at poor Dzień. God, he hates rain." The Mustang looked her way, then dropped his head again. The only thing that perked him up was the occasional bunch of grass he found while fossicking in the mud.

"He's a desert pony. I can understand, nobody likes it. Sorry, Dzień," Xavier said. The Mustang shook his head and water flew sideways.

"Is THAT YOU, Xavier? I'd recognize Charro anywhere," a grizzled man called out as he stood in the open doorway of the stage stop.

"Sure is, Elisha. I'd like you to meet my wife, Aleksandra."

"Welcome, both of you. Put the horses in the barn, plenty of room." He glanced at Rogan. "Two stallions? Put them in the two stalls in the front of the barn—my mare's at the back. I'll get some dinner on."

Aleksandra smiled her thanks in his direction. They raced for the barn as the heavens opened and a bolt of lightning lit the sky behind them.

They were warmer after unsaddling and rubbing the horses down, and warmer still seated in front of his splendid fire, their stomachs filled with hot stew. Each of the men shared a bit of their lives since they last saw one another. All too soon, it was time to head out into the rain again. They talked about the high rivers and Elisha's forehead furrowed when Xavier told him their plans to take a riverboat to San Francisco, but he only wished them well.

"Goodbye! *Hasta luego*," Xavier called. Aleksandra waved as they rode out of his yard and headed on down the mountain.

It was still pouring by the time they rode through the town of Rocklin. "Over there," Xavier pointed, is Joel and George Whitney's Spring Valley Ranch. When I was last by their place, he was talking about importing all sorts of animals and plants and growing them on his huge holdings."

"What sort of plants and animals?" Aleksandra wrinkled her brow at him.

"He wanted to import sheep from Australia, Shires from England, and loads of citrus—oranges, lemons and limes." He stared around his friend's ranch for a time, then shook his head. "By God, looks like he's done it!" Xavier laughed, pointing at the rows of dark green trees, and the white dots scattered over the pastures. "He was also trying to bring plenty of his countrymen over for an English settlement. By the look of all those houses on his place, he's probably done that, too."

The sun came out and they shed their soggy jackets, but a quarter of an hour later, it started pouring again. Another hour through the drenching wet found them at Grider's stage stop.

'High Sierra View Ranch,' said the sign beside the trail. A pack of barking dogs ran out as they rode up to the log cabin. Beside it stood a clapboard house, with ruffled curtains in the windows. The dogs grinned and wriggled as Aleksandra spoke to them and dismounted.

"Well, if it isn't young Xavier. How are you keepin', boy?" a tall, muscular man said, as he stepped out the office door.

"Mr. Cirby, it sure is."

"George, if you please," he said, then in an aside to Aleksandra, he added "makes me feel old, it does."

Xavier introduced Aleksandra, who nodded to him as he took her hand.

"Come on in, out of the rain. Looks like old Charro's got some friends. Tie 'em in the barn for now, then we'll sort the other horses to make room, that is, if you're staying?"

Xavier nodded. "If you please?"

"Good. Settled. Now you just hand me your bedroll, Aleksandra, and I'll take it in." Dzień was unloaded, and Charro, and they led them into the barn.

"So did you work here, too?" Aleksandra shook her head. "Either you were here for a long time, or you ran from job to job."

Xavier laughed. "A little of both, I think. Different ranches needed help at different times, and they sort of shared me around. Met a lot of people and ate a lot of fine cooking."

"Ah, food…the currency of the teenaged male," she said, and returned to her vigorous rub of Rogan's dripping, muddy coat.

"Xavier, it's been years, boy. What have you been up to? Heading back to California now?"

He nodded, seemingly not sure which question to answer first. He started with the last one. "Yes, going home seems the right thing to do."

Cirby shook his head. "I hope you don't plan on heading west anytime soon."

"Floods?" Xavier grimaced.

"Yep. They say it's looking to go over the stop banks in Sacramento, not that they're high enough to do anything, anyway."

"True," Xavier conceded. "They're only about three feet high, aren't they? I once spoke with an Indian, a *Maidu*. He said his family'd been telling the settlers not to build so close to the river, but they thought they knew more than an Indian." He shook his head.

"Bet he's laughing now."

"Another Indian I spoke with last week in Grass Valley said his whole tribe moved up into the mountains a month ago," Aleksandra said, and leaned over to pick out a hoof. "They knew this was coming." All were silent for a moment. "They watch the signs from the animals, the earth, and the stars. They knew."

"Amazing to think not so many weeks ago all of us ranchers and farmers were praying for rain, after two dry decades," George said, and removed Dzień's halter. The pony shook his head and headed for the hay rack. "I don't think any of us had *this* in mind. We've already had a full year's rainfall, not to mention snowfall, even down here, in the past two weeks."

"That's why we're making a dash for it now," Xavier said. "The storms in the Sierra Nevada have turned warm, and I'm afraid the snows will keep melting—and we might not get back for months."

GEORGE COCKED A BROW AT HIM. "You've got a point there. You're trying to get to your family's *rancho* at San Francisco, aren't you?"

"We are," Xavier said. "The riverboats are still running, aren't they?"

"As far as I hear, they are. If this rain keeps up, though, I don't know how long they will be. Anyway, come on in and meet the family."

"You've got a family now?" Xavier said, with a grin.

"A wife and three children already," George said, puffing out his chest, as he led the way back out into the storm.

His wife already had the door open as they ran up to it, a newborn clutched in one arm and a toddler clinging to her leg. "Come in, come in," she said, and held the door wide.

George introduced them to his wife, and then he picked up a baby of about one year old from a cot and held him aloft. "This is Jason, and this," he grabbed the two-year-old's hand, "is Sarah, my eldest, and my wife is holding baby Nell."

Aleksandra and Xavier made the appropriate noises. She shrank away when he handed the little boy to her, but then something inside made her reach for him and hold the child close. He stared up at her, his big green eyes so trusting, and she forgot to be afraid. She looked up and locked eyes with

Xavier. He smiled, and bit his lip. She looked back down at the boy and put her fingers in front of his tummy. He grabbed one finger and clung to it with surprising strength. A giggle escaped her, and she took a deep breath and looked back at Xavier. He was beaming now.

"Go on and take a seat by the fire, Mrs. Argüello."

She did, and sat the little boy up on her lap, where he entertained her until the meal was set upon the table. The rain outside became a downpour. Raindrops that made it all the way down the fireplace hissed as they touched the burning wood.

"I'm sure glad to be in here by your fire. Thank you so much for having us, Mrs. Cirby." The woman put the boy back in his cot and they sat down to a nice supper.

"So I hear they want to put the railroad through here," Xavier said.

"Yep. Judah was up here a couple years ago, surveying for the Auburn Branch of the railroad from Sacramento," said George. "It's his dream to continue the railroad straight through to Truckee. He's been trying to get the lawmakers to make a bill up since then, but now with the Civil War, it's been put on the back burner."

"Might be a while, then." Aleksandra said.

"So you're really going to try to make it to San Francisco, are you?" Mrs. Cirby said, her brows wrinkled.

"I want to make sure my family's OK," Xavier said, "and the *rancho*. I hear there's already flooding down that way."

"Can't say I blame you," George said. "It's still pretty risky, though the riverboat captains won't go if they don't think it's safe."

"We'll go down to Sacramento and see what it looks like, anyway, but we won't take unnecessary risks."

George and Mrs. Cirby exchanged a glance, and a grimace. "You two just take care, eh?" he said. "My wife will show you to your room. You'll be wanting to leave at first light?"

"Yes sir, we will, and thank you."

⌒

IN THE MORNING, they headed out, waving their new friends goodbye. If the wagon trail had been muddy before, it was a quagmire now, and the horses slipped and slid in the clay. A short time after they left the Cirby's, they came upon a muddy and frothy river.

Xavier blinked. "That's meant to be a stream. It's usually so small, they call it Dry Creek."

"Well it's not dry now," Aleksandra said, "and it looks like we might have a bit of a time crossing it."

They studied the torrent for a while and finally found a place where the water was wider, slightly shallower and a bit slower. The horses stared and balked, but they eventually went through and continued down the road. As the day wore on, what should have been a three hour ride to Sacramento became nearly four, although thankfully all downhill.

"What is *that?*" Aleksandra said, staring down the hill as a roaring sound echoed from further down the mountain.

43

"It's a river," Xavier said.

"Where is it?" Aleksandra frowned.

"It's miles away."

She stared at him and rode onto the crest of the next rise, then stopped, stunned. The brown, swirling liquid monster was miles and miles wide, moving slowly at the edges and faster in the center, with whole trees bobbing in the current like so many matchsticks. In the distance, out in the middle of the inundation, was a city. Her mouth dropped open, and she snapped it shut. "I take it that's Sacramento."

He nodded.

"And we're to catch a boat there?"

"Not anytime soon, it would seem," Xavier whispered.

They rode closer to the city. By the time they reached the first buildings, the water was up to their horses' fetlocks. Aleksandra and Xavier locked eyes for a moment, then went on. Worried people sloshed through the water, placing filled feed and flour sacks against doorways, then climbing in through their house windows to sit with the rest of their frightened families. Several rats half swam, half ran through the water. The place stank to high heaven, the sewage channels already well-overflowed.

A man hurried past, his arms full of packets, and a young woman ran up to him. "You were able to find food?"

"Yes, it will feed us for several days. This water should be down by then," he said, patting her hand. When she turned to head back toward what must be their house, he caught Aleksandra and Xavier looking at him, and winced, shaking his head.

They gave him a wave and carried on their way.

By the time they reached J Street, where the riverboats docked, the water was part-way up the big horses' forearms, and touching Dzień's belly. There were no riverboats in sight, only stunned people staring from their upper story windows at the muddy water filling their city. A stench hit Aleksandra's nose and she turned slowly, gagging. A bloated cow, likely several days dead, floated past and moved off toward the main body of the river, and Dzień snorted.

"Aleksandra," Xavier said firmly, "come this way."

She turned to follow down a street marked 2nd Street. Rogan tripped on something beneath the surface of the muddy water and nearly went down on his knees, slipping on the cobblestones as he tried to keep his feet. She stroked his neck, as much to calm herself as to calm him. This was, by far, the biggest city she'd ever seen. It left Salt Lake City in the dust. "How big is Sacramento?" she asked Xavier.

"I heard the census last year said there were over 13,000 people here."

She could only stare. "And it's all going underwater. Why ever did they build it down here?"

"Who knows? Likely Sutter thought this was a good place to put it, for trade, at the junction of the American and the Sacramento Rivers. His fort is just a little south of here."

She shook her head. "They should've listened to that Indian."

"They might be thinking about that right now. Anyway, here's the old Pony Express station. It's a stage stop now," he said, dismounting. "Can you stay with the horses, please? I don't want to leave them in this."

She shuddered. "You go ahead. I'll be here when you get back." She called Dzień to come closer and he pressed his side against Rogan, staring around him at all the water. He didn't like getting his feet wet at the best of times, but this would top it. He looked pretty miserable right now. "Well pony, that makes two of us."

When Xavier returned, he didn't look so happy either. Aleksandra raised a brow at him. "There haven't been any steamers through for a few days, but they're hoping one might come later this week, maybe just after," he winced, "Christmas."

She took a big breath and held it, letting it out slowly. "So, do you have a plan?"

"Working on it," he said, looking around.

"Do they have that much trouble with thieves?" Aleksandra asked, looking at the iron shutters covering most of the long, vertical windows throughout the city.

"The shutters, you mean?" Xavier said.

"Yes."

"After most of Sacramento burned to the ground a few years ago, they replaced all the wooden shutters with iron ones to make fires harder to spread, and they rebuilt the city from bricks, instead of timber, both of which also makes the buildings harder to rob, as you mentioned."

"It doesn't look like the river has have much of a problem 'breaking in'."

"Unfortunately not." Xavier sighed heavily. "I've found a hotel further along the banks of the American River, a little way up the hill. It's currently above the waterline. I suggest we go up there for the time being. There are others there who want to go to San Francisco, and the stage depot will send a runner," he closed his eyes for a moment, and the corners of his mouth up turned slightly, "or at least a swimmer, to let us know when a steamer comes."

"I'd be happy to stay somewhere in one of the upper stories here, but we can't leave the horses standing in water for that long," Aleksandra said.

"I agree." Xavier led the way past brick buildings, their first floors flooded, some with people in the upper stories, some abandoned, dead animals and bits of wood floating where gardens should lie.

An hour of slog later, they arrived at the hotel. A holiday wreath decked the front door, above the floodwaters. Aleksandra looked at Xavier. "What's the date?"

"I don't know, but that bit of greenery says it'll be Christmas soon."

Aleksandra winced. "I'm afraid I haven't thought about Christmas much."

"Me neither. Shall we worry about that once we get to California?"

He gripped the handle and turned it, then opened the door for Aleksandra.

THE COMMON ROOM was warm and past full to capacity. "I think this is the only hotel above high water," Xavier muttered in her ear. "Let's see if they have a room."

"I'm sorry, sir," the hotel owner behind the desk brushed the hair back from his face and took a deep breath, "but we have no more rooms. People are bunking down on the floor in this common room," he nodded at the milling crowd, "or in the barn."

Xavier looked at Aleksandra and she nodded. "We have three horses, do you have three stalls?"

"Can't they go in together?"

"Two of them are stallions."

His mouth formed an 'O', and he took another deep breath and held it.

"If you have three stalls, we can stay with the horses," Xavier said.

Aleksandra smiled her best smile at him, and he blushed.

"That will be fine, if that's all right—"

"It will be fine," Aleksandra said. "Is there somewhere we can get meals, or shop and cook?"

The poor man just stood with his mouth open, overwhelmed.

"Shall I go to the kitchens and ask?" Aleksandra said.

He nodded.

"Xavier, if you take care of the horses, I'll find out about food."

Xavier glanced around at the mixed crowd and frowned. "I don't like leaving you alone with all these people."

"I'll be fine. I'll be out in just a moment."

"I've heard that before," he said, then turned and disappeared.

The cook was nearly at her wits end, too. "I don't know how I'm going to manage all this, but if you'd like to help out for a short time each day until the steamer comes, I can feed you and your man at no charge."

"Sounds like a good deal, and I've nothing else to do, anyway." Aleksandra said, to the harassed woman.

Her beatific smile was all the thanks she needed.

"I'll be back soon," Aleksandra promised.

⟋⟍

SEVERAL DAYS LATER, it *really* poured. For two more days. The local newspapers announced that Christmas was cancelled.

Christmas never really happened, other than the prayers they offered to mark the day, but no one had the heart to do more than that.

"The steamboat will never come upriver in this," Aleksandra said, pummeling the huge mound of bread dough before her. The cook had no answer for her.

Xavier came into the kitchen, his face set. "The floodwaters are part way up the third story of the stage building, where the Pony Express ran from." He wiped a grimy hand over his face.

"Third story?" Her heart clenched in her chest. "Then... is the town gone?"

"No, but it's not looking good. Most everybody was asleep in bed when the biggest water came up last night."

She set her jaw. "And we're taking a boat down this?"

"That's the aim." He looked straight ahead.

"Would we be better to ride?"

"Where? The whole place is flooded. Until the rains stop for a few weeks, maybe more, that's not going to change. The whole Central Valley of California is flooded, and much of Oregon and Utah."

They stared at each other in silence for long minutes, then he pulled her into his arms. "It's not looking so good down here. I'm sorry I dragged you into this."

She shook her head at him, kissed his lips and returned to her bread. "Come sit down by the fire and get dry."

Xavier had made himself useful chopping and carrying firewood to the kitchen and the common room for the past few days, as well as lifting and carrying heavy pots. The cook couldn't feed the two of them enough goodies. She was cooking for three times as many people as she normally did, but she smiled as she she bustled around the kitchen.

Xavier returned from another trip outside with an armload of—wet— wood. After dumping it into the wood box of the kitchen stove, he looked up at Aleksandra. "Down at the docks today," he paused, "the water had risen ten feet since yesterday. It was over twenty-two feet above the low water mark, up to those third story windows. Even if there had been a steamboat there, I don't know if I'd want us to be on it, with all the wood frame houses, dead sheep, cows and horses, not to mention whole trees floating down the river. Sound like a recipe for disaster."

Aleksandra closed her eyes for a moment, then resumed pulling off pieces of bread to form into loaves, working in silence for long minutes.

"Oh, and Aleks," Xavier asked, "guess who I just met in the common room?"

She raised a brow at him.

"Leland Stanford."

"The new Governor? What's he doing here? Thought they just settled into some fancy mansion in Sacramento."

"They did, but so has the flood. Leland and his wife are staying here."

Aleksandra raised a dubious brow at him. "With all the commoners?"

Xavier laughed. "He's not so bad. He and his wife have been friends of my family, or my mother, anyway, for many years. He invited us to his inauguration, on the tenth."

"The tenth?" she managed to squeak.

He looked at her with a crooked grin. "We have no idea when we get to leave, and it might be fun."

She sighed, and kept kneading the heavy mass before her. "OK, if we're still here, it might be fun." She managed a grin in his general direction.

"They'd like to meet you, when we're not in the kitchen."

"We'll catch up with them tonight then."

LYING in the straw of Dzień's stall that night, Aleksandra snuggled closer to Xavier. Snores all around them bespoke a large human population in the stable tonight. "They were nice, actually, the Stanfords," Aleksandra said.

"You sound surprised."

"Well, I would've thought a man of the law, and a politician, might be a bit full of himself."

"Sometimes he is, but he was in family mode tonight, so we'll just enjoy it while it lasts." Xavier chuckled. "Stanford likes the land around the *Rancho*, and Charro, as well. He's tried to buy both several times, but neither is on the market." He grinned. "There's a big ranch just south of us he's been trying to buy for years, as well. He likes racehorses, and says someday he might have a racehorse farm. Imagine that, a whole farm just for horses."

"Papa worked on a Lipizzaner horse farm in Europe." She jumped at a thunderclap that sounded right on top of them. "Goodness, listen to the rain out there," Aleksandra whispered with a shudder. "I find myself wondering… if it's ever going to stop."

"It has to stop, someday," Xavier said. "You'll have to tell me about that farm sometime." His fingers moving in long, smooth strokes down her body, making her forget the storm outside, drawing all her attention to the one kindling within her. "Right now, we need to go to sleep," he gave her a lazy grin, "or…perhaps something more interesting."

'Something more interesting' sounded a whole lot better than sleep Aleksandra slid her hands beneath his shirt and tugged it off over his head, as his hands slid up her ribs. She gasped as their world spun down to a tiny circle, snug in the warmth of the barn.

THE TWO DAYS before the inauguration held possibly the greatest rainfall anyone could ever remember. One riverboat came up from San Francisco, but there were so many people wanting to flee, there was no room for three horses. They would wait.

They arrived on the tail end of a hot conversation when they met up with Leland and his wife in the common room that morning. "A carriage is out of the question, my love."

Aleksandra saw the governor-elect bite his cheek to stop from laughing, as his wife, luckily turned away from him, scowled.

"So how do you intend to get there? In a boat?" she spat.

"Unless I plan to destroy this suit, that was the intention."

"I'm not going in any boat through the capital city," she growled.

" Are you sure, my dear? Do you wish to miss it, after you've worked so hard in the campaign?"

"Well…"

"The rowboat is big enough to take," he looked around and waved at Aleksandra and Xavier, grinning, "all of us, if nobody moves around much."

"Well, all right. I'll go in the boat." Her smile appeared to be won at hard cost.

It was almost festive, bobbing in a boat through the middle of Sacramento to the Capitol Building at Seventh and I Streets, but for the dead creatures and tipped over buildings floating or lying everywhere. The water was still up to the third story windows of those buildings lucky enough to have three stories, a full two streets back from where the currently invisible port stood.

The streets of the city were usually sixteen feet above the low water mark, but a crusty old man they met in town one day told them it wasn't really all that abnormal.

"I've been trapping here for the past twenty years, and at least once every four or five years, I can row my canoe through what's now Sacramento," he'd said, then torn another chunk from the bread loaf in his hand.

"Maybe the city fathers should've taken the hint," Xavier had said.

Aleksandra's stomach turned, more than once, at the smells and the dismally sad sights. Only Leland seemed happy and excited. Mrs. Stanford looked like she was about to burst into tears, sitting in her frilly best dress in a little rowboat splashing through the mud and refuse. Aleksandra reached out and gripped her hand. The new governor-to-be's wife smiled past well-bitten lips, and held on tightly until they reached the site, when she had to release Aleksandra's hand and disembark the vessel to follow her husband out onto the steps of the Capitol Building.

The ceremony went on and on, while the rain began to beat down in earnest.

"It would've been even longer," Xavier whispered in her ear, "but most of the visiting dignitaries couldn't make it here from San Francisco, so consider yourself lucky."

She grinned at that. "At least we don't have to stand up there with Leland, as Mrs. Stanford does."

The couple finally returned to the boat and managed to climb back in without capsizing it. "Governor," Xavier nodded and doffed his imaginary hat, then took up the oars again.

Leland grinned like an idiot. "I've waited for this for a long time," he said, with a laugh.

"You really do need to do something about the water in this town," Xavier said. "I'm sure it's been discussed. Any idea what might be done to solve it?"

"First off, the existing levee, and the railroad embankment have to go.

The levee is too low in several places, and the embankment doesn't allow the water coming into the town from the flooding American River to leave. Then when the river drops, the water in town is at a higher level than the Sacramento river, but there's no way to let the water out unless we breach the levee. We may have to do that as soon as the rivers drop. Second, we could try to divert the river, but we really don't have the manpower or the equipment."

"I heard they raised the buildings, sidewalks and roads in Chicago," Aleksandra said. "Apparently, it was built in a similar situation to Sacramento, near a big river in a swampy floodplain."

"Raised the buildings?" Xavier blinked.

"Yes," Aleksandra said, "they set jack screws all around the perimeter of the city, including several hundred buildings, and then raised them nearly twenty feet. They added walls to create basements, then raised the roads with brick buttress supports. If I hadn't seen pictures in the newspaper, I wouldn't have believed it."

"Yes," nodded Stanford, "we've been looking into that and I've requested the same Chicago engineers to come out here and give us a quote, so we can put it before the state government. Hopefully, they can help us get us started and teach our workers what to do. Nobody wants to spend the money, but we really don't have a choice." He sat quietly for a moment. "We have serious problems with the rivers and flooding throughout California right now, not just here. There have been many lives lost and the true cost of this inundation, even in Sacramento alone, won't be discovered for years."

"News this morning from Placer County isn't good," Xavier said, his face falling. "At least forty-five Chinamen were swept away, still in their cabins, at Oregon Bar. A thousand Chinamen at Long Bar drowned when their shanties disappeared into the floodwaters. They stayed in their rooms, as they had done during previous floods, until the waters rose too high and wild for them to escape. Nearly every building in Knights Ferry and Mokelumne Hill has been washed away, the bridge wiped out by another bridge from upriver, and a big landslide in Volcano killed seven people. And this is just what we know right now."

It was a silent trip after that, other than the drumming of the incessant rain.

44

Somehow, later that week, the captain of the steamboat *Gem* managed to float his boat upriver to Sacramento without having it blasted to kingdom come by the odd house or two.

"We've been hit by quite a few trees and dead cows, but she's good solid oak," he said, slapping his hand on the railing as he spoke. "We'll be leaving in the morning and we've room for you and your horses. Mind you, this isn't my normal route, but we've lost a ship and I've taken this run over."

Aleksandra and Xavier gave him their profuse thanks and made their way back through the pouring rain to the hotel. They had a party in the kitchen with the cook and her husband, the stressed man at the desk, who treated them to the best the kitchen and bar had to offer. They fell into bed early, to be ready to leave at the crack of dawn.

They were going home. It wouldn't be long now, rain or no rain.

THE HORSES WERE NOT AT ALL IMPRESSED by the deep water. Rogan, fresh from his enforced inactivity, bucked and bounced all the way to the deeper water where the boat 'sat'—a relative term—with her ropes tied to several of the tall trees which normally lined the river.

At the pilot's wave, they swam the horses out to the river stopbank, now only four feet under water. One at a time, each horse was fitted with a cargo harness. Dzień laid his ears back, but didn't move a muscle while the straps were tightened. Annoyed, but quiet, he hung in the harness with his head down, as the ship's boom lifted him aboard.

Rogan was a different story altogether. He kicked and shrieked like a banshee when he was hoisted from the deep water onto the deck. Dzień, already on board, mustn't have been impressed by his antics because he snapped at the colt when he barged toward him after being released from the straps.

Like Dzień, Charro was a gentleman throughout the ordeal and stood alert, but quiet, once he was on board.

"Riverboat rides are old hat for him, though he's always been able to walk on board from a dock," Xavier said, as he backed the gray into a tie stall near the stern of the steam paddler.

Shouts rang out and metal clanged on metal while the crew worked feverishly to release the anchoring ropes, and then the ship bounced into the racing current.

"They're reasonably content with their nosebags," Xavier said, with a nod at the chewing horses. "Shall we go up to the wheelhouse? We need to see if the pilot can stop by Benicia Barracks so we can deliver the Governor's message to the commander."

The pilot was struggling to steer the boat in the raging flood, jaw tight and fingers white on the wheel.

Aleksandra glanced behind them and her heart nearly stopped. "Captain, erm, Pilot, sir, look behind us," she said, as calmly as she could.

The pilot glanced back over the huge stern paddlewheel, then paled as he spun the wheel. A two-story wooden house rocked in the current behind them, headed straight for them. The blast of the steam whistle rent the air as he yanked on the cord. "More steam!" he yelled down to the men standing beside a coal bin. "Now!"

The men raced to their stations, shoveling for all they were worth. The *Gem* slowly, but surely, pulled away from the out-of-control house.

"I wish I knew where the riverbanks were," said the pilot. "All I have to follow are the tops of the tall trees that normally line the river banks. I think."

Aleksandra's and Xavier's eyes met and they winced as one.

"This isn't my regular run," the pilot continued, "as I said. Me an' *Gem* usually work between Sacramento and Red Bluff, but we've lost a boat on the run and they thought this old girl would be best suited for this trip. The water seems to be dropping, anyway."

The water level must have dropped by many feet already, evidenced by the bodies of bloated cows, dogs, cats, rats, and the occasional human, each in varying stage of decomposition, hanging snagged in branches above the water or beached on higher muddy islands near the ship's path. Aleksandra's stomach was usually steel-clad, but she gagged at the smell and blocked her nose.

"Despite what we're finding out here, I'm sure staying in Sacramento wouldn't have been healthy, Aleksandra said softly. "A perfect breeding ground for typhoid fever—all that standing water and human waste."

Xavier squeezed her hand. "*Dios mío*, that's a ranch over there," he said, pointing at a cluster of treetops surrounding the roof of a farmhouse. Several people perched on its apex, waving their arms. Their shouts could be faintly heard on the breeze.

"Captain?" Xavier nodded in the direction of the stranded farmers.

The pilot clenched his jaw and hesitated for a moment, then with a glance behind, and to the side, spun the wheel and headed for the roof. Swearing a blue streak, he managed to position the ship downriver from the house. "Throw ropes to them. They'll have to jump. We've nothing to tie up to." He gave them the ghost of a grin. "The last thing we need is to be attached to a loose house."

They rescued six people, two dogs and an extremely angry cat.

Two of the children were crying, but the older boys were so excited they could hardly stand still. "James and Sam," barked their mother, "you two make yourselves useful and go tie those dogs up somewhere. Sarah, hold on to that cat, before she hurts someone." Aleksandra ran to help, offering their spare lead rope. Out of sight of their distraught mother, they grinned at each other, and at the Aleksandra, once they figured out she was onto them.

"Oh man, what an exciting day," young Sam said, and his brother nodded.

"Were you farming out there?" Xavier said, coming up behind her.

Both boys gulped. "Yes, sir." Sam replied, and paled, then looked down at his feet. "Cows and vegetables," he mumbled. "I guess they're all gone now."

James closed his eyes as he whispered, "all of them." A tear rolled down his cheek.

Sam gulped. "Even our pet milking cow, Racy. She just washed away. They all washed away."

"Maybe she'll find a high spot," James glanced over the railing at the endless sea of muddy water and faltered, "somewhere." He sat abruptly on the slick boards of the deck and wrapped his arms around both dogs. His brother joined him, and soon the wagging and panting dogs were licking away the boys' tears as fast as they fell from their eyes.

Aleksandra moved to stand beside the mother. "They're as fine as they are going to be for a while. Can I help you with anything? Are any of you hurt?"

She gripped Aleksandra's offered hands. "We're all fine now, thank you. We've lost our stock, but our family is alive, thanks to you people." She turned to the pilot. "Thank you sir, thank you with all my heart. We never considered we needed a boat upstairs in the house," she said, with a crooked grin, through her tears. "We don't quite know what to do next." She looked askance at the pilot.

"I don't think there'll be anywhere populated and above water where we could set you down before we get to the Benicia Barracks, other than Suisun City. Do you know anyone there, or in San Francisco?"

"My father and sister live in San Francisco, if you don't mind taking us there...I don't know how long it will be before we can pay you." She hesitated before continuing. "They'll take us in; that is, I hope so," she whispered, uncertainty written all over her face. "Thank you, again. I'll go see to my family now."

Aleksandra gulped.

There but for the grace of God go I.

She went to check the horses, keeping her eyes peeled for floating or stationary obstacles in the brown, churning water.

"I think this is it..." the pilot murmured as the treetops ahead divided into two paths before them. He pulled the wheel hard to the left. "We'll be taking Steamboat Slough to San Francisco. Normally," he cocked her brow at them, "we'd take the Old Sacramento, but there are...usually fewer obstacles to negotiate through the slough. Unfortunately, today all bets are off."

"Confidence inspiring," Aleksandra murmured and gritted her teeth, as her eyes scanned the water. "Nice table. Pity we have nowhere to put it." She waved a hand at a massive polished oak tabletop floating beside them, sunlight glinting off its shiny surface.

The pilot shook his head, then locked his jaw and took a deep breath.

The lump chilling in Aleksandra's stomach turned to ice. "What is it?" she muttered. "How do you find your way in this delta, with all these different pathways, even though they're just treetops?"

The pilot gulped. "It's a bit tricky. I'll thank you to please keep your eyes up ahead, looking for where all these little byways converge into one, in about half an hour."

"What if we take a wrong turn and miss it?"

He didn't answer.

45

The pilot's lack of reply was answer enough. She and Xavier both watched like hawks, as the iceberg inside Aleksandra grew by the minute.

"The pilot of the *Chrissy* set a new record for this run on New Year's Eve," he said, never taking his eyes from the water in front of his ship.

Xavier raised a brow at him. "Let me guess, that was downriver, at full flood."

"The *Chrissy*, is that the *Chrysopolis*?" Aleksandra said.

"Sure was. Made that trip in five hours and nineteen minutes."

"They didn't have room for us, and the horses." Xavier paused for a moment. "Is her boiler still intact?" he asked dryly.

"Should have been," the pilot laughed, "he probably didn't need to use it, at the speed the river was running."

Aleksandra shook her head. "We're just not in that much of a hurry, so you needn't try to beat that record on our behalf."

"I love my old *Gem* too much to blow her up."

"Can't say but I'm glad to hear that," Xavier said, pulling Aleksandra back against him and wrapping his arms tightly around her.

The great sea of treetops of the delta began to narrow, then the greenery outlining the outlet of the slough narrowed to only one path, and Aleksandra let out the breath she didn't know she'd been holding. She turned in Xavier's embrace and wrapped her arms around his neck, then kissed him long and hard.

"We'll get out of this," she said.

"You always seem to, whatever trouble you find yourself in."

"At least this wasn't of my own making." She quirked her lips at him.

"We're not out of the woods yet, get your eyes back on the river," Xavier said, turned her around firmly and kissed the top of her head.

Scarcely half an hour later, they passed Suisun City, which was, for the most part, situated high above the river. No one waved from the bank, so they continued on.

"I can't believe all this water," Xavier said, his face stricken. "There are ranches and farms all through here. Where are all the people, and the stock? Have they all drowned?"

"By the number of animals I've seen drowned, not to mention people, I'd say a fair few," the pilot said. "They would've had only an hour's notice in some places, of the biggest floods. Without a pretty big boat, they wouldn't have been able to save many."

The path between the treetops widened further and further over the next hour, until none showed at all along the sides, only smooth hills rising from the muddy water.

"This is Suisun Bay," Xavier said. "The Benicia Barracks and Martinez are right at the end of this bay, in the narrow strait between there and San Pablo Bay."

"That strait's why we have the delta we just passed," the pilot said. "It's too narrow to let the big flood waters through, and the water has to go somewhere, so it spreads out into the delta, and on down through the rest of the Central Valley of California. 'Specially when there's been as much rain and snowmelt as we've just had."

There wasn't much to say to that, either.

"I haven't been down this way for quite a while," the pilot continued, "and I don't remember the configuration of the docks at Benicia, but I'll give it a go."

"Look," Xavier said, "the top of the wharf pilings are clear of the water by nearly two feet."

"It's not much, but it's enough," the pilot muttered as he fought the wheel, trying to dodge a big tree trunk while lining the steamer up to dock.

A small group of men in uniform stood on the bank, just past the barely-visible wharf.

"The welcoming committee," Xavier murmured.

"With rifles, no less?" Aleksandra cocked a brow. They held their rifles to the ready, looking anything but friendly.

"Halloo," the pilot shouted.

"You know there's a two hundred yard boundary," one shouted, as they came closer.

"Permission to dock, sir," the pilot returned. "Man to see the commander."

The soldiers conferred and one ran for the buildings up the hill.

"OK, but watch your step," barked the same soldier. "Cannon are trained on your hull."

"We're just here to see the commander, no need for that. I'll stay with my ship and these two'll come ashore."

Jaw tight, the speaker motioned with his rifle to Aleksandra and Xavier, standing at the rail.

Xavier handed Aleksandra out onto the pier, its timbers trembling from the onslaught of the current.

"Hadn't realized how much I missed standing on dry ground," she said, over her shoulder, with a wry grin.

"I have news for the commander from the governor in Sacramento," Xavier said to the leader of the soldier as they neared them.

The man's eyes boggled and his nostrils flared. "Well, then..." he stumbled over his words, "why didn't you say so, sir?" He spun on his muddy heel and set a brisk pace up the hill.

Aleksandra and Xavier shared a glance, and she smirked behind her hand.

"So you've come down from the capitol, have you? Is it as bad as they say?"

"Sure is." Xavier said shortly.

"Is Captain Moore in residence?" Aleksandra asked.

"He is. He arrived last week, ma'am."

"Would we be able to see him please?"

"He's with the commander, so you should be able to see him right away, as well."

He led them up the hill toward a group of buildings. They passed some long, windowed, two-storied buildings, so new their painting hadn't been completed.

"New buildings?"

"The new barracks for the arsenal. We're the staging place for this whole coast. There are so many volunteers we couldn't accommodate them all, so we're building new barracks to house them properly." The young man puffed out his chest. "A sight better than the wet tents of the soldiers over the rest of the country, especially with this rotten weather." He led them to an expansive red tile-roofed building. "Headquarters," he said, as he held open the huge oaken doors beneath the elaborate entryway that reached to the top of the second story. He knocked on the door of the commander's office.

"Come in," roared a deep voice.

"Xavier!" Captain Moore stood from the map table. He turned to the commander and made introductions while Xavier passed over Stanford's letter.

"Nice new barracks, sir," Xavier smiled at the commander.

"They're getting done, and just in time. If you'll excuse me, I'll leave you with Moore. Good to meet you, and thank you for the hand-delivery." He nodded at the missive in his hand.

Captain Moore turned to them after the door closed. "My apologies to you both, but I've not been able to find hide nor hair of O'Rourke, though I fully intend to keep trying. Please let me know if you hear anything yourself."

They made their goodbyes and returned to the ship, the same soldier chatting happily all the way back to the dock, now they were no longer under suspicion.

The *Gem* waited until they jumped aboard and the ship was underway within moments. The town of Martinez slipped past them on the south side of the strait, and within twenty minutes they floated into the wide San Pablo Bay.

"Nearly home." Xavier smiled from ear to ear and let out a big sigh. "You should see it the way it is normally, a big blue expanse of glittering diamonds when the sun shines upon it. From here, we go straight into the San Francisco Bay…and home."

Aleksandra didn't think he could smile any wider. She wrapped her arms around him and squeezed with all her strength.

"Do we get off at San Francisco, or closer to Rancho de las Pulgas?"

"We disembark at the San Francisco docks, then it's just over five hours' ride from there. We should be able to get there by dark." Xavier's eyes lit up.

"That's good," she said, glancing at Rogan. The horse was beginning to shuffle around a bit, while his stablemates dozed. "By then, Rogan will have burned his extra energy and be ready to greet the family like a grown horse."

SURROUNDED by hills which gradually rose from the muddy water, the expansive San Pablo Bay was so big it took them nearly an hour to cross it. As the sides of the bay narrowed to an outlet, Xavier nodded at the town of San Rafael to the right.

"We're on the El Camino Real, or 'The Royal Road.' It connected the old Spanish missions and presidios. It runs all the way from Baja California Sur, the Baja Peninsula south of California, north past our rancho, past the Mission San Rafael Arcángel, just over there," he pointed to the right, "and finally ends at the Mission San Francisco de Solano, north of here. The Presidio, which we'll see soon, was built on the south side of the Golden Gate to provide support for the missions…but that support mostly consisted of keeping the mission natives in line." He winced. "The Indians were ostensibly there to be converted to Catholicism and learn new ways, but they were mostly slaves for the missions. They couldn't leave. If the Indians chose to return to their home villages, the soldiers dragged them back."

Aleksandra cringed. "It never really ended, then, did it?" She took a deep breath and turned her gaze full on him and he squeezed her hand. "How far is that, to Baja California Sur?" Aleksandra asked.

"Probably about six hundred miles, extending down into what's now Mexico."

"One road, that whole length?"

"Yep." They were silent for long minutes, as the hills of gold, covered by the remnants of late summertime grass, slipped by. He lifted a hand toward a white mansion glowing against the tan hills to the left of the bow. "That's the Rancho San Pablo. Juan Bautista de Alvarado built it when he was the governor of California, twenty years ago."

"Is it as big as it looks?"

"Sure is. I've been there once. And over there," he nodded at the headland just after the Alvarado adobe, "is Point Richmond. My private marker to let me know I'm nearly home." He beamed. "You'll like this one. That point over there?"

"The one with the sharp tip, with an island beside it?"

"*Sí.* That's *Punta de Tiburon*, Shark Point. I don't know if it's named that because of its shark-snout shape, or because of the plentiful sharks."

She shuddered. "There are sharks in this water?"

"Sure are. That island next to *Punta de Tiburon* is Angel Island. Once we're past that," he shook his head at himself at the butterflies in his stomach, "it's only Alcatraz to go, then we dock!"

Half an hour later, he turned her to the right and pulled her back against him, then waited in silence.

"What is it?"

"Wait for it," he murmured in her ear and kissed the top of her head. A heavy mist obscured the hills to their right. As they watched, it lightened. A narrow chasm appeared between the steep mountains to the north and a cluster of white buildings high on the cliffs to the south.

"What is it?" she breathed.

"It's the Golden Gate."

"The beginning of the Pacific Ocean?"

"*Sí,*" he whispered, past the lump in his throat. "Those adobe buildings are the Presidio. Fort Point, out at the tip of the Presidio," he pointed to high walls on the cliffs above the water at the south side of the Golden Gate, "guards the bay. The government's been trying to get its hands on the northern point there for another fort, but even after ten years, they still haven't been able to wrench it from its owner."

"They just finished Fort Point last year and put the first cannons into the gun emplacements," said the pilot, "and Johnston filled it with soldiers."

"What's that little island," Aleksandra pointed, "and all those buildings on it?"

"Alcatraz."

"What's an alcatraz?"

He laughed. "It was originally called *La Isla de los Alcatraces*, or 'Island of the Pelicans'. When the United States took California from Mexico," he said, "the army chose the island as the best strategic position for the defense of San Francisco Bay, and started to build the Alcatraz Citadel." He pointed at the three-storied brick building. "Complete with a moat, drawbridge, barracks, cell blocks and batteries. They only finished it three or four years ago. It was designed to hold two hundred men and enough provisions to withstand a four month siege."

Aleksandra's brows shot up and her eyes widened. "Look at all the cannon."

"Yep, nearly a hundred. There were eleven when Johnston took over as Commander of the Department of the Pacific, but just before he resigned, he stocked it with the rest of the cannon, soldiers and something like 10,000 muskets and 150,000 rounds of ammunition. It's probably the most powerful fort west of the Mississippi."

"They're calling it 'Fort' Alcatraz now, and it's become a war camp," the pilot cut in.

Aleksandra narrowed her brows at him, a question in her eyes.

"A prison for captured Confederate soldiers, or those who stir up trouble for the Union Army," he added, then checked his compass and changed their course slightly.

"Back to its origins, then." Xavier grinned, "The *Ohlone* Indians believed evil spirits lived there. Seems they banished those who violated tribal rules to the island." He quirked an eyebrow at Aleksandra. "All good, except they gathered eggs and seafood from Alcatraz too, so who knows, maybe the evil spirits were just a story they used to keep others away from their food-gathering spots."

"It's pretty secure," the pilot said. "Nobody's ever escaped from there. It's a long swim, in shark-infested water."

Aleksandra exchanged a look with Xavier. "The sharks will be in their element, with all the dead animals this month." She gulped.

"Is the water level here high from the floods?" Xavier asked.

"Not a lot, maybe three feet, but the water's muddy, and it certainly doesn't usually have dead stock and trees floating in it," he said, with a grimace as he glanced around. "There are fewer bodies here than upriver, but I've certainly never seen any in the San Fran Bay before today."

Xavier turned to Aleksandra. "If the water's only up a little, we should be above the waterline most of the way home, and only have to go inland a little way."

"That'll make a change from the last month or two. I was thinking I'd need to grow webbed feet," she said, her lips turning up at the corners.

She turned toward the approaching docks and froze.

A sea of masts and a veritable army of people scurried around the wharves. The houses and warehouses seemed to go on forever. Her nostrils flared, as the color drained from her face.

46

Xavier stepped close to Aleksandra and put an arm around her waist. Even from this distance, the noise of the busy docks rang across the water.

"Yes, it's a big city. Noisy and big, but you'll be all right. We aren't staying there. Stay close and you'll be fine."

She gave him a wan smile and leaned back against him. Her pulse raced at her throat, and he held her tight, willing her to calmness.

"We'll put in at Meiggs Wharf, where the ferries dock now," the pilot said.

"Where's the old dock?" Xavier asked.

The pilot laughed. "Where all old docks and abandoned ships go, under the city."

Aleksandra turned to stare at him. "Pardon?"

"Look at all those ships. Most have been abandoned."

He was right. Gulls circled overhead, screaming, as the boat drew nearer to the docks. They began to pass ships with sails in tatters, their metal fittings rusting on the decks and masts. The sun bleached, neglected decks and railings were covered with seagull droppings.

Xavier winced and pulled Aleksandra in close.

"Where have all their owners gone?" she whispered. "It looks like a ship's graveyard."

"The gold rush. They came and went for gold, or their crews jumped ship and the captains either went with them or couldn't sail them alone, so they left them," Xavier said.

"They've beached hundreds of the hulks," said the pilot, "dumped yards and yards of dirt and rock on top to fill in most of the shoreline hereabouts, like Yerba Buena Cove, and then drove pilings and put planks down...and built more city on top of them. Sold 'water lots', lots out in the water, which are now 'land', or 'fill', anyway, but part of the city. It's a disaster waiting to happen."

"One of my first jobs was carting fill for them," Xavier said, with a shudder, "until I found Abe's Cobweb Palace." He jerked his head up to the man at the wheel. "Is he still open?"

"Yes, and you're in luck, it's at Meiggs." The man smiled.

"How could I forget," Xavier's eyes almost rolled back in his head for a moment, "chowder, hot toddies and cracked cra—" he jumped "—wait, is it crab season?"

The pilot laughed. "November to March, you're in luck, boyo. I take it that's where you're having dinner?"

Xavier grinned. "Right, you are." He turned to Aleksandra. "You won't believe this place."

When she turned to him, her color was back and she was smiling. She faced forward again.

"I can't believe all the ships, just dumped...and look at all the docks!"

"I wouldn't tie up to any of those, the old rickety bits of junk," the pilot said. "There's ours," he pointed to an L-shaped pier extending nearly half a mile into the bay. "That's Meiggs."

A few paddle steamers were docked there already, but there was plenty of room. The smell of the city hit him as soon as the mooring ropes were thrown. Decay, rotten food, and worse turned his stomach. Aleksandra gritted her teeth as she let go of her nose.

"Smells pretty bad, eh?" he said, and she nodded.

"The horses will be pleased," was all she said, as she began untying Dzień. Taking the Mustang's lead in her left and Rogan's in her right, she followed him and Charro off the ramp, waving goodbye and thanks to the pilot. The rescued family were dead to the world, sleeping in a huddle. "I wonder how long they were clinging to that roof?" she whispered to Xavier as they walked down the dock.

A huge building stood at its end. "That's Abe's place," he said, with a huge smile.

They watered the horses and tied them behind Abe's Cobweb Palace. Xavier entered one of the sheds and returned with hay for the horses.

Aleksandra looked at him sideways in silence.

"Yes?"

"You know your way around here, too. Did you work here, as well?"

He blinked. "Well, yes. The food was too good to be working anywhere else."

She laughed. "Lead on. Let's see this magical place of yours."

She stopped, dumbstruck, just inside the door.

"I'll have a rum and gum. What'll you have?" Aleksandra jumped as a voice screeched loudly, just beside them.

"Oh Warner, up to your old tricks again?" Xavier said to the parrot, on his perch beside them. The bird bounced his whole body in place, the pupils of his eyes widening and narrowing as he danced. The miscreant screeched some other words he didn't recognize, and Aleksandra gasped.

"Rude bird!" Her eyes were wide, and she walked over to him. "You can't say that in public!"

"What did he say?" Xavier asked him, interest piqued.

"It's not repeatable. In German. How many languages does that bird know?" Aleksandra giggled, and the bird flew away, screeching more foreign obscenities, by the way she held her hands over her ears and shook her head.

"That'll be four."

"Pardon?" Aleksandra's head shot up and she stared at the man behind the bar, and the three monkeys sitting on it.

"Four languages. He swears in four languages. Most educated parrot I've ever met."

She laughed. "Wherever did you find him?"

"He came in with a sailor who couldn't keep him." He turned to Xavier. "Welcome back, just in time for your crab, Argüello. Have you come back to work for me?"

"Abe," Xavier took his hand and shook it warmly, then introduced Aleksandra. "Sorry, but we're on the way back to the *rancho*. I've been away since I last saw you, but I couldn't go past without seeing you."

"Without my chowder and crab," he grinned at Aleksandra, "more like."

"Well, there is that." Xavier laughed. "Digger, is it?" The old monkey held his arms out to Xavier from the top of the bar and leapt into Xavier's arms.

Aleksandra's eyes glowed as he cuddled the monkey.

"He's gorgeous," she said, slowly reaching a hand out to him. Digger took hers and pulled her closer. She took a deep breath and held out her arms. He climbed over Xavier's arm and into hers. The monkey and Aleksandra stared at each other for long moments. "He's lovely, Abe."

"That he is, he's been with me a long time," the crusty old barkeep said, "a long time. Digger, why don't you show the lady around?"

Digger pointed to the far side of the room, and Aleksandra started walking.

"What'll you have, Xavier?"

"Crab for three, it looks like." He grinned at Aleksandra and her new friend.

Xavier walked behind Aleksandra as she and Digger moved along the countertop, gazing at the scrimshaw beneath the glass top and then at the Japanese masks, South Pacific war clubs, and all sorts of stuffed animals. The monkey pointed to another wall and Aleksandra's eyes widened, then she stared, before turning back toward him, her cheeks pink.

"Aah, come over this way, look at the Alaskan totem pole," he said, pulling her away from the huge expanse of Abe's favorite nude painting gallery. "Look, there's a kangaroo, from Australia!"

She flashed him a smile of gratitude and rushed away from the paintings. She stopped to gaze at the animal coming toward her. "They swing, rather than walk, don't they?" she said, wonder in her voice as she took in the unfamiliar creature, its tiny forelimbs contrasting with its massive hindquarters and tail. It, too, nuzzled her for a treat.

"Xavier, supper's up," Abe called.

"I couldn't eat another bite." Xavier groaned as he pushed away from the table. "Charro will never forgive me."

"My first crab and chowder, and sourdough bread like I've never dreamed of tasting before." Aleksandra shook her head. "I'll be back, Abe." Digger, still on her lap, waved his bread crust and clung to her.

"Looks like you'll need to come visit, or that monkey might run away from home with you," Abe laughed and plucked the animal from her arms, as they readied themselves to leave. "We'll see you both soon, then?"

"You have my word on that," Xavier said, and Aleksandra agreed.

The horses looked keen to get moving. After another drink at the trough, they saddled them and headed up Powell Street. "We'll go past the old mission on the way."

The horses' hooves clip-clopped on the wide wooden-plank roads between two storied office-cum-warehouse buildings. Men working the docks glanced at their horses, and at Aleksandra, with raised brows, but turned away at a look from Xavier. The wooden road continued south around the base of Russian Hill.

In the distance before them rose a cluster of buildings. Some whitewashed adobe buildings stood out against the dark wood structures surrounding them in a big flat valley running down to the sea.

"The Mission San Francisco de Asís, more commonly known as Mission Dolores," Xavier said. "Unfortunately, the mission lands have all been sold and it's become the entertainment area of San Francisco," he said, through gritted teeth. "The mission house still stands, but lord knows what it's being used for now. It's that tall adobe with a tiled roof and the low buildings attached to it."

As they approached the old mission, two drunken men wobbled from one of the adjacent buildings and a saloon girl followed them out. She took them both by an arm and led them up a nearby street.

"I guess it's a saloon now," Xavier said under his breath, and scowled. He looked around them as they rode. "Those are probably immigrant worker shacks," he pointed out some ramshackle buildings near the mission. "Poor beggars probably can't afford digs any closer to their jobs in the city."

Some Indians worked in a small picket-fenced garden beside the building. They took no mind of them as they passed. "Mission Indians?" she murmured.

"When I was last here, there were only a few here, I'm surprised any are left. The fathers used to have small homes with gardens around the church, but I don't see many there now, if there are any at all."

"What's that?" she stared at a big hole in the ground with a stout fence around it, while the horses shied sideways away from the structure. It reeked of blood and gore.

Xavier's jaw was tight when he answered. "A bear-and bull-baiting pit. Can't believe they're still doing it. And the old racecourse is still there too," he nodded at it.

"Let's get out of here," Aleksandra couldn't resist a shudder. "Trot time."

Rogan was only too happy to accommodate. Overfed and underworked, he was a bit hard to hold, but they were soon well away. The plank road ended and the packed-mud road began.

"Mud or no, this is the driest ground I've seen in months," she said.

"El Camino Real continues on that way," Xavier waved a hand to the right, "but we're taking the coast road for now. We'll join it again a bit further south."

Sea birds called and swooped as the horses made their way from the town down to the marshlands at the edge of the bay, and soon only the open road greeted their eyes. The glittering, if brown, San Francisco Bay guarding their left hand. The land to the west was rolling, but their road followed the tidal salt marshes of the bayside. It was level, and a good track to ride.

A short way along, Xavier pointed left. "That's Hunters Point. I went to school with the Hunter boys in San Francisco. When their father split up the place, they were meant to sell their pieces, but I think they've stayed there to farm it."

"Sounds perfectly reasonable to me," Aleksandra said.

The point was solid ground, but after that, as far as she could see were salt marshes. Flocks of birds took off and landed in the spiky vegetation, and near the edges of the marsh, long-legged birds pecked for food. "What are those birds, Xavier?"

He looked. "I see stilts, *many* stilts, a white egret, and a pair of blue herons, along with the ever-present seagulls."

"The swamp doesn't exactly smell fresh, but it beats San Francisco hands down." Aleksandra reached forward to scratch Rogan's neck. "Shall we have a little run? I'll let Dzień off first."

The wind in her hair was exhilarating, and the horses wanted to run forever. They passed a few solitary riders and a few wagons carrying freight, but for the most part they were on their own. When they stopped for a breather, she asked Xavier about it.

"Most of the traffic uses El Camino, because this road gets pretty muddy when it's wet. El Camino goes up through those hills," he pointed west, "but comes down near the water again."

A roadhouse, with carriages and horses standing outside, appeared on their right. "Stage stop?" Aleksandra asked.

"Just a roadhouse, 7 Mile House. It isn't a stage stop, because the stages stay up on El Camino too."

"Was this land a Spanish land grant, like Rancho de las Pulgas?"

"All of this land was. This was part of the "*Rancho Cañada de Guadalupe la Visitación y Rodeo Viejo* grant.""

"What a mouthful." Aleksandra blinked.

He laughed. "It goes all the way from San Francisco through to Millbrae, further on, and includes that big San Bruno Mountain." He pointed southwest at a set of mountains.

Soon they passed another roadhouse, 12 Mile House, and a short while later, a third, 14 Mile House.

"That's some creek," Aleksandra said, eyeing the wide body of water. "Is it tidal?"

"Yes. That creek is the other reason the stages go the other route. They'd get mighty wet."

"Dzień won't like it, but he'll live. Let's go boy," she said, with a pull on the Mustang's lead.

"Water...it had to be water," Xavier said, mimicking Dzień's probable comment.

The pony laid his ears back and leapt straight in.

"Best get it over with," Xavier continued, and she shook her head.

Seabirds flew up at the pounding of the horses' hooves as they continued along the marshes, loping, trotting and walking as the mood took them. Soon their trail beside the water joined again with El Camino Real, and their road became more crowded with other travelers.

"This is Millbrae. It used to be the old Sanchez place, but it was bought by Darius Mills and his family years ago," Xavier said, and flicked at a fly on Charro's rump.

Half an hour later, Aleksandra gestured at an outcropping of firm land extending a short way past the marshes into the bay.

"Coyote Point. That means we're *truly* nearly home," Xavier said, in a nonchalant voice, but the telltale signs were there. His voice bubbled with increasing effervescence every time he pointed out something new, and he kept flicking his hair back with the back of his wrist.

Yep, excited, for sure.

Aleksandra smiled.

"This is San Bruno, just starting here." He was nearly jumping out of his skin.

Three miles on, there were more and more people on the road, and the towns came in quick succession.

"This land here, from San Bruno to San Mateo, is part of the old *Rancho San Mateo*. A banker named Ralston owns it. He wants to buy it all up, but he's not getting ours," he hesitated for a moment, his brow creasing, then added, "yet."

She smiled and reached for his hand.

"See that cluster of trees up there on the hill?"

"Yes," she tilted her head and looked at him. He quivered with an air of expectancy.

"There's a creek there. San Mateo Creek. That's home." He stopped, and a tear ran down his face. His voice shook when he continued. "It's our northern boundary."

"You didn't think you'd see it again, did you?" Aleksandra said, softly.

He shook his head and bit his lips together.

"Well done, then, coming home, *mi querido*," she said, in a stronger voice.

"Without you in my life, it wouldn't have ever happened, I hope you know that. I have you to thank, *y mi madre*."

"*Y su madre*," Aleksandra whispered, and squeezed his hand.

He looked down at her. "Your *Español* is coming along, *Querida*."

She grinned. "I thought it might come in handy, if I were to live in the house full of *Californios*."

"*Sí, de veras*," he said with a smile.

"Is your horse tired?" he asked, with a glint in his eye.

"Don't be funny," she said, narrowing her own at him. "Rogan's born ready, and Dzień can't wait to get that pack off and be done traveling." She whistled up the pony. He looked up from grabbing a choice morsel beside the road, and whickered, then came at a trot. "Let's go!"

She clapped and hooted when they crossed the creek onto Rancho de las Pulgas territory, startling a handful of birds from the brush beside them. Rogan shied, but Charro snaked his teeth in his direction, and the colt straightened up and loped on.

El Camino Real barely skimmed the edge of the marshes. To the west were rolling grasslands, and further back from the bay the grassy slopes sported the occasional trees.

"Go right at the next wagon road," Xavier shouted, from behind her.

She turned off and they pulled the puffing, snorting horses to a walk. Dzień raced on past and headed for the nearest grass. "He'll turn into a butterball, that pony," she grinned at the Mustang. "This Utah pony's never seen this kind of grass before."

"We'll have to watch him."

She nodded. "I've always had to, even in Utah, when we went up into the mountains."

Aleksandra took a deep breath as a shiver run up her spine. "We're really here, aren't we?"

"We are. It's just a little further." He gripped her hand. "Nervous?"

She nodded.

"So am I," he said, "but Mama has enough love for everyone." He rolled his eyes. "I keep telling myself that. I'll believe it soon."

As the road cut west across pastures and climbed the foothills, the landscape changed from the rough sea marsh flats to close-cropped pastures. Beef cattle and deer lifted their heads from their grazing to watch them ride past.

"Nearly there." Xavier motioned to the right with his head.

"That track?"

"*Sí*, it goes to *la hacienda*."

They turned off the road and headed southwest, through golden rolling hills dotted with clusters of ancient oak trees. The hills were framed by a deep green forest that capped the distant mountain ridges behind.

"I've never seen anything so beautiful," she shouted into the wind, an ache in her heart.

"The ocean is only three days distant," he called back, "or maybe two days for you, across that range and down the other side. Our *rancho* runs from the shoreline behind us to the base of those hills, and for another eight miles to the south of *la hacienda*."

"Rancho de las Pulgas" she said, tilting her head, "what does it mean?"

"Ranch of the Fleas." He shot her a wry grin, and pulled Charro to a trot.

"Fleas." She wrinkled her nose and followed suit. "Romantic. Not at all what I expected."

"It was originally called *Los Cochinitos*, 'The Pigs'. Maybe there were more fleas than pigs, *quien sabe*? Who knows? Whatever the name, my grandfather didn't look a gift horse in the mouth when he was offered the biggest and best land grant on the San Francisco peninsula, and so it was named. When the United States took over California, they promised previous land grants would be honored. Unfortunately, the grant holders had to reapply to the Public Land Commission, and Mama's applications were refused for five years. In Carson City, she told me she has a new lawyer, Señor Mezes, and he's finally had her grant patented—at nearly double the size of the original 'one league by four league' grant. Well worth the land Mama paid to the lawyer for handling the patent process."

"How scary would that be," Aleksandra shuddered. "At least it's done now. Doubled, eh? Not a bad lawyer."

"No, he did a good job."

"How far away are we now?" She edged Rogan closer to the big gray stallion.

"Very close, *Querida*." He smiled down at her and reached out to softly graze her cheek with his knuckles and they slowed to a walk.

"I'm so glad you met with your mother in Carson City."

"What a difference it's made to my life, and it wouldn't have happened without you," he breathed, and leaned across to kiss her. She stood in her stirrups to meet him halfway. The depth of the kiss drew forth an ache in her core and she reached a hand up to touch his face. He ended the kiss and touched his lips to her forehead. Lifting his head, he glanced forward. "Look there, Aleksandra," he nodded between Charro's ears, "*La hacienda, y la casa grande*."

She turned and inhaled sharply. As they rounded the bend in the trail, an expansive ranch came into view, its mansion surrounded by lush gardens, smaller houses, stables and barns. A stream tumbled from a gully between the two hills sheltering the homestead, and flowed down its rocky course past the house.

Aleksandra shook her head and looked up at Xavier.

"I could never have imagined a place like this." A tear ran cold down her cheek. "It's beautiful."

"Not as beautiful as my wife. Mama will be ecstatic to meet you."

"She'll be even more pleased to see you," she countered, "although I'm not sure she'll ever forgive us for marrying without her." Aleksandra looked up at him with huge eyes and bit her lip.

"I promise you, it will be fine." He chuckled. "I'm trying to cheer you up. Really," he said, as he took her hand. "She will understand."

Aleksandra was looking down at Rogan's mane. Xavier sighed, let go of her hand and dismounted, then supported her as she slid from Rogan's back.

"Let me assure you, *Querida*," he lifted her chin with his fingertips and spoke slowly and deliberately, "I love you and you alone, forever. You have my heart, whatever anyone else ever thinks or says."

She smiled now, her cheeks hot. "And I, you, *mi querido*," she whispered.

"Furthermore," he said, kissing her again, "Mama will forget about all of it when we start a family to keep the Argüello dynasty alive." He waggled an eyebrow at her.

A dark chill descended at that, and she gulped and shivered with it.

"What's wrong now?" he said, stroking the hair back from her eyes.

"I don't know if I can do... keep a baby..."

"Aleks," he pulled her against him, hard, "it will be fine. You will be fine. We will be fine. We have help here. You, me and our babies will be fine. Trust me."

He held her against him for a moment, turning her slowly toward *la hacienda*.

"They have seen us." He nodded toward the big house. "They are gathering...with smiles and a cold drink, to welcome us home."

He took her hand and together they led the horses toward *la casa* to meet their family, awaiting them with open arms.

PART IV

1862 ~ RANCHO DE LAS PULGAS, CALIFORNIA

47

January 1862, Rancho de las Pulgas, San Francisco Bay, California

"YOUR MOTHER IS MORE lovely than lovely," Aleksandra said, slightly muffled, as Xavier slipped her buckskin shirt over her head. "And Adelita, Jose, all of them…" she hesitated, then continued, "though Sancho might take some getting used to." She tried to smile, then tugged the string of her trousers and they fell to the floor. "They were all so welcoming."

"You're something special to welcome, my love."

A silence fell, then she looked up to find him staring at her. "What is it?"

"What did I ever do to deserve you, *Querida*? You fit in here like no one else ever could. I love you so much." He enveloped her in his arms and held her close for long moments.

"Was this your room?" she asked, gazing around at the stark manliness, yet warmth of it.

"Yes," he said, and looked about him as well. He swallowed hard. "It's just as I left it, but probably cleaner." He let his arms fall from around her and grabbed her hand, leading her to a framed photo on the wall of a young boy on a massive horse. "Mama helped me break this horse and train him in advanced movements. He was magnificent." His eyes filled, but didn't quite spill over.

Aleksandra reached out and touched his face, and he turned toward her.

"He was my horse before Charro. He died…in an…accident, my stepfather said, but it was no accident. He was aiming for me with his knife, and stabbed the horse. He died of that wound weeks later."

"Oh, Xavier." Aleksandra didn't know what to say.

"But it is over. The man is no more, and the world is a better place for it," he managed. "Charro has filled the gap in my life, and more. Mama helped me with Charro, as well."

"And a magnificent beast he's turned out to be. You've done so well."

"Let's get to bed. It's been a long day, week…month, but we're here now."

"You hadn't noticed the bath?" Aleksandra lifted her brows at him and pointed to the steaming tub on the other side of the bed.

"We couldn't possibly get into that clean bed like we are, could we?"

"Absolutely not," she said, as she began to strip off his shirt. He wriggled when she left his arms high in the air and slid her fingers slowly down his lean, hard torso and slipped the drawstring on his trousers, then slid the snug pants down over his hips. His interest was piqued, if his growing erection was anything to go by.

"It you keep that up, we won't even make it to the bath, *Querida*," he said from inside the shirt.

She giggled and reached up to tug his shirt the rest of the way off.

"Into the bath with you. Get clean and I'll rub your…back," she managed between kisses as he lifted her in his arms and sat in the tub with her in his lap.

She hoped there were plenty of towels…the floor was going to get very wet.

Quite some time later, floors none the worse for their cleaning, they slid between crisp, fresh sheets. Xavier slid close behind Aleksandra and pulled her in, his fingers on her breasts making her anything but sleepy. It had been a long day, and the night wasn't going to get any shorter.

He rolled over on top of her, onto his elbows, and nibbled at her earlobe.

"And tomorrow," his lips slid down her neck, "I take you to see your new home," and lower, until his mouth found a hard-pebbled nipple, "and introduce you to your people."

If he said anything else, she missed it. His words disappeared. There was nothing but his mouth, hands, and her soft cries as they rolled in each others' arms.

He'd have to tell her again tomorrow.

"XAVIER, a letter came for you last month from someone in Australia," his mama said.

"Australia?" He took the letter she offered. "It's from von Tempsky. I met him in the California goldfields many years ago. We've kept occasional contact, but I've not heard from him in many years." He opened and scanned it while his mother checked the bubbling pots on the stove and stirred one. "He thinks we should come to New Zealand. He's in Australia right now visiting his wife and children, but he's going gold mining in the North Island, at a place called Coromandel. He got the claim for a song, and would be interested in my becoming his partner there."

"That's half a world away, Xavier."

"Yes, a long way from Las Pulgas, now I'm back." He smiled at this woman, who had so very much faith in him, both now and not so long ago, when he had none. Her visit to find him in Carson City had been the start of his new life, both with his family and with Aleksandra. He could never repay what she'd offered him that day, his own heart. "I'm back, and here we'll stay, Mama. Thank you again for what you did for me that last visit. It's made all the difference in my life. I can't ever hope to repay it."

"Your having love in your life, for yourself and your woman, and for your family is all the thanks I could ever desire, *Querido*." She kissed him on the cheek and swatted him on the rear. "And where is that lovely girl of yours this morning, anyway?"

"I imagine she's out with her beloved horses."

"A woman after my own heart," she said. "Charro's looks *fantástico*, you've done well with him."

"Thank you, Mama," Xavier said. "*Buenos días*, Sancho," he added, as his brother stepped into the kitchen.

Sancho nodded curtly, then glanced at his mother. "Morning," he said belatedly.

"I'll be off, then. Sancho, is there anything you need done?" Xavier said.

"No, everything's done, *hijo*," Maria said. "Jose has gone to see when he can get passage to *España*, or at least to South America, from where he can get a ship to Spain."

Xavier's brows shot up. "Already?"

"He says he's waited too many years already to see the world," Sancho muttered. "He's only too happy to leave the *rancho* in your…" he hesitated, "…capable hands."

Xavier could swear Sancho gritted his teeth. Was he jealous? His eyes narrowed at Sancho. Maybe he was being overly sensitive. "Surely there's enough *rancho* for all of us?"

His brother grimaced and turned away.

ALEKSANDRA GROANED and raced from their bed, barely making it to the chamber pot before she emptied her stomach, again.

Xavier got up and poured water into the Wedgwood basin on the bureau and wet a cloth, handing it to her as she sat up from kneeling on the floor. He pulled her hair back and tied it with a ribbon, then stroked her hair until she turned to face him, cheeks pink.

"Feel better now?" he murmured.

"Getting there," she said and took his hand. He pulled her to her feet and she followed him back to bed.

It was already hot, despite the hour, and sweat beaded her forehead.

"Let's get this off you, eh?" he said, grasping the hem of her nightgown and lifting it over her head. His gaze fell to her breasts.

Yep.

Her nipples, normally rosy-tipped, had darkened. He reached his hands out to lift both of her breasts. Heavy.

Yep.

She followed his gaze downwards, then gave him a tentative smile.

He shook his head and wrapped his arms around her. "Congratulations, Mama," he whispered into her ear.

"How long have you known?" she asked shyly.

"I've wondered this week, but this morning clinched it."

"I feel better now," she said.

"That's good," he said, lying still.

"Shouldn't we be getting out of bed?" She sat up beside him.

"I think you should stay in bed and rest…"

She regarded him sideways. "Rest?" Her gaze warmed.

"Mmmm hmm," he mumbled, as he pulled her down beside him. "I can be restful if I try," he said, and propped himself up on one elbow to trace a finger from her lips to her ear, down her throat, to encircle a nipple, then down, down. She shivered and he rumbled deep in his throat at the brown nipples hardening into tight nubs. His lips followed the tracks of his finger and she whimpered.

"If I didn't know I was pregnant before, I would by now," she whispered. "Always so hot."

"Never so hot as when you are," he agreed. Footsteps approached down the hall, then stopped.

She flicked a glance at the door. "We should—"

"—no, we shouldn't. We're doing all we should be right now."

She gripped his shoulders and pulled him on top of her. The footsteps resumed their soft tread and disappeared. "Please, Xavier—"

He grinned. "—in time, in time," he said, and bent his head to the task.

"I CAN'T WAIT to begin preparing the nursery *por su bebé*." Maria beamed as she gripped Aleksandra's hand.

The warmth of her new family nearly filled the hole in her heart.

"You should have plenty of time to do it while I'm gone," Xavier said, his fork halfway to his mouth.

"Where are you going?" Maria's brows shot up.

"I need to go back East to pick up two colts from Utah and check on Aleksandra's family's cabin."

"That's a long way to go for a few horses." Maria's brow wrinkled, as she picked up her china cup and took a sip.

"They're Charro's first get." Xavier grinned at her.

"Ah, that's a different kettle of fish," she said, her eyes glowing.

"*We* need to go," Aleksandra said, through gritted teeth, with a sideways glance.

Maria nearly snorted her coffee out of her nose. She looked at the table for a moment and set her cup down, carefully considering the pattern on the bone china before she spoke.

"Nearly eight hundred miles there and the same back, on a horse," Maria said testily, her voice growing in volume as she went on, "over the Sierras, not to mention the Great Salt Desert, never mind you were a Pony rider, nor the Indians, and *pregnant*?" She lifted her gaze to Aleksandra, black fathomless eyes, then at Xavier. "You cannot be serious."

Xavier swallowed hard, and looked at Aleksandra. "We've discussed this and I thought you agreed."

"*You* decided," she said.

No one said a word.

Maria glared at her daughter-in-law and then at her son.

Xavier stood and crooked a finger at Aleks. She ignored him for a moment, then slowly got to her feet.

"If you will please excuse us, Mama?" He said, and fairly dragged Aleksandra toward the door.

Sancho chose that moment to stumble in the door.

"Bloody Yanks, slaughtered us at Shilo." He muttered. "That damn Yank Grant is making mincemeat of our troops."

"What?" Xavier turned to him, still gripping Aleksandra's arm. "Oh. Your Confederates, not mine," he barked. "Keep a civil tongue in this house, *hermano*. Your treasonous talk's not welcome here. Now get *out*."

Sancho stared at him like he'd never seen him before, turned and stumbled out into the hallway.

Xavier tugged Aleksandra on up the stairs and into their bedroom so fast she had to trot to keep up.

He slammed the door behind them, dropped her arm and turned on her. "I thought you wanted this child."

"I do." She glared back at him, her chin high.

"Yet you'd risk it? Like last time?"

Silence.

"I was trying to save my child's father," her chin held high in the air.

"Well this time, I don't need saving," he growled. Closing his eyes, he leaned back against the door. "*Uno, dos, tres, quatro...*" He counted softly in Spanish to at least twenty.

Aleksandra cringed. She was *so* in the wrong, but nobody was going to tell her what she could or couldn't do.

He finally turned to face her. "While I appreciate your coming to my aid the last time," his clipped words chilled her, "this isn't like last time."

She gulped and stared at the ground.

"Well, is it?"

"No," she whispered.

"Do you want this child?"

"Yes, more than anything," she blurted out.

"Then why do you insist on having your way, to its almost certain detriment? I nearly lost you as well, the last time," he said, and gripped her arms tightly enough to make her whimper.

"You're hurting me, Xavier." She winced.

He inhaled sharply and lightened his hold, but he didn't let go. "I cannot bear to lose you," he said. "If I have to—"

"—I'll stay home," she breathed, her heart in her throat. "I was being stupid, and childish."

"You want to know your needs and desires are considered, but they *have* been, have they not?"

She shuddered. "Yes."

"Can I do anything more to prove what you mean to me, to my family, to everyone on this whole damned *rancho*?"

"Forgive me, Xavier? Please? Love me, just love me." She buried her face in his chest.

He pulled her in tight, then lifted her chin with the side of a finger and kissed her eyelids, then her mouth. Tears flowed hot down her cheeks as she stood before him.

He pulled the slipknot of the drawstring from her blouse and the linen slid to the ground.

Their heightened anxiety lent a fierceness to their lovemaking, and by the end, both were spent, anger forgotten, new bonds forged in the flame.

"I'll miss you terribly. Will you take someone with you?"

"*Sí*, I'll be fine. I'm taking Carlos. It's you, I worry about."

"I'm pretty hard to kill," she said with a chuckle, then sobered, realizing it was far from true. She could fight a single person with a *shashka*, but more? She gripped his hands. "I promise to care for myself and your unborn child until your return, and thereafter, so help me God."

"And I, for myself." He let out a huge breath. "Now we've missed breakfast, but maybe Adelita has saved us some?"

"Let's go—and you'll have to find your brother."

His gaze darkened. "Not so sure what to do there," he said, sitting up.

"That makes two of us."

"It seems most of the *Californios*, especially down in southern California, are truly in favor of the Confederates. I've spoken with several of these ranchers, but I didn't want to worry you. Funny," he gave her a twisted grin, "in light of the fact the Confeds are offering the squatters land for joining them as well. They certainly can't give the same land to them both."

"Not much we can do now, Xavier. Let's go down."

He nodded and stood, then pulled her up and kissed her again.

"Xave, let's get some more *dzhigitovka* lessons into you before you go. I'd like to know you can fight from horseback, if you need to. I won't be there to save you," she said, with an impish grin over her shoulder.

"And I can only miss my holds and fall off so many times, so you'd better teach me a lot, soon," he grumbled, as he pulled his shirt on.

48

It was a long wait, longer than Aleksandra had imagined it could possibly be, until Xavier returned. Maria was kindness itself, and Adelita shared even her favorite secret family recipes, in exchange for a working knowledge of sourdough biscuits and *żurek*. She kept the horses in work, but avoided *dzhigitovka* and took care to take someone along when she rode to check stock on the far reaches of the *rancho*.

"A letter for you, *señorita*." Miguel handed her the well-worn envelope he'd collected in town.

"From New Zealand, yet?" Thanking him, Aleksandra took it into the kitchen.

"New Zealand? Whomever would that be from?" Maria's brows shot up.

She eyed it, then opened the missive.

"From Gustavus von Tempsky, addressed to Xavier and I. He and his wife, etc. etc., congratulating us on our wedding." She smiled. "That was a long time ago. He's now in New Zealand, writing for a newspaper." She stared at the letter, frowning. "Xavier said he was originally from Polish Prussia, became a mercenary, went to Australia to mine for gold, and was heading for the Coromandel in New Zealand to mine as well." She looked up at Maria. "In his last letter, he offered Xavier a share in his New Zealand mine, but now he's a newspaperman? That's a strange career change."

Maria's brows drew together and she sat down heavily. "Xavier told me about him when Mr von Tempsky's last letter arrived. As I told him, it would be difficult to run the *rancho* from half a world away. Is Xavier considering it?"

"I don't think so." She smiled at her mother-in-law. "He's happy here, and so glad he's come home."

Maria breathed again, a tear escaping from one eye as she gripped Aleksandra's hands. "And without you…"

"He'd have figured it out," Aleksandra murmured, but she knew it might never have happened. "How is your heart, by the way?"

She looked away for a moment before answering. "In truth, as long as I try to stay calm, don't worry, and eat well, don't drink wine or beer," she grinned, "or *tequila*, the palpitations stay away." She regarded the coffee before her. "And I limit the evil drink of coffee."

"*¡ESTAN viniendo, estan viniendo* Xavier *y* Carlos!" The stableboy's voice rang down the hall.

"*Gracias*, Jesús." Aleksandra yanked her apron over her head as she followed him out to the yard.

Not only Xavier and Carlos, leading the two glorious colts from Doc Faust, but Molly and Sebastian as well. Tears streamed down Aleksandra's face as she ran. At the white-eyed glances from the two young horses, she dropped to a walk to greet them.

Molly cried, too, as they hugged. Aleksandra gripped Seb's hand in welcome, and headed for her husband.

Carlos took one look at her as she came his direction, en route to Xavier, and blushed. "I'll just be taking them for a drink," he said, and backed his horse away, dragging the two colts with him.

He thought you might kiss him," Xavier laughed, "but I'll take his." He slid from the saddle and into her arms. The two-month kiss took long enough for Molly and her son to dismount and untie the saddlebags from their horses.

Molly laughed at them when they finally pulled apart, spent. "Congratulations to you both," she said. "You've been well, Aleks?"

"Never better. A good thing my husband left me here." She grinned at Xavier from beneath her brows. He shook his head and unlaced his bedroll from behind Charro's saddle. "Stopped by Virginia City and Molly wouldn't let us go without taking her and Seb with us."

"Thank you for bringing them both, with all my heart." Aleksandra beamed at Xavier. "And the colt are magnificent. Thank you for collecting them," she breathed.

Maria came down the steps, welcoming everyone. Aleksandra made introductions, while she held the horses for the travelers to unload.

"I'll take them," Xavier said, gathering up their reins, "and you can get

Molly and Seb settled, please." He kissed her again and turned toward the barn.

Aleksandra bent down to pick up his heavy bedroll.

"Don't," Xavier's growl came from behind her.

"I'll get it, Uncle Xavier," Seb said, and shouldered it with a grin at her.

She'd have to get used to being taken care of again, now Xavier was back. She sighed.

It will be worth it.

Her cheeks warmed at the thought, and she caught Molly's grin. "It's so wonderful to have you here. Thank you for coming out." Aleksandra gripped Molly's hands.

"I'm happy to welcome you here, too." Maria smiled at the newcomers. "Come, come, into the house. There's hot chocolate waiting." She hustled them up the stairs and into the kitchen. "Aleks has told me so much of you," she said, as she closed the front door. "And you, too, Seb. It'll be good to have a young man around the place again, now my boys have all grown up."

Seb puffed out his chest and stood taller, while behind him, Molly smiled.

When they were all seated, their drink and bowl of *chili* before them, Xavier came in.

"That was fast." Aleksandra smiled.

"Miguel took Charro and kicked me out of the barn," he said, and pursed his lips, then laughed. "Charro doesn't care, he just wants his stable and hay."

Maria handed him a bowl and bussed him on the cheek. "Welcome home, *Querido*," she murmured. He squeezed her hand and kissed her cheek in return.

"So Molly," Maria said, "Aleks mentioned you might wish to practice your midwifery here?"

"I would like to, very much."

"I'd be only too happy to take you around to the *ranchos* and the women in town to introduce you. You'll create quite a stir." Maria's eyes sparkled. "There are no midwives hereabouts."

"Oh, would you, Mrs. Argüello? I would appreciate that."

"If tomorrow suits, I'll be ready to go after breakfast," Maria replied.

Molly beamed. "I especially wanted to get here for February," she glanced at Aleksandra, "and needed to cross the Sierras before the snows came, or I wouldn't make it before the birth."

Aleksandra blinked. "I'd forgotten about the snows. Glad you remembered."

"Excuse me, Xavier," Seb looked up at him, "Carlos asked if I'd help him in the stables. Would you mind?

"You're a good hand with a horse, Seb. I'm sure your help would be valuable. Thank you," he replied.

"Aleks, I've brought a copy of the *Territorial Enterprise* back for you." Xavier tossed it to her. Aleksandra jumped on it and scanned the front. "Oh, stories by Samuel Clemens."

"I thought you'd enjoy it," he said.

"You men are back just in time for haymaking," his mother said.

"That's what we were aiming for."

"I'm ready," Seb said.

"We hoped you'd come this week. Your new Buckeye mower is here, Xavier."

Xavier nearly leapt out of his seat and Maria laughed. "It'll still be there after we eat. Would you like to tell the men we'll start at dawn?"

"Will do." His eyes glowed with anticipation. "I'd hoped it would be here before we needed to cut hay. I'll go over the other equipment this afternoon to make sure it's all ready. Is Sancho here?"

A silence fell over the table.

Aleksandra plucked up an answer. "Haven't seen him this morning. Come to think of it, haven't seen him for a few days. Maria, any word?"

She sighed and looked at her plate.

"His trips away are getting longer," Aleksandra said softly, into the gap, "and he's not looking well when he returns."

Xavier gritted his teeth and let his breath out slowly, then exchanged a glance with Aleksandra.

"The stock look well, though," she added, with a wry grin.

"Thank Christ for that," Xavier said, his voice heavy. "What's the weather been like?"

"Occasional thunderstorms," Aleksandra said, "but dry, overall. The hay's well grown, or so Marcelo told me when he showed me around the hay fields last week."

Xavier smiled at her. "Learning a lot?"

"It's a whole new world for me."

"You're doing well, Mrs. Argüello," Xavier said, and kissed her.

The front door slammed and there was a heavy thump in the entryway.

Maria started to jump up, but Xavier motioned her down. She sat and waited, her face frozen.

Sancho entered the kitchen and glanced around the table, his brows briefly lifting at the sight of Molly.

"*Buenos días*," he said, and half-bowed to Maria, and to Molly. "You're back." He nodded at his brother.

"Good morning, *hijo*," Maria answered, and got up to hug him. "We've missed you, Son."

A grimace appeared fleetingly beneath his bloodshot eyes as he presented his cheek dutifully to his mother. He turned his attention to Molly as Maria introduced them. "Welcome to Las Pulgas," he said, and helped himself to some coffee.

Aleksandra blinked at the alcohol fumes emanating from her brother-in-law, as he walked past her to sit beside Molly. His clothes, never the cleanest, would likely stand up on their own if he shed them now.

Molly edged infinitesimally away from the newcomer and attempted a welcoming smile. Sancho didn't seem to notice. He just sipped his coffee.

"We're making hay tomorrow, Sancho," his mother said.

Sancho winced and buried his face in his mug.

"I'll take my bedroll up, then I'd best be off to check the equipment for tomorrow." Xavier stood.

"*Gracias por el desayuno*, Adelita," he said, then offered his hand to Aleksandra and led her from the room.

"*De nada*, Xave," Adelita called after him.

Hefting his heavy bag, he motioned Aleksandra up the stairs and followed. Dropping it just inside the door, he pulled her into his arms. "I've so missed you, every day, every minute," he murmured. "I almost wished you'd come along," he grinned, "and now I'm too filthy to do anything about it." He pressed her against his length.

She could tell he'd missed her, against her own hardening belly.

"And how's our—" he slid his hand between them to caress the young life inside her.

She held his hand still. "Wait for it," she whispered.

He blinked at the tap, and his smile and eyes grew wider by the second. "When did he start kicking?"

"Just the other day," she whispered, and gripped his shoulders. "I'm sorry I was so horrible. I couldn't risk its life like that. I promise I won't do it again."

"It's hard to change the habits of a lifetime. Thank you for trying and thank you for giving me, *us*, this gift."

She threw her arms around his neck and clung like there were no tomorrow. Her kiss promised more. "Go see to your mowers, I'll take care of Molly and Seb. We might have an...early supper," she finished on a low tone, and slid her hand down from his earlobe, fingers light over his ribs, along the soft skin of his groin, before kissing her fingers, and then his lips.

"If you don't stop," he quivered, tight as a bowstring, "we'll never leave this room." His eyes raked her and she shuddered.

He drew slowly away and laughed, then opened the door, pulling her with him.

"I'll see a bath is set up," Aleksandra raised a brow at him. "You could use it."

He laughed. "I'd have bathed in the rivers, but I didn't want to scare Molly," he said, and smacked her on the bottom, sending her down the stairs.

ALEKSANDRA TRIED to focus her eyes in the semi-darkness of their room.

"You stay in bed, *Querida*," Xavier murmured, leaning over her. He kissed her forehead. "No need for you to get up, yet."

"But I can help," she said, turning over to see the early dawn light, barely peeking through the trees outside their bedroom window.

"You can help by staying right here."

"I can at least check the stock." She eyed him sideways. "I've been doing it every day until you came home, Dr. Argüello."

He hesitated for a moment, then breathed out. "So you have. Well, OK, but can you please be careful?"

She smiled. "Of course."

"Of course," he said, with a twist of his lips. "Butter wouldn't melt, would it?"

"Never." She sat up. "I'll be right down." She made little shooing motions with her hands, then slid out of bed to get dressed, inhaling sharply as her feet hit the cold floor.

EARS PRICKED, Rogan eyed the blond stranger with his back to them. The bay sidled a bit as Aleksandra pushed him, her legs firmly on his sides, toward the man.

The blond spun at the last moment, leveling his Enfield at her. When he saw his target, his eyes opened wide and he dropped the muzzle, then stood there in silence.

"What are you doing here?" Aleksandra frowned at him.

He raised a brow. "Ummm, what does it look like? Hunting."

"This is private property." She looked past him, at the fields of the Cañada de Raymundo, and at the Alta Sierra beyond, then hardened her gaze back on him. "Do you have the owner's permission?"

"Of course."

"Whose?"

"Ummm," he gritted his teeth, "I don't rightly remember, but I met him one night at the tables."

"The one who can give you permission doesn't gamble. I'd ask you to leave now."

He narrowed his eyes at her while he perused the horse she rode. He bit his lip, then his gaze fell on her *shashka* and he laughed. "That itty-bitty sword gonna make me?" He shot a look at her face, and backed up a step. "Well, since you asked so nice, guess I'll go." He slowly turned away and started walking.

She held Rogan still where they were until he was gone from sight, then shook her head. "Idiot," she growled and turned the horse back toward the *hacienda*.

A rifle shot, close at hand, ripped the stillness of the *cañon*. Rogan spun and shied sideways. Aleksandra cursed as she felt the saddle slipping from beneath her seat. She grasped at the mane flying in her face, but the thin handfuls weren't enough to stop her from falling, reins slipping from her hands as the ground came up to meet her with a smack, dirt and grass filling her mouth, the taste of blood, pain in her chest, and then darkness.

49

"What's Aleksandra up to today?" Xavier quirked a brow, as Molly handed him the water dipper. "Has she managed to stay out of trouble?"

She smiled. "She went to check stock. Said she'd be back soon."

Xavier frowned, then forced a smile. "She didn't go alone, did she?"

Molly laughed. "She said you'd ask. She also said to tell you she'd be fine."

He sighed. Something didn't feel right. "When did she go?"

She shook her head. "Just a little while ago. If it will make you feel better, I'll send her out with the water as soon as she gets back."

"OK, then." He gritted his teeth, and returned the ladle. "You'll send her with someone—"

"—of course." Molly cut in. She shook her head with a wry grin. "Good to know she's loved."

"Thanks," he said, stifling his fear, and went back to help the others turn the drying hay.

A few hours later, hoofbeats caught his attention. His heart froze as Molly galloped up to him on a lathered Rogan, one broken rein knotted between the bit and Molly's hand.

"He came back alone, trailing what was left of his reins. Miguel's saddling Charro for you now. Can you get up behind on Rogan?"

Xavier glanced at the bay, his eyes rolling white in his head. "Best we don't try it. No use both of us getting tossed. He's not used to two."

"I'll walk back and follow on Dzień. You take him." She flung herself from the saddle and held the dancing horse for him to mount.

"Let go," he barked, and vaulted into the saddle as Rogan struck up a canter. "Thanks, Molly," he called back. Aleksandra's *dzhigitovka* came in handy after all. His lips twisted into a parody of a grin as they raced back to the *hacienda*.

What could have happened?

Plenty. It could be anything.

He made it back to the barn in minutes flat. "Miguel, can you ride Charro? Rogan's not used to anyone but Aleks and I, and Molly, it seems. We may need both of us," he said. "Which way?"

Miguel pointed and swung up as Xavier loosed the bay's reins and they shot away, Charro only a few lengths behind. Miguel wasn't their head stableman for nothing. The man could ride.

"Do you know where she was going to check stock?" he shouted over his shoulder to the man.

"It was her second trip out, and she should've been out to the west boundary *en la Cañada Raymond, cerca de la laguna.*"

He swallowed hard. In the big *cañon*…near the little lake…she could be anywhere, through a rough and rocky *cañon,* to the furthest northwest corner of the property—in any of dozens of small side-*cañons,* looking for stock, or —a little voice crept in—she might not be there at all.

He shook off his fears and focused.

"Maybe Rogan will take us there," Miguel said.

Xavier sighed. "The only things that interest this horse are supper and mares," he growled, and let him run. The bay shook his head and ate up the trail. "You look left and I'll look right," Xavier yelled into the wind, getting a mouthful of mane for his efforts.

Cows and calves resting beneath oak trees scattered in their wake as they galloped past, but nothing walked on two legs or lay on the ground.

They shot into the big *cañon*, twisting and turning, avoiding the biggest of the boulders littering its floor. "Aleks… Aleks…ALEKS!" Xavier shouted at the top of his lungs.

Only the echoes of the two big horses' hooves answered, and they rode on. It was a good six miles to the end of the *cañon*, and another four to the *laguna.*

They shot out of the valley into the full glare of the setting sun and nearly missed her, a small ball of buckskin and white just to the right of their path.

As they approached, her hand began to fly to her *shashka* and she shrieked.

"Aleks, it's me," Xavier called, sliding from Rogan's saddle, as he slid to a halt. He threw the reins to Miguel and ran to her side.

"What are you doing out here by your—" he growled, then saw her face, white where the tears tracked down through the dirt. "*Querida?*" he whispered.

She shook her head. "Collarbone," she mumbled. "Head," and brought her left hand up to cradle it. "And I think…I'm bleeding."

"Just lie down," he murmured, gently supporting her back onto the ground. "Let's see what's up here."

He stared into her eyes, as she'd taught him. "Close them," he said, and she complied. While her eyes were closed, he peeked at her trousers and his breath locked in his chest at the blood staining the leather at the junction of her legs, and he bit his cheek to keep from groaning himself. He opened one lid at a time.

"One pupil's a little slow to react," he said, then felt over the rest of her. "Can you move your fingers and toes? "*Gracias a Dios*," he muttered beneath his breath, when she wriggled them all.

"Just don't make me move my right arm," she said. "My collarbone's sore." She winced as he examined it gently.

"Hopefully it's just cracked. It's not overriding, thank Christ. Can you walk?"

"I don't know. I only tried to move after I heard you." She swallowed hard and looked up at the men. "Thank you both for coming to get me."

"I'm going to take you back on Charro. Six miles is too far for you to walk," Xavier said, trying for a grin.

Not sure he made it. Not at all.

"At least riding Charro is like sitting on a cloud," she said, groaning as Xavier picked her up from the ground, "his gaits," she let her breath out slowly and continued, "are so smooth." She gave up talking and gritted her teeth.

"*Señor*," Miguel said, "I will ride the wild thing," he nodded at Rogan. "You give the *señorita* to me and get up, then I'll hand her to you."

She smiled gratefully at the man through her tears, and bit her lip as he handed her up to Charro's great height.

"*Con permiso*, I will ride back and tell *Señora* Argüello. She will make the necessary arrangements."

He was gone before Xavier could answer. He tightened his grip on his wife and she inhaled sharply. "*Lo siento*, sorry *Querida*. I'll have you home soon."

"A walk is fine," she managed, between tight lips, smiling briefly before falling into a doze.

His heart thudded in his chest, hoping his mama would send for the doctor and that Aleks would be OK, again.

He couldn't live if she died.

He shook his head and she winced in her sleep.

She awoke when they were halfway home. "Did you see the man?"

"*What man?*"

"The one with the rifle."

Xavier thought he'd scream, but schooled his tone. "There was no one there when we got to you." He looked her over more closely as they rode. "Did he touch you?"

"I don't know. I don't think so. He was hunting. Fired a gun."

"At you?"

"I don't know," her brow furrowed. "I'm trying to remember. Blond man, said he had permission to hunt here."

"Whose permission?"

"Said someone he met gambling."

Xavier was silent for long moments, then took a deep breath. "What else can you remember?"

She told him what she could, and he growled. "No one will hunt here again. No question about that." He tried to slow his racing heart.

"I'm sorry, Xavier, I didn't mean to—"

"—you did right. You rest now."

She slept.

Hoofbeats on the track sounded soon after. Maria drove her team, with Molly beside her, much faster than the rough road allowed, and Xavier held his breath until they stopped beside Charro. He held up a finger to his lips.

"*Está bien?*" Maria whispered.

"She's asleep," he mouthed.

"I've sent for the doctor, he should be *en la hacienda* soon. I'll go back and prepare, if you're all right with her."

"She's bleeding," he wrenched out and gulped, "and probably has a broken collarbone. And a concussion."

Both women in the gig paled, and Maria drew the shape of a cross on her chest. She waved her fingers, turned the horses, then set off at a flying trot for home. Molly stared back at them over her shoulder, knuckles white on the back of the seat and tears streaming from her eyes while Maria drove as if pursued by the hounds of Hell.

THE DOCTOR AGREED with their diagnoses. He prescribed bed rest, and as he made his exit, murmured soothingly about plenty of good food and absolutely no riding. The door clicked shut behind him.

Aleksandra glanced at Xavier and opened her mouth to protest, then slapped it shut again.

"Plenty of time for that later," Molly agreed, handing her a cup of hot chocolate. Aleksandra started to reach out with her right and shuddered, then took it with her left.

She sipped the hot liquid and handed it back. "I promise," she whispered, then gave the ghost of a grin. "Don't you love the way Mexicans make hot chocolate?"

Molly rolled her eyes. "I'm going to have to find myself one, a Mexican, just to have this chocolate for the rest of my life." She turned to go. "Oh, and one of those chocolate beaters, with the rings."

Aleksandra smiled faintly. "A *molinillo*, it's called. One of the first Spanish words I wanted to learn."

"You sleep now," Xavier said, after her mug was empty, "and when you wake up, I'll bring you some nice supper."

She looked up at him, all big eyes in her wan face.

"What is it?" Xavier returned to the bedside chair and gingerly took her hand.

"Flan?" she whispered hopefully, "that is, if Adelita wouldn't mind making it?"

"I'll bet she's already got some in the oven for you. She'll not have forgotten something like that." He carefully felt her forehead. He tried for calm, but everything in him screamed to find out the story behind the rogue hunter. He'd get to the bottom of it, if it killed him.

SUPPER WAS DONE. In between trips tiptoeing upstairs to peek into their bedroom to see if Aleksandra had awakened, he sat at the kitchen table, drumming his fingers. After Adelita pointedly raised her brows at them for the third time, he tapped his boot on the floor, instead.

His brother still hadn't returned by the time he'd fed Aleksandra and she'd gone back to sleep, but he could wait.

From far away, he heard the Spanish sing-song coming up the drive. Despite its lashing of alcoholic overtones, Sancho still had a good voice. Xavier shook his head. Lot of good that would do him in the next fifteen minutes. He stood and flexed his muscles, stiff from haymaking and sitting in one place for too many hours. His fist itched to do damage to the one responsible for Aleksandra's state.

He met him in the barn.

Sancho turned slowly, one boot dragging on the ground.

Fantástico.

He was potted.

"*Aiee, hermano*, but you surprise me. My good friend Jack said..." he hesitated and frowned, then tried again. "He said..." He stopped again.

"Where's that bitch of a wif—"

That was as far as he got.

He hit Sancho with all the hours of pent up fear, frustration and rage in his body and he dropped like a stone.

Xavier stepped back, still itching for a fight, and considered the limp form on the ground. He closed his eyes and shook his head.

Would've been good to at least find out the name of the idiota *with the gun before flooring him. Smooth move, Xave.*

He turned and walked away. The rats could have him, for all he cared.

ALEKSANDRA WAS IMPROVED in the morning, judging by the fact she'd consider something other than flan to eat.

She looked at his hand, then her eyes narrowed as she flicked them up to his. "That wasn't from haymaking. Who'd you hit?"

"No one of consequence." He looked away.

"Xavier," Molly's voice floated up the stairs, "are you up?"

"I'll be down in a minute."

"Your brother's passed out on the ground in the barn and I can't wake him," she called.

Aleksandra's eyes bored a hole in his back and he turned. She looked at his hand again. He nodded. "Bastard deserved it, and high time. He won't continue to make the place unsafe for my family. If he wishes, he's welcome to go."

She stared at him, but said nothing, then gave him a weak smile.

He kissed her again. "*Te quiero, Querida.*" He turned on his heel and left.

Between the hangover and the broken nose, Sancho was not a happy man.

"*Mi amigo*, Jarome Jackson, said he was kicked off Las Pulgas yesterday, and by a girl. He was pretty upset. I had to buy him many drinks to make up for it, so you owe me, Xavier," Sancho said, and glared at him over his coffee. To Sancho's credit, and his health, today he refrained from referring to his wife in the terms he'd used last night.

One saving grace, he didn't remember coming home.

"I still don't remember getting hit in the face—stupid horse probably ran under a tree again."

"While I wouldn't be surprised at that, that's not what happened."

Sancho looked up at him with still-glazed eyes, his brow raised. Blood had begun to trickle from one nostril, and he wiped at it with the back of a hand already stained dark with dried blood.

"She's upstairs, pretty broken. While I realize that won't likely concern you, it should. Your invitation has caused pain to someone I care for deeply. I suggest you find *su amigo*," his voice dripped sarcasm, "and ensure that he, and anyone else you've allowed to hunt or merely trespass on this property, never do so again. If they do, you'll answer to me. A broken nose will be the least of your worries, plus you'll never be welcome here again. *Comprendes?* You understand?"

Sancho was awake now. He stared, eyes wide. He gulped, then stood stone still for a moment, before finding the sense to ask after his sister-in-law.

"Alive," Xavier growled low, "no thanks to that bastard Jackson."

"But he said—"

"The hell with what he said. He's responsible for injury to Aleks. He'll pay."

"But—" Sancho whined, grabbing Xavier's arm as he strode past him.

Xavier shook him off and aimed another punch at his face, but Sancho ducked.

"It's not worth it, Xave, just go find Jackson," Maria said, steel in her voice.

From the barn door, he glanced back to see his brother dragging himself up the stairs beneath Maria's grim perusal, her arms crossed and lips pursed. He'd not be likely to get sympathy from that quarter.

He found Jackson. By the time Xavier left him, the man was under no delusion about his welcome back at the *rancho*.

He surely wouldn't come near the place again.

Xavier's vision cleared slowly on the ride home. The darkness had begun to descend again but he'd kept it, for the most part, at bay. He needed to look at the Las Pulgas accounts—it didn't look like Sancho would be around for long, and he didn't want any surprises when he finally did leave. He'd talk with him about it tomorrow.

50

"I didn't think it possible, Xavier, but Sancho seems to have turned over a new leaf, or taken a new lease on life, or something." Aleksandra frowned. "I can't really believe it, though."

He raised a brow at her, then sighed. "I'd like to believe it, but I'm finding it hard, too."

"Maybe the broken nose made him think about it. Stranger things have happened. He's even staying away less and helping more."

"True," he said, grudgingly, "but he'll bear watching."

Weeks passed, and though Sancho continued to stay away overnight, he didn't come home drunk, and his attitude improved.

"Maybe he won't be going anywhere after all. I thought I needed to get familiar with the books, but perhaps it won't be necessary." Xavier shrugged, but didn't look entirely convinced.

"It would be good if he stayed nice. Your mama's been happy with the changes."

He gave her a faint smile.

"I don't hold much hope for it either," she said, "but I'll continue to work with him if he's willing to try."

"Anyway," he placed his hand on her belly, "have you had any more bleeding? You're looking well."

"It seems to have stopped, and Molly's satisfied everything is fine with both of us." She winced. "Just my arm."

He raised his eyes sharply. "I'm glad. I was so worried for you. For *us*," he corrected, then closed his eyes. "I can't wait to hold you again," he gave her a faint smile ,"without hearing 'ouch'."

"You will be able to—soon," she said, carefully moving her arm. "It's hard enough for *me* to keep from hurting it." She gave a little snort. Laughing hurt too much.

He sighed and gritted his teeth.

"What?"

"My brother, the Confederate."

"What now?"

"He's ranting about Lincoln's 'Emancipation Proclamation'."

"I guess it'll change the focus of the war from the preservation of the Union to the abolition of slavery," she said.

"That's a bonus, if you're against slavery, but it'll only free slaves in the rebel states, not the Union ones. How's that supposed to work?"

"Maybe it's Lincoln's answer to making things difficult for the Southerners by offering freedom to their slaves. It'll affect not only those supporting or fighting in their armies, but also those left home to keep the plantations running," Aleksandra said, and bit her lip.

"I heard the other day that England and France were thinking again about supporting the Confederates, but after the Southerners were pushed out of Maryland at Antitam," Xavier brushed his hair off his face with the back of his hand, "they're not keen to put their weight behind the losing side."

"Thank God for small blessings," she murmured.

"Anyway, I've told Sancho to keep his traitorous opinions to himself, and he's shut up."

"More small blessings."

"Anyway," he rubbed his hands together, "haymaking is done, and it's time to get ready for winter. I'm already a month behind, so I'm off to cut firewood today. What are you up to this morning?" he said, pulling her toward him and wrapping his arms around her with care.

She sighed. "I won't be coming with you, so I guess I'll work on baby clothes again, and Christmas presents," she smiled at him, "since we missed it last year, and since I'm zero use on the farm. My timing is immaculate, once again."

"It wasn't your fault. *Qué será, será.* Just think, our baby will have clothes. Otherwise he would be naked." He grinned and kissed her goodbye. "Take your time. Breakfast is ready when you are."

She blew him a kiss as he left, and the door clicked shut.

Reaching into her chest beside the bed, she pulled out the shirt she was making for Xavier. Never had she bothered to take such care in her sewing. He'd be pleased. She hummed as she took tiny stitches, then began thinking of the infant kicking around inside her. She had to take care of herself—and this baby.

Time I grew up.

For once, it didn't make her feel deprived, just very grown up. *That* made her smile.

"*Feliz Navidad*, Merry Christmas, *mi querida*," Xavier breathed, and ran fingers down from her shoulder, along the side of her breast, then further, to smooth the skin over her belly.

"Ahhh, Xavier. I love you. Merry Christmas." She could only smile, her heart fit to burst.

"You're the best present to wake up to every day," he said, as his lips moved down her body, tracing his fingers' previous path.

She jolted when they found a nipple and sucked gently. A twinge deep down. "More, harder," she whispered, "please."

"Your wish," he said, from the side of his mouth, "is my command, *princesa*."

THEY WERE VERY LATE for breakfast, but Maria's eyes lit up at their arrival. "*Feliz Navidad*," they called, and a chorus from the table returned the greeting.

"*Huevos Rancheros para la Navidad*, mmmm," Xavier handed Aleksandra into her seat, then took his.

"That baby needs its sleep, no?" Maria's eyes twinkled with mischief.

Aleksandra's face heated, then she grinned at her. "*Sí, Mama*," she murmured.

Maria laughed. "Merry Christmas to you both, or to all three of you."

A small box in tissue paper sat beside Aleksandra's plate.

"Go ahead, open it," said her mother-in-law. Aleksandra unwound the cord and unwrapped it, folding the paper aside. A necklace of pearls and sapphires lay on the bed of purple velvet.

She could only sit in stunned silence, staring at the beauty before her.

"It was my mother's, then mine, and now it is yours." She glanced at Xavier and nodded at Aleksandra. He stood and carefully removed it from the box, then clasped it around her neck and locked it.

Molly and Maria beamed at Aleksandra, who opened her mouth, but still nothing came out. Finally, she said "Maria, thank you, but I could—"

"Nonsense. It stays in the family. You will give it to your daughter, or to the wife of your son."

Aleksandra's eyes met Xavier's and he nodded. "It is so," he said, with a heartwarming smile.

"Well, then, thank you with all my heart," she said, glancing around at everyone at the table. Only Sancho wasn't smiling. He just looked at his plate. When he flicked his gaze up to her, it was with such venom that she stared for a moment, then looked away. Her stomach fluttered and she shuddered. When she looked at him again, his bland smile was back in place. Had she imagined it?

She hoped so. She *really* hoped so.

THE STORM WAS RAGING OUTSIDE, but they were snug and warm beside the kitchen fire.

"Is someone at the door?" Xavier said, getting up.

Then she somehow heard, above the rain pelting the tile roof, the dull pounding of a fist on wood. Xavier jumped to his feet and strode to the front door.

"Stanford, what are you doing out in this?" Xavier shouted over the tempest through the open doorway. "Are you staying?"

"That would be," he wiped his hand over his dripping face, "appreciated."

"Let's go put your horse up. We'll be in soon, Aleks. Would you please put something on to heat for Leland?"

"No problem," she said, shoving the door closed behind them against the driving wind and rain.

By the time they returned, *tortillas* and beans were on the table.

"Mmm, my favorite. Adelita remembered." He winked at the cook, who fluttered her lashes at him. "Thank you."

As he steamed before the fire, he regaled them with stories of Sacramento. "You call this a storm?" He waved his hand at the window, rattling in the wind. "You wouldn't countenance it, but the floodwaters didn't go down last year until nearly March."

Aleksandra spun to stare at him. "You cannot be serious, all that time?"

"Yep. And they are jacking up the downtown, like you suggested, as we speak."

"That, I'd love to see," she said.

"You could, if you two come up for the groundbreaking ceremony for our new railroad." His grin stretched from ear to ear.

"Which railroad?" Xavier asked.

"The Transcontinental. It's really going to happen."

"I thought the government was broke and couldn't foot the bill," Xavier said.

"We're paying for it ourselves."

Aleksandra and Xavier stared at him.

"We?" Aleksandra cocked a brow at him.

"Some business associates of mine. They're calling us the Big Four," Stanford said, with a grin. "Huntington, Crocker, Hopkins and I, though we'd rather be known as 'The Associates.' A bit less ostentatious, you know."

She chuckled. Knowing the man, she was sure he liked being called one of the Big Four. "Thank you for the invitation, but does it look like I'm traveling over the Sierras anytime soon?" She looked at him from beneath her brows and glanced at her growing abdomen.

"Well…no," he quirked his lips, "but soon you'll be able to even go over the Sierras in one of our carriages, tender condition, excuse my rudeness, or not." Stanford laughed.

Aleksandra tried to paint on a smile for their guest.

What would it do to the peaceful mountains, and the plains beyond? And the Indians?

"Progress," he barked. "Nothing like it. We'll open up the West, and the middle of this great country like never before."

Aleksandra swallowed hard and exchanged a glance with Xavier.

"What about the Indians?" she finally ventured.

"The Indians?" He looked at her blankly. "My partners and I are taking care of them. They won't kill our workers, not if we have anything to say about it."

"You don't understand me. What will happen to them, with this 'progress', and the lack of food, and taking their land?"

"Their land? There's plenty of land for everyone in this great nation. Speaking of land," he turned to Xavier, "I wanted to talk with you about land again. I'd really to buy some of that land in the southern part of your property."

"Sorry, Leland, it's not for sale," Xavier said stiffly. "I could speak with the next *rancho* to see if they're interested in selling."

He frowned. "I'd make it worth your while."

"Thank you, but no," he repeated firmly.

"Well, then, I'd like to speak with them. Perhaps tomorrow?"

"We can do that, if you wish," Xavier said, "if they're home."

"If they're not, I can return another time."

"Was land the purpose of your trip today?"

"Sure was. Can never have enough land, and I've always liked it down here. Close enough to San Fran for business, but far enough to really get away. If I ever retire, I might just like to do it down here."

"Well then, we'll take a ride tomorrow," Xavier said.

How CAN he be so callous about the Indians?" Aleksandra was nearly wailing.

"Some people just don't see what we do, *Querida.*" He pulled her close to spoon before him. "Here, put a pillow under that baby of ours," he said, handing one to her.

She began to cry, then to sob. Incoherent words jumbled together. He made out 'Indians', 'Dancing Wolf', 'Golden Hawk', 'starve', before her words became totally unintelligible.

"Shhh, shhh," he murmured, stroking her hair, her body, anywhere to make her stop.

Nothing.

He went to the door and called for Molly. She came at a run.

"Aleks, you need to stop. This isn't good for the baby," she said, and gave her a little shake.

Adelita came up the stairs with a cup of something warm. "To help her sleep," she said, pressing it into Xavier's shaking hands.

"Drink this, *Querida.* Adelita made it for you," he said. She drank it, between hiccoughing sobs, and gradually, with Molly and Xavier stroking her, she slept.

"Overwrought." Molly shook her head. "All that talk about the Indians. She'll be fine by morning. You cuddle her and get some sleep, Xavier," she whispered, as she backed out the door.

It clicked shut and he was left with his thoughts. It was a long time before he slept.

XAVIER LEFT ALEKSANDRA sleeping in the morning and sought jobs close to the house, until he was sure she was OK. He put down his tools to go inside when he heard the creak of the stairs and through the open doorway, saw her making her way to the kitchen.

She was seated at the table when he entered the room, and he placed a kiss on her neck. "All good this morning?"

"Yes, thank you." She seemed cheerful enough, but looked pale. He stood behind her and rubbed her shoulders. "Mmm, that feels good," she said.

"Ready for breakfast?" Molly quirked a brow at her.

"I'm not sure. Maybe some chocolate," she murmured.

"Not even some custard?" Xavier joked.

She closed her eyes for a moment and her pale face turned green. She started. "What about Leland?"

"I made him a map and sent him on his way to look for land. Wasn't willing to leave you."

"Good." She reached up and squeezed one of his hands

He sat beside her and watched as she closed her eyes for a moment and took a deep breath. "How's that little one, bouncing around?" Xavier winked at her, and she swallowed hard.

"He-she's still asleep, it seems," she frowned. "Unusual."

"Ah well, long night," he said lightly, but turned to exchange a worried glance with Molly.

Aleksandra suddenly hunched over and wrapped her arms around her abdomen.

Xavier slipped an arm across her shoulders. "What is it?"

"I don't know, cramping, maybe just kicking," Aleksandra said, her face draining even of its greenish tint.

He looked up to see Molly and his mother sharing a look, their frowns telling him all he needed to know.

She still had three weeks to go, so far as he knew.

They looked at him and nodded at his glance toward the stairs. "Up you come, my love. Let's go have a lie down."

She winced again and hunched more. "But I just got—" cut off as she tucked herself tighter into a ball around her belly.

"Get her upstairs, Xave, we're behind you."

51

Xavier carried her to their room and laid her on the bed. If it was morning, why did it seem so dark, like the middle of the night? She was in her own little world. Then the pain began coming in waves, and all other questions dissolved in the mist. The baby wasn't kicking—was he all right?

She gripped Xavier's hands, her only lifeline. Her mind wandered—sometimes she was in the bed with soft, smooth sheets, but at others, lying in the grit of the Utah desert, where she'd fallen and aborted the last time. It filled her mouth, until Xavier held a cup to her mouth to rinse it.

I cannot lose another baby.

It spun through her mind, round and round.

Murmurs from the end of the bed— "again," "too much excitement yesterday," "those heavy pots—she shouldn't have been..."

Then the pain, the final pain, and a thin cry as her baby was ripped out of her warm cocoon into the cold world.

She looked up to see Xavier's stricken face, which began to smooth only when Maria brought their daughter to them.

She looked so tiny, and so very upset, scrabbling with her hands at the air and crying.

"Poor wee darling," Aleksandra murmured, "I'm so sorry to drag you out of your warm nest, and so early." She didn't know how she knew, but she pulled the infant toward her and placed her at her breast. They both fumbled until Molly took one of Aleksandra's breasts in one sure hand and the babe's head in the other. She thumbed the little jaw downwards and latched the infant on. The baby took an experimental draw, then began to suck with a vengeance. Aleksandra flinched at the strength of the pull, then relaxed when tiny hands wound themselves in her long mane, and she settled back against the pillows Maria had fluffed behind her. A moment later, the cramping began again. She flicked her eyes to Molly.

"It's OK, the suckling causes the cramping. It'll bring the rest away." Molly smiled a tired smile. "You've been doing all the work, but I'm worn out. Congratulations, darling. She's lovely."

Maria stroked her brow with a cool cloth, then Xavier reached over to kiss her lips. "She's perfect," Xavier breathed, then paled again at the sight of the blood in front of Molly, at Aleksandra's nether end. He sat down abruptly in the chair beside her.

"We're OK," Molly said, with a touch upon his shoulder. "It's normal. She's a little early, but everything seems to be fine."

"Why don't you go get something to eat? You're been in here all day," Maria said, with a smile. "Perhaps the others would like to know there's a new Argüello."

With a kiss for Aleksandra and his daughter, and a last haunted look at the foot of the bed, Xavier exited.

"He's done pretty well, really," Molly grinned at Aleksandra. "He never winced at your death grip on his hand, and never left. The blood after, and the rest," she waved her hand at the now-balled up sheets and towels, "I wouldn't expect any man to handle well. Would you like us to leave you alone with her for a while?"

At Aleksandra's tired nod, she replied, "I'll return soon with something to eat. What would you like?"

A pang from the past. Her mama always brought custard. "Flan, please?" she asked.

Maria smiled and slipped from the room after one more whisper-light touch on her granddaughter's golden downy head.

A wave of sadness washed over Aleksandra, that her mama couldn't be here today, but she tightened her jaw. She'd give this baby all the love Mama'd given her. "Thank you, Mama," she whispered to the heavens, and returned her gaze to the infant in her arms. Soon the pressure of the infant's mouth on her breast dissipated and the nipple slipped from her perfect little lips as she fell asleep. Aleksandra closed her eyes for a moment and knew no more.

MELISSANDRA, as the little brown-eyed girl was named, grew quickly. Sancho made himself even more scarce, but after his anger and threats in response to their loving questions concerning his health, no one complained. They let him go his own way.

A month after the birth, Aleksandra began riding once again. Melissandra was an easy baby, only too happy to feed regularly during the day, and at night, in their bed. She was comfortable with her *abuela* Maria, Molly and Adelita, so Aleksandra was free to help out on the *rancho* again.

"I'm sure glad we came home," Xavier smiled at Aleksandra, as she rode beside him to check stock on the far side of the *rancho*.

"It's been wonderful." She looked down and scratched Dzień's withers. "*Your* family—"

"—*our* family," Xavier corrected.

"*Your* family has become mine, and I'm so grateful."

"They feel the same about you—and they know you're the reason I'm here in the first place." They held hands as the horses strode down the trail. "I have to take a herd up toward Sacramento soon and bring some calves back down here. With the drought, they need the meat up there, and *rancho*s between here and Sacramento have no grass for their calves, so I'll be bringing many head of young stock back here to graze. Luckily, we have the fodder."

"I can barely imagine a drought after the floods last winter."

"That flood water killed a lot of grass—and I can hardly believe all that water is actually gone."

"How long will you be away?"

"I expect it'll be a few weeks. The calves will slow us down a lot."

"We'll be OK. I'll miss you," she waggled an eyebrow at him, "but we'll be fine." Her face heated, thinking of their lovemaking the previous night, the first since Melissandra's birth.

He rode closer and took her hand, as she looked into his glowing eyes.

"I'll be back as quickly as I can. Wouldn't want to miss another day of you." He leaned across and their lips met, both insistent, both wanting. He pulled back and glanced around them. "I've been wanting to take you to my special place," he said, his voice throaty. "It's just ahead. No one will find us there."

At his tone, her abdomen quickened and her breasts twinged. She looked down to see stains on the front of her loose *camisa*.

"Never mind," he said, and his voice caressed her, as his splendidly work-roughened hands would soon also do. "I'll take care of the horses," he said, and she was lost. She dropped the reins and let Dzień follow the big gray up the little canyon to Xavier's hideaway.

ALEKSANDRA SIGHED. The house was quiet, with Maria and her maid gone to San Francisco for a few weeks to visit Maria's best *amiga*. Her mother-in-law had stayed close to help out for the months before and after Melissandra was born, but it was time she took some time away.

"You don't want una *abuela de edad*, an old grandmother, in the way all the time," she said, grabbing Aleksandra by the shoulders and kissing her on both cheeks. "You and Molly enjoy some time alone *con la niña*." Maria smiled and waved as she and Luisa drove away behind her pair of fine grays.

"*Hasta luego, que le vaya bien!*" Aleksandra shouted after her.

"You're blessed to have a mother-in-law who loves you like that." Molly sighed. "So lucky. Not everyone is."

"I appreciate it every day," Aleksandra said, as they turned back to the house.

"Molly, do you mind watching Melissandra for a little while? I need to check some stock."

She smiled. "Of course not. You go right ahead, as soon as she's had a feed. I miss having a baby to hold. Seb only wants cuddles when he's hurt, now."

"I'll go saddle Dzień, then come in to feed her, so I won't waste valuable baby-sleep time."

"See you in the house," Molly said.

Aleksandra rode out as soon as she'd fed Melissandra. The cattle in the higher valley out the back of the *rancho* had strayed, but she and Dzień found them all and put the wanderers back where they belonged. On the way back home, she smiled, pleased with herself, despite the uncomfortable tightness in her breasts. Melissandra was bound to be awake and hungry. As they neared the *hacienda*, Dzień's ears pricked and he screamed his loudest whinny, then broke into a trot toward an oncoming horse and rider.

The other horse, a pinto mustang, trumpeted back and broke into a lope toward them. Aleksandra shook her head. She'd thought she might never see him again, but here he was, in California, of all places.

"Dancing Wolf!" she shrieked, as she leapt to the ground and ran to him. "You've come, you've really come!"

The Indian slid to the ground and embraced her quickly then held her at arm's length. "So what news?" He looked down toward her flat stomach. "You should have had your baby by now."

"Yes, yes! Melissandra was born last month."

His brows narrowed as he looked about Aleksandra. "But where is she?"

"She's in the *hacienda*, with Molly." She scrunched up her forehead. "But how did you know about her?"

"You would be amazed at the things I hear," he raised a brow at her, then he relented. "From Ephraim Hanks."

"Of course, Ephraim." She smiled. "And how is your family?"

His face fell. "We'll talk about that later, eh?"

Aleksandra froze. "Oh, Dancing Wolf."

"I've come to see your little Melissandra, as well as you and Xavier."

Aleksandra took a deep sigh and hugged the Indian's pony. With Dzień's reins in one hand and Dancing Wolf's hand in the other, she half-dragged him to the back door of the house.

"Molly, Molly!" she called out, as they neared the door. Somewhere inside a door slammed, then the back kitchen door opened.

"Is everything all right, Aleks?" Molly said, as she came down the steps, her eyes narrowed at the tall Indian by Aleksandra's side.

"Molly, this is Dancing Wolf," she smiled up at him, "the man I told you about. He's come to visit and to see Melissandra. Is she awake?"

"No, sorry Aleks," she ducked her head and hunched her shoulders, "we were playing and she's only just gone to sleep half an hour ago."

"That's OK, we'll just put the horses up. Could you please organize something for us to eat? I'm starving." She glanced up at Dancing Wolf. "Are you?"

"You know me, I'm always hungry," he said, turning his horse around. He glanced around as they walked toward the barn. "So where is Xavier?" he asked.

"He's away with one of the hired hands delivering a herd of steers to some new buyers near Sacramento. I expect he should be back in about three days. How long will you be here?"

The man frowned. "I'll probably miss him then. I must be back in Benicia on the day after tomorrow."

"I'm awfully pleased to see you, what are you doing in California?"

"I've been asked to interpret in a trial involving a few young men from another *Shoshone* tribe." He stared at the ground, then looked up at her, his brown eyes showing nearly black. "Have you heard they're using the Alcatraz Citadel as a prison for Confederate supporters?"

"Yes, but what does that have to do with the *Shoshone*?" Aleksandra slipped Dzień's bridle over his ears and replaced it with a halter. She glanced at Dancing Wolf, then stopped and stared. She'd never seen him look so worried.

"It seems some property near Great Salt Lake was damaged by white men of the Confederate cause and they're trying to blame it entirely on a few of the young braves who were accompanying them. My father sent me to help them, if I can."

"And they're out on Alcatraz Island?" She winced. "How long have they been there?"

"For a few months now."

"Months? On that cold rock in the middle of the bay?" She slipped the cinch and slid the saddle from her pony. "I wish I'd known, I'd have tried to help." She took a deep breath and turned to him. "So when is this trial?"

"Day after tomorrow."

"Oh no, so soon? I'm not sure how to manage by then…there's no one to oversee the place." She flicked the saddle over a rail and turned the saddle blankets upside down over it. "Xavier's mother is away too, and his…brother—"

Dancing Wolf glanced up at her tone, then Aleksandra continued, more lightly.

"—his brother—is not, shall we say, much use." She stopped in her tracks, considering. "I could do it, but I'd have to take Molly along to help with Melissandra—"

His eyes were wide, and completely black now. "Oh no, *Kwahaten*, you cannot be thinking of taking a newborn infant to Alcatraz." Each word was enunciated from between gritted teeth as he led his Mustang into the stall she'd indicated. He shook his head and glared at her. "I forbid it, and I can imagine what Xavier would say." He cocked an eyebrow at her. "Am I correct?"

"But the men—" Her words dwindled to silence.

"The men. I will do my best for the men. That is what warriors are for. Like it or not, it is not women's work, especially when the women are doing the important work of caring for our next generation."

He was right. Xavier would not be pleased—not at all. He tolerated her waywardness most of the time. This would not be one of those times.

"I have only this afternoon to spend with you. I'd hoped to see Xavier, but perhaps we will meet up with each other on my way back north."

"Not likely, as you'll probably be on riverboats headed in opposite directions."

He nodded in acquiescence, then took the water buckets from her hands and moved in the direction of the indicated barrel.

Aleksandra turned at the sound of footsteps entering the barn, hoping upon hope that Xavier had returned early. Instead, his brother Sancho stood in the doorway, his gun hand halfway to his holster.

"*No*, he's a friend!" she screamed, drawing her *shashka* as she ran for him.

Dancing Wolf, his rifle still mounted on his saddle on the far side of the barn, ducked behind a partition for a moment, then followed Aleksandra.

"Drop it or you're dead," she gritted out. His Smith & Wesson thumped dully onto the dirt floor. She had him in a headlock with her left arm in seconds, her sword just touching the skin over his jugular vein. "He—is—a—friend," she said, in much the same tone Dancing Wolf had just used with her.

"*Bien, bien*, let me go." He shook her off as she let go.

"You would have just shot him?" Aleksandra growled. "Someone you don't even know, and who is not threatening you?"

"He's an Indian."

"And you're a *Californio*. Should I shoot you? This is Dancing Wolf. We grew up together and my father was his blood brother."

"And is that supposed to mean something to me?" His jaw was tight, as he tried to stare her down.

"You are 'supposed' to be my brother-in-law. Perhaps it should mean something to you."

"You know *nada*, nothing, *de nuestra familia*."

"I know that the *rest* of your living family is caring and lovely. You are being given every chance. What is your problem?"

He growled and muttered something in Spanish beneath his breath as he turned on his heel and slunk off toward the *hacienda*.

"There's trouble to come from that one. You'd better watch your step with him around. Who is here to protect you?"

"My *shashka*," she patted the scabbard, "and Molly."

"Molly...ah yes..." He gazed away from her for a moment, then his eyes snapped back to Aleksandra, the muscles of his jaw like a bowstring. "What was Xavier thinking to leave you on your own, with that poisonous snake of a brother, and only a woman for protection?" he growled, as he picked up the gun and handed it to Aleksandra, butt first.

She sighed and shoved the pistol into her belt beneath her shirt. "My husband doesn't see that side of Sancho. When Xavier is here, he is nice as pie. I've tried to tell him, but he thinks I'm jealous of his brother, for some odd reason."

"I'd thought he would have learned to trust your intuition about people after the incident with Vladimir."

"I guess not."

"Anyway, let's get these horses fed and go in. Your baby might be awake and hungry."

Her face grew warm. She was still embarrassed at the normal motherly things that were so new to her, and would be doubly so if she had to feed her baby before Dancing Wolf.

Aleksandra took a deep breath and climbed up to the loft for hay. She fed each horse an armload, while her old friend picked up the discarded water buckets and filled them, then they headed in.

Upon entering the kitchen, they found Adelita had already placed two dishes on the long kitchen table and stood at the other end, patting out *tortillas de masa harina*.

"Adelita, *el se llama* Dancing Wolf, *un amigo especial. Gracias por la cena.*"

"*Hola, hola, señor,*" she bobbed at him, smiling from ear to ear. *De nada, it is nothing,*" she murmured to Aleksandra.

"*Hola, señora.*" Dancing Wolf nodded in reply.

"*Sientate, sientate,*" she urged, waving at the long benches beside the kitchen table.

"*Gracias,*" Aleksandra said, as they sat to enjoy her trademark meal of *Chiles Rellenos con Queso.*

The front door slammed and Aleksandra jumped to her feet and dashed to the window. In time to see Sancho swing up on his horse, spin him about, and gallop away.

Molly slipped into the kitchen, Melissandra in her arms, her brow furrowed. "That was odd. What's with Sancho?"

"He pulled a gun on Dancing Wolf as soon as he saw him in the stable, and I threatened him with my *shashka.*"

"And put a headlock on him." The Indian raised a brow at her. "Was that really necessary?"

"Only if you wanted to stay alive. He would have used that pistol."

"And now he's a true enemy of yours." The Indian gritted his teeth. "He was very angry when he left. I don't like leaving you alone here."

"I have Molly and Adelita."

"And Dzień," he said dryly. "Don't forget Dzień."

Aleksandra's brows narrowed at him. "Not you, too."

"I wouldn't say anything if I didn't care."

"Well, I'm concerned," Molly cut in, "and not for you, Aleks, but for Melissan—"

"—what's the matter with Melissandra?" Aleksandra cut in as she jumped to her feet, reaching for the sleeping baby in Molly's arms.

"She's fine," Molly looked down at the sleeping child, "but I was just now getting some clothes from her closet when Sancho entered Melissandra's room. From behind the door, I saw him glance back out the door, then he reached his arms out toward her."

Aleksandra inhaled sharply.

"So I just watched him. The hair stood up on the back of my neck, but I thought I should be happy he wanted to give her some attention, after never having done do before. When he saw me there behind him, he swore, turned, and raced down the stairs and out the door. He just galloped off on his horse."

Aleksandra's mouth dropped open, her core turning to ice. She shivered, and sat down heavily on the bench.

52

"I don't want to leave you two here without protection." The Indian paced back and forth in the sitting room as Aleksandra fed Melissandra beneath a blanket.

"We'll be fine," Molly said, staring out the window at the driveway leading from the house. "When Sancho leaves, he tends not to return for a week or two. Xavier should be well back by then. We're not sure where he goes, but it must be far away."

"How do you know it's far away?" Dancing Wolf wasn't convinced.

"No one locally hears of his escapades, nothing like we used to when he drank and gambled closer to home," Aleksandra said.

"Oh, like that, is it? That's worse than I thought." His face darkened even further.

"We'll be fine. Molly and I will be right next door to each other."

"If I didn't have to leave for this hearing, I'd stay until Xavier returned," the warrior growled. "At least place one of the stablemen on guard here at night."

"You always worry about me," Aleksandra scowled. "I can take care of myself."

"You forget, I've heard you say that more times than I can count…and I've dragged you out of more scrapes than I could have believed existed." His lips slightly curled up at the ends, breaking the tension.

"See? Now you're smiling. It'll all be fine. We'll be fine, your trial will go…" she gulped, "fine, I hope. Do you think you can get them off?"

"I really don't know, but I'll do my best." Dancing Wolf glanced out the window. "We're losing light. As much as I hate to leave, I must," he said, a tic appearing in his clenched jaw.

"Really, we'll be fine," Aleksandra shook her head. "Truly."

Dancing Wolf's face fell as he looked out the window and a tic appeared in his clenched jaw. "As much as I hate to leave, I must."

Adelita scurried in from the kitchen. "*Señor*, I have food *por su viaje*," she said. "Will you take?"

"Of course, *gracias, señora*," he replied, and stood, bringing the ladies to their feet.

"You will take care, Dancing Wolf? These are bad times. Please leave a message with someone to let me know—no, I'll send a man with you. He can watch your back and let me know if anything goes wrong. You've brought no one with you, have you?" Aleksandra frowned.

"That I would appreciate, Aleks. There was no one to come with me."

She turned and stared. "What?"

"There was no one to come with me."

At the look on his face, Aleksandra's stomach turned over and she grabbed at the doorway to keep her balance.

So I'm not much use, eh?

Sancho's blood boiled at his sister-in-law's comment. They'll see just how useless he could be when they were looking for their baby. He wouldn't miss the next time, and he'll take out that damned Molly as well. Aleksandra's Indian friend wouldn't be there tonight, anyway. Sancho listened long enough at the barn door to ascertain that.

Mr. Ryan wouldn't even mind that he'd fumbled today's attempt to snatch the kid when he succeeded in the attempt tonight. He smiled. It was going to be a good night. He rode on to the barn at the back of the *rancho* where Ryan and his gang waited, then entered and seated himself at the makeshift table, his legs sprawled before him as he sat his hay bale.

The leader smiled after Sancho finished his report, but his eyes glittered and made little quivers in Sancho's stomach. The *Californio* reached gratefully for the whisky shot before him.

"Hold on, Sancho." Mr. Ryan's smile became more of a grimace, and he moved the glass out of reach with the back of his hand. "We need to talk a little first."

"*Sí, sí*, what is it you wish to know?"

"That brothah o'yours, he still gone?"

"*Sí*, he is."

"So y'didn't git their baby. That's not good. We need t'make some othah plans." Ryan gritted his teeth, and Sancho bit his lip.

"It's OK, I have another plan," Sancho said, jumping to his feet.

"Siddown." Short, abrupt.

Sancho sat.

"About this Indian," Ryan continued. "Ya say he's a friend o' the girl's from th' past…is he good lookin'? Are they close?"

"Very close. Too close." Sancho grinned.

"Maybe after th' Indian leaves, y' kin kidnap both th' girl and the babe, deliver her 'n th' babe to me, then go back 'n apologize to 'em, maybe say ya were embarrassed 'bout not havin' been a bettah uncle t' the babe, 'n that y' caught the Indian 'n Aleksandra togethah in th' barn, talkin' 'bout runnin' away t'gether. That should do it. He might not even come after 'er."

"But why do you want Xavier's wife?" he eyed O'Rourke sideways, "and why…a, and why the babe?"

Mr. Ryan hesitated, then cleared his throat and gulped. "Xavier'll dump 'er after y' tell 'im she ran off with th' Indian. He won't want t'stay at the *rancho* aftah his wife deserted him there. You'll git full control o'the Rancho de las Pulgas back. Y' want that, don't ya? Y' said you did th'other day. We got a whole room o' men heard that. Ye'r part of it now." He turned an evil grin upon him.

Sancho wavered, but tried not to show it. Something was wrong here, but he couldn't put his finger on it. He didn't remember saying any such thing. Maybe he'd been drunk, if he said it at all. How did this man even know about Aleksandra and Xavier, other than his mention that they were *en nuestra familia*? He looked around at the leering faces of the group of half-drunken men and realized they could, and would, make him do their bidding if the leader of this wolf pack howled in his direction. He squirmed on his seat.

Sancho rather liked the way the *rancho* had been going, before. There was plenty of money for gambling, but since Xavier returned, it hadn't been so easy. His brother had no idea of the man Sancho had become, but Sancho could control him, on his own. Aleksandra knew, though. He'd seen her watching him, assessing him. She knew. The idea of her absence was sounding better and better. His brother wouldn't find out about his debts if his bitch of a wife were gone.

He leaned back against the rough wooden wall, considering his sister-in-law. His hand slid toward his holster, then he swore. He'd left his gun in the stable. *Her and that sword of hers.* White dots flickered before his eyes, then everything started going dark. He took a few deep breaths.

This wasn't going to be as easy as he'd—

"—well, whaddya think?" The ringleader barked at him.

"*Lo siento*, I'm sorry, what did you ask?" Sancho gulped.

"'Bout yer next move to free yerself of the bothe'some sister-in-law and her brat, as well as get the family *rancho* back fer your own, the one ye've slaved on fer years, only to have to give it up to Xavier when he decided t' prance back in," he said, one brow raised, a sardonic grin on his face.

"Oh," he replied.

"T'night."

Sancho gritted his teeth. He'd had that very idea himself, but now he wondered if she slept with that sword of hers. Maybe she was watching now. Maybe the Indian would stay, now Sancho had shown his hand today. "'Mmmm…they might expect trouble now—" he hesitated for a moment, "—and that Indian might still be there."

"Y'all said he was leavin'." He raised a brow at Sancho. "We'll be right b'hind ya. Not gettin' cold feet now, are ya? It's a bit too late fer that. Y'owe me far too much after those last few card games t'let it go much longah. Ah think it'll be t'night." He nodded at Sancho. "All ya have t' do is go in there, git the girl and the babe, an' git 'em out to us. We'll all be waitin' just outside the entrance t' the yard. Y'all drop the pair, go back t' the house, stumble up th' stairs like the drunken sot ya are, and go t'bed. In the mornin', ya can say what I said b'fore 'bout them in the barn 'n mention ya saw the Indian 'n someone on a light-colored horse trottin' out the far side o'town when ya left the saloon t'night. Easy as pie. Ya go t' the kitchen 'n get whatever ya normally take fer a hangover 'n go back t'bed while the rest unravels. No one kin blame ya in the least."

"But—"

"Best of all, this li'l favor'll take care o' yer debts t' me. Ah'll even sweeten it up a little fer ya. I'll send ya five hunnert more when we clear the Golden Gate."

Sancho's eyes snapped up to his, and then he dropped them again, but said nothing.

"That oughta take care o' yer other debts, won't it?" He stopped and gave Sancho a hard stare. "What's th' problem?"

"She's deadly with that—"

"Yer afraid of that little *girl*? Asleep?" He shook his head and nodded to one of his men, who walked out the door and soon returned to hand O'Rourke a small sack, out of which he pulled a glass bottle and a pad of cotton. "Take this. Ya'all know what it is?"

The *Californio* shook his head.

"Chlor'form. Ya pour some o' this on th' cotton 'n hold it over 'er nose till she passes out."

Sancho swallowed noisily. "Can someone help—"

"By God, boy, yer th' weakest, lily-liv—" Ryan closed his eyes and took a deep breath. "Look," he said in measured tones, "y' owe me a not-in-substantial amount o'money. It's time t'buck up afore I take it out o'yer hide instead. Clear?"

"*Claro...* clear," he whispered, took the bag the boss offered, spun about, and fairly ran from the barn.

He heard laughter behind him as he swung up on his mount and bolted back toward the *rancho* in the gathering darkness.

"WHERE ARE THEY?" Aleksandra whispered.

"We were at the Bear River winter encampment, at the Bear River Massacre," Dancing Wolf said, through gritted teeth.

Aleksandra just stared at him, speechless. Molly stood like a statue in the kitchen doorway.

"At the time you left, the Indians were struggling. After a few hard winters, with the settlers' invasion and destruction of our food sources and livelihood, we were starving and destitute. Some of the young braves took to stealing to help the tribe survive. There were attacks from both sides." He took a deep breath and looked at the floor.

"Dancing Wolf," Aleksandra whispered, "why didn't you come find me? Maybe I could have helped—"

"—early the next year," the man resumed, ignoring her question, "the Superintendent of Indian Affairs, James Doty, spent four days in Cache Valley. After seeing the conditions there, he tried to get the government to create an Indian reservation in Cache Valley and to furnish us with livestock so we could become herdsmen instead of beggars. The government, of course, didn't listen." He scowled, and was silent for a moment. "Instead, five weeks ago, Colonel Connor from Fort Douglas made a surprise attack on our winter encampment, at the same time as the chiefs were in great Salt Lake City negotiating peace on behalf of all the Northwestern *Shoshone*. Luckily for us, it wasn't a surprise. We'd prepared. We had screens and rifle pits dug into the banks of Beaver Creek and the Bear River, but their numbers were greater than we expected. Connor split his soldiers and marched many of them during the night on their approach." He stopped again and Aleksandra led him back to a chair to sit. "When they came, before dawn, after the coldest night anyone can remember, we were ready for them, or so we thought. Their big guns on wheels were stuck in the snow far away, but even so, they had more ammunition than we did. When our ammunition and arrows ran out, they slaughtered most of our people, raped the women who remained alive, and bashed in the children's heads. Their official report says they killed 246 *Shoshone* warriors and left 160 women and children, but I counted nearly 500 dead, including the women and children." He stopped and closed his eyes. "There were not 160 women and children left in Cache Valley, not alive anyway. Some of us got away afterwards, but many others were wounded and captured."

Silence reigned for a long minute.

"And your mother and father..." Aleksandra heard herself say, as she let out her breath.

"She has gone to the spirit world," he whispered. "My father wishes he had gone too, but he was away with Chief Sanpitch attempting to negotiate a truce." He gritted his teeth and closed his eyes. "The young men I'm trying to get off of Alcatraz are some of those who got away, to another area. They haven't yet been recognized as having come from that battle. I only hope they haven't told anyone, otherwise they're dead men. As it is, they're some of the few remaining braves from our village."

"Oh my God, Dancing Wolf." Aleksandra struggled for words. "What can we do?"

"I'll try to get them out, and we can join with Chief Sagwitch. He is negotiating with the Mormons for some of us to begin farming with them, or hide in the hills, or go to the cities to find work, if anyone will have us, or—go to the Fort Hall Indian Reservation."

Aleksandra gripped his hands and her tears dripped onto their conjoined fingers. "Is there nothing to be done?"

He let go of her hands and tipped her chin up. "The government wants the West settled. Troops are sent in place of aid to massacre my people. No, I think short of getting these boys out of jail, there is indeed nothing to be done." She'd never heard him sound so bitter.

Aleksandra gritted her teeth and stood. "I will find someone to go with you."

"I've already done that," Molly said as she approached and held out her hands to Dancing Wolf. He held them for a moment before she hugged him tightly about the neck, then ran from the room in tears.

"*Señor, su cena...*" Adelita's brows were drawn tightly together, and she bit her lip as she handed him a bulky, muslin-wrapped packet. She hadn't understood the whole story, but she knew enough to feed a man when he was down.

Dancing Wolf smiled and kissed the top of her gray head. "*Gracias, Adelita.*" He turned and walked from the kitchen and Aleksandra followed to the barn. She bridled his pony and rubbed him in his favorite place under his forelock, then hugged Dancing Wolf.

"*Que le vaya bien, Querido,*" Aleksandra said, "Go well, my dear one. I hope we meet again...soon."

He shook his head and grinned as he swung up. "Can you doubt it,

Kwahaten? You will always find trouble, so I must continually seek you out. You know this."

She shook her head. "Take care, my friend. I hope you can rescue your Braves. Santiago," she nodded at the young man mounted on a bay horse before the barn, "will accompany you."

"Aleks, it is not necessary to take him. I do not wish to endanger any more lives. I appreciate your thought, but please?"

She took a deep breath and let it out slowly. "I understand." She turned toward Santiago. "You don't need to—*Gracias* Santiago, *pero no tiene que ir.*"

Santiago nodded and dismounted. She turned back to Dancing Wolf, who waved and rode away, not looking back.

53

Sancho's heart pounded as he stood watching Aleksandra's darkened window. He'd seen her practicing with the *shashka*, riding that yellow pony of hers. She was lethal. He had a general contempt for women, other than, of course, for the only thing they were really useful for, but he could buy that. This one, though, was different. He wondered how he could detest her, and at the same time become aroused anytime she was near. And she was his brother's. Just like this *rancho*. The thought of it burned bitter in his mouth. For years, he had worked this place. All Xavier had to do was waltz back in, and it was simply handed to him. It didn't sit well. This plan of Mr. Ryan's might be the best thing that ever happened to him—*if*—he survived. He swallowed hard.

He wondered, as he heard a weak cry from the infant, then the sound of metal striking flint, what *Señor* Ryan actually wanted with her. As a lamp began to glow in the room above, he reflected that he was in no position to start asking questions. Without this opportunity, he was sure he would end up in the bottom of the bay, tied to a big rock. Luck hadn't been with him lately at the tables. He knew it would get better, he just needed a little more time to find the money he owed several big men in San Francisco, and better luck.

As Sancho edged closer to the house, his view diminished, so he moved further away again. He stumbled over a heavy stick, caught himself, and picked it up with a smile.

"*Gracias a Dios*," he whispered, and crossed himself.

He could see only the back of Aleksandra's head over the top of her her chair, as it rhythmically rocked. She must be feeding the child, since it wasn't making any more noise. Eventually, the rocking stopped, but the back of her head still showed, behind the lace curtains. No sound came to him on the cold night air.

Hoping she was asleep, he tiptoed across the porch, careful to miss the boards he knew creaked. This sneakiness had become a habit, with the life he led.

Thinking of his mother, he squirmed. She'd tried to raise him well, but she just didn't understand how good gambling and drinking made him feel— like he was on top of the world. It let him forget, if only for a little while, his position as the unentitled youngest son of the Arguellö Dynasty. He'd show her—he'd show her he was just as good as Xavier, as soon as his luck turned.

The house was dark as pitch. Sancho closed the parlor door and slid toward the stairs, then grunted as he tripped and fell full-length on top of a body.

"¿Cómo?" The body muttered. A man. He must have been sleeping there.

Sancho froze, his hands shaking, then he swung the stick in his hand toward the noise. A heavy clunk sounded as the man hit the floor, and the body moved no more.

Holding to the banister, he held his breath, listening for any sound from upstairs, his heart clutching in his chest. In the silence, he mounted the stairs, two at a time. Ahead of him, light shined to one side of Aleksandra's and Xavier's door.

"Dios mío, gracias" he breathed, at the slightly ajar door.

Praying the girl would be asleep, he pressed the door open with two fingers and listened for any sounds. He heard only her even breathing. Slipping his head around the door, the side of her head appeared, turned away from him as she slept in the rocker. He took a step back into the hallway and eased the cork from he bottle. His stomach turned at the sickly-sweet smell emanating from the open bottle as he soaked the dirty cotton Mr. Ryan had provided with the liquid. He didn't know long it would take, nor how long he could hold onto her. He only hoped her grasp on the child in her arms would restrict her ability to fight back.

Remembering her arm lock from the barn earlier in the day, he grinned. She'd placed herself in the only position from which he had any advantage. He quickly took it, stepped the three strides to the back of her chair and locked his arm around her neck, then held the sickening rag over her face. She fought, even managing to reach one hand back to gouge his face with her nails, but short of throwing her child onto the floor, she didn't have a chance. He managed to cling onto her, bucking and jerking, for several minutes until she finally stilled. He wasn't sure if she passed out from lack of circulation from the headlock, or from the chloroform, but something had worked.

He stood frozen for a moment, listening, and watching her and the babe. If Molly was indeed in the next room, she must be a sound sleeper indeed. Aleks had clearly been feeding the infant, because the front of her muslin nightdress was untied and both of her breasts were displayed, just for him to see. As he watched her, the *bebé*, which had been half-awake and mewling a bit as she struggled, snuggled against her belly and went back to sleep. His hand stretched out, of its own volition, and touched the white flesh with its rosy tipped peak. He hardened, and wondered if he had time to sample her before he turned her over to Mr. Ryan. His guts clenched as he squeezed one of her breasts tightly, then broke out into a cold sweat. Mr. Ryan's men waited just beyond the *hacienda* gate. No doubt, they had approached and were watching him even now. Bed springs creaked on the other side of the wall, and his breath caught in his throat.

What could I have been thinking?

He tucked his shirt tightly into his belt and slid the baby inside, against his chest. He hadn't planned how he would get the baby and the girl out of the house, but this should work, as long as no one woke up. He reached forward and around the girl's hips, then tossed her over his shoulder. With one arm under the baby and one arm around her thighs, he made his way out the door, then somehow closed it and got down the steps. Hoping the man at the bottom of the stairs was still unconscious, he stepped carefully over his prone body and out the front door.

The girl's Mustang was already tied to his horse. If he was going to make it look like she'd left with the Indian, the horse had to go too. He tried mounting a few times with her over his shoulder, but finally gave up. He dragged his horse to the side of a wagon and dumped Aleksandra unceremoniously into the wagon bed, then climbed up. He planned to seat her astride before him, but if he was going to take the baby as well, that wouldn't work. He tried holding her seated across the horse, facing the opposite direction to the infant. The men shouldn't be far off, and then he could hand the pair to them. Their delivery would guarantee his debts with *Señor* Ryan were paid off, and if he played his cards right, he'd get enough money to pay the rest of them off as well. He smiled. Not a bad night's work.

The baby wriggled against his chest and the forearm of his rein hand, and he felt an unfamiliar squeeze in his heart. Maybe he wasn't doing the right thing. This baby girl, after all, was his own flesh and blood.

No! Do this. The girl has created all the trouble in your life. Without her, Xavier would never have come home, and the rancho have been yours, forever.

He gritted his teeth, shut his eyes and inhaled deeply. The girl in his lap begin to stir, and he clutched for the chloroform rag in his pocket, hoping it hadn't all dried out. He'd dropped the bottle when he dumped Aleksandra into the wagon, and the liquid had spilled out. He held the rag against her face with one hand, its musty sickliness smelling cold in his nostrils. He turned his head away, not wanting to pass out as well. He turned the bend in the road, and the buckskin snorted and threw up his head. The six mounted men stepped out of the trees and stood across the roadway.

"You've done well, Sancho. There doesn't seem to be any sign of a ruckus back at the house."

Sancho could only sigh with relief.

Mr. Ryan himself stepped forward from the rest of the men. "You know what you have to do now. I'll take her and you, Johnno, can take the baby. Come closer, Sancho."

Sancho gave the reins of Aleksandra's Mustang to one of the men, then moved his horse side-on to Mr. Ryan's. The ringleader reached out for Aleksandra's limp body and Sancho handed her across with grim satisfaction. A big burly man urged his horse forward and motioned for Sancho to hand over the babe as well.

Sancho had a momentary fit of madness and clutched the little girl to his chest, not wanting to release her. The feeling soon faded, and he pulled her from his shirt and handed her over, but his chest was tight and he struggled to draw a breath. Closing his eyes, he shook his head. This couldn't be him, *Sancho,* feeling something for the little brat. The burly man turned his horse and walked away.

"I'll need that chloroform bottle," Mr. Ryan said, reaching out his hand.

"Ahh, sorry," Sancho muttered, "I dropped it when I was trying to subdue her."

"Tell me you have the rag, at least," Mr. Ryan growled.

"Yes, it's here." He passed it over.

"Well, Sancho, it's been real nice doin' business with ya." Sancho heard the smile disappear from the man's face with the next words. "Not a word about this night's work, or you're a dead man." The blue-gray gleam of his pistol as it slowly made its way north to Sancho's forehead left him in no doubt he meant every word.

Sancho spun his horse on its haunches and bolted back toward the barn, then took a deep breath and slowed to an amble as he neared the stable doors. He couldn't believe his luck. The house remained in darkness. He clumped up the stairs and in through the front door, dropping his coat and boots with a clunk.

"Ahhh..." The man on the floor groaned and the wall clunked as something heavy hit it.

Sancho lit a splint of kindling from the coals in the fireplace and touched it to the wick of a lamp he found on the sideboard, turning it up and sending a warm glow throughout the room. By its light, he saw he'd knocked out the *rancho* foreman.

"Marcelo, what happened to you, and what are you doing here?" Sancho knelt beside the man, who was clutching his head in his hands. His gut tightened at what he'd done to a man who had always been his friend.

"I'm here to guard Aleksandra from you, but I don't know why," he muttered.

"From me? But I've only just returned from supper with friends, and found you right here in the hallway with a nasty bump." He felt the man's cracked pate, with blood seeping from it. "Whatever happened to you?"

"I was sitting here. I must've nodded off, and now I've woken up with a sore head."

"What hit you over the head?"

"I don't know, but I'd best go check on the *señorita*," he said, pulling himself to his feet by the staircase banister railing.

"Can I help you? I'm sure she's fine. Don't you want to go home to bed?" Sancho asked.

"No, I'm to stay with her and make sure she's OK."

"Is everything all right down there?" Molly called, her voice sharp. "Aleksandra?" she said, tapping at her door.

There was no answering sound from her room. Sancho heard only silence, and then Molly ran to the head of the stairs.

"Aleks, are you in the kitchen?"

Silence met her and she raced down the stairs, frowning at the two men as she approached them. "Where is Aleks?"

"*No sé*, I don't know. I just got home and found..." he waved at Marcelo.

Molly frowned at the foreman and raced on to the office, then out to the kitchen. "ALEKS!" she screamed, and waited in silence. "Where is Aleks?" she asked Sancho.

"I told you, I haven't seen them."

Molly stared at him. "Them." Her eyes narrowed. "How do you know it's 'them' missing, and not just Aleks?"

He stared at her. "Well, if one is..." He stopped.

"You!" she shrieked into his face, "what have you done with them?"

Sancho backed up, his hands up to protect himself. "*No sé, no sé nada*, I don't know anything, Molly. I just got home and found Marcelo with a very nasty cut on his head at the bottom of the stairs."

"Where could they have gone?" Molly wailed.

"I saw that Indian heading north out of town, and someone was with him—on a little horse that looked like Aleks' pony."

Molly stopped stock still. "When was this?" she said quietly.

"A few hours ago."

"It cannot be," she whispered. "She wouldn't just leave like this. We'll never find them now."

"Maybe she just likes that Indian more than Xavier," he said, and looked down to hide his eyes. He was unprepared for the very un-feminine fist that slammed into his jaw.

"Don't you ever cast aspersions upon Aleksandra's character ever again. She has more worth and morals in her little finger than you have in your entire body. I suggest you get on your horse and leave right now, and don't come back until you've either found them, or Xavier has returned."

"You'll not tell me what to do on my own *rancho*, or it was until Xavier came..." He broke off at the look returning to Molly's face.

Shock turned to calculation. "What are those scratches on your face?" She whirled around, raced upstairs and slammed the door.

Sancho reached up and fingered the four scrapes down his cheek. "Must've happened when the horse went under those willow branches. The beast nearly knocked me off."

"Sancho, *tal vez* you should come sleep in the bunkhouse with me tonight," Marcelo said, "Molly's very upset."

"And don't come back until you found her!" Molly shrieked from upstairs.

"Don't you think we should go look for her?" The older man's mouth tightened into a line as he gazed at Sancho, who looked away first.

Sancho returned his gaze to him and pursed his lips. "You really think she wants to be found, if she went with her Indian?" He turned away, hiding a smile, thinking of the debts that had been wiped and the money he'd be getting as soon as *Señor* Ryan cleared the Golden Gate.

Marcelo looked sideways at Sancho as he led him to the bunkhouse and frowned. That same Indian Sancho just spoke of told him to protect Aleksandra, and from Sancho himself. He twisted his neck carefully. His head throbbed and felt like it might fall off.

Sancho had grown up on the *rancho* under Marcelo's eyes. Marcelo trusted the young *serpiente de cascabel* about as far as he could kick him. How did Sancho get the new, bloody scratches on his face? No branches Marcelo ever met left him looking like that.

He bowed his head and a tear rolled cold down his cheek. He was fond of Xavier's new bride, and of the *bebé*.

He was in no condition to ride tonight, but as soon as Sancho was asleep, the stableman would go. Armed and on their fastest horse. He would find Xavier or Aleksandra, whoever he caught up with first.

This wasn't something he'd let wait until morning.

54

"*Not a word...knights...circle...*" Voices drifted in and out of her mind as Aleksandra rose to the surface. Cold wind, clammy darkness. She clutched her arms together to stay warm. Why was she so cold?

More voices. "John said...skiff at the marsh dock...deep water... schooner...leaving before dawn."

Aleksandra took a deep breath and shook her head to clear it.

Bad dream.

The arms surrounding her weren't Xavier's...her heart raced...and she was seated sideways on a horse. She kept her eyes squeezed shut while she listened.

"Watch out...Revenue men." A voice, from a short distance away.

"You know what to do with anyone interfering with the Knights' business, eh men?" a familiar, yet disconcerting voice that she couldn't quite place rumbled against her side.

Aleksandra tried to keep her breathing even, while she strained to hear every sound.

Melissandra. Where is she?

Images shifted in Aleksandra's mind. Her bedroom, an arm around her throat and mouth, a Spanish-accented voice whispering for her to keep quiet or her baby would die. In the lamplight, her own arms holding her infant against her body, feeling the helplessness, not being able to fight her way out. The musty-sweet smell of chloroform. Slipping Melissandra down to grip her between her knees so she could claw at the face behind the arm choking her down, then nothing, until now, jolting on the front of a horse, alone.

"... get a move on...outgoing tide," another voice. "Mazatlán...won't wait."

"She'll wait. Captain has his orders, we'll be there in time. It's the *Oregon* we don't want to miss. She's carrying two mill in gold and silver. The Knights want it, they want it bad. We can capture the ship as soon as we get out into open water, out of sight of the Golden Gate."

A mumble from behind. "Plenty o'money 'n guns our Confederate brothers need so badly back East," another man said.

"What about the guards at Fort Point?"

"They'll nevah catch us, not in the *Chapman*."

A mumble from behind that she didn't catch.

"Where? The *Oregon*? She'll be sent to Vancouver fer refittin'. Anothah privateer fer us. The other one they're still buildin' at Victoria—"

"Yep, the *Thames*. Should b'ready soon too. Soon we'll control th' seas off this coast 'n the Union'll have to kiss California goodbye." Her captor's Southern drawl deepened as he spoke.

O'Rourke.

It registered, with a cold shock, who held her on his lap. Aleksandra finally connected the voice to the man, the only one in the world for whom she felt real hatred.

So he was heavily involved with the Confederacy—but what did that have to do with her?

The men's voices were no longer blurred, but she still wasn't thinking clearly.

Melissandra.

She listened hard, but she couldn't hear her baby and her heart clenched. She couldn't wait any longer—she had to know. "My baby! Where is she?"

"Quiet down, an' you'll see her again."

A plaintive cry rose up from somewhere behind her and Aleksandra struggled upward, twisting around to try to see her in the darkness. "Give her to me," she growled.

"Tsk tsk. Yer temper'll no longa be tolerated," he said shortly, as his hand clamped tightly on her swollen breast.

Pain shot through her body, bringing her fully to her senses. "Where are you taking me? I'll be still, just please give her to me," she said, freezing until he released his searing hold upon her.

"That's bettah. Ye'll learn."

She tried to control the shaking that began in her core. Fighting her way out wasn't an option, when her month-old infant was being held by someone else on a horse, trudging through the night. Melissandra's mewling cries became a wail.

"Shut that kid up," her captor hissed.

"I'm trying, Boss, but I don't know what to do. I've never held one before," a gruff voice said behind them.

"We'll just have to leave 'er behind," O'Rourke said.

"No, give her to me, please. I'll do as you ask—I promise," Aleksandra whispered. "Only give her to me, please." She tried to look behind her, but all she saw was a small horse being led beside them. "Dzień!" she said in a low voice.

He whickered and snuffled at her leg with his nose.

"Get back," O'Rourke growled, and swung a foot at him.

Aleksandra felt warmth invade her very cold heart, that her Mustang was beside her still. But why? How was she here, with O'Rourke, her child, and Dzień?

Her brain slowly cleared.

"Bring th'brat up here so she kin shut it up."

Aleksandra let out the breath she didn't know she'd been holding and reached for her baby as the other man rode up beside them. She plucked her from the man's all-too-willing hands and gripped her to her breast. The thin muslin of her nightgown felt suddenly too thick. Melissandra's wails turn to mewling cries as she hunted for a nipple.

"Can we stop so I can feed her?" Aleksandra asked softly.

"No time fer that now. Shut it up 'r leave it behind."

"Where, here?" Aleksandra peered around in the darkness. Nothing but moonlight glinting off water in the distance and some stars in the sky above. *The bay, then?* No lights or civilization in sight.

"Heah. Try me 'n see."

Aleksandra bit back a reply and put a finger up to Melissandra's mouth. She grabbed at it and sucked hungrily. The silence would only last so long.

"Where are we going?"

"We're takin' a li'l trip. I'm sure yer husban' won't mind. He'll think you've run off with your Indian friend. Bet he won' even come lookin' fer ya."

"Not highly likely," Aleksandra growled, but her heart sank as she fought a rising panic. If she fought or made a fuss, he'd leave Melissandra behind. The infant wouldn't live through the night, easy prey for a coyote or wolf. No, she must await her chance.

She hugged her baby to her chest and waited.

"Here." A man rode up beside them and threw his coat over the front of Aleksandra and Melissandra. "I don't need it, it's getting warmer," he said. Not looking at his leader, he returned to his place behind them.

Aleksandra couldn't see how many men were behind them. She felt more naked without her *shashka* and knives than she felt in only her muslin nightdress. Seabirds squawked overhead even before she smelled the marsh. The horses' hooves squelched now and again as the wind grew stronger. She huddled down into the coat and clutched Melissandra to her, trying to inch herself as far from O'Rourke as possible without raising his ire. Peeking over the edge of the coat's collar, she saw a boat waiting at a small dock she didn't recognize, its white sail the only clear evidence of its presence in the indigo night.

A sob escaped her as her captor handed Dzień's lead rope to one of his men. The pony looked back at her, ears pricked, and tugged against the rope, but the man had already dallied it around his saddle horn. He had no choice but to follow.

"Where is he taking Dzień?"

"Who?" O'Rourke said.

"Dzień, the Mustang you were just leading."

"Ah, the buckskin. He'll be hidden away fer a while, 'till we're well away. Wouldn't want t'let anyone in on our li'l secrets," he said with a laugh, and reached around her to touch her breast. She recoiled and raise one arm to swing, but he just squeezed it tighter instead, until she stilled again. "None o'that, now 'r ever," he said, his eyes gleaming in the darkness. "I'd hate t'mark yer pretty hide, but ah'll do it if y'keep askin' fer it. Stripe it 'till y'beg fer me t'touch ya. Until y'beg. Remembah that."

She would remember. Until his dying day, she would remember.

THE COLD WIND whipped Rogan's mane back into his face. Miguel exulted in the sheer speed of the young stallion. He raced north along the El Camino Real as if his life depended upon it.

Señorita Aleksandra's just might.

The stableman kept a close eye about him. Xavier could be anywhere between here and Benicia by now, so it could be a long ride. Miguel hoped Xavier would be camped with a large enough herd that he could see him by the roadside.

Topping a rise, Rogan's ears pricked and his head shot up, flared nostrils sniffing the air. He screamed the trumpet of a full-grown stallion, flattened his ears and flew even faster. An answering high-pitched whinny streamed back to him through the darkness. Automatically, the man switched both reins to his left hand and grabbed a handful of mane, leaving his right free for his gun.

Miguel and Rogan were nearly on top of the man leading Dzień before he even saw them. The man was scrabbling for his pistol, while trying to hold both his mount's reins and the lead of the buckskin pony, who was trying to jerk it from his hand. The Mustang broke free just before the man fell from the saddle, stunned by a crack on the head from the Miguel's pistol butt.

O'Rourke dismounted and pulled Aleksandra from his saddle at the end of a short dock. She stumbled as her feet hit the ground, then recovered, gripping Melissandra hard against her body. He hustled Aleksandra across the uneven boards toward the sailboat moored at the far end of the dock and thrust her into the hands of a man waiting on board. The sailor pushed her toward an open hatch and dropped them through it, onto a pile of something soft, but rigid—sails? The wooden hatch cover banged shut, then groaned as if they'd placed something heavy upon it.

"Don't make a sound," O'Rourke hissed, from the deck above.

Aleksandra closed her eyes and took a deep breath, instantly regretting it, as the smell of mold and decay hit her nostrils. She moved her foot and it slipped off the fabric into a puddle of icy liquid in the bottom of the hold. She jerked it back. A scurrying somewhere in front of Aleksandra told her she wasn't the only occupant of the chamber and she crushed her infant tighter in her arms. Glancing up again, only darkness met her eyes.

This might be the only chance she had to feed Melissandra. She untied her gown and let the ravenous child latch on. When the baby let go and began to cry, Aleksandra latched her back on and leaned against the pillar behind her, trying to relax so her milk would let down. Despite the smell of the bilges, she forced herself to breathe deeply as ropes thumped on the deck. The little boat rocked harder, as more and more waves slapped against the hull under her feet.

Melissandra drank her fill and drifted off to sleep. If nothing else, her over-full breasts finally stopped aching. Whispered voices sounded above. How long? It seemed they'd been in here forever, but it was probably only an hour. The dull bump of wood upon wood, then the slap of water against something solid. The hatch opened and a shadowy face appeared against the starry darkness above.

"Stand up girl. Not a sound, 'r that baby o'yers'll go swimmin'" O'Rourke growled.

He jerked the baby from her arms and she shrieked, but one of his men put a hand over her mouth and pulled her out, then clamped an arm about her waist. She lifted a foot to kick him, but he wrapped his leg around hers, pinning her against him.

"I mean it. B'have and you can have 'er aboard ship," O'Rourke hissed beneath his breath. He reached the baby high above his head to a waiting sailor leaning over the side of a big schooner. "Now climb."

Aleksandra shook herself loose of the man behind her, stumbling as he let her go. He chuckled. She spun and shot daggers with her eyes and his grin faded as he stepped back a pace.

"Git on with it if y' wanna see yer baby again," O'Rourke said, and shook his head at his man. "Scairt of a little girl, Smith? And she ain't even armed. Seems I need another new lieutenant." The man stood taller and puffed out his chest. "No sir. Ah know my job...sir."

Aleksandra gathered her nightgown and knotted it below her hips, her jaw tight, then climbed the rope ladder on the side of the ship. She wished she had the guts to kick O'Rourke in the face as he climbed the ladder behind her, but she knew he wouldn't hesitate to drown Melissandra.

"Where's the captain's cabin?" O'Rourke barked toward a group of sailors huddled beside the mast. "And where's the captain?"

The accompanying sailors' brows rose, then one nodded his head toward a dimly lit dock in the distance. "I'm the first mate, sir," he remarked.

"Where's the capt'n? I'm requisitionin' his cabin," O'Rourke growled.

"Um, he...didn't make the tug last night. I understand he was celebrating his last night in port. He gave orders for us to have her out in the stream to wait for the breeze to come up. He's coming out on the first morning tug."

O'Rourke's eyes narrowed. "Who's payin' fer this ship? We need t'leave, and I expect mah orders t' be obeyed." He glanced back at the Pacific Street Dock, where men moved about, even at this early hour. "Wind should be up soon 'n we can't wait any longer. I'm yer acting capt'n, men. I've no great patience right now, s' just show me the cabin, then prepare to sail."

Gritting his teeth, the mate spun on his heel and led the way.

The sailor holding Aleksandra's baby followed the mate across the deck of the schooner and disappeared into a hatchway as she followed, with a glance around her to ascertain the layout of the deck. She tripped over a coil of rope on the deck before her, but O'Rourke gripped her arm again. He half-pulled, half-dragged her through the opening and down a narrow passageway.

The officer unlocked the door and stepped out of the way with barely concealed fury. "And who is this?" He looked sideways at Aleksandra and the whimpering infant squirming in the sailor's arms.

"A visit'r who'll be travelin' with us. Y' don't need t' know her name."

Aleksandra bit her lip and ducked her head. Melissandra wouldn't last five minutes in the cold waves lapping the side of the ship just below, if she made trouble now.

O'Rourke stood beside the door tapping his foot and looked pointedly at the officer until he dropped his eyes and left the cabin. O'Rourke took the infant from the tar, who bolted as soon as he was free of his burden, kicked the door shut and leaned against it until it clicked. He reached around behind him and locked it, then stared at Aleksandra, his eyes roving over her near-nakedness in the thin muslin gown with only his man's jacket over her shoulders. He licked his lips and walked toward her.

Aleksandra tried to stop her shiver of revulsion and wrapped her arms about herself to keep from gouging his face and ripping Melissandra from his arms.

"Not so high and mighty now, are we, Aleks?" O'Rourke laughed and handed the baby over. "Where's your fancy sword?"

Aleksandra said nothing, just hunched her body over her daughter. Melissandra wound her fingers into the long tendrils of Aleksandra's hair and sighed. It was cold and the rocking sea just outside the porthole didn't help the roiling fear in her gut. She couldn't fight her way out of this one with a one-month old baby in her arms.

"Answer me when I speak to you, girl."

What was...

"Your accent," Aleksandra stared at him, "it was a fake?"

His brows narrowed at her, then he grinned. "Wondered when you'd notice. I was at West Point, and I'm as Northern as they come. My daddy'd roll over in his grave to see me and my brother turn coats, but there's a lot more money in it. Be that as it may," he slipped deeper into a nasal New England whine, "you'd best find some manners. It'll be a long trip around the Horn," he said.

That got her attention.

55

Dancing Wolf sat upon a barrel, leaning back against a warehouse wall. The waves, rhythmically smacking against the pier below, had lulled him into a half sleep, but he couldn't let consciousness go. The situation he'd left behind at the Rancho de las Pulgas, and the one into which he would step from the boat on Alcatraz had him on edge.

How could he have left Aleks to the whims of Sancho, without her husband to protect her?

Despite the blanket wrapped around him, he shivered in the foggy night, awaiting the dawn, when the Indian Affairs-assigned counsel to the boys in the clink would meet him at the Clay Street Wharf.

The metallic ring of horseshoes on cobblestones at a gallop echoed down the street, between the high buildings of the San Francisco wharf district. Dancing Wolf shuddered. A man would have to be in a big hurry, or drunk, to risk his and his horse's necks in this way.

The hoofbeats came closer, and he looked up to see a powerful gray running full tilt toward the docks.

Charro!

"Xavier," he called out, and the horse clattered to a halt.

"That you Dancing Wolf? Where's the hell's Aleksandra?" Xavier growled as he threw himself from the plunging stallion and ran straight for Dancing Wolf, his fist heading for his head.

The Indian sidestepped and waited for him to return. "I left her, against my better judgment, at the *rancho*," he gritted out from between clenched teeth as Xavier rounded on him again. He swung and connected with Xavier's gut, then stepped back while the *Californio* recovered.

Xavier dove and grabbed him around the waist, then slammed him against the brick wall. "Where is she?"

Dancing Wolf threw him sideways and they fell to the cobbles. By the time he landed, a knee on either side of the *Californio's* chest, his knife was across his throat. "I should ask you the same question, my friend. I left her at your home."

"My brother said he saw you leaving with her—riding on Dzień." Xavier said, through gritted teeth. "Where have you put her?" He tried to flick Dancing Wolf off his chest. " I wanted to trust you, but you took advantage—"

"—if you refuse to listen and don't hold still, I will slit your throat and find her myself. There may not be much time."

That got Xavier's attention. In the lamplight, his eyes opened wide and his mouth fell open.

ALEKSANDRA'S HEAD whipped up and she stared at him. "The Horn."

"Yes. There will be plenty of time for us to spend together, my dear. Get used to the idea." His eyes glittered as he looked her up and down once more. He continued to watch her as he slowly turned and unlocked the door. He exited the cabin, the lock clicked, and his boots clumped away down the passageway.

Aleksandra sank upon the bed, letting the repressed shaking finally take hold of her. After a few minutes, she took ten deep breaths, then tucked Melissandra into the captain's bed, beneath the down and woolen blankets.

She looked around her. O'Rourke hadn't checked this cabin.

Mistake. He must not have been at West Point for long.

A search revealed a revolver in the bottom desk drawer, and she smiled for the first time in many hours. It was loaded and tin boxes of powder, balls, wadding and percussion caps sat beside it. She pocketed them all. Her spirits rose further when she found, hanging on the wall, a gold-tasseled ceremonial sword. Its blade was dull, but in the captain's glass keepsakes case, beside a piece of whale-tooth scrimshaw, was a piece of scoria, flat on one side. Small, but it did the trick. She listened to noises on the deck, but kept sharpening. Soon the blade's new edge and tip gleamed with a dull sheen in the hint of dawn's early light peeking through the porthole.

The sword was sharp enough to split the captain's tablecloth, anyway. From half of the fabric, she made a sling for her daughter like those used by the Mexican women on the *rancho*, then cut smaller pieces for swaddling Melissandra's bottom and wrapping the sword blade. On a shelf was a pair of the captain's woolen trousers. She pulled them on, sighing with their welcome warmth, then slipped the sword inside them. Her nightgown was never designed to be used as outerwear, especially on a damp ship.

A knock came upon the door and she froze.

"*Mevrouw?*" came a voice through the door. The voice of a woman.

"Yes?"

"*Hallo.* I haf brought to yoo some food," she said. A faint scraping and the lock turned. A slight woman entered and locked the door again.

"How did you get the key?" Aleksandra stared. The woman held a basket with bread, cheese and a few apples. She was familiar, but Aleksandra couldn't place her.

She looked at Aleksandra from the corners of her eyes. "*Meneer* O'Rourke, he told me to bring it to yoo. *Alstublieft*, here you are," she said as she held the basket out to her.

Aleksandra raised a brow at her and nearly refused the food, but she couldn't make milk without it, so she reached out her hand for the proffered bread and cheese.

"*Eet smakelijt*, enjoy," the woman said, her eyes following the food.

"Are you hungry?" Aleksandra asked the young woman.

"No, *mevrouw.*" She looked away.

"No, seriously, are you?" Aleksandra persisted.

She raised her eyes to Aleksandra's and took a deep breath. "*Ja, ja*—yes, I am."

"Well, eat then." Aleksandra pushed the basket towards her. "You look familiar, what's your name?"

"Esi, *mevrouw.*"

"Have we met, Esi?"

"Ve vere on de vagoon train togeder, for some little time, anyvay." She gulped and turned away. "And," she whispered, "yoo vere kint too me vhen de Sooderners, dey shot mine man back in Udah."

Aleksandra stared, and finally saw her. The bedraggled calico dress the woman wore now could be the same one she'd worn on the hillside near Ephraim's house, and on the wagon train, walking beside O'Rourke's wagon

"You helped Xavier when he was prisoner of that monster, didn't you?"

Esi only nodded.

Aleksandra reached out and hugged her. "Bless you, and thank you with all my heart. How long have you been with O'Rourke?"

"Forefer, it feels like." Esi looked into her eyes. "Years. Much too longh."

"Do you want to stay with him?"

She raised an eyebrow. "His slafe, I am, but his voman, I am noot," she said, with a short mirthless laugh.

"Would you like to be free of him?"

"Yes *mevrouw*, but hoow?"

"My name is Aleks, please call me that," she said, and the woman nodded. " I don't know yet how, but we'll find a way." Aleksandra showed her the pistol and her eyes lit up. "Do you know how to use one?"

"I've noot doone it, but I was oon de slafer foor many years, Aleks," she tried the name out. "Dere vere many guns." Her eyes glittered.

"This one is fairly new, so you might not have seen one like it before, but it's already loaded. You have six shots. Do you know how to load it?" She handed the Remington to Esi, who looked it over with care. "I've got a sword. My weapon of choice."

Esi only had eyes for the shiny new gun. "I've seen dem loaded, but I haf nefer doone it.".

"That's OK. I have the rest of the ammunition." Aleksandra stood silent for a moment, then went on. "I don't know if Xavier knows we're here, but the longer we are in port, the more likely he'll find us. I wish I knew a good way to detain the ship."

Esi's head shot up. "I do."

Aleksandra stared at her.

"Oon de slafer, de rudder, it wood soometimes jam with flootsam."

"Down in the water?" Aleksandra blinked. "There are sharks in that bay."

"I'm a good svimmerr."

"But how would you get down there, much less back up?"

"Leave it to me. Foor now, hoold on to de gun. She voon't voork so good vhen she's vet."

"Are you sure?"

"*Ja, ja*. Nefer been moor sure. Sure I doon't vant to spend another night vid dat bugger, much less de rest oof my life." She reached for a last chunk of cheese and swallowed it. "I vill return soon."

"What is your native language, and how do you say good luck?"

She listened at the door for a moment, then replied. "It is Dutch. I coom froom Dutch Vest Africa. It is *sterke*. To vish somevone strengt," she whispered, then she slipped the key into the door.

"*Sterke*," Aleksandra whispered as Esi slipped out the door, locking it behind her.

"ENOUGH?" Dancing Wolf growled.

"*Sí, basta,* enough," Xavier said, though every muscle in his body was tight as a bowstring.

"If I let you up, will you talk like a civilized man?"

Xavier's scowl melted a little at the reference.

"Now tell me what you know," Dancing Wolf removed the knife from Xavier's neck, but stayed sitting where he was.

"She's been taken, and the babe as well. Sancho put the word out that she was seen leaving town with you."

"If that were true," Dancing Wolf spat out, word by word, "she would be here with me now. As it is, she loves you and was waiting at home. I want to slit your throat for leaving her in danger from that snake of a brother of yours."

Xavier took a deep breath as his face drained of color.

"Yes, he is a snake, regardless of what you think of him. Did Aleksandra not warn you of his intentions and attitude?"

Xavier still said nothing, then finally answered. "She was concerned. I told her it was nothing...again..." Xavier stared heavenward and took a deep breath, "I didn't listen to her. Last time it was Vladimir, this time Sancho. I hope I get another chance to listen to her."

"That's more like it. Do you have any idea where she might have been taken?"

"No. Our stableman found me on the road. Our *rancho* foreman was attacked when he sat at the stairs guarding Aleksandra. I'm not sure why he was there," Xavier's brow creased.

Dancing Wolf glared at him. "I set him to it. Specifically to protect her and your baby from Sancho. There was an 'incident' while I was there."

Xavier stared. "What happ—"

"—we don't have time for that now. Regardless, your stableman rode to find you, and?"

"And he found a man on the road leading Dzień. Let me up, I'm done," Xavier said and took a deep breath as the Indian climbed off him.

"Who was this man, with Dzień?"

"*No sé,* I don't know," Xavier swept his hair back with one fist, "but when he woke up after being hit on the head, he mumbled something about a ship called the *J.M. Chapman,* set to leave San Francisco at dawn. The man wasn't going to talk initially, but he became more helpful after losing part of his ear, under the threat of losing his family jewels."

Dancing Wolf turned and faced the bay. "There's a lot of activity down at the next dock, for this hour." He nodded his head at a three-masted schooner with a long row of cannons down the port side, lying just in the stream.

"Let's go then," Xavier said, but Dancing Wolf was already running as fast as only an Indian could.

"THEY'RE PREPARING TO GO, men. That's my ship, and they're leaving without me!" The man's uniform and demeanor screamed captain, but his attire and person were disheveled and stained like the lowest ship's boy.

"If that's your ship, why're you still on the dock?" a man asked the captain in a familiar voice.

Xavier's head shot up, then he hustled his way through the crowd toward the questioning man, an old friend from his school days in San Francisco and current head of the revenue department.

"I was having a bit of a celebration—we'll be away from port for a while," the erstwhile captain said, looking at his feet.

"And where might you be headin'?" the revenue agent continued to question him.

"Aaah...I'm not at liberty to say...sir." The captain gulped and seemed to shrink.

Xavier's friend nodded to three police officers positioned near the captain. The rumpled man threw glances around him in desperation, but seeing no help in the crowd, went quietly when the policemen led him away by the arms, up Clay Street.

"Xave, long time no see, what's up?"

"I might ask the same, but I'm in a hurry. I've been told my abducted wife might be on the *J.M. Chapman*. Do you know any way we can get out there. Was that the captain?"

"Sure was. That's the schooner right out there." He pointed to her. "Matter of fact, we're on our way out there as soon as they head out."

The grinding sound of an anchor being winched up carried to them from somewhere close at hand. Movement on the deck indicated it was the *Chapman*.

"They're ready to go?" Xavier flicked his hair back with one hand and spun back toward his friend.

He nodded. "Now's our chance. We've been watching that ship for weeks. Think it's been outfitted as a Confederate commerce raider, as well as carrying troops and weaponry for the damned traitors."

Dancing Wolf and Xavier looked at each other. Xavier froze and struggled to breathe.

The revenue officer glanced at the Indian beside Xavier and raised a brow as he looked him up and down.

"He's with me," Xavier growled under his breath.

"Oh, pardon me," he said, and introduced himself to Dancing Wolf with an apologetic smile.

"He's a friend of my wife's," Xavier looked up at the Indian, "and hopefully, mine."

The corner of Dancing Wolf mouth lifted for a fraction of a second, then the warrior was back.

"Would you be looking for any volunteers, sir?" Dancing Wolf said, his jaw set.

"Thought you'd never ask." He grinned at Xavier. "Just like old times, eh? We're boarding in a few minutes—compliments of the warship *Cyane*.'"

Xavier returned the smile briefly, then gritted his teeth. "What's our—" he jerked his head up as the rattling of a released anchor chain sounded across the bay from the direction of the schooner. "—strength?" He swallowed hard.

"We'll have plenty of men on board the sloop-of-war, and the captain's holding two small boats of heavily armed men at the ready. I've the tug *Anasha* chartered and ready. Captain Lees of the Police Department and Port Surveyor Dr. McLean await me on the tug already, but if you'd like to come along, you're both more than welcome, especially as you have a vested interest." He reached out a hand to shake Dancing Wolf's, then Xavier's hands. "Good to see you again, buddy."

"They've dropped the anchor again?"

"Something odd's been going on. A small sailboat came from the south earlier, and some people came aboard, but the ship sailed back south. We've sent someone to intercept them when they're out of sight of the *Chapman*. Less than an hour later, there was a splash in the water near the stern, and a dark shadow moved around the rudder. Soon after, it looked like the anchor chain was moving, but no one was on deck around it, and then all hell broke loose, albeit quietly, on the deck. Looks like they beat someone up after that. I'd sure like to know what that was about. Then you arrived."

"Then they winched up the anchor and now they've dropped it again?"

"Appears so. Not sure what they're doing." The revenue officer frowned. The ship faced them bow-on now, with the turning of the tide. "We'll have to wait until they move. Want this to be clean and tidy. No mistakes. You boys armed?"

A nod from both Xavier and Dancing Wolf seemed to satisfy him. "We want the traitors, you get your woman."

"And my daughter."

His eyes goggled. "You have a daughter? How old is she?"

"One month. I figure Aleks would have fought her way out already, otherwise."

"Guess we won't be blowing any holes in the side of the schooner, then," he said dryly, as he led them toward the huge warship before them. "I'll go see Captain Shirley and ensure no cannons are fired." He headed off at a trot.

Dancing Wolf took one look at Xavier and wrapped an arm over his shoulders, gripping hime tightly as they neared the gangplank. "She'll be OK. She always is. She just needs a little help to get out of this one, with the little one."

"I only hope we're in time. This has the stink of O'Rourke all over it, and I trust him about as far as I can kick him."

56

The to-ing and fro-ing Aleksandra had been hearing from the deck above intensified. How Esi would accomplish her mission was something she was afraid to even contemplate. Melissandra awoke and she put her to her breast. Every time Aleksandra thought of Esi going into the cold water surrounding the ship, Melissandra's tiny lips let go and she mewled in distress as her milk supply dwindled.

Aleksandra finished changing her baby's wet diaper and laid her now-sleeping infant back upon the bed as a great clanking sound began. Anchor chain? She tried the door. Locked. What of Esi? The chain continued its grinding metallic sound as it was wound up. Her heart sank as the ship began to rock a little. They must be on their way out of the harbor. Where was Esi?

There was a banging toward the bow of the ship and raised men's voices. The sound of an anchor chain rattling as it ran back into the water, and then the boat stilled. Aleksandra headed back toward the bed.

A great pounding of feet to one side of the ship stopped her in her tracks. Men growled in low voices and the ship listed a little to one side, then shortly after, a woman's scream, bitten off.

Was it Esi? What were they doing to her? Aleksandra fingered her blade and tried to stay calm. Nothing could come of hysterics.

The sound of heavy footfalls and something being dragged down the passage to her door. A key grated into the lock and turned.

"Rudder was jammed, but we're on our way." O'Rourke dumped Esi, dripping wet, into the corner and turned to Aleksandra. "Stupid woman, must've jumped into the water. Not a good way to escape. You won't do it again, will you?" he shouted in her ear. "It's put us behind but we should be in time to meet up with the *Oregon.*"

The anchor chain began to creak once more as it was wound up and the schooner soon rocked in the waves again.

"Excuse me, sir, but the captain's shrieking from the dock, wants the tug to go back and get him," the First Mate said, through the door.

"He was too drunk to make it back last night, he can stay ashore. I'll captain her."

There was silence from the other side of the door, then footsteps as the officer walked away.

"Besides, it saves me from having to do away with him," O'Rourke added beneath his breath.

Aleksandra shuddered, then flicked her gaze up to him as the boat lurched. "Let me go, you don't need me anymore."

"I have no time for this, Aleks. We have an appointment with a ship."

"Maybe you could leave me with the other ship you're to meet?" Aleksandra made herself give him a smile, but it almost cracked her face. "If it's money you want, I'm sure my husband will pay ransom."

"He won't. He knows you ran away with that Indian friend of yours. He won't even be looking for you. Even if he did come, I couldn't be happier." Evil glinted in O'Rourke's eyes. "I want to hand him over to the Confederates. You can watch. They're mighty upset at what he did to our camp near Churchill. The Mexican owes us. He owes us a lot."

Aleksandra stared at him, the cold feeling in the pit of her stomach turning icier by the second, but she held on. "He'll know it's not true."

"That's not what I hear. I hear he's just dumped you. Couldn't care if you die, by all reports, which is just what you're going to do, as far as he's concerned. You're going to disappear."

Her heart shattered. *Impossible.* She shook her head. Of course it *was* possible—*this was O'Rourke.* "Where are you taking me?"

"None of your concern. You'll go wherever I want you to go. Your precious life is no longer your own. It's mine now and if I have to beat the wayward spirit out of you," he looked across at the negro woman huddled on the floor in her dripping muslin dress, "I will. Just ask her."

Esi didn't even lift her head.

"I've got things to do now," his eyes roved over her body, lingering on the swell of her breasts above her nightgown, "but I assure you, I'll be back when we've dealt to these Yanks and have the gold."

Her brows narrowed at him.

"Gold destined for the Union cause, which will soon be mine. Then we're out of here. The Yanks are crawling all over this coast—it's not safe for a

Confederate ship out here anymore, so we'll be going." He slammed the door and the bolt slid home with finality.

Aleksandra stepped to the door and tried it, but its solid oak didn't even rattle when she shook it with all her might.

No way out.

The walls closed in and she stood with her back against the door, then slumped to the floor. There wasn't a way out of this one. She was, for the first time in memory, in the complete control of another—and an evil one at that —and what was to come of Melissandra? The baby whimpered and she crawled to the bed and dragged herself up, then enveloped her in her arms. Opening the front of her dress, she fed the infant until she slept again. She must have needed the comfort—she only fed for a few minutes and never fully opened her eyes at all. Aleksandra laid her down on the bed again and covered her closely, frowning at the musty dank smell of the blankets, then looked across at Esi, watching from the corner.

Aleksandra drew a breath and got to her feet, then offered a hand to the woman, who hesitated. She finally took it and let Aleksandra help her from the floor. They crossed to the window seat beside the porthole, gripping each others' hands. Esi winced as she sat down.

"Maybe we can escape when we reach the other ship," Aleksandra whispered.

"*Mevrouw* Aleks, dese men, dey are pirates—dey'll kill all doose people on de ooder ship—dere voon't be anyvone left to save us."

"But—"

"Nooboody" She said, her voice hard as granite. "Best get ust to it. Ant obey. He'll kill you, but verst, he'll make you vish you vere det."

Aleksandra frowned at her. "What's happened to you?" she said, "you thought we could get away before, before you went to jam the rudder—"

"—he haf reminded me of vhy I shoould nefer try to escape him," she cut in.

"Escape?"

"Dat is vat I tolt him—dat I vas trying to escape. If dey knew my real purpose, I'd haf gotten more dan dis."

The hairs raised on the back of Aleksandra's neck as Esi stood and lifted her skirts. Her gorge rose at the angry red welts, some seeping blood, across her thighs, bare buttocks and back. "Did they just do that?" she whispered. "Oh Esi, I'm so sorry," Aleksandra said and reached toward her to hug her, but she shrank away into the corner.

"Dey do it vhen dey tink ve neet it—but if dey knew vhy I vas in the vater…do you tink dey vould have stoppt dere? Any idea hoow you't feel after he gived you to de crew for a few nights? And vhat of your baby? How are you to protect her if you're hav det? *Ja*, just you gif in. Vorth it, it is not. You're his noow, like he sait. Dat man of yoours, he voon't be cooming. Already ve het for the big Pacific Oocean. Dere is nooting between here and Soouth America to stoop him and all thoose big cannons on dis ship. Not a ting."

Aleksandra knew she should fight, but how? The marks on Esi's body were bad enough, but her total submission terrified her. She'd do anything it took to protect Melissandra, whatever that was. She still had the sword, but what would that gain her? Her head sank to her chest, and her heart to somewhere lower. Esi was right. Out in the middle of the ocean—against a ship crew and its mad captain—it couldn't possibly be enough, if she wanted Melissandra to live, and to see Xavier again.

Xavier...she closed her eyes and prayed. He wouldn't be coming, even if he could. Her insistence on keeping her friendship with Dancing Wolf had ensured Xavier would believe what O'Rourke told him. How he knew, she had no idea. Would Dancing Wolf be locked up by now with his Indian braves on Alcatraz? Dead? All her fault. She'd always just said full speed ahead and damn the consequences. It clearly wasn't the way to go, but why did she have to wait until now to find that out?

She reached for Esi and gently put an arm around her shaking shoulders and just held her.

Esi dropped her head.

"You're not alone anymore. I'm in it with you now. Whatever comes." Her words sounded brave to her ears, but in her heart, she knew they were both already dead, or would be by the time the ship next docked.

She let the tears flow.

A CRASH, followed by the creaking and groaning of the ship's timbers, nearly knocked Aleksandra and Esi to the floor and shouting broke out on the deck above. Heavy footsteps pounded to stop just outside her door. A metallic scrape of a key in the lock, and the door burst open. O'Rourke slipped into the cabin and kicked the door closed behind him. He spun to face her, his breathing fast and color high. He glanced at the baby on the bed and at Esi, cringing in the corner.

Aleksandra lifted her head, tears cool on her cheeks, and quirked a brow at him.

"You're going to save me and this ship," he replied to her unasked question, then grabbed her left arm and twisted it behind her back. He shoved her toward the door and thrust her down the passageway toward a group of men milling around the deck.

"Tell me what's happening," she said from between gritted teeth.

"We've been boarded, and you're my ticket out of here," he said, as they burst out into the dawning day. "Gentlemen," he announced, "I'm sure we can come to an agreement. You let us go, and the lady lives. You don't... and she dies as she stands here."

Uniformed men carrying boarding axes stood all about the deck, clustered about a group of others already in handcuffs. They eyed each other at this new development. Aleksandra lifted her gaze past the milling men to a massive sloop-of-war rising high above the schooner's deck, its dozen cannons blocking out the pinkening sky.

No wonder there wasn't a fight when they boarded. We'd have been blown to kingdom come if we'd resisted.

She shuddered. Surely the three of them in the captain's cabin would have been dead by now if the ship were fired upon.

"If this girl dies," O'Rourke continued, "you'll have every *Californio* standing against you. They're already for the Confederacy, but this will sway those currently undecided. Who is she? Why, of course, she's the wife of Xavier Argüello, of the Rancho de las Pulgas. You wouldn't want that on your heads, now, would you?"

57

While O'Rourke spoke, Aleksandra stared out at the crowd, but knew no one would be there for her.

Then her heart slammed against her ribs and her face heated at the sight of not one, but two of those dearest to her in the world standing off to her left. She held herself rigid, all but her brows, and Xavier and Dancing Wolf both gave a faint nod. Xavier stood, his face drained of blood and his hand on his pistol butt, but the Indian showed no emotion whatsoever. His face could've been cut from a slab of mahogany, but Aleksandra knew better. His eyes dropped to her side, where the sword was concealed, and she saw the edge of his lips quirk up. Aleksandra splayed all five fingers of her right hand, then made a fist, then repeated the action. Dancing Wolf turned his head toward Xavier and his lips moved for only a moment.

O'Rourke finished his pretty speech just as the ten seconds were up. The Indian gave a bloodcurdling screech at the same time as Xavier fired his pistol into the air. Her captor's attention shifted to his left, Aleksandra threw her body forward to release the arm lock and whipped the ceremonial sword from the slit in her gown, but he held on. The air rammed out of her lungs as her body hit the deck with the O'Rourke's full weight on top. When his weight shifted and disappeared, she gasped for air and tucked up her legs, twisting around to see the scene behind her while she scrabbled blind for her dropped blade. Dancing Wolf had her captor about the waist and gripped his left arm, but O'Rourke still held a knife. Xavier made it to Aleksandra's side and picked up her sword, then lunged for O'Rourke as the fake Southerner threw his knife. The *Californio* pivoted and stepped out of the path of the knife, as he sliced the sword diagonally across O'Rourke's exposed throat. The wound spurted blood with every heartbeat from the severed vessels. Crimson bubbles spewed from the edges of his lacerated windpipe, and Dancing Wolf let him go and watched him sink to the deck. His scream became a whistle as he sank to his knees in a widening pool of his own blood.

Another gunshot rang out and a man slumped against Aleksandra's legs, shot through the head. A knife clattered onto the deck beneath his hand in the sudden silence.

She stared. It was the man O'Rourke called his lieutenant. He indeed had O'Rourke's back, but someone else had just saved either her or Xavier.

"Who shot that man?" a man in a police uniform called out.

Silence.

She wondered, but then Xavier was there, holding her, while Dancing Wolf herded the authorities away, talking all the while.

"*Donde está*—where is Melissandra?" Xavier clutched Aleksandra to his chest, his eyes searching hers.

"She's in the captain's cabin. I need to go to her." Aleksandra took a deep breath and glanced sideways at the approaching officers.

"We need to speak to you for a moment, madame."

"My baby, I need to get my baby!" She pulled away from Xavier and ran.

"We will return in a moment, sir. Our baby is unattended in the captain's cabin."

"Very well, be sure you return immediately."

"Look, Dancing Wolf knows as much of the story as I do. My wife and I will return presently," Xavier said. "That will have to suffice."

Xavier stopped dead in the doorway to miss colliding with Aleksandra, then wrapped his arms around her and pulled her against his chest. They stood together in silence and watched Esi crooning to Melissandra in Dutch as she rocked her against her breast. The baby was asleep and there was a longing on the woman's face as they entered the room.

"*Meneer, mevrouw* Aleks! I vas praying you vould both come back. She is now sleeping. She voke up vhen *Meneer* O'Rourke took you, and I vas tinking of vhat I vas going to do to keep her alife if everyting vent bad out dere. You're here, so I guess *Meneer* O'Rourke, he is gone?"

"He is, and not a moment too soon." Aleksandra went to the woman, who made to hand the baby over, but Aleksandra shook her head. "Xavier, this is Esi, the woman who fed you at the rebel camp and helped me delay this ship."

"Thank you with all my heart, Esi." Xavier took one of her hands and kissed it.

"Esi, do you still have the revolver?" Aleksandra said. "One of O'Rourke's men was about to knife one of us, but he was shot, and no one knows who did it." She looked at Esi hard.

Esi looked at her with wide eyes that glittered. "Is that soo? It is unfoortunate the man ov the *Meneer* vas soo hard oon my man back in Udah. I have learned is good to be kind to people, *ja*?"

"*Ja*," Aleksandra said. She raised a brow at her and returned the Remington's loading materials back to the drawer. "I'm sure it'll be found again in the captain's desk drawer. Fully loaded and wiped clean. I never saw a gun."

"Vas there a gun? Really?"

Xavier looked from one to the other as understanding dawned on his face.

"Would you please hold her for a few minutes more?" Aleksandra touched Melissandra's cheek with the side of her index finger, "We must speak with the authorities. They have many questions, and they will wish to thank you for delaying the ship." She hugged the woman tightly. "Thank you, Esi, with all my heart," she whispered.

"I'd be happy to, *mevrouw* Aleks." Her smile, as she gazed at the tiny girl, said it all.

"Thank you, Esi." Aleksandra smiled at her and squeezed her shoulder. "I believe there are some dry clothes in that closet, if you want to change. We'll be some minutes."

"Mrs. Argüello, something odd happened before the ship left. Can you explain it?" Dr. McLean said. "It appears someone was in the water near the stern."

"Yes, sir, that was Esi. She is a slave, and when I asked if she had any ideas to detain the ship in case anyone," she paused and looked at Xavier and Dancing Wolf, "was trying to come and save us, she did. She'd been on a slaver for years and knew a rudder could be blocked, so she did it."

"In that freezing water? That would explain the dark shadow we saw. The woman deserves a medal."

"I'm sure she would rather have her freedom. She certainly deserves it, and she was the slave of O'Rourke, so she deserves it more than most."

"I'll see what we can do about that. It seems a small price to pay," the port surveyor said. Can you bring her up top, or would she rather see us below?"

"Perhaps below, for now. She's with our baby."

The assembled surveyor, police captain, Aleksandra, Xavier, Dancing Wolf and Esi met below in the captain's cabin. It was a tight squeeze, but decidedly cozy. By the time they finished, it appeared Esi would be returning to the *rancho* with them for the time being, while her emancipation was finalized.

Aleksandra leaned back against Xavier upon the captain's bed, watching the proceedings with a sleeping Melissandra in her lap. "I knew you'd come. O'Rourke kept saying you wouldn't, but I knew you would."

"Sometimes we all need a little kick to remember what's real," Xavier murmured into her hair and caught Dancing Wolf's glance. He nodded his thanks to his Indian friend and squeezed his wife tight. He'd never let go again.

58

"And so, Mama, Esi is a heroine and soon, free," Xavier said, smiling at the African woman, who ducked her head at the attention. "Again, my thanks. Without your delay, we might have not found Aleks and Melissandra before O'Rourke did something stupid—or something even more stupid." He squeezed Aleksandra's hand.

The *maître d'hôtel* of the sumptuous Occidental Hotel in downtown San Francisco cleared his throat and all turned to him. "Would you like to place your order for supper now, Mrs. Argüello?"

They ordered, while admiring the unique new supper room.

"I thought you were staying with your friend, Maria," Aleksandra said, shifting Melissandra to a more comfortable position on her lap.

"I was, but this lovely new hotel was so entrancing, I couldn't resist staying here for just a week. They'll be opening the new grand staircase tomorrow."

Aleksandra chuckled. "We'll see it, then. Thank you for inviting us to stay with you tonight." She stifled a yawn. "I could use a night in a bed."

"And what a bed!" Maria's eyes lit up. "So big and so fluffy, it's like sleeping on a cloud."

Xavier laughed. "We'll have to get one for you to take home."

"Miss Esi, I've been thinking, would you like to be employed on the rancho until you decide what you wish to do with your life?" Maria asked, reaching a hand out to her.

"I vould lofe to do dat, *Mevrouw* Argüello."

"What would you like to do, and what are your skills?"

"I vas born at de Elmina Castle, and dere I vas traint as a ladies' mait vhen I vas a young girl. I should be happy to do dis, if you vould like. I vould not like de stable vurk."

"*Muy bien*, that would be perfect, especially as my longtime maid would like to stay in San Francisco with her family," Maria chuckled, "and we have other people better suited to work in the stables."

"And Dancing Wolf, what are your plans?" Maria asked.

"I've arranged for the release of the boys from Alcatraz, and we leave for Utah tomorrow. I'm not sure where we'll go next, *señora*, but I will keep you informed." He glanced at Xavier, then at Aleksandra, who bit her lip. He gave her a lopsided grin. "We'll be fine, Aleks."

Aleksandra took a big breath and changed the subject. "The men in charge were appreciative of their help, Maria." Aleksandra winked at her mother-in-law.

"And how could they not be? My boys are wonderful. All of them. Will you be one of my boys, Dancing Wolf? You are always welcome back at Las Pulgas." She reached a hand out to both of them and they beamed, then Dancing Wolf turned to Aleksandra.

"Without that ceremonial sword inside your skirt, Aleks, things might have gone very differently, however," the Indian said quietly, "and without you, too, Esi, we might have lost some of our family to O'Rourke's lieutenant, so I give thanks to both of you for your part in this."

Aleksandra looked down at her hands upon Melissandras's shoulder.

"Hear, hear," repeated around the table. When it died down, Aleksandra picked up her head.

"Oh, Esi and I met with the judge you recommended today, Maria," Aleksandra said, "and while we were there, he told us what they found in the hold of the *J.M. Chapman*."

"What was in there?" Xavier returned his gaze to her.

"Beyond the crew of four above deck, there were fifteen or sixteen Confederate soldiers secreted away in the hold, two brass twelve-foot boat howitzers, complete with carriages, twenty rifles, two hundred loaded shells, powder and ammunition. They were, of course," she grinned, "packed and labelled as machinery, which they claimed were for Mexico. There were also papers and oaths of secrecy, many of them torn in pieces and chewed up, in connection with the Confederacy. Oh yes, and over seven hundred flasks of quicksilver and other legitimate freight, which it seems they planned to dump once out to sea to make room for a rendezvous where supplies and more men were waiting."

There was silence at the table.

"Some freight," Xavier said.

"They estimated it at thirty-three thousand dollars," Aleksandra added, "and then they planned to rob and sink the Oregon once they were both outside the Golden Gate, beyond the help of Fort Point. The Oregon carries two million dollars-worth of gold on this trip."

"*Dios mío*," breathed Xavier. "Big plans."

"Their big plans got them a place on the rock, Fort Alcatraz," Dancing Wolf said. "I was out there today. They had to put the Johnny Rebs in solitary confinement, so the other inmates couldn't get at them."

There was silence at the table for long moments.

"We were all very lucky," Dancing Wolf said, then turned to Aleksandra with a frown. "Aleks, do you think you can stay out of trouble for a few months, perhaps?"

"I'll try," she said, and winced.

Laughter and applause broke out around the table. Maria nodded at the hovering *maitre'd hôtel*, who ushered in two waiters with chilled champagne.

"A toast," proposed the matriarch of the Argüello clan, "a toast, to the Union, and its stalwarts right here at this table. Thank you, to all of you. People like you are why we're going to win this one."

"This bed really *is* like sleeping on a cloud," Aleksandra stretched luxuriously. "I could stay here all day."

"That could be arranged, though we might have to slip downstairs to see the opening of the grand staircase, and see the manager about shipping one of these mattresses home." Xavier grinned as he climbed out of bed and reached for his shirt. "Now, about this staying in bed all day, shall we start with breakfast in bed? I'm sure even that can be arranged."

She turned to check Melissandra was asleep, then gave her husband a glance designed to melt steel.

His jaw dropped and the shirt hit the floor with a whisper of linen.

"Come here," she said, reaching out a slender hand to him.

The day looked set to disappear into oblivion.

The End

EPILOGUE

"I'm not looking forward to this meeting with Sancho," Aleksandra said.

"Neither am I." Xavier pushed the hair back from his eyes in a quick gesture, as they rounded the last bend in the drive leading to the *hacienda*.

"Melissandra's still asleep." Aleksandra peeked inside the *rebozo* that she'd fashioned from Xavier's serape. "She seems to like riding better, now that she's not inside me."

"I want to know what happened here. I hope Sancho's home," he said, "then I won't have to go hunt him down."

The dogs barked, and Molly shot out the door.

"You're back, you're back," she shrieked, as she ran toward them, traces of tears down both cheeks. "What? Who..." She stopped. "Come on in, give her to me so you can get down," she said, reaching for the baby.

"Yes, Molly, we found them." Xavier looked straight at Sancho, who'd come out onto the porch. "They'd been kidnapped."

Sancho seemed to be doing his best to look at them, but kept dropping his eyes.

"Sancho, *hermano*, what do you have to say?" Xavier said, his voice low and deliberate. "I'm told you pinned it on Dancing Wolf."

His brother swallowed and his jaw tensed. "I'm sorry, Xavier, I admit I was wrong. I was so sure it was him."

"Why would you think that?"

"Well," he was silent for a moment, then "he and Aleks seemed such good friends, too good, really, if you know what I mean." He looked at Aleksandra with defiance and flinched at Molly's sharp intake of breath.

"No, I don't know what you mean, brother. Perhaps you could explain yourself," he said, as he took one step toward Sancho.

"In the barn, and then in the house, they were…" Sancho stumbled over his words. "I just want to protect you, *mi hermano*," his voice dwindled. Sancho may not have been keen to talk, but Molly had plenty to say.

"I was there the whole time in the house, Sancho," she said, between gritted teeth. "What can you possibly mean?"

"Well, while they were talking," Sancho murmured, "she hugged him. That is just too bad for words."

Molly scowled at Sancho and shook her head. "So did I. He was relating the story of how nearly every member of his village was just slaughtered. I'd even give *you* a hug if that happened to you, Sancho. You're a snake." She whirled and fled into the house with Melissandra.

"I don't know what's going on in your head, Sancho, but you'd best clear it out. Did you have anything to do with the kidnapping?" Xavier didn't really trust him, but he wanted his brother to be clear of doubt, if he were innocent.

Sancho stared at Xavier. "Of course not. I was at the saloon and came back after they'd been abducted. I thought I saw the Indian leave town, with someone on a light colored horse. It was dusk, so I could be forgiven for thinking it was your wife."

"I'm not in a very forgiving mood right now. I'm settling a few things here. You have an apology to make, or rather, quite a few of them."

Sancho's head jerked up. "Please give Dancing Wolf my apologies."

"And what of your sister-in-law?" Xavier glanced at Aleksandra.

He hesitated. "I'm sorry you were kidnapped."

"Is that all?" Xavier's heart gripped tight in his chest.

"Ummm… I'm sorry I doubted your friend." Sancho ducked his head. "I've got to go check some stock," he said, and headed for the barn, then stopped in his tracks and slowly turned. His brows were nearly touching. "Who…where did you find Aleks, and the baby?" he said, past tight lips.

"They were on a Confederate schooner that was captured in San Francisco, just off the docks."

His brother's face turned an ivory color and he opened his mouth to speak, but nothing came out, then he pivoted and continued on his way.

Xavier stood watching Sancho's retreating back for long minutes. For the first time, he saw his brother's snakeskin, the same one his new friend and Aleksandra had described. He didn't like it, not one bit. And what was that last exchange about?

Time would tell, but his brother would bear watching.

"ADELITA, I'm off to town, not sure when I'll return," Sancho said.

Her brows drew together and her lips pursed. "*Su cena?* I have your meal ready."

"*Está bien*, that's OK. Leave it out for me and I'll eat it when I return."

The woman stood still and watched him go. She wasn't really ashamed of him, just worried. That made two of them. His worry was bigger, though.

What happened last night?

Xavier's answer about where they'd been found was useless to him. It offered no opportunity to ask from *whom* he'd rescued the pair, and he hadn't dared ask.

Damn.

He dragged his mount from his corral and flipped the saddle onto his back.

He couldn't very well bring up Mr. Ryan's name, and ask where he could find him. He wasn't meant to even know the man. Some of the gangleader's boys should still be hanging around the old barn or the saloon where they'd first met. He headed out the back gate and up into the rolling hills behind the *hacienda*.

A quick trip to the back of the *rancho* offered no hint of their whereabouts. He gritted his teeth. He might need to go up to San Francisco and find out where Ryan, and Sancho's promised money, had gone.

Double damn.

He wanted to go for an overnight trip to the big smoke to find out, but what if one of Ryan's men showed up and talked with someone at the *hacienda* while he was gone?

He sat at a table in the back of the local saloon, scowling to himself, and ordered a double whisky. Maybe one of Mr. Ryan's men would show. Half an hour later, he had another one for the road.

This was not turning out as he'd planned.

A WEEK LATER, life was returning to normal on Las Pulgas. Even Melissandra finally settled after her harrowing experience, and would let Aleksandra out of her sight without shrieking the house down.

Aleksandra and Adelita kneaded bread at one end of the long kitchen table.

"*Yo voy a la casa.*"

"*Sí.* Now try 'they go to the house'."

Aleksandra considered for a moment, then took a deep breath and tried. "*Ellos van a la casa.*"

"*Muy bien.* Now," as the front door slammed, "Sancho goes to the house."

"*Sancho va a la casa.*"

"Very good. Those verbs for 'go' are not easy."

Aleksandra looked up to see Sancho, the worse for a few nights away, stumble into the kitchen and slump onto a chair by the door.

"*Hola*, Sancho," Aleksandra said.

He blinked at her, but didn't reply. He leaned forward a little, lost his balance, and fell face-first onto the tiles.

Adelita and Aleksandra looked at each other and shook their heads as he sang a little song in Spanish. He stopped, then began to speak.

"Rancho de las Pulgas should be hers, *pobre niña*," he mumbled from his place on the floor, words slurred with *tequila*. "It is too bad she was born out of wedlock."

"What did you say?" Aleksandra squinted and shook her head, but when she opened her eyes, he was still there. "Sancho, could you repeat that?"

"Out of wedlock, Melisssshha—" he said, then his head lolled to the side and he slept.

The End... again.

THANK YOU

Thank you for joining Aleksandra and Xavier in
The Hills of Gold Unchanging.
They will be returning in *A Sea of Green Unfolding*

Enjoyed the story? Want to read more?
If you loved it, a short review on Bookbub, Goodreads and your favorite
eBook retailer would sure be appreciated.
I'd be grateful for your help in spreading the word!

Sign up for Lizzi's VIP Club to hear about new releases and specials, plus get
your free sampler gift here!

www.lizzitremayne.com/VIPHills/

FIND EBOOKS & PAPERBACKS

Find eBooks

at your favorite online retailer via buy links at www.lizzitremayne.com/books/

Find Paperbacks

New Zealand and Australia

My signed print books are available in standard (and some in large format) print. Contact the author via her website at:

https://lizzitremayne.com/contact-lizzi/

New Zealand Schools

Available from Wheelers and AllBooks (print and digital)

Other Countries

Print books are available in paperback from most online retailers and in select bookstores around the world.

If you cannot find them, contact the author via her website at:

https://lizzitremayne.com/contact-lizzi/

LIZZI TREMAYNE
BOOKS

COMING
SOON!

BOOKS DETAIL AND UPCOMING RELEASES

The Long Trails Series

Book One: *A Long Trail Rolling*

A dangerous job. Is it a convenient escape route...

or a death trap?

Winner of True West 2016 Best Western Romance, Romance Writers of New Zealand: 2014 Pacific Hearts Award and 2015 Koru Award

UTAH TERRITORY, 1860. *Alone.* Aleksandra has spent her whole life training for the inevitable. So when a brutal Cossack tracks down and kills her father, she knows what she must do. She flees, disguised as a Pony Express rider, in an attempt to keep her pa's killer from discovering their family's secret.

Xavier has kept the world, especially women, at arms-length since he ran from his troubles as heir to his *Californio* rancho family. As a Pony Express Station Keeper, having a girl riding the Pony out of his station wasn't ever part of his plans... but somehow it happened, blackmail being what it is. Curiously, he didn't want to let this one out of his sight.

They begin to let each other into their hearts, but the cards are stacking against them as the minutes tick by and Aleks rides full speed into the Indian Paiute War. Can they learn to trust in time to escape the Indians, evade the killer, and save both their love and Aleksandra's family legacy?

Book Two: *The Hills of Gold Unchanging*

As the Civil War rages, secessionists menace California. The Confederates want the state and they'll stop at nothing to they'll stop at nothing to take it.

UTAH TERRITORY, 1860. On a wagon train headed for the Golden State, Aleksandra makes a dangerous enemy of a gun-running Confederate when she fights her way out of his unwelcome embrace.

After a late-night poker game, Xavier's new friends realize he's heard too much to be allowed to live.

Embroiled in the Confederates' fight to drag the new state from the Union and make it their own, can Aleks and Xavier survive? The secessionists mean business.

Book Three: *A Sea of Green Unfolding*

They set sail for the peace and calm of New Zealand, but they hadn't counted on murderers, mutineers, and a land war in paradise.

SAN FRANCISCO BAY AND NEW ZEALAND, 1863. Aleksandra and Xavier have finally found happiness on their Rancho de las Pulgas, but tragedy and death strike far too soon. Sickened further by the U.S. government's treatment of their Native American friends, they only want out. Of everything.

They are thrown a lifeline by an old friend of Xavier's from the California goldfields. This Gustavus von Tempsky, with his shadowed past, is now a newspaperman in Coromandel, New Zealand. His invitation draws them to a new start, with a part to play in the development of the peaceful young country—but by the time they arrive in Aotearoa, everything has changed.

Aleks thought mutineers and scoundrels aboard ship were the worst of their worries, but she hadn't planned on disembarking into a turbulent wilderness and befriending the helpful local Māori, only to find von Tempsky leading the colonial troops into the bush against the natives who'd saved her life.

Box Set: *The Long Trails Box Set*

Can an orphan, with only her Mustang and a Cossack sword, survive alone on the frontier?

From the deserts of Utah, through the gold mines of California, to the turbulent wilderness of Colonial New Zealand, Aleksandra rides, loves, and fights—with only her Cossack skills to keep her alive.

** From multiple award winning author Lizzi Tremayne **

UPCOMING: *The Tatiana Series*

(with links to The Long Trails series)

Book One: *Tatiana I*

Stableman's daughter Tatiana rises to glamorous heights by her equestrienne abilities—but the tsar's glittering attention is not always gold.

MOSKVA, RUSSIA 1842. Tatiana and her husband Vladimir become pawns in the emperor's pursuit of a coveted secret weapon. While Tatiana and their infant son are placed under house arrest, Vladimir must recover the weapon or lose his wife and young son. With the odds mounting against them, can they find each other again— half a world away? *Coming soon!*

UPCOMING: *The Somewhere Series*

(also with links to The Long Trails series!)

Book One: **Somewhere Called Home**

Highlands to Waterloo—can love prevail over fate?

SCOTTISH HIGHLANDS, 1813. Lachlann is disowned for refusing to become clan tacksman after his father and heads for the city, alone, to build a life for himself and his beloved Annis. Annis' waiting turns to despair when her mother buys safety during the clearance of their village—leaving Annis at the mercy of the laird's degenerate son. Lachlann emerges from the hell of Waterloo wanting only to see Annis again... and his father. *To be released soon.*

The Once Upon a Vet School Series

Drama and humor abound as Lena pursues her childhood dream of becoming an equine vet—and beyond—in this upcoming, unique series of

six independent novella sequences:

~Junior Years~

After Lena hears she needs good grades to become a veterinarian, things start to get tricky. Even her pony doesn't get out unscathed. (Middle Grade) *USA 1972-1976*

~High School Days ~

When your high school counsellor says vet school's too hard for you and your HS sweetheart offers you a dream life of farming, writing, and babies, what do you do? Is vet school really the be-all, end-all? (Young Adult) *USA 1976-1979*

~College Nights~

How can you have a life when you need an A in every class for four years to get into vet school... on top of 800 hours vet practice work? Something's got to give. (Young Adult and up) *USA 1980-1984*

~Vet School 24/7~

Now they're in, the pressure for grades is off and vet school social life is upon them... there's only the tsunami of 200 years of veterinary knowledge to pack into their heads. Can Lena and her friends stay afloat? (Young Adult and up) *USA 1984-1988*

~Practice Time~

Finally graduated, prima ballerinas of the university, Lena and her vet school classmates disperse to far-flung practices... and real life. What could possibly go wrong? Late nights on-call, mud, blood, and finally, a light at the end of the tunnel... unfortunately, it's only the penlight of a dictatorial vet technician in Lena's eyes after she passed out on the floor. (Women's Rural Fiction with Romantic Elements) *USA & New Zealand 1988-2012*

~Long in the Tooth~

When Lena suffers another catastrophic back injury in New Zealand, what's she to do to feed her family and keep the farm? She can't breathe around cats or birds and what good's an equine vet who can't hold up a horse's leg? Time for Lena to go back to school. Again. (Women's Rural Fiction with Romantic Elements) *New Zealand 2012- ...*

Currently Available Reads:

~Vet School 24/7~

Fifty Miles at a Breath

Horses bring them together and their future looks rosy—it's the present they can't handle.

When equine veterinary student Lena and veteran pilot Blake fall in love, vet school and the past intrude. Add in a long-distance relationship, and things get just plain hard. A grueling endurance race forces them to draw on their strengths and face their fears—together.

Lena Takes a Foal

She needs help... he needs to stay away...

Lena's got a problem—one that might prevent her from graduating. When her horse flips over and lands on her, it has to be the dashing resident, Kit, who finds her. Luckily, she's sworn off relationships after her last debacle and sea-green eyes and rugged good looks are the last things on her mind. Besides, to a veterinary school faculty, relationships between residents and students are like oil and water.

They just don't

mix.

~Practice Time~

Greener Pastures Calling

A new country, a great job, and a good Kiwi bloke. Life couldn't be better.

Until it gets worse.

Newly emigrated to New Zealand, Lena wants a 'good Kiwi bloke', but they're elusive as their nocturnal namesake. Nigel's avoiding females, unless they're cows, horses, or his mother after his first marriage. Sparks fly when they meet—but not the first time, over the dirty instruments in a filthy cowshed. They seem to be made for each other, until Nigel remembers where he first saw her. And then the questions start.

<u>Understanding Modern Vet Med for Owners</u>

The new series of veterinary books for horse owners to let you use what vets know to keep your horses healthier and happier. *First volume due out soon!*

Sign up for Lizzi's VIP Reader Club to hear about new releases and specials, plus get your free sampler gift at

www.lizzitremayne.com/VIPHills/

AUTHOR'S NOTES

A few clarifications may be helpful:

Aleksandra's hero Xavier, is a *Californio*, an old Californian of Spanish descent, and as such his name is pronounced 'HAV-ee-air.'

Aleksandra, Xavier, and several others in the story are completely fictitious characters, but the incidents portrayed are not. Many of the historical figures included were real people, however, and I have taken artistic license to describe their actions. I have utilized actual people and incidents to offer history to some who may never pick up a book of historical nonfiction, while attempting to offer history buffs historical figures in a different light. Some of the dates have been altered to make a story work, but otherwise I have presented the history of the events and the people as best I understand them from the historical record.

While my research has uncovered no precedent of female riders of the Pony Express, in light of the prevalence of women who followed the guns of the American Civil War in the same year, it is not impossibility.

Sumner sent troops from Ft. Churchill to quell a Confederate uprising in Virginia City, but I've directed them to "Dixie" instead, which was renamed Unionville, its current name, after it was cleared of Southern sympathizers. For years, the Northerners and Southerners segregated themselves on opposite sides of the main street. The date for the formation of the town of Dixie was pulled back by one month to June from July 1861 to make the scenario work.

The town currently called Nevada City, in California, was named 'Nevada' at the time of this story.

Empire Cottage, the beautiful English manor home described in the story at Empire Mine, still stands. It was built, however, after the time of this story. It was used by the mine's owner, or at least by the man with the biggest controlling interest in the mine. It was designed in 1897 by architect Willis Polk. The main floor holds the kitchen, service rooms, living room, dining room and a reading room. Four bedrooms and two baths are on the second floor. The servants' rooms and a bathroom were located above the kitchen. It's exquisite. Go visit it.

Julia Burette was the darling of the Comstock, popular with both the miners and the firefighters. She was an honorary member of Virginia Engine Co No. 1. While she didn't move to VC until 1863, she was such a colorful character, I couldn't leave her out.

At the time of the story, the real Maria Soledad Ortega de Argüello, mother of the fictitious Xavier, had already sold the remains of *Rancho de las Pulgas* and moved to Santa Clara County to live with her son.

In 1976, the City of Redwood City renamed a downtown plaza at the intersection of Broadway and Argüello Street as Argüello Plaza. A bust of her was erected in September of the same year in that plaza. The bust is on the edge of the train and bus depot, next to the Broadway train crossing.

I hope you enjoy your foray into my world of historical romantic suspense. If you liked it, help others find it by leaving reviews and comments where you purchased it, on Goodreads, and on my webpage. If you want to pass on a comment, please find me via my *Connect with Lizzi* page.

Warmest regards,

Lizzi Tremayne

GLOSSARY

a charaid (G) ~ a friend

Allez (F) ~ Go, or begin (fencing)

Alstublieft (Du) ~ Please, or reply to 'thank you'

Basta (S) ~ Enough

Bien (S) ~ Good, OK

Amigo/ Amiga (S) ~ Friend masc/fem

Bebé (S) ~ Baby

Buenos días (S) ~ Good morning

Camisa (S) ~ Shirt or blouse

Casa grande (S) ~ Big house, mansion

Californio (S) ~ Spanish California colonist/ descendant

Cena (S) ~ Evening meal

Chiles rellenos (S) ~ Filled chiles

Claro (S) ~ Clear, clearly

¿Cómo? (S) ~ What? How?

Con permiso (S) ~ With your permission

Con todo (S) ~ With all

Da ow agato (Wash) ~ Lake now called Lake Tahoe

Datsa' shut (Wash) ~ Lake now called Donner Lake

Desayuno (S) ~ Breakfast

De veras (S) ~ It is true, the truth

Dios mío (S) ~ My God

Dzień (P) ~ Day. Pronounced 'Zshen/Jean/Jen'

Dzhigitovka (R/P) ~ Cossack military show riding

El Camino Real (S) ~ The King's Road/ The Royal Road

Eet smakelijk (Du) ~ Bon appetit, enjoy your meal

En nuestra familia (S) ~ In our family

En garde (F) ~ Prepare (fencing command)

Está bien (S) ~ It's okay, fine

Estan viniendo (S) - They are coming

Estás loca/o (S) - You are crazy (fem/masc)

Far, Far, kom med mig (Da) - Father, father, come with me

Gracias (S) - Thank you

Gracias a Dios (S) - Thank God

Hacienda (S) - Ranch house, estate

Hallo (Du) - Hello

Halte (F) - Halt (fencing)

Hermano (S) - Brother

Hijo mío (S) - My son

Hombre (S) - Man

Huevos rancheros (S) - Eggs with salsa on tortilla

Ja (Da/Du) - Yes

Kielbasa (P) - Spicy polish sausage

Kwahaten (Shos) - Antelope, Shoshone name for Aleksandra

Lo siento (S) - I am sorry for it

Maître d'hôtel (F) - Head restaurant waiter

Mange tak (Da) - Many thanks

Meneer (Du) - Mister

Mevrouw (Du) - Mrs.

Mi corazón (S) - My heart

Mochila (S) - Pony Express mail carrier, leather, fits over saddle and is transferred from horse to horse.

Moskva (R) - Moscow

Niña (S) - Girl

No sé (S) - I don't know

Opłatek (P) - Traditional Wigilia wafer

Pemmican (Cr) - Fat and protein dried food, AmInd

Perdón (S) - Pardon me

Piececitos (S) - Little feet

Pierogies (P) - Polish dumplings

Pobre niña (S) - Poor little girl

Prêt (F) - Ready (fencing)

Que le vaya bien (S) - (I hope) that you go well

Qué será, será (S) ~ What will be, will be

Querida/querido (S) ~ My darling/love (fem/masc)

Rebozo (S) ~ Mexican baby carrier made from shawl

Recuerda (S) ~ Remember

Shashka (R) ~ Single-edged, guardless, Caucasian, then Ukranian/ Russian saber

Schlachta (P) ~ Polish noble

Señora (S) ~ Married or older woman

Señorita (S) ~ Girl, miss, familiar for young, +/- married woman

Serape (S) ~ Latino shawl/blanket worn as cloak

Serpiente de cascabel (S) ~ Rattlesnake

Sí (S) ~ Yes

Siesta (S) ~ Afternoon nap in the heat of the day

Sientate (S) ~ Sit down (command)

Sterke (Du) ~ Wishing you strength/ luck

Tak i lige maade (Da) ~ Thanks, in like manner

Tal vez (S) ~ Perhaps

Te quiero (S) ~ I love you or I want you

Tiene que ir (S) ~ Have to go

Welganuk (W) ~ Place now called Truckee Meadows

Wiglia (P) ~ Polish Christmas supper

Zakwas (P) ~ Rye sourdough starter

Żurek (P) ~ White borscht, traditional Polish stew

Key:

Cr: Cree Indian / Da: Danish / Du: Dutch / F: French / P: Polish / R: Russian / S: Spanish / Sh: Shoshone / W: Washo language of Washoe Indians

RECIPE: CHILES RELLENOS CON QUESO

Chiles Rellenos, ("chee-leh rrreh-yeh-nohs kohn keh-so": stuffed chiles) are Aleksandra's and my favorite Mexican food. They are a bit time consuming to make, but the flavor is worth the effort. This recipe will feed 3-4 (or two very hungry) people.

A few words to the wise suggest working in this order:
1-make the sauce and put on to simmer
2-prepare and stuff the chiles, then dip in flour to coat and stick the slit closed
3-make the coating
4-fry the coated chiles
5-top with salsa and garnish.

Salsa de Jitomate
(sal-sa de hi-toh-ma-teh: Tomato Sauce)
½ cup onion, chopped
4 cloves garlic, minced
oil for frying onions and garlic
15 oz (400 g) canned (whole/chopped) or preferably, fresh tomatoes, roughly chopped
½ c (175 ml) water
¼ tsp salt
½ tsp oregano, crumbled

¼ tsp salt
small pinch chile powder

Sauté onion and garlic in oil until golden. Stir in tomatoes and the rest of the ingredients. Simmer for 15 minutes while stuffing chiles and making the sauce.

Chiles

8 Poblano or Anaheim, mild, fresh green chiles, blistered and peeled
Find instructions online if want to try using fresh chiles. It's tricky, but worth it for the taste! Remove seeds and pith from inside, then cut a slit in the side to put the cheese in. Leave the stem as a handle for cooking.

OR

8 Canned Anaheim or Ancho green chiles
Rinse and use as below.

½ - ¾ pound (250-500 g) jack, colby, or cheddar cheese, cut into long sticks (~ ½ in x ½ in x length of chile)

About ½ cup flour

Stuff chiles with 1 stick of cheese into each chile (into top of tinned ones or through slit side of fresh ones). Overlap the chile sides a little to prevent cheese loss, and roll in flour to coat and stick the slit closed then gently shake off excess.

Puffy Coating

3 eggs, yolks and whites separated
4 Tbs flour
1 Tbs water
¼ teaspoon salt
salad oil or butter for frying

Beat egg whites until they form soft peaks. Beat the egg yolks separately with flour, water and salt. Fold yolk mixture into egg whites.

Making the Rellenos

Coat and fry chiles by putting oil or butter into a frying pan over a medium heat.

Mound up about ½ cup of the coating in an oval shape in the HOT oil, and immediately lay a stuffed chile in the center of the mound and spoon another ¼ cup coating over the chile to just cover it. Use more if needed. You can cook as many as will fit in the pan. Cook for 2 to 3 minutes on one side, then carefully turn them and cook for another 2 - 3 minutes longer, or until golden brown.

Top with hot *Salsa de Jitomate* and grated cheese or sliced green onion tops.

Enjoy!

ABOUT THE AUTHOR

Lizzi grew up riding wild in the Santa Cruz Mountain redwoods, became an equine veterinarian at UC Davis School of Veterinary Medicine and practiced in the Gold and Pony Express Country of California before emigrating to New Zealand. She has two wonderful boys, a grandson, and an awesome partner in that sea of green. When she's not writing, she's swinging a rapier or shooting a bow in medieval garb, riding or driving a carriage, playing in the garden on her hobby farm, singing, cooking, teaching, or looking into a horse's mouth in her equine veterinary dental practice. She is awarded and multiply published in fiction, nonfiction, special interest magazines and veterinary periodicals.

With her debut novel, Lizzi was:
Winner 2016 True West Magazine
Best Western Romance
Winner 2015 RWNZ Koru Award
Finalist 2015 Best Indie Book Award
Winner 2014 RWNZ Pacific Hearts Award
Finalist 2013 RWNZ Great Beginnings

CONNECT WITH LIZZI

I'm looking forward to hearing from you!

Join conversations and find story excerpts, buy links, and more here:

www.lizzitremayne.com/VIPHills
www.lizzitremayne.com
www.horseandvetbooks.com
www.bookbub.com/profile/lizzi-tremayne/
www.facebook.com/lizzitremayneauthor/
www.instagram.com/lizzitremayne/
www.tiktok.com/@lizzitremayneauthor
www.twitter.com/LizziTremayne/
https://www.youtube.com/channel/UCylITovsoX1H1E17lJZTxTQ
www.goodreads.com/LizziTremayne/
https://nz.pinterest.com/lizzitremayne/

ACKNOWLEDGMENTS

My most profound thanks to...

Matthew, for giving me your love and the encouragement to write; Mum, for your constant enthusiasm and encouragement; Stuie, Elliot and Tamiee, for giving me a reason to keep progressing; Bhiannon Fritz-Hammond, for her map of my heroes' travels and for keeping me sane during final edits.

The many who assisted in my research, especially: Patrick Hearty, National Trails Chairman and Past President of the National Pony Express (PX) Association, his wife Linda, and the whole family for their hospitality, help and horses for the Pony Express Re-Ride last year; the Librarians at Hauraki District Council libraries; Greg at the Utah State Archives Office; Tami at the County Clerk's License Office; Carol at the San Mateo County Library; Chaun Owens-Mortier at the Truckee Donner Historical Society; the lovely ladies at the San Carlos Museum of History; and a massive thank you to Archivist Carol Peterson of the San Mateo County Historical Museum for providing me with a copy of the *Map of Rancho de las Pulgas Land Grant Title,* from which one map was drawn.

Those who contributed to the craft: The Quartz Cafe and The German Bakery, of Waihi, for letting me spread out my notes and scribble for endless hours; Gracie O'Neil, for help with my synopsis; Lena, Tiggie, Maya, and Pandora, for my writing sanity; Amy Taylor, my son Elliot (again), Blue Mist Shemaya (Maya) and Sonny, for giving up half of a Saturday for cover photos: Amy lives to compete, but Elliot hadn't been on a horse in years, much less bareback.

My lovely beta readers: Jude Knighton (who read the entire manuscript during its last edit at *past* the last minute and provided indispensable critical insights plus kept me in one piece over the pagination of the paper copy), Matthew Mole, Annie Featherstone, Kate Anderson, Ngaire Phillips, Danielle Louise Hadfield, Shelagh Merlin, Kirsten Davidson, Tanya Sherborne, and Jackie Ward. Without your great criticism and ideas, this book would not be half what it is today.

Those other unwitting victims upon whom I foisted the odd chapter and too many supportive RWNZ fellow-writers to even count. You are an amazing bunch of people.

The many others who have helped, not only in my pedantic search for detail, but in so many other ways, not the least your everyday encouragement to finish this story and get it out!

Thank you all. I couldn't have done it alone.

xx
Lizzi

EXCERPT FROM A SEA OF GREEN UNFOLDING

November 1863, East Coast North Island, New Zealand

"I'M THINKIN' we be in the Aucklan' Current," Jacob confided that evening, over the supper they shared in the hold. "This time o'year it run to the east o'New Zealan', down past Poverty Bay and heads fer th'South Islan'."

"So you think we're headed for New Zealand, then? The captain doesn't know where we—"

"—this 'cap'n' ain'a real cap'n," Jacob interrupted, "and don't know sh—"

"—I understand," Aleksandra cut in, flashing him a grin. Dzień shuffled his feet and even the little rustling of straw sounded loud to her ears.

"Jus' so we understan' each oth'r." He smirked.

"So how would I find Coromandel Town from that coast?" Aleksandra muttered into her salt pork.

"Coro? I don' be likin' yer chances, Mrs. Argüello."

"Jacob, you can call me Aleks, remember?"

"Aleks, then. Some awful big mount'ns a'tween that'n East Coast n' Coro Town. Y'll need'n t' find a mission house'n ask 'em fer help. They c'n prob'ly find y'a native guide," he whispered, blowing crumbs of hardtack with his words. "There be lots'a boats comin' up'n down th'coast, all a time."

"Jacob, we owe you more than you can ever know. If we get out of this alive, please come find us, wherever we are. We're seeking a man called von Tempsky. He's from Poland, where my family comes from. Xavier met him in

California, and he's a bit bigger than life, so I'm sure you can find him, and through him, us. When you tire of the sea, you'll always have a place with us."

The boy's eyes shone wetly in the dimness, and he ran a sleeve across his eyes.

"Thank'ee, Mrs... Aleks." He gulped. "Ain't no one never said nuthin' like 'at a'fore. My thanks. I'd best be goin' now. I'm thinkin' yer land'll be 'ere soon. I seen alb'trosses las' night, an' it smells like land. T'morro', mebbe?"

"Thank you, Jacob, from the bottom of my heart. Now go." She gave him a little push. He turned and dashed up the ramp, his light footfalls barely audible over the munching of many beasts.

Louder feet, heavier ones, irregular, came down the ramp and she looked up, heart in her throat.

"And what was all that about?" Broadhurst strode in, the collar of Jacob's shirt in his clenched fist. "Why did the boy run out of here, and why were you two talking together so quietly?"

Aleksandra looked down at the ground, as her guts churned and her face heated. How could they get out of this?

"Well, sir," she put her hands over her face, "I do believe I embarrassed the lad, being frank with him about a woman's needs..." She rubbed her eyes and whimpered a little. "With my man not available, why, I just wanted a little closeness, but... but the boy's as good as his word and I'm a married woman... a bad, bad married woman. Please, please don't tell my husband I've been unfaithful in my heart," she got out, between sobs.

"That true, Jacob?" Broadhurst growled.

"Well, yessir. 'Tis," he said, in a small voice.

ALEKSANDRA PEEKED BETWEEN HER FINGERS. The boy was biting his cheeks, his lips quivering.

"Aleks." She awoke to Jacob's voice beside her ear and his touch light upon her shoulder.

She bumped into Dzień's muzzle as she sat up in the darkness and reached out to the boy. The Mustang whickered softly at the diminutive seaman, then nuzzled the back of Aleksandra's neck, his whiskers tickling her fully awake.

"Good save yest'day, wi' the cap'n'. He just'n 'bout found ye out," he whispered. She could swear he grinned in the pitch-darkness. "I smell'n land fer sure. It's jus' aft'r midnight, but I smell it and I hear some o' them li'l owls them have, them'r callin' 'em moreporks."

"What do you want me to do?"

"First light, if'n it's safe, I'll knock on th' deck above ye four times. Ye come out 'n ride fer yer life. I'll have m' men ready so's ye don' get shot while yer swimmin', but there won' be much'n time. If'n it gets t' be no safe, I'll bang three times. Ye'll have to do summat else, mebbe use th' two horses'n like we talked 'bout."

"OK. I'll be ready," she said, her stomach already knotting.

"I'll be tellin' yer man how ye went," he whispered, and they clasped hands before he melted into the night.

Sleep came hard, but she got some, in fits and starts, as the ship rocked through the night.

"It must be near to dawn," Aleksandra murmured to Dzień as he nuzzled her hair and shifted his weight to his other hind leg.

She sat with her skirt loosely tied over her short trousers, arms clasped around her knees. Aleksandra's knapsack remained hidden and Dzień's bridle stowed with it. No sound had yet come from the boards above.

At the sound of footsteps, Aleksandra looked between the planks lining Dzień's stall and she frowned. This wasn't their plan.

"Over here," she whispered.

"Expecting someone, were you?" Broadhurst sauntered into view.

"Only wishful thinking," Aleksandra said, and pulled her blanket up under her chin to better cover her fully-dressed frame. Her heart pounded so loudly she was sure he'd hear it six feet away.

"Better get used to the idea your husband won't be coming back to you. He'll be hanged for what he did to Symes. Remember that," he said. His footsteps retreated toward the ramp.

"Thank you for the visit," she said, sarcasm dripping from her voice.

"Just a reminder. I'm watching you," he said, not bothering to stop.

How she wanted to bury her throwing knife between his shoulder blades.

Four knocks came through the ceiling boards and the captain's footsteps stopped.

"What's that?" he growled, his shoes squeaking as he spun around.

"It's still dark, you've woken me up from a sound sleep, you hear noises, and you ask me what they are?" Her voice raised as she railed at him, making sure it reached maximum volume by the end. "Good night, Captain Broadhurst," she shrieked at him, her hands clenched at her sides.

He took a deep breath, then resumed his walk topside.

Two minutes later, three knocks sounded and repeated.

Aleksandra assembled all just beside the door and went for a walk to see the lay of the land. She walked the long way to the privy. It gave her a view all around the ship as she walked, slowly and a bit unsteadily, as if still groggy from sleep. She turned a corner to see the captain headed back toward the galley and Rach's old cabin, then a door clicked closed. Ducking into a narrow space where she couldn't be observed, she strained her eyes to starboard. There, rising from the straight line of the sea.

Jagged lines of mountains, glorious mountains, broke the horizon. She bit her tongue to keep from crying out as she quietly opened, then slammed the privy door shut, and slipped back the way she'd come. No one else was out walking at this hour. As she entered the hold, four faint knocks sounded on the wood above.

Aleksandra smiled. Jacob was on the job.

Dzień took the bit she proffered, then her fingers flew as she slipped the crownpiece over his head, buckled the throatlatch, and flicked the split reins around his neck. Slinging the knapsack onto her back, she strapped it on tightly. One tug on the string of the waistband of her skirt and it slid to her feet. She stepped out of it and shivered, goosebumps raising against the thin men's trousers.

Leading her pony from his tie stall, she swung up and they dashed away, up the ramp from the hold to the 'tween decks. She turned the corner toward the top deck and Dzień slid to a halt as a shadow rose up before them, hands held high.

"Stop," Broadhurst barked.

The captain dropped his hands and walked toward them, shaking his head.

"Stupid, stupid. That's the oldest trick in the book." He grinned as he reached for Dzień's reins.

Next Chapter

Aleksandra's father hadn't spent years training her and her mount in the Cossack ways for nothing. She drew her shashka as Dzień rose up on his hind legs in a levade, tucking his forelegs up to protect his rider and free her to swipe at Broadhurst. He dodged, but not before he received a slice across the inside of his right forearm for his efforts.

The captain's fingers jerked backwards and he screamed.

Desperately hoping Broadhurst shot his pistol right-handed, she called out to Dzień and he swerved around the man crouching before them, holding his arm and screaming.

Dzień galloped the rest of the way up to the deck. She turned her head to sight the five-foot-high bulwark, topped by the even higher gunwale, and lined the Mustang up to give him the longest possible run. Reaching behind her, she shoved her shashka into the pack then loosed the reins and called to Dzień as she aimed him for the solid wall. Her heart sang as he raced toward it like he'd been shot from a cannon. The Mustang gave a great grunt as his forelegs left the ground and he shoved with his hindquarters. Then his hind hooves, softened by the long trip in the damp hold, slipped.

Heart in her mouth, Aleksandra held her breath and kept her eyes up, her legs clamped firmly on his sides. She'd never jumped this high, much less bareback. Dzień swung his hind legs sideways to miss the rail and his hind hooves clipped the top of the gunwale, but then they were over, and falling, falling until they hit the dark water.

Find this book here!
https://books2read.com/SeaOfGreenUnfolding

EXCERPT FROM TATIANA

M*id-1842 Moskva, Russia*

BY THE TIME I was fifteen, and Vladimir sixteen, we were inseparable. No longer did he clean stalls as punishment, but to help me before his Training School classes began. This gave us more time to fit ourselves and prepare our combined *džigitovka* performances. We had been selected as part of the team to perform for the Tsar on his next visit to Moskva from St. Petersburg.

The tsar's creepy messenger, who came to our door with increasing regularity for no seemingly good reason, had delivered the invitation for our group to give the performance. His terse smile showed through the lace curtains as he stood before the door. I managed to talk Papa into answering it, claiming I couldn't leave my cooking pot.

The messenger, whose name I never asked, but he told me anyway, was Sambor Andropov. Due to his frequent visits, I had taken to ignoring anyone knocking on the door when I was in the house alone. His mere eyes on me made my skin crawl, and I felt I was being undressed before his eyes. Although a servant of the tsar could not be ignored without serious repercussion, if he didn't know I was there, all would be well. If the message was important, he would return, or Mrs. Bagrov would get the door if she was in.

I had the grace to be embarrassed when I realized he had carried such a special invitation to our door after I had avoided him. It was just that men and boys in Papa stableyard never looked at me like that, so perhaps I was being overly sensitive. I vowed to be kinder to him when I saw him next. He was, after all, just doing the tsar's bidding.

After this missive, our training intensified. We only had a month to prepare our troop for our presentation before Tsar Nicholas and his Empress Alexsandra Feodorovna.

There were eleven men in our group, plus me. We were drawn from the wider area around Moskva, but bragging aside, Vladimir and I were the stars of the show.

We had a joint act, with a quadrangle, jumping and shashka work, but our own little act was the best one. It began with Vladimir and I standing in Sarda's saddle, with me just behind him, one hand in the air, waving at the audience. We would then do a lift, ending up with my standing upon Vladimir's shoulders—at a full gallop.

It was a truly tricky maneuver, and one that few ever attempted. We lived, ate and breathed *džigitovka*. In any spare time, we worked out together — running, press-ups, sit-ups— we needed all the strength we could muster, and on the day of the performance for the Tsar Nicholas and Tsarina Alexandra Feodorovna, we triumphed.

During our bows to their Excellencies, the Empress Alexandra Feodorovna beckoned us closer.

"Your skills," she said, "for such young people are to be rewarded. I should like to see you both again." She paused for a moment. "Perhaps," she glanced at the tsar, who lifted an eyebrow at her, and then turned back to us, "you would like to attend the ball at the Kremlin tomorrow night?"

I swallowed hard.

"We should be honored, your Excellencies," Vladimir said, his voice smooth.

"We will see you there." The tsarina nodded and turned back toward her husband, dismissing us.

I curtsied as gracefully as I could, holding a pair of reins and wearing jodhpurs and boots, lacking the essential skirts. Vladimir drew me to my feet and escorted me away.

"A ball at the Kremlin?" I blinked and took a deep breath. "However will I find a ball dress before tomorrow night?"

"You have none?" He looked at me, jaw dropped.

I peered from beneath my brows. "How many balls have I attended since we met?"

He stared at me. "Well..."

"Exactly. I attended the end of year cadets ball with you last year, but that dress will hardly be suitable for an audience," I indicated my breeches and boots, "other than this, of course, with the tsar and tsarina. It's easy for you. You simply need your Training School dress uniform."

"Sisters. Yes, that's it." He spun to face me. "Olga and Sonja will have a dress to fit you."

My jaw dropped. His sisters were elegant young ladies. I'd been introduced to them before, but they hadn't seemed impressed by the stable girl performing with their brother. "But they live a full day's ride away. I'd never be able to ride there and return and still take care of my stable duties."

"I'll go. I can get one of the other lads to do my work for me, if your father permits."

"I permit," he said, walking up in time to hear the end of the conversation.

"Thank you, sir. I have three sisters, most of them close in size to Tatiana. With your permission, I will leave as soon as I cool out my horse."

"We'll take care of that and inform the headmaster. Well done, both of you. Your performance was without equal," he said, taking the reins of Vladimir's horse and leading him back toward the barn.

"Papa," I said, and he turned. I reached out for Sarda's reins. "Thank you, for all you've done for me, for us." I glanced at Vladimir's retreating back.

He handed them to me and hugged me, his eyes glistening with unshed tears. "You have made me so proud, both you and Vladimir. What a team you make."

"We could've never done it without you."

"Soon he will be finished here and must enter the tsar's army." He took back Sarda's reins and together we began walking the sweating horses. "Have you considered what you will do then?" His eyes looked at me—through me—and I shuddered, then swallowed and looked at the floor.

"I honestly do not know, Papa."

"A life of horses is hard for a man, much less a woman, and I won't be around forever."

My eyes snapped up to his. "What?" For the first time, I saw his weathered visage, the grayness of his skin at the edges, and my stomach clenched. "Papa, are you ill?"

He took a deep breath. "I'm not sure, but my heart, it does funny things sometimes. Not badly, but it's enough to give me pause—to question and to ensure you are provided for."

The walls of the Kremlin swayed around me. Papa was my rock, although I'd been increasingly leaning on Vladimir as we had become close friends, and now, it seems, something more.

"Have you been to a doctor, Papa?" Knowing he hadn't.

"No, but there is little they could do."

"You don't know that..."

"Trust me, I know. Anyway, *princessa*, you will be going to the ball and dancing the night away on the arm of your prince.

"Will you becoming?"

"The invitation was only for the two of you, but I will be awaiting your return with bated breath." I offered the horse a few sips of water from a bucket then pulled Sarda away and we resumed our walk.

"This will be my first ball without you, Papa..." I searched his face, seeking to know the extent of his sickness, but nothing showed.

"My *solnishko* has grown up." New tears in his eyes threatened to fall. "You will be the loveliest woman there."

Woman.

I'd never thought of myself as that...it would take some time to sink in.

Due out soon! Look for it!

THANK YOU FOR READING AND SIGNUP

Thank you for reading.
I hope you enjoyed The Hills of Gold Unchanging!
To join Lizzi's VIP Club and hear about new release and specials, plus get your free sampler!

It's right here:

www.lizzitremayne/VIPHills/

www.ingramcontent.com/pod-product-compliance
Lightning Source LLC
Chambersburg PA
CBHW031022030726
47497CB00004B/969